ENCORE

Books by Monique Raphel High

THE FOUR WINDS OF HEAVEN
ENCORE

"Dancers were allowed to give two or even more encores; there were no restrictions. But when the Tsar and Tsarina were present, if the audience demanded a third encore, we had to turn to the Imperial Box and wait for a signal from the Emperor and Empress. . . . When she nodded her consent, I curtsied low and reembarked on my coda to a veritable storm of applause."

MATILDA KCHESSINSKAYA, *Dancing in Petersburg,* p. 116

ENCORE

Monique Raphel High

DELACORTE PRESS/NEW YORK

Published by Delacorte Press
1 Dag Hammarskjold Plaza, New York, N.Y. 10017

Manufactured in the United States of America
First printing

Designed by Laura Bernay

Library of Congress Cataloging in Publication Data

High, Monique Raphel.
Encore.

I. Title.
PS3558.I3633E5   813'.54   80-26120
ISBN: 0-440-02351-3

For Robb, whose book this was from the beginning.
And for all the ballet lovers of the world . . .

"If two lives join, there is oft a scar.
    They are one and one, with a shadowy third;
One near one is too far."

ROBERT BROWNING, *By the Fireside*, xlvi

Foreword

One of the abiding mysteries of the arts concerns the birth of trends. Why do certain writers, sometimes separated by oceans, cultures, and tastes, happen to seize on a common subject at the same time, creating a body of work that then becomes "fashionable," like this year's hemlines? Recently there has been a rebirth in fascination with ballet dancing, and with the Diaghilev ballet. Perhaps, above and beyond my quite personal reason for choosing to write this book at this particular time, a greater hand has guided me, hiding its motives from my conscious mind.

Encore takes place within the confines of Serge Diaghilev's Ballets Russes. In researching the history of my Russian family, the Barons Gunzburg, about whom I wrote in *The Four Winds of Heaven*, I unearthed a plethora of loose threads that at first seemed intriguing only if taken one at a time as individual anecdotes. One could hardly use such tidbits for a major work. And then it struck me that there was a connection: At the center, taking shape, Diaghilev and his cohorts were emerging! In particular, my great-great-uncle, Baron Dmitri de Gunzburg, had been an intimate of Diaghilev and his principal backer during the years of the Ballets Russes: It was he who had translated the shipboard proposal of Nijinsky to Romola de Pulszky, a proposal that had repercussions throughout the artistic world of the epoch.

Encore is a love story set against this rich tapestry. It is a work of fiction based on true happenings that occurred within the ballet. Although Count Boris Kussov was not real, I cannot deny that he was largely inspired by the actual Baron Dmitri de Gunzburg. But this is true only in regard to his involvement with the Ballets Russes. Beyond that, Count Boris, like all my characters, is his own person.

I have attempted to simplify the Russian names, and as a result the pet names that were in fact used are not found in this book. Although this method does destroy some of the authenticity (Diaghilev's friends actually called him "Seriozha," and Nijinsky was known to his intimates as "Vatza"), it prevents the reader from becoming overly confused.

In regard to my other characters, I would like to plead forgiveness from the *balletomanes* who will doubtless be shocked at the liberties that I have taken. In order to form my central figures, I have allowed them to usurp the roles of actual dancers, painters, and choreographers who made the Ballets Russes famous. Thus, well-known works by Bronislava Nijinsky, Picasso, Larionov, Gontcharova, as well as parts played by Karsavina and other illustrious ballerinas, have in this novel been assigned to my protagonists. This was done in tribute to the Masters and Mistresses of the Ballet—not as a theft of their great talent.

I would like to thank Andrea Cirillo, my superlative editor, who gave me sustenance throughout the project. I also want to thank Dorris Halsey for her comments and her corrections of my German. Aliza Sverdlova went over the Russian for me, and two dancers and teachers, Barbara Chesney Schmir and Robin Sinclair, proofread the dance sections. I am particularly indebted to Ms. Schmir, whose wealth of information and indefatigable research proved invaluable to my own work. My gratitude goes to my dearest friend Walter Wolin for my jacket photograph. And last, but hardly least, Ellen Edwards, my assistant editor, deserves to be called for an *encore* after the long hours she put into this endless manuscript.

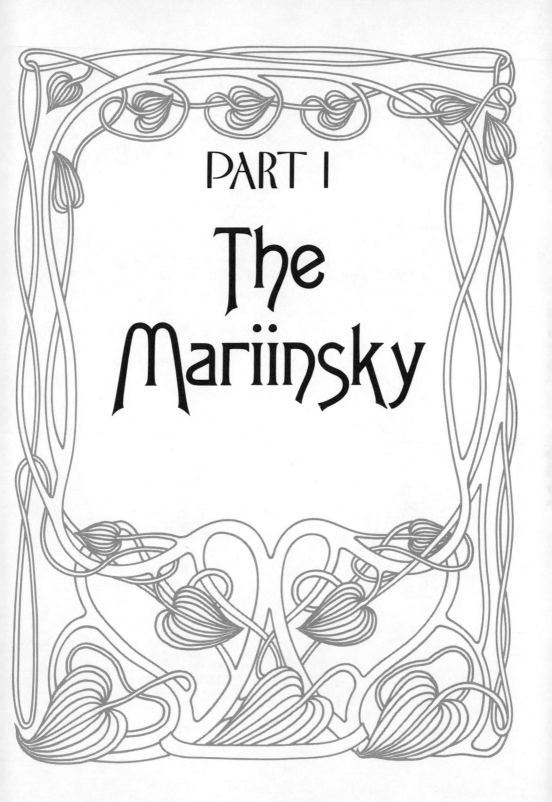

PART I

The Mariinsky

rom the outside, the Mariinsky Theatre appeared elegant and stately, a palace of smooth Grecian lines where it seemed fitting to produce flowing performances of the Imperial Ballet. Boris Vassilievitch Kussov, however, knew the edifice from the inside out, and now, hurrying through its dark corridors, his mind passed over his interview with the director, General Teliakovsky. They had discussed many matters regarding the current state of unrest at the Ballet. The younger dancers wanted more autonomy and were demanding changes. But Teliakovsky was of the old guard and did not think that lesser members of the company had the right to pit their own small experience against that of the Mariinsky's choreographer, Marius Petipa, who had been producing splendid ballets and revivals for half a century. He had asked Boris Kussov to confer with him because Count Boris was an important patron, respected by all concerned. But little had been accomplished.

All at once, however, Boris Kussov's thoughts were interrupted by a small invasion of students from the Imperial School of Ballet. Ah, yes, he thought, stepping aside to let them pass, they are coming here to rehearse for the Christmas production of *The Nutcracker*. Then his eye, casual and amused, was caught by the girl who headed the little procession. She was older than the rest but wore the same blue-gray uniform of the student dancers. She was small and slight, and her compact young body at first reminded him of a boy's. In the semi-

4   darkness of the corridor, her tender heart-formed face glowed, translucent as skim milk, the blue veins in her temples gently throbbing. Her eyes were almond-shaped and very brown, almost russet. They met his own without shyness, only curiosity. Her nose was too long and thin, and her lips had a sculpted delicacy, sharply defined and rather bloodless. But it was the neck that made him look twice: A smooth, vulnerable line, it proudly supported her head with its bun of fine mahogany hair.

"Excuse me," the girl said, and then she was gone, her receding figure hidden from him by the group of younger pupils. He forgot her: just another ballerina in the forming, not as extraordinarily ethereal as Anna Pavlova, or as blooming and fresh as Karsavina or Lydia Kyasht. The directress of the ballet school, Varvara Ivanovna Lithosherstova, graduated girls like these every spring, and it was impossible to predict which ones would rise to stardom and which would remain ensconced in the *corps de ballet*. Count Boris Kussov raised the astrakhan collar of his coat and steeled himself for the bleak December winds of Theatre Street.

As he spotted his carriage, he thought gloomily: It is almost Christmas again, but why, then, is joy eluding us? The last two years snapped into focus, first the war with Japan in '04, which had decimated the Russian navy, and then the year now coming to a close, 1905. For over a month, a workers' strike had virtually immobilized St. Petersburg, his lovely city. Nearly a year ago on Bloody Sunday, armed Cossacks had fired upon a peaceful procession bearing a petition to Tzar Nicholas II. The Tzar, who was not Boris's favorite member of the Imperial Family— his own intimate friend was the Tzar's uncle, the Grand-Duke Vladimir, expansive and a lover of the arts—had not been at the Winter Palace, where the procession of innocents had been headed. But Boris's own victoria had nearly been overturned in the mêlée, and his coachman hurt. And now even in the rarified atmosphere of the Mariinsky there hung clouds of unrest, germs of dissent.

"Home, for God's sake, Yuri," he said to the driver as the latter bundled him into the warmth of his carriage. Abruptly he recalled the girl's white face, her autumn eyes, and an odd

thought occurred to him. "You, too, have not known joy," he
said to her remembered image. She was so young, and very
nearly beautiful—but somehow incomplete, somehow tarnished. And then he smiled ironically. What a fool he was,
speaking to himself! . . .

When Count Boris Vassilievitch Kussov entered his bachelor
quarters on the Boulevard of the Horse Guard, not far from the
Winter Palace where the Tzar resided, he was heartened by the
orange-red flames that crackled in the fireplace. The thick quilt
that his coachman had placed upon his lap in the victoria had
not kept him warm in the subzero weather, and he was cold to
his very bone. His valet removed the fur coat, and now Boris
stood with his back to the fire, surveying the charming living
room, the only place where his restive soul ever felt at peace.
His intellectual friends mocked his taste for personal luxury but
had to grant him excellent marks for decoration. Small tables
with delicate inlays stood beside Louis XV chairs and love seats,
and Renaissance paintings made interesting contrasts with
sketches by his friend, Léon Bakst, and the green and gold hues
of a Cézanne. Boris touched the Della Robbia enamel medal-
lion hanging above the alabaster fireplace and felt revived. "Do
I have an appointment, Ivan?" he asked rather absently.

The valet cleared his throat. "Yes, Excellency. The young
man from the Academy of Fine Arts is coming here in fifteen
minutes. Pierre Riazhin."

"Riazhin? I had forgotten. But I did finance his studies,
didn't I? And now he's graduated? Probably a jaded young man
who paints with the constipation of all the Academics." He
raised his eyebrows quizzically. "Or maybe he's rebelled and
joined the Ambulant school—then he's probably crude and intense, as befits the son of a liberated serf, out to educate the
mujiks. Ah, well, Ivan, prepare us a lavish tea. But without caviar and such. This Riazhin comes at a bad time. I'm exhausted."

When the servant had departed, Boris walked to the large gilt
mirror and examined his reflection. He was indeed tired, but
his fatigue in no way detracted from the artistry of his elegant
figure, which was like one of his own beloved works of art. The

6   mirror did not reveal his tall stature, his slender hips, but it captured the symmetry of his straight shoulders and narrow waist,
of his poised neck and long face. His eyes, a light, metallic
blue, made him look cold, and his hair, pure Florentine gold
interspersed with an occasional thread of gray, was brushed back
from a high forehead. The creases at the outer corners of his
eyes, coupled with the somewhat lopsided smile of his rather
thin lips, hinted at irony rather than mirth. His nose was
aquiline, with nostrils that quivered like those of a nervous
Thoroughbred. He put a fingernail to his waxed mustache, then
gently scratched beneath his neatly trimmed beard. People had
told him he resembled his mother, who had died in his youth,
and Boris was pleased, for Countess Kussova had been one of
the great beauties of Tzar Alexander's court. One of Russia's
treasures, he thought with wry amusement. His friend, Serge
Diaghilev, had created quite a stir earlier that year by setting up
a massive exhibition of national masterpieces at the Tauride
Palace: What a shame that he had not had a portrait of the
deceased countess at his disposal. . . .

The doorbell sounded, gently muted, and presently Ivan entered, announcing Monsieur Pierre Riazhin. Boris did not think
he had ever met the young man, for over the years he had supported many artists and musicians during their education. Boris
felt in the artistic endeavors of other men a vicarious catharsis
that filled a void in his own being. Now, he looked up to see
Riazhin enter—and at once, he registered surprise.

Pierre Riazhin was not elegant. He was young, perhaps
twenty-two, and if Boris had not seen him face to face, he
might not have noticed any quality to set Pierre apart from
others. But Boris saw the vitality in Pierre's face, square and
strong with high cheekbones healthily flushed, from which dark
eyes beneath thick black brows moved with instant attention
over the delicate furnishings of the room and over Boris himself. Riazhin's body was compact and quick, and his host
thought: He is a black panther out of its element, sniffing at a
strange lair. But the young man's clothing denoted, above all,
spare means. He clasped a large portfolio beneath his arm.
"Sir," he said. He gave a quick jerk of a bow, and Boris was
suddenly glad that he had not said "Excellency." He himself

said to the valet: "We *shall* have the caviar sandwiches, Ivan."

Boris Kussov motioned his caller to a small settee facing the fire and sat down in an armchair on the side. "My dear Riazhin," he began, with a charming smile, "I have forgotten your patronym. You are Pierre . . . ?"

"Pierre Grigorievitch Riazhin. I have come to you for several reasons, sir. First of all—"

"Yes, yes, we can dispense with that. You want to thank me, of course. I accept your thanks. But I am curious as to what sort of brushstrokes I have set in motion, so to speak. When did you finish at the Academy, Pierre Grigorievitch?"

"In the spring. I then returned to my native Georgia in the Caucasus and have attempted to put together the best of my work. I wished to show it to you in this small collection, for I know that your opinion is valued by painters whom I greatly admire."

"Ah. And who may they be?" Boris accepted the large portfolio and laid it open on his lap. An intense splash of color drew his attention, and he forgot the young man and instead concentrated on the riot of magentas and oranges on the page before him. Riazhin had depicted a girl, a gypsy or a peasant, Boris could not be sure, but a girl of the wild, of the Steppes. Her look was defiant, maybe angry, certainly proud. To Boris she resembled the young man in his sitting room.

"I can see why you planned a trip to your homeland," Boris said, slowly stroking his mustache. "I do not know that area well—the Caucasus. But you belong there, in full costume: a long red tunic closed with gold braid and a sling of cartridges around your chest, your rifle at your back, black trousers stuffed into high boots of fine leather. With a fur cap upon your black curls, to complete the effect. Certainly a vast improvement over your present attire, I dare say."

But the young man did not smile. His eyes blazed offense.

"Is it true then that Caucasians punish the slightest affront with a shot in the back?" Boris continued, mockingly.

Riazhin clenched his fists in his lap, then regarded the older man with disconcerting directness. "Not quite, sir. When a guest offends us, we smile so long as he remains within our premises. He may kill our brother or rape our sister, yet that

8   does not alter our obligation as hosts. But when he bids us farewell, and we escort him out, hospitality ceases the minute he crosses the boundary line of our domain. At that point, revenge is ours. It is possible, sometimes likely, that we may shoot him then. We are savage, cruel but proud. In the capital we learn to adjust, but when we are children, we are taught to ride wild horses long distances, and so we grow up as centaurs, half man, half beast." The young man was smiling, revealing large white teeth between full, sensuous lips.

"Your work reflects your origins, Pierre Grigorievitch. But your name is too tame, too civilized. You should be called by some noble Georgian appellation, such as . . . maybe 'Khadjatur?' "

"If you do not think much of my sketches and paintings, then I shall go," Riazhin said tightly.

Boris burst out laughing. "Right now *you* are *my* guest. It would hardly do to shoot your host. Do not take such small jokes to heart. I find your art quite extraordinary—powerful, real, yet also touched with the fantastic. In short—you could become another Bakst. Or—I could be entirely wrong—a Cézanne. Now, who were those friends of mine whom you claim to admire?"

"You mentioned one of them: Léon Bakst. Then, naturally, there was my old teacher, Valentin Serov. Also Somov, Benois—although I am not given to landscapes of his tenderness, my own work being somewhat more—"

"Fierce. Yes. Serov taught you at the Academy?"

"Briefly. He resigned because of his outrage over Bloody Sunday, and since then I have not seen him. That was why I came to you, and not him. I would not have known where to find him, or whether he remembered me. Naturally, I had also wished to thank you—"

Boris smiled. "You would have come last spring, had that been all you wished. No, you are an ambitious sort, Pierre Grigorievitch. You came to be introduced to my groups of friends, the ones who used to put together the *World of Art* review. You knew that I had been a part of those people. You also remembered that I had money. Everyone remembers that in reference to me: Count Boris Vassilievitch Kussov, whose good taste we may flatter so that he may untie his purse strings. Oh, I am hardly blind to such machinations, but surely a man of your directness would be ashamed of employing flattery as a tactic? I am disillusioned."

"Sir—"

"You may address me as Boris Vassilievitch. You are not my servant. If I am to sponsor you—ah, here comes Ivan with tea! I hope your appetite matches your talent. I am famished, myself."

Pierre Riazhin opened his mouth and started to rise, but felt Boris Kussov's gently restraining hand on his arm. He sat down uncomfortably and regarded his host, and this time the black eyes seemed almost to plead for an explanation. Boris's own blue eyes softened, but he said nothing as Ivan laid a magnificent tea upon the table. The young painter's expressive face had made him recall the girl in the hallway of the Mariinsky. How different those two faces were, and yet how liquid the eyes! He sighed, and felt the weight of his thirty years. Riazhin was in his earliest twenties, and the dancer? Sixteen, at most? Two very young people who did not need money in order to expand into creativity, two people with urges that he had never felt, would never feel. And yet he was surprised that the girl had not already slipped from his memory. . . .

"Tell me, Pierre Grigorievitch," Boris asked, "do you ever attend performances of the ballet?"

"Once or twice from the gallery," the young man replied. "I can't afford it more often."

"Then you shall have to come as my guest. I have a stall. But please, do justice to Ivan's teacakes—the ones with sesame and honey are succulent, and nobody can resist them."

The Imperial Ballet School closed around Natalia Oblonova like a cocoon of pure but compact silk. Alone in the large, sloped rehearsal room, she pulled up her thick, ungainly leg warmers and went to the *barre*. Dawn was just beginning to break, its pearlescent pink peeking between the gray skies of St. Petersburg. She was completely alone. Should one of Varvara Ivanovna's governesses awaken and find her there, privileges, scarce as they were, would be taken away. For she was not yet a

senior student. Rules were rigid, similar to those of a convent—
or so the fifteen-year-old girl thought, knowing nothing at all of
convents. But she knew the school, and she felt protected
within it. Hurt lay beyond its graceful eighteenth-century walls
of white and yellow stone. Degradation did not penetrate
Theatre Street, whose entire left bank was comprised of the
various Imperial Theatre Schools. Bounded by the elegant and
well-traveled Nevsky Prospect, and by the pleasant Fontanka
River, this little street lay ensconced in the heart of the city but
secluded from its general activity. The students, each and every
one sponsored by the imperial purse, were completely hidden
from life except when they performed at the Mariinsky.

Exercising at the *barre*, making the blood flow to the tips of
her fingers and toes, the small, slender girl with the heart-
shaped face could feel herself come alive. For a moment, a picture passed in her mind's eye of a field of red poppies, wind-
swept with the scent of fresh hay. She increased the width of her
rond de jambe to chase the thought away. It belonged to a
previous life, when for brief instants she had felt the same fire of
excitement in the core of her being that she now felt whenever
she danced. Her face, not beautiful but delicate in its molding,
was set into lines that belied her youth and took all gentleness
from her features: Now she looked like an antique Russian icon,
proud and ruthless. She stopped her movement slowly, winding
down, then sank to the floor and began to execute limbering
motions, forming a line with her extended legs, then bending
her head first toward one knee, then toward its opposite. The
muscles in her back loosened, and she breathed deeply. Thinking was bad for her.

Yet her thoughts kept intruding ungraciously. She had once
been a Dew-Drop, and later a Bon-Bon, in *The Nutcracker*
productions at the Mariinsky. Then, the previous year, she had
been chosen to dance Clara, the little girl who, with her magic
Nutcracker-Prince, undertakes the magnificent journey to the
land of Snow and the Kingdom of Sweets. This year it had
been announced, in a matter-of-fact manner, that she was to
take the part of the Sugar Plum Fairy, an honor most often
reserved for a member of the Imperial Ballet. To dance the
Fairy, dressed exquisitely in pink finery, lifted by her male

partner in sweeping gestures, moving to Tchaikovsky's music in the blue and silver theatre crowded with members of the aristocracy—she lived for this and this alone. Others had surely helped, but she had essentially created herself, and she intended to become the famous Oblonova, just as the daughter of a Jewish laundress had made herself the incomparable Pavlova.

Natalia could not remember the taste and color of love, and she thought it a somewhat pretentious affectation. She cared for Katya Balina, her classmate, and even for Katya's family, who had taken her in during the first year, before she became a boarder at the school. She was fond of them, especially of Katya's mother, who always struggled to keep neat and forever failed, a laughing, witty woman who kissed her children and husband in front of the fire, when all the family would take turns reading from a Chekhov play.

The Balins were an alien lot to Natalia, and she knew that they had held her in some awe—this child who had never been a child, whose laughter had never tumbled out of her in spasms of delight, who had never allowed anyone to see her weep. Natalia had never once received a Christmas package, and she was sent only chance letters scattered throughout the year. But the Balins had listened to Katya, who told them that Natalia's dancing was like no other, that in her movements there was life itself.

Katya was soft, round, and pretty, and talked all the time about her feelings; when an older girl snubbed her, Katya was hurt. Natalia could not comprehend how Katya could care so much for the outside world, for meaningless arrows from the slingshots of meaningless people.

Natalia did not carefully ponder these ideas now as she exercised. Sometimes months went by without a thought like this, but now her bends and stretches could not block out her memories. She recalled the Crimean countryside, so fertile and magnificent in its vibrant hues, aromatic scents, and gentle climate. She remembered the farm on which she had first lived. She did not concentrate on her parents, but they were there: Dmitri Oblonov, the embittered second son of a second son of a very minor squire in Simferopol, a man whose holdings were so scant that he had married Elena, thin and brittle, only because her father had been a fairly comfortable leather worker and she his only heir. They had lived on the farm, always bemoaning poverty, always beholden to the local landowner, Baron Gudrinsky. Elena had complained. She had wanted to live, no matter how meagerly, in Simferopol, and she still daydreamed about tea with the wives of the local gentry. Dmitri had hated his wife and "made do" with the little maid who helped in the house. He had been—and probably still was—a magnificent man, his auburn hair tinged with red, a tall, massive man with good color and brilliant blue eyes that were obscured by envy and lust. His wife might have been pretty once but had long since aged into mean, petty frailty and ill health. He had loved no one; she had loved Vera, her older daughter, who had inherited Dmitri's handsome looks and features. Elena had seized on Vera's beauty as a vicarious means to small gentility, for Vera, placid and not too intelligent, would marry properly through her fair attractions. Natalia—mousy little Natasha, who was neither feminine nor pleasing of character—would never become anything worthwhile. Natalia was willful and thin, like a small, furtive animal: No man worth more than a few kopeks would settle for such a creature. Elena had resolved to ignore her younger child—and she had succeeded.

But even now, Natalia did not hate her mother. In her heart, instead, was a total absence of sensation, as if Elena had never been a part of her existence. She was not taking anything away from her mother, for Elena had placed nothing there with which to start Natalia's life. Natalia had reared herself; her sister, too soft, girlish, and fearful, had not been close to her either. But Dmitri had been there. Sulking, violent at times, envious of others' wealth and ease, he had run his small farm, and his younger daughter, to whom he had barely acknowledged parenthood, had followed him, dogging his footsteps in admiration of his bestial beauty. Had she loved her father? Was that love, to watch a man work a land he detested, feeling excitement when he raised his strong arms or pushed aside a cow, but in no way feeling connected to this strange, defiant creature? Yet she *had* felt a slight connection: She had absorbed his desire to flee, his fury at his bondage. She had sensed his animal will and felt a similar strength within her own small self.

She had imagined Dmitri as a tramp, combing the roads of Russia, befriending drunkards and whores—and had envisioned him happy, unfettered. One could not blame a man for wishing to rejoin the elements. Unwittingly, he had taught her that.

She had loved the Crimea in her own way, while realizing, even as a toddler, that the land did not bind her to it; she had loved it in the same free manner as had the children of the rich landowner, Baron Gudrinsky, who visited each summer from St. Petersburg, knowing they essentially belonged in the capital. Yet the land had expanded her soul, linking her to something greater than herself, greater than her own small-minded family.

And so she hugged the trees and rolled in the soft earth and emitted wild cries, leaping over brooks and attempting to fly, failing gloriously. Baroness Gudrinskaya had seen her one day, and during the annual festivity when she gathered together all the people employed on the vast estate, as well as those who, like the Oblonovs, provided her family with services and goods, she had asked Elena if her daughter had ever expressed the wish to become a dancer. "But Baroness, she is only a goat, that Natasha!" her mother had cried, shocked and bewildered.

"Goats scamper on mountain rocks that no one else can reach," the baroness had stated, amused.

"A dancer? But where would she learn? That would be too costly, in any event."

"I was thinking of the Imperial Ballet School," the squire's wife said. "The children spend seven or eight years there, at the Tzar's expense. Then, upon graduation, they enter the Imperial Ballet. But of the two hundred girls who come for the entrance examination each summer, perhaps six are chosen. It is a great honor, Elena Alexandrovna."

Elena had shaken her head. "Natasha has no talents. And besides, we lack the means with which to send her to St. Petersburg."

Baroness Gudrinskaya was growing bored with this recalcitrant farmer's wife. Her summers were long, and she was at loose ends. She enjoyed the ballet, and the notion of sending this wild child to the capital to audition at one of the country's most prestigious institutions had at first appealed to her. She liked performing good works. But now her amusement was waning. The mother did not think her child had talent—so be it. The child was ugly, anyway.

And then, strangely, the challenge had returned in the form of Dmitri. His ears had perked up at the thought of ridding his household of one mouth to feed, and he went to the baroness. "About Natasha and the Ballet School," he began awkwardly. "How certain would we be that they would accept her?"

"Not certain at all. But I think you and I can make a bargain, my dear man. The auditions are in August. That is when my servants return to the capital to reopen the house. Your daughter could travel with them; and in return you would lower your price on next season's produce."

"And if she is rejected, Baroness?"

"Then she would work one year in my household, as assistant to my seamstress. She would quickly learn how to sew. And you would not have to feed her for that time, of course." The baroness had secretly smiled, knowing that the man's greed would now win him to her side. The idea of scoring a victory against the town's most unpleasant individual appealed to the baroness's vanity: She was only a woman, and an aristocrat, yet she had won a round with a merchant of sorts, a barterer. Her friends in Petersburg would be thrilled to hear this tale—how daring, and how brilliant, to have come down the social ladder, thus, and to have braved a man known for his intensely bad manners and violent temper! The child was no longer the object of the game, but the man had been cowed.

Elena had professed herself pleased. Now Vera could afford new lace with which to make a series of inexpensive dresses. Dmitri had been pleased, too: Had he not hoisted one of his three burdens to the shoulders of this refined and empty-headed city woman, and perhaps even of the Tzar himself, should the chit, by sheer luck, pass the examination?

Natalia would never forget the day that she had learned she was to travel to the capital. She had never been farther than Simferopol. At ten, untamed and unstyled, she could not imagine Petersburg. She had only thought: I am to dance, to spend my lifetime dancing! She had never seen a formal ballet and did not think one had to be trained to espouse the motions of the wind as it wrapped its breath around the barks of frail willows. She was glad to leave what had never felt like home.

In her simple cotton shift and bright red kerchief, Natalia had taken her place beside Masha, the baroness's maid. There were ten carts and wagons in the Gudrinsky procession bearing goods and servants to the train station several hours away. The August heat had scorched the small girl, who had sat proudly beside the sulking maid. Masha had hardly spoken to her: She probably resented the added burden of having to care for a child during a long journey. There was no true road, only ruts of wheels in the burned grass. Then they had arrived at the little town with its crude sidewalks of thrown-together wooden planks. Natalia had seen her first train: enormous, lumbering, wide. Masha had pushed her into a third class compartment with hard wooden seats, and two bulky men had squeezed her next to the window. She had not wanted to sleep, watching the scenery change from province to province, the lushness of the Crimea giving way to more barren land, and then cities.

When they were hungry, Masha unfolded baskets of provisions, but Natalia tried to ignore her hunger pangs, for she did not want to owe the Gudrinskys for more than the barest necessities. At ten years of age, she had already learned pride, perhaps because her mother had been so blatantly devoid of it and her father's had been false. Each time the train stopped at a large station with a restaurant, Masha would descend to refill her teapot from the steaming samovar inside. At night, the controller would send away all but four passengers and would raise the backs of the wooden seats to form two upper bunks: Russians, no matter how poor, could not conceive of sleeping without lying down. Several times Masha made Natalia climb down, bringing all the baggage with her, too: They were changing trains. But Natalia learned that Russian trains paid scant attention to schedules: Sometimes, while the Gudrinsky staff was still waiting for its connecting train, night would fall, and they had to make do with benches in the waiting rooms for bunks.

Natalia was mostly silent. Slowly, the unkempt, unacknowledged child of the Crimea, Natasha "the goat," was being

16   shed, and a clearer, more defined character was emerging: that of Natalia who wanted to win a place at the Imperial School of Ballet. She did not think this so impossible; maybe the baroness had begun this adventure as a lark, as a joke upon an unfortunate family unpopular in the town. But she, Natalia, had always felt that something would occur to free her from her sister's destiny. She was not beautiful, but she was intelligent, though unschooled, save in the crudest manner. Even the majesty of the Orthodox religion had been denied her, for her parents, disillusioned nonbelievers, had rarely made the effort to send her to the village Sunday school; it had been otherwise for Vera, in the hopes that the parish pope might help to make her more eligible for decent matrimony.

As a farm child, Natalia had seen death many times and was not frightened by it. She knew that death was acceptable. Far worse a commonplace existence, which was a denial of the divine side of man, of his humanity. She did not know then that money might have saved her, had she possessed it; for, as with love, she had never known money. Hence she must rely on herself. If she were to emerge with dignity, if she were to accept herself, she must do so alone, with whatever gifts might lie within her. At ten, she did not reason this out—but she knew it instinctively, with a keen sense of self-preservation.

Now, alone in the rehearsal room, covered with sweat, Natalia thought: I shall never bear a child, never. It destroyed my father, took his freedom from him and beggared him to the Gudrinskys. And love? How could I love a child when I despise the notion of living for someone else, as Katya's mother does, or as mine did with Vera? And a child should not grow up as I did; it costs too much in pain. I am afraid of joy, except the one pure joy of dance, this exhilaration brought on by embodying beauty with my own straining tendons. If I admit joy, then I shall admit pain with it.

Katya is a fool: She loves the governesses, she loves the boy who sends her notes during ballroom dancing class, she loves the babies in the parks. Yet while she loves, she laughs and is joyful. Why? What lies forever beyond me, who am intelligent but within easy reach for Katya, whose mind is simpler than mine? Why does she pray to God, while I know He does not exist?

Pink light flickered through a dismal cloud, and she stopped to watch it grow into a crimson flare. Daylight. Natalia quickly executed two *pliés* and cursed her poor turnout. She had chased away the ghosts, and now, golden and warm, she remembered her first glimpse of this school that she felt was hers. The architecture from the days of Tzarina Elizabeth, daughter of Peter the Great, was simple and noble, with the Alexandrinsky dramatic theatre, topped with its three equestrian statues molded in bronze, bordering the Nevsky Prospect at the end. Theatre Street. A guard had let her and Masha pass into the Ballet School, and in the enormous rehearsal room—this very one!—she had seen more children than she had ever before imagined. One hundred fifty boys and two hundred girls had been lined up, the mothers and guardians standing against the walls to await the outcome. First, the doctor had examined her, then she had gone before the masters seated around a long table. A beautiful lady with dark hair had been there, and when Natalia had walked, jumped, and turned, this lady had exclaimed: "She's a single continuous line, isn't she?" Natalia had thought: I have failed. Later, she had learned that the lady was Matilda Kchessinskaya, *prima ballerina assoluta*, once the Tzar's mistress before his marriage and now the consort of his first cousin, the Grand-Duke Andrei. The words spoken by this great lady had been complimentary, not critical.

During the grueling day, the children had taken a break and had tea. Sitting alone, not thinking, Natalia had felt a hand upon her arm. Alarmed, she jumped up, but it was only the blond-haired girl who had been behind her during the testing. "Hello," she had said, and her voice was different, with an accent that jarred upon Natalia's ears. "I'm Katya. Ekaterina Nicolaievna Balina. And you? What's your name?"

"Natalia. Oblonova."

Katya, a well-groomed child whose mother had trimmed her hair with care around the ears so that it curled gracefully, would not be put off. "You will be chosen," she had said. "You're very good. Better than I."

Natalia had known that was true. She had smiled for the first time. "You're not bad. But for you, dancing is not your life. For me—it means being able to stay here, being able to be a person, a real person. . . ."

"I think dancing's the most beautiful thing I've ever seen," Katya said. "Have you seen many ballets?"

"I haven't seen any yet. In the Crimea I lived on a farm. But I want to learn. I'm not afraid of being tired, and my body wants to grow, to make beautiful shapes. In the country I used to run, and move, and stretch—and then I was happy."

They had both been selected in the final analysis, along with six other girls. Then Katya had asked: "If you're from so far away, Natalia, where will you live the first year? You can't board at school, you know, until they accept you for the second year. Why don't you come and live with us? I have four brothers, and I'm the youngest. Mama won't mind—she loves children."

Madame Balina had, indeed, not minded. Baroness Gudrinskaya, swept up by her own part in her protégée's good fortune, had made the arrangements with the Balins, the school, and the Oblonovs. Dmitri had been told that since his daughter's future was now assured, a family of moderate means had offered to board her the first year. In return, he was to send them produce from the farm every season. He had grumbled; but after all, as Elena made him understand, if Natalia had been turned down by the Ballet School and become apprentice to the baroness's seamstress, she might have proven unsuited for her work and returned home after a year or two. This way, the Tzar ensured eight years of bills, and a few sides of beef and fresh vegetables were well worth the bargain. Dmitri grunted and promptly forgot that he had ever fathered a second child. Vera's wardrobe increased by two tea dresses. And Natalia found herself with a friend, although she had never thought herself in need of one before. But perhaps this was the custom of St. Petersburg; for she quickly noticed that most of the girls talked in pairs, laughed in pairs, practiced in pairs. Katya Balina protected her from curious glances and from taunts of provincialism; for Katya was a Petersburg girl, and she generously bestowed her city upon her new friend.

Natalia was finished with her warm-up. She ran from the rehearsal room, aware that the bell was about to ring and that she must not be caught out of bed. She reached the dormitory in time, and slipped noiselessly onto her cot. A shiver of pleasure raced through her, and her skin tingled from the exercise. She closed her eyes. She envisioned the Mariinsky and herself in her Sugar Plum costume. And then, abruptly, she remembered the elegant blond man with the ironic smile whom she had encountered in the corridor the day of the rehearsal. What an odd expression on that princely face. "I don't like him," she murmured, not realizing that she had spoken out loud.

"Who's that?" Katya demanded from the neighboring bed.

"A living statue with a top hat and scented hair," Natalia replied.

Katya began to laugh.

The palace of Count Vassily Arkadievitch Kussov stood on the French Quay among the embassies, a cream-colored structure of simple, flowing lines that always pleased Boris whenever he came up to its enormous oak door. His father had neither chosen nor furnished it; he was a sturdy, uncomplicated man, happiest in his summer residence near the town of Dunaburg, on the train line to Berlin. There he possessed a vast stretch of fertile land around a lake, shaded by pleasant Mount Cavallo, where he liked to hunt in the company of other hardy men like himself. His palace in the capital had been selected by his own father, Count Arkady Kussov, a man whose delicate tastes had skipped a generation and resurfaced in Boris. Count Vassily's wife, long-deceased, had added many treasures from France, Italy, and the Orient to the original furnishings. Of all Count Vassily's four children, Boris most resembled his exquisite late mother in looks and temperament, and his father's father in the eclectic nature of his interests.

The liveried Swiss doorman bowed and opened the doors for Boris, whose cloak of black seal was instantly removed by a discreet *maître d'hôtel*. "Is my father waiting?" Boris asked pleasantly.

"Yes, Excellency. In his study."

Boris nodded and rubbed his hands together to dispel the

ungodly chill of a Russian winter. When the servant had departed, he stood hesitantly in the hallway, then could not resist the temptation to take a quick look around the salon. He fingered a sculpted lamp base of opaline, representing a Chinese woman with stiff headdress, and gazed lovingly at a small boulle secretary. He straightened his back and consulted the gold watch in his waistcoat pocket. He stepped away from the salon into a corridor illumined by a chandelier of shimmering Venetian crystal, and stopped by a door which was ajar. Crackling sounds of a fire reached his ears from inside the room. He knocked, paused, and said: "Papa?"

"Boris!" Now the younger man strode joyously across an Aubusson carpet of soft pastel hues. In front of a large mahogany desk stood a portly gentleman with hazel eyes beneath bushy brows, red bristles gleaming through darker sprouts. His fleshy nose curved toward a magnificent walrus mustache—in fact, he actually resembled a well-fed, elderly walrus still fighting to retain a grip on his prime. There was little gray mingling with the brown and red of his hair, and his paunch was hard, as if possessing an entity of its own. This was Vassily Kussov, whose intimate friendship with Tzar Alexander III had made him a familiar at the court of this now-deceased sovereign.

Boris embraced his father, and the two men sat down by the fire. "I hear much of your activities," the older man commented, drawing on a briar pipe. "You and your artistic friends. When I do not see you, I can always rely on Grand-Duke Vladimir to keep me apprised of all your doings. Not all, actually: only those with which he is acquainted as president of the Academy of Fine Arts."

"Come now, Papa, you sound as though I have been neglecting you," Boris chided gently.

"You don't come often enough to suit me, my son. The girls are dutiful and attentive, but what can I say? Daughters are not always a blessing. That, in fact, is one reason why I bade you come today. To discuss your sisters."

"What have they done? Or rather, who has done what?" Boris half-smiled and raised his fine golden eyebrows.

"The two younger ones are getting themselves married, that's what. Nina's court wedding last Christmas to Prince Stassov has already yielded one daughter, and I am pleased: The union is solid, for he's a good man. Nadia is being seriously courted by young Savin; and now Elizaveta is receiving attentions, too, the little chit."

"Lizotchka? I had no idea! She's only eighteen."

"At that age your mother was married. Liza seems to have attracted that Moscow lad, you know the one—Alexei Leontiev, the general's son."

"But surely you do not have objections, Papa? I am not personally acquainted with this Alexei, but I know the Leontievs— and there is no better family in Moscow. As for Nadia, and Nina . . . what troubles you, Papa? Are you sad that your chicks are all leaving the nest at the same time? But they won't: Certainly Liza will wait a while, at the least. And Nina lives so close by. . . ."

"I wouldn't mind if they took all their fineries and left tomorrow," grumbled Count Vassily. "I was not made to be the father of daughters, let alone three of them. And I confuse their suitors. I call Stassov Savin, and Savin Leontiev, and the girls wreak havoc on my head afterward."

"You do it on purpose, to put them off. I know you too well. But what is the problem? Surely you did not summon me to write you memory cards, did you, Papa?" Boris began to laugh, and got up to stoke the lazy fire. His father sat glaring at his back.

"Boris, you are irresponsible. You spend money as if it were limitless, but you seem to forget that you have sisters, and with two more weddings on top of Nina's, there will have to be two other large dowries. Your own income cannot remain the way it is, but your tastes are as extravagant as ever. I have this monstrosity of a household to keep up, as well as the summer estate, and there are the usual expenditures accruing to all members of the imperial court. Already, you have blithely consumed more than half the fortune left to you upon your mother's death. And your artistic friends bleed you dry. How much did that Diaghilev fellow borrow for his Exhibition of Russian Portraits? No, don't tell me: It was a gift, of course, from the bottomless purse of the bountiful Kussovs." The old count snorted, and his nose twitched. Small red veinules seemed to swell over his cheekbones. "Damn it all, Boris! You will have sons, too, one day, and I shall not have you squander their inheritance before they are even born!"

The young man turned around, his face merry. "So that's it! You worry that, as with Pushkin's fisherman, my luxurious predilections will cause the magic fish to turn my palace back into a hovel. But you forget, Papa, that the fisherman started out poor, and that it was his wife's boundless greed that finally irritated the little fish. I have never wished for more than I had; I am not a gambler and have no debts. I merely live well, as Kussovs have always lived since the days of Ivan the Terrible. Am I so different from the sons of your good friends?"

The older man glared at Boris, then puffed silently upon his pipe. "Yes!" he finally stated, his voice rising to a dangerous bellow. "God in heaven, yes! A mistress, even an expensive one—even two expensive ones—can only exact so much per month. But art . . . ! Someone was telling me—I can't for the life of me remember who—that you have a new protégé, yet another one—a young painter this time. And your travels— other men buy baubles, but you! Silks from the Orient, Renaissance paintings, first folios, Meissen figurines—it never ceases. Even Kussov money dwindles down. There is only one solution, for you are my only son and I refuse to beggar my daughters. You must marry, Boris. You must make an advantageous union with a woman of standing who will bring you a considerable dowry. You are too old for bachelorhood."

Boris was quiet. He fingered his mustache, his beard. "I love you very much, Papa," he remarked after some thought. "But one no longer weds to please one's father. Isn't that a rather antiquated notion?"

"I am asking for your sake. A dowry would not hurt your extravagance. And . . . one does not have to deny oneself certain discreet pleasures, my boy. If you loved someone, then all the better. But if you are forming a bond of convenience, there are means of easing the pressures. And those means are augmented by a second fortune."

"Do you have someone in mind, Papa?"

"Indeed. Do you remember Princess Marguerite Tumarkina, the niece of the provincial governor of Kiev? Her father is an important sugar plantation owner there, and Marguerite is his only child. I saw her father at the Brianskys' home last night. He asked me pointed questions about you, and from my own inquiries of Count Briansky, I gather that the Prince wishes to find a husband for his daughter."

"Why can't she find one herself? She must be at least twenty-three. Why does her father travel to the capital to marry her off?"

"He was here to see a minister. Don't be an idiot, Boris. And don't condemn this girl. Kiev does not possess the possibilities of the capital, and surely her father would wish the most advantageous life for her. As for you—you know all the unmarried women in St. Petersburg, yet you have chosen none. Perhaps you should search outside for a suitable bride."

"I simply do not wish to marry. I have three lovely sisters, and would rather be loved by them than by a wife. Besides, I am not without female companions, Papa. Princess Marguerite is thin, nervous, and sickly, from what I remember. Do you not recall the rumors several years ago? She suffered a nervous collapse and was sent to Switzerland. Besides, she upset my constitution when I last saw her. It was when I made that trip across Russia in search of unusual icons—and I visited the provincial governor. Marguerite and I met then. It was quite enough, thank you."

"She is coming to Petersburg, Boris. Her father is sending her, to enjoy the remainder of the winter season. She is to stay at the Brianskys'. I should appreciate it if you called upon her and took her somewhere. The theatre—wherever. I see in her an excellent possibility. You do not need a flamboyant hostess, for you are sufficiently flamboyant yourself. She is not a bad-looking girl, and her family is excellent. In short, I would be pleased to have her bear your sons. I would have preferred a truly unique woman along the lines of your late mother, a charming, witty beauty, as was the dowager empress in her youth. But short of that, a cultured, aristocratic girl, a bit shy and provincial, will do. The Tumarkin connections cannot hurt a Kussov in court circles, and Nina's Stassov would like that. He does business with Marguerite's father."

Boris's eyes had half-closed to slits and now the irises shone between his lashes like bits of blue glass. He had intertwined his fingers so that his hands were gripped together like taut vines. His father regarded him with a scowl that turned into a look of surprise, then of dismay. Boris resembled a carved alabaster statue of compressed anger and restrained force. The two men remained wordless as the flames rose and fell listlessly before them, sending out no warmth.

Then the study door was opening, and gay female voices filled the room, dispelling the aura of electric static between father and son. Three young women greeted their brother, their curls and ribbons bobbing in front of his face, their scent filling his nostrils with perfume of lilies and attar of roses. Boris seized the wrists of the youngest girl and tumbled her into his lap, where she collapsed, laughing. Count Vassily closed his eyes, crossed himself in the Orthodox fashion, and touched the wedding ring on his finger as though it were a soothing icon. The flames in the great ebony hearth had subsided to dying embers, and the brass tong stood forgotten near Boris's chair.

atalia awakened in the middle of the night from a vague dream of Christmas trees growing and children playing with life-sized toy soldiers. While she had been dreaming, her conscious voice had spoken out, telling her that the children were only an illusion, that the tree was a fantasy teasing her, that she herself was really in bed, sleeping. She had awakened with a jolt, and now, sitting up, she thought: My God, yes! That is the secret—so simple, after all! We do not have to take *The Nutcracker* seriously, for it was meant to be a dream within a dream, a joke. The spectators all know it is a fairy tale. Then why can't I dance the Sugar Plum as though I am on their side, as though I, too, know I am merely an illusion for their momentary pleasure, for Clara's pleasure? I will be an intelligent, humorous Sugar Plum who enjoys the game while knowing full well that it *is* a game.

She could not go back to sleep, although she had often been told that it was essential to rest properly before a performance. She was so excited at the notion of dancing her unusual Sugar Plum that she could not relax. She had never felt so wonderful.

In time for the performance, the black, hearselike carriages used to convey dance students from the school to the Mariinsky took Natalia's group the short distance between the two buildings. Natalia and Katya, who was to be an older girl at the Christmas party in the first scene, went to the dressing room reserved exclusively for members of the school. Katya chattered continuously, but Natalia said not a word, her thoughts riveted on the movements that she would have to perform. She put on her costume of pink tulle and her small headdress. A spot of rouge on each cheekbone, and that was that. Natalia fretted, and yet she yearned to feel a part of the Mariinsky, longing for the moment of almost nuptial blending of herself into the company of dancers, when she would cease to be set apart as a student and finally become her true self. Impatiently interrupting Katya, she said: "I must go to the water closet." Quickly she turned on her heels and left the room, which had begun to oppress her.

Natalia leaned against the door of the students' dressing room and shut her eyes. Red dots moved on the inside of her lids, and her mouth tasted of iron. She looked around and, seeing no one, ran on tiptoes through the corridors of the Mariinsky Theatre, in search of the room where she knew dancers of the *corps de ballet* must be preparing themselves. Now, for the first time, she did not want to be around other students: She wanted to see and be a part of the real world of ballet, to smell real makeup and listen to bona fide dancers as they gossiped before a performance.

She stood on the threshold of the dancers' dressing room, a very small, slight girl in a pink tutu, with a delicate, heart-shaped face and large almond eyes. Women were sitting at tables in front of mirrors, applying white powder and rouge to their faces and helping each other adjust wigs and climb into elaborate costumes of moiré silk and brocade. The heady odor of female sweat mingled thickly with that of musty clothes and cosmetics. Natalia watched, bemused, as large thighs gleamed before her, strong female thighs, less dainty than those of the younger students. Immodest bodices were exposed in ways that would have shocked the governesses of the school. Yet Natalia did not feel as though she were witnessing an improper sight. She felt, somehow, that here, and here alone, was reality. One pretty young woman whispered to a companion: "Are you being taken to Cubat for supper tonight, Marie?" And Natalia found herself yearning, from deep inside herself, for the privilege of being asked that question in such an easy manner. To belong!

So engrossed had she become in the women's conversation that she did not notice the approach of a tall, black-haired woman dressed as Clara's mother. "Well," the woman said in an undertone, " 'tis the spirit of the Sweet, I see."

Natalia looked up and saw a long face with strong features, not at all beautiful but distinctive, unforgettable. The woman had black eyes and a Roman nose. Natalia smiled. "Not at all sweet. Only the costume," she said.

"Ah. Good. I am allergic to sugar; it gives me indigestion."

Natalia began to laugh. She wondered if this woman would also be going to supper at Cubat, and if she shared Natalia's secret irritation with the symmetrical classicism of Petipa's ballets, considered beyond criticism at the school; and also, had she seen the American prodigy, Isadora Duncan, who had danced for St. Petersburg in her bare feet the previous year? The stranger belonged to the hallowed halls of the Mariinsky, while she herself was less than nothing, still half-formed. Yet this tall woman made Natalia feel welcome and accepted. Presently she said: "This is my first big role, but I am not going to dance the Sugar Plum Fairy sweetly. I have to understand her, or else I won't be able to be her. And I must enjoy myself."

"You're very self-confident for a student," the woman replied.

Natalia opened wide her brown eyes. "Not at all. I'm terrified. That's why I couldn't stay with the others. I might have been ill."

"No, you wouldn't have, or they'd never give you another important dance. What's your name?"

"Natalia Dmitrievna Oblonova. And you?" Suddenly Natalia felt shy. She would have preferred anonymity.

"I am Lydia Markovna Brailovskaya. I am a *coryphée*, and that, my dear, is what I shall remain to the end of my dancing days. Why I was ever raised from first line of the *corps*, I shall never understand. I loved it and performed adequately. Now I am allowed to dance in smaller groups, but I won't ever rise beyond that to soloist of the second degree. But you will. If you're to dance the Sugar Plum tonight, your teachers must already have singled you out. Whose class are you in? Guerdt's? Cecchetti's?"

"Guerdt's. Maestro Cecchetti is next year. Was he your teacher, too?"

"He is old enough to have been everybody's teacher. Now you must excuse me, Sugar Plum. The Party scene begins the action, and my wig is askew."

Natalia watched her companion mingle with the other dancers. Someone bent over the loose tendril of Lydia Markovna's wig and adjusted it, laughing. Natalia felt a pang of jealousy. Lydia could have asked her to do it, but who, after all, was Natalia Oblonova? Not even the lowliest member of the *corps de ballet*. And then she thought: But in five years, I shall be more than all these women; I shall be a soloist of the second degree. And with this thought to console her, she pushed aside the pain of being excluded.

Pierre Riazhin sat uncomfortably in the elegant stall overlooking the stage of the Mariinsky. His stiff back was hurting him. The tuxedo fit him too snugly, and the side part in his curly hair caused a bang to sweep over his brow, annoying him. He felt acutely ridiculous and resentful of Boris. Why had he listened to this dandy, and why had he allowed him to purchase this costly outfit as a gift? To be aided in one's career, when one possessed talent but no funds, was one thing; but to accept personal favors was quite another. It went totally against his grain.

There were other spectators in the Kussov stall, but Pierre refused to join their airy conversation about *entrechats* and Trefilova. He gathered that the ballet critic, Valerian Svetlov, was most fond of this ballerina, but that Boris preferred somebody called Egorova. Svetlov was seated on Boris's left, while Pierre was on his right. Boris was so engrossed in his talk with Svetlov, who sported a tuft of white hair that glistened from the chandeliers of the theatre, that he had carelessly thrown his right leg over his left, so that his right knee touched Pierre's thigh. Pierre attempted to move his own leg, but Boris's stubborn knee would not budge. Pierre yielded, annoyed. Everything was conspiring to prevent his relaxation.

The Mariinsky pleased him with its blue and silver decor, and Pierre was not above enjoying the luxury surrounding him. He could scoff at it when it was out of his reach, but when able to sample its splendor, he found it quite wondrous. He loved all that was beautiful, and with his opera glasses he scanned the other booths, relishing the sight of unknown ladies in *décolletés*, their diamonds ablaze. Pierre forgot his discomfort and his boredom with Boris and Svetlov by shutting out all but his sense of sight. He conjured up a vision of this assembly in parody: the ladies less dignified, their tiaras tilted on their lascivious heads, holding out sweets from delicate fingers to gentlemen who ate them on their knees. But Boris was speaking to him now, in low tones: *"The Nutcracker* is a delightful piece of fluff choreographed by Lev Ivanov. It's meaningless and sweet and a good beginning for you. The first woman with whom you dance should be like this ballet: utterly beautiful, marvelously synchronized, and not too intelligent. Good practice."

"I have seen other ballets," Pierre replied defensively.

"Well, so you have. But from a stall one can define the ballerina's movements in a totally different fashion. Valerian says that a student is dancing the Sugar Plum tonight. Rather an honor for her, I should say. I have never heard of her: Natalia Oblonova."

Trefilova, Egorova, and now Oblonova. Pierre smiled, but Boris misinterpreted the expression and patted him on the knee. The lights dimmed. The curtain went up, and Pierre sat transfixed. The stage setting glared back at him: Christmas tree, fireplace, sturdy furniture of the Biedermeier genre. He would have done this differently, with lighter touches denoting the fairy tale elements of the story. His tree would have spread out in delicate branchings and been covered with minuscule balls of colored foil, giving the impression of a myriad of diamond chips. His furniture would have been totally un-Germanic: ottomans of bright silks and velvets, matching vivid wall hangings and exotic curtains.

In spite of himself, Pierre was fascinated. The Party scene glittered, and the small children pirouetting before the assembled guests made him feel strange. Christmas had always been so simple in the Caucasus! This was a Hoffman fairy tale, but it also suggested the wonder of the Russian capital in its excessive sophistication. Contrary to the spontaneity of life itself, ballet was the most sophisticated art form, and it drew him by its perfect development, by its harmony. Yet the young man knew that these well-heeled gentlemen and perfumed ladies of

Petersburg had not come merely for the pleasure of watching children parading before a Christmas tree. His expectation grew, and he leaned forward, waiting.

All during the first act Pierre Riazhin waited. He began to fret. "The decor is heavy, like a burgher's wife," he finally whispered to Boris Kussov. He had rehearsed his words and was upset when the other laughed with easy irreverence. "What do you know of burghers and their spouses, my dear Khadjatur?" his elegant host murmured. "Have you ever visited Germany?"

"No, and you know I haven't," Pierre retorted, his pride stung. After that, he would not look at Boris and held himself aloof, while his impatience quickened. Children! Had he come merely to witness a battle between dressed-up mice and a giant nutcracker, to watch a small girl hurl her slipper at the Mouse King? And then, almost taking him by surprise, the curtain came down and the brilliant lights of the Mariinsky bloomed overhead. Pierre blinked, disillusioned.

During the intermission Boris, resplendent in his well-tailored tuxedo, his gray spats shining and his ruby and black pearl stud lending a strange distinction to his stock, rose rapidly and scanned the amphitheatre for familiar faces. "My sister is here," he said to Pierre. "My sister Nina, and her husband, Prince Andrei Stassov. I am going to Dumas, the French confiserie in the square, to purchase some candied fruit to take to her in their loge. Will you come with me?"

"If you don't mind," Pierre replied somewhat rudely, "I should like to stay here and watch the audience. There are so many interesting faces. . . ."

The other members of the party all followed Boris Kussov from the stall. But Pierre was not bored. He had not found the first act inspiring. Russian folk tales appealed to him far more than German and French, for, he thought, they possessed more passion and originality. The costumes of the party guests had upset him. They were too staid. He now sat with a small pad of paper and a pencil, both of which never left him, and started to sketch. He imagined settings, scenery, costumes, then strange faces from the stalls. He had become so preoccupied that a deep voice surprised him. "Where has Boris disappeared to?" a man asked.

Pierre turned around and saw a tall, powerfully built man with black hair in which a single lock shone completely white. He was immaculately dressed and wore a monocle. "Boris Vassilievitch has gone to pay a call upon his sister, I believe," Pierre said. He stood up awkwardly.

"Ah. I am Serge Pavlovitch Diaghilev. Why Boris wanted me to join him tonight is beyond me. I've seen a dozen *Nutcrackers*, and Teliakovsky's productions are in the worst possible taste. Tell me, who are you?"

"Pierre Riazhin. I—am a guest of Boris Vassilievitch. I am pleased to make your acquaintance, sir." Pierre regarded the other with a mixture of awe and pride. So this was Diaghilev, who led the group of artists known as the World of Art committee, named after the periodical which they had produced several years before. Diaghilev was a controversial man, a dilettante, a master of no single art yet able to pick out great artists in all fields. An opinionated man, he was the sworn enemy of Teliakovsky, director of the Imperial Theatres. Some said that he, not Teliakovsky, should be holding this position. Pierre had wanted to meet him almost more than he had wished to meet Léon Bakst and Constantin Somov, painters whom he admired and who were also part of the group to which Boris belonged. It was Diaghilev who welded all these artists together. Boris had been dangling the promise of this meeting before Pierre as though it were a golden apple to be earned: Though how Pierre was supposed to earn it, he had still not discovered. Boris was an enigma for the young Caucasian.

A thin young man had entered behind Diaghilev, and the older man said: "Alexei Mavrin, my secretary; Pierre Riazhin. Are you not that young painter about whom Boris has been telling me? Serov's student?"

"I did not know that Boris Vassilievitch had mentioned me," Pierre remarked. He appeared humbled.

"Now I know why Boris inveigled us to come tonight! A casual encounter. Truly, Boris must see some good in our meeting, and—we missed the first act. What do you think of what you've seen?"

Pierre sat down beside Diaghilev and began to tell him his impressions. As always, he was most confident where his work was concerned. He no longer felt ill at ease, or in awe of the other. This time his painter's eye put him in charge. When Boris and Svetlov returned, laughing, Pierre was showing his sketches to Diaghilev. Boris looked pleased, but he said very little, merely taking his seat between Pierre and Svetlov. But Pierre was suddenly touched: With what finesse Boris had arranged this encounter, allowing Pierre to meet Serge Pavlovitch as a fellow guest, equal to equal, rather than in Diaghilev's apartment in front of all the other members of the "committee"! He felt embarrassed and cleared his throat. "Boris Vassilievitch," he murmured, his voice unusually melodic and gentle, "I want to thank you."

Boris raised his fine golden eyebrows and nodded. He was holding a small box, which he now laid unobtrusively on the floor. But the curtain was rising once more, and silence descended moments before strains of Tchaikovsky's music filled the theatre with sound. The Land of Sweets was displayed, a candy box wherein the Sugar Plum Fairy was queen and mistress.

Natalia came out among the small pupils, the various sweets that peopled this land of fantasy. All at once calmness diffused through her from head to toe. Her nervousness had stilled, after its first quick flare-up behind the scenes, and the lights blinded her view of the spectators. She felt at ease forming the familiar steps. The Nutcracker-turned-Prince arrived with small Clara, and she thought: I know him, he was a senior last year, but I can't recall his name. The Prince did not smile at her; with singular sympathy she could understand why. She did not smile at him, either.

All at once they were performing their *pas de deux*, the short piece that was this ballet's dessert. In the Kussov stall, Pierre Riazhin suddenly came alert. He focused his opera glasses on the small billow of pink tulle swept into the air, horizontal above her partner, who was holding her by the thighs. Her tiny, boneless arms were like wings, her head reared up as though poised for flight. This was a teasing, impish fairy: translucent, ethereal, yet conspiratorial. Pierre began to smile. Next to him Boris had stiffened, and in the absolute stillness even Svetlov and Diaghilev seemed to have stopped breathing. Pierre's heart soared, as it had when he had ridden his beloved stallion bare-back in the Caucasus. Through the glasses he could define her face, the face of a figurine, with disproportionately large eyes, chin too small, and the nose perhaps too long. He wanted to cry out, but instead he bit his lip and regarded Boris. His patron had risen in his seat and was now flinging something from the stall, his features concentrated on the stage and the little ballerina.

Natalia saw nothing of her public, for the stage lights separated her from them, but at the back of her mind she was aware that flowers were being cast from the loges to the dancers' feet. She had been told that the dowager empress, Maria Feodorovna, was present, but this fact was meaningless to her moving limbs. She had blended with the air, created a momentum that made her magic. During the playing of Tchaikovsky's favorite instrument, the delicate celesta, Natalia even ceased being aware of her partner: He had become as separate from her as an icicle from red-hot fire—odorless, sexless, ageless, as distant as an angel from the human heart. This feeling of separateness created a disorientation that, added to the lights, made her dance with yet a stronger appeal to the unseen public. She seemed to say: Play with me, believe in me, but don't think that I am made to last!

It was over with the abruptness of an awakening. She curtsied to the bejeweled people in the stalls. Looking up briefly, she was startled to recognize the tall blond stranger whom she had encountered in the corridor of the Mariinsky. More luminous than the others, radiant as a bright bird, he could not be missed. Through a blur, she saw his raised arm; something was floating through the air over the heads of the orchestra players. It landed at her feet. Her Prince had seen it, too, and was now bending with infinite grace to retrieve it. He handed it to her with a courtly, sweeping gesture, and she executed her final *révérence* and disappeared as swiftly as a frightened doe, her face tingling, her limbs trembling. Behind the stage she did not stop, continuing her steps to allow the momentum to decrease naturally. Then it was over, truly over. She could hear the ovations from the theatre but already she had blanked them out.

No one had found her yet behind the scenes, and she

34 crouched down, touching the bouquet of rosebuds that the stranger had hurled to her. They lay nestled among soft leaves. She counted fifteen rosebuds, white, pink, red, and yellow. And then, curled between two sprigs of baby's breath, she saw a stiff card. Surprised and intrigued, she pulled it out, and saw a family crest embossed with a calligraphic name: Count Boris Kussov. Was the name familiar? He had scrawled below it: "May these herald full-blooded roses at the peak of their bloom." Suddenly she felt the presence of someone behind her and turned abruptly to face Lydia Markovna Brailovskaya.

"All alone, our Sugar Plum?" Lydia asked. "Finished with the *encores?*"

"Did you like it?" Natalia broke in hastily. "The way I danced her?"

"Infinitely better than I liked Clara," Lydia said and laughed. "You were adequate, lovey."

Natalia said nothing, but the color drained from her face. Lydia's eyes softened. "You were much more than that, and I think you know it. You were the most spirited Sugar Plum I have ever watched." Then, quickly looking away, she noticed the roses. "What's this?" she cried. "Your first admirer?"

"I'm not sure," Natalia responded hesitatingly. She handed Lydia the bouquet with its card. The other read it carefully, then raised her eyebrows quizzically and gave the flowers back to the young girl.

"The praises of Boris Vassilievitch are worth a mountain of roses," she commented wryly. "He is a true balletomane. He follows his favorite dancers to Moscow when they go. They say he organizes claques to applaud his pets, but I don't believe it. He's Svetlov's friend—you know, the ballet critic."

"Do you know him?" Natalia queried.

"I've met him. He's a magnificent man, yet I've never heard his name linked with a woman's. Perhaps he is discreet. He is much coveted in society. The Kussovs are an old aristocratic family, friends of the court ever since there's been one in Russia. But none of the Kussov men has ever worked to increase the fortune. Oh, there is a great deal of wealth—but I have heard that Count Vassily, Boris's father, is becoming worried. He is marrying off his two younger daughters, and Boris spends more money than any man in Petersburg. Soon, he will have to find a wife."

"But—why?"

"Ah, you are naïve, love," Lydia said. "For men such as Boris Vassilievitch Kussov, wives mean handsome dowries to recuperate funds lost by marrying off sisters. Although I don't suppose he'll have much trouble finding a lady to his taste—there are so many who would wish to be selected!"

Natalia began to laugh. "Well then, let's wish him luck!" she cried. "And I shall keep his rosebuds, for they have brought me luck, too, haven't they?"

In Boris Kussov's victoria, Pierre Riazhin, his cravat untied, his eyes wild and glowing like a cat's, was laughing. He had never felt such ecstasy in his twenty-two years of life, and the champagne that had flowed at the Aquarium nightclub had only improved his already ebullient mood. He had consumed it like water, and now his head spun round and round. "The Paris exhibition!" he cried over and over, remembering that Diaghilev had been impressed with his sketches and ideas, and had suggested that Pierre come by his apartment to show him some of his more serious work. He might include Pierre's work in the art exhibition which he was planning at the Grand Palais in 1906. Pierre could hardly believe his infinite good fortune.

"Naturally, there are no guarantees," Boris was saying somewhat cruelly. "Serge's taste—and that of our friends—is very particular."

Pierre's effervescence seemed to subside. He did not understand why his patron was placing a damper on his enthusiasm—he who had arranged this meeting with such apparent care. But Boris said: "Well? Are you going to accompany me to Prince Lvov's gathering?"

Pierre shook his head. "I don't think so, Boris Vassilievitch. I—have work to do." He glanced uneasily at his sponsor, whose fine profile seemed tightly drawn at this late hour.

"Work? Now?"

"Yes. I could never settle down if I tried to sleep. Too much excitement." He felt awkward about admitting what was on his mind. He had seen the loveliest creature in the world, an airborne sprite defying human limitations, and he wanted to rush home and commit her to paper. She was the sweetest, most mischievous fairy, a brilliant dancer. Svetlov had said so, too: "That is the first time I have seen a Sugar Plum with a sense of humor." And although he had added criticism of her *port de bras*, Pierre had felt that he had done so only to preserve his reputation for tough judgment.

Clearly, Boris had agreed with this approval. Pierre realized that the count had purchased flowers during the intermission, but that he had not thrown them down until the end. He had even written a few words on one of his visiting cards. Well prepared, Boris Vassilievitch: a bouquet in case he should become transported with enthusiasm. Pierre sorely regretted not having possessed his patron's foresight. Thinking about the ballerina, Pierre's former euphoria returned. "I have never seen anyone so wonderful as little Oblonova," he said. "Don't you think so, too?"

Carefully appraising the young man, Boris replied: "Ballet is still new to you. But yes, I agree. She combines character with fluid grace. That is very rare. However, I shall have to take you to a performance of the greats. Pierre, Kchessinskaya is too staid these days, but you will enjoy our new ballerinas: Pavlova, Karsavina, Kyasht."

Pierre shook his head in sudden animation. With profound emotion, he countered: "No, Boris Vassilievitch. As works of art, perhaps I shall appreciate these ladies, but for me, no one will ever surpass the charm, the absolute beauty, of Oblonova. I—I could love her."

"Oh? Tell me, Pierre—what do you really know about love? It seems to me you're being somewhat childish. Talented, yes: Of course, she's that. But—love?" His mouth turned down in a smile of irony, but he could feel his throat constricting. Boris smoothed his mustache in a mechanical gesture and looked out the coach window, past the blur of nighttime mist. "Love . . ." he intoned pensively, almost to himself. "Come now, Pierre. One doesn't love a woman from afar."

With sudden stubbornness the younger man resisted. "Then, I'll arrange to meet her." He glared at Boris. "Why should you

care, Boris Vassilievitch? Clearly you already know all the ballerinas and could make love to any one of them!"

Boris's stomach turned. He pressed a hand to it, containing
the crippling pain. Turning from the window, he stared directly
at the young painter, his eyes intense points of metal, sharp and
cruel. "Don't be an ass, Pierre," he said. "Let's drop this discussion, shall we?"

But the other refused to let go. Something in Boris's tone, a
verbal dismissal, had hurt his pride, and now he cried: "I see it
now! You're incapable of love, and so you envy me! You could
not understand my feeling for Oblonova. In my place you
would simply want her for a toy, to be displayed at your convenience. You fancy that artists are your friends, but you can't
grasp our fundamental soul, what makes us live and breathe! If
you ever felt love, it would not be the love we feel but something else, something tarnished, a need to *use*. Well, Oblonova
is not a mechanical doll that can be wound up for your pleasure. She is an artist, and only another artist can really be
touched by her performance. If I could meet her, I know that
she could love me, too. She would understand what lies in my
heart, and she would identify with my conception of the
world."

Boris now turned toward Pierre, and the young man suddenly
shivered. The count's face was distorted into a mask of Greek
tragedy, tight and ugly. He jabbed the young man in the chest
with an extended forefinger that seared like a talon. "You, my
friend, are going to pay for this," he whispered. "And may God
damn you straight to hell."

The coachman was now stopping in front of the shabby
building where Pierre rented a small apartment. Before the
horses had fully halted, the young artist pulled open the door
and jumped out. Boris watched as he ran into the building
without looking back. The points of fire in his stomach refused
to subside.

Chapter 3

rincess Marguerite Tumarkina sat very quietly next to Boris. She was a small, thin girl with a bust too large for her petite build. Her face was plain, with pale blue eyes, a small upturned and rather pleasant nose, and very slight, bloodless lips. Her hair was a dull blond, and too thin, so that the elaborate pompadour that dominated her head was always threatening to come tumbling down. Tendrils curled around her forehead, and she looked uncomfortable with herself, as if her natural state beneath her finery was one of shy simplicity and dull predilections. Or so Boris thought, speaking with her.

"You do not like Italian opera, Marguerite Stepanovna?" he now asked.

"I—I do not know enough about it for discussion," she replied and bit her lower lip. She was embroidering a cushion in petit point and now averted her eyes to look intently at her work.

"That is fine artistry," he commented, taking a corner of the material and examining it. "Marguerite Stepanovna, you must see the jewel that is our Mikhailovsky Theatre—all orange velvet and silver. I shall take you there to hear *La Traviata*. Our singers are magnificent—Battistini, the baritone, and the Swedish soprano, Arnoldson. You will be enchanted."

She looked at him then, the color gone from her thin little face. I'll be damned, he thought. She resembles a scared rabbit cornered by a hunting dog! He enjoyed his own analogy. But she smiled, and tiny green and gold flecks shone in her eyes, and a spot of pink jumped into her skin where it was tightly drawn over her cheekbones.

"If you would like to go, of course I shall be glad to accompany you, Boris Vassilievitch. You—are so attentive. But you do not have to feel obligated to take me. The Brianskys have been most kind to me, and I am not bored. You—mustn't worry."

Good God, he thought; but he inclined his head and smiled. "It is my pleasure," he murmured. "I never forgot our encounter in Kiev years ago." Indeed no, he added wryly to himself.

She blushed to the very roots of her hair, and did not answer. Presently he took out his gold watch and exclaimed: "Dear Marguerite Stepanovna, you must forgive me! I am late for a meeting."

"But of course. An artistic meeting, Boris Vassilievitch?"

He appeared surprised. "Why, yes. Had I mentioned it?"

She shook her head, which was top heavy and garnished with a thick comb of mother-of-pearl. "Count Briansky told me that you are a great patron of the arts. He says that you have helped painters, and that you love the Imperial Ballet. I have done some water colors, and play the piano, of course—but I do not know any artists." She looked wistfully at him, and he thought, Now she will want to play me a sonata, to please my artistic tastes. . . . Damn Briansky!

"I truly must leave you," he stated, and bowed over her frail hand. His senses were rebelling against his rational mind, which argued that she was not, after all, such a bad sort. But reason could do little to dispell the revulsion he was feeling toward Marguerite.

She was drab, timid, not as cultured as a girl of her station should have been—but perhaps that was due more to a deficiency in taste and intellect rather than education. Other men had wives such as this one stashed away in elegant palaces on the Quays—and surely this little rodent of a girl would hardly be bold enough to impose her own predilections upon the furnishings, or bemoan his absences. Still, his entire being shied away from Marguerite Stepanovna, and it was with physical relief that he stepped outside the Briansky mansion and into his waiting victoria. He began to hum an aria from *La Traviata*, then stopped suddenly. He had committed himself to escorting her to hear the opera, and he would choke rather than bring the agony closer by association.

He was going to meet Walter Nouvel and the painter Léon Bakst, friends who had been associated with the Diaghilev projects for many years. Boris had known Nouvel during their adolescence at the May Gymnasium, although the other man was five years his senior. Bakst had joined the group later. He was a red-haired, elegantly attired Jew who had been born "Rosenberg" and had adopted the name of his maternal grandfather; Bakst was nearsighted, and his small mustache matched the high color of his hair. His background was very different from that of any other member of the group. He did not possess a university degree, but not because, like Diaghilev, he had abandoned his studies; indeed, he had never begun them. As a Jew, he had not known the easy, aristocratic life of his companions during early youth; his social class was rooted in commerce. Young Pierre Riazhin had most attached himself to Bakst; not only did he admire the vivid tone of his work, but having begun as an outsider, too, Pierre felt drawn to him.

They were to have met at Boris's apartment, and now, because of Marguerite, he was late. Ivan had settled his friends in the sitting room, with a plentiful supply of tea and cakes. He joined them. Bakst had brought some samples of the gold brocades with which he planned to hang the icons in the Salon d'Automne of the Grand Palais during the exhibition of two hundred years of Russian painting, concerning which project Diaghilev was in Paris making further arrangements. "And is Pierre going to contribute anything?" Boris asked nonchalantly.

"Several pieces," Bakst replied. "One is most interesting—of a ballerina. Have you seen it? Nothing so dark as Degas's works. This one is full of joy, incandescent. I have never heard of this girl, but after seeing Pierre's rendition, I am much intrigued."

Boris regarded his friend with a level gaze. "I dare say," he commented dryly. He was somewhat shocked: Pierre had never shown him the canvas in question. Yet Pierre always came to him first. If this was to hang at the Paris exhibition, then surely the boy must have known that Boris would see it then. Why then, and not now?

Walter Nouvel, who was most knowledgeable in music and had straight, intelligent features, now said: "Boris, there is a slight problem. Serge's calculations fell somewhat short, and the patrons—Grand-Duke Vladimir and the others—have already clinched their various contributions. We shall need a loan."

"Oh? A Kussov loan, I presume?"

Nouvel smiled. "We have all given what we could. You have more at your disposal than the rest of us."

Boris frowned. "But at this moment, I have less than usual. Damn it, Walter, you know it isn't a loan that's needed, but a donation. Do you remember my sister Nina's wedding the Christmas of '04? It now appears that my father intends in the near future to marry both my other sisters off in similar pomp. Even the Tzar's own marriage was no more extravagant. Why Liza couldn't have waited—well, in any case, my yearly income will be smaller because of these family expenditures. Father would not understand that our needs are more important than placing his three daughters on display in Petersburg. One day the girls will die, but Russian art will continue. Tell that to him!"

Bakst touched the bridge of his pince-nez spectacles and smiled. "And your princess from Kiev?"

"I can't stand her. Forget that idea, Léon, once and for all."

"Your father hinted to the grand-duke that you were not indifferent to the girl."

"Certainly not indifferent. My father is attempting to force my hand." But Boris had no wish to pursue the issue. He compressed his anger within him until it had become a bar of fired metal, but he continued to converse, offering cakes to his two guests. They left with the question of the donation unresolved.

Boris went into his bedroom and stood absorbed in front of the small fireplace. Gnawing at the insides of his mouth, pressing his hands together dryly, he thought of his friends—of Serge Diaghilev, the artistic entrepreneur, of dapper Walter Nouvel, of Bakst, with his amusing flights into romantic involvements. He had willed himself aloof from them, and from the others—Benois, Somov—so many times since his first encounter with them as a youth at the May Gymnasium. Their families were good, his was better. In education and culture he equaled the best of them. Yet they were creators, and he had never held the illusion of being able to wrest art from himself. Still, that art lay at the very core of his being, and so he knew that he needed them more than they needed him, that the funds they required of him were nothing compared with the loss that he would feel if he were suddenly to be free of them, of the magic of their visions. Why was peace so impossible for him to attain, and especially to hold onto? The fire mesmerized him, hypnotized him until the bar of metal dwindled slightly in his stomach. But the depression would not lift.

Marguerite wore a cloak of pale blue velvet lined with white ermine, its hood covering her small head beneath its pompadour. It was really too cold for a walk, but Boris seemed to need the brisk exercise, and she had not wished to refuse his request. He appeared disturbed, and she, who absorbed others' moods like a sponge, was growing nervous. The Summer Garden stretched before them; they were like moving figures in a still life, and she thought that the large statues seemed grotesque replicas of a time when the sun had shone and blood had coursed through human veins. Now, only she and Boris traversed this lovely French-styled park, only he and she existed in this frozen landscape. In Kiev there were the sugar plantations, enormous stretches of flat ground. But she had pictured more movement in the capital, and the emptiness gave her a headache.

What was it that Boris wanted? She sneezed and tried to keep pace with his long strides. She was certain that her father was concerned for her, and that he had forced her to come here for a reason. She had never before wanted to leave the safety of her home—not since that awful year when everything had turned into a dark hole and she had stopped sleeping. Even now the memory of Baron Revin made her eyes burn. He had not loved her—had not found her worthy. Or had someone told him stories of her frail constitution, of her fainting spells? Because she was genuinely sickly, nobody knew how frequently she had enlarged on this weakness and literally made herself black out or attain heights of hysteria when she rolled on the floor—to frighten her parents or her nurse into granting her fulfillment of a wish. She had wanted Revin, had wanted somehow to bind him to her, and in the effort Marguerite had become very ill. But Revin had returned to Moscow without proposing marriage. She had set her mind to win him and had failed. Even her considerable dowry had failed. After that her parents had sent her to the rest home in Switzerland. And since then she had been afraid to appear much in public. She knew that some of her former friends in Kiev said that she was crazy, that there was a streak of insanity in her that could resurface at the least provocation. But the Brianskys were most kind to her, and as for Boris—who could have hoped for a more enviable escort?

Suddenly she did not want to hear what Boris had to say. She already knew what it would be: He had not wanted to mislead her, but he did not care for her. Somebody must have told him about the sanitarium. She clasped her hands together until they hurt. She had not allowed herself to want a life, any kind of life outside her calm existence in Kiev—until now. Going out into Petersburg society with this handsome, intelligent man—she did want this, desperately. She remembered wanting a ruby necklace once in Geneva and sitting down in the middle of the street with her arms crossed, while coachmen maneuvered, cursing, around her, until her father had been forced to give in and purchase the gems. She had been barely twelve years old at the time. No, most decidedly, today she did not want to hear Boris's excuses. Marguerite uttered a small cry and started to run, light as a sparrow, across the snow-covered park.

At first Boris watched her erratic advance in bewilderment. Then, with annoyance, he ran after her. His steps were longer, quicker than hers, and soon he had reached her side. "What on earth—?" he began, then stopped, for the small pale face turned to look at him with an intensity of emotion that robbed him of speech. She bit her lip until it was almost bleeding, and he saw that the rims of her pale eyes were red. "What is it, Marguerite Stepanovna?" he asked. Her expression was so strange that he felt ill at ease so close to her.

She took a step toward him and stood right in front of him, her hands touching the lapels of his coat. "Do you love me?" she whispered.

He thought he had surely mistaken the question. "I beg your pardon?"

"I said: 'Do you love me?' Because you see, it is essential that you love me. I *need* your love! Now you must propose marriage to me."

Boris felt that he had entered a dream, or rather a nightmare. "Marguerite Stepanovna—" he began, but she interrupted him, putting a finger on his lips.

"Don't speak unless you love me," she said. Her cheeks were flushed. Boris thought: Perhaps the sickness has resurfaced and she is truly becoming insane. Had his own father done this to him? What was he to do? Such a wave of revulsion swept over him that for an instant Boris thought he would vomit. Then the nausea drained away, and when he regarded Marguerite once more, she too seemed to have calmed down, returned to normal. She had stepped back a decorous distance from him, and her face was pale and reserved, if somewhat embarrassed. She said, tremulously: "It's all right, Boris Vassilievitch. I am sorry."

But the incident could hardly be erased. He gave her his arm but could not help trembling with ill-concealed repugnance. They resumed their promenade, each silently locked with his own thoughts. She was, in actuality, too afraid to think. But he was pondering the question of the loan, or the donation, to the committee of friends. What would happen if no one came up with these funds? And afterward? There would be further shortages, further demands. He had absolutely no illusions: His friends liked him well enough, but among all these gifted people, his most important contribution was money. And he needed them more than they needed his money. He lived through all of them, and if he were to be excluded from their enclave— It was better not even to formulate the thought.

And Pierre. Pierre was going to exhibit some work in Paris. His future reputation might be made at such a show. Pierre had not shown him the painting of the girl, the dancer, and Boris knew exactly why. Pierre was learning to play the game by Boris's own rules, and this was not good; it was even dangerous.

Children, or those endowed with the naïveté of children, should not be permitted to manipulate events to suit their own fancy, to play at being gods. Pierre had to be allowed to go to Paris—for the sake of all concerned. The Tumarkin dowry would amply cover the expenses of the exhibition, and no Kussov funds would need to be probed: His father would be relieved, Pierre would be grateful, and the Sugar Plum would reenter the realm of a simple artwork. Because it could be no other ballerina but that one, he knew.

Before he had a chance to regret it, Boris turned very rapidly to Marguerite and said thickly: "You were right, and there is no need to apologize. This is the moment to ask for your hand in marriage. Will you permit me to take the first train to Kiev in order to speak to your father? For we must be married soon, my dear. We cannot wait."

"I had no idea your feelings were—so deep," she stammered. And then, piteously, she burst into tears.

Right after their wedding in Kiev, Boris took Marguerite to Moscow for a honeymoon trip. He had not wanted to take her to Paris, for Serge Diaghilev and their friend Alexander Benois were there, preparing for the exhibition. He did not want to be seen by his friends with his new wife. And to travel with her to Rome, or to the Greek islands, such spots of charm that seemed to spell romance, would have been a violation of himself and of these places. So he selected Moscow. It was interesting and not too far. He would not feel cut off from the world there, alone with her, or forced to provide for her every need. Consequently, they took the train and spent their first night together in a spacious Pullman. He settled her politely into her berth and returned to the compartment only after she had turned out the light. If she was disappointed, she did not say; he did not ask. But in Moscow he knew he would have to face this dreadful error he had made.

He liked this city: It was typically Russian, with wide streets, mostly unpaved, bordered by lovely houses of one or two stories, with façades of delicately wrought stone or graceful pillars.

Moscow possessed four hundred churches, as well as museums and historical monuments. The Kremlin was a city unto itself, with its own churches, large and small palaces, houses built at various epochs and of different architectural styles—a heterogeneous conglomeration that was nonetheless imposing. Boris took his bride to visit it as soon as they arrived. Then he brought her to the Slavinsky Bazaar, a restaurant where the waiters were clothed in white, their collars and cuffs adorned with embroidery, and a wide, supple belt cinching their waists. He ordered a traditionally Russian meal for her: borsht, *pirozhkis* filled with cabbage, chicken, and for dessert, kissel, a fruit-and-sugar compote. They drank kvass, the ordinary peasant drink made from fermented wheat. Marguerite thought the dinner a vast success and laughed nervously during its progression. Her cheekbones were very red and she clenched and unclenched her hands a dozen times.

He had reserved the bridal suite at the Hôtel de l'Ours, and when he took her upstairs, he said: "I think that I should like to walk around a little, my dear." While he was gone, she readied herself, but he did not return as quickly as she might have expected. He had gone downstairs then out into the city, his mind a fog and an angry blur. She rang for the hall maid and expressed concern: It was past one in the morning, and it was cold outside. But he had forgotten the time, willing himself to forget it. It was only when the church chimes in some godforsaken neighborhood rang two o'clock that he shook himself from his stupor. Nobody could help him now. God had long ago stopped caring, for Boris had himself left religion behind him in his adolescence. And who else would have brought comfort to a man of thirty-three, fit and able?

He retraced his steps, hoping that Marguerite would have possessed sufficient sense and modesty to have gone to sleep. He entered the sitting room and received a jolt: The chandelier was brightly lit. He heard her moaning slightly, and there she was, on the threshold of the bedroom, her long, thin blond hair spread like a mantle over the bony shoulders. "Oh, Boris!" she cried. "My darling, are you quite well? What happened?"

Attempting to avoid her eyes, he said with annoyance, "I am not accustomed to being watched, Marguerite. I've lived too many years as a bachelor for you to expect me to change my ways so quickly. I merely stepped out, that's all. If you become hysterical every time this happens, I shall not be able to tolerate it."

"But this is our wedding night!" she exclaimed. Her shoulders drooped. "Boris—please. I'm your wife now. The train—"

At this he suddenly became very red and glared at her. "Are you, or are you not, a lady?" he asked her roughly. "If you are, then pray behave as one. I took you to be modest." And abruptly, trembling all over, he turned away. There was a decanter of Napoleon brandy upon the sideboard in the sitting room, and he tried to pour himself a thimbleful. His hand could not stop shaking. He spilled the liquor. Marguerite watched him, truly terrified now and also ashamed. She began to whimper.

He turned to face her, and thus to face his own demons squarely. Her large breasts, unsupported in the frail lace of the nightgown, loomed ominously in his field of vision, and he felt a surge of illness. If only she had been compact, well muscled, and small. Her bones showed in the wrong places, and the breasts—oh, God! the breasts! He swallowed down a spew of bile and clutched the sideboard for support. After all, it couldn't be worse than the cocottes of his early youth. Remember that: It couldn't be worse. At least she was not vulgar, as they had been.

He followed her into the bedroom, attempting to summon his strength of character, recalling phrases he had heard concerning his strength. Men wished to remain on Count Boris's good side, for he was a fierce opponent. Men were afraid of him. He possessed a will of iron. He wanted to laugh and to follow that with countless bottles of vodka. Instead he watched her lie quietly upon the coverlet of the magnificent bed. He removed his coat, his jacket. He went into the bathroom and undressed completely. Too late for the bath that his body craved. He placed an elegant maroon dressing gown over his nudity, tied it securely, and emerged into the bedroom once more.

Then he came to her and sat down upon the bed, while the lights still blazed in the lamps. He pulled the silk gown from her shoulders and looked at her, fully. The stomach was nearly concave, with the pelvic bones showing. The breasts flopped loosely. She had shut her eyes in misery, aware of his scrutiny and not understanding. Tears formed in the inner corners of her eyes, but he had no pity for her. In one swift move he took the coverlet and pulled it over her. Silently he left the room, reentered the bathroom, and donned his dinner clothes and his shoes. He took three bills from his wallet and left them on the sink. He was not fully conscious of performing these tasks, knowing only that they could not be avoided.

Then Boris Kussov slipped from his bridal suite into the corridor, and from the corridor into the early Moscow dawn. He hailed the first coach he saw, and told the driver to take him to the station. There he purchased a first-class ticket to St. Petersburg.

More and more frequently now, Natalia did not spend her Sunday leaves with Katya's family. Their predictable gaiety and teasing, their large meals interspersed with gentle stories about old Russia, and their summers in the country seemed oppressive now that they were no longer new. It was almost as if the Balins had two daughters, and she was one of them. They fretted and fussed about her health, about her occasional sad moods, about her abstraction. They tried to teach her to be a lady, with mild manners and a kind, sweet disposition. Natalia had lived sufficient years without the benefit of parents; now their efforts bored her somewhat and made her impatient. Instead, she visited Lydia Markovna Brailovskaya.

Lydia lived alone with her old nurse in a small apartment not far from the school and the Mariinsky. It was on a side street, pleasantly shaded in the spring and rather dark during the winter. Manya, the old nurse, was devoted to Lydia but had grown too old to be of much use to her in the house; she had remained because Lydia loved her, and because she was the only person who represented "family" to the *coryphée*. Natalia liked the old peasant woman, and found her gruff, superstitious admonitions amusing and touching.

Lydia was the daughter of a *premier danseur* at the Mariinsky, a friend of Pavel Guerdt and Enrico Cecchetti. He had died several years before, and though he had not bequeathed his talent to his daughter, she had inherited his friends. Lydia was invited places by members of the Ballet, by Chaliapin, the *basso profundo*, and by the French actors who played during the winter season at the Mikhailovsky Theatre. She knew everyone in this varicolored world of theatre folk. She also learned St. Petersburg gossip more quickly than anyone. Natalia found her biting wit a challenge: Here was a person who was interested in Natalia's thoughts, in her own irreverence. And Lydia did not treat Natalia as an inferior because of the ten years that separated them. She recognized that Natalia had bypassed childhood.

By Lent, the scandal over Count Boris Kussov's marriage to Princess Marguerite Tumakina had erupted full scale, and Lydia said to Natalia: "Your admirer has certainly engendered a mess. At court people have formed two camps—the Kussov one and that of the Tumarkins, Princess Marguerite's family. It must be difficult for the Imperial Family. The Kussovs are old court retainers of the highest aristocracy, but Princess Marguerite is the niece of the provincial governor of the Ukraine. A fine stew!"

"You know more about this than I do," the girl replied, shrugging. "At school we hear virtually nothing intriguing."

"I remember what it's like. Well, this is the crux of the issue: Count Boris claims that the marriage was annulled because he had not been properly informed of her previous bout with mental illness, and that insanity was starting to manifest itself during the wedding trip. Hence, he claims that the Tumarkins duped him on purpose. They, on the other hand, say that he abandoned her on their honeymoon without consummating the marriage, and that, therefore, the annulment was procured on their behalf. All these humiliating details have been brought to the surface because of the matter of the dowry. If indeed he married her in good faith and discovered that she was not in total possession of her faculties, then he should retain the money. But if she was the wronged party, then naturally he must return it in full. The Tzar, I'm told, thinks that Count Boris should keep half. I presume the judge will agree with this settlement. That way, nobody comes out stronger than anybody else."

Natalia raised her fine, arched brows. "She was a fool to subject herself to marriage in the first place. She could have used her income to travel—to see the world, to enhance her education. Now what will become of her? Or is she really—debilitated?" She motioned to her forehead.

"I wouldn't have the slightest idea. There must be a grain of truth in it somewhere, or Count Boris wouldn't have the temerity to state it. But—do you know?—they say she's already engaged again—to someone else, of course. To a Prussian man, Baron von Baylen—he's first secretary at the German embassy. Clearly her parents want to speed up this wedding so that people here will forget the other scandal. I've never formally met the woman, but I saw her once at Cubat with Count Boris, before their marriage—if one can call it that. She's a rather nondescript little person, but not really bad looking. He resembled a peacock next to a moorhen. He is splendid, isn't he? But not a nice man."

Natalia grinned. "Oh? That makes him distinctly more interesting. Do you think either of them will stay in the city after this? I mean—wouldn't you think each of them would want to escape for a little while before coming back to court and everything?"

"Count Boris is planning to be in Paris for the art exhibition. In the meantime, I don't believe he'll go out of his way to appear at functions attended by the Tzar and Tzarina! Alexandra, especially, is very straightlaced, as was her grandmother, Queen Victoria."

Natalia yawned. Queen Victoria was definitely not a pet subject of hers.

On Palm Sunday, the ballet school held its annual performance at the Mikhailovsky Theatre. Natalia had the most important role of the evening, although she had not been told that her masters intended to judge that very night whether she should be allowed to complete her schooling the following year, in May 1907, rather than a year later with the other girls in her class. She was sixteen now and would be young if they granted her this rare permission. Varvara Ivanovna, the school directress, was doubtful. She kept her girls under strict supervision and held praises at bay. Exceptions made her acutely uncomfortable, and she did not want little Oblonova to lose her levelheadedness.

Natalia was to dance Aspitchia in an abbreviated version of *The Daughter of Pharaoh*, the ballet that had marked the start of Marius Petipa's stint as choreographer of the Imperial Ballet. This ballet had also turned back the style of dance from the romanticism dominant in Europe during the twenties to that of classicism. Now the younger dancers criticized Petipa for his unwillingness to change to a more natural fashion of ballet; some had actually formed a coalition during the politically troubled end of 1905 in an attempt to break the rigid dominance of the French Petipa and his assistant, Lev Ivanov. But their efforts had come to nothing. Natalia had ardently supported them in her heart, but had been too sheltered at the school to aid them in person.

Lydia had told Natalia all about it, for she had been involved in the committee meetings. She had told Natalia that much promise lay in the young *premier danseur*, Fokine, and that he should be watched; also, that Pavlova was keenly jealous of Karsavina, who was a gentle creature, and a lady.

The Daughter of Pharaoh was an opulent Nubian drama that offered one of the best opportunities for miming that Natalia had ever encountered. The entire ballet revolved around Aspitchia; in fact, when it was shown in its entirety, this character did not leave the stage for the entire four acts. Petipa had provided an exercise in virtuosity, while transforming a Russian girl into a Nubian princess. Natalia loved the dramatic challenge of this character change and liked the Eastern abstract patterns of her long tutu embroidered in gold thread.

The annual performance of the ballet school was not only attended by family and teachers, but also by the most ardent devotees of the dance, such as the critics Svetlov and Skalkovsky. Members of the court came as well, most frequently represented by Grand-Duke Vladimir. Among the students would be found future *prima ballerinas* and *premier danseurs*, and the connoisseurs wished to be the first to discover new talent. Natalia stepped out onto the well-watered floor of the little theatre and looked out to her public. The grand-duke was in the imperial box; but, to the girl's utmost surprise, next to him sat the Tzarina, her pale red hair setting off the milk-white features beneath it. Natalia was suddenly very apprehensive. She had never seen Alexandra Feodorovna from so close.

Then again lights glared and Natalia ceased to see faces before her. She entered the body of the passionate Aspitchia, in love with Taon. Pugni's music carried her like a wave. She had studied this part so long and thoroughly because she had to mime her story to the audience, and she liked Pavel Guerdt, who had coached her, and wanted him to be proud of her. She had forgotten the Tzarina but not Guerdt, whose watching eyes she could almost feel. Behind her danced the *corps*, Katya among them. They were Natalia's own Greek chorus, underscoring her drama.

In the third act she perspired a great deal, for this was a Petipa extravaganza to show off her skill on *pointes*. She could feel a muscle contracting strangely as she rose, leaped, and turned, but the cramp did not set in, as she had feared. She felt so relieved that sheer primal joy coursed through her: She was vanquishing the difficult piece, taming her recalcitrant body by the sheer strength of her will.

Amid pyramids, palaces, and a fisherman's hut, Natalia danced, her face red and glistening. At the end, when she had successfully convinced the King of Nubia to allow her to marry her lover, exultation shone through her performance. She had triumphed. Aspitchia had won, and so had Oblonova. Natalia made her *révérence* and went offstage, her eyes tingling, stars shining before her. She stumbled. A gaping black hole sucked her inside it, and she collapsed at the feet of her teacher, Guerdt, who had come to give her his approval.

She came to in a small room, and found herself on a narrow cot, surrounded by men and women whose faces she could not place but who spoke loudly in her ears so that their voices rang. Somebody was applying ice water to her temples. "It's all right, *ma petite*," Pavel Guerdt said, and, recognizing him, she closed her eyes again. Somebody fanned her. Then a female voice burst in excitedly: "Quick, get up, Natalia! The Tzarina is coming!"

The next few minutes seemed like a collage of haphazard

images to Natalia. The door swung on its hinges, and she saw the cold, clear features of the empress. Natalia sank down in a profound curtsy and did not rise until a thick hand tilted her chin upward. She gazed with consternation into the large face of Grand-Duke Vladimir. "So," he remarked, as though he had been on speaking terms with her for many years, "the little flower wilts before we can see it."

"I am sorry, Your Excellency," Natalia stammered.

"Pah! Sorrow is for the dead." His jovial laugh surrounded her as a warm blanket.

"You were lovely, Natalia Dmitrievna," the Tzarina said. "I wished to present you with this trinket in memory of today." She handed the girl a small box decorated with her portrait in painted enamel. Natalia's fingers shook as she received it, and she curtsied again, unable to utter a syllable. Then the door opened, other people entered, and the Tzarina and her husband's uncle departed with Varvara Ivanovna. Natalia wished desperately to be alone, and in the tumult of voices in the room she slipped onto the floor, mingling with the legs of her well-wishers. She leaned her head against the post of the cot, and allowed the conversations to float above her. Nobody seemed to notice her there, and she felt better.

Slowly the room began to empty, the din to recede. The door opened once more, and Natalia, her feet tucked unceremoniously beneath her tutu, saw the blond man whom she had encountered months before in the darkened corridor of the Mariinsky. "Count Boris," she intoned with amazement. It was not a greeting but rather an exclamation of surprise. The people in the room turned to him with interest, some executing curtsies. She did not move, her entire body as heavy as stone.

He bowed, his mocking smile for her alone. "I see you know my name," he said.

"I couldn't help but know it." The implication, impolite in the extreme, made him wince. She cleared her throat. "I should not have said that."

"No, indeed. But you did, so why retract it? My own reputation is much tarnished these days, I'm afraid. Yours, however, is on the rise. My friend Svetlov finds you quite marvelous, Natalia Dmitrievna."

"Monsieur Svetlov has my profound gratitude." She was still stunned and knew that her conversation, directed as it was from her position on the floor, contained an element of absurdity.

"Your Aspitchia was a most intelligent young woman," Boris commented. "But I prefer your funny little Sugar Plum Fairy. In that ballet you were quite remarkable. Perhaps, when you finish with this nunnery, you will accept an invitation to have supper with me. I should like to toast you properly with the best champagne."

"You are most generous, Count Boris. But I am not to graduate for a long time." She could not help smiling at the idea of drinking wine with this elegant man suggestive of scandal. She said impulsively: "Your rosebuds have brought me good luck. Thank you."

"And did you press them in your Bible?"

"I don't read the Bible," she replied with some asperity. "But yes, I pressed them. I am not a sentimental fool—but I am a dancer, and they were a memento of my first serious performance. Even Satan's wife would have found something to save from such an occasion!"

In her confusion she had become angry, and he burst out laughing. "That is very good! Satan's wife. I shall have to remember that one and tell it to my friends. But here, I have brought you something this time, too, although as a nun you won't have much use for it, I'm afraid. But it was made by Fabergé—or rather, the oysters made it, and he put it together."

He leaned toward her, extending his finely manicured hand in a mock courtly gesture. She shook her head, bewildered and a little frightened, opening wide her brown eyes to encompass the red velvet case he was holding. "Don't be silly," he admonished. "Open the damned thing."

She took it gingerly. The velvet felt softer than anything she had ever touched, like a rose petal. She moved the little gold button in the center, and the case opened. She was staring at a row of perfect pink pearls held by a ruby clasp. Her lips parted, and her breath stopped on a sudden intake. "I can't," she said.

"Why not?"

"Because there is no reason for this. I have never seen anything like this necklace. It is exquisite, and I have done nothing to deserve it. I—" She reddened, swallowed, then plunged in, looking him in the eye: "I am not your mistress."

This time he had to grasp the doorknob to keep from falling down with laughter. Natalia rose, holding out the box. He shook his head, no, but her eyes suddenly hardened with determination, and she did not slacken her arm. They had begun to draw the attentive glances of the others in the room. His blue eyes narrowed, became very cold. "Take it," he ordered, and she shivered slightly. "Take it, little girl, and don't cause a scene. I can afford such a gift, and if you knew anything at all about me, beyond tawdry gossip, you would have learned that I love all the arts and all good artists. What is the difference between the roses bought with hours of toil by a poor man in the gallery and these pearls purchased by a Kussov? I assume you would accept the former."

She remained speechless. He adjusted his cravat, and his expression changed back to one of mirth. "However—consider this, Natalia Dmitrievna: Many men will ask you to bestow your favors upon them. But before you decide to—shall we say— 'become a mistress,' remember me. You owe me first priority."

He walked out of the room, closing the door behind him. The red velvet case was still in her hand. Natalia could not think. The room began to spin, and she faltered toward the cot, falling upon it blindly. Tears filled her eyes, overflowed, and filled them again. A sob was wrenched from her chest, then a second, a third. Uncontrolled trembling passed over her body in great, tumultuous waves. A woman came to her and touched her hair. Natalia felt as though she were in the very eye of a tornado.

The pearls slipped from their case onto the floor, where the yellow light captured their myriad hues—blue, green, pink, gray. Natalia did not see them, for she was weeping. She wept as never before and did not know why. But her body seemed to warn her of a cataclysm before which she knew she possessed no power.

Later that night, Boris sat fingering his mustache. He would have given half of his fortune to have seen Pierre's portrait.

August in the Netherlands was not as suffocating as it would have been in Russia, Pierre Riazhin thought. It was such a small country, and so near France—but how different, how self-contained! A tiny paradise of clean, bright charm, with its planned canals, its varieties of tulips in bloom, and its neat red-brick houses with pots of colored flowers in every window. It might be the 1600s—except, of course, that I never lived then, Pierre reminded himself with sudden amusement. I remain solidly anchored in 1907.

He was strolling with Boris along the quiet streets of The Hague. Now his companion turned to him and, catching the smile, said, "I can see that this trip has done you some good, at least. You seem less bored than the diplomats, I must say."

"The countryside is beautiful, Boris Vassilievitch—a place that could spawn the Great Masters and Vincent Van Gogh could hardly bore me. The peace is almost soporific—I could remain here forever. Though perhaps after some years I might grow restless."

Boris stroked his mustache and idly contemplated the symmetrical perfection of a small town house. "You can dispense with the patronym, really now, Pierre. We are friends, aren't we? No need for formality. I shouldn't say this—God forbid that it should leak back to good old Nelidov!—but if it weren't for the refreshing atmosphere provided by your artistic appreciation of this little flatland, I, on the other hand, would wither away from lassitude. For the life of me, I cannot understand what possessed Nelidov to ask for me to join his delegation to the Peace Conference."

Pierre looked at the blond count in his elegant gray suit with its stiff collar and stock, gaiters, and gold cufflinks. "You are the picture of a dapper diplomat," he answered, smiling.

"It's all a front. Underneath, I couldn't care less." Boris burst out laughing, his mirth so engaging that Pierre, although somewhat reluctantly, had to join him. The young man was still wary of his elder. Now Boris said pensively: "Nelidov and my father are friends. Nelidov, you know, doesn't believe in this second Hague Conference. Neither does the Tzar. Peace will not be accomplished by a lot of stuffy little men who purposely choose to skirt the very heart of the peace issue: a slowdown in armaments. Yet you mention the words and these men pale, cough with embarrassment, and change the topic very rapidly. Poor Nelidov did not wish to be president. I suspect that he did not know whom to bring along for pleasure and so chose me because I can amuse him between sessions."

"Yes, and my role is the same, isn't it?" said Pierre. "You amuse Nelidov, and I amuse you. The men behind the scenes."

Boris appraised the young painter shrewdly, thinking that he detected a note of bitterness in the repartee. "If I had to be pulled away from more interesting pursuits," he replied, "and get stuck with two hundred fifty pedants inside a musty hall of the Dutch Parliament, surely your lot is not comparable. A pleasure trip to help broaden you in your field—now isn't that the traditional gift of a patron to a talented artist? Cheer up, or I shall regret my investment. Rembrandt wouldn't have complained."

They walked along in silence for several minutes. Presently a man approached them, and Boris visibly paled. Pierre saw a middle-aged gentleman, tall and thin, with gray-blond hair parted in the center and pale blue eyes that squinted slightly. The man came up to Boris and bowed very stiffly. "You are Count Kussov, of the Russian delegation?" he asked. He spoke a guttural French, clipped and unmelodic.

Boris had regained his perfect composure. He smiled and inclined his head. "Baron von Baylen, am I correct?"

The other nodded. Switching to Russian, Boris said: "Baron, may I present Pierre Grigorievitch Riazhin? Pierre, Baron von Baylen is here with the German delegation, but he is the first secretary at the Petersburg embassy, where I met him several years ago. It's been a long time, hasn't it, Baron?"

"Indeed it has. You are taking a constitutional?"

Boris laughed. "Just enjoying the scenery. My young friend is a painter and has had a better time here than I. Than any of us." They began to walk again, three abreast, and Boris commented: "A strange time for such a conference, don't you think? The Kaiser is not well disposed toward peace, is he now?"

"Unlike the Tzar *he* was not recently defeated, both abroad and at home. Not that the Tzar did not succeed in quelling the rebels in '05—but that was a close call, wasn't it? The Kaiser wants to be a friend to the Tzar—they are cousins by marriage, aren't they?"

Pierre thought: For gentlemen, smiling and bowing graciously, they are not mincing words. He wished he were back in his room, near his palette. Why had he agreed to come to the Netherlands with Boris?

Baron von Baylen said smoothly: "Ah, but there will be no war. Look at this world, at this European continent! Prosperity, everywhere prosperity! Right here, see that incongruous motorcar in this Renaissance town? Yet in several more years we shan't find a single coach to ride, I'll wager! Russia will always lag behind, I'm afraid, because of its icy winters. Motorcars won't properly invade it for a while . . ." He turned to Pierre: "And you young artists! Flourishing! The French Expressionists have captured my fancy, so bold and bright! You creative spirits will not permit war, will you?"

Pierre did not know how to reply. Instead Boris said: "My friend, like most artists, lives in a glass tower removed from politics and economics. But I am certain you have seen the clouds, Herr Baron. Right now they are still fluffy white lambs, but one day in the not-too-distant future, they will turn gray and hide the sun from our eyes. For the moment, I prefer to avert my gaze—to the Ballet, for example. Do you enjoy our Imperial Ballet, Herr Baron?"

Later that day in their hotel, Pierre asked Boris: "Do you really feel that the Conference is a waste of time?"

"Undoubtedly. We shall all disperse soon to our various home grounds, rubbing our hands with great smugness. But to no avail. Ah well, my dear boy, let us not be gloomy. That damned Baron was like a cup of warm water on an empty stomach—I still have not gotten him out of my system."

"Who is he?" Pierre questioned.

Boris drew back his lips from his teeth. "My ex-wife's new husband. I wish to God he'd kept away."

Pierre raised his eyebrows and laughed. "It's so unlike you," he said, sudden mockery in his voice, "to allow another lowly mortal to disturb your equanimity. I must admit, it does my heart good to see a touch of human vulnerability in you!"

"You don't think of me as human, then, Petya?" Boris asked.

For a moment there was silence, a palpable discomfort. "You play with others' emotions," the young painter finally said, looking away. There was an edge of resentment in his words.

"And you, *mon cher?* You don't?"

The silken tone, with its undercurrent of irony, was like a slow tease. Pierre wheeled about, suddenly angry. "How can I?" he asked. "Only the very rich or the very powerful can manipulate their retinue. The rest of us have to learn to survive, and that's difficult enough!"

Boris folded his hands together behind his back. "Pride is a dangerous commodity, Petya. We can only handle it if we're willing to use it responsibly. It seems to me you use it at will. It's easy to act the protégé, dear boy, when you want to obtain a favor or two. But what of the attendant responsibilities? They exist, you know."

The two men stood examining each other, Boris a tall, haughty exclamation point, Pierre on the defensive, his nose twitching, sweat beginning to bead on his forehead. "Goddamn it!" he finally cried, the first of them to break. "What do you want of me, Boris Vassilievitch? A display of loyalty?"

Boris inclined his head in mock approval. "Gratitude," he enunciated carefully, the syllables ringing like cool bells in the night. "A little bit of gratitude. I could suggest something, perhaps. You have a masterpiece in your possession, and I want it. Now, it would make a perfect gift of thanks to a beloved patron—but I shan't ask that much of you, Petya. You're too poor, as you so eloquently reminded me just now. I shall pay you for it. I'm speaking of your portrait of the Sugar Plum Fairy."

Pierre's black eyes widened, his lips parted. "But—it's not for sale!" he exclaimed. Rage constricted his throat.

Boris raised one golden eyebrow and smiled. "Oh? Well then, I'm doubly honored. Thank you, *cher ami.* I shall accept your gift after all. And I shall tell everyone about the generosity of my protégé. You are a dear boy, and I shan't forget your largesse."

As Pierre stood open-mouthed before him, his face drained of color, Boris said lightly: "Come, it's time to dress for supper. I'll be by in twenty minutes." He walked out of the room, humming an aria from *La Traviata*.

On his way to his own quarters, Boris ran his dry hand through his hair and thought: It's his own fault. He's still an innocent, but he keeps trying to pretend he's not—and until he learns the rules of the game, he'll always be the loser. But the hollow sensation within him contradicted his conscious mind and spread like ink upon a blotter over his sense of triumph.

Chapter 4

On September 1, 1907, Natalia Oblonova officially entered the *corps de ballet*
of the Mariinsky. Before the summer
she had made her debut in a tableau
from *Swan Lake*, then had left the Imperial School for good and gone to live
with Lydia Brailovskaya in her apartment. Katya Balina still had one year to
go before graduating, and although her
parents had begged Natalia to make her
home with them, she had preferred the freedom that Lydia's
offer gave her. Katya found this decision somewhat shocking;
Lydia's spinsterhood, and her lack of family, had given many
proper Petersbourgeois the impression that the *coryphée* was
only slightly removed from the *demimonde*. Only the presence
of the old nurse, Manya, reassured them. But to Natalia, there
was no shame in the *demimondaines*, who were richly kept by
members of the aristocracy. She found them more honorable
than women who allowed their families to hand them over with
a dowry to men who would later betray them in the beds of
more assertive females. Marriage, she thought, stripped women
of their humanity and turned them into serfs forced to bear
children. At least, when a *demimondaine* gave her body to a
man, she did so honestly, and by choice. Or so Natalia believed
at seventeen.

Her last year as a student had been marked with much professional excitement. Her performances as the Sugar Plum Fairy
and as Aspitchia had brought her to the attention of Michel
Fokine, the young dancer who aspired to choreograph more

fluid, less contrived ballets than those of Petipa. In February he had staged a benefit performance at the Mariinsky for the Society for the Prevention of Cruelty to Children. His selection of Natalia to appear in his lyrical accompaniment to music by Chopin, entitled *Chopiniana*, had been strangely appropriate. Natalia had danced with fifteen other women, and her own part had not been spectacular. But she had felt the "rightness" of Fokine's simplicity, his rejection of extravagant effects.

Afterward, patrons had come backstage to congratulate the dancers, and Natalia, young and unknown, had been virtually eclipsed by the stars: Pavlova and Siedova. They were all to be fêted at Cubat, but she, still a student controlled by Varvara Ivanovna's rigid rules, was not to be included. She had been fascinated by the admiration lavished upon the other dancers and had unobtrusively drawn near a cluster of bejeweled *grandes dames* to look and listen as they praised her more illustrious seniors.

All at once one of the ladies, a woman whom Natalia had never seen before, had noticed her, and touched her friend on the arm. "Look, Ludmilla Karlovna! It's the little ballerina from the Grand Palais! Isn't that so?" The other had nodded with enthusiasm. Natalia had blushed in complete bewilderment. "What's your name?" the first woman had demanded.

"Oblonova. Natalia Oblonova."

"Well, young Riazhin certainly captured her, didn't he? Is he a friend of yours, by any chance?"

"I don't know anybody called Riazhin, madame," Natalia had demurred.

"But there can be no mistake. Your portrait hung in the Grand Palais in Paris last year. We all noticed it. That young artist, Pierre Riazhin, made quite an impression. All the Russians who were in Paris for the art exhibition fell in love with your portrait. Didn't you know that it existed?"

"No," Natalia had answered, perplexed and silent. The women had made quite a fuss, and then Natalia had been taken back to the school. She had asked Lydia what this meant—but her friend had only told her that there was indeed a new artist called Riazhin, a follower in the frenzied steps of Vrubel and

Bakst. Lydia had not seen his work—he was only just beginning to become known in St. Petersburg—but she assumed he must have painted a ballerina who bore a vague resemblance to Natalia. Yet Natalia was a woman: She had not forgotten, or dismissed the incident so easily.

That April there was a school performance of another Fokine production, *Les Gobelins Animés,* in which Natalia danced in a *pas de trois* with another girl and a boy. Then in autumn, she became a professional at last. Now, at seventeen, she experienced a change. Lydia and the other dancers treated her as a peer, and all at once no restrictions existed. She could take a walk without asking permission; she could choose her own clothing. Away from Varvara Ivanovna's influence, she saw that another reality existed outside of dance. She entered it with caution.

Natalia had never taken the time to consider the character of those around her. The governesses and masters at the school had simply been there, to be pleased, avoided, or humored. Katya had been so close to her, expressing each thought and feeling that occurred to her, that it had been unnecessary to wonder about her inner being. Natalia had never thought that by failing to display her own heart she might have been hurting Katya's gentle nature, so trusting and sharing. Lydia had been the mirror image of Natalia herself grown wiser and more cynical, without the driving force and the talent to set her apart. Natalia had lived the most egocentric of lives, yet without the experience to know that she was shutting out others. She had concentrated only on her body.

Now the world began to intrude upon her in numerous ways, and at first she fought its challenges. The first time she danced alone as a member of the Mariinsky, and a group of eager young men in the pit began to clap, she felt jarred. They had intruded into her life: They were no longer part of her anonymous public, but her "claque"; every time she reappeared before them, they cheered her. She realized that she owed them the excellence of her performance, much as a dutiful wife owes her husband her sexual consent. But she was uncertain how to accept this new responsibility, for she had always lived a life devoid of debt: What she had was hers alone, obtained by her own means. "Don't complain," Lydia told her. "Only the most inspiring dancers have claques. No one has ever noticed me!"

Natalia had thought of herself as a finely tuned instrument, to be kept in shape, but not as a woman with female charms or emotions. Similarly, she had been an avid reader and a good student but had merely considered this a vital necessity: She was a nobody and needed to survive. Her intelligence would get her by where others used their family connections or their social graces. But that she might one day be important to anyone but herself, in anything other than her dancer's role, she had simply not considered. Natalia's shutting out of the world had gone this far: Not wondering about others, she had never thought that others might wonder about her.

She earned sixty-five rubles a month as a member of the *corps* and contributed to the upkeep of the apartment and to the cost of food. Her clothes were simple, for she had no social life during those early working days. She had met other dancers, but their lives seemed far removed from hers, with families and friends she did not know. Lydia, of course, knew a great many people, but her older friends did not know Natalia and had no reason to include her in their reunions. Lydia invited some of her acquaintances to the flat; but when she met them, Natalia remained quiet, listening to this outside world that sounded no gong of recognition in her own experience. "Why do you saddle yourself with little Miss House Mouse?" one of Lydia's friends mischievously asked her one evening. "Are you growing charitable in your old age?"

"She's a great deal more than you think," Lydia retorted. "Watch her."

And then, one day in the early part of November, the old nurse greeted Natalia at the door with an ivory-colored envelope bearing her name. The young girl was puzzled. She thought that the handwriting looked familiar: elegant, petulant, vain. She frowned and slit it open, removing a stiff card. "What's a *dîner de têtes?*" she finally asked Lydia.

Her friend was intrigued. "That's something French; it isn't usually done in Russia. It's a dinner where the guests come in fancy headdresses. I suppose the Parisians have them instead of costume balls. For a supper, one could disguise one's head alone, but of course not for a ball: That would look a bit ridiculous, don't you think? Formal gown and strange headdress?"

"It seems I've been invited to one," Natalia stated evenly. She handed Lydia the card. "At Count Boris Kussov's. What an odd man he is: the pearl necklace, then nothing—and now this. I wonder why he suddenly remembered me?"

"Boris Vassilievitch Kussov does nothing lightly. He is good at recognizing talent. Surely you do not think you will remain in the *corps* for long? Everybody knows you will soon be a soloist. Perhaps our fair count wants to give you a foretaste of the society that a Petersburg ballerina is supposed to keep. But this *dîner de têtes*, now. You will enjoy yourself. Boris Vassilievitch is a magnificent host, and if he has decided that the French have a good thing, then we must believe him. He forecasts trends before they become fashionable. The *dîner de têtes* will be a society staple within the year—mark my words."

"But I won't go," Natalia replied lightly. "I am not a commodity, a display piece. I am a dancer."

"You, my friend, are only a fool," Lydia said. "A scared fool, too. You must go, and you must look beautiful and be clever. If you're afraid of people, then you must face them squarely and overcome your terror. Human beings eat up those who are frightened of them, and you can't avoid the world forever. A dancer cannot soar above herself if she does not know how she fits into the larger framework. Do not be afraid that those who touch you will automatically violate you: That is emotional frigidity."

Natalia stared at Lydia, her great brown eyes wide with outrage and panic. She felt as she had after the performance of *The Daughter of Pharaoh*, eighteen months before: like a cornered wild animal. But Lydia shrugged her shoulders and grinned disarmingly. "We must think up a head for you," she said.

As he had written on his invitation, Boris sent his covered troika to fetch Natalia on the appointed evening. She was sitting stiffly in the small parlor, her young body sheathed in a low-cut crimson gown that revealed the tops of her breasts and her graceful arms. Around her long, slender neck lay the pearl necklace. She had chosen to wear a traditionally Russian headdress, the *kokoshnik:* a diadem of rubies, sapphires, and emeralds worn at the coronations of the Tzars. Lydia had found it at the Jewish market, and of course the stones were clever imitations. The gown had been sewn by the old nurse. Her entire appearance was striking: the pale, smooth skin, the enormous eyes, the gilded headdress on the shining brown hair, the brightness of the cloth over her small shapeliness. She looked at once very young and frozen with apprehension—detached and aloof, regal and imposing.

During the drive over the snow-covered pavement, she did not move. The darkness outside hypnotized her, and the horses' hooves reverberated inside her head. But when the Swiss doorman of the building on the Boulevard of the Horse Guard opened the front door, and when, at the entrance to the huge apartment, she heard the noise of laughter, a shaft of pure pain pierced through her. She had never felt so oddly set apart as now. The door opened, and a servant removed her wrap; she fancied that he disapproved of it, for it was old and out of fashion. At last she stood in the brilliant room.

She stood there for a full minute before she was noticed. Then she saw strange heads turn toward her—Napoleon in his tricornered hat, a bewigged Louis XIV, Mary Stuart. She noticed the room with its intimate silks and velvets, its oil paintings, porcelain vases, and lamps of opaline and jade. It was all a dream. Louis XIV was coming toward her, executing an elaborate bow, and he said in the ironic voice of Count Boris Kussov: "A charming sight. Come, *ma chère,* I shall introduce you."

There was nothing to say. So many faces thrust at her, so many names—names that all meant something to her. There were singers, actors, painters, statesmen, names from books and periodicals, names whispered in gossip. There were ballerinas present, too, but none with whom she was personally acquainted. She could barely speak, but Boris kept her arm in his, and was murmuring to her, with a certain familiarity that she found puzzling. She did not belong here at all, any more than her mother had belonged in the salon of Baroness Gudrinskaya.

"You see, dear Mala," a gruff voice said jovially, "our little dove is in awe of you tonight, but I assure you, one day she will provide you with some interesting challenges." Beneath the Louis XIII plumes, Natalia saw that the speaker was the Grand-Duke Vladimir, and that the woman he had addressed so lightly was his son Andrei's acknowledged mistress, Matilda Kchessin-skaya, the *prima ballerina assoluta* of the Imperial Ballet. Natalia had no idea how to accept this compliment with grace: She wanted to die, and executed a deep curtsy. Then, thankfully, Boris brought her to yet another luminary.

Alone in the corner Pierre Riazhin waited. Tonight he resembled a figure from a painting done by Frans Hals in the seventeenth century. His dark face, with its serious black eyes, seemed *à propos* beneath the Dutch hat, so large, imposing, and classical. His fingers closed around the thin stem of his champagne glass as he watched Boris and the girl. How proprietary Boris looked. The girl seemed removed, in a stupor. He could well understand. It had taken him two years of exposure to learn how to be clever in society, and as it was, he was most often rude and unable to conform to polite and witty rituals. She was so beautiful, he thought, and something inside him swelled with pain. Pierre suddenly hated the girl for being slim and pale and wide-eyed; he wanted to strangle the life out of her, to obliterate the vulnerability and empathy that she brought to the surface in his own heart.

Boris had brought Natalia before a *zakuski* table set against the wall and laden with hors d'oeuvres: meat-filled pastries, tongue, stuffed mushrooms, caviar, smoked whitefish, and salmon. He heaped a small dish of Sèvres china with various foods and handed it to her. "You see," he was saying, his smooth tones easing her over the difficult moments, "King Edward charmed the French. Centuries of enmity—blood hatred—were somehow conquered by this English monarch, and if he can do it, so can we! A season of our robust Russian opera. Quite a change from Italian!"

"Why is it so important to spread our culture to France?" Natalia questioned. There was an edge to her voice because she was nervous.

"Why does anyone want to go beyond himself? This is the

human secret. I don't know, my dear. Why did you decide to become a dancer?" He quirked one fine blond eyebrow, smiling ironically.

"I was too young to be a courtesan," she retorted with asperity. Then, abruptly, she blushed. It had been an impulsive, defiant answer born of fear.

But Boris laughed. "Nevertheless, you wanted to be loved! Whether as Oblonova the ballerina, or, if you like, as Madame de Montespan, whore to Louis XIV"—and he looked into her eyes with calculated mirth—"you did not wish to remain an anonymous woman. A country is the same. Russia wants to be loved, by the French, by the British—because we are a vain lot."

Pierre Riazhin had been watching them closely, and now he put down his glass and strode to them rapidly. There was a jerky quality to his movements, a half-repressed passion manifested in his limbs. Boris glanced up at the intruder with annoyance. "Ah, we have here our young genius, Pierre Grigorievitch Riazhin. Have you come to meet this charming lady?"

"I do not need an introduction," Pierre said, looking directly at Natalia. She was so small, close up—small yet strong, compact, athletic. And grave. He liked her seriousness, which contrasted so vividly with Boris's careless ease. Suddenly Pierre wanted to be very rude to Boris, to lash out at him. Instead, he said to Natalia: "I wondered if you would be so beautiful in person. I see that you are."

Her brown eyes took him in, with his absurd Frans Hals hat, his earnest black eyes that seemed bottomless, his quick face, massive carriage, and slim waist. She shook her head, bewildered. "What do you mean?" she asked. She saw the dark, crisp hair, the large hands with their well-shaped, blunt fingers, the wide nostrils. She could almost breathe him. He smelled of maleness, a strange, unfamiliar scent that threw her off. She shivered, thinking of a Crimean wheat field swept by southern winds.

"He is paying you a compliment, Natalia Dmitrievna," Boris laughed pleasantly. "But ignore the boor. He has all the delicacy of a young panther on the prowl."

"No," Natalia said, looking at Pierre, "it was the way you said

it—as though you had seen me before. But I do not know you."
Yet something was eluding her, something in the not-too-dis-
tant past—the women after the performance of *Chopiniana!*
"Riazhin," she intoned with wonder. "Yes, you are a painter.
But we have never met."

"You have never met me, but I did meet you, two years ago.
I saw you dance the Sugar Plum Fairy. I have never forgotten
that night."

"I was only an insignificant ballet student," she stammered.
The feeling in the black eyes that bore into her was disconcerting. She had never spoken to anyone like this young man,
whose probing intensity dismayed her. She had not yet learned
to parry compliments and was uncomfortable. "Please," she
said, and her voice trembled. "I am honored that you remembered me, but—"

"Pierre loves all beautiful things," Boris commented. His
fingers closed over Natalia's delicate arm, but his eyes were lev-
eled at Pierre Riazhin, and the girl stepped back, watching black
eyes hold blue in an incomprehensible deadlock. She should
have stayed at home. Here were Louis XIV and a seventeenth-
century Dutch baron sparring. Around them floated the room,
with its Renaissance medallions juxtaposed with artifacts of the
Chinese Sung dynasty and laughing voices. Matilda Kchessinskaya, Feodor Chaliapin, and the minister of education. She
felt ill, and unconsciously found herself leaning on Boris's arm
for support.

"There now, Natalia Dmitrievna," he said to her, "are you
faint?"

"I'm quite all right, thank you, Boris Vassilievitch," she replied.

"But you, Boris, are being neglectful of your other guests,"
Pierre said. "Why don't you leave Natalia Dmitrievna to me? I
can entertain her." Natalia thought: How rude he is, and yet
what a relief it would be for Count Boris to leave me . . .

"Yes, please, Boris Vassilievitch," she interposed. "I should
not like to think that I were keeping you from more illustrious
and amusing company."

Boris Kussov gazed at her through narrowed eyes, then at the
young man. Natalia felt cold. Without a word, their host turned

away and merged into the crowd of odd faces and hats. Natalia started to laugh nervously. "You were unkind," she commented. "Are you not afraid to displease Boris Vassilievitch? I have heard that it is dangerous to upset him, and he did look somewhat . . . upset."

"Yes, well, so much for him. Let us talk about you. When will you have another solo role? I would like to see you."

"I'll dance in the *Pavillon d'Armide pas de trois* on the twenty-fifth," she replied.

An awkward silence ensued. He said irritably: "Do you like society?"

"If you could imagine how much I would like to die right now!" she cried, then bit her lower lip. "But that is most ungrateful, isn't it? Somebody told me about you, Pierre Grigorievitch. You took part in the Russian exhibit in Paris last year, didn't you?"

"Yes. I wanted—I'd hoped—" Suddenly he looked away from her in confusion. "Come with me," he ordered. He offered her his arm, then walked rapidly from the drawing room into a small corridor. Away from the noise of the other guests, he faced her. "I must show it to you," he murmured. Then he led her mystified, past a door into a square study upholstered in Cordova leather. A fire in the hearth burned orange and gold. Only a single lamp shone in the room.

"There," Pierre announced, indicating the wall farthest from the door. Natalia looked up and started. A large oil painting hung in an ornate gilded frame, and she saw herself, small, wistful, mischievous, in her pink tulle outfit from *The Nutcracker*. It was unmistakably her, and not merely a resemblance. "Had anyone told you?" he asked, scanning her face for a reaction.

"Yes," she whispered. She turned to look at him and stiffened. This was all so bizarre, so unforeseen. "Who are you?" she demanded. "Why did you paint me?"

"I am an artist, like you. Why? Why does there have to be an answer?"

"Because!" She moved away from him, suddenly fearful. "You have taken me and put me in a frame, and I don't know anything about you!"

He took a deep breath, and his nostrils flared. She knew she had made him angry. "You know more about me than anyone," he stated. "Or you could, if you wanted to look. Look, then! I have put myself inside this frame as much as I have put you there, but you are too blind, too self-centered to notice! And yet the Sugar Plum Fairy was not self-centered. She was real!"

"You are the strangest man I have ever met!" she cried back.

They stood opposite each other, pent-up nervousness exploding, anger being released, unacknowledged emotions rising to the surface. His hands clenched into fists. They stared at each other in shock and surprise, as if suddenly naked and exposed. Then she stepped back, her lips parting in fear, and he moved forward, unthinking, elemental. He grabbed her shoulders and shook them once and then he bent toward her, roughly, his face flushed, hers white and drawn.

All at once the door swung open, and the sarcastic voice of Boris Kussov said: "Supper awaits, my dears."

On November 25 the première of *Le Pavillon d'Armide*, an expansion of Michel Fokine's *Les Gobelins Animés*, took place at the Mariinsky. Natalia danced in the *pas de trois* as she had in the former ballet. The choreographic innovations were well received by the aristocracy of St. Petersburg—so well received, in fact, that the composer, Tcherepnine, the designer, Benois, and young Fokine were all called forward for an ovation.

This presentation had been the culmination of much hard work. Fokine was a high-strung perfectionist, and his methods were so different from those of the classical choreographers, Petipa and Ivanov, that many of the ballerinas could not follow him well. Wills clashed more than once, and tempers were strained. But Natalia was the most junior of the ballerinas and knew how to hold her tongue. This was a marvelous chance for her, not one to be wasted. She avoided the troublemakers and practiced relentlessly.

Natalia now had access to the established and more prestigious of the Mariinsky's ballerinas. The management recognized that she would rapidly be promoted to *coryphée* and then to soloist of the second degree. Had she not graduated a year early, she could not have skipped the entire process of joining the *corps*. She danced in small groups during most performances and sometimes had a minor part of her own. She now got dressed with those who had achieved a certain measure of distinction and was learning from experience what to expect of whom: Pavlova was the least tractable of the ballerinas, prone to jealousy that took the form of hurtful comments; Tamara Karsavina was intelligent and agreeable, and one could ask her questions; Olga Preobrajenskaya was a true professonal, and kind. And Matilda Kchessinskaya, if one did not challenge her supremacy, could be witty and charming. But her ego was even more fragile than Anna Pavlova's, and Prince Volkonsky, the previous director, had been forced to quit his position as a result of a disagreement with her. Her Imperial lovers made her a matchless enemy for anyone.

Natalia thought that *Le Pavillon d'Armide*, an uncontrived ballet with asymmetric pieces, was more difficult to dance than the traditional Petipa fairy stories. But what most appealed to her was that the pace of her movements changed during her special dance as one of Armida's confidantes. The other female dancer, Karsavina, possessed a gay, light role that did not parallel hers. The male dancer of the *pas de trois* was a young man who had graduated the same year as Natalia. His name was Vaslav Fomitch Nijinsky, and he was small and airy, with Oriental features reminiscent of a woodland animal's. When he leaped, he remained suspended above the stage far longer and more gracefully than Natalia had ever seen anyone else soar. The critics called this talent "ballon."

Natalia's eyes had wandered to the stall where she had noticed Boris two years before, magnificent in his black and gray evening suit. This time she picked him out at once. Next to him was Pierre Riazhin—a rather defiant Pierre, if she could judge by the way he held himself apart from Boris, his feral head proud and aloof. Then she began to dance, paying them very little attention. Still, what attention she did pay them was too much. Her concentration was broken ever so slightly, and she was angry, angrier than she had been over the claque. She knew that Pierre had come for her, placing her under greater obligation than ever before to be excellent for *his* eyes.

Undressing afterward, her fingers trembled. It had been several weeks since she had met Riazhin, but in her imagination she had frequently relived that moment in Boris's study when Pierre's hands had seized her by the shoulders. His fingers had been round, hard; his eyes black, ringed with thick black lashes. His black curls had fallen over a wide brow, and his body had conveyed a sense of boundless strength, of danger. He had smelled of danger. Better to keep away from him in the future, she suddenly decided.

But would she be able to? She bit her lip and smoothed back her fine brown hair. There was to be a dinner at Cubat for the dancers. Would he attend? If so, what then? Inexplicably, her eyes filled with tears, and she wanted to run outside in the cold and find her way home. She was behaving like a child, and so she breathed deeply and continued to dress.

She was always somewhat dazed by these celebrations. Nobody knew her yet, and if someone spoke to her, it was generally as one does to a naïve beginner. The *basso profundo*, Feodor Chaliapin, had tapped her hand, and Kchessinskaya had called her a "sweet little dove." What did they know of her? She was somewhat disgusted. Yet Lydia had told her that a dancer was not merely the instrument of her body—that she would have to learn about public and private life. Therefore, she went to learn—about good food, wit and intellect, and deportment, all that she had never come to know as a child. There was wonder in the outside world, and strange light, new odors. The problem lay in sorting through the sensations afterward and in not feeling alienated at the time.

When she stepped outside, a figure darted from the darkness and confronted her as she was turning toward the carriage. She looked up, her throat constricting with fear, and saw Pierre Riazhin. He was wearing a tuxedo, yet his barely contained frenzy belied the formality of his attire. His head was bare, the curls spilling over, and his face was pale. "Natalia Dmitrievna," he said.

"Are you coming, Natashenka?" a gay voice called out from the carriage.

"That is my car," she said.

"Let it go without you. Please! Let us go somewhere together.

I would like to talk to you." He placed a hand—one of those hands which she had dreamed about—on her sleeve. "I beg of you."

"No," she replied forcefully. "There is no reason for us to talk. And—and—it wouldn't be right."

"Do you care what people think?" he asked with incredulity.

"Right now I do. Let me go, please." But, to her dismay and growing despair, the carriage door was closing, and the coachman was raising his whip. She gazed wide-eyed at the hand on her arm and jerked free. "You are a nuisance, Pierre Grigorievitch," she cried. "Now I shall miss the supper! What do you want? Why can't you leave me alone?"

He stiffened. All at once he stood upright, unflinching, tall and broad in the night, the lights of the Mariinsky casting gold reflections on his hair. "As you wish," he said tightly. He turned with almost military dignity and started to walk away with long, angry strides.

Feeling the wind lift a strand of her hair, Natalia stood alone. The audience had long since departed, and now even the dancers had left. Her cloak billowed around her, and she shivered. A tremendous feeling of gloom pervaded her, which she could not shake free. She looked at Riazhin's retreating figure, and thought, I did it! I've sent him away. But instead of triumph or relief, hard-edged misery flowed through her. She took one small step, then another. In the night she called out: "Wait! Please!"

He had already melted into the shadows, but she saw him stop and turn, his face relaxing from its taut white lines. He waited for her. For a moment she remained uncertain. Small pricks of sharp emotion pierced her consciousness. He waited, and then she ran, light and airy on the tips of her toes. She ran to him and then, face to face with him in the cold November night, she felt embarrassed. She was there. Now what? Why had she come? Had she not won and sent him away, this odd man who had painted her vulnerability upon a cloth canvas, who had shown her to unknown eyes in a city halfway across Europe, who pursued her with an intensity for which she was unprepared? She did not like him, but he did not appear to like her any better for all his admiration of her work.

Lydia had told her about the golden youth of Moscow and St. Petersburg, wild young men who wasted fortunes on gypsies at the Aquarium, who possessed women with single-minded intent. When they met a woman of virtue, they attempted to buy her services, their blood lust unabated by the difficulty of the challenge. Was Pierre Riazhin like them? He failed to fit the picture. Surely he did not lack mistresses of far greater charms than Natalia herself. She was small with plain coloring, hardly vivid or sensual. Her breasts were small, her calves well developed like all dancers. And Pierre? He was not a gentleman—a painter, not a wealthy scion of society. Nothing made sense.

"Are you afraid of me?" he asked, his dark eyes probing hers.

"I do not understand you," she replied. But the sound of his voice had reassured her, had reestablished normality between them. "We do not know anything about each other, and yet you have staked a claim. But what sort of claim? Do you want me to pose for you? I don't know how. Painters are a mystery to me."

"I occasionally work on commission," he said. "But rarely. I do not like to paint people as they see themselves. I have my own ideas, you see. I do not ask my subjects to sit. I prefer to think about them, and then paint. That is how I did the Sugar Plum portrait. They liked it, in Paris."

"It is cold," she said. "Do you have a carriage?"

"We'll have to hail a coach. I came with Boris Vassilievitch, but I—did not want to return with him." He suddenly smiled. "I had a bouquet of asters for you, from a Swiss florist on Morskaya—but I forgot them in the stall. The first time that I was organized, too! But I did not want to miss you as you left the building, and so the flowers are still waiting beneath my seat."

She laughed. A landau for hire passed in front of them, and Pierre stopped it. He opened the door, and she climbed inside. He gave the coachman his own address, then joined her. As the horses started, he said: "I am taking you to my flat. I could not think where else we could go. Your party will be at Cubat. Besides, Paris has brought me certain customers, but my means are still limited. Do you mind terribly?"

"You have already totally ruined my reputation," Natalia answered. "There will be an empty place at the long table, and when somebody asks, the girls will say I was detained by a strange man. They will wait awhile and then assume that I have gone to his rooms somewhere!" She shook her head, her brown eyes luminous: "I do not really care what people think. There is nobody whose good opinion I treasure, you see. I am not what you would call a lady."

"No. You remind me of the wild horses in the Caucasus— beautiful, graceful, and totally unfettered. But also somewhat scared. I wanted to tame the fright out of them."

"Is that why you waited for me in the dark? I do not like it. You take me by surprise and throw everything off kilter. Yet you still have not explained yourself at all." But somehow as she leaned against the soft upholstered cushions of the carriage, she felt a new elation. This was an adventure and anything was better than another painful dinner with the company. At least, this way . . . She looked at his profile, strong and clearly defined, and suddenly realized that this was the first time she had ever been alone with a man. Her panic returned. She wished she could stop the horses and get off, in the middle of the road— anywhere! She had been mad, reckless, and childish—not for accepting the ride but for having called him back into her life.

But the landau had come to a halt, and Pierre took her hand to let her down. She trembled slightly at his touch and once again pictured his fingers: large, strong, not gentle. He opened a massive oak door, then led her up a flight of musty stairs. He removed a key from his pocket and opened a second door. They stood inside an unlit room, moonlight filtering through the curtains onto the carpet. Pierre walked into the room and turned on a yellow light. Natalie blinked and started, motionless. They were inside a small enclosure bound by extremely high walls leading to a beamed ceiling. On the walls, hung one over the other, were what appeared to be canvases of differing sizes, depicting subjects that were as varied as their colors. "All yours?" she whispered.

"Yes. I have seen your work and understood you. Now you can see mine and know me. Would you like some tea?"

She shook her head, mesmerized. "I could not eat or drink,"

she murmured. "Usually a performance makes me hungry, but tonight I could not consume a thing. I would have made a valiant effort at Cubat—but no, thank you."

She did not look at him or consider that she was being most unconventional, coming to his flat without company. Hesitating, she asked: "You do not have a servant, Pierre Grigorievitch?"

"No," he replied. "I can hardly afford one, although Boris Vassilievitch sometimes sends me Ivan. Ivan is—what do they say?—a pearl. But he does not approve of me."

So there was no one. She walked to one of the walls and examined a green and gold pasture interspersed with crimson and indigo. She touched the canvas. It felt hard. She ran her finger over it and felt ridges of color. She wet her lips, blinked. Then she went to the next painting. Her senses seemed strangely short-circuited, the hues cramming into her brain, fighting for space. She stepped back to see the wall as a whole, and her cheeks glowed. Her scalp beneath the soft chignon tingled. She felt physically assaulted by a surfeit of brilliance.

In front of her was an unfamiliar world: sharp, dry, abrupt mountains, with rivers that cascaded from snow-covered peaks to the turbulent sea; close-ups of water hitting the sides of a narrow, deep gully; a pasture full of peaceful cows; vineyards, wine presses, orchards of flowering peach, pear, apricot, and apple trees; fine shady beaches. "Where is this?" she asked, turning to Pierre.

"It's the Caucasus, the most magnificent country I know. It is a world unto itself. From the Caspian to the Black Sea, everything exists there: the most arid mountain range—you should see the Kazbek, dominating the world!—and then, green fields, beaches, and Tiflis, the most charming city you can imagine. The panorama changes before one's very eyes. I have not stopped painting it."

She noticed the bright light in his eyes, the nervous excitement in his strong legs. "Why did you ever leave it?" she asked.

He sat down on a low stool next to where she was standing, her blue velvet cape trailing on the floor. She could not read his expression. "I wanted to expose my paintings, to speak through them to a multitude of people. I wanted to see great cities and meet other artists. I felt as though I had outgrown my country. I was wrong, though. It's still in my heart, and I shall paint its landscapes forever."

"But—you're sorry, then, to be here?"

He shook his head. "Ill at ease, perhaps, but hardly sorry. I was built one way, and here I must adapt to another pattern of thought, to people who are not my own people. Sometimes I cannot stand the constriction—but if I am to stretch myself as an artist, I must also try to reach beyond my small reserve of experience. If Antokolsky had remained in the Pale of Settlement, he would have spent a lifetime hewing Jewish shtetls out of limestone and would never have sculpted his marble busts of the Tzar and Tzarina. Isn't that true?"

"Are you an ambitious man, Pierre Grigorievitch? Does it interest you to mingle with important men?"

He shrugged somewhat impatiently. "I do not know whom you mean by important men. I have met artists of reputation, yes, and have learned—am learning—through their influence. If you mean statesmen and financiers and members of the aristocracy—well, I suppose they are important to an extent. Without patronage a man could never win acceptance these days—not a pleasant fact, Natalia Dmitrievna, but one which I have had to learn here in the capital. Struggling along, one relishes one's pride, and that is a wonderful feeling—but an unseen painter is like a voice crying in the desert. Anything is better than that— anything! An artist, after all, is primarily an exhibitionist. We perish in closets, away from the world with which we seek to communicate."

Bitterness twisted his features. She felt a sudden surge of sympathy, thinking of Matilda Kchessinskaya, empress of the ballet. How far would she have climbed had she not first been the Tzar's mistress, and later that of two of his cousins? And yet . . . "Is this why you associate with Count Boris?" she asked.

Pierre said coldly: "He is my patron. I did not know him while I was at the Academy, but his scholarship helped to support me during my student days. When I met him, he took an interest in my career. He has been most kind."

Almost instinctively, Natalia touched the pearls around her

neck. "Is he always generous with artists?" she asked somewhat breathlessly.

He did not miss the gesture. "As generous as with you?" he demanded, and now his tone was sarcastic and unkind.

She winced. "You knew then, about his gift to me? What was wrong with it? Others have received similar presents, no doubt."

"No doubt. But yes, I knew. Boris is a strange man. He wanted me to know. Perhaps to prepare me for his taking on a new protégée."

"And you were jealous?"

He started to laugh, but the sound was harsh and it jolted Natalia. "Jealous, yes, but not in the way you assume. I had been hoping to meet you, you see. He simply reached you first. It was all planned, I assure you."

Natalia carefully sat down on a hardbacked chair that faced Pierre. "I wasn't even out of school at the time," she said in measured tones.

"But he saw you as the Sugar Plum Fairy. Svetlov was with us. You were a unique dancer, even then. Signaling his interest at that time was a stroke of genius: No one else could lay claim to you afterward, when you fulfilled your initial promise. Boris is like that—a most exclusive man, who lives through the creativity of others by controlling their very souls. You must admit that in itself, despicable though it may be, that is supreme creativity."

"I find it diabolical—and nauseating," Natalia said. "Why don't you shake him off and stand alone? After Paris—"

"After Paris I am still a shadowy figure. Boris has lifted me from obscurity by introducing me to Bakst, Benois, and Somov. He has aided my career by bringing me to the attention of Serge Diaghilev. But without his continuing support, these men would quickly stop bothering with me. He is the key to everything I want—everything! He is the final link between artists and society, between those who will critique my work and those who will buy it. Don't you see?"

Coolly, her brown eyes appraising him, she replied: "No. I see a caricature of a painter—a man of talent and vision, who has bartered his pride for a few connections. Frankly, I have more respect for Count Boris. He has helped you willingly. You treat him badly. I saw the way you spoke to him in his house. But if you sold yourself to him, you sold him spoiled goods. A serf, defiant and ill-tempered, is a bad serf."

Pierre half-rose, shaking with anger. "And you?" he cried. "Are you going to let him buy you for a necklace of pearls? How different are you from Kchessinskaya, or from Anna Pavlova, who seeks patrons in every man with clout? Or from Valerian Svetlov's Trefilova? All whores, in one way or another! Whether you marry for influence, or become a man's mistress, or simply curry for his good word in the proper circle—all that is prostitution!"

"Yes, and I admire a clever prostitute, if she is honorable. Honor demands that she pay for the favors she obtains. That is where you err, Pierre Grigorievitch. What does your patron demand? Friendship? Fealty? Attention? What does Boris Vassilievitch demand of you?"

"I do not know," Pierre said. All at once he fell back upon the stool and mopped his brow. "I do not know," he repeated. "Maybe that is the key to my resentment. If only he would make things clear between us, I would know if I wanted to continue this odd relationship. I would gladly be his friend— though why a man such as Boris would want it is beyond my comprehension. He possesses countless friends, all more intelligent, cultured, and cosmopolitan than I. His serf, you ask? No, never that. The one who listens to his ideas? Perhaps. Or maybe he simply enjoys raising others to heights to which he himself aspires. It is his sardonic humor that I cannot bear. I cannot help thinking that somehow he is using me, although I cannot tell how. It is maddening!"

She stood up and picked up her cloak. "I am tired," she said. She looked once more around the room, at the streaks and stripes of color. Somehow it seemed unreal after this conversation. The young man in front of her, with his chaotic emotions, seemed unreal. Her leg muscles hurt. For the first time since arriving at this impoverished little flat, she remembered that she had danced that night. "I must leave now," she said.

Pierre rose too, a flicker of sadness in his eyes. She regarded him with a momentary fear, threatened by his overwhelming physical presence. She was so small and slight, he so imposing in his height and stature. When he had touched her at the *dîner de têtes.* . . . Yet now he was like a wounded panther. She found it difficult to empathize with him, to feel for him. "Do not bother to find me a coach," she said. "I can find one myself. I think I'd like to be alone now."

His magnificent black eyes held her, pleading. "Why must you go? Don't you trust me?"

"I have never trusted anyone," she replied seriously. "But dancers must rest, or we get cramps in our limbs. Good night, Pierre Grigorievitch."

With elfin swiftness she disappeared from the apartment, and he went to the window to watch as she left. There she was, a billow of blue velvet, frail and tiny . . . evanescent. He shut his eyes and uttered one anguished, guttural cry. Over the city the winter stars blinked their indifference.

Pierre had to admit that nothing in his life brought him the joy for which he had hoped. He thought again about Natalia's question: Did he, in fact, regret leaving the Caucasus? He had never been more miserable nor in greater turmoil than now. Petersburg had caged him, tamed the savage pride of his people from his heart, and turned him into a despicable excuse for a man—a sniveling little boy whose talent, as she had said with such cruel justice, was threatened by burial under the burden of his weakness.

Yet he could not change the contradictions in his nature. He resented the decadence of this glamorous capital, but he admired its beauty, its imperial splendor. He disliked Boris Kussov, yet at the same time he was exhilarated by the man's intelligence and by the company he kept. He hated himself for yielding to his patron's superior will but was intrigued by the privilege of this friendship. Paris had been glorious, but especially because of the attentiveness of Boris, who knew it well and had escorted Pierre, a callow provincial, to the places that were dearest to him. Together they had visited the various museums, and Pierre had reveled in Notre Dame and lost his head at Versailles. They had gone to the Opéra, and dined at the most fashionable restaurants: Larue, Diaghilev's lair; Weber; Sirdar; La Coupole, with its wall frescoes. They had fed pigeons near the Arc de Triomphe and watched children's puppet shows in the park. Boris had taken Pierre to meet his Parisian friends and had not left him alone for one minute. The young man could not speak French, as did the better-educated Russians in their entourage; and, upon their return, Boris had begun to teach him the language, taking infinite patience to clarify its Latin rules. Yet this friendship was not the same easygoing one that he saw Boris sharing with Walter Nouvel, Diaghilev, or Alexander Benois. Was it because, as his patron first and foremost, Boris still "patronized" him?

The fact remained that this relationship deeply disturbed Pierre. And now Natalia Oblonova disturbed him, too. He thought of her constantly these days, and after being with her tonight, he knew that she would become a veritable obsession for him. She had been here, in this very room, and he had insulted her, upbraided her on account of that necklace, that miserable pearl necklace that Boris had purchased as he might a pair of cufflinks for Pierre or another one of his friends. Boris loved to make magnificent, opulent, perfectly timed gifts to those around him. Yet little Oblonova was not around Boris to stimulate his impulse to give, and Pierre felt fresh resentment for his patron, because of the pearls. How could anything that he himself might offer her compare with Boris's lavish present?

But surely Boris did not want her as he did. Surely the pearls had been symbolic, of admiration, encouragement, possible patronage. Pierre had known of other dancers whom Boris had patronized—yet no one would have doubted the purity of his intentions toward them. Why did Boris's motives with Oblonova matter so much? Pierre knew the answer, of course: because he himself wanted her and considered Boris a rival. It had physically hurt Pierre to see the pearls around her neck tonight—as well as that first night at the dinner. She had worn them because she was poor and owned no other jewels—yet Pierre hated her for having accepted the gift and Boris for having offered it.

He found his desire to possess her bewildering, and unsettling. He had felt strongly attracted to many young women before her, and because of his physical charms, most had suc-

cumbed without second thoughts. He had never wakened thinking of them. Yet this girl troubled him, haunted him. She was
far less beautiful than most of his passing fancies had been.
There was no color in her thin cheeks, and her slender nose was
too long for symmetry. She was too delicate, yet slightly thigh-
heavy. Her brow was too large for her tiny chin, and her breasts
were boyish in their smallness. What was it, then, that appealed
so strongly to him?

He thought of her as a shaft of pure light, simple, straight,
and proud, good but not virtuous, totally devoid of pettiness or
frivolity—stripped bare. Did he like her? He was not sure. She
saw through him, was more powerful than he was, more able to
control her own weaknesses. Yet she was only seventeen, nearly
eighteen—hardly what a sophisticate would call a woman. Boris
had singled her out, too, and this in a certain ironic sense justified Pierre's own feelings. Boris wasted no time upon medi-
ocrities of character or accomplishments. If he was going to
champion her among today's fresh batch of talented dancers,
then Natalia was worthy of attention—Pierre's and other people's.

Pierre was not good with verbal concepts, with organizing his
thoughts. He merely felt them and sometimes wondered about
the strength of his feelings afterward. Now, all at once, he pictured his mother in her youth. His father had been a Georgian,
his mother born of the Tcherkess, a fierce and beautiful tribe of
the Caucasus. Tall, with dark braids that reached below her
knees, she had never wept in front of him. She had been loyal,
passionate, and unafraid. He remembered having seen her
dance the *lezhinka* among her people: a man in front of each
woman, dancing in small rhythmic steps that grew more and
more frenzied, the men hitting the floor with the heels of their
boots. At last the men had unhooked their daggers and one by
one had hurled them into the floor boards, while the women,
still smiling, had continued dancing, unafraid. They had
trusted their men's aim. His mother had carried this philosophy
of blind faith into her private life: She had never questioned his
father, never opposed him. Yet she had been the strongest person Pierre had known. His father, who had raised grapes for

wine, had spent his days riding, a splendid man welded to his white purebred. Yet Pierre had known that his mother, not his father, was the stronger person.

Was Natalia like his mother, who had accompanied him to the train station when he had left this final time and, as a farewell, had given him a small icon to take with him to the city? He did not think the girl was religious, like his mother. She was strong, yes; indomitable, like the Tcherkess women; passionate, like the Tcherkess dancers. But not wise like his mother, not wise enough to place her man first, to obliterate herself for him. Natalia needed to shine, to triumph. She was an exhibitionist and an artist, as he was, in no lesser measure.

Without her dancing, Natalia would be another colorless provincial girl. Pierre was twenty-four, almost as young and inexperienced as she was. What could he offer her? What could Boris offer her? Everything, of course. Why should this lovely young woman be denied an ideal patronage? Why could she not accept Boris's patronage as well as Pierre's love?

There, now, was the word, the word that Pierre had been avoiding. Love! He hardly knew Natalia, and she was not attracted to him, or she would not have left his flat so easily. She was probably a virgin, and proud of it. But this did not disturb Pierre. She had been alone with him in this very room, and he had not touched her. Why? Why did he fear Boris—and his interference?

She is not what I need, Pierre thought. She is not a gentle woman. She is too selfish and not supportive enough. She could never give me the attention I receive from Boris, for example. Boris plays with me, but he also cares deeply about my paintings, the progress of my work, because there is nothing in his life to take precedence over this. But Natalia? She would not play games, and that is good; but she also might not care, or care less than she would about her own dancing. Damn! Can I never stand alone, without needing others to reflect my own worth?

He left the window and sat down, his head in his hands. To marry Natalia Oblonova. Someday—quite soon, in fact—he would become well known. Riazhin would become like Serov and Bakst. Then he would have a life to offer this girl, a life that would tame the selfishness out of her. To be the wife, the companion, of a famous painter! She would meet interesting, cultured individuals, and she would not need to place him below herself. But would he still love her if she gave up her own ambitions so easily? Did he really admire his mother beyond all women? Or had his mother's hardness created an overwhelming need for female softness and gentleness? He wanted Natalia because she was strong and talented, but also because of her hidden vulnerability. He did not know her background, but he instinctively understood that they were both nobler and more savage than city people, yet oddly deprived of affection and nurturing. They were alike in that regard, and this was good.

Pierre felt exhilarated: to marry the girl! But he hardly knew her. She did not like him. She was still so young. He thrust his fingers into his thick hair, overwhelmed. It would never work. He would have to exorcise her from his mind—and from his heart, too. He had never felt such bittersweet yearnings for anyone, such creative stirrings, such a need to combine his essence with that of another person. Natalia, Natalia, he thought. I shall never let you go, though you do not yet know that I have captured you.

Chapter 5

At the New Year Natalia was unexpectedly summoned to the office of General Teliakovsky, director of the Imperial Theatres. He motioned her to take a seat, and smiled paternally. "We are pleased, *ma petite*," he announced. "And so, before your contract is to be renewed, we are promoting you to the rank of *coryphée*."

This was a tremendous, unprecedented honor. Natalia was elated, but contained the joy inside her, for she did not wish to appear arrogant to the senior dancers. Tamara Karsavina came to her, and, putting her arm around her, said: "Congratulations, Natalia." But Anna Pavlova clenched her small, delicate fists and screamed: "You have little talent, and fewer looks! You'll see, nothing will last! Svetlov will write bad things about you—and you will be finished before you ever become a ballerina!" Natalia looked away, her profile haughty and dignified. It did not matter. She had learned long ago that nothing anybody said really mattered.

The *coryphées* danced in small groups, smaller than those of the *corps*. Sometimes one was asked to perform a solo role. Natalia danced another fairy, the Lilac Fairy in *The Sleeping Beauty*. It was a small but charming part, and she appeared at strategic moments, if not for long. Then she danced one of the three main Shades in *La Bayadère*, a Petipa ballet about an abandoned, betrayed fiancée who dies and enters the ghostly Kingdom of Shades. Natalia's ethereal ghost was a single fluid line, and Valerian Svetlov wrote that young Oblonova danced "like magic quicksilver." She enjoyed the role: It was sad and haunting and as different from any of her previous ones as sorrow can be from joy.

Natalia was no longer an unknown dancer. In February she turned eighteen. In a single year so much had happened! She received a small corsage of roses from Teliakovsky and chocolate creams from Karsavina. When she arrived at the flat, Lydia's old nurse, Manya, gave her two packages. One was small and flat, and when she opened it, Natalia found a pair of pearl earrings to match her necklace, each one a pearl teardrop with a ruby. Her heart seemed to race into her throat: It was impossible not to guess who had sent them. She read the message: "Terpsichore is a woman now. Your admiring B.V.K." Ah, she thought, and what does that mean? What should be different now?

The second package was larger, but also flat. She tore the paper in an effort to get around its unwieldiness, and saw the back of a painting. Canvas and wood— *Why?* she thought, suddenly anguished. Why can he not leave me alone? What does he think I owe him? She placed the canvas down and tore the wrapping from its front.

The frame was ornate gold leaf, like the one hanging in Boris's study. She was essentially a simple person, and was somewhat put off by this richness. Then she saw the subject: a woodland scene, with wild animals from mythology—unicorns, a white bull, a golden fish out of water, and a bird with fiery plumage. There was a nymph beneath a tree, and it was, of course, herself: Natalia with tresses flying, a veritable Botticelli's Venus, yet scantily clad in forest leaves. Peeking from behind the tree was Pan. Examining him, Natalia saw he was Pierre. She started to laugh. The colors were of earth, wind, and fire, but the theme was amusing beyond words. "I shall hang you up in the drawing room," she said. "He would have preferred the bedroom, no doubt. Still, he knows our sex: Every woman needs a reminder that she is at the root of mythology."

The painting pleased her. In some small measure it proved to her that she had traveled long distances since her day as "ugly and strange little Natasha." She had read enough about society to know that throughout the ages women larger than life had been immortalized by the pens of poets and the brushes of painters. She knew, inside, that she would one day become famous. But today? A small thrill burst within her. Someone had told her that Riazhin had sullenly refused to paint a portrait of the French ambassador's daughter. Yet this was the second one he had done of her—obscure, impoverished Oblonova. She would hang it in the living room and stun Lydia's guests—some of whom still treated her as her parents had done in the Crimea.

She could not sleep. Everything was happening at once—the praise of an outstanding critic such as Svetlov, this promotion, the gift of costly and incredibly beautiful jewels from one of the court's most prominent members, a leading patron of the arts in St. Petersburg. Had Svetlov been at all swayed by Count Boris's kind outlook toward her budding talent? And Pierre: However much he disturbed her, the fact remained that he was growing in stature as one of Russia's developing young painters. He had been asked to help design the set of a new production at the Mariinsky, *Nuits d'Egypte*. But she was still the lowest dancer among the soloists, if she could even include herself among them. Pavlova still spoke about her rather than to her. And her pay was barely sufficient to provide her with the essentials of life. She was blessed with peaks of glory but still lived on a relatively barren plain. Mystified, Natalia found growing womanhood a mixture of inexplicable signals. Was her life progressing well? She did not possess sufficient experience to know the answer.

Nuits d'Egypte was to be given at the Mariinsky as a charity performance. It was a voluptuous Fokine fantasy of a world that had collapsed centuries ago. Natalia was to be Tahor, another betrayed fiancée, to Michel Fokine's own Amoun. Her role was secondary to that of the languid, sexual Cleopatra—but it was one of desperation and pathos, a good interpretive role.

A week before the show Natalia received an invitation to attend a supper at the home of Count Boris Kussov. As always, she hesitated. Her conversation with Pierre still rankled: She was angry with both men for assuming situations and for playing charades to her. Yet Boris had treated her with the utmost gallantry—as a kind patron. He interested her: She admired his quick mind, his rich culture, his perfect appearance. It was flattering to be included in the circle of his acquaintances. He knew all the ballerinas: Kchessinskaya was an old friend, and he had heard the confidences of Pavlova and Trefilova and boosted Karsavina's sometimes sagging self-concept. Yet Pierre had said he was a man who lived as a vampire from the blood of others.

Was Pierre going to be there, too? Boris was Pierre Riazhin's golden angel—everybody knew it. Pierre's attentions toward Natalia were becoming more insistent—and this was a problem. A man had never cared for her before, and she did not understand. Did he like her? Did he want to sleep with her? Or did he admire her as an artist? Pierre was all tangled emotions, all darkness, while Boris was light and cool. But Pierre reached something deep inside her, so that sometimes she thought of him with strange poignancy. The feelings he inspired in her were fearful and odd, but sometimes she felt that if he were in the same room, her will would melt and she would turn into an animal and do strange things. She did not know what those strange things would be. She found the young painter unlike any human being she had ever met, and still she did not know if she liked him.

Count Boris Kussov's landau came again for her. She had spent more time preparing herself for this occasion than for any previous one, a knot of fear having gathered at her throat. Natalia had always tried to hide her flaws and weaknesses from those who might hurt her—but this time she had gone a step beyond, and granted more importance to her appearance as well. She had purchased peach-colored silk, and the old nurse had made her a gown of her own design, admirable in its bold simplicity. The slim skirt sheathed her hips and legs and widened at the ankle, and the neckline went straight across her collarbone, showing the rounded tops of her shoulders. A ruffle fell over her breasts and shoulders, so that her bust appeared larger than it really was. She had parted her hair in the center and puffed out the sides, bringing it up into a topknot decorated with a single coral rose. She wore the pearls in her ears and at her throat.

The elegant apartment was filled to capacity with men and women about whom Natalia would not have dared to dream during her Crimean childhood. She could not help but feel awestruck. She wished Pierre Riazhin would come to speak with her, but he was in a corner with a woman bedecked in diamonds and emeralds. Boris came. He lifted her small hand to his arm and kissed her lightly on the cheek. "I have a surprise," he told her. "In fact, I will show it to you at once. The others can wait to see it later."

Silently Natalia permitted her host to lead her to his study. The memory of Pierre flashed vividly before her, and for a rash moment she wondered whether Boris might not want to make love to her, too. But when he opened the door, she stood hypnotized on the threshold. Four large trunks lay open, with brocades, muslins, satins, and rich velvets spread around the room. "Come in," he commanded. "Touch my little treasures!"

She did so, gingerly. The materials had been fashioned into ancient robes, and shoes—men's exotic apparel such as she had never seen anyone wear, even in Petersburg. There was also burnished jewelry with encrusted semiprecious stones. Boris held a tunic of gold threads intertwined with bright purple strands across her neckline. "True loveliness," he commented. There was irony in his blue eyes, but also, she thought suddenly, a tinge of real appreciation.

"What is all this, Boris Vassilievitch?" Natalia asked. "Where does it come from?"

"India, Egypt. If you wondered what kept me from your last performances, it was a voyage that I undertook for the Imperial Ballet. I have taken a great liking to Fokine—and it is difficult for him to be duly recognized by our conservative balletomanes. Also Pierre is designing—has designed, now—the set for *Nuits d'Egypte*. This is his first effort at set design. Teliakovsky has taken an interest in developing our Russian painters in this direction, but, being a Muscovite, had been employing men from his city, Korovin and Golovin. Now it's Pierre's turn, thank God. But, to return to my part in this: I thought that this opulent Egyptian production needed something extra—so I took Pierre up the Nile to find genuine costumes."

Natalia blinked. She looked at Count Boris's fine features, at his exquisite nose and eyes, and thought: To love artists so much! "I am sorry," she said. "My own impoverished child-

hood is still too close for me to fully comprehend the extravagance of such a gift to the Ballet. The trip alone! It makes me
think of *The Thousand and One Nights.* Did Pierre enjoy the
new worlds to which you introduced him?"

"Pierre needed to see the Orient. An artist must understand
and participate in other cultures, other vistas. Yes, he was wide-
eyed, much as you are now simply hearing about it, Natalia
Dmitrievna." Boris had caught the quick rush of color into her
cheeks at the mention of his protégé, and now he examined her
through half-closed eyes.

But Natalia had abruptly thought: So that is why I received
no word between that night in November and my birthday. She
met Boris's look and said: "You must have great affection for
Pierre, to do so much for him."

Boris stiffened. "Indeed," he replied. "Pierre is a genius of
sorts, but he is young and provincial. If I can help—then of
course I am glad to do so." He looked toward the door. "Shall
we go now, Natalia Dmitrievna?"

Panic rose in her. "Please," she said in a small voice, "would
you allow me to remain here for a little while longer? I am to
dance Tahor—and if I could just look around . . . ."

Formally Boris nodded, "Very well. Suit yourself. When you
are ready, look for me. I have seated you on my right and
should like to take you in to dinner."

When he had left, she sat down, stunned. On his right? But
the Grand-Duke Vladimir was here—and Kchessinskaya—and
Lady Buchanan, the wife of the British ambassador! She found
Boris a most bewildering man, and her own part in this gathering even less understandable. She thought of Pierre and remembered that he had not greeted her at all. Had she offended him?
Yet she had sent him a most gracious letter of thanks for his
marvelous woodland scene—a sincere letter of admiration. She
had thought—what had she actually thought? That he would
call upon her in her home to see the painting in its new haven.
But what did his indifference matter? Why was she hot and
flushed in this room filled with exotic fineries, some of which
she herself would wear at the Mariinsky?

"Boris is a rogue, keeping this from us!" trilled a voice from
the corridor. Natalia quickly rose and touched her topknot. It

was Matilda Felixovna Kchessinskaya and the critic Skalkovsky. The *prima ballerina assoluta* tripped into the room, her dark hair a mass of attractive curls, her small, well-shaped body resplendent with magnificent jewels. "Ah—Natashenka," she said. There was a curious tone of displeasure in the greeting. "What are you doing here all alone?"

"Boris Vassilievitch brought me here moments ago," the girl replied.

"Oh? What attentiveness, don't you think? You have quite charmed the gentleman. But oh! What beauties lie here! So like a miracle. Don't you agree?" she asked, turning to the critic.

"Frankly, Matilda Felixovna, I find all this excessive. The Fokine ballet is only for a single charity night, and he is not an official choreographer. I do not like his work—it reminds me of Duncan. What we need today is more of your virtuosity, *ma chère*. The newfangled ballets fail to employ the full resources of our dancers' training."

"And Michel Fokine is a slave driver," added Matilda Felixovna. "An ambitious young hothead with no due respect for those of us who have paid our dues. I did not like Teliakovsky's putting on *Nuits d'Egypte* for this benefit. I think I shall have a talk with the Grand-Duke Vladimir. It is time he wielded his influence to have us put on *La Fille Mal Gardée* instead, which allows me to perform my special variations. The public comes primarily for me—does it not?"

"Naturally, Matilda Felixovna. You *are* the Ballet. I myself follow you to Moscow every time you dance there," Skalkovsky said, touching his mustache with a careless finger.

Natalia stood listening, the muscles in her body tense and taut. "But, Matilda Felixovna, *Nuits d'Egypte* has been rehearsed, the sets are ready, and publicity has been made. Surely you would not have it changed at this late date?" she asked.

Kchessinskaya breathed deeply. "*Coryphées* should not have an opinion," she intoned.

"We have all made valiant efforts for the new ballet," Natalia continued. "Fokine deserves a chance, even if he does lose his temper and treat us all badly, like naughty schoolchildren. Please! Boris Vassilievitch and Pierre Riazhin took a special trip

to India and Egypt. Would you have had them travel in vain?"
Natalia's pulse raced. She would not think of the consequences
of speaking up like this. These things must be said!

Matilda Kchessinskaya looked away from Natalia around the
room. Her fine eyes landed on Pierre's picture of the girl as the
Sugar Plum Fairy. "I see," she said. "Your boldness is a display
of your protected status. I did not realize that Boris had included you under the mantle of his patronage. Or is it more,
my partridge?"

"It is nothing like that," Natalia replied, her brown eyes clear
and wide with defiance. Words came tumbling out of her: "I do
not require a well-placed man's protection before professing an
opinion." It was too late to swallow back the implication.

Matilda Felixovna took two steps toward Natalia. Without
speaking, she raised her right hand and slapped the young girl
on the cheek, where the red imprint of her fingers remained
etched in pain. Then, proudly, Kchessinskaya took Skalkovsky's
arm, and, without looking back, they strode from the study.

Natalia stayed prostrated on the chair, her face in her hands.
She felt the hot tears spill from between her fingers onto her
gown, her lovely apricot gown. The room with its brocades and
jewels lay about her small misery, oddly clashing with it. She
heard footsteps but did not heed them. Then two strong hands
were laid upon her shoulders, and she looked into the dark face
of Pierre Riazhin, kneeling in front of her. She attempted to
draw away, but in urgent gasps, he said: "It isn't worth it! Stop
crying, my darling. She does not matter, only you matter—you
and I!"

"Wh-what do you mean?" Natalia asked, startled. Her panic
was returning.

"Who cares about Kchessinskaya? She is an old bag, passed
from one grand-duke to another! I heard about what happened
between you—she was telling everyone—but it doesn't matter! I
shall have a great future soon now. You must—you must marry
me, Natalia Dmitrievna. Say that you will!"

Natalia stared at him, totally devoid of feeling. Then a tickle
began in the pit of her stomach and traveled inch by inch up
her throat. It exploded, like a magic bubble—and she sat shaking with laughter, hysterical wails of laughter that could not be

controlled. Pierre's hands abruptly dropped from her shoulders. "I never expected *this!*" he said, rising.

The bubbles of laughter died down at once. She looked away, embarrassed, ashamed, feeling ugly and naked. "Forgive me, Pierre Grigorievitch," she whispered. "It was the tension . . ."

He wet his wide, full lips. "Then, will you marry me?" he asked again. "I want this very much, Natalia Dmitrievna. I want you. But I shall not humiliate myself by having you mock me again."

They looked at each other, and her lips parted. She clasped her hands together, then shook her head, a tendril falling out of her topknot. "No," she said. "I would not mock you. But I cannot become your wife—or any man's. You see, I—marriage—it wouldn't be the right way for me to live."

"I am not good enough? There is someone else?" The black eyes would not leave her face.

She bit her trembling lower lip. "Please!" she cried. "Can't a woman simply prefer to live alone?"

His face had grown pale, and there were circles under his eyes. He looked suddenly much older, hurt, defeated, and rebellious as a result. She wanted to move to him but could not. "I do not believe you," he said simply, and walked out of the room.

Music reached her ears from the salon, strains of a waltz. She leaned against Boris's boulle secretary and steadied herself. She did care. Something inside her had leaped with yearning when she had heard his voice, felt his hands upon her. It had been wonderful but terrifying, and now she had averted the danger. She felt sick, tired, and empty and sad. Was it Pierre, with his absurd proposal, or was it the scene with Kchessinskaya that had sapped the life from her?

"You are going to take my arm like a good girl," Count Boris was saying. "There now, that's better. And remember this, Natalia Dmitrievna: I too possess influence at court. You are not going to shame me by not appearing beside me."

General Teliakovsky said: "I am sorry, Natalia Dmitrievna. The pressures upon you have undoubtedly been too strong to

bear. You are very young. Varvara Ivanovna kept you very quiet
at the school, and now—without a family—"

"But I do not need a family!" she exclaimed. "Why? I have
not been late to any rehearsals. I have been in wonderful
health."

"That is what you fail to grasp. Your health is not so good.
You are rapidly becoming hysterical here in my office, and the
report was worded very strongly: You lost your temper and
nearly went out of your mind, Matilda Felixovna said. She was
most concerned. She should be able to recognize the first signs
of strain. You are working too hard, and it has been my fault.
Lopokhova can take over your role in *The Little Humpbacked
Horse*—and Pavlova shall dance Tahor. You will go home and
rest for the remainder of the month. Come to class, that is all."

Natalia took a step toward the great mahogany desk. "But
none of this is true!" she cried. "I beg of you, General—let me
explain!"

"If you continue this, I shall have you forcibly removed," the
director interrupted her. He stood up, tall and imposing. "I
mean it: One more word, and I shall fine you. Go home,
Natalia Dmitrievna."

"You aren't being fair with me," she said evenly, not moving.
"You are not allowing me to defend my own position. I am a
good dancer and do not deserve this suspension. I have never
disobeyed you. I have never been temperamental. Yet you have
singled me out because of something that does not have anything whatsoever to do with the Ballet."

Teliakovsky sighed. "Oblonova, five rubles shall be withdrawn by the management from your next six months' salary. I
warned you, and you did not listen. Now are you satisfied?"

Natalia did not tremble anymore. She nodded humbly and
turned around. The door stood before her; she turned the knob
and passed silently into the corridor. This was not real. No one
could be so vindictive. Kchessinskaya was proud but not mean;
petty, but not cruel. And kind, paternal General Teliakovsky?
No, no, this was a farce, a Russian fairy story without fairies, a
Hoffmann fantasy ending in . . . God only knew how this
would end! She went into the dressing room, which was empty,

and began to gather her possessions. Almost a full month! It was incredible, farcical.

Someone had entered behind her, and she turned to see Anna Pavlova, her frail shoulders sloping delicately like angel's wings. Natalia stiffened. "So," the other woman said, "you did not think that your luck would hold out forever, did you? You are a nobody from the Crimea. Everybody knows all about you. I remember the day that you took the exam, when your mother brought you. The maid of Baroness Gudrinskaya. Hidden away on some Crimean farm! Tell me, love, who is your father?"

Natalia stared at her with utter shock. She could not make a sound.

"In any case," Pavlova continued, "a girl must play her fair share of the old classics before being permitted to dance the modern ones. Michel Fokine did not really want you. Your bones show. How voluptuous is a bony Egyptian? You are audacious and impudent. Nobody likes you here. You are only tolerated because of Boris Vassilievitch. People are afraid to offend him, and for some bizarre reason he seems to like you."

Natalia folded a pair of leg warmers carefully, and placed them inside her bag. Since she refused to look up or reply, Pavlova shrugged and went to her own dressing table. Natalia walked out of the large room, holding her head rigid and doll-like. Pavlova ignored her exit and sat down, humming to herself.

Outside the Mariinsky, Natalia stood uncertainly. Answers, retorts burned in her head. But of what use would they have been? She started to laugh, a small, trembling laugh filled with tears: the daughter of Masha, that sullen maid! It would all have been amusing, if it had not been coupled with the fine and the suspension. No one worked longer hours than she—nobody! Nobody sublimated all her desires in work, in strain. She had always known that the world was not a fair place, but to have come so far and lose it all—her only chance to make something of her life!

For the first time since she was ten years old, Natalia Oblonova did not know what to do. There was no comfort anywhere. She began to walk, telling herself that it did not matter if she overstretched her leg muscles, since she could not dance anyway. It was a warm day in March, and the streets were thawing. Clouds of tiny mosquitos rose from the ugly, oozing snow, but the Anitchkov Palace shone orange, the spire of the Admiralty white and gold. Natalia walked and walked, as she had not walked since living in the Crimea.

Toward dusk she found herself in a side street, in front of a low, run-down building. Had she intended to come here? She was exhausted, dazed. She knew this area, this apartment house. It was where Pierre lived, Pierre Riazhin. She was here, then, for a reason.

She could not think things through; her mind refused to function. Hurt, angry, disbelieving, her thoughts remained blocked, obtuse. She knew that she was dirty—grimy from the streets, perspiration clinging to her neck—but still, she pushed open the large front door and walked laboriously up the ramshackle staircase. She knocked on the wooden panel beneath his name, but there was no answer. She sank to the floor, weeping soundlessly, settling helplessly on the floorboards.

She did not notice the passage of time. At some point she realized she was hungry, but then the pains abated, and only weariness remained. The hallway light went out, fizzing and spurting before expiring in its ceiling socket. Horses' hooves resounded on the pavement. Natalia propped her knees up and tucked her skirt beneath her feet because it was cold. She laid her arms upon her knees, and her head in her arms. Intermittently, she dozed.

Then the front door was banging open. A carriage horse was being whipped into action outside and there were footsteps on the stairs. She raised her head and was taken aback. Pierre, in full evening regalia, his black silk top hat in one hand and an elegant silver-headed cane in the other, was bounding up the stairs, his ebony cape unfurling picturesquely behind him. He resembled a prince of darkness, Pluto returning from the cavernous depths in which he had imprisoned Proserpine. He did not belong in this building at all, but rather in a palace upholstered in black and crimson velvet, filled with large, baroque mirrors. She forgot her misery and cried: "How wonderful you look, riding the winds!"

He halted, staring at her in amazement. Then his face became younger, gayer, lighter. He extended his hand to her, and pulled her up. "You came," he said. "I hadn't hoped—"

She merely shook her head, turning up the palms of her frail hands. The misery and hopelessness of her situation came clear as her physical fatigue overwhelmed her. He unlocked the door, held it open for her, and she passed into the flat in front of him. He turned on a light. "If I had only known—" he stammered. "I wouldn't have gone out. The opera. *Sadko.*"

"Yes. Chaliapin transports a person out of his depths. Do you know him?" she asked, awkwardly standing in the small room where the paintings hung.

He was removing his cape, hanging up his cane and hat. "Yes. He and Boris are quite congenial. We had supper with him afterward. He tells a good story."

Now he stood in his tuxedo, a strange sight in the small, badly furnished room. She thought: Boris Vassilievitch has taught him how to dress, has probably loaned him the use of his tailor. Pierre did not look as rough and provincial as the first time she had met him. Perhaps the city was etching its indelible imprint upon him. Was that good? Or were people like Boris Kussov too refined, too rarified, too effete? She looked at Pierre quite frankly from her wide, clear eyes, brown and limpid. It felt warm, pleasantly tingling, to appraise him thus.

He appeared to enjoy the strength of his body, his well-proportioned thighs and shoulders, his powerful agility. Now he looked at her, and she was suddenly embarrassed. I'm so dirty, she thought, and wanted to take to her heels and forget that she had come, hoping that he would forget, too. With whom had he been, apart from Boris and Feodor Chaliapin? Beautiful, scented ladies of the aristocracy? Divas from the Opera? *Demimondaines* at the sinful Aquarium? A shiver of repulsion swept over her, and she imagined Pierre placing his hands upon a woman's thigh, upon her bodice.

They had both stopped talking and in the soft glow of the yellow light he extended both hands to her, and she took them in her own, fingers to fingers. Neither wished to break this sudden intimacy. She was tired, hungry, and wanted to cry, but she was also exhilarated. Then he took her in his arms and kissed her, a rough movement that tilted her head back in an uncomfortable position. She could not breathe. She wound her arms around his neck and returned his kisses, uttering little moans of unexpected delight. Then he stepped away from her and asked, "You will marry me, won't you?"

Frantically, she seized the lapels of his dinner jacket and thrust her face into his chest, like a lost animal of the forest. She felt his heart beat, the life of him, the miracle that was the life of him! Tears came to her eyes. She raised her face and touched his cheeks with gentle, tentative fingers. "I don't know," she whispered. Then, shaking her head, her curls tumbling out of the French twist which had been holding them in place, she exclaimed: "Don't talk about it now!"

Pierre Riazhin saw the anguish in her face and knew that something terrible had happened. But it was not the time to ask her about it. She had said, "I don't know," and that was closer to consent than anything he had heard from her before. Tomorrow she might repeat her former refusal, which he could not understand. If there were another man—Boris, and his damned pearls?—then she would not now be kissing him so passionately, with so much love. "But you do love me, Natalia?" he asked, a gnawing fear seizing him that she was somehow using him as substitute for something, someone else. "I have to know," he added urgently, gently shaking her shoulders.

She nodded, biting her lower lip with perfect white teeth. Tears were streaming down her cheeks, and she looked pale, haggard. She tried to smile, but the smile was crooked. She reached his lips with hers, standing on her tiptoes, and this time he did not question her, but lifted her from the floor and carried her into his bedroom. She said nothing when he placed her tenderly on the bed, or when he removed his jacket. Keeping her eyes on his, she began to unbutton the front of her bodice, and her long, fine fingers were fast and sure. His own eyes filled with tears and he thought: Dear God in heaven, let me love her enough.

Natalia sat against the pillows, her brown hair around her like a gentle halo. He briefly wondered at the power in that young, strong female body, the muscled thighs, the small, round breasts, the shoulders that sloped into well-formed arms. He had not imagined she would be so firm, this small, frail girl with the wide eyes and vulnerable mouth. He had simply forgotten that this woman danced every day of her life, that dance had kept her apart in much the same way that convents secluded religious women with unfathomable rigors. Now he was confronted with this new Natalia, this firm but yielding body that lay exposed before him. She felt his eyes examining, appraising her, and all at once she made the timeless gesture of Eve, and covered her breasts with one hand and her pubis with the other, and turned aside, waves of embarrassment washing over her. She would have done anything to escape, to be done with this man and with this bed and with her own confusion and shame. She was ashamed of being human, of being a woman.

Would there ever come a time, he thought with sudden compassion, when a girl would be able to display herself naturally, without this ancestral guilt, this fear of judgment? But she was looking at him now, and the brief flush had seeped away, and she was very pale, as if bewildered. "You're very young," he murmured softly, knowing that she had never seen a man's hardness before, and that the very first time wonder vied with a certain revulsion in most women. They simply did not come prepared. He came to her and knelt before her, so that his head was level with hers, and so that his maleness was hidden from her for the moment. When he touched her cheek it was very cold, and he knew she was numb with shock. Part of the numbness was desire, the other part an elemental fear, the fear of being opened up to this man, of being violated. After tonight she would never be the same again, never whole and her own.

Her throat constricted, tears clouded her eyes, and suddenly she began to cry soundlessly. He buried his face in the crook of her neck and held her to him, and she wept into his hair, rocking with him. It was all right this way, it would be all right. Then, with the hunger of his own impatient youth, he kissed the softness of her swan's throat and crept downward with his lips, seeking the tips of her breasts, and she could feel his teeth around the puckered skin. Her lack of experience confounded her, and she grasped his hair with a sort of desperation, twirling her fingers through the thick locks. Then he pressed her down on the bed and she knew that she must confront him, the newness, the shock, the strange ugliness and fascination of his maleness. She lay back and watched him lie down next to her, and then, horrified, she wrapped her nakedness in a side of the blanket and shrank to the edge of the bed, unthinking and trembling.

Tentatively he touched her shoulder, and, to his surprise, she turned to him, her eyes wide open. "It's not new to you," she whispered. It was a statement, oddly quiet after the weeping. She touched his face, caressed his cheeks, went lightly over the tulip softness of his eyelids, one after the other. "Please, please turn off the light."

"But I want to look at you," he answered softly.

"Why?"

"Because it *is* new to me. It's never been you before—never Natalia. Let me make love to you properly. Don't make me grope for you in the dark. It's a sacrament, you know."

"You're breaking into me," she said. "All of me—all of me at once. There's no comfort in this."

"No, there's no comfort," he agreed, putting his arms around her and gently drawing her to him. "There's no comfort anywhere, Natalia. Don't come to me for safety, because I can't bring it to you. I love you too much."

Then she kissed him and smothered herself in the smell and taste of him, and when he touched her firm taut stomach, she was still, and waited. He placed her hand over his hardness and she did not cry out. She felt it curiously—this something that she did not know, that was altogether too solid to merge into her. He was a man and the whole concept was electrifying, terrifying, mesmerizing. When finally he shifted his weight to his knees and moved on top of her, she closed her eyes and clenched both hands over his forearms, to steel herself for the assault. "Don't fight me," he said, as if she could have known what he meant, as if she could have known how much it would hurt. Instead she felt the searing pain, and he saw in her eyes the shock, the betrayal. They'd all felt like that, all of them. "It won't ever hurt this way again," he told her, watching her white face and feeling guilty.

For a while there was nothing—simply an adjustment to the tearing inside, then a numb warmth. Something moved inside her, and she breathed again, slowly at first. He kissed her cheek, her chin, her lips. "There've been so many others in your life," she whispered, almost accusingly. "Why did you want it to be me, if for you this is such a normal thing?"

"Because it's different when you love," he replied. "You still don't believe me, do you?"

"I want to like it," she whispered. "But it feels as if you've wounded me."

The words, wondering and tinged with resentment, whipped into his consciousness, and he began to slide inside her, up and down and softly sideways. Her mouth relaxed. He could see her arms reaching up to him, her hands wrapping around his neck. "I'm sorry, I'm sorry," she murmured, pressing her breasts against him, the nipples hard and warm. She could feel the tip of him way inside her, pushing against the edge of the womb. The pain stayed with her, the burning sensation, but now there were other sensations, and the rhythmic flow of his body was like a dance—that was it, like a dance. But too quick, too hard. Part of it felt very good, very fine and mellow, but then it would begin again, the thrust too sudden. It was like a dance. You had to learn, you had to practice. It was like taking on a new dancing partner—you had to learn his style, his tempo, and adjust your own.

Then she knew she wanted this breaking open of her, this merging, this deep penetration to the core of her being. She held him tightly and began to lift her legs to allow him further access, and a great joy took possession of her, the joy of wanting another person, this person, Pierre. She called his name, "Pierre, Pierre," like a declaration, a fondling. He was making her beautiful, making her human, making her a woman. When his face contorted into a grimace of pain and pleasure, and he cried out, incoherent animal moans that at first profoundly frightened her, she realized that it was different for him, different for men, that the passion overrode the searing and the burning and maybe even the love. But it was all right. He was young and he was hers, and he had made himself vulnerable, by crying out, by letting go. She loved him for it, more than for the kisses, more than for his beauty.

Afterward it was he who wept, not she, and she did not understand. "It's not fair," he said. "I love you so much more than this, and it's too soon for us, you're not used to it."

"But I want to try again, because I can't seem to stop loving you back," she murmured, moving to the crook of his arm. "I've never been in love, and I'm still afraid of you, Pierre. My beautiful Pierre." But he had fallen asleep, and so she closed her own eyes and allowed herself the luxury of floating into space, hypnotized by the cadence of his breathing and by her own exhaustion. She wanted to laugh and sob at once, but she was too tired. At last she raised herself on one elbow, turned down the wick in the lamp, and welcomed the darkness.

She awakened drenched with perspiration. There had been a beach, and the sea, and suddenly a wave like a pillar, blue-green and ominous, coming toward her. She had felt pressure in her throat, a strangling and a suffocation. She sat up, gasping for air, her eyes distended. Relief flowed her over like balmy breath: She had escaped, she was alive. It had only been a dream.

When she lay back upon the pillows, she realized that she was not wearing the high-necked negligé in which she usually slept. She felt the soft grain of her skin—her arms, her knees, the small mounds of her breasts. She was completely naked! Goose bumps spread over her. Slowly she turned her face toward the left and saw his tousled curls. His large back lay next to her, and she felt it tentatively with her finger. He moaned in his sleep. Shivers, tremors passed over her then, one after the other. Horror, joy, fear, remembered pleasure—all these sensations struggled within her half-awakened consciousness, and she sat up again, willing the night away.

Then misery overwhelmed her. The previous day came to mind, and every nerve cried out in agony. What was she to do? She looked at Pierre and was afraid to touch him. The broad back, the pronounced muscles, the strength, the manhood of him—what wonder, what beauty, what strange sensations they provided! But what had he to do with her predicament as a dancer? What of the Mariinsky, the suspension, the shame? Was she finished at eighteen? She shut out the tears with her eyelids and clenched her fists. She could not stay, she must not succumb to his presence, his smell, the way one thigh straddled her effortlessly—the way he had tried not to hurt her but to relax her, gently, unselfishly. She would never have suspected his kindness. She would have thought him brutal and self-serving with a woman. Not at all— But if she stayed with him she would not be able to think, to plan, to dance, to sort out her life.

She threw back the covers and jumped to the bare floor. Quickly she found her scattered undergarments, the drawers, the corset, the corset cover. There was no time to waste. She had to leave before he awakened and claimed her again, before he looked at her with his ebony eyes that dragged her soul into his, that closed the narrow gap separating them. Hastily, she stuck the tortoiseshell comb into her topknot, buttoned the top of her blouse, and grabbed the bag stuffed with her belongings from the Imperial Ballet. She did not think to leave a note. Pierre had become a demon now, one from whom she must flee as rapidly as possible. Only outside in the bitter cold of the early morning did she think, with a sudden pang of dreadful yearning: But when shall I see him again? Will he ever speak to me again?

It did not occur to her to feel ashamed of what she had done, or to fear Pierre's subsequent rejection. She knew that he loved her, that they had bound themselves to each other completely—and that it was this very commitment that had to be broken, for it went against all that she had spent her lifetime achieving: her sense of self, her independence. With renewed trembling she thought, Pierre could eat me alive. It would do no good to ask herself if the half-life to which she might consign herself without him was worth the sacrifice. Her young life had already been paved with many sacrifices.

Gently, Boris knocked on the door. When there was no answer, he turned to his manservant and said: "Open up then, Ivan." The other, in his black broadcloth, the very symbol of his calling, deftly removed a key ring from his pocket and, without a moment's hesitation, inserted the correct one into the lock and turned it. Boris passed into the small hallway and sniffed: "This place smells of sleep—and of sweat. Also of something else. What is it, Ivan?"

"A lady, Your Excellency." Ivan turned on a light, and preceded his master into the room with the paintings. He was carrying a small basket and a large bag, and now he began to empty the latter. He placed floor polish, furniture wax, and dustcloths of the finest chamois on the floor. Ivan then took out a freshly baked poppy-seed cake, and a small box of Calville apples and Muscat grapes.

Boris stood with his erect, graceful back to the wall hung with paintings. He had clasped his hands behind him and appeared lost in thought. The manservant observed him from hooded eyes and wondered at the taut skin over the cheekbones, the small wrinkles around the eyes. His master wore a tragic mask this fine morning. He cleared his throat and said delicately: "If there is a lady, Your Excellency, should I still awaken monsieur?"

"That wouldn't do," Boris replied, the words dripping like icicles from his tight lips. "No, Ivan—a lady would faint if you were the first sight to greet her in the morning. I would be infinitely more suitable."

"Quite, Your Excellency. I shall make the coffee." Boris watched Ivan carry the foodstuffs into the tiny cubicle that was Pierre's kitchen. He waited, listening. Then, almost in sprightly fashion, he shook himself into action and walked to the doorway of the bedroom.

Before looking, Boris closed his eyes, a sudden quick pain flashing through his stomach—the burning warning of anxiety that seemed to tear his body in two. It passed, and he breathed deeply. He tugged on the lapels of his light brown Norfolk jacket and touched his waxed blond mustache. Pierre lay sprawled in his bed, and Boris entered, blinking. The elegant tuxedo was on the floor—the ruffled shirt, the pants, even the undergarments. Boris scooped to pick up something that gleamed: a gold cufflink emblazoned with a topaz, his own present to the young man. Boris sat down on the edge of the bed, watching the other breathe, and his jaw set tightly. But he did nothing to disturb the scene.

At length the sleeping figure stirred, feeling a foreign presence. Pierre's hand groped on the neighboring pillow, and he turned his head toward Boris. He mumbled something, and Boris stiffened, then bent forward to catch the words: "Darling, darling." Still he did not speak. Like all heavy sleepers, Pierre was taking his time to bridge the gap between dreams and reality. He was opening his eyes, searching. "Natalia?" he said.

"She's not here," Boris replied clearly. It was better this way, knowing. He shut his mind to the searing in his stomach lining and said calmly: "Wake up now, Pierre. It's past ten. Breakfast time, you know."

Pierre sat up and rubbed his eyes, the gesture of a small boy. "Boris?" he intoned. "I don't understand. What—?"

"You forgot Ivan, then," Boris answered lightly. "How can anyone forget Ivan? He came to clean this hellhole. It's Friday. I promised you Ivan's services on Friday. And then I thought: 'Knowing Pierre, after the supper party last night, and the opera, he will sleep late. Why not share a breakfast with him when he rises?' Was it a bad idea?"

Pierre's face grew red, and tendons stood out on his neck. "For god's sake, Boris!" he exclaimed, fully awake now. "Without warning? You come at all times of the day and night—I tell you, I can't stand it! This is my home, for whatever it's worth— mine, not yours! You may own the rest of the world, but not this hellhole, as you call it. You can take Ivan and—"

"And what? Would you discard my friendship in one fell swoop?"

Pierre's mouth worked silently. The hand that he had raised fell on the coverlet. "Damn it!" he cried. He glared at Boris, then seemed to remember something and searched the room with his squinting eyes. "How long have you been here?" he asked.

"Ten minutes. I told you, she's not here. She hasn't been here since we arrived. Little Oblonova?" Boris raised one fine golden brow and smiled.

Pierre's black eyes halted upon his friend's face. Boris read in them pain, bewilderment, love. The nakedness of this expression hurt him. Pierre shrugged. "No, someone—inconsequential. But still, damn it, if she'd been here—"

Boris started to laugh. "Go on, get up and conquer the world.

Ivan is preparing coffee—though I wouldn't want to guess with what! Did you also forget that Fokine and Benois wanted to see you today? At Serge's flat."

Pierre stood up, tall, massive, golden brown, and reached for a dressing gown. For a moment he hesitated, sensing eyes upon him, but when he wheeled about, Boris was idly examining the cufflink in the palm of his hand. Pierre thought: I shall think about you later, Natalia—when I am alone once more. But he did not understand where she could have gone, or why.

Count Vassily Arkadievitch Kussov stared at his son from beneath his bushy brows, and puffed on his pipe. "Why?" he asked. "Why is it so difficult for me to reach you these days? Your behavior troubles me, Boris. Believe me, I understand about Marguerite. They were not truthful with us. Even the Tzar understands now and has taken your side. Giving back part of the dowry has not hurt you much, I can see that. But still— there are other reasons why a young man should marry. It almost seems as though you were relieved that Marguerite possessed a flaw, instead of outraged, as any bridegroom should have been! But all that is past history. Today, you should be planning to leave heirs. You are thirty-three now."

"That is young enough, Papa," Boris replied. He was sitting on a love seat in the magnificent living room, with its chandelier of Venetian crystal and its delicate rose lamps and tapestried walls. His massive parent occupied a large armchair across from him.

"Perhaps. But Boris, there are other things that disturb me. Your friends. All fine young men, all aristocrats, except for Bakst, the Jew. But some of them have reputations. Teliakovsky tells me that several years ago when Diaghilev worked for Volkonsky, his predecessor at the Imperial Theatres, there was quite a scandal. Some of his colleagues gave the young man a powder puff to show contempt for his sexual preferences. And Lvov— Pavel Dmitrievitch—how well I know that family! There is none better in Petersburg. But the parties he gives—all for his male friends, his lovers! I find this very distressing. Why do you associate with men such as these?"

Boris sighed, then smiled and shook his head. "Really, Papa!

I am certain that some of Nina's friends, or Nadia's and Liza's, may be committing adultery. One continues to see one's friends because they are interesting, talented, or simpatico. Besides—today homosexuality is not seen as the great shame it was once considered in Petersburg. Truly, it has become—like adultery. One knows homosexuals and adulterers, and while one may not approve of what they practice behind closed doors, one pretends one doesn't know. It's that simple."

"For lower echelons of the nobility maybe, or for those who do not dwell among their kin. Diaghilev's family is from Perm. But Lvov has brought pain to his people, that is a certainty. And while we may not be like the English, who condemn outright, we have our standards, nevertheless. Your proximity with men of dubious morals has brought me sleepless nights. If you were married, tongues would not wag."

"And my other friends? Benois is a happily wed father, and Nouvel, too. Bakst adores women. Why are the majority of my companions forgotten for the marginal minority? You are not making sense, Papa. Should a man marry in order to move freely among talented men who amuse him, simply because not all of them conform?"

Count Vassily sat up, suddenly stern and imposing. "Boris, you are glib with me, and satirical! Keep whatever friends you wish. I do not question your own integrity or your morals, only your well-being. Is there a reason why you do not pay court to any particular woman of society? Are you afraid she may turn out to be like Marguerite? Tell me about yourself. I am your father, and you shut me out! Talk to me. You are my own comfort in life. Your sisters bore me. It's not their fault—but they are women, and that, for me, is foreign territory. Talk to me!"

The old count's strong voice reverberated in the delicate room. Boris sucked on his upper lip. At length he said: "There is someone I care for, enough so that I do not want to marry another woman. Marguerite—what a disaster that marriage was! I admit that I gained from it, financially. My part of the dower settlement can support several years of artistic endeavors without my needing to touch the balance of my personal income. It helped, with the two weddings within eighteen months of each other. But now all my sisters are well married, and there is no further need for me to form an alliance based on greed, shall we say. So I shall not marry at all."

"But why can you not marry this woman? Is she already married?" his father asked.

Boris looked at a painting of a Madonna and Child by Raphaël. The Madonna was young, with enormous soft brown eyes that reminded him of someone, and the picture was round, encased in a frame of blue lacquer. He stared at it pensively, then appeared to make up his mind. "No, she isn't married," he said. "But she isn't of our sort. She is lovely, gifted, brave, but not a gentlewoman, as you would say."

His father's eyes rounded. He smiled. "I see. In other words, marriage to her would bring nothing more to you than you already have. I can understand that, Boris. A mésalliance would surely be wrong. I pity you in your predicament. And yet—what if a child should come?"

"I would not worry if I were you, Papa," his son replied. "However, should the unexpected occur, I would do right by her. I would certainly recognize the child and make it my heir. Does that satisfy you?"

"Naturally. You are an honorable man. Shall I ring for tea now?" The older man bent toward his son and patted his hand. "Still," he added, "the whole affair's a damned shame. I would have preferred it otherwise. But then, so should you, so should you."

Boris nodded, but he thought: How could I have permitted him to trap me into a corner like this? Now what am I to do? The Madonna was looking at him, and now he fancied her mocking. He welcomed the tea tray because food and warm liquids always relieved the burning in the pit of his stomach. But his fingers on the glass shook slightly.

Ivan cleared his throat and repeated: "The young lady is in the salon, Your Excellency. I took the liberty of bringing some fruit and tea. She seems at her wits' end."

Boris stood in his bathrobe, drying himself. "You did well, as always, Ivan. Please tell Natalia Dmitrievna that I shall come out as soon as I can." He waited as his servant removed the empty pitcher and the bowl of sudsy shaving water. Then he poured some toilet water into his hand and splashed it over his neck, into his hair. He was smiling. There was a silk dressing gown ready for him on the small settee, and he put it on. She had come unexpectedly: Let her, too, be surprised! When he stepped out, he resembled a splendid bridegroom on his way to the bedchamber.

He found her in the living room, eating an apple. She was very small, ensconced in the large Louis XV armchair. Her brown hair was in disarray, strands escaping from her topknot. There were purple circles beneath her large eyes. Her attire was, if not shabby, then certainly hastily chosen and donned. She seemed like a waif from the pages of Dickens, and he smiled. Then he felt a flash of cruelty: He knew where she had been this morning, and if she was now suffering, so be it. He took a deep breath: "Natalia Dmitrievna! I thought you would have been rehearsing today!"

She jumped to her feet, and his anger diminished. She was a pathetic little bird. "I—" Her eyes took in his dressing gown, his still wet hair. Suddenly, she laughed. "Truly, I'm sorry," she said. "My timing . . ."

"Your timing was off. You should have come sooner. I would have received you during my bath. Quite an enjoyable experience." He twinkled at her, taking delight in his shameless speech. He wanted to say: There now, don't be embarrassed. After all, I know all about you. But even in his meanness he felt a flash of compassion. "What is it?" he asked, sitting down near her.

She looked away and blushed. "I should not have come," she began. "I should not—but I did, for there is no one else who might help me. Boris Vassilievitch—General Teliakovsky has suspended me. I am still not certain whether *Nuits d'Egypte* will be shown at all. You see—it's Kchessinskaya. She wants to dance *La Fille Mal Gardée* instead, and she is angry with me, angrier than I ever thought she would be, because of the argument we had in your study."

Boris's eyes had widened. "No *Nights?* Now that's absurd! Surely you are exaggerating, my dear."

Natalia's face crumpled like used tissue paper. "I don't know what to do!" she cried, wringing her hands. She took a deep breath, composed her face, and added more quietly: "Forgive me, Boris Vassilievitch. This outburst—"

"This outburst is sincere. But Natalia—I may call you Natalia, may I not?—this is petty and childish on Mala's part. What would you have me do?"

"I don't know! Perhaps—perhaps you could reason with her, Boris Vassilievitch. You have been so kind to me in the past. I thought that maybe— Was it presumptuous? I would do anything, anything at all, to continue my career, to dance again as before. I am afraid that if no one intervenes, I will be allowed to return to the Mariinsky at the end of the month, but my progress will go no farther. Pavlova saw me and said some dreadful things—all untrue, but rumors do not help a sagging reputation. Do you understand what I am telling you?"

Yes, he thought, I understand. His mind went back to his father. "My poor Natalia," he said. "There may indeed be someone I can see. But not Mala Kchessinskaya. Only a member of the Imperial Family could influence her. I shall have to go to—yes, I believe that is whom I must see. Excuse me, *ma chère*. You stay here. Ivan will make you comfortable. I must go now but shall return later."

Impulsively, she took his hand and brought it to her lips. "Thank you!" she whispered. His eyes swept over her with amusement. It was essential that *Nuits d'Egypte* be saved, and if, in the process, he could also manage to indebt this girl to him . . .

Yes, he thought as he tied his four-in-hand in front of his dressing table, it has to be *this* girl. His jaw tightened when he thought of Pierre and the tuxedo thrown haphazardly on the floor. He rang for Ivan. "Send a card to the Tzarina, please, with this message: 'Your humble servant begs for a short audience with you, and so on, and so on.' Have Yuri bring it over now, while I am dressing. Let him bring back her reply. This is not a special afternoon for her, as I recall."

To those who knew Boris Kussov well, nothing was a surprise, save, perhaps, his wedding to Marguerite Tumarkina. His impeccable appearance, his good taste, his generosity toward the artistic community of St. Petersburg—all these helped to create the impression of blond perfection, of intellectual and cultural nonpareil with which he clothed himself. But very few knew the inner Boris, what he thought and how he thought it. Now, in his carriage, he did not have to wonder what he would say to the Tzarina. He already knew. He had racked his brain for facts that might prove useful to him and had remembered Alexandra Feodorovna's schedule. This afternoon she would have time to receive him. She was the single person most able to help him accomplish his aim.

He was admitted to one of the smaller sitting rooms, for the Kussovs were received in court as friends. When he had first been introduced to her years before and seen her frigid, proud, and frightened profile, two thoughts had assailed him: That, as a foreigner who was not well liked by her father-in-law's court-iers, she would doubly appreciate those of the aristocracy who did befriend her. Also, that as Queen Victoria's granddaughter she would have a tendency toward harsh morality. She had con-demned him, he knew, for his scandalous marriage. Had she had time to put it behind her?

"Your Majesty was most kind to grant me these moments of audience," he said, bending over her hand. "I am most grate-ful."

"Please sit down, Boris Vassilievitch," she countered. "The pleasure is mine, I assure you." She seemed stiff, but he knew that she was shy, and when she smiled he felt renewed con-fidence. "How is your father?" she asked politely.

"Papa is fine, and begs to be remembered to you. He sends you a basket filled with compliments and eulogies, to be deliv-ered by me."

"How charming, Boris Vassilievitch! Now tell me, what is troubling you? How can I be of help?" She leaned forward ever so slightly, and he thought, She cannot break through her re-serve, but she tries.

"I have come to Your Majesty on behalf of some friends of mine," he said. "You have always been such a balletomane—so has the entire Imperial Family, of course." He watched care-fully as his innocent words registered on her. Then he pro-ceeded: "There is to be a benefit performance at the Mariinsky, on the twenty-first of this month. It was to be a new ballet,

Nuits d'Egypte, choreographed by young Fokine, with designs by some excellent people, among them a painter called Riazhin with whom you are probably not yet familiar. One of the dancers is a good friend, but she is eighteen and impetuous. In defending this ballet, she managed to insult Matilda Felixovna. It was all so innocent, I assure you! She feels absolutely miserable about it!"

"Indeed." Alexandra Feodorovna sat gravely looking at Boris. She did not betray her emotions. "Please continue, Boris Vassilievitch," she simply said.

"To shorten this tale of youthful woe, our young *coryphée* has been suspended for the duration of the month and fears that her brilliant career will stop before really beginning. She is talented, Your Majesty. She is as good as Karsavina—and such a considerate person, too. But Mala is adamant—her pride has been wounded. It also seems she may talk Teliakovsky into canceling *Nuits d'Egypte* altogether."

He stopped, tactfully. Alexandra Feodorovna was pensive, abstracted. "Yes," she said at length, *"Nuits d'Egypte.* Our uncle, the Grand-Duke Vladimir, told me that you had traveled to Egypt and India to purchase marvelous materials for the costumes and sets of this ballet. I should be distressed to learn that your trip was in vain. But tell me: Who is this young ballerina in whom you have taken such an interest? Have I seen her perform?"

"You may have, Your Majesty. Her name is Natalia Oblonova. She—"

"Why yes, Oblonova! Little Aspitchia! She is graceful and nervous as a springtime doe. I do remember her. She was also in *Le Pavillon d'Armide,* the *pas de trois* with that remarkable young man, Nijinsky. Two very unusual dancers, and both so very young." She paused. "I shall speak with my husband and my uncle. Surely so great a dancer as Matilda Felixovna can choose to overlook such a peccadillo. I can promise nothing, of course. But I hope, Boris Vassilievitch, that Natalia Oblonova will be most grateful to you for intervening on her behalf. Not every dancer can boast of such a devoted patron."

"Thank you, Your Majesty. Not every patron can boast of the

sympathy of such a gracious monarch." He rose after her, and bowed once again over her proffered hand. She gave him a brief half-smile and accompanied him to the door of the receiving room.

"Boris Vassilievitch," she said clearly, "you behaved in a most cruel fashion toward your wife. I was disappointed in you. I would have thought that you, of all men, would have been kinder. Why, I have received Marguerite Stepanovna in my own chambers, and I do not believe that she is more than nervous, poor thing. I do not think she possesses the strains of insanity within her."

Boris bowed again. "I hope for her sake you are right in your charity, Your Majesty. But I had grave doubts, which disturbed me greatly, and I had to think of possible children. One can hardly bear to imagine the guilt incurred by those who pass on, or allow their spouses to pass on, bad blood."

The Tzarina inclined her beautiful head of gold-red hair. "I had not thought of the situation under such a light," she remarked. She smiled. "I shall not forget our talk, Boris Vassilievitch."

Natalia was summoned once again to General Teliakovsky's office, but this time he smiled at her benevolently. "Matilda Felixovna tells me that in her concern she may have misinterpreted a momentary nervousness on your part and overblown it. You are a sweet girl, Natalia Dmitrievna, and a responsible member of the Ballet. I feel that if you tell me you are not suffering from strain, then I can trust your own evaluation. You will take two days' rest, to make certain that all is well. Then, you will resume your rehearsals. Lopokhova and Pavlova will give you back the roles that were yours to begin with."

Healthy color rose to Natalia's cheeks. "I am infinitely thankful," she murmured. "I shall not disappoint your faith in me."

"Indeed not. But I shall not rescind your fine. After all, you cannot lose your head in my presence and question my fairness. I did what I thought was best, as I am doing now. The fine, you understand, is a matter of principle."

Natalia cried, "Yes, of course, and I am sorry!" but she

thought: Who cares about the five rubles? Money is only money, but I am to dance, and that is everything to me! She bowed her head, curtsied, and left. How different today was from the last time she had been called to Teliakovsky's office!

On Natalia's way out of the theatre, an elegant figure nearly collided with her. It was Matilda Felixovna Kchessinskaya. Natalia looked aside, but the other woman placed a cool hand on her arm. "Ah, Natashka, Natashka," she said. "What a pretty child you are. Let us be friends, shall we? For I do admire you, I do!" Her beautiful eyes twinkled. "You are almost as good a dancer as I was at your age," she said, and then her gaze hardened. "But never forget that I am not your age." She walked away, and Natalia shivered slightly in her shadow.

Natalia closed the door of her small room and sat down at the secretary, tears in her eyes. She took out her pen, dipped it in the inkwell, and began to write on the crisp white paper:

My dearest one,

Surely by now you are furious with me, and also surprised. That I should have left so abruptly, coldly, and not sent any word till now . . . I am sorry. I simply could not—cannot—face you. You represent a part of me that I did not know existed. Joy and love—these things were never in my life before, and above all, I want you to know that I love you. But I shall not marry you and cannot continue to see you alone. It is you, or myself. In your arms or in your heart, I could not remain myself, a woman standing unafraid. You see, this is even more important to me than that new, that lovely part of myself that I so recently discovered. You will think it is my ambition to be a great dancer that stands in our way. But you see, dance is the best way I know of expressing myself—this self of which I write to you now. I do not deserve your love, for I am too self-centered, as you can see, but still, this one last time, I send you the kisses of my heart.

NATALIA

She raised her head, swallowing her unshed tears. Then she folded the note and began another.

"Dear Boris Vassilievitch," this one read,

> Your generous intervention has brought me back to grace. However can I thank you? I am not adept with words, but I shall dance for you, that you may know for whom you pleaded. Your most grateful Natalia Oblonova.

The sun gleamed copper on the horizon, and she rolled down the top of her secretary. Slowly she went into the little drawing room and fetched a hardbacked chair. She removed her shoes, then stepped on the seat of the chair and reached up to the wall. Her frail fingers closed around the edges of a painting frame, and she took it down, turned the canvas to the wrong side, and wedged it between a bookcase and the door.

I have never been a dreamer, she thought, and went out, carrying the letters.

Chapter 6

atalia did not receive an answer from Pierre. His anger upon receiving the note was profound and violent, like an unleashed deluge. He uttered a wild cry and tore the paper in half, then hurled dish after dish of his inexpensive plateware against his bedroom wall. His face was congested, purple, and the muscles in his neck stood out, taut and swollen. As much as he had loved her, he now hated her—with passion and abandon. At the gala of *Nuits d'Egypte* he saw her. His black eyes bored into her face, mesmerizing her, so that she could not look away from the pure hatred in them. All his humanity, all his gentleness, seemed to have been drained away and replaced by untold bitterness.

She had spent the first few days fighting the hope that he would disregard her words and come to her. She had known the persistent, insistent lover Pierre. She had not guessed at the implacability of the vindictive, rejected Pierre. Now she finally encountered him and shuddered: *She* had done this to him. But even then, at the back of her mind, she thought: There is still time. If I go to him now, he will accept me again, he will forgive me. But she could not. Her dramatic, pathetic Tahor, betrayed by Amoun for Cleopatra, was magnificent. Why must men make me suffer so in my roles? she wondered, and did not go to Pierre. In her dancing, part of the pain in her own heart showed through, and she felt sublimated, almost whole again. Later she asked herself whether her frenzied desire to achieve had not removed her from the very pulse of life—but her answer always confirmed the rightness of her decision. She could accept love, revel in it, but it would kill her if she did not then retreat from its total immersion, to protect her innermost self.

One night late in April Count Boris Kussov invited her to dine with him at the restaurant Medvyed, in one of the private rooms off the elegant gallery. This was not the first time she had supped with him. He was a gracious, witty host, and his attentions were flattering to a woman as young and unworldly as Natalia. She sharpened her own mind on his, and he appeared to take pleasure in teaching her the finer points of culture that endowed life with a softer, gilt-edged finish. She questioned him freely. He was a cynic and thus appreciated her own view of the world, her unabashed distrust in Providence, her boundless curiosity, her keen intelligence. They talked. That these were never personal talks did not detract from the agreeable quality of their conversations.

Yet each was wary of the other. She sensed that a game was being played, recalling Pierre's statement of months before, that his mentor lived by controlling the souls of others. Boris realized that Natalia was not merely a good dancer, a provincial girl whose head could be turned in an instant. He could understand now why Pierre had loved and wanted her. She was bright, sensitive—and strangely wise. If he were to manipulate her for his own purpose, he would have to use the utmost finesse. And in so doing, he was prepared to enjoy himself.

That evening Natalia appeared more striking than usual. She wore a very simple gown of emerald green, which heightened the delicacy of her features and figure. Boris thought, If only Marguerite had resembled her. The tiny breasts, the firm body. There was nothing loose-skinned, flaccid, or colorless about her except her pale complexion. He remembered his first impression of her in the corridor of the Mariinsky: She had brought to mind a young boy, a proud Athenian youth. She wore pearls— his pearls—at the throat and ears. "I shall have to give you some emeralds," he said lightly.

"Oh, no, Boris Vassilievitch. People already exchange naughty thoughts about us. Everyone in the Ballet seems to be observing us."

He laughed, throwing back his graceful, golden head. "And this disturbs you?"

"I would much prefer being linked to your name than to be thought the illegitimate daughter of a country servant," she said, smiling. "But some people are envious. In a sense you have become my unofficial patron. You spoil me. Your other friends in the Ballet feel that you are forgetting them because of me. I am only an upstart, you see."

The waiter entered, bearing an enormous platter covered with a silver dome, which he removed. "Pheasant!" Natalia cried.

"Yes. I am to leave Petersburg soon, and so I thought we should celebrate before then." He smiled at her, his odd half-smile that meant that in some manner he was making fun—of her, or of himself. They were silent while the waiter served them. A wine steward entered during the proceedings and wheeled in a small tray with a bucket and champagne. "Always take the *brut* kind, Natalia," Boris advised paternally. "When you give your first reception, don't forget that. Dry champagne is cloying to the palate and not really 'dry' at all!"

"And besides, it's *déclassé*," she added impishly.

They were alone again. "Well, yes," he agreed, pretending bashfulness. "But look—I was telling you about my trip. I am going with the opera singers to Paris. Diaghilev is exporting *Boris Godunov* and Chaliapin. The painting exhibit was so well received that he and Nouvel wanted to bring Russian music to France this season."

She looked into the translucent champagne glass in her hand. Of course, she is wondering about Pierre, Boris thought. "It is stupid to pine for him," he commented acerbically.

Her head flew up, startled. For a moment she said nothing, blood rushing to her cheeks in embarrassment. How did he know? Had Pierre told him? Then she shrugged, admitting defeat. "I was thinking, he will be accompanying you, won't he?" she murmured simply. "I can't help it," she added. "Sometimes, I do think of him."

"I don't know what happened between you, but I do know this: He certainly is not wasting *his* time thinking of *you*!"

Natalia started. She looked at Boris with amazement. Her

fork, laden with roast pheasant and truffles, remained in mid-air between the table and her parted lips. "What a cruel man you can be, Boris Vassilievitch!" she said at length.

"Not cruel, realistic. You and Pierre Riazhin would be ridiculous together, with nothing to add to each other. Let's face it, sweet girl: You are both immensely talented in your own fields, but apart from that, *c'est tout*. Neither one of you possesses sufficient clout to help the other. Both of you need rich patrons, people of influence. If he can make a princess fall in love with him, it will boost his career. As for you, the upward climb will be easier. Society dandies adore ballerinas. You must simply learn how to take advantage of that. You are a Crimean nobody, and Pierre, the son of an obscure vine grower in the Caucasus. Your decision not to pursue this relationship—"

"How did you know that the decision was mine?" she asked.

"I guessed it. Pierre does not discuss you with me. I regret to tell you that there are other matters on his mind these days."

"You make everything sound so ugly, Boris Vassilievitch!" she cried. "But there was never any relationship. He is free to consort with whomever he pleases. Why should I care? I do not want a binding union with any man. Perhaps you are right: Pierre Riazhin and I would not bring each other good luck. But still, you make talent seem so unimportant compared with connections. I don't agree. A woman does not need a famous lover to be lifted to fame. That is an antiquated notion."

"As you wish," Boris replied lightly. "You had wanted to learn whether Pierre would go to Paris with us: Yes, naturally. For him it will be a vacation this time. Perhaps one day soon, I shall take *you* to France. It is a sublime country, filled with charm, though not a grand country, such as our own, or a precious, intricate, fragile one, such as Italy. France is beauty, France is grace. I suppose that sums her up: grace inherent. You must enjoy her wine country, her châteaux, her rivers—and Paris, of course."

"Yes. Someday I should like to travel. But Petersburg is probably as far as I shall go. From the Crimea, it seems like China!"

They ate in silence after that. She was thinking: Surely for some women love can coexist with selfhood. But not for such a nobody from the Crimea. She thought of Paris, her dreams of it and paintings she had seen of it. Boris Vassilievitch possessed it all: the taste, the wealth, the connections. But for her—and for Pierre—life was a constant struggle.

Boris went over bitterly what he had thought almost three years before: that his own soul was empty, bereft of the creative gift. This exquisite young girl would be remembered by posterity—but who would give due credit to the patron behind the scenes? Dear God, each time I hope to attain release, and lose it before ever finding it, he said inwardly.

There was a gentle knock on the door of the intimate cubicle in which they sat. A *maître d'hôtel* appeared. "Someone to see you, Excellency," he announced, covertly examining Natalia. A man's shape filled the doorway. He entered behind the *maître d'hôtel*. Natalia saw his tall, well-built frame, the monocle, the trim mustache, and the lock of white hair in the dark head. She had seen him before. As he strode to embrace Boris, she recognized him.

"Join us for a cognac," Boris said gayly. "Tell me, Serge, do you know Natalia? My dear," he addressed the young woman, "this is Serge Pavlovitch Diaghilev. Serge, Natalia Dmitrievna Oblonova."

Diaghilev smiled and bowed gracefully over her hand. They were two of a kind, she said to herself, one blond, one dark, both with infinite charm. "But of course, I would know her anywhere," he murmured to Boris. "I have been watching her since she danced the Sugar Plum Fairy. In fact," he added, "it was she I first noticed tonight, when you both walked into the gallery. When somebody eclipses you, Boris—need I say more?"

Natalia smiled, wanly. She still did not know how to receive a compliment with poise. Flattery sat ill with her. Never having received it as a child, it was still too new, too foreign. She watched Diaghilev and Boris. So this, then, was the man who had been Teliakovsky's rival for the position of director of the Imperial Theatres. Pierre admired the man, found him alternately charming and harsh, encouraging and manipulative. He was a genius at putting together artistic endeavors, much as Boris was one at finding new talent.

She listened to the two men, sitting in her chair, her back upright, her long neck straight and graceful. There was so little for her to say! Then she recalled something. "Serge Pavlovitch," she said, "you have been planning this season of opera for a long time now, haven't you? I can remember hearing Boris Vassilievitch talking about it months ago. Why has Russian music been so slow to spread to Western Europe? The Italian opera is well known here, and the French troupe comes every winter for a season of plays at the Mikhailovsky. Boris Vassilievitch says that countries, like people, are vain—that cultures want to conquer one another. Why have we Russians remained such an enclave unto ourselves?"

"There was never a Serge Pavlovitch to bridge the gap," Diaghilev replied, his eyes twinkling at her.

Boris raised his glass to her. "*Ma chère,* how you have changed since that conversation! Imagine, Serge—Natalia was most angry with me. She assured me that Russian opera would do very well without spreading anywhere—that we did not need France. Now she wonders why we didn't go there sooner!"

Natalia blushed, suddenly feeling awkward and out of place. But Serge Diaghilev remarked, draining his own glass: "We were all like that in the beginning. Boris is cruel. He was a born and bred Petersbourgeois, whereas I only came here for law school—which, naturally, I abandoned for more interesting vistas! We are all parochial at first. I only enjoyed the music of Glinka and Glazunov! How mercilessly my better-rounded friends teased me! But, Boris, to a man or woman from a smaller province, the capital itself seems a foreign country. Doesn't it, Natalia Dmitrievna?"

She nodded. "Boris Vassilievitch was telling me about Paris. I do not think I shall ever go there. As you said, Serge Pavlovitch, St. Petersburg seems a cosmos in itself to someone like me. Still . . ."

"Still," Diaghilev said, "I would not close my mind to the West if I were you."

Both men regarded her intently for a moment, and, embarrassed and confused, she glanced at her hands, at the roses on the table. She felt she had made a bad impression, that the emerald dress was too stark. She wished Diaghilev would go away now and that Boris would leave her alone. She did not belong with men like these.

When the Mariinsky season ended, and Natalia was given her new contract for her second year, she received a shock: She had been promoted to solo dancer of the second degree. Old Enrico Cecchetti, who ran the classes for the soloists, said to her: "We shall have to work together on the *port de bras, carina.* Much, much work. Do not pay attention to your admirers—too much admiration is as bad for a young ballerina as excessive criticism. It dulls one's perception of one's own work." She smiled at him: To be trained by him was in itself an honor. She was the youngest of the official soloists.

The long, hot summer stretched before her. Katya graduated and would enter the *corps de ballet* in the fall. Meanwhile, there was little to do in the suffocating city. Lydia was going to Poland on tour with a small group of dancers. Natalia thought: I am betwixt and between. No one is offering me anything. I have gone beyond the *corps* but am not yet a soloist—and so, I fit in no touring company. No one knows me well enough to like me; they think I'm too reserved. I don't fit in anywhere: I am not a lady, and I am not a star. Yet, I am no longer a nobody. She felt proud of that. There were times now when someone would recognize her—not yet by name, but from some previous role.

She caught herself thinking of Pierre. The glow of her small successes, of her promotion, had heightened her awareness of life. She wondered if he would ever forgive her, if any other man would ever touch her. She wondered about Boris: What did he want with her? What was he doing in Paris? She felt small, inconsequential and unwanted. Boris was not really her patron. True, he had intervened in her behalf and escorted her to fashionable restaurants. But he was Pierre's patron. He was taking Pierre, not her, to France—for the second time. Then the full weight of her nothingness fell upon her, staggering her. Perhaps, she wondered miserably, she would always be dull, ugly, strange little Natasha.

Katya invited her to the summer house which her parents were renting in Imatra, just outside Petersburg in the Finnish countryside. There the air was cool, the breeze sang songs in the blue-green pines, and she felt momentary peace. But all the time she thought: He—they—are in Paris. Pierre is probably learning French, and visiting the château country with Boris. Oh, to be in the Loire Valley instead of Imatra! To listen to Boris, or to Serge Pavlovitch, discussing the poems of Verlaine, or the art of Vuillard, rather than hear Madame Balina extolling the virtues of cornstarch in kissel!

She lay in her little bed at night, while Katya slept across the room, and clasped her hands together. Come back, come back! was the refrain which echoed in her mind. Come back, take me into your lives, into your wonderful world, which you have shown me from a distance. I want to learn, to touch, to feel comfortable in other surroundings besides the theatre. She was stupefied at the unexpected turn of her thoughts and at their vehemence.

Then came the opening of the new season. Natalia no longer felt stabs of discomfort around Pavlova and other ballerinas. She was the youngest, the despicable beginner, and after new performances she was frequently greeted by a torrent of criticism. She was learning to sort through these volleys of words to discover what was valid and what was not. She no longer resented her admirers in the gallery. It was pleasant to receive ovations. But something was missing.

Katya, in the *corps*, was her protégée. They had been equals, and best friends in school, but one year in the real world had separated them. Katya was so naïve. Lydia Markovna Brailovskaya did not like her and told Natalia: "That girl is a simpering child. What do you see in her?" Natalia smiled, remembering that only a single year ago Lydia's own friends had wondered, too, why Lydia had put up with Natalia.

She watched out for Katya warily, nervously, for Katya was indeed a rosy-cheeked child. She saw the young man from the male *corps de ballet* who made eyes at Katya, who sent her bonbons and fresh fruit. His name was Grisha Marshak, and he had dark hair and blue eyes, like a doll's. She told Katya: "He's distracting you. If you want to become a *coryphée*, don't let him come to the house every night. He is stronger than you and does not seem to show the strain as you do. You need your rest."

"Boris Vassilievitch Kussov does not appear to drain your resources," Katya replied stingingly. She resented Natalia's dislike of her beau and did not understand it.

"Boris Vassilievitch? I have hardly seen him since his return. Besides, he is only a friend, a sort of mentor, whereas Grisha loves you, doesn't he?"

"Yes," Katya answered meekly, "he does. And I love him back. Is that such a crime?"

One day in October Katya came to Natalia, her face red and glowing, her eyes the color of fresh cornflowers. "Grisha has asked me to marry him!" she cried. "I have said yes, of course. He is so wonderful and will go far. And do you know, Natalia, General Teliakovsky told me today that I could become a *coryphée* next fall, if I work hard."

"That's marvelous!" Natalia cried.

"But I told him I didn't want to. The *corps* is fine for me. I shall dance for a few years while Grisha gets started as a soloist, and then I shall have babies. That is what I really want to do."

Katya's eyes pleaded for approval, for understanding. Hadn't Natalia always advocated the saying: "Live and let live?" Why was it so necessary for Katya Balina to emulate Natalia, to do exactly what she had done? Wasn't Katya allowed to live her own life with her own priorities? Why was Natashenka crying, then? Why did she behave as though she had been slapped in the face? "Oh, sweetie, sweetie," Katya crooned, putting her arms around the other girl. "Are you sorry? Was there somebody you turned down and didn't tell me about?"

"Tell him," Natalia repeated to Lydia, "that I am absolutely unable to receive him. He'll have to leave." She was lying on her bed in her chemise, her hair in disarray on the pillow.

"But surely it would do you good—"

"No, it wouldn't." She sighed, and closed her eyes. Lydia walked out of the room. Why? Natalia thought. Why had he come? Briefly there was a sharp pain in her chest, and she said to herself: But Pierre will never come. He is bad for me, an egotist who does not think I am as important as he. He wants a wife, not a dancer. Now she was being unfair to Count Boris, but that was too bad, because she was angry with everyone, including Boris Vassilievitch, whose friendship was so puzzling, who catered to Pierre because he thought that Pierre, not she, was the up-and-coming talent of St. Petersburg. She had never felt so confused and upset.

She was so angry that she did not hear him until he was in the room, standing over her bed. She screamed and drew up the sheet. "Lydia!" she cried. He was laughing, as though he had caught a child hiding stolen sweets, when actually she was a full-grown woman in her chemise with unlaced corset stays, and her hair unpinned. "It's all right, don't blame Lydia," he said. "I pushed past her. I had to see you, you know."

He was dressed in a loose-fitting suit of dark blue serge, with a high, stiff collar and a four-in-hand. A sapphire gleamed at each wrist. He held a cane topped with a gold handle. He was certainly a man of the times, slender, graceful—and out of place in this room. "Boris Vassilievitch, I don't feel well," she said. "Please let me be.

Instead, he sat down nonchalantly on the edge of the bed and took her hand. "I am growing tired of calling for you here in this miserable apartment and finding that half the time you are gone, and the rest refusing to receive me. Are we not good friends?"

She was taken aback. His blue eyes shone intently on her, double sapphire rays. She crouched back on the pillow. "Friends," she repeated. "Yes. But—"

"Something has been brewing in my mind. I like you, Natalia. I need artists around me. For some reason, they are necessary to my life. I myself have never been capable of creation. I can help you."

She listened to the quiet, grave words, spoken not in his customary ironic voice but in a gentler, older one with which she was unfamiliar. Something stirred within her. She replied, softly, a little hoarsely, "Yes, I know. I know that about you." She had a momentary glimpse into his life. "You have already helped me," she added.

"But when I help you, it is I who benefit more. You are so young, so lovely, with so much glory in your future—"

"And so," she said, "you wish to play a part in my destiny. But you know that you have already done much to enlarge my mind. What have I done for you in return? What can I do for you?"

He did not answer. He looked at her directly, scanning her face. She was oddly not embarrassed by her lack of appropriate attire. For some reason this man was familiar to her, someone who could read her thoughts. But was he a friend? "What is it?" she asked him.

"I should like to set you up in my home among beautiful works of art. I should like Ivan to serve you on my Meissen porcelain. I should like Yuri to take you anywhere you want to go in the landau or the victoria. Come home with me, Natalia."

She was speechless. Her eyelids fluttered, her nostrils quivered. An absurd desire to laugh rose in her throat as when Pierre had offered her marriage. She coughed it down. "Boris Vassilievitch," she asked, "are we back to the incident with the pearls? Or is this—is this—a proposal?"

He smiled, but not his usual, ironic half-smile. This one was rather wan and brought out the fine wrinkles at the corners of his eyes. "Not quite," he said. "I am not asking for your hand in marriage, if that is what you mean. However, aside from that, I am asking for the same thing: For you to 'come live with me, and be my love,' as the English poet says."

"We *are* back to the pearls!" she cried. Now she could no longer contain her amazement. "Boris Vassilievitch, this is silly. You do not love me. You do not love me at all, I know it! All the time you have been kind to me, you never once behaved as a man who is courting a woman but rather as the good friend you are, older, more learned, better traveled. You have guided me, teased me, helped me—but certainly not loved me. A woman does feel a man's love—or even his desire. No, you definitely do not desire me."

"Desire is the last thing you want from me," Boris retorted. "You do not want a man's love, either. You want space around you, and most men are not willing to give that to the woman for whom they care. I am different. To me, your beauty, your primary beauty, is your virtuosity. Also, your character. Oh, Natalia, I do not always like you. There are even times when I dislike you intensely. But I never stop admiring you. I admire you sufficiently to offer you the sort of life that I know you need: my care, my protection, my connections, my worldliness, without the restrictions another man might impose. You do not have to love me. I want you in my life, but I do not wish to *be* your life."

"What you ask is for us to be lovers," she said, "but without your marrying me and without my loving you. Yet what man wants a mistress who does not love him? I shan't grow to love you, Boris Vassilievitch. Yet you are quite right. I do not need a man in my life. I despise marriage. Why, then, should I allow myself to be openly kept, which means the same thing?"

"Because," he explained, "I shall show you the world, and you do want that. I shall never prevent you from dancing but shall help you in any way I can. I shall shield you from that other force that frightens you, call it what you will—men, love. You can be honest with me, Natalia. I have felt your fear. Yet, around me you are not afraid, because you do not feel threatened. I shall not ask to share your bed. I know you would not want this. Just come and let us make a life for each other."

For a moment she felt blinded and put a hand out to shield her eyes. Then she felt Boris placing his arms about her, holding her up. His arms were strong, calm. He smelled of spearmint and clean lime. To be free, free of her obsession with Pierre. To dance without fearing Kchessinskaya, or Pavlova's evil tongue. Was she so strong that she could resist Boris's proposal? And why should she? Who but Boris had ever gone out of his way for this child of the Crimea? To go from being despised, unwanted by her own parents, to becoming the acknowledged consort of a member of the Tzar's own court. . . . To live in beauty, without struggle. . . . To see Paris. "But you?" she asked. "What would you receive from this arrangement?"

"A man can be born to great wealth and to an illustrious name," he murmured into her hair. "But to be allied to loveliness and talent is the ultimate goal. Be my princess. To be sure, other men will envy me. Soon the name Oblonova will be famous."

She shivered, remembering something else that Pierre had told her. Boris staked out his claims before anyone else even took notice: "No one else could lay claim to you afterward," he had said. She thought of Pierre and their love—a useless love. What had Boris said? "You and Pierre Riazhin would be ridiculous together, with nothing to add to each other." She sighed.

Laying her head wearily on his chest, she murmured, yielding: "So be it, Boris Vassilievitch. I shall go with you."

Above her soft brown curls he smiled, and his sheer blue eyes shone like an azure banner in the sky. Pierre would not want her now, his little Sugar Plum. There would be no further trysts between them, no more late-night encounters. But Boris would be acquiring the most promising protégée of the Mariinsky stage. He had killed two birds with one stone, and perhaps this time he might put his own pain to sleep for a while. Of all his intimates, of course, his father would be the least surprised. Boris thought of the brown-eyed Madonna and touched Natalia's hair.

Natalia thought: I have changed, my life has changed. In many ways this was true. She had at first felt like an intruder in the vast apartment on the Boulevard of the Horse Guard. Ivan, the *maître d'hôtel*, was more polished than she, while the young chamber and scullery maids came from families like her own. All these servants had resided for years under Count Boris's expert command. They ran the flat according to the orders of the immaculate, intuitive Ivan. In the beginning Natalia had to find a place in this strange family. She had to be careful not to do anything to embarrass Boris.

She had her own bedroom and boudoir, and her own maid-servant to comb her hair and set out her clothes—an entire new wardrobe, which had been made to order by the team of seam-stresses employed by Princess Nina Stassova, the oldest of Boris's sisters. "We shall hire you a seamstress of your own, by the by," Boris had casually declared. But this is absurd! she had thought. I need no more than the few gowns I already own.

All her life she had earned whatever she possessed, and now, such luxury was placed at her disposal that she did not know how to react. Boris wanted her to wear the emerald tiara, and wanted to take her with him to select an Aubusson carpet of rose, violet, and cerulean blue for her boudoir. He insisted on inviting guests for lavish six-course suppers on Thursdays, to give her a day's rest after her performance on Wednesdays. The guest of honor sat at her left, and she was expected to be a gracious, intelligent hostess. Across the table from her sat Boris, regal and golden. Whenever she made a salient point or expressed a strong, witty opinion, he would smile, narrowing his eyes. This meant: Good, good. You are not disappointing me. You are doing your job well.

But, in effect, what was her job? She sometimes even wondered who she was. At the Ballet, she noticed a different attitude among the dancers. Tamara Karsavina and Olga Preobrajenskaya continued to be unswervingly kind, the former in a gentle, discreet manner, the latter, who was older, in a more protective way. Anna Pavlova observed Natalia covertly and often avoided her, but she was no longer rude. Natalia saw many of these women at social gatherings. She had even been invited to Kchessinskaya's palace, as Boris always had been in the past. Kchessinskaya never referred to their disagreement and was animated and agreeable with Natalia, in the vein of an older sister. After all, were they not both concubines of influential noblemen?

Even the upper echelons of the aristocracy did not reject her, as she had expected. The gentlemen passed her from arm to arm as one would an enchanting exotic pet, a rare jewel to be displayed. To be sure, some of the ladies scoffed about her position in Boris's life, the same ones who criticized Kchessinskaya. But for the most part, she was well accepted.

Furthermore, she was now one of the soloists at the Ballet, and she soon learned that artists were thought to have rules of their own, created by the unusual needs of their genius. Not everyone regarded her with such lack of moral prejudice, but Boris protected her from those who did not. Her main concern was: What am I doing in his life?

She had overheard her young maid, Luba, talking one morning with the French cook. "No, it's true!" the girl was saying. "Madame has never slept with His Excellency. I would have noticed if she had. There is never so much as a cufflink in her room, or a hairpin in his. Besides, they both have their scents. Madame's is attar of roses, and it's unmistakable. Her odor has never been mixed with his—in either room."

"Hush now, Luba, and mind your business," the cook had interposed.

But, of course, it was true. Boris treated her with consideration, even affection. Now there was a new expression in his eyes when he regarded her: Sometimes the old irony, so often tinged with cruelty, would mingle with a certain pleasure, or praise. He approved of her. He even liked her. He would casually leave a gilt-edged volume of Petrarch's poetry, bound in crumbling antique Moroccan leather, by her armchair, remarking that he had enjoyed it and perhaps she might, too. That was his way of indicating a new area for discovery. She had learned French during her rigid courses of instruction at the ballet school, but only in basic, cursory fashion. Now he had found her a pleasant middle-aged French widow to come to the flat and speak with her, suggesting reading to improve her fluency and general culture. She learned quickly, so that by the middle of the winter season she could hold conversations in French with their guests, most of whom spoke it in the manner common to the Russian aristocracy since the days of the Empress Catherine.

She was never bored with Boris—but she was baffled. At first she had tensely listened for his footstep by her door at night. But evidently he intended to respect his promise not to intrude as a man into her life. She was relieved. She still thought of Pierre and could not lie still remembering the night that she had spent in his arms, the joy, the sweet pain. She did not feel the same way about Boris. Her skin did not tingle when he drew near her, and she did not feel lightheaded and dizzy when he entered a room. She thought of Boris as a cool wind, a peaceful landscape that brought repose and loftiness to her existence.

Lydia often came to see her, and amusement glittered in her black eyes when Ivan bowed to Natalia and called her "Madame." "Fancy that," she would say. "Our Manya would look askance at us in this loveseat, with our tea glasses mono-grammed with the Kussov *K*. Manya is shocked, Natalia. She wholeheartedly disapproves of this illicit arrangement of yours." Natalia knew that such criticism was unavoidable. The enlightened members of St. Petersburg could afford to be more liberal, both in the matter of their own conduct and in accepting hers— but the middle classes and the peasants considered her no better than a whore. Katya practically never saw her now, except at the Ballet; her family had expressed such utter condemnation of Natalia's life that the young woman's own opinions had been shaken, to the point where she could not feel comfortable with Natalia. Natalia accepted this censure as inevitable. She had gained so much from Boris that the loss was minor in comparison.

He had set up a bank account in her name, "so that you will not feel under obligation to ask for every small thing," he had explained. She had been touched by his consideration. In return, it did not occur to her to tell anyone the truth about their relations, even if this might have rehabilitated her reputation in certain circles. She was, then, for all intents and purposes, firmly established as Boris's companion—his mistress.

At the Mikhailovsky one evening they encountered his father, Count Vassily. He bowed over her hand, and said: "I have watched you at the Mariinsky, my dear. I am not a bal-letomane, but in you I saw the loveliness of which my son has spoken." What did she see in his expression: approval? complicity with Boris? The old man was rather paternal. For a member of the old guard, he behaved decently and kindly.

So did Boris's sisters, the two that she met, that is, for Liza, the youngest, lived in Moscow. Princess Nina Stassova invited her to tea and praised her great talent. When she thought that Natalia was out of earshot, she told Boris: "She is charming, absolutely charming. What a pity you can't marry her. I like her a lot more than I did Marguerite, for all her superior breeding." Sometimes Princess Nina brought her small daughter, Galina, for a quick visit to Natalia—and Natalia knew that this was an unspoken sign of acceptance. A Stassov did not expose her three-year-old child to women of bad influence. Galina was tiny and golden, a fairy—and Natalia often thought with amazement that women's lives could be so different, her own devoted to her art while Nina was dedicated to her family. In a sense Natalia had exchanged Katya for Nina Stassova. For a person who had always relied on her own resources, an exchange of one friend for another was not a trauma but a nonchalant affair. Nina was a friendly acquaintance who wanted to like her because she loved Boris; whereas Katya had been dependent on Natalia. In actuality, neither of these women made a vital connection with Natalia's heart and soul.

I have but one real friend, Natalia pondered: Boris Kussov, a strange, essentially lonely man, whom I am afraid to try to reach. She felt compassion for him, as she had never felt toward another human being. Whatever he sought, he was not finding it. She would go to him in the study, and sit with him by the fire, not speaking. She knew he was unhappy, but there was nothing she could do. She wanted to say "Thank you," or to cry out to him that she was there, another person, someone who cared. But she could not. Instead, she took his hand, and when his startled eyes flew to her face, she quickly kissed it, turning away—knowing that for this gesture he would deride her.

"What have we here," he would say, "a romantic little *bayadère?* Come now, *Liebchen,* let us not become maudlin before the ripe old age of nineteen."

"Say what you will, Boris," she replied. She picked up Voltaire's *Candide* to resume her reading. Her face, small and austere, was as impenetrable to him, she realized, as his Grecian features remained closed to her. Theirs was a decidedly odd friendship—yet real, nevertheless.

With all her will power, she had blocked her small, persistent questions about Pierre. She never saw him; Boris never mentioned him, and she never asked. Yet many times when Boris left her to go to meetings of Diaghilev's committee of artists, she thought: Yes, he sees Pierre. Pierre and he could not have stopped seeing each other because of me. Pierre was central to Boris's life—what had happened to all that? Still, she did not ask. It was better to pretend to have forgotten. She sensed, too, that Boris would be very angry if she mentioned Pierre—he had certainly discouraged the slightest relationship between them in earlier times.

One of the aspects of her life with Boris that she most appreciated was their mutual respect for each other's privacy. If she kept the door to her boudoir open, it was a signal that he could come in and chat with her. He would frequently enter in his silk dressing gown, while she would already have donned hers, trimmed with Belgian lace and ruffles. Their lack of embarrassment seemed to indicate: We have gone beyond all this, haven't we? But he never intruded if the door was shut, and it would not have occurred to him to come into her bathroom during her nightly preparations. Neither did she ask him where he went alone. Presumably Ivan knew, but she was not even certain of that. Their comings and goings were clothed in courtesy and delicacy.

One afternoon, upon arriving at the Mariinsky for a rehearsal, she met Nicolai Legat, the *premier danseur* who led a class of soloists and sometimes choreographed, too. "Tell your coachman not to leave, Natalia," he said to her. "We've reorganized this week's program, and Kyasht will be dancing Aurora this Sunday instead of you. Next week, you're to do *Giselle*, and I didn't think you ought to strain. Go home and rest. A day off won't hurt you."

She inclined her head. How different life was from six months before, when an enforced rest had meant the possible end to her career! There were still many steps to go before becoming a *prima ballerina*, but the one from *coryphée* to second soloist was the crucial gap to bridge, the one most often missed by female dancers. She was not quite nineteen, but secure now at the Mariinsky—in part because of her talent and hard work; in part, too, because of Boris Kussov's patronage.

Yuri took her back to the boulevard in the warm carriage. It was winter again. Christmas was coming, with its bright memories of the Sugar Plum, her first triumph. It had been three years ago—more like an eon. She had matured in that time, firmed up. Even her face had acquired a sensitive beauty, or maybe it was only that Luba knew how to dress her hair in a more becoming fashion.

It was freezing in the stairway. When Ivan admitted her, she indulged herself by letting her mantle drop to the floor in one long shudder, crying delightedly: "I know, you're not expecting me home so soon! But I can smell the fire in the salon. Is His Excellency in?" Before the surprised Ivan could reply with his customary deference, she ran in little leaps into the sitting room, calling: "Boris! I have a free afternoon!" The thought of Christmas had turned her back into the small girl she had never been, but could still become, at eighteen.

Suddenly the mirth vanished from her face. She became a pillar of marble, her lips parted, her heart racing beneath her blouse. Die now, something told her. Faint, do anything. But don't look, don't look.

Pierre was alone in the salon by the red and gold fire. When he heard her voice, he rose quickly, upsetting the portfolio of drawings which lay on his lap. He rose instinctively in a swift, savage motion, his face reddening. There was such an aura of danger around him that she was filled with fear, and for a panicked moment she considered calling Ivan. Instead, she entered the room, slowly, carefully. There was no escaping him, no escaping the questions that had nagged inside her—no escaping the knowledge that in spite of her pretense, Pierre continued to live and breathe in this world.

She walked up to him, but he drew back fiercely, as though afraid she would contaminate him by her proximity. The etchings lay scattered at his feet, ridiculously vulnerable on the Persian carpet. "You came to see Boris," she said finally, to fill the electric air.

"I didn't know you would be here," he said, looking away.

"Then I shall go to my room and have Ivan call Boris."

"He isn't here!" Pierre cried. "D'you think I'd wait in this house if it weren't important?"

"Then, you never come here?" she asked.

"Never! The idea of you—of this place—it makes me ill to think of it, to think of you."

Hardly daring to breathe, she whispered: "You hate me that much?"

He looked at her and for a moment said nothing. His eyes were like flaming orbs, surrounded by black lashes. "You can ask me such a question?" he said.

Tears stung her eyelids. "You ask, then, Pierre. Ask whatever you want. Do whatever you want. You can't kill me with questions."

"I have only one question," he said. "Why? I wanted to marry you. You wrote that there was no room in your life for a man. But he—he overcame that reticence, didn't he? I know all about you. The jewels he gives you could purchase my father's vineyard. You used to despise me for not breaking a friendship that was oppressive, my friendship with Boris. But you! When will this stop? When he has made you three illegitimate babies?"

"Don't!" she cried. "Stop, you don't know what you're saying. That isn't at all how it is between us."

"Then you tell me. Is he a better lover? Is that the secret? What is it, Natalia, that has turned you into this man's whore? I want to know. God, how I want to know! You have killed me, both of you. But you, especially. At least he never knew how I truly felt about you. I never actually told him. It may have amused him to win, thinking it was an inconsequential game with me too—but I think he was friend enough that had he known for sure, he wouldn't have done it. But you? To do this? With him?"

"He's not my lover!" she exclaimed and burst into tears. "Ask him, if he's your friend! He—and I—we've never—"

"I don't believe you," Pierre said. He sat down on the sofa, his hands trembling. He bowed his face into them, and horrible, muffled sounds came through his fingers—dreadful, inhuman sounds from the bottom of his gut, from the hollows of his chest. She was silenced, then bewitched by this open pain, this agony that wracked him in front of her eyes. She could not move. She could not go to him, touch him, undo what had been done.

"You shall please leave us, Natalia," said a quiet voice at her back. It was the voice of normality, Boris's voice. Mutely, she nodded, relieved. He would take care of this, do something. She turned and fled to her room.

Presently Luba came in with a tray. "Camomille tea, madame," she said, pouring it. "It soothes the nerves. There now,

let's get you into bed. Let's get your head up on those pillows."
But Natalia could not close her eyes.

Boris sat alone with Pierre. The dying fire provided the only
light in the room, darkened early in the Petersburg winter.
Pierre seemed oblivious of the older man, and Boris sat opposite
him in a wing chair, his chin propped in the palm of one hand,
staring at the weeping figure and thinking. His impatience
showed in occasional twitches, the biting of his lower lip. At last
he rose and went to the sideboard in the far corner of the room.
From a bottle on a silver tray, he poured a thimbleful of white
liquid into a small glass, then walked to the sofa.

"There," Boris said in his quiet, clear voice, placing a hand
on Pierre's shoulder. "Drink this." It was such a cliché that for a
second a glint of amusement pierced his blue eyes. With more
compassion he added: "Pierre, for God's sake, no woman is
worth dying for. Not even Natalia. Drink the vodka, it will restore your sanity, put some fire into your stomach. Then we can
talk."

"What's there to say?" Pierre asked. He looked up, accepted
the glass, and drank it down in a single gulp. His shoulders had
stopped heaving, but he was tired, so tired, as if the life had
been drained out of him. He wiped his eyes with the back of his
sleeve. "I should go home now—home to Tiflis. The whole
thing was stupid. I'm stupid. A bloody fool." He stood up unsteadily. "I'm going now. The sketches—"

"The sketches be damned!" Boris stood up too. Putting a
hand upon Pierre's arm, he said: "Look, let's go somewhere for
dinner. We should talk. I won't have you speak nonsense because you've had a shock. Let's go to the Aquarium. It will distract us. I tell you, there's no one like a pretty *tzigane* to soothe
a wounded heart. To hell with the world!"

"I loved her," said Pierre. "And you are hardly my friend."

"We can discuss it in the landau," Boris cut in peremptorily.
He put his arm firmly around Pierre's shoulders and pushed
him forward. "Ivan!" he called, before Pierre could recover
from his torpor and change his mind. "Tell Yuri to meet us in
front. Quickly, please."

138   Under the thick quilt in the carriage, sensation began to return to Pierre's limbs. He blinked. "Couldn't you have picked
someone else?" he exclaimed angrily, turning to Boris. "Another dancer? You did know—you knew from the beginning.
There isn't a thing in Petersburg you don't know, so tell me the
truth!"

"What truth?" Boris demanded, suddenly harsh. "All Petersburg knows I've been living with Natalia. Don't tell me you
were the only innocent around!"

"To know is one thing, but to see is quite another," Pierre
said, his voice trembling. "One can brush aside rumor—but not
this! This is a betrayal!"

"You can't blame me for your troubles," Boris replied. His
eyes were narrowed and he seemed quite severe in his evening
apparel. "You never thought fit to share your feelings with me.
I merely thought we were both admirers of the same woman.
Even she is not reason enough to question our friendship. No
woman should be worth that. A man who puts a woman at the
core of his life is less than a fool—he is a thoughtless animal. In
their proper place women can add a dimension to our life—but
they can never truly understand a man. We remain strangers to
them forever, and the more we beg for a connection to their innermost being, the more we demean ourselves in their eyes."

Pierre said nothing. At length Boris continued: "Does it occur
to you that perhaps that very thing happened to you and Natalia?"

"How can you speak about her so glibly?" Pierre cried,
outraged. "What does she mean to you? You would not marry
her—but I would have, then. Not now—"

"No," Boris remarked. "She is a lovely, intelligent girl, but I
have not surrendered my soul to her—and neither should you.
She isn't worth such an outpouring of emotion. You are an artist, Pierre. Put your feelings into your work. Let women alone.
Natalia is not in love with me, if that's what bothers you—but
she doesn't love you either. She is in my life precisely because
of that: She is a wise girl, who knows better than to waste her
creative urges on a man. I can accept that—but you can't, and
you know it. To have her on those terms would sap the very life
out of you. Perhaps today was necessary: You needed to come to

terms with who she is, how she acts, what she does. I can accept her, all of her—but for you it is either black or white, pure or impure, wife or whore. Natalia operates in the gray areas of life—my kind of areas, not yours. Yes, you needed to come and see her and face the facts as they are, not merely as you chose to interpret them."

Again Pierre did not utter a word. Boris turned to him. "There is no going back," he said. "Pierre, you are the most important being in your own life, not this woman. Respect yourself! Have a good time, play—but don't waste your precious heart on a self-centered young girl with whom you had a single night! If it could make a difference—if she were right for you, or if she cared for you—I would tell her to go to you, I would release her willingly. Pierre, friendship is more important than this senseless blood lust. But no—she isn't right. Let this sink in, though it may be a harsh lesson to swallow: she wouldn't go. She—would—not—go—to—you."

The carriage was stopping, and Yuri was opening the door. A sheet of snow blew into their faces, hard flakes that stung their skin. The Aquarium stood outside the confines of the city, and the drive had been long, tortuous. The two men went in, shaking out their pelisses.

The main hall was gaily lit and warm. It was still early for the after-theatre crowd of Petersburg's golden youth, but Boris was well known, and they were settled at a small table where they ordered supper. But Pierre was not hungry. So much had happened, so many confusing emotions. A group of *tziganes*, beautiful dark-haired gypsy women clothed in flowing, clinging cloth-of-gold, undulated in sultry, langorous dances. They had throaty, velvet voices. "Isn't that one splendid?" Boris asked. "That's Mashenka."

Pierre looked around him. He could not help being sucked into this atmosphere of sensuality, of abandon. He could not eat, but he could drink the champagne that was brought in great quantities to their table. Boris sat back, observing him, a thin smile on his tan face. Finally Pierre said: "No, she isn't worth it. I'll be damned if I'll return to Tiflis because of this!" Then, almost as an afterthought, his black eyes filled with tears.

Boris placed his hand on Pierre's: "Come on," he said, coaxingly, "pick out the one you like and let's go upstairs." He signaled to the waiter: "Set us up in a private cubicle," he murmured.

Upstairs were a series of small, enclosed rooms, and Boris and Pierre found caviar and more champagne awaiting them. Boris noticed that Pierre seemed to be reviving. His eyes were bright, his cheeks aflame. He had had too much to drink, but then that was why they had come, that was precisely what was called for. The waiter stood discreetly by the door. Boris said: "Summon Mashenka and Rosa." To Pierre he added: "Since you could not choose, I did it for you."

The two gypsies who entered were fluid and dark, amber-skinned and heavily scented. They began to sing. The sad undertones of their music filled the air with poignancy. Pierre felt a knot in his throat. He wanted to cry out, "Enough!" but could not. The melody became rich and vibrant with unspoken promises. Pierre leaned forward. Mashenka's body was moving, swaying before him, her heavy breasts entrancing him, soft and round like her hips. Rosa sat on Boris's lap, and whispered something in his ear. Boris and Rosa left the room. Mashenka went to the ice bucket, withdrew the fresh bottle of Dom Perignon, and poured it liberally into two glasses. She handed one to Pierre and kept the other for herself. Still she sang and swayed, sang and swayed.

Suddenly a frenzy seized Pierre, and he finished his drink and threw the glass into the large mirror in front of them. It splintered. Mashenka began to laugh, a marvelously deep and resonant laugh, and handed him her glass. He threw it against the other side of the mirror and laughed, too. Mashenka examined the champagne bottle: It was empty. She handed it to Pierre and it, too, was hurled at the shattered mirror. She threw her arms around his neck, and pushed him back against the velvet settee. He rolled her over, covering her mouth with his own, searching for her breasts with his blunt fingers. It did not matter anymore that she was not Natalia, or that Natalia had betrayed him.

The flat was discreetly lit, with several lamps shining soft pink and green in the salon and the dining room. The servants had gone to bed. Boris supported Pierre, who, being heavier and more muscular than Boris, was somewhat of a burden. Boris laughed. "You'll have to learn how to drink, Petrushka," he said. "Come, let's get you on a bed."

A single light shone in Boris's bedroom. The two men entered, stumbling. Pierre uttered a silly laugh. "There now," Boris said. "This—is—a—bed, and we lie down on it. Good, that's better." He moved him onto the pillow. Pierre opened his eyes and looked about him in bewilderment. Boris sank down on one knee and removed the young man's shoe, then the other. "For God's sake," he said, "help me get these things off. Don't act like the helpless idiot you are." His tone was congenial, amused.

"Idiot? Yes, yes . . ." Pierre mumbled. He sat up and let his pelisse slide off. Boris stood over him and loosened his cravat. "It's all right now," Pierre said thickly. He fumbled with the buttons of his shirt, and unhooked them.

"Very well, then," said Boris. "I'm tired. I'm going to change." He left the room. Pierre methodically, ploddingly continued to remove his cumbersome clothing. He had to be a good boy, help Boris. Boris couldn't do it all himself, Boris wanted Pierre to go to sleep, Boris was giving Pierre his own room, good night, good night. He dropped his clothes on the floor feeling dizzy, not distinguishing the shapes in the room, their edges blurring. Mashenka? A large looming breast, no face, just one breast. He laughed a little and lay back on the pillow. Sleep. Pain? Yes, pain. Seeing the other one. Boris saying what now? "She isn't worth it, she wouldn't come to you," something like that, the whore, the damned bloody strumpet, Natalia, Natalia. Forms swam before his eyes and he closed them, closed out the world.

Boris looked into the room. Moonlight fell on Pierre's naked body. Stealthily, he turned off the lamp. There was a quilt at the foot of the bed, and he pulled it up to cover the young man. Pierre mumbled something indistinct. Boris sat on the edge of the bed and looked at him: pure, linear, strong limbs, the strength and beauty of him! Boris clenched his hands together, reeling suddenly with his agony, his manhood, his unassuaged desires and needs. Dear Lord in heaven, he thought, and hot tears came to the back of his eyeballs, burning them. Boris moved forward on the bed, toward Pierre, and touched the muscular back, gently, gently, with new fingers. Thickly, from a dream, Pierre said: "Who, Natalia?"

"No," Boris whispered, "she doesn't love you. I do."

Silver moonlight danced over the two perfect male bodies, one strong, massive, asleep, the other lean, long-limbed, still young. Boris lay down next to Pierre and buried his questing lips in the crook of the other's shoulder, thinking: Don't mention her name, forget that she ever existed. And he alchemized his pain into pure, fiery joy.

Toward dawn Natalia awoke, her entire body distressed, kinks in her arms and legs. She had slept fitfully, dreaming of fires, storms, and men lurking in passageways, ready to kill her. Misery filled her. How impossible it was to live a simple life, to choose a safe existence with a man who demanded nothing of her. Damn Pierre, damn him! She had dreamed of him, too, dying of a knife wound, dripping blood in Boris's salon, accusing her of murdering him. Natalia's hair clung to her temples, and she got out of bed, nervous as a hunted doe. Ivan and the cook kept biscuits and apple cider in the pantry. Maybe some food would soothe her nerves, calm her down. If only Luba were awake . . .

She opened her door and went into the hallway. She wondered when Boris had returned home. She had imagined noises—probably another nightmare. She turned on a light, walked into the pantry, and found the biscuits, the cider. She placed her snack on a tray and carried it gingerly into the salon. There she hesitated: Something was wrong.

She looked around her, turning on more lights. A small stand on which Ivan stacked the art periodicals to which Boris subscribed had been knocked over. But Boris never got drunk; he could drink gallons of Dom Perignon or bottles of vodka, and they never even clouded his mind. She straightened the stand, rearranged the periodicals. A rectangular rug caught her eye, its corners turned under. She smoothed it down. What had Boris been up to?

Concerned now, she walked back into the corridor. Boris had

left the light on in his bathroom. She turned it off carefully. There was a small candle in its holder and some matches on the table. She lit the candle: It would provide enough light to make sure everything was all right, but not enough to awaken or alarm Luba or Ivan, if they should hear her footsteps at this hour and stir in their sleep.

Natalia tiptoed to the door of Boris's room. It stood slightly ajar. She thought: I can't intrude, but if he's ill, or if he needs me . . . She remembered stories of men who had suffered heart attacks in the night and been unable to call for help.

She gently pushed open the door and went in quietly, holding the candle. She could hear breathing, but it was odd, almost as though there were two people in the room, not one. She stiffened: But no, if he had wanted another woman, surely he would have gone to the woman's residence and not humiliated her, Natalia, his *maîtresse officielle*, in front of the servants. A tremendous curiosity swept over her, quelling her scruples. She had to see! She lifted the candle, and looked at the bed.

As if sensing her presence, Boris awakened, sat upright, and blinked in the candle's glow. At that moment horror overtook her, and she screamed, one loud, piercing shriek. The candle fell to the floor, and Boris, naked, jumped out of bed to retrieve it before it could start a fire. Pierre stirred, mumbled something, and rolled over. Boris held up the candle, and Natalia saw Pierre's own nudity. She fell against the wall, her fingers groping behind her for support. Soft moans escaped from her parted lips.

Boris said, "Natalia—" and the urgency in his voice broke through her realization, pushed back the reeling pain, the elemental passion of her reaction. She jumped up, fiercely. Pierre had opened his eyes and sat staring at her and Boris in disbelief. She put her hands out before her face, as though to protect herself from both of them, and then she finally cried out:

"You have called me a whore? You? Filthy, filthy men, you have used me, used me, made a mockery of me, a mockery of the act of love—" She ran from the room, sobbing, slamming the door behind her. She ran into her own room and threw herself across the bed, shaking over and over with utter horror.

144   Wave after wave of disgust assailed her, pinning her down. She leaned over the edge of the bed and vomited bile. Some things could never be forgiven, or forgotten, even if in remembering them, she relived the end of an era in her life. She was vomiting up her youth, her naïve stupidity; they would never again be part of her.

PART II

New Decor

ong ago, as a child of ten, she had made the right decision, choosing dance. There was ecstasy in dance, and, unlike love, dance could not betray. And so she went to rehearsals, and sat stone-faced among her companions until it was time to take over the stage. Then she lived again, and for a while the agony that tore at her insides was transformed into a spiritual force, like the magic of worshiping God, or the martyrdom of the saints.

When Boris had found her packing her bag that morning, he had said to her: "You are not thinking, Natalia. You are young, naive, inexperienced, and so you shut your mind to life as it really is. Running away from me will not help any of us. If you leave, where would you go? Back to Lydia? Do you realize how much harm such a move would do you? Petersburg would whisper, 'He has thrown her out.' You would be finished! But if you stay, I will help you—your career, your social standing. You know I will."

"And Pierre?" she asked.

"For Pierre I can do a great deal, also. I have already done much to further Pierre's dreams, to make them a reality. But if Pierre breaks off with me, he will find me a most powerful enemy. He still needs me. Do you think my friends would employ him or commission works from a man I reviled? There are other bright young painters—just as there are dozens of Oblonovas at the Ballet. Do not forget the incident with Kchessinskaya: She is a woman who knows exactly how to obtain what she wants out of life!"

Natalia had put down her clothes and examined him— elegant, trim, with chiseled features, golden hair, impeccable manners, and an ironic half-smile. "Obviously your threats have worked with Pierre," she said, and then, tears rising to the surface, she turned away, her face twisting unattractively. "Because I know—I know he would not have done this otherwise! He enjoyed it too much with me to choose this sort of life of his own volition. You have manipulated both of us so that we can never be together again! I shall never have anything more to do with Pierre Riazhin. But—I do feel sorry for him."

"Hysteria does not become you," Boris said. "So you feel used. In life, little girl, people do make use of one another: It's a basic fact of life. Few of us are born happy. We all die alone. In the meantime—well, we each must try to get a little bit of happiness where it's possible, because there's too little to go around. For every Natalia Oblonova there are more than one hundred Katya Balinas and Lydia Brailovskayas—and for each of them, one thousand girls rejected the first day at the examination. Perhaps you should feel guilty about having usurped *their* happiness."

"But that was a just and open competition. You and Pierre waged some kind of game where I was the playing piece. I had already turned my back on Pierre. It was not necessary to use me this way. Why did you have to involve me at all?"

"Don't cast the first stone," Boris retorted dryly. "You have not exactly received nothing in return. Pierre was not the only reason for my coming to you. I won't try to deny that he was certainly a part of it. But there was you. Someday, when you're in a better mood, I'll try to explain it to you. Now unpack, and grow up a little. I always took you for a realist, who knew that nothing in life is fair, that nothing is a gift. I admired you for that almost as much as I admired your genius onstage."

She had stared at him, stunned by his lack of apology, by his bitterness, and by his sarcasm. So must the Medicis have been, and Machiavelli—ruthless, secure, mocking. One had to admire a person like Boris, who bent the rules and shaped the course of events. She thought: He is right, of course. What can

I do? I need to dance, and if he wants to, he can ruin my career. It is my own fault for coming here in the first place—but it was Pierre's fault for upsetting my life, for making impossible demands of me and forcing me into a corner. She turned her back on him and unpacked her clothes.

She took the pearls, the emeralds, the various fineries that he had given her, and wrapped them in tissue paper. She placed the package on his bed without a note. During the days that followed, she appeared at dinner but would not speak to him.

The disgust that she felt was so strong that, for the first few nights, she could not sleep. Burned on her memory was the candle flame illuminating the two of them in the bed, nude. She had loved Pierre, been obsessed by him, given herself only once to a man—to him—and he had defiled her. No, she had to remember, remember it always, and never trust, never love again. She had learned this so well as a child on the farm. How could she have forgotten this lesson for even a single moment?

Pierre's notes kept arriving, and she tore them to shreds and threw them fiercely into the fireplace. She would burn him out of her thoughts. She did not really understand about him and Boris, but if she were to ask Lydia, everything would come out, the shame of it, her own stupidity.

One evening in January, she was taking tea alone in the drawing room. Boris had not appeared for dinner, and she had preferred a light snack after her bath. She was weary, discouraged, defeated—tired of fighting her eternal round of bewilderment, anger, outrage, opposition, and resignation. Ivan came in bearing the silver card tray and told her that Serge Pavlovitch Diaghilev was waiting to see her. She sat up, and glanced at his scribble on the card. Her face was pale, her hair flowing down her back, her gown plain and comfortable. There was no time to prepare for this unexpected visitor. "Bring him in, Ivan," she said, "and fetch us some caviar and smoked salmon."

"Natalia Dmitrievna, forgive me for intruding," Diaghilev said. There was something soothing about playing the well-defined role of a gracious hostess to this man. He was Boris's friend. But hadn't Lydia mentioned something scandalous about him, once long ago?

"It's very simple so I'll come right to the point," he said,

150 crossing his long legs and looking at her intently. "Do you recall our last conversation, months ago at the restaurant Medvyed? About Western Europe? Paris?"

He had a charming smile beneath the pencil-thin mustache. "Yes, of course," she replied, intrigued in spite of herself. Laying a slice of salmon over a round of brown bread, Diaghilev said: "I am—we are—putting together a Russian Season of Ballet and Opera to be performed in Paris, in May. I have just begun to approach possible members of the troupe, singers and dancers. I am about to leave for Moscow to see whether Vera Karalli, Mordkin, and the Feodorovas would be interested—and I thought, why not first stop and see Natalia Dmitrievna? Or has Boris already discussed this with you?"

Her pulse began to race, and her heart thudded beneath her chemise. "Boris? No, he did not tell me about your plans. But, please elaborate, Serge Pavlovitch. How could I fail to be interested?"

"The French have responded favorably to our art and music. They wept last year when they heard Chaliapin and want to hear him again. Several of my friends—Boris at the forefront, naturally—have been pressing me to organize for dance what I did for painting and opera. I have interested Michel Fokine. If you come with us, you would dance in his *Chopiniana*, only this time you would have one of the three principal roles—and you would perform again in the *Pavillon d'Armide pas de trois*. Is the West still too far for you, Natalia Dmitrievna? Pavlova and Karsavina will not deem it too far for themselves!"

His eyes twinkled at her, and all at once she felt tears on her cheeks, laughter in her throat. Paris! To dance there, to dance Fokine's ballets, to be among great ballerinas, keen intellects, beautiful palaces, awesome museums, and sunny boulevards bordered with white buildings. France! She gasped, and exclaimed: "Oh, Serge Pavlovitch, I would go with you if you were offering me the job of floor waterer—or of scene duster! I am truly, truly honored." She knew she sounded silly and inexperienced, unworldly and childish.

Bowing over her hand, he said: "Well then, that's settled. I shall discuss your contract with Boris after my return. And please do not talk of this with your colleagues. I shall have to approach most of them after Moscow."

She remained in a daze, her pulse fluttering in her throat, her cheeks flushed. All at once she thought: But Boris and Pierre will be there. They will be together; and I? Yet to refuse because of this obscene business—to lose this opportunity after my years of training and dance— No, I shall not. I will go to Paris, and—what? She pushed away the tray of delicacies and fell against the soft velvet armchair, burying herself under several embroidered cushions and throw pillows, unable to think or move. One of the maids discreetly removed the tray and turned down the lights, but Natalia stayed hidden and withdrawn.

Hours later she heard a footstep and glanced up. It was cold; the fire had died. Boris stood in the hallway, looking into the room directly at her. She sat up and smoothed out her brown hair.

"Isn't it time we talked?" he asked quietly. "Serge tells me he was here earlier. He thinks highly of your talent. Surely you realize you are precious to me, too."

"So this, then, is your doing?" she cried. "He only brought me this offer because of you?"

Boris took off his evening cloak and folded his opera hat. "Do not demean your own worth by such stupid talk," he said roughly. "He would have come regardless of me. But he would have come *after* Moscow, after he had obtained his most important stars. My contribution is slight—but yes, it's there. Do not think me an absolute demon, Natalia. There is some good in me. One of the things I do best is to champion artists—but only if they are truly excellent, and worthy of me. As for Serge—he listens, and sifts through recommendations, and then he does exactly as he chooses. Each of us is our own man, just as you are your own woman."

Natalia did not reply. Boris sat down on the loveseat, passing a weary hand over his brow and into his hair. As he closed his eyes and bowed his head, he looked like Atlas with the weight of the world on his shoulders. Watching him in a cold and detached manner, Natalia perceived his unhappiness and felt a mirror pang inside herself. She had recently suffered much and could recognize the same misery in another. But she did not know how to broach the subject with him. Neither of them was capable of laying bare his heart, for each had spent a lifetime guarding its secrets.

She was not sure whether she really wanted to bridge the anger and resentment between them; she did not know what could be forgiven. She cleared her throat. "My mother," she murmured, "was an inconsequential woman who was worth neither love nor hatred, and not even contempt. My father did not love me. If he died now, I would not go to him, I would not grieve. Perhaps I would feel better if I could—but I am not a kind, gentle person. I don't go back to the past."

He was silent. "Why do you love Pierre?" she asked.

Boris raised his head to meet her grave young face, and for the first time he regarded her with candor, his intense blue eyes captivating her, holding her. He held his fine gloved hands in his lap with agonizing dignity. She was suddenly piercingly ashamed to have asked. "It doesn't matter," she said and looked away, embarrassed.

"No, of course it matters. You think I wanted you to find out. I may have wanted to keep you away from him—but not this way, Natalia. What is there to say? Perhaps that with you things might be different, that if I were ever to go to a woman, I could go to you, because of your infinite loveliness, your cleanness of spirit and demeanor, your honesty and courage, the way you face life without squeamishness or false pride. The rest—that he wanted you too—that is beside the point, isn't it? Why do I love him? For the same reasons you once did. It is not something I can help. It's there, and that's it: I have to live with it."

"It's always been that way?"

He nodded. Somewhat startled, she thought: But he is not ashamed! As if reading her mind, he cut in somewhat sharply: "Come now, Natalia. You lived as you pleased and did not conform to the dictates of a society that you hardly respected. Why should the rules be different for me? I did not choose to be 'that way,' as you so quaintly put it. God, Natalia—sometimes I wonder whether the provincial air will ever be cleaned from your soul! No, I happen to prefer men to women. How it began, I don't know. I have forced myself to make love to women at various times in my life—and I suppose I might find one that would please me. I had entertained that hope—with you. But there is no shame in loving someone. Pain, yes. To want a person who may never return that love, to always feel shortchanged—that, my dear, is agony. It is far worse than to incur humiliation. Think of it that way: It helps, you know!" He smiled at her, shaking his head.

She rose and took a few steps toward him. He looked up, somewhat startled by her approach, and she stood over him uncertainly. Hesitantly, almost grudgingly, she extended both hands to him, and when he took them in his own, she whispered: "What's to become of us? Can you tell me, Boris?"

He shook his head and stood up. She searched his face, anxiety welling up within her. He placed his hands on her shoulders and drew her gently to him, enveloping her frailty with his arms. "How to untie the knot," he murmured. "No one can do it. But we're all part of it, like strings of a cord, all meshed together."

The months that followed became a changing kaleidoscope of events. An unspoken understanding had developed between Natalia and Boris. Natalia knew that somehow she belonged in his home, that he needed her; although there was still pain and anger, most of it was directed at Pierre. After all, Boris had never pretended to love her, and neither had she loved him. But Pierre was an altogether different matter, and she was adamant in her refusal to acknowledge his existence.

On February 22, 1909, the Grand-Duke Vladimir died. He had been a supporter of Diaghilev's endeavors for many seasons, and his loss was felt as a sudden shock. One evening Boris burst into Natalia's boudoir in a state of great agitation. "The Tzar has withdrawn our subsidy," he announced. "Without the promised hundred thousand rubles, we may be finished before we start."

She was sitting by her vanity brushing out her hair. "What happened?" she asked quietly. Boris did not usually share the problems of the committee with her; she knew he wanted her to dance without concerns. It was one of his ways of "taking care of her."

"It's Mala Kchessinskaya, no doubt. She isn't really the sort of dancer we've had in mind to dazzle Paris. She's been there before and was received rather tepidly. This is our chance to show Fokine's new works, and she is not suited to them. Nevertheless, how could we leave her out?"

"But she's to dance Armida," Natalia countered. "Surely that's a large role?"

"She wanted several ballets, so that the Grand-Duke Andrei influenced the Tzar to abandon the project."

Natalia looked at Boris carefully. He was nervous and angry, but alive and brimming with energy. "You thrive on chaos that needs to be sorted through," she told him. "Remember how you saved the season of Russian art in '06?"

"Ah, yes, the season of art." Both were silent, sobered by memories—the painting of the Sugar Plum Fairy, Pierre Riazhin. "For starters," Boris said, "I am going to write a check to Serge for twenty-five thousand rubles."

Natalia raised her fine eyebrows but did not reply. She was thinking: How much of this is for me, and how much for *him?* Pierre's involvement in the season was considerable: He and Bakst had been making the set designs and costume preparations for the revised version of *Egyptian Nights*, to be called *Cleopatra*. But she merely remarked: "Your father will be appalled."

"My father is used to this. Besides, my dear, he likes you. He likes it when I take proper care of you." They smiled in tacit understanding, then sadly remembered Grand-Duke Vladimir, who had been similarly fond of his own son's mistress, Kchessinskaya.

Grand-Duke Vladimir had been able to obtain imperial permission for the dancers to rehearse in the Little Hermitage Theatre, where performances were put on solely for members of the court. Those who had been asked to participate in the Paris season met there, in the small white theatre with its columns of roseate marble.

The Paris repertory was to be a medley of Fokine ballets and adaptations. He was to be the *premier danseur* of the enterprise, as well as its choreographer. But other male dancers, particularly young, sloe-eyed Vaslav Nijinsky, would share the limelight. Moscow's elite would mingle with that of the Mariinsky in a perfect blend of styles and physical characteristics.

Natalia was exhausted from double rehearsals for Paris as well as for her regular Mariinsky roles. But she felt honored: Pavlova was a *prima ballerina* and Karsavina a soloist of the first degree, yet, though she only had a junior position, Diaghilev and Fokine had awarded her parts in three of the proposed ballets. She would be one of the witch Armida's confidantes, was a leading sylph in *Les Sylphides*, and would play the heartrending role of Tahor, the abandoned fiancée, in the opulent production of *Cleopatra*. When Pavlova arrived in Paris at a later date, because of another engagement elsewhere, she would take over the Egyptian role from her younger colleague. For after all, Natalia had to accept the proprieties of hierarchy in the Ballet. But with two other coveted parts, how could she complain of fatigue? She was only nineteen and filled with strength and health.

At the Hermitage Theatre, the dancers practiced and the painters worked. Natalia felt smothered in this proximity, for she could not avoid seeing Pierre frequently. His eyes sought her face, and there was tragedy in them. Well, he has made his bed, but I shan't share it with him, she thought harshly. She would not speak to him or read the notes that he persisted in sending. After a while he stopped sending them.

The Moscow contingent was not able to practice at the Hermitage, since their own engagements were keeping them in that city until the end of the spring season. But Ida Rubinstein, who was not a ballerina and did not belong to a company, joined them. She was the daughter of a well-to-do businessman who had catered to her desire for the stage by taking the advice of their friend Bakst and enlisting Fokine's services in teaching Ida to dance. Still, she did not perform classical ballet. She mimed and moved in indescribable ways, langorous and sensual. She was sultry and tall, and, although her bones showed, she made her thinness an asset and danced to show it off. The costumes that were being designed for her by Bakst and his young protégé, Pierre, were alternatively loose or clinging, and altogether revealing. Natalia watched her from the corner of her eye and thought: Here is a girl who loves herself and wants every man to do the same. In each movement she invites lovemaking. Apparently, Pierre was responding.

Neither Boris nor Natalia talked about Ida Rubinstein and Pierre Riazhin. Yet Natalia thought: He is doing this to defy us both. What can Boris do about it? But Boris was thinking: Pierre will never again come close to Natalia, and another woman must be a poor substitute. So be it.

The entire world was upside down. The new *régisseur*, Sergei Grigoriev, manager of the company, had his hands full, and Alexei Mavrin, Diaghilev's secretary, spent his time running back and forth delivering frantic messages. Natalia examined Mavrin closely whenever she could, for Lydia had told her that Diaghilev was "like Boris," as Natalia now called it to herself. Mavrin was his contant companion. Yet the young man seemed quite ordinary to Natalia, as did Serge Pavlovitch himself.

On April 2, Natalia was nearly knocked over by a frenzied Mavrin, who seized her by the shoulders unexpectedly. "Natalia Dmitrievna!" he cried. "Get your belongings! We've been driven out of the Hermitage Theatre and have to move ourselves down to Catherine Hall on the opposite side of town!"

Shocked, Natalia hastened to the rehearsal room and gathered together her costumes, her dancing shoes, and her leg warmers. The dancers and painters stepped into a convoy of carriages. Somehow Natalia was thrown in beside Pierre. Jammed between his thigh and the door, she could hardly breathe. Goose bumps rose on her flesh. He whispered to her: "I didn't want any of this to happen. Don't you understand? I was drunk, I didn't know what he was doing."

She felt a surge of bile rising in her throat. "Always blame someone else," she hissed back sarcastically. "But I've long since stopped caring what you do."

"I don't care what you do, either," he said then, quite audibly. "Your biggest role is as his foil. The glitter that hides the filth."

She faced him squarely, and there was such passionate hatred in her brown eyes that he recoiled. He would never forget the condemnation in her silent expression.

Catherine Hall was a large mansion, and when the carriages disbursed their passengers with their materials, Natalia rushed out into the confusion, grateful for its bustle and commotion. Boris was standing at the door, smiling. She came up to him quickly, with something like relief. Putting his arm casually around her shoulders, he said: "The Tzar does not like our self-sufficiency. Since he won't let you practice at the Hermitage, we had to find another location at once. This was the best I could come up with."

"You? But how?" she asked.

"It's a German club. I simply went to the German ambassador. He's an old acquaintance. I told him that if this season is a success, I don't see why we couldn't go to Munich sometime soon."

Natalia looked up at him, feeling tiny beside him. He was watching the members of the *corps de ballet* struggling with boxes. A sudden flame of anger shook her. Surely Pierre must realize and appreciate all the trouble, all the agony this man was going through to ensure the success of the ventures in which the young painter was involved. She bit her lower lip and shook her head slightly. "I am still a provincial fool," she murmured. "I don't understand very much. I don't know if I shall ever forgive you, Boris. But I am grateful."

"That's a step," he admitted with a rueful grin.

Chapter 8

Natalia had dreamed of Paris and pictured it in her mind, but still it was not as she had expected. She stepped into wide boulevards lined with graceful plane trees, horse chestnuts, and maples. The sun shone over the white buildings, over the open-air cafés where elegant women drank tea and watched the passers-by. Paris was not golden and soaring like St. Petersburg with its spires and cupolas: It was simple and gracious, a serene yet gay city. Driving by the Seine, she saw the Île-St.-Louis and the Cathedral of Notre Dame and felt that Paris was the Middle Ages, the Sun King, romance and moonlight all rolled into one. Boris said: "I did not tell you that we have a home here. Everyone else is dispersing into various hotels, but you and I are moving to our own house."

She was amazed. Boris was forever revealing surprising possessions; part of his character was always hidden beneath veneers and poses. She would never know the man, she realized. She was silent in the coach that took them through the majestic avenues. She looked out the window and marveled. Everything was quiet, reserved, and elegant. "We're in the sixteenth district," he explained. "As befits the aristocracy," he added with his satiric half-smile of self-deprecation.

They passed the Museum of Man and its twin, the Museum of the Navy, and Natalia saw the Eiffel Tower in the midst of the wide field called the Champs-de-Mars. It seemed out of place, a steel needle among graceful, low buildings. "It's a year older than you are," Boris told her. "Don't you like it?"

"It's like Isadora's dancing; it takes getting used to," she answered, amused.

Passing by the Bois de Boulogne, Natalia exclaimed out loud. The large lake, the islands, the small lake—the scene was peaceful, sun-filled, a dream. But the coach would not stop. She shut her mouth, feeling unsophisticated and childish. At nineteen, women of Petersburg society knew Paris as well as they knew their native city. Boris would find her excitement embarrassing. But he was laughing.

The car finally stopped not far from the Bois that had so captured Natalia's fancy. They were on a large avenue, the Avenue Bugeaud, in front of a two-storey mansion of white stone. "I'll show you the garden first," Boris suggested. While their bags were being unloaded and brought inside, he led her around to the back of the house. There was a large square of trim lawn as deep as the house itself, bordered by begonias, poppies, and rose bushes and enclosed by a twelve-foot wall covered with ivy. Trees and manicured bushes were scattered over the lawn, and strolling to the farthest wall, which ran parallel to the house, Natalia discovered that it was adorned with a bronze high-relief.

Boris guided her toward some large, low steps that led from the garden to a terrace. "It's like the countryside," she marveled in a hush tone. He was opening the glass doors into the salon. It was enormous, upholstered in delicate mauves and pale greens, the walls hung with ancient tapestries depicting unicorns and huntresses. "But we won't live in this room," he told her, pushing her gently toward the right.

She passed ahead of him into a smaller parlor comfortably decorated in an English country style, airy and informal. The knickknacks on the tables and shelves were priceless. She noticed at once several black ashtrays and bowls adorned on the inside with real Brazilian butterflies of extraordinary hues. Across the hall was the dining room, designed in classical, symmetrical Louis XVI fashion.

On the way upstairs Boris took her past the entrance gallery, with its bronze statue and potted plants. On the second floor the rooms were smaller: a master bedroom, three smaller bedrooms, three baths, and the boudoir. Natalia could not believe her eyes: The latter was totally Chinese, with red-lacquered walls adorned with gold metal and black designs. Even the flowers were exotic: orchids and red camelias in low, bright bowls. "And so," she said, turning to him, "where is my bedroom?"

"Pick any one," he replied easily. She wondered if she had said something wrong, but no, he was appraising the boudoir with ironic nonchalance, his customary expression.

"It's beautiful, Boris," she said. "It's like a museum, only one feels life here—one isn't afraid to touch. I must say I prefer it to our flat in Petersburg. When did you buy this—or have you always owned it? It seems to suit you so well that I can't imagine your father living here before you."

His eyes were narrowed, his expression becoming withdrawn. "No," he answered, "it's mine. I purchased it the summer of '06."

For *him*, she thought, and felt momentary nausea. How could she ask "Where did he sleep?" so that she wouldn't pick the same bedroom? Oh, God, there was no escaping it, no avoiding it. "Put me wherever you prefer," she said. "You know me best, my particular tastes."

Without waiting for his reply, she turned and ran down the stairs, seeking the freedom of the garden.

There were only two weeks to prepare for Opening Night, with two different sets of dancers who had never before practiced together, the Petersburg and Moscow contingents needing time to meet and adjust. Vera Karalli, the leading dancer from Moscow, had replaced Kchessinskaya as Armida, after the latter had refused to participate in the Paris season. The old Châtelet, where they would perform, was like an aged Cinderella being fitted for the ball. Natalia got headaches from the constant clanging and banging of the carpenters who were transforming the pit into stalls. Fokine's nerves were even more frayed than they had been in Petersburg. He shouted at the dancers, upbraiding them for their deportment or lack of it, telling Natalia that she was a shame to this production, with her dangling arms.

Exuberant society people came to watch the rehearsals because they were friends of Diaghilev, Benois, or Boris. Misia Edwards, the young Polish-Belgian wife of the publisher of the daily newspaper *Le Matin*, was charming, feminine, and round, with upswept burnished hair and pouting lips, a woman with a romantic past. Natalia particularly liked her, because she was quick and open-minded. She gave receptions in her apartment on Quai Voltaire, where Natalia met Marcel Proust, ill and greenish-skinned, and the young artist and writer Jean Cocteau. Boris knew the Comtesse Elisabeth Greffuhle, Madame de Chévigné, and the Rothschilds. Sometimes they came to watch the rehearsals, too, upsetting Fokine. "We are here to work," he would cry, "not to entertain bored members of the idle classes!" But since the critics also came, Diaghilev calmed him down. He did not wish to lose good publicity.

The Parisian press had been alerted, and the intelligentsia and nobility were expectant and excited. Natalia was tired, overworked, her nerves on edge. She had to keep in mind all the personalities around her and hold herself in check, accepting Fokine's abuse without breaking down. And Nijinsky—aloof, withdrawn—he was best kept at arms' length. Actually, he and Natalia got along quite well, for she too was reserved and did not mix well with the other dancers.

She enjoyed her colleagues but could not feel close to them because of Boris. Everyone knew of their relationship and understood that she was privileged because of his protection. With Pavlova not here yet, there were no vicious tongues. Natalia had learned that every creator had an ego, which was tender and easily bruised. She was considerate and cared only that the end result be good, that she perform her roles well.

There was also Pierre. He had settled into the same roominghouse as Benois, on Rue Cambon, but he attended many of the same functions she did. He worked in the Châtelet, but they avoided each other. At Misia's open houses, it was more difficult. There were no set groups: Enclaves formed and reformed in a constant pattern, an ebb and flow of conversation and relationships. Misia took her aside one evening and said: "Natalia, my dear, do not go to the opposite side of the room when that young painter walks in. We all know that he painted you in '06. Be kind to him. He is a genius, and he adores you."

Natalia had replied, quite coldly: "He is not my type. Besides, the painting was commissioned by Boris." It was a convenient lie since the painting hung in Boris's study.

Misia had raised her eyebrows and changed the subject. Pierre was popular among the French. He was so Russian— dark, strong, bold and sometimes uncouth; besides, they had met him before, two summers in a row. The ladies whispered that he was painting Ida Rubinstein—in the nude. But Natalia thought: This year *I* am Boris's companion. What are the people thinking? Does anybody know about the two of them?

The night of May 18 was the *répétition générale*, a preview in full regalia of the première on the following night. This was to be as important, if not more so, than Opening Night. Diaghilev and the impresario Astruc had organized everything with such perfect showmanship that the result was nothing less than dazzling. In the front row of the first balcony, or dress circle, Astruc had placed the fifty-two most beautiful actresses of Paris, alternating blondes with brunettes so that the effect was of a basket of flowers. From then on, this area of the theatre would be called the *corbeille*, or basket, to commemorate Astruc's genius.

The *tout-Paris*—everyone who mattered—was represented: French diplomats and statesmen and all the aristocracy. The list was varied and long, not the least prominent figure being King Edward VII of England. Even Isadora Duncan was present. Diaghilev and Astruc had drawn the choicest spectators.

This first night there would be only three productions: *Le Pavillon d'Armide*, the Polovtsian Dances of *Prince Igor*, and *Le Festin*. Natalia's stomach twisted. This was different from Russian audiences, and even the refurbished Châtelet seemed unfamiliar. Nijinsky practiced offstage. He was simple and remote, an odd fellow, but no one with whom she had ever danced could master the air the way he did, floating upon it in fantastic leaps, undulating in a way that was neither masculine nor feminine, more spritely than human. He glanced in her direction and briefly nodded. She nodded back, gravely. They understood each other, the professionalism that allied them. They did not need to be friends to work well together.

The conductor for *Le Pavillon* was its composer, Tcherepnine, and when he rose to the podium to lead the Moscow orchestra, Natalia thought: It has begun, there's no going back. It was a dream to be here, to perform before an audience whose. singular composition could never be matched. The Armida story was unfolding, Mordkin and Karalli had taken over the stage, then the fantasy took shape. The diamonds of the women in the theatre blazed, their cheeks glowed. It was time for the *pas de trois*.

Natalia went onstage and felt the response as she had never felt it at the Mariinsky, in spite of the balletomanes and the claques. Paris was ready for Fokine, for the Russian dancers, for Benois's costumes of grace and lightness. She began her number: slow, then faster, with pauses for effect. She heard cries, applause, and a lump rose in her throat. Boris sat in his box, surrounded by elegant people: Misia, the comtesse Greffuhle, Diaghilev. Natalia gave herself up to her interpretation. There was gold inside her veins, wine and ambrosia. Karsavina and the sublime Nijinsky joined her, and their movements were filled with joy, three youthful bodies, three souls, mingling, joining, reaching the audience, making the supreme connection.

It was over. Natalia was bathed in perspiration, but, as Karalli and Mordkin went to take their curtain call, as the tumult in the stalls and rows resounded like a volley of gunfire exploding close at hand, Karsavina put her arm around her and they fell back, exhausted, laughing, triumphant. It was time for their own *encore*. They stood on either side of Nijinsky. The others would have to dance again, in *Le Festin*, but for Natalia it was over, the evening was finished. It was time to change and join the others in Boris's box.

Already people were pressing backstage, not even waiting for the next number. Natalia made her way to her dressing room, and before she could reach it she saw the bejeweled ladies with their tuxedoed escorts, forming a crowd. Someone touched her, grabbed her, hugged her. "*La jolie* Oblonova!" she heard, and grew dizzy, smelling the expensive scents, reeling from the refractions of sapphires and rubies. *"L'inoubliable* Oblonova!" another cried, and then a strong male voice said: *"Laissez-la passer, laissez-la donc, nom de Dieu!"*

It was Boris, it had to be; he seemed to turn up in places like these. She tried to reach his extended hand, found it, grasped the fingers. He was holding her, supporting her, almost carrying her, and then they were in the dressing room filled with roses and boxes of chocolate. She smiled at him, her lips trembling, and he said urgently: "You've won! All of you—the Russian Ballet, the designers, the musicians. It's the most marvelous success I've ever witnessed!"

She took his hands. "We wouldn't have reached Paris without you," she reminded him. "It's your success too." Her eyes were limpid and wide.

He kissed the top of her head. *"Les français t'adorent,"* he said. And then, growing authoritarian, he added: "Hurry up. I don't want to miss the Polovtsi tribe in the throes of violence!"

Boris took the newspapers to her in the morning and made her read aloud from them, saying, "I didn't spend all my money on these French lessons for nothing, did I?" He sat on the small ottoman while she read. Praises for the Russian dances, for the choreography, for the ballerinas and Nijinsky. Praises for Diaghilev, praises for Benois and Tcherepnine. And then she came to it: a photograph of her, Natalia.

"Robert Brussel says that I am 'a return to ancient Greece, where the women knew how to live, love, and feel,' " she exclaimed with a little laugh. "Oh, Boris—*L'Oblonova est un oiseau immortel, une femme-oiseau.'* An immortal bird! What a kind, generous thing to write, don't you think?" She was red with embarrassment and also with excitement and pleasure.

"He hasn't seen you yet as Tahor, or as a Sylphide. And in the meantime, let us see if you can improve for the première. Most of the official reviews don't come out till after then, you know."

He had made her no extravagant gift, nothing with which to celebrate the triumph. Ah, then, he was waiting for the première tonight. And Pierre? Unable to stop herself, she asked, her pulse racing, "Was anyone else in the box with you, before I came?"

Her question broke up the atmosphere like a snowball hurled into a hothouse. She regretted it immediately. Boris stared at her distastefully. Rising, he tossed the newspaper, which she had laid on his lap, onto the Chinese carpet. "Don't be a fool, Natalia," he said in a clipped tone. "If anyone had been with me, he would have stayed for the rest of the show. And last night would have been a more appropriate time to ask me, don't you think?"

Pierre has stopped caring for me and Boris can't, she thought desperately, her bright joy fading to a purple ache. The review lay on the carpet like a forgotten relic.

Natalia would never forget the night of the première. The atmosphere backstage was joyful, a tense joy that bound everyone together in a winning team. There was also fear: What if something went wrong? What if the critics turned against them? The *répétition générale* had been like an engagement party: There was still the wedding to come, and the lengthy marriage between the Parisian public and the Russian artists.

Once on stage Natalia felt confident. The Russians were the exotic jewels with which the French, hungry for new and more exciting experiences, were adorning themselves this season. She felt a flow of love for them, wanting them to love her too, wanting their extravagant praises. This was the release, the fulfillment—this was exactly why she had put aside her life in order to dance, why she had told Pierre that marriage was out of the question. Katya Balina Marshak would never experience this oneness with hundreds of people. It was not at all like loving a single man. She felt swept away, exultant, febrile, alive—as if she would never die, never feel fear again.

She knew that she had never danced so well. It was the start of a new season, a new vigor, a new femininity and virtuosity. She glowed. She went into her dressing room to change, buoyed by her taut joy and vibrant nerves.

When the performances ended and Boris took her arm to leave the Châtelet, she heard Diaghilev say: "Natasha, you are the new Taglioni. Wait until tomorrow's papers!" She wanted to cry but didn't. It was a time for celebration. He had called her Natasha, the little mouse Natasha, ugly, odd little Natasha. What would her parents have said about her tonight? It did not matter: She was free of them, exultantly free, a woman at last.

Outside on the pavement, she felt Boris's arm tense up. Glancing up, she saw that he was rigid in his evening wear, tall and frozen. A pang of fear shot through her, a premonition. She clung to his arm, wanting to infuse her own life into him. He stood looking at a woman, and now she looked too, curiously and with apprehension. It was a young woman with dull blond hair piled ridiculously high with curlicues, a woman with a pert nose, a small body, and an enormous white fur cape. Natalia blinked back wonder, but Boris did not move, and the woman stared at him too, her blue eyes widening. Natalia whispered, "Come on, Boris. Serge Pavlovitch is holding the car for us. The supper—"

But now the other woman stepped forward, until she stood barely a foot away from Natalia and Boris. People had begun to form a circle around them, mystified by this strange approach. The woman held her finger out, pointing at them, and then she began to scream in a hysterical voice: "That's her, that's Oblonova! That's the whore who took my husband!"

Horrified and disbelieving, Natalia grabbed Boris's arm and shook it, shivering under her coat. "What's going on?" she whispered. "Who is that? Please, please, let's go!" she pleaded. All around her people had stopped, hearing the name Oblonova. "Yes, yes, that's l'Oblonova!" they said, trying to touch her. Boris drew her closer to him but still would not budge.

The woman paled and cried, hoarsely, wildly: "Do you see her, everybody? She took my husband from me, the common prostitute! He left me on our wedding night to go to her, the strumpet, the whore, the whore!"

The commotion had drawn a larger crowd. Suddenly a man jumped out, a distinguished though nondescript man of middle age in a tuxedo and opera hat. He took the woman by the shoulder and began to whisper to her. He was murmuring in Russian: "Marguerite, it's all right, it's all right, don't think of him, let's go." Then he said the same words in French. Diaghilev came running, having heard the hysterical voice.

A policeman drew near, and the crowd began to disperse, whispering loudly and angrily. Diaghilev seized Boris's arm in an iron vise and brought him to the waiting car. "Why didn't you go, damn it?" he hissed. "Do you think this sort of publicity does us any good?"

"But who was she?" Natalia repeated, her head spinning.

"It was Marguerite von Baylen, Boris's ex-wife," Diaghilev told her. His voice was cold and nasty. "That's all we needed, all we needed!"

"I had no idea she was here in Paris," Boris murmured, his voice hushed and toneless. "I'm sorry, Natalia."

But Diaghilev could not be contained: " 'Sorry, Natalia!' It's the reputation of the Russian season you should be sorry for. Thank God her husband will do something about her, send her away or something. But you, Natalia: You have to return to Petersburg tomorrow. I can't afford to have our season besmirched by scandal!"

Natalia's eyes grew round, her throat constricted, and her palms began to sweat. "Return to Petersburg?" she cried. Angry tears rose to her eyes. "No! I'm part of this season. They approved of me. Brussel liked me! Boris!" she exclaimed, turning to him. "Do something! Say something! You can't let this happen!"

"There is absolutely nothing he can say," Diaghilev replied quietly. "I do regret this, Natalia. But if you think about it, you'll see the predicament this situation has put me in."

She burst into tears, sobbing loudly and without restraint. Boris placed a hesitant hand on her head, and Diaghilev stared grimly out the window into the night. She continued to cry, brokenly, raucously, she who cried so rarely and then, so discreetly. Finally Boris murmured, "There is a diamond brooch, at Van Cleef's, Place Vendôme, which I wanted to give you— which I had specially made for you."

She raised her head, and looked at him from tear-stained eyes. "It won't make up for this," she whispered. "Nothing will ever make up for this."

They had stopped at an intersection, and, without warning, Natalia pulled open the door and jumped out, her cape opening like an umbrella around her. When they peered outside trying to find her, she had disappeared completely from sight.

Serge Diaghilev told Pierre Riazhin what had happened. The two men had nearly collided in the lobby of the Hôtel de Hollande, where a group of celebrants were meeting before going to a late supper. Boris had kept the carriage to look for Natalia. It was a pleasant spring night and she might be wandering aimlessly through the city. Already she knew it well, and had spent much time walking through its avenues and parks, and along the Seine where the booksellers and painters set up their open-air stalls.

Diaghilev had to abandon the search, for he had people to meet. Pierre wondered why the entrepreneur had chosen to tell him of all people about Natalia. Did he know about his feelings for her? Serge Pavlovitch did seem to possess an uncanny sixth sense relating to the undercurrents of relationships among "his" people. Or else he might have remembered the painting of the Sugar Plum Fairy . . .

But Pierre did not waste time in pondering this thought. He grabbed his cloak and ran hatless into the wide avenue. There, disoriented, he tried to imagine where Natalia might have gone. He began to walk briskly, a light wind caressing his thick black curls and rustling the silk of his evening pants. It did not occur to him until he had walked to the Place du Trocadéro that he should have hailed a cab—but where would he have told the coachman to go? He was better off on foot.

What a crazy girl, running off into the night this way! he thought. At first nervous energy kept him going. Then, on the marble square that separated the Museum of Man from that of the Navy, he began to laugh. A young couple, snuggling together on a bench, the plumes of the woman's hat blowing in the breeze, turned from contemplating each other to stare at him, his black eyes sparkling with dots of red, his hair wild and unruly beneath the stars. The irony of it! Natalia having to pay for Boris's sins; Natalia being accused by the deserted ex-wife!

He wondered what Boris had said, how he had handled it. Pure hatred filled him, and Pierre thought: I hope to hell he botched it, made it worse!

Pierre concentrated on the sixteenth district. Toward dawn he had to admit defeat. He fell on a bench and removed his shoes. His feet ached. He laid his head in his hands, and thrust his fingers through his hair. It was no use. The damned girl! Well, perhaps Boris—or Diaghilev—or someone else had already found her. That was the pattern of his luck to date: to reach her too late, after someone else had laid claim to her.

He was hungry. There was a bakery on Avenue Kléber, near the Trocadéro, which he knew stayed open all night so that partygoers could pick up pastries before going home and workmen could purchase breakfast rolls just prior to work. Having come full circle in his search, he went to the bakery and bought a bag of hot croissants. When he walked outside, he found that a pink cloud had risen in the distance: dawn.

He was exhausted and his emotional state had reached its lowest ebb. Still, this was Paris, a Paris with which he had become enamored two summers before, and he thought: The Bois is so close that I might reach it before my legs give out. An artist can't always create in comfort! He dreamed of the park's color in the early morning light, and of strolling through its garden patches all alone, preparing himself for a painting when he returned to his rooming house. He should not waste this time— Natalia had eluded him, but there was his work. He might still make use of his exhaustion to produce something fantastic, a Parisian scene dredged up from the night's peregrinations. Munching on a croissant, he made his way to the Bois de Boulogne, near which he had lived for two years with his benefactor and friend, the man who had then defiled and used him and wrecked his dream.

Pierre found her when he reached the bank of the large lake of the Bois. He had already scattered some crumbs to the ducks in the water, when he looked out toward the romantic island and saw the little rowboat, and the lone figure crouched inside it. The blue cape, the delicate form, the haphazard pile of smooth brown hair were immediately recognizable. His heart lurched: She was so pitiful, so appealing, so waiflike in her little boat, alone in the dawn! How could he reach her without frightening her off?

He waited, sitting on a bench, eating his rolls. Presently, she turned the boat around in the water and returned. Evidently she had convinced the attendant to let her go out before opening hours. He saw her moor the boat with the others, and hop out, a light gazelle upon the pier. Then she began to walk, slowly, with apparent aimlessness, along the edge of the water. She had not seen him on his bench.

He approached her gently, not wishing to break too harshly upon her solitude. He placed himself in her path, and when she looked up to see who was blocking her way, she did not seem surprised. They resumed walking, side by side, smelling the dawn, the lake, listening to the awakening birds calling to one another. Hesitantly, he placed her small hand in his own, still without a word. The springtime buds were bursting on the brown branches of the tall trees bordering the path.

At length they sat down, and he broke the final croissant in two and handed her half, although it had grown cold. She ate, suddenly very hungry. Then she looked at him full in the face, and smiled a small, wavering smile. "Why are you always here when I think that my career has washed away?" she asked.

He didn't answer. Instead, he cupped her pale face in his strong hands and tilted it upward. He kissed her eyelids, her nose, her chin. Then, with mounting thirst, he plunged his lips into hers, merging himself into her coolness. She did not fight him, but she was tired, drained, and disoriented. When he rose to the surface again to breathe, she said: "But there will always be this doubt between us, won't there?"

For a moment he was angry, disillusioned, poignantly hurt. But he saw that she was right. He loved her—he adored her— but would he ever cease to wonder how she had sold herself to Boris? He could understand her own lack of trust as well: She would never be sure of what had happened between him and Boris.

They rose simultaneously, no longer touching. A zigzag of pale yellow was reaching across the horizon, and he caught his breath at its beauty. Yet he knew he would not paint it when he returned to his room. A lifetime had evolved since the night when he had found her on his doorstep. He felt old.

When they drew up to the white stone house on the Avenue Bugeaud, the front door opened from within and Boris, pale and drawn, with purple circles under his eyes, stood like a specter in the hallway. With a weary sigh, Natalia went in. By the bronze statue she stopped to look at them, the tall blond man holding the door, his eyes narrowed and hard—and the young man on the steps, his nostrils flaring, his black eyes iridescent in the morning light. She shivered slightly, then turned away. It would be best for her to go to bed at once.

Chapter 9

That summer, Boris spent a great deal of time thinking. He had rented a villa in the aristocratic resort of Pavlovsk, not far from St. Petersburg and a bare fifteen minutes by carriage from Tsarskoïe Selo, where the Imperial Family had its Summer Palace. Pavlovsk was pleasantly wooded, the villas snuggled within immense bowers of fruit trees and flowers.

He had selected it because of Natalia's state of mind. After leaving Paris in May, she had been so withdrawn that he had not known how to reach her. The reviews after the première spoke of her as a mistress of the plastic arts, an elf, a sprite, a modern virtuoso in the vein of La Camargo or Taglioni. But reading them to her would have made matters worse. He was only relieved that she had come home and not done anything foolish. He was furious with many people over this debacle, but mostly with himself. He should have checked on the whereabouts of that madwoman Marguerite! Yet never in a million years could he have predicted such an outburst. It had been humiliating, undignified—and the result, so unjust! Why hadn't that new husband of hers, the Prussian diplomat, done something about her?

Natalia had buried her tremendous anger under a total passivity that frightened him. He had come to understand her pride, her wounds, her defenses—but this complete remoteness was new and impenetrable. The gift from Van Cleef and Arpel's, a splendid diamond sunburst, had left her indifferent. He knew that if he had taken her to Vienna or Switzerland in this mood, she would have remained unseeing, seemingly unfeeling—a pillar of stone, beyond emotion. Yet he sensed the hurt inside her, which she refused to allow to surface, of which she was ashamed. He had rented a villa near the Russian capital, hoping that at least she might rest in the golden sunshine.

Now, lifting his eyes to the blue-green pines that spread like parasols around the villa's terrace, he pondered over the complexities that faced him. He remembered the look of pure hatred on Pierre's face, that morning after Natalia had run away. The blood pulsed inside him like a waterfall, and his stomach burned. To love so much and be hated in return—to have gambled everything on this love, and to have lost every chance.

Well, maybe not every chance, he countered silently. His eyes became slivers of steel. He had more control than Pierre, poor innocent. Pierre would twist the knife in his gut, but Boris still held Natalia. Her return that morning, when she might just as easily have gone with Pierre, proved the strength of his own hold on her. Yet there was more to Natalia than that. She had become a part of him, and he could no more conceive of letting her go than he could imagine voluntarily stripping himself of his keen intelligence. What was it about the girl? She was not very pretty—at times, beautiful, opalescent, something out of the Grecian past, but otherwise just a small, trim girl of nineteen. Pierre's love for her had made her more valuable to him, that was certain. But that had been in the beginning only. Now she possessed an essence of her own, an entity—yes, he needed her.

Then it came to him: This little dancer with the brown and white tones of an old postcard was the single person who had seen him stripped of his veneer. Although a provincial girl, she had accepted him, as he knew his own three adoring sisters would never have been able to, had they, instead of Natalia, learned the truth about him. Now they would never learn—of this he felt certain—mostly because of Natalia, because she had played the part so well, so naturally and convincingly.

He remembered the scene in his father's study before his quick, disastrous marriage to Marguerite. Nina, newly a mother to three-month-old Galina, the Princess Stassova come to have tea with her parent and siblings . . . Nadia and Liza, both engaged to scions of the highest aristocracy . . . And the old man, blunt and virile, always baffled by his artistic son but loving him with the strong faith of the blood tie . . . Boris felt a sudden spasm of anguish. If he had loved them all any less, if he had been a casual profligate like his friend Prince Lvov—or even if, like Diaghilev, he had resided far from his close relations—then he might not have cared so much, and life would have been easier, with fewer lies and fewer restraints. There were those who shared his predilections more openly, and surely they were the lucky ones. But the Kussov blood had burdened him with a need for the most stringent discretion, and Natalia's presence had stopped certain questions from ever having to be asked.

He smiled ironically. He was drawing odiously close to sentiment, and that was an absurdity not to be considered. So— Natalia was a fine dancer and loyal to him; furthermore, in her, he possessed something Pierre wanted. Having her was a fit manner of revenge. Yet, how long could he hope to hold onto her? She was drawn to the young painter by the most elemental magnet: sex, old as the ages. And the disaster of the Paris season had not endeared him, Boris, to her in the least. He knew, in fact, that she was furious, outraged; she still blamed him for what she considered the downfall of her career as an international dancer.

Poor Natalia! He had not even known her when he'd married Marguerite! Oh well, there was nothing he could do now about the lost Parisian season. But he might be able to do something about the next one.

Yes, Serge had known how to protect his new company from the slightest blemish of scandal. And God knew that enough of it had occurred after their departure. He had to smile, malevolently: Mavrin had run away with one of the Feodorov sisters from Moscow! There was justice in this, too: Serge had lost his lover to a woman! Poor Serge. Yet Diaghilev had had his eye on Nijinsky before then, anyway. Still—to be left for a woman—that was a stab at one's pride as well as at one's heart, and Boris knew exactly why his friend had told Astruc not to give a single kopek to his disloyal secretary, although he had owed him back pay. For Serge was always behind in his remunerations. Then, of far more serious consequence to the Ballet, Vera Karalli had run off with the tenor Sobinov.

But Boris was amused rather than disturbed by Diaghilev's problems. He was also coldly angry. There was something humiliating about how Serge had dismissed Natalia, something that had nothing to do with her at all. It had been a means of showing Boris that this enterprise was his alone, not Boris's or anyone else's. It was exactly what he had later done with *Cleopatra*, pitting Pierre against Léon Bakst, friend against friend, so that in the end only he kept the whole thing together. Boris smiled: He knew this tactic well, having made use of it many times—but to have had it used against Boris himself was an even greater insult. He had saved Diaghilev's hide so often with gifts of money. But this time, although Astruc kept writing desperate notes concerning thousands owed to him by his entrepreneur friend, Boris would not lift a finger to help. Natalia had been used, and if she could not reap the glory due her, then he would cease to aid Diaghilev's adventure. Perhaps there was another possibility . . . to separate Natalia from the Diaghilev enterprise altogether.

Boris turned his thoughts to Pierre, who persisted in being childish. Pierre wanted to hate the only person who truly loved him. Turning against Diaghilev would also give Boris the delectable pleasure of impeding Pierre's growing career, to watch him suffer as he himself was being made to suffer by the young man.

Boris thought again of Natalia and turned to regard her in her chaise longue across the terrace from him. How it must hurt her to know that Karsavina and Pavlova had replaced her in every role, that they had conquered Paris while she sat here nursing her wounds. He examined her covertly, thinking: Her career means everything to her—but still she wants Pierre. I can't ever let the two of them come together again—not ever. He thought of Diaghilev's affairs, of his friend's despair over lovers' abandoning him. Only marriage could prevent desertion, could provide the ultimate bond. If Pierre and Natalia were ever to marry . . . He could not finish the thought, for bitter sadness twisted his insides, and the desire for revenge, for salvation, for the end of pain all tore him.

"If I could promise you the best roles to dance, and the most agreeable working conditions, what would you say, Natalia?" he demanded carefully, walking toward her.

"There's only so much that even you can promise," she replied. "There was Paris, remember?"

He stroked his mustache. "Yes. That was my fault. Protection is not enough. If you'd been my wife, no one could have touched you with the hint of scandal—and of course Serge would never have dared send you home. But—if you *were* my wife—think of the possibilities!"

"An Oblonova doesn't marry a Kussov," she said dryly, suddenly smiling. "Even the Tzar could not marry Kchessinskaya!"

"But we are only nobility, Natalia—not royalty. I could marry you. In fact, I rather think I should. It would strengthen our bond, and I owe it to you."

"I don't believe in marriage, and besides, you're teasing me," she countered, beginning to sit up. "Why do you speak this way?"

"Because I've been thinking. We live together, and in that sense, we're already married. I don't want children—so I don't need a woman of aristocratic blood. What I do need is an artist in residence, if you will—an everlasting, understanding friend. And how could it hurt your status to become the Countess Kussova? There are those who would sigh with relief in society and open their palaces to you." He said the last with his twisted half-smile of irony, and then laughed. "Wouldn't you like to shock them, Natalia? Wouldn't it be fun?"

"We have an adequate arrangement," she said stalwartly. "You don't need to question my friendship."

"I don't. But you questioned mine, in Paris, with Diaghilev. Marry me, Natalia. Things won't change between us—but to the world, things will have changed a great deal. That's important to me, for my own reasons."

She turned her rich mahogany eyes to him, and her face was very still. Paris. Pierre. The walk back to the house on Avenue Bugeaud. The end of a shattered, childish, impossible dream.

To clinch it for good. She thought, with sudden shock: Of course! It's on his mind, too—that's his reason. But she would never marry Pierre, that part of her life was over. Should she marry Boris? What he had said was true: In the most important sense—their cohabitation—they were already married in the eyes of their acquaintances. And yes, he did owe her something—something to help assuage the old betrayal, something to formalize her role in his life. She had helped protect him by hiding his secret, and surely it was silly now to resist the honest compensation. In any case, theirs would not be a true marriage, not the suffocating, destructive relationship she had always vowed to avoid. Then she would be able to put her memories of Pierre behind barriers that the live Pierre would never be able to cross.

"All right, I accept," she stated, wondering why her voice was firm and clear, so unemotional. She felt him kneel beside her chaise longue, smelled the spearmint of his breath as he kissed her forehead—and all at once tears came, and she trembled. What had she said? What was she doing?

"You will be the new Taglioni, my dear, the new Sallé," Boris was murmuring. "You'll see!"

Now Boris Kussov sat in the Restaurant Weber, on the elegant Rue Royale, in Paris. It was October, and as he lifted the goblet of wine to his lips and planned his next words carefully, he once more saw the image of Natalia on their wedding day, a month before. He had not wanted an extravagant affair that would remind him of his marriage to Marguerite; but his father had argued him out of a quiet ceremony, emphasizing that the first event had taken place in Kiev, and that members of the court would be more likely to forget that debacle in a wash of champagne in honor of the new bride. Boris had smiled to himself: Certainly some people had been shocked that a Kussov had actually allied himself to a simple girl from the Crimea, but others had envied him the new soloist at the Mariinsky.

Boris tasted the wine, an excellent Mouton Rothschild, and recalled his wedding. It was odd what stayed in one's mind from the important events of one's life: the smell of the chapel; the melodic voice of the metropolitan bishop; kissing the Eastern

Orthodox cross; kneeling on the velvet cushions with that waif of a girl, all wrapped in lace and silk yellowed with the age of thirty-five years. It was his mother's wedding dress, with tiny pearls scattered over the lace and in Natalia's hair, his sister Nina's *kokoshnik* on her head. He had lifted the veil for the chaste nuptial kiss. Then the wedding night, quiet and graceful: a parting of the ways by her boudoir, another small, dry kiss on her forehead, as he might have given to his small niece, Galina.

Boris put down the goblet and folded away his thoughts of Natalia. Today he was dining with Gabriel Astruc, the impresario of the Societé Musicale, who had secured the Châtelet and provided all the publicity for the first Parisian season of Russian opera and ballet. "Of course, a second season was foreseen," Astruc said. "The success of the first was inevitable"—he smiled, inclining his head toward his companion—"given the fact of our participation, *mon cher* Boris. However, Serge has treated us both shabbily, I should say, and I shan't stand for it any longer."

"No, indeed," Boris commented. He took a forkful of partridge. "These are succulent," he said. "But tell me more about the Opéra. Serge is arranging to take his company—or rather, I should say, the company that he gleaned from the Moscow and Petersburg Imperial Theatres—to the Opéra next year, but has failed to include you in the negotiations?"

"No. And you are aware that he owes me a great deal of money from the first season. Two and one-half percent, that was all I asked for! Well, he owed me fifteen thousand francs as of several days ago, and I intend to collect this time. I need to live, too! He overspends so that he is always operating at a deficit—but that is no longer my problem. My real problem is this: If he goes ahead and brings the Russians to the Opéra on the proposed days in May and June, he will be competing directly with me, for I have booked Caruso into the Châtelet at that time. It is a very unpleasant situation. Without me, the last season would have been a disaster, and Serge is the most ungrateful man I know."

Boris remarked acidly: "Not quite. But perhaps, Gabriel, I might be able to do something to help you. I was not at all happy with the way he treated my wife. She was unwell for several months after being dismissed."

"And how is Natalia now?"

Boris smiled. "She dances *La Fille Mal Gardée* this week at the Mariinsky, an old Kchessinskaya role. This little talk is giving me ideas, in fact. But Natalia is fine. I shall be sorry to miss her performance."

With a sparkle in his eyes, Astruc retorted: "She will doubtless be sorry to miss yours. What exactly do you have in mind?"

Boris placed his elbows on the table and leaned forward. "Listen to me," he urged quietly.

When Boris returned from Paris, the winter season was in full swing. He surprised Natalia by announcing that they would give an important dinner, and that the guests of honor would be Kchessinskaya and Chaliapin. "You are not to concern yourself with this," he told her. "Ivan will help you plan it, and the seamstress will make you up a splendid new gown. I would have brought one back from Pacquin, or Worth—they still have your measurements to make to order—but this time I did not want you to outdo Mala. It is of utmost importance that she feel the star of the evening."

Natalia said nothing. This strange man was her husband now, but she was still not certain what to make of him. She had agreed to marry him—for only this way would she impose the final check on her instincts, barring even the possibility of Pierre's interference in her career plans. Boris would not force himself upon her sexually, leaving her magically untouched. But what of him? How had she possibly been able to add to his life? He had actually been prepared to defy his father in order to marry her, although that had proven unnecessary. She could feel his protectiveness, his respect—but she also knew he did not love her. Yet she had been chosen over women with family and funds—and there were times when she could not comprehend it.

Reflecting upon her marriage made her think how her life had changed because of a single official ceremony. Now she was the Countess Kussova. She was received at court. But she knew better than to mention this within the ballet company. Among the artists tempers flared, jealousy erupted at the slightest provocation. Kchessinskaya, not yet a married woman herself, treated her affectionately and had even helped to train her for her own favorite role in *La Fille Mal Gardée*, a classical comedic ballet of the eighteenth century. Pavlova seemed less openly hostile. Why, even General Teliakovsky, still paternal, found a nice word here and there when he encountered her in the passageways of the Mariinsky. Natalia thought: They are hypocrites. To them I've become a passageway to Boris.

Now there was this dinner. As usual, Ivan and Boris had outdone themselves, leaving very little up to her. But, she thought with a certain amount of pride, she was learning. She was learning how to place her guests, how to speak to them in the finest French. That was a bitter pill to swallow: her perfect French, for which Boris had provided the lessons, and which she had learned for Paris. She braced herself: She would not allow self-pity to destroy her. Diaghilev was already hard at work planning a second season for that summer, in 1910.

On the night of the dinner Natalia looked around her, surveying guests and servants from her hostess's vantage point at the head of the long table. The supper was delicious: clear consommé with meat-filled *pirozhki* pastries, followed by salmon in a thick velouté sauce, with white wine. Chaliapin sat on her left, and, laughing at one of his innumerable funny anecdotes, she wondered: I am at ease with him. He can tease me and I no longer wish to die of embarrassment, as I did two years ago. Then her thoughts returned to the pork roast with prunes, baked apples, and an enormous salad of exotic greens and fresh vegetables. If she concentrated, she could hear strains of conversation at Boris's end of the table. Drinking her Bordeaux wine, Kchessinskaya was saying, in her melodic but rather loud voice, which carried effectively: "He told everyone in Paris at the Châtelet and the Opéra that he was a representative of the *Tzar?* Why, the gall of him, the nerve of that despicable man! Wait until I tell Andrei. What an impostor!"

Boris was replying quite seriously for a spirited dinner conversation: "Perhaps it was only a misunderstanding, Mala, darling."

A gigantic duckling, piquant with grated lemon peel and a lemon sauce, with roasted onions and potatoes and baked tomatoes *à la provençale*, was being served, with a rich Madeira wine. Natalia barely sipped it; her head was beginning to reel, and she did not wish to consume excessive amounts of food and wine because of her dancing weight and fitness. Boris was saying, "Poor Astruc does not know what to do. It seems so unjust, after all his hard work."

"I gather," Kchessinskaya remarked with a pert toss of the head, her eyes glinting with mischief, "that you, my love, are not going to offer to pay the fifteen thousand francs? Not even out of compassion for Astruc?"

Boris took her hand and bowed over it with mock gallantry. "My dear," he said, "I have a wife to support now. Remember?"

Across the yards of white linen spread with silver goblets and crystal bowls, and lined with hand-painted china from Sèvres, the *prima ballerina assoluta* caught Natalia's eye and waved gaily. Then another guest leaned across the table to ask something, and Kchessinskaya and Boris were obliterated from her view. Natalia was intrigued.

The servants came in with chocolate and orange ices. Champagne was presented. Then came the fresh fruit trays and the sweetmeats. At long last the supper was over. One by one, each man took the arm of his dinner companion, and in twos they came to congratulate Natalia on her splendid meal. This was a gracious tradition honored by all members of Russian society, but Natalia still felt awkward about receiving thanks, especially since she had had so little to do with planning the evening. But she was Boris's wife, and the hostess: There was no evading this ceremonial finale.

In the drawing room Ivan had set up the coffee table, and Natalia sat down to serve the hot black beverage to her guests. In France this, too, was handled by servants, but Natalia preferred the Russian custom of more personal hospitality. She liked to have something to do with her hands. Boris was dispensing liqueurs to the gentlemen, and Natalia listened to the conversation going on around her. She felt a pleasant afterglow from the meal.

To her right the man whom she still hesitated to call her husband was murmuring something in a low voice to the charming Chaliapin. "Feodor," Boris was saying, "Caruso's reputation among the French—among all the Western Europeans—has been established for a long time now. Even if he's a tenor and you a *basso profundo*, he is your sole rival in the world of opera, in terms of attracting an audience. For you to try to challenge him so soon after conquering the French would be sheer folly! Wait several years. In the meantime, go to Paris as much as you want, but not at exactly the same time as he. Put some distance between you."

"Yes, of course, Boris," Chaliapin replied, thoughtfully. Here was another conversation with ominous undertones, Natalia thought.

When everyone had left, Boris seemed in extremely high spirits. What a handsome man he was, she had to admit. Blond and fine and priceless, like an antique. Joy made him buoyant, alive, and his skin seemed ruddier than usual. He put his arms around her waist from behind, and rocked her quickly back and forth, a strange, mesmerizing dance. "A perfect evening," he commented.

When she turned around with a quizzical expression on her face, he shook his head. "This is not the time for explanations, my pet," he told her, and touched the tip of her nose with a playful finger.

In the early part of December Diaghilev called on Boris at his Petersburg apartment on the Boulevard of the Horse Guard. Boris was in his study, perusing some first editions of artistic works on Christian iconography. He wore a maroon smoking jacket and was nonchalantly holding a pipe. A fire blazed in the hearth. His friend appraised him shrewdly and commented: "You are the very picture of comfort."

Boris's eyes narrowed. "And you, Serge, look like a network of exposed nerves. Won't you have a cognac?"

Diaghilev shook his head, drew up an armchair, and sat down, rather heavily. "What game are you playing now?" he demanded.

"Game? Why, my dear fellow, life's too serious for games. I

play for my share of flesh and blood, like Shylock." Boris puffed on his pipe and reclined in his seat, his elegant, lanky body conforming to the cushions. He smiled slightly: "What's on your mind?"

The two men stared unabashedly at each other for a full minute. They were no longer smiling. Finally Diaghilev broke the silence. Dramatically, he burst out: "Years of devoted friendship! Years! You were still at the May Gymnasium when I met you—a boy of sixteen! That's half a lifetime ago, do you realize that? Nearly eighteen years of being your guide, your mentor—including you in all my endeavors! You needed me, for you do not possess one ounce of personal talent!"

Boris nodded. "Indeed. Neither do you, Serge. You find it, and I finance it. Two sides of the same coin. Symbiosis. It seems you've needed me too in your time."

Diaghilev waved these words aside as though they were annoying flies buzzing around his head. "At first I thought it was a mistake, a network of impossible, unfortunate coincidences. The Tzar's final, unequivocal refusal to subsidize our enterprise, now and forevermore. Then Feodor's telling me he won't sing in Paris next year, when he's pivotal to our season. Then your lame excuses for not lending me funds with which to get that goat of an Astruc off my back. Bits and pieces of conversations came back to me. Kchessinskaya's sudden friendship with Natalia. And so it occurred to me that all this can be traced back to her—to Natalia and the scandal that I luckily averted in Paris last May. Yet somehow I believe there's more to the issue. You are trying to ruin me—but not just me. What is it, Boris?"

The insolent ease with which Boris had been listening to his friend was replaced by an alert tautness. Boris leaned forward. "You've used me before, Serge," he said in a low voice. "Often. Flattering me, coddling me. You knew that I realized it was a ploy to obtain Kussov money. I played along, and you knew that I was playing along. I truly think we both enjoyed the game, and each other's cleverness. But there was no need to involve Natalia."

"So you think, if Natalia is to be avenged, then the whole Russian season must be wiped out, discredited. Actually, I wanted Natalia for some very important roles in '10. Regardless of your role in her life, she is as fine a dancer as Karsavina, and while she was in Paris, the French adored her. I need Natalia! And Pavlova won't be back this year, so I shall need her even more. I also need you. Why should I deliberately alienate you? To make a display of authority? That would be childish, wouldn't it? No, there's more to this. You've been using me in an attempt to do something quite different."

Boris burst out laughing. "What do you want, Serge?" he asked.

"The question is, what do *you* want? I am prepared to name you co-director of this enterprise if you could see fit to be part of it again. You—and Natalia, of course."

"And in return? I am to pay Astruc?"

Diaghilev smiled. "That would be nice, yes. You might also speak to him about a reconciliation. We could go to Paris together to see him."

Boris shook his head. "That is not enough. Natalia will be pleased, I'm sure. The money would have to be paid in smaller lumps, and as a legal loan, so that I could collect from you if you should default. You would have to find other financiers for this project, as I can certainly not be responsible for all of it on my own. My fortune is not inexhaustible, as my father has oft pointed out. There are the French Jews—the Deutsch de la Meurthe brothers, the Rothschilds, the Gunzburgs; we could certainly try to inveigle them to donate funds. I would be more than willing to help you, as your ability to wade through financial matters is nil. But, as I said, that won't be enough to tempt me back."

Diaghilev scrutinized his friend and did not say a word. Presently Boris spoke, his tone offhand, casual. "How well our first encounter worked out," he said. "Now all the Paris salons are wearing the wild colors of our friend Bakst—and all the *grandes dames* are undulating in vaporous gowns like Ida Lvovna Rubinstein's. And Benois—the delicate pastels of his *Pavillon d'Armide!* Our artists have outdone themselves."

"Indeed," Diaghilev asserted. He leaned forward and waited. Boris smiled.

"But artists are extravagant, Serge. Their montages always

turn out to be more expensive than in the original proposals. We shall have to cut expenses somehow, my dear fellow."

"You just said that Bakst and Benois have enriched both art and fashion with their confections," Diaghilev countered. "How would you trim their budgets?"

"Oh, not theirs, exactly. I would trim ours. Why do we need hangers-on, not-quite-there young artists such as Pierre Riazhin? He's been disappointing, Serge. I expected him to make miracles, and instead he's merely tried to copy Léon Bakst—at his worst." He paused. Then in a low, barely trembling voice, he added: "We can't afford him anymore, dear friend. Not anymore."

Diaghilev raised his eyebrows and nodded ponderously while he took in this information. He looked at Boris, smiled briefly, and stood up. "And Feodor? Will you woo him back?" he asked.

Boris shook his head. "Feodor is best left out of this. Let's have a season of pure ballet this time. Besides, do you want to ruin him, pitting him against Caruso?"

A momentary flash of anger came into the eyes of Serge Pavlovitch. "We shall see," he said.

Boris rose too and came across the room to his friend. They smiled at each other and opened their arms. Then, laughing, they hugged each other. "Co-director! That's not half bad for a ploy, Serge," Boris said. He slapped his friend on the back. "Come by to see Natalia," he added cordially, escorting the other to the door. "You flatter her by your presence. She's still a charming child at heart."

"It's interesting how you find these rustic young geniuses," Diaghilev remarked lightly. He slid his arms into the sleeves of his coat, which Ivan was holding out for him. Boris's expression did not change. Diaghilev shrugged lightly and said: "Goodbye, dear boy."

The door closed on Diaghilev's back. Ivan unobtrusively disappeared. Boris slammed a fist into the palm of his other hand and ground his teeth together. He imagined Pierre standing before him, his large black eyes glowing in the firelight, his tense young thighs taut with nervous energy. He saw him sitting at Diaghilev's table, eagerly expounding ideas for settings, for costumes. But there had been the still life on the steps of the house of Avenue Bugeaud, the look that had passed between them. It did no good to go back, to reevaluate. Boris had never made it a habit to retrace his steps, and he was surely not going to do it now. "Ivan!" he called. "I shall be going to Paris next week. Prepare my bags, will you?"

Chapter 10

At the end of the spring season Natalia was promoted to soloist of the first degree. She was twenty years old and beginning to shine among the ballerinas of the Mariinsky. Her career seemed to be steadily progressing. Boris thought: It was wise to have secured her for my wife. He began to plan for the summer season with Diaghilev.

In the midst of helping to create new ballets he took time to have his principal assets transferred to France. There were bad seeds in the wind, unrest in Russia, disquiet at Kaiser Wilhelm's court in Germany. Boris clearly remembered the small Revolution of 1905 and the disaster that had preceded it, the war with Japan. The French, he felt, were less likely to turn hysterical, and in that country the Kussov fortune might grow faster than here, where Tzar Nicholas paid no heed to his people's cries. Whether war came or another small revolt, the Russian economy would be the first to suffer.

When this transfer had been smoothly accomplished, Boris felt a wave of relief. He could resume his concentration on the finer things in life, the arts, the dance. The 1910 ballet season came upon the Kussovs as a small whirlwind. Natalia was enjoying herself. Diaghilev's dancers went from Germany to France, and in neither country did Marguerite appear. Everywhere Fokine's choreography was applauded and the ballerinas acclaimed. Both Karsavina and Natalia took turns partnering Nijinsky, whose ability to stay in the air like a magic bubble was already becoming a legend. Natalia was given the chance to

188   demonstrate her own virtuosity as never before: She danced in a new production based on a vivid Russian folk tale, *The Firebird*, to unusual, strident, and dissonant music by a young composer, Igor Stravinsky, whom Diaghilev had discovered. The score was arresting, unsettling, and hinted at the supernatural in every phrase.

In her Firebird costume Natalia was, indeed, a plumed being endowed with magic powers. Her brown and white coloring had been transformed into a turquoise transparency, with jewels in her hair and threads of gold twisted into her locks. When she begged for her release from her captor Ivan, her entire being pulsated, throbbed, and the feathers danced with her in sweeping arabesques. The audience clapped and cheered, and the men stood up with excitement. That evening, in her Chinese lacquered boudoir, Natalia looked at herself in the mirror and wondered whether she would ever dance another role so perfect for her temperament as this magnificent Russian folk bird, proud, vulnerable, passionate, and graceful. She truly was the Firebird, where she had only played at being the Sugar Plum, Aspitchia, or Columbine.

The Firebird pleased Diaghilev because it was his first full-length original ballet, but Natalia sensed that her unqualified success had irked him, wounding his pride and hurting his single-minded championship of Nijinsky. She was thoughtful as she combed out her long, silken hair, so fine on her shoulders. She "belonged" to Boris, and Nijinsky "belonged" to Serge Pavlovitch. Did neither of the two mentors realize that, in spite of their youth and lack of worldliness, the young dancers possessed souls and wills of their own? It was almost as if, in their odd rivalry, Boris and Diaghilev had wound up two mechanical dolls and pitted one against the other. Her friend Karsavina was independent, and suddenly Natalia envied her. She had a life of her own!

This, then, summed up Natalia's problem: Her professional existence was dependent on Boris, but she had no life aside from her work. Boris had turned her into a magnificent plumed firebird, spoiled by his wealth and by the roles that he obtained for her. But she was a woman, and this fact stood between them as no other could. He owned her but did not possess her. It had been so long since a man had wanted her enough to try to possess both her body and her soul, to want her not for *what* she was but for *who* she was. Pierre had consumed her, and she had fought the demanding pressure of his ardor—but Boris lacked all ardor, and in her heart there was a dryness, a thirst—a vague longing. With unexpected ferocity, she posed the question that had been nagging her for an entire season: Whom had Pierre offended that he was still in Russia, that no one dared to voice his name aloud in the Ballets Russes?

Perhaps it's better this way, she thought, closing her eyes. With him in Russia I won't be reminded of him. When we are in the same city, that knowledge alone is enough to set me back, to make me remember. Onstage and at the rehearsals, at the lovely receptions where she was fêted, Natalia could reduce the memories, crush them with the toe of her ballet slipper. But not alone, at night . . .

She was wretched in Brussels, envying Karsavina's freedom from the oppressions of patronage and jealous also of her colleague's happy marriage. A life of her own offstage! Perhaps her old friend Katya had been less stupid than she had once judged her to be.

During the next year Natalia seemed to acquire new color, a rose tone that gave her more beauty, more delicate reality than her previous paleness. Her arms and shoulders were rounder. There was little doubt now that she was a beautiful woman, no longer a frail young girl blending into the background. But she did not notice the appreciation in others' eyes. Her life had been spent training her body, and she still remembered the years on the farm when she had been the ugly daughter, ignored and deprecated. These memories still rankled within her. Her mother had finally written her, complimenting her on her brilliant marriage. The Gudrinskys were wondering when Natalia planned to come to the Crimea to show off her handsome count. They wanted to entertain the Kussovs at their family mansion if Natasha and Boris came during the summer hiatus. The entire community was agog with expectation—and Elena claimed she had always known her younger daughter was destined for glory. Natalia crumpled the letter into a small ball and felt the hot sting of humiliation. She dismissed her parents from her consciousness. On their Crimean farm they did not know that they had died for Natalia long ago.

Back in the Russian capital Natalia was at once swept into a flurry of rehearsals. It was difficult to believe that Diaghilev was growing tired of Fokine's choreography and had told Boris that it was old-fashioned, with its emphasis on times gone by and romantic, colorful places. At the Imperial Theatres Natalia still danced mostly classical ballets, with perfect symmetry in the *corps de ballet* and herself on *pointe*, showing off her prowess. Boris had also told her that Serge Pavlovitch was eager to form his own company, instead of waiting for the summer when vacationing dancers of the Moscow and Mariinsky Theatres would be free. Diaghilev—and Boris, too—were always surprising her with their ambitious ideas.

Toward the end of January 1911, Natalia and Vaslav Nijinsky performed the lead roles in *Giselle*. Alexander Benois had confectioned a short tunic for the young man when he had danced Albrecht in Paris, and now, instead of a more concealing outfit, Nijinsky insisted on wearing this costume, without undergarments. Teliakovsky was away, but Krupensky, his assistant director, immediately registered his opposition. But Nijinsky was most stubborn: He would dance Albrecht only in his Parisian attire.

During the intermission Boris was on his way to visit the dowager empress with a box of sweets when he encountered Matilda Kchessinskaya in the corridor. She seemed particularly excited, her eyes sparkling. "What do you think of all this nudity?" she demanded.

"Whose nudity, my dear Mala?" he asked, suddenly wary.

"Why, Vaslav's, of course. Maria Feodorovna was very upset. I've just been in her box. As the Tzar's mother, she felt personally insulted by this unashamed display of . . . male attributes. Placate her, will you, darling?"

"I will try. But something tells me you're up to mischief. And it isn't subduing the offended sensibilities of our honored dowager empress."

Matilda Kchessinskaya kissed the tip of her finger and laid it lightly on Boris's cheek. "Silly man," she said archly, moving away in the opposite direction. She left him strangely unsettled.

The following day Diaghilev informed Boris that Krupensky had asked Nijinsky to apologize for his indecent accoutrement, but that he, Serge Pavlovitch, had advised him to refuse and to stand by his artistic decision. Krupensky's response was immediate: He dismissed the young *danseur* from the Mariinsky. "And now," Diaghilev said, smiling, "I can form a full-time company of dancers. Vaslav will not have to finish his five years of compulsory service in the Mariinsky."

"And Matilda's role in all of this?" Boris demanded dryly.

"Oh, she had no idea that she'd be playing into my hands. You did such a fine job convincing her last year of my ill will toward her that she was trying to organize a faction against me. She thought getting Vaslav fired was a good first step. But I've been waiting for just such a chance! If this hadn't happened, he would not have been allowed to quit until May of next year."

"The five-year prison term, indeed." Boris stroked his mustache. "Natalia is still bound until then. No one will see fit to fire her, will they?"

"You could hire Matilda to plot something. Remember the *Egyptian Nights?* Perhaps you could revive her animosity toward Natalia. One never can tell."

Boris shook his head. "How we do dig up the past, don't we, Serge? But it's the future that counts, isn't it?" There was a sharp edge to his tone. Then he shrugged. "Congratulations, *mon cher,*" he added, inclining his head toward his crony. "Good work!"

They began to laugh together, but their rivalry remained a palpable presence between them, thick with memories.

On the eve of her birthday, in February, Natalia was alone. Boris had gone to a meeting at Diaghilev's flat to help plan the new season. Sitting down at her vanity, she felt depression settle heavily upon her. It was so strange how little Vaslav Nijinsky had been dismissed. Now his beloved mentor was forming a company with him at its base. She was glad for him. After all, if Kchessinskaya had made problems, if she had used the Benois attire to fabricate a reason for ridding herself of a rival in the public eye, the boy had been cruelly used. There was no more fantastic dancer than Nijinsky, with his ambiguous voluptuousness, his incredible leaps. If Serge Pavlovitch could turn the dismissal to the young man's advantage, then all the better.

She did not feel strongly about the real Nijinsky underneath the artist. He had an ego, yet he held himself apart from others so that no one truly knew him. She thought, with surprise: I don't seem to find fault with them anymore, these men "like Boris." They possess different instincts from my own, but then, so does Katya, who has stopped dancing to have one child and then another. This is the world of artists: They do as they please, according to their own rules.

So why was she depressed? she wondered. It was frustrating to know that Vaslav Nijinsky, Diaghilev's "Vatza," was going to travel and dance modern ballets while she remained at the Mariinsky, redoing the same Petipa classics and being kept in check by the *prima ballerinas*. But that was not the real reason for her lassitude. Nijinsky and the Ballets Russes of Serge Diaghilev had brought to mind the strange triangle of her life with Pierre and Boris. She and Boris lived as man and wife in every way but one, and, as she did not want children, she could not complain. But what did Boris think about when he was alone? What thoughts haunted him? Once he had confided in her—but that was long ago. She suspected that what was for her a barren life imposed by the nature of their relations was not quite so barren for him, that sometimes when he dressed for the evening and did not invite her to accompany him, he was meeting someone with whom to alleviate the frustration. Was it Pierre, or had their relationship died long ago? Or, as the young painter had tried to tell her on the way to Catherine Hall, had it never really begun? But she had seen them! And if Pierre did not love Boris, did Boris still love Pierre?

These thoughts were like sores on her mind, and she told herself to stop, for every way she turned there was pain. But the fact remained that she was unhappy and that she could no longer hide behind her roles at the Mariinsky. Unwittingly Vaslav and Diaghilev had pointed out the unsuitable nature of her present screen. If she had to hide, let it be behind a nobler screen, a challenging screen. And that was no longer the Imperial Theatre's.

Tomorrow she would be twenty-one. Suddenly she rose, and went to the small room in the back corridor near the vast kitchen where the French cook was chatting with Luba, her maid. Crates of old belongings stood there gathering dust—old periodicals, clothes that were no longer fashionable. She sneezed and reminded herself to tell Ivan to have the place dusted. There it was, against the back wall, in its crude wrapping. She pulled it out and carried it back to her boudoir.

In privacy, she undid the strings and set it face up on the carpet. The woodland scene. Three years old now! He must have loved me then, he must have! she thought frantically. Where is he now, that we have not heard from him in so many months?

She closed her eyes and saw herself again in the Bois, walking beside him. She could have chosen to go with him then, to trust him. But she knew that, no matter what, she could not have left Boris to go with Pierre.

Luba knocked discreetly at the door, and Natalia hastily jammed the painting beneath the love seat. The maid entered and asked: "Will Her Excellency be wanting her supper now?"

Natalia stared at Luba, brought back to the present, to the silk texture of the boudoir walls, and the cocooned existence in which she had been ensconced for three years. All at once her longing, her restlessness, became untenable. Even as the maid blinked, wondering at her mistress's confusion, Natalia came to a resolution. She had to act now, before she lost her nerve, before Boris returned, before his presence once again imposed its elegant passivity over the elemental side of her nature.

Natalia stood up. "No, no," she replied, her cheeks crimson and her breath short. "I think I'll go out, Luba. My friend, Lydia Markovna—I think I shall pay her a visit this evening."

"Shall I lay out your dress?" Luba asked.

"No, I can take care of it. But Yuri can bring me in the troika. Serge Pavlovitch sent for the Count, didn't he, with his own carriage?"

When the maid had left, Natalia went to her closet and carefully selected a simple gown of gray silk, high-necked, with demurely puffed Bishop sleeves that entirely covered her arms. She hesitated near her jewel box, then deliberately did not open it. She pinned her hair into a simple pompadour with topknot, and tied a gray silk ribbon around it. She met Ivan in the hallway and had to accept the splendid white ermine cape which he held out to her. She could not have explained her preference for a simpler overcoat.

Yuri took her to Lydia's apartment, and she dismissed him at the door. He wanted to wait, as was his custom, but she said, "It's cold, Yuri, go home and rest. Lydia Markovna will send me back in a coach. I don't know how long I'll be, as His Excellency will not need me at home. You know how late those sessions last at Serge Pavlovitch's!"

Now she ran up the stairs to her former apartment and was let in by the old nurse Manya. Natalia kissed her. She went into the living room and watched Yuri drive away. Lydia appeared in a dressing gown, her black hair down her back. "So you've come to pay your dues. Fancy that!" her friend exclaimed.

Hastily, Natalia propelled Lydia into her bedroom. "I'm sorry," she began, in an undertone. "I should like to stay tonight, but I can't. I need to find a coach . . . to go somewhere."

"Oh." Lydia's small black eyes widened, but she said, "I have a small carriage, which I drive myself. I could let you use it, if you'd like. One of your people could drive it back tomorrow."

"That's kind of you, Lydiotchka. It would make sense, wouldn't it, to let me drive it home after my visit."

"Yes. Well, it's downstairs. A modest affair compared with the Kussov *équipages*. Take good care of it, as it's the only one I can afford."

Natalia gave her friend a wordless hug. Then she left, bypassing an incredulous Manya. The carriage, a simple two-seater, stood in back of the house, and she had little trouble hitching the single horse to it. It reminded her of her childhood on the farm. It was cold in the open air, while the covered troika had been warm. She drew her knees under Lydia's thick blanket, gritted her teeth, and headed toward Pierre's building. It had to be done, she had to see what had become of him. Her skin was numb with frost.

The light was on at his window. She was trembling with cold and hitched the horse to a lamppost, hoping it would not begin to snow. Yuri would have been appalled at her lack of care for the poor animal, but she had so little time! She ran up the stairs and then, in front of the door, a deathly stillness came over her. A lump rose in her throat. Resolutely, she knocked, and the sound was like a death knell. She clasped her hands together and waited, not thinking.

When he opened the door, she went inside without looking at him, without allowing him to speak first. A smell of dust and rancid oil assailed her nostrils, and she turned to him, surprised. His hair was disheveled, and there were circles under his dark eyes. His dressing gown hung loosely on him and appeared used and ill cared for. She stopped the question on her lips and instead walked into the room with the paintings. Motes of dust flew up at her entrance, and on the floor she saw an old canvas caked with paint, but only half finished. She wanted to cry out: Why have you turned this place into a sty, and yourself into a pig? But she bit her lower lip and hugged the ermine cape around her, shivering. The fire had gone out in an incredibly dirty hearth.

"Once, years ago, I offered you tea and you turned me down," Pierre said. "Could I make some for you now?"

She shook her head. "No, I shall make it." She went into the tiny cubicle that was the kitchen and gasped. Dirty dishes lay piled on the sides of the sink, on the counter, on the small round enamel stove, strangely empty. Angry tears came to her eyes. "My God, Pierre!" she cried. "What's happened to you?"

He shrugged, and she noticed that his strong shoulders seemed to have shrunk inside his dressing gown. She examined it and saw the initials *BVK* on one of the lapels. Boris's old bathrobe! "It doesn't matter, does it?" Pierre said. "You are the Countess Kussova, a soloist at the Imperial Ballet. You stand here in your fur coat and look at me with disdain, as one might look at a rat in a gutter. What do you care, Natalia?"

She thought: Then *he* hadn't seen him in all these months. Boris is too fastidious to have permitted this squalor. She circled the small samovar with caution and peered at the coals in the tubular pipe, long grown cold. "When was the last time any one cleaned this?" she asked. Without waiting for what she knew would be a stinging reply, she emptied the old water from the copper instrument and scrubbed its insides, soaking her delicate hands in the filthy liquid. She dried it with a cloth that she found on the counter, and said to Pierre: "We need some embers from the fire. Not that what you find will be very hot, but your stove is completely empty in here."

There was a harsh, nagging edge to her voice, and she tried to repress it when he brought her two warm coals still tinged with red. She dropped them down the long pipe that served as a chimney for the samovar and filled it with hot water. She put the small iron teapot on top of the coal pipe to keep it warm. "We'll wait for this to boil," she told him, and went into the sitting room that was also his studio. She knew she sounded pettish and matronly, like a country schoolteacher, but she could not help herself. She had expected anything but to have to perform cleaning chores in an abode of stench and grit. At least she could do this work without thinking, and for this she was grateful.

Now, they sat face to face. She removed her cape, and he looked at her dress without expression. "Come now, Countess!" he said. "No gems from your dear husband's coffers?"

She did not answer, but looked at him directly without flinching. "Why didn't you go to Berlin, and Paris, and Brussels?" she asked.

For the first time his black eyes flashed, and his hands became fists. "Because I wasn't asked!" he burst out. "The favorite has lost his appeal, isn't needed any longer. What did you think, Natalia? Your husband was bound to tire of me someday, only I never thought he would turn everyone else against me too! Diaghilev, Bakst, Benois—no one invites me to committee meetings anymore, and no one has commissioned any new paintings. I can't sell any of my work in Petersburg. The rich society ladies who were clamoring for Riazhin portraits suddenly have their afternoons full with other, more important, sittings. Bakst has turned Paris into a Persian harem with his settings for *Schéhérazade*, while I—oh, never mind. Who is Riazhin, anyway?"

With a swift motion she rose and cried: "I cannot bear this self-pitying streak in you! We all suffer from occasional bad luck. Why must you blame Boris for it? He helped get you on your feet, didn't he?"

"Yes, and then he deftly knocked me down. He is a master at construction but also at destruction. Boris Vassilievitch! I hope he is happier than I am. He has systematically taken from me everything that was mine."

"No," she said softly. "You are wrong there. He has not, and never could, take your talent from you."

In the kitchen her hands trembled when she placed the teapot under the faucet of the samovar to fill it with the now boiling water. She found two cups, some loose tea, sugar, and a lemon, which she sliced. She could not find any spoons, and instead put two forks on each saucer: They would have to do. She placed the teapot with its tea and hot water on a large dish, and crowded the cups and saucers around it. Then she carried it into the other room. Her face was pale and her eyes loomed enormous.

Pouring the tea, she said: "Pierre, I don't understand, not any of this. I'm sorry about your work. You're a great artist. Boris—"

"Boris can go to hell!" Suddenly Pierre regarded her with animosity: "Did he send you here?" he asked.

She laughed, a short, harsh sound that held no mirth. "No one knows I'm here," she told him. She examined her hands, bit her lip. "Please, Pierre," she said, "don't give up. It wouldn't be right. I was looking at the painting you gave me when I turned eighteen—and it's wonderful, full of life and fantasy. You mustn't give in to hopelessness, to living this way. Hasn't anybody at all been here to see you?"

A sudden vision of him in his opera clothes, black opera hat, and cane came to mind. She winced. Pity was a dreadful emotion. She was embarrassed for Pierre, for herself, and at the thought of the horse downstairs, shivering in the winter cold. What have I done? she thought, appalled.

"You have truly become his wife," Pierre remarked then, and there was amazement in his voice. "You have forgotten all of it, all about us, and remembered only your splendid new life, your new position. Why, you are even loyal to him! If you think I betrayed you, surely what he did was less than honorable."

"But he loved *you*. You said you loved *me*."

"And of course you persist in not believing my explanations. What sort of love is that? And your marriage to him? Never even explained!"

Stiffly, she said: "I did not owe you any explanations."

"Nor did I. You had left me long before, when you sent that note of refusal. Marriage did not mesh with your need to dance, to be an independent individual. Still, today you are a married woman. Logical, Natalia? Or merely money-hungry, like the rest of us? A better marriage may not necessarily mean a better man. Tell me, does he sleep with you?"

Without even thinking, she cried out: "Of course he sleeps with me, I am his wife!" Then, suddenly, she burst into tears. She stood up and sobbed for several minutes, then dried her tears like a child, with the back of her hand. She picked up her coat and put it on.

"It's you!" she cried. "You have killed it! Killed me, killed yourself, and killed Boris, too! You never loved me, you never loved him, and both of us were fools ever to care, to care so deeply for a sniveling little man such as you've become! How could you do it, Pierre?" Tears flowing down her cheeks, she added: "What a waste of our love."

She left her teacup half empty on the little table. Small, dejected, yet suddenly aware of a liberating truth, Natalia walked toward the door and did not look back.

atalia was preparing for the spring sea-
son of 1911. Boris had left her to ac-
company the newly formed "Ballets
Russes de Serge de Diaghilev"
to Monte Carlo while she finished off
the season at the Mariinsky. In early
May she would meet him in Rome,
where she had never been, and then
together they would proceed to Paris,
and from there to London, where the
Ballet was scheduled to perform at
King George's Coronation Gala at Covent Garden.

In planning her wardrobe, Natalia called on Princess Stassova, Boris's sister. At twenty-eight, Nina Vassilievna Stassova
was poised, thoughtful, gentle, and very close to her brother
emotionally. They bore a striking resemblance, inherited from
their mother, and Nina's daughter, Galina, carried it through
to the next generation. She was a small golden butterfly, an
engaging child.

Watching her, Natalia experienced a strange sensation. Truly
the girl could have been Boris's own child, and, in an inexplicable way, this created a bond between them. Almost against her
will, an idea began to form in Natalia's head, and one afternoon
she asked tentatively: "Nina, has anyone ever painted Galina's
portrait?"

Her sister-in-law shook her head. "Not yet," she replied.
"Why?"

Looking down at her fingernails, Natalia said: "I was just
thinking. She's a striking beauty, and I know a man who could
bring her spirit to life on canvas. He was once a protégé of

Boris. Someone told me that he's had a reversal of fortune, that his work hasn't been much in demand these days. But he's really very good."

"I could have her painted for Andrei's birthday," Nina suggested.

"I'm sure our friend would be grateful. But Nina, don't tell anyone about this. He'd be humiliated if he thought I'd recommended him—and Boris would be upset to learn that he's come upon hard times. It would be better for the artist's pride, and for Boris's peace of mind, if you pretended to remember his work from before, when he was popular. He was the man Boris took to Egypt—he designed the costumes for *Egyptian Nights*: Pierre Riazhin."

"Ah, yes," Nina assented. "I remember the name. I shall call on him within the week."

When the tall Princess stepped into his messy sitting room, Pierre remained framed in the bedroom doorway, his shirt open at the neck, the blood pulsing in his throat. He could not help blinking. The woman and child were too much like Boris, and so were too hateful for words of politeness, or gallantry.

Nina ignored the clutter, the room's dust, grime, and sadness. Galina moved closer to her, her small nose wrinkling. "My husband and I have been searching for the proper portraitist to commit our daughter to canvas," Nina offered gently. "I remember your vivid oils, Pierre Grigorievitch. I should like you to paint Galina."

"I don't think so, Princess," he replied harshly. "I don't paint children. They can't sit still."

Nina smiled nervously, fingering the lace on her cuffs. The small girl stepped forward, right up to Pierre's thigh, and stopped abruptly, rearing her golden head. "You were rude to my mama," she said in a high, clear voice. "I don't like you. Besides, I'll bet I can sit quietly better than you can!"

Stricken with embarrassment, Nina said nothing. She was thinking: Poor man, how bad luck makes one bitter sometimes! But still, at that moment she wanted to return home to her clean boudoir and her lady's maids. Then she looked at Pierre and found a curious expression on his dark face, which had ap-

peared to her animalistic and harsh. He was staring down at the
child in wonder. Now she thought: Why, that man is handsome, in a brutal sort of way! She felt a small thrill of fear and
pleasure run up her spine. She was remembering. Hadn't there
once been a famous painting, of a ballet—of a ballerina—years
ago? By this man, Riazhin? The painting Boris had hung in his
study—

But Galina was saying in her singsong voice: "Sit down so I
can climb on your lap. You smell of resin, like the forest."

"I smell of turpentine because I've been painting," Pierre retorted, reddening. "And you can't sit on my lap. I'm full of
oils." But in his eyes there was a new lustre, a certain softness.
He was not seeing Boris anymore, or thinking with hatred of
Natalia. He was remembering his own childhood in the Caucasus. And Galina was not at all afraid.

Several weeks later Nina said to Natalia: "I wanted to ask a
favor of you. Andrei will not be going away this summer.
There's been a business crisis—nothing serious, only he can't
leave the city for a few months. I should like to remain here
with him, but there's Galina. We'd been planning to go to
Switzerland this year, and Petersburg in summer is no place for
a youngster."

"Then I shall take her with me to Rome," Natalia answered.
"Don't give it another thought. Boris adores her and so do I.
Will you come with me, Galina?"

The small girl's face became flushed with crimson, and her
blue eyes shone suddenly. "Oh, Aunt Natalia!" she cried. "May
I, really?"

"I can't thank you enough," Nina was murmuring, wrapping
her sister-in-law in a warm embrace. Natalia smelled the soft
lilac scent of her hair, felt the slight moistness of her cheek, and
thought with a sudden surge of panic: What have I done, bringing a child into my life? I'm going to Europe to dance, not to
play house! But the words died in her throat.

During the voyage to Italy, Natalia wondered why she had
panicked at the idea of taking a child along. Galina was easy to
handle; besides, her governess, Fräulein Weisskopf, had helped

with some of the more complex travel arrangements. Natalia admired her little niece's inbred refinement, her lack of wildness, and something painful stirred in Natalia's consciousness: She could not relive her own childhood through Galina's, for worlds stretched between the child she herself had been and this cherished, well-tended little princess. For an instant a preposterous thought flashed through her mind: If ever she were to bear Boris a son or daughter, her own heredity would show through and he would find this offspring wanting, not quite on a level with Galina. Natalia found this a jarring, painful thought.

Boris was awaiting them in Rome with the Ballets Russes. Once settled at the hotel, Natalia felt the city beckon to her in the splendor of its historic contrasts. Renaissance palaces of marble spread their ornate façades next to crumbling ruins from the days of Caesar. Such an easy comradeship bewildered and delighted her senses. She felt dwarfed by history, yet somehow part of it. Roman matrons and their bustling children congregated in bright daylight around the alabaster Fontana di Trevi, where one could throw coins to make wishes come true. In the moonlight Boris took her there and she threw in a Russian kopek. "What did you wish for?" he asked. But she shrugged; she didn't know what to wish for anymore.

The ballets they gave in Rome were fitting to the spirit of the city: the fairy-tale romance of *Le Pavillon d'Armide*; the graceful, soulful *Sylphides*; and the lustful, violent Polovtsian Dances from *Prince Igor*. Natalia performed in the first two, in her usual roles. She felt that one danced to the Italians, and to their Royal Family, with one's heart rather than one's brain or one's feet. The Italians loved her, wanted to cherish her and protect her delicacy. She received a profusion of poetry from her admirers but did not laugh. Unsentimental by character, Natalia found the Italians lyrical in a way that touched her deeply.

In the golden sunshine Boris took her and little Galina to the churches and museums. Sometimes, in the afternoon, Galina and the Fräulein would play on the Pincio, a steep hill topped by a park, the Villa Borghese. Their hotel garden had potted orange and tangerine trees, and Natalia and the little girl ran down to pick the fruit, for neither of them had ever seen it growing on trees before. In Russia oranges were only to be found in baskets!

The Italian sojourn felt unreal to Natalia, tinged with pale rose and gold thread. Somehow performances seemed to be put on in slow motion. She awakened each morning to soft strains of a plaintive adagio that never left her brain. She felt at once very fluid and very slow, as though she had become a trickle of thick, golden honey. Only Galina forced her out of this mysterious trance, and then only for brief intervals, like intermissions. She thought of the Kingdom of Shades in *La Bayadère*.

Perhaps it's the city's sheer beauty, she thought, picturing the vast enclave of the popes, the Vatican, and the stained-glass windows and mosaic floors of St. Peter's Cathedral. Or perhaps it's regret—I'm feeling old suddenly, without ever having been young. She glanced at Boris, who was regarding her with that shaded irony that saw through to her core. More and more frequently now, she found him examining her—undressing her emotions, she thought with swift, hot resentment and shame.

One afternoon, near the Spanish Steps, the bright copper sun dappling the aged cobblestones, she turned to him and said: "Don't you ever feel it—the days weaving into one another, without any joy except from one's work? It's wonderful here— but the people are happy, and I'm not. I'm on the outside of a pane of glass, and they're all inside, celebrating."

A little boy, nut-brown and agile, handed Boris a red carnation, which he exchanged for a lira. Boris placed it among the cluster of curls at the back of Natalia's head. They stood looking at each other, their shadows mingling on the pavement. If she had been afraid that he would laugh, his quietude surprised her. He touched her parted lips with the tips of his fingers, and her hand held them there for her to kiss. The touch, the kiss were as butterflies playing with the velvet petals of a pansy: gentle, hesitant, longing, and afraid. A breeze lifted a strand of her hair, the sunlight shone through his, yet they remained strangely intent upon each other, like glimmering statues.

After Italy came the Paris season, and then the first official visit to Great Britain. King George V was being crowned on

June 22, and the night before, the Ballets Russes were to perform at Covent Garden. This was the first time that an entire Russian company had come to England; the British had hailed Kyasht, Karsavina, and Pavlova separately, when each of the great ballerinas had come to display her individual talent. These dancers had broken their country's noble tradition by performing in music halls, along with vaudeville acts and circus acrobats—and there they had been duly fêted like their predecessor, the ballerina from Copenhagen, Adeline Genée.

The British responded to the Ballets Russes with their personal brand of restrained enthusiasm, and Natalia smiled to herself after the performance of Opening Night. The following day, Coronation Day, the critics praised her for her "eloquent grace." There was no performance that day, June 22. Boris had driven back with her to Ashley Park, the lovely Cromwellian palace they had rented for their stay, after the celebrations had terminated the preceding night. In the old black Daimler that belonged to the owners of their mansion, the drive lasted only an hour; Brighton, the chauffeur, could make the vehicle glide more smoothly than a troika on ice.

Natalia awakened very early and, parting the curtains of her bedroom window, looked out onto the pasture to the right, where Galina and the indomitable Fräulein Weisskopf were strolling among the animals. The small girl stopped to crouch by a cluster of flowers and picked a long-stemmed weed bursting with yellow petals. She ran toward a young colt and, unafraid, stuck the mongrel bloom right underneath his quivering nostrils. Natalia smiled. There was something elemental in this scene that struck a chord in her own breast: The animal, the child, the flower—they were, somehow, "right."

She laughed at the ridiculous sentiment and got dressed. Boris had evidently not yet risen, and there were no guests. Natalia sat alone at the long dark table, and two servants appeared, ready to serve breakfast. A double Bunsen burner stood at the opposite end of the table on which lay a platter of hot porridge, and another of fried fish. With impeccable style the young male servants dished out the hot food and set out the white bread with its soft crust, which to Natalia's robust Russian palate tasted strangely like rubber. Hiding her smile, she helped herself to the never-changing strawberry jam and orange marmalade. There was no fresh fruit, no fruit compote. Ivan would have been frankly aghast. "Will m'lady be wanting eggs?" the *maître d'hôtel* asked.

"No, thank you, Lacey. But if my husband comes down, please tell him I've gone for a walk."

Since the advent of cars, the sole animals kept at Ashley, apart from the farm cattle and plow horses, were Galina's colt and two dogs. The smaller of the two, a Seidenpincher resembling a terrier, came running out to greet Natalia at the door. "Ah, Dreadnought!" she said. "Are you restless too?" Together they went out onto the vast, flower-bordered lawn, the frail young woman in her long blue linen dress, and the small brown dog with his fringe of bangs and fluffy tail. Dreadnought had fallen in love with Natalia the first day. Or perhaps he sensed that they would naturally wend their way to Galina. There had not been a child at Ashley for many decades.

Natalia and the dog walked first to the stables. There were no thoroughbreds there now, perhaps because the owners were too old to ride. The car was kept there instead, as well as the batteries and flat-wheel engine that made electricity for the large estate. Dreadnought was apparently old enough to remember other days, for he sniffed and yapped around the old Daimler with distaste. Natalia was as unfamiliar with house dogs as she was with children: in the Crimea she had known only mangy, functional farm dogs that helped with the animals in the pasture.

They strolled out into the cool silver sunshine. She felt a pervasive contentment seeping through her. The life of an English homesteader had the appeal of down-to-earth reality. She was tired of fighting the eternal questions within her, that unabated search for who she was and why.

Galina came hopping and skipping toward her, her blond curls flying behind her like gold streamers. "Aunt Natalia!" she called out. "We found a shortcut to the woods! Come see!"

Behind her, gasping for breath, came Fräulein Weisskopf. Natalia started to laugh. "It's all right. Dreadnought and I were getting bored. Why don't you rest for a while, Fräulein? Galinotchka can show me the way. I spent my childhood in wideopen spaces such as these. It will do me good."

"It isn't indicated for dancers to run, madame," the governess stated with misgivings. Natalia found her an annoying woman and felt a burst of pity for the child. She turned to Galina and took the small, plump hand that was stretched out to her.

"This is fun, spending time with you and Uncle Boris," Galina said as they clambered up a green hill, Natalia holding up her long skirt. "Papa is a nice man, but he isn't like Uncle Boris. No one is quite like my Uncle Boris. He is like the Prince in the *Sleeping Beauty*. Have you ever danced the Enchanted Princess? Mama took me to see it last year at the Mariinsky! Oh, it was wonderful! Like my Uncle Boris."

Natalia smiled. How she talked on and on, the thoughts merging and then separating, the high voice lilting prettily with the effort of sorting out images and ideas in her six-year-old mind. She said to Galina, "You are like your Uncle Boris—a golden girl." But Galina is happy, she thought, unlike Boris.

Galina broke in upon her thoughts. "Aunt Natalia, the man who painted my picture—is he a very mean man? He didn't seem to like me at all, when Mama first brought me to his house. Do you like him?"

"I'm sure he's a very nice man, Galina," Natalia replied. Her pulse pounded in her throat. "Sometimes people are not well, or not very pleased with themselves. Sometimes something has happened to annoy them, something that has nothing at all to do with you. I'm sure he liked you, darling." She added, seriously: "Galina, did your mama tell you that we must not tell Uncle Boris about the painting? It's going to be a surprise for your papa's birthday."

"And the man is poor, and Uncle Boris would feel bad if he knew. Yes, Mama told me. Maybe that is why the man is not well: He is poor."

Ah, so the child is wise, too, Natalia thought. But her temples ached from the flow of blood that rushed through them. She looked intently at Galina, but the little girl had already forgotten about the painting. "There we are!" she cried. "The shortcut!"

Natalia was preparing herself for supper. She knew that she had shocked her British chambermaid, Crowley, by showing her figure in its small, flat brassiere, while the majority of proper British women still wore corsets. But the maid had adjusted the straight tunic gown, so simple and elegant in its shades of ashes of roses. She had pinned a single rosebud to her mistress's hair and then left the room.

Natalia could imagine Boris waiting for her. She felt a sudden need for his approval tonight. She needed to sense it. Now, as she descended the stairs to the long, formal dining room, her heart beat in her throat and at her wrists, and her mind was oddly cleared of thought. It was like living inside a dream, as if, since that day in Rome near the Spanish Steps, she had penetrated closer to that self-contained man who was her husband in name only.

He stood at the foot of the winding staircase, looking up, and for a moment she closed her eyes, hoping he would not be in a flippant mood. It was so difficult to predict how he would act from one minute to the next, and she knew she would deal badly with his cruel cleverness tonight. But, slender in his close-fitting suit of blue-gray summer linen, he greeted her with a thoughtful expression on his face.

"How charming you look!" he said, giving her his arm. "Like a long-stemmed lily."

She smiled up at him but fought an inward pang that made her wince. I have to look like a boy to please him, she thought, and was surprised that it hurt. In that odd way he had of appearing to read her mind, he remarked casually: "The styles are so much more feminine this decade, aren't they? The couturiers are finally awakening to the fact that a woman's form is decorative of its own nature, without needing contrived additions."

Slowly she blinked with self-consciousness. The blood was beginning to beat in her ears and throat, and she felt a moment of dizziness.

The dining room was not comfortable. At least when Galina and her governess took their evening meal, it was still daylight and less gloomy. Natalia, at one end of the long oak table, was dazed by the cavelike atmosphere of this room, with its dark walls hung with equally somber portraits of the owners in solemn expressions and high, stiff collars. The chandelier above the center of the table shimmered with reds and sapphire blues over an expanse of white linen and pewter candlesticks. The table stood out like a white jewel, leaving the edges of the room devoid of light. Far across this field of white Boris sat with his pompadour of golden hair and his brilliant blue eyes so grave and serious tonight; he seemed like an Olympian descended to earth for a brief visit.

"You are so quiet tonight," he said to her, and his voice in the magnificent gloom rang out to touch her.

"I have nothing to say," she replied simply.

The first evening at Ashley they had been merry at dinner and exchanged amused glances over the well-done, unsalted roast beef with its mint sauce and boiled vegetables—children playing at being country squires, pretending so as not to shock the vigilant servants. It was a charade, really, this formality to be kept up in front of maids and butlers, this sanctity of upright decorum put on for the benefit of the hired help—as though the vast Cromwellian palace belonged to the servants and not to them. But this evening, over the enormous, tasteless leg of lamb, and later, over the chocolate-covered milk-and-rice pudding, they did not smile. They ate in virtual silence, and now and then she noticed that he was looking at her, and she quickly bowed her head, a sweep of blood pulsing to her cheeks. Her fingers trembled slightly.

After supper they went as usual, arm in arm, to the morning room for coffee, but she did not look at him at all. Her eyes stung. The morning room was the most pleasant area of the house. Two sofas stood back to back in the center, one facing the fireplace while the other looked out toward the park. A single lamp illuminated the expanse of well-trimmed lawn, the gracious white gazebo. Boris's presence unnerved her.

She knew that he was watching her and felt confused and uneasy. His clever eyes took in every line, every fold of her gown, of the limbs outlined beneath it.

How pure and lovely she is! he thought. How graceful, like a statue that moves and pulsates with life! He found himself unable to look away, mesmerized by her proximity, by her thigh, her arm, the soft gold hairs on her arm, the straight line of her nose. It was as though he had been afraid to look at her before. No, it isn't that, he said to himself, passing his tongue over his dry lips; it's that she's changed, grown up, defined herself. Or maybe it's I who have changed. As if I could!

"Natalia, look at me," he said, and when she turned her face to him, he could see the fear in her wide eyes and quivering nostrils—a fear that matched his own. He was thirty-six years old, yet he could not ever recall having felt such a constriction in his throat, not even when Marguerite—

Abruptly, he stood up and went to the piano. He sat down on the stool and rolled back the top. Without giving himself time to think, he brought his fingers down on the keyboard and began to play a Chopin nocturne, the plaintive notes lifting like human cries into the night. Her head came up in bewilderment, for she had never heard him play like that, nothing of this sort, only ironic bits and pieces, parodies of Rimsky or Glinka. But this was so personal, so naked—so unlike him. She felt as though for the first time since she had known him, he was offering her a glimpse into his inner being. Oh, he had done so once before, but that had not been meant for her, only an explanation due her because of her discovery. This, on the other hand, was for her. She could feel each note reaching to sink into her very heart, and tears came to the surface of her eyes, trembled, and spilled onto her pale cheeks.

Yes, she thought, he is more frightened than I, and so it is I who shall have to come to him. And she rose as in a dream in slow motion and walked hesitantly on the tip of her toes to the back of the stool where he was sitting. Her hands felt like lead, but she forced herself to raise them, then bring them gently down like folded wings over the slope of his shoulders. She felt him tremble slightly, and his fingers stopped playing. Complete silence hung in the room, silence sparked with tiny motes of electricity like red dots in the air.

Then he looked up, his blue eyes meeting her unflinching brown ones. She held his gaze and wondered, with sudden panic, whether he would not now flee from her. Her chin quivered. If this was a mistake, they would never be able to continue, to backtrack. But his arms were reaching round to encircle her waist, and she bent her face toward his and covered his lips with her own.

Chapter 12

The British season ended in December, giving Natalia, Boris, and Galina barely sufficient time to return home for the holidays. New Year's Day was a special occasion among the socialites of St. Petersburg. It was a time for all the ladies to be "at home" and for the gentlemen to call upon them one by one. Boris donned his cutaway and accepted from the ever-thoughtful Ivan a stack of engraved cards for those ladies he might miss, and a large purse of coins to tip doormen and butlers along the way. Natalia was sitting down to await her first well-wisher when her husband departed to start his rounds.

It was a freezing day, and a blizzard was blowing. Boris had saved his sister Nina for the end of his rounds, knowing that this would be one visit he would enjoy. There had always been a solid understanding between the two of them. It was not that his sisters Nadia or Liza loved him less; in fact, they rather idolized him. But between him and Nina there existed a true friendship. She saw him as a man rather than as the hero that he seemed to be for the younger girls.

By the time Yuri drew the covered troika up to the stone mansion on the Boulevard of the Big Stables, where the Stassovs lived, Boris was chilled to the bone. All afternoon, he had been alternating between the warmth of elegant sitting rooms and the sub-zero temperature of the snowy streets. He had not stayed long anywhere, sometimes merely dropping off his name card as was the custom, and now he longed for the comfort of a pleasant visit near his sister's hearth.

She was in her blue and gold sitting room, serving tea and cakes. It was rather late, and two elegant gentlemen were preparing to make their *adieux*. He waited at the side, smiling. When they had left, she threw herself with a small moan into his arms. "I'm so glad you're here," she said. "What a bore and a trial these New Years are. I'm ready to drop! Tea, my dear?"

"Yes, very strong. If you're going to complain, don't do it until I've had a turn. You, at least, stayed in one nice warm room all afternoon. I envy womanhood."

He sat down beside her and accepted the tall glass with its amber liquid. She looked up at him, smiling: "I'm glad you saved me for the end, like dessert," she remarked. She took his hand. "D'you know, it's a joy to see you these days. There's something—I don't know—something very 'at peace' about you. Natalia isn't *enceinte* now, is she?"

He laughed, and a sudden redness came over his cheekbones. "Don't tell me you're embarrassed, Boris," she chided him. "After all, it's a perfectly natural thing for a married woman. Well? Is she?"

"No. You know she's not the motherly sort. She wants to dance too much."

"Still, Boris, didn't Kchessinskaya dance till her sixth month? Isn't that what most of them do at the Mariinsky? You'd have a nurse, and then a governess. Why, Fräulein has worked wonders with Galina. And you know how much Natalia loves Galina. You can't tell me she wouldn't love her own child— yours—even more."

"In May Natalia's contractual five years will be over at the Imperial Theatres. We're going to be traveling all year round then, Nina. I don't know if dancing throughout the globe would be advisable if she were expecting."

"Well, it'll happen someday," Nina said soothingly. "You'd like it, wouldn't you? And Papa would be ecstatic!"

Boris kissed his sister. "How peaceful to be you, my love!" he commented with amusement, shaking his head at her. "You've analyzed the world into a straight line, from A to Z! Amazing girl."

But Nina sat pensive next to him. The fire danced red and orange in its marble setting, but she did not reply. She had not spoken to Natalia about what they should do once the portrait of Galina was completed. She bit her lower lip and at length said, with forced cheerfulness: "Boris, I'd like to let you in on a secret. I had something made for Andrei's birthday in two weeks—but it's so beautiful that I want you to see it now. Come."

He followed her down the corridor to her boudoir and she pushed open the narrow door. They passed into the small room with walls of gray silk, and she opened a closet door and pulled out a large canvas framed by the enamelist jeweler Fabergé. "Look," she said. "It's Galina."

Indeed it was. Golden Galina, pink and plump in a dress of white taffeta, white ribbons in her unruly hair. Boris felt as though someone had stabbed him unexpectedly from behind, and his hands began to tremble. The touch was still there, the marvelous imperfect lines, the Vrubel colors that seized and held one right inside the frame. His sister turned to him, the smile dying on her lips, for he stood rigid and white, with two hard lines on either side of his tense mouth. He stared at her with a stillness that frightened her, so that she brought her hand to her throat. "Boris," she asked, her voice shaking. "What on earth's the matter? Don't you like it?"

"It's a Riazhin, isn't it?" he said in a tone he had never used with her before. She had heard him speak this way to some of his associates when he was crossed by them—but never to her, his sister.

"Yes," she answered, feeling absurdly guilty. Remembering, she added: "You see, he did such a splendid job with *Egyptian Nights!* And I remember people praising him after the Paris exhibition."

"It's all her doing," Boris cut in sharply. "I should have known! You're a terrible liar, Nina, so you may as well stop. Oh, I hardly blame you. But now I'm going to go home and deal with Natalia. This isn't something I'm about to forget!"

Nina cried loyally: "Natalia had nothing to do with this! Stop it, Boris! I have no idea what this is about, but you're being horrid, and you've ruined my New Year and Andrei's present! Oh, go away. I don't feel like being around you when you're like this—beastly!"

She turned to him with tears in her eyes, but he had already left the room.

Ivan had never quite witnessed anything like this. His master pushed past him without a word, hurling his overcoat on the floor. The white rage on his face had distorted his chiseled Greek features. He strode through the hallway toward his wife's room and burst in without knocking, and Ivan, who had been with him many years and thought that no man possessed more self-control than Count Boris Kussov, heard the beginnings of an angry shout before the door slammed shut.

Natalia was sitting at her vanity, and now the tortoiseshell comb which she had been inserting into her raised chignon fell to the floor. Her lips parted, and the blood drained from her face. She half-rose in her chair, but he pushed her down and held his hand roughly on her shoulder, bruising the tender flesh.

"Nina showed it to me!" he cried, and the twist of his mouth made him look ugly for the first time since she had met him. "And now you're going to explain to me why you did this!"

She could not speak. Terror froze her very thoughts. It was unbelievable, what was happening, after all the good that had come to them. She felt dizzy and nauseated. Finally she whispered: "What are you talking about, Boris? What have I done?"

"The painting of Galina! Nina told me she went to him on her own, because of the set designs of *Egyptian Nights*. That was four years ago! Nina's memory isn't that good, and one does not choose a portraitist for his scenic decor! When did you see him, Natalia? And why involve my sister?"

A flood of comprehension rushed over her, and, at the same time, dreadful apprehension. She licked her lips. "Boris," she said as calmly as she could, given the pounding of her heart through her dressing gown, "you must listen to me. I haven't seen him. I haven't seen him! It's just that—just that"—and now sudden panic erupted within her—"someone else saw him, my friend Lydia. Lydia Brialovskaya. She saw him, and she told me—this was last February, Boris! Last February, before— before— She told me that he was in bad straits, that he was not working, and that he was living in squalor. And when Nina said she had thought of having Galina's portrait painted, naturally— I mentioned Pierre, because it's not right, is it, for someone with his talent to let it all go to waste?"

She felt as though she were being smothered, choked. "I don't know why this is so important to you!" she cried. "I didn't do anything wrong! Tell me!"

"It wasn't your job to find him work!" he said. "I can't explain it any better than that. If he was starving, you should have let him! Don't you see that?"

"No!" she retorted, "I don't see at all! I thought you would have wanted to see him work, after all the effort you went to on his behalf! I didn't think you'd want to imagine him that way."

"At one time I would have given my life to him. Now I wish he were dead! I thought he was dead, for you! Tell me, do you still care? I thought, Natalia, that that was over, before the summer!"

She jumped up, pushing his hand away from her shoulder, and cried: "But don't you see that it is—and was? I wanted him out of our life as much as you did! Those memories bring me nothing but pain! I do not want to resurrect him for either one of us—but you're the one who's dredged it all up! Why won't you let it lie? Boris, for God's sake—let it lie! For *our* sake!"

She fell silent and dropped her face into her hands. The crimson fury that had shaken him now seemed to be waning, although his face was still a distorted version of itself. He looked at the red bruise on her shoulder and gritted his teeth. He was shaking. She raised her head from her fingers and said: "Boris, what does it matter whether he paints Galina or anybody else? How could it possibly matter to us—to you and me? Love and hate, Boris, are really the same thing, after all. If you hate him this much, then you must still love him, and the obsession is still there inside you. Is it, Boris? Answer me!"

He shook his head. "I don't know. I don't think so. There are things one doesn't forget or let go. Bitterness dies hard."

"But it has to die! It died for me, with my father. Don't you remember how I let him go, at long last? I don't hate him anymore. He has simply ceased to play any role whatsoever in my life. But Pierre is a great artist, with true talent. Our feelings should not have any bearing on his work. Let him create, Boris! You don't have to love or hate someone to let him go about his own existence!"

Hesitantly, she reached up and touched his cheek. "You don't own the man," she said gently. "If you do, then your own heart is not free, and this obsession with Pierre will keep festering within you. Boris—I don't want that. I can't take that! Not now!"

He made a helpless gesture, half shrug, half futile question, and turned away. "I'm sorry, Natalia," he whispered.

He felt her arms go around his waist from behind, and her head lean on his back. "Don't leave me, Natalia," he said, and his voice caught.

For a moment they remained entwined, and then, slowly, he turned around and faced her. The soft hair was falling gracefully about her shoulders, and now he touched it, tentatively. A tremor passed through him. Natalia moved closer, so that he could feel the pressure of her firm young breasts beneath her dressing gown, and then, in one sudden motion, she shook the gown from her shoulders. It slid to the floor in a heap of silk, and he thought, amazed: She wants to make love now! and wondered briefly if all women were this impatient, their eager young bodies held tensely in waiting. The horrible quarrel still rang in his ears, strangely quickening his own pulse, and when he enveloped her firm nudity in his arms, he found his own need matching hers. He carried her to the bed, his temples pounding. It was not until he kneeled naked before her that he noticed there were bright tears glistening in her eyes.

She held her arms out to him and caressed his neck and shoulder. As always when he approached her, there was hesitation, almost a pulling away at the last moment. She was attempting to quiet that tension, to ease him to her, to bind herself to him in small gestures. Her fingers touched his nipples, circled them. Her hand lingered along his lean, long torso. He was elegant even in his nakedness. Natalia drew him over her and wound herself about him sinuously, so that he could smell her hair, its soft scent of attar of roses. "Don't ever doubt me," she murmured over his shoulder. And he thought, with wrenching pain: But I shall always doubt myself.

Boris regarded his pipe with an ironic detachment he did not feel. He was almost thirty-seven, and the other side of his life stretched ahead of him, more ponderous challenge than the first. One attacked the years of one's youth with the voracity of a predator, but before the second half of life, one paused to consider more carefully. Here, in Budapest, one of his Slavic glooms had descended, and he found it difficult to rid himself of the dead weight. In addition, there had been the death of his friend, the painter Serov, only months after the assassination of the Russian prime minister, Peter Stolypin. Boris still mourned these men.

Alone in his hotel room, he sat stroking his mustache. A kaleidoscope of visions passed through his mind. Vaslav Nijinsky, irritated like a raw nerve ending, was rehearsing his first choreographic work, *Afternoon of a Faun*. Diaghilev was excited over his protégé's creation: Vaslav had to be more than a mere dancer; he had to explode into composition in order to fulfill his promise to the world. But Michel Fokine had heard of these secret rehearsals conducted behind his back and was threatening to quit the Ballets Russes. He'll go, Boris thought grimly: Serge has seen to it by crushing his pride.

Abruptly, Boris thought of Romola de Pulszky, a young blond Hungarian debutante, whose mother was the leading actress in Budapest. Romola's interest in the Ballets Russes had at first amused him and irritated Diaghilev. She was ostensibly an admirer of the *danseur* Adolph Bolm. She was taking ballet lessons and wanted to be a dancer of some sort. Natalia, a real dancer, lived and breathed her movements day and night, and somehow Romola's excessive zeal seemed off-key, beside the point.

Absentmindedly, Boris tapped the bowl of his pipe onto the edge of an ashtray. He was still pondering the issue of Romola. I shall use that girl, he said to himself. With Fokine's departure, there would be only Vaslav, and Natalia. Always, at the center

of his plans there was Natalia. But not now, later. He began to
laugh, a low, hearty chuckle.

"As long as I can practice my craft, I am glad to do so,"
Pierre said. He raised his black eyes to his subject, seated on the
dais, and cleared his throat. "An honor," he added self-con-
sciously.

"It is we who are honored that you could come to Kiev for
this setting," the gray-haired Princess Tumarkina said, lifting a
strand of her daughter's limp blond hair and securing it behind
the comb of mother-of-pearl. "Marguerite comes so rarely to
visit us, now that her husband is with the Foreign Ministry in
Berlin."

"Well," Marguerite interjected, spots of pink appearing on
her cheeks, "if Pierre Grigorievitch had not been able to come
here, I would have insisted that he come to me in Germany."

"Hush, dear," her mother said. "If you excite yourself, he
will make your color look quite vulgar." She moved to the side
and smiled at Pierre. "There now, isn't that better? More se-
date, for the wife of a diplomat. You won't be too inexact, will
you, Pierre Grigorievitch?"

"Mama," Marguerite said, "Pierre Grigorievitch is known for
his freedom of line and for his bright hues. I do not want to
look like a sepia-colored *Hausfrau*, do I?"

The old princess sighed. "What can I say? I am *vieux jeu*.
Well, I suppose I shall leave then and see to your father,
Marguerite. *Au revoir*, Pierre Grigorievitch."

"Your Excellency." Pierre bowed, thinking, as he always did,
that manners were a confounded nuisance, especially when
they got in the way of his work. He stood back and examined
the canvas: a pale face with blue eyes that he had tinted with
sea-green, a pert nose that he had rendered bold, and blond hair
massed on top of a wide forehead. How could he add character
without adding . . . madness? A delicate question, one which a
master of the dialectic might handle better than he. His jaw set.

"Pierre Grigorievitch, you painted for the Ballets Russes,
didn't you?" Marguerite asked, and he saw that her eyes had
become curiously distended.

"Yes, Your Excellency. But that was before they became the Ballets Russes, when the company was composed of borrowed dancers from the Mariinsky and from Moscow." He did not smile, and his breath came hard for a moment. "I haven't been a part of that enterprise for quite some time."

"It's an abominable group, all of them!" Marguerite cried. "Do you know Count Boris?"

"Count Boris Kussov. Yes, I am acquainted with the man. I must tell you that I am aware of your own connection with him.

"Well, then, tell me what you think of him!" Marguerite demanded. Pinpoints of hysteria pierced her voice.

Pierre laid down his brush. "We were friends once, and he did me much good. Now, however, I could not answer your question: The reply would not be fit for a lady's ears. Enough said, Baroness?"

"No!" she answered. "Never! I am married to such a nice man, Pierre Grigorievitch. Such a good, kind man. But I did not want him. I did not wish for a life with a Prussian diplomat. I wanted Boris, and he tried to have me put away as a madwoman. Now I think it is he who is mad. Tell me—do you know the ballerina whom he married, after me?"

"Baroness, I must ask you to sit quietly, or I shall not be able to capture your natural expression," Pierre cautioned.

"You can do it later. Tell me—"

Pierre left the canvas and strode over to Marguerite. He stood over her, almost ominous in his massive strength, his black hair and black eyes gleaming under the overhead light. "I have come all the way from Petersburg to make you immortal," he said. "Now, perhaps you will find me a boor to mention it, but if immortality does not appeal to you, I shall go home at once. I am not good at conversations, Baroness von Baylen. I am only good with oils. So if it's talk you want, I have wasted a trip and you are wasting a commission."

Marguerite uttered a small laugh and threw her hands up to cover her face. "I'm sorry!" she cried, and laid her hands down. "It's just that no one wants to be made a fool of, don't you see?"

"Yes," he said, "I see. Now look serene, a little more to the left—ah, perfect!"

Poor woman, he thought, settling himself behind his painting again. Then he felt a surge of old pain sweep through him. No, truly, he was not a politic man, or he would not have allowed his life to slip so far. The old days: the committee, Bakst, Benois, Diaghilev—Boris; Egypt and France and The Hague; palace hotels and golden cufflinks; intelligent conversation, good food, a lesson in manners and savoir faire. And the silver hope of Natalia. Now there were faded society ladies, little children, and half-mad wives of Prussian diplomats. But it was a step up from where he'd been before the Stassov work.

That small blond Galina Stassova—it was difficult to reconcile her sweet nature with the fact that she was Boris's niece. She looked exactly like him, but soft and gentle. He had wanted to kiss her, to pet her, and instead, he had glared at her like an ogre, remembering her parentage. Princess Nina was another good, kind soul, but devoted to her brother. Damn them all! Boris had ended up with everything, everything! How could he not hate the man? Boris had given him everything and then withdrawn it all. Better to have stayed on the periphery and never been helped at all.

I should have listened to my instincts, Pierre thought fiercely. Never take, so that you will never owe. The mystique of the golden Boris. Still, Natalia was right: Pierre had his talent, his genius. He would rebuild his life, trusting in his own abilities. Why should he always seek out pillars on which to rest? He had let Petersburg corrupt his soul; in the Caucasus he had never relied on others.

Or had I? he wondered. There had been his mother, indomitable, a silent tower of will and support, as he had wanted Natalia to be. Natalia was right! Pierre thought with angry self-condemnation. I would never have been happy with her. She is too separate, too complete, and I could never have allowed her to stay that way. I would have consumed her, used her to fuel my own creative energies. She did what was right for herself.

But I shall never accept it, never.

He suddenly asked: "Do you miss Count Boris, Baroness?"

Marguerite blinked. "Miss him? No. That is not it at all," she replied with some asperity. How did one explain the anger after a theft? One did not necessarily miss the robbed goods. "How can one miss a person like Boris?" she added. "He is conceited, selfish, acerbic, cruel— What is there to miss?"

"Those very things, I suppose," Pierre replied. "He is, as you claim, a wicked man, often an odious one. But he also has the most diverse interests. He is never boring."

"I did not know him well enough to judge," she replied with a shrug.

Pierre uttered a short laugh. "This sitting would amuse him. His ex-wife, and his ex-protégé! This is the ultimate irony."

Marguerite announced: "I shall make you a household name in Berlin, Pierre Grigorievitch. My husband, the baron, loves artists. You shall have to come for a visit—and paint my friends."

Pierre felt a momentary spasm of disgust. He had never wanted to be a society portraitist, and the notion of visiting the dull von Baylens filled him with horror. He remembered the gallant dinners at Boris's, the elegant Petersburg aristocrats who were not afraid to mingle with real artists. He knew that if he went to Berlin, it would be as a hired hand. How things changed!

"Thank you, Your Excellency," he replied, lifting his brush to the canvas.

In early May Natalia resigned from the Mariinsky, much to the disgust of General Teliakovsky. Taking her hand, he said softly: "I was going to promote you to *prima ballerina*. We need you here, my dear. Karsavina still dances with us and manages to fit in Diaghilev. Or is it your husband? Does Boris Vassilievitch wish to hold you back from your Petersburg admirers?"

She hesitated: Why, indeed, was a choice so necessary? But the die was cast, and she packed her bags to go to Paris for the spring-to-summer season. Vaslav Nijinsky wanted her for his first ballet, *Afternoon of a Faun*, in which she was to dance one of seven woodland nymphs. The entire production would last only twelve and one-half minutes, but Diaghilev had told her that the innovations his protégé was instigating would be revolutionary for the world of ballet.

Now, days later, Boris and Natalia were seated on the terrace of their home on the Avenue Bugeaud in Paris when the maid came out with the tea tray. She deposited it on the table in front of her mistress, bobbed a curtsy, and retreated. Boris looked attentively at Natalia from half-closed eyes. She had lost some weight, and her glossy brown hair did not hold its form as well as usual. Her eyes seemed to have taken complete possession of her small, pale face.

He said nothing, but when she seized the teapot, he noticed that her fingers were trembling. She steadied the pot with her other hand and poured. She handed him his cup, then lay back in her chair, closing her eyes. "Are you ill, Natalia?" he asked.

Her whole body jerked to attention. In a low, tremulous voice, she said: "If you really want to know, Boris, it's that damned Nijinsky! I can't take it another day, I swear I can't! Nobody else can, either. Karsavina, Nelidova—we're all sick of him, sick to death of his impossible requests. When your body's been trained for over twelve years to make only certain kinds of movements, it's inhuman to expect it to flatten itself into a single dimension, like the figures in those drawings of ancient times! You know—the ones on your Greek amphoras and on those Egyptian parchments you brought back. But we're real women—ballet dancers!"

"New concepts are always hard to work out," he said softly. "And Vaslav can't express himself like other people. Serge has always been his mouthpiece. He isn't a verbal person, and in his frustration he may say things he doesn't mean. You must rise above that, Natalia. You, of all people."

"But why? If Michel Fokine leaves, I do not want to stay with the Ballets Russes! I'd rather return to the Mariinsky and accept Teliakovsky's offer. As a *prima ballerina*, I could have much greater freedom of choice than I had as a soloist of the first degree. I might not see as much of other countries—but we could travel during the summer and accept engagements at that time."

Boris was silent. She sat back and poured a cup of tea for herself. Her face had grown pink with animation, and now she seemed spent. He regarded her keenly, then said: "Natalia, if there were no solution, I would not subject you to this. But I'm going to ask you to do something for me. Learn to work with Vaslav Nijinsky. It will pay off in the end. You will be far happier than with that ass Teliakovsky."

"What do you mean?" she asked, suddenly alert.

He shook his head. "Nothing as yet. Simply what I've told you. I know, it's a small ballet, and you're not the lead. But it's important."

Her lips parted on a question, but she stifled it. She had learned long ago not to ask him what was brewing in his mind. Instead, she sighed. "All right," she replied, with weary resignation.

On Wednesday, May 29, 1912, the *beau monde* of Paris went to see Nijinsky's first effort at choreography. Based on Stéphane Mallarmé's poem, "Prélude to the Afternoon of a Faun," this short work was a collaboration between the young Russian dancer and Debussy, whose score was graceful airiness, breeze, and flow. Nijinsky had taken the theme of woodland eroticism and made a tableau of flat, friezelike nymphs moving in furtive steps around a Faun, not quite man but more perceptive than beast. Seven Nymphs danced one by one, watched by the Faun, stimulating his nascent desires. The last one was Nelidova, tall and angular, the only one not dancing in bare feet. They wore headdresses of gold braid and long white skirts heightened with splotches of red or blue, and the Faun wore an off-white body stocking marked with brown spots. At the end all that he was left with was the scarf of the tall Nelidova, and, taking it to his promontory, he made love to it in strange masturbatory movements.

The French public was shaken to its foundations by this short ballet. Cries erupted at its conclusion, and people stood in their seats, shouting. "This isn't dancing!" some cried. "Give us back our money!" And: "Such an obscenity, on the French stage!" But other yells were veritable ovations. During the days that followed, newspapers devoted entire columns to heated rebuttals, and France took sides for or against Nijinsky.

Serge Pavlovitch was jubilant. "Think of the publicity!" he exclaimed and rubbed his hands together.

Boris said to Natalia: "Vaslav's a genius. It comes from a subconscious well inside him that defies intellectual comprehension. But sometimes the world can be too much for people like him. They aren't practical enough and certainly possess no analytical perceptions."

She looked at him quizzically, but he simply shook his head and stared into space.

Sometimes the dancers were exhilarated by the nomadic quality of their touring company, but at other times they felt like cattle being shipped in boxcars for inspection at county fairs. At Christmas the Ballets Russes were once again in Budapest, and, following that visit, young Romola de Pulzky was indeed accepted into the *corps*. Boris befriended her, to Natalia's slight irritation. She could not fathom why this society girl had attached herself to a company of professional Russian dancers. The Hungarian had joined them in London.

Now, in March, another trip, another language, another country: lilac-and-jasmine-scented Monaco, on the Riviera. The dancers decorated the lovely town, from its harbor to its craggy tops. Wearing wide-brimmed hats, the Russian ballerinas discovered little alleys covered with vines and sipped tea *chez Pasquier*. Natalia liked the evenings best of all: In the indigo sunset she felt a completeness, a comfort, an inner joy.

Overlooking the blue-green bay of Monaco, Boris and Natalia stood on a high rock, the falling dust spreading about their shoulders like a magic cloak. A light breeze caressed her hair. "I think I like it best here," she murmured softly. "It has the poetry of Italy and the grace of France. It is a hybrid town, in the hills. When we are old, Boris, you will have to build me a house here, with fruit trees in the garden and a terrace that faces the sea."

"It seems almost like a miracle to hear you say that: 'When we are old.' Do you really think we shall grow old together?"

She turned her face to him, like a flower opening its velvet petals. "How else would it be?" she asked and placed her hands on his shoulders.

"I don't know, Natalia. A gust of wind could suddenly blow you down into the sea, or Sinbad the Sailor could send the Roc to collect you in its beak. You're very fragile, you know. Anything could happen!"

She laughed. "I'm as sturdy as an old farm horse. Look at me!" And she twirled around on the tips of her toes, her skirt billowing out around her. He thought, she is twenty-three, and I, thirty-eight: almost eight years of two lives that have meshed in and out like two recalcitrant threads, at length intertwining. Eight years, five of them under the same roof, two of them together as man and woman.

He fought the overpowering sentimentality that had suddenly seized him and attempted to laugh. But something in his throat blocked the sound. She was still dancing, round and round, her wide hat a halo surrounding the brown hair. But when he reached her, she stood still, and then, light as an evening breeze, she pretended to collapse in slow motion into his arms. She smelled of apricot and rosewater, fresh, unadulterated by confectioned perfumes.

Leaning his head into the crook of her shoulder, Boris said: "Natalia, we could make 1913 last forever, couldn't we?"

She blinked slowly. "But how?"

"We could make each other the gift of a child."

She stiffened, and her eyes grew very wide. "I didn't know you wanted one," she said, and her tone was distant suddenly, and a little hurt.

"I didn't know I wanted one either," he replied. "But it's all right, I understand how you feel."

She bit her lower lip, and said nothing. Then she murmured: "No, you don't know how I feel. It isn't that. It's . . . I don't know how to put it. I feel silly and female, and . . ."

He began to laugh and tilted her face up to him. "I suppose you're right," he remarked. "I never did say the actual words, did I? I love you, Natalia. But you knew I felt it, didn't you?"

"I know you feel it now," she answered, her voice trembling. "Before—I could not be sure. I thought—yes—but . . ." She shook her head lamely and held out her hands in a gesture of helplessness.

Then, in the gathering darkness, she wound her willowy arms around his neck and fit the stem of her young body to the birchlike firmness of his. Tomorrow he would laugh at the schoolboy romance, but there it was, the peace which had eluded him for a lifetime. It did not matter that he had spent years protecting himself against the pain, years storing up the memory of every slight aimed at him. There had been pain, and humiliation. For her too, years and years of them, of loneliness, distrust, and fear.

"I love you, Natalia," he whispered into the softness of her hair. And then again, "I love you." Yet, even as he said the words, the image of Pierre's strong limbs etched itself over his memory like a faded blueprint. His hands over his wife's hips tightened, his fingers trembled slightly, and he thought fiercely: Yes, we must have a child.

Chapter 13

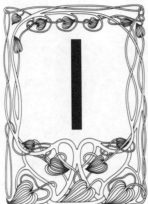

In May 1913 Nijinsky once again surprised the Parisian public. He had formed his own choreographic style, all linear planes, stark and savage. In *Games* he depicted a highly stylized confrontation between a boy and two girls, one of whom was Natalia. The boy had come upon the young women as he was searching for his tennis ball, which Bakst had designed as big as a grapefruit. The second ballet was *The Rite of Spring*, an elemental bacchanalia that hailed more from the days of the Druids than from those of civilized Attica. Natalia danced the frenzied, dervishlike sacrificial virgin who at last expired from breathless exertion. At the end of this performance the gracious French public turned into a mob, screaming, standing in their seats, outraged, offended, and uplifted in turn.

As with *Afternoon of a Faun*, the newspapers once again took sides for or against the young choreographer. Natalia lay in bed the following day, white with exhaustion. Certainly this was a momentous landmark in her life as a dancer, but she did not yet know how to interpret it. What had Boris said after *Afternoon of a Faun?* He had seemed to ask: "Can such a genius last in this world?" Surely Nijinsky was a genius, although intellectually he could hardly express himself. He was subliminal, surprising, and almost impossible to connect with as a person. Childlike, aloof, he did not encourage friendship. Yet beneath it all one felt a heart that did not know how to assert its needs.

Nijinsky was a phenomenon. He was Diaghilev's creature, yet ingenious enough to produce unique ballets. Still, without his patron lover, the sloe-eyed young man would have alienated the entire company. He did not know how to handle people, how to make them work for him toward a common goal. *I would know*, she found herself thinking, suddenly fierce. *I would know*, but nobody's asked *me* to plan a ballet.

All at once she knew that this was the direction she wanted her career to take. Entering the master bedroom, she confronted Boris, who had been reading at the table. Color had risen to her cheekbones, points of crimson fire. Her hand trembled on the doorknob. "I could compose a ballet," she stated, her voice low and tense. "I could bring new ideas to the Ballets Russes!"

She could not tell whether he appeared surprised. He put the book aside with care, taking time to set the ribbon to mark his place, and then he looked up, his eyebrows quizzically arched. "An intriguing thought," he commented dryly.

"Why not? Because I'm a woman? Isn't that unfair, Boris? For centuries women have been the backbone of ballet dancing. Yet never a choreographer among us!" Her brown eyes were flecked with golden dots of anger.

He shrugged lightly. "I'm not disagreeing. But Serge has been trying to bring out the male *danseur*—you know that. This is hardly the proper time to bring up the matter of fairness to women!"

"Then you won't talk to him?"

He looked away. "No, Natalia, I won't. But not because I don't believe in you. Because I have other plans."

Her lips set, and she breathed deeply. "I see. At heart, then, you still agree with Diaghilev—with all that he is and stands for. I had thought differently." She turned her back on him, slim and proud, and left the room. His mouth worked silently. He clenched and unclenched a fist—and then, abruptly, he slammed it down on the oak table with a vehemence that made the book slide to the very edge. His face glowed stark white with tension.

In mid-August, Natalia went on her first ocean cruise. The Ballet was leaving Europe for an initial foray into the unfamiliar

228   continent of South America, and Serge Pavlovitch had left the running of the company to Boris, who was a better sailor— Diaghilev had a superstitious fear of the ocean—and whose taste for territorial variety exceeded his own. Dressed in a cream-colored linen suit, Boris looked resplendent when he came on deck of the S.S. *Avon*. The trip began with panache in Southampton. Boris had had baskets of fresh flowers delivered to all the ballerinas in their second-class deck.

He and Natalia shared a first-class cabin, paneled in rich wood, with a small bathroom adjoining it. He thought this a splendid arrangement and ordered champagne for those members of the company who, like themselves, were in first class. Karsavina had taken another ship that traveled faster. But Adolph Bolm; the *chef d'orchestre*, Rhené-Baton, and his wife; a *corps* dancer called Kovalevska, whose exalted status came from having been mistress to the Aga Khan in Monte Carlo; and Diaghilev's Polish secretary, Trubecki, and his own wife all appeared in the Kussov cabin to toast the voyage. Little, blond Romola de Pulszky came, too. "This is so exciting!" she cried. "But where is Vaslav Fomitch?" Nijinsky's absence did indeed stand out.

"He will join us at Cherbourg," Boris replied easily. "He and Serge and Benois have been dreaming up a ballet to music from Bach. I suppose our young genius will be most absorbed in this project."

In Cherbourg Vaslav Nijinsky came on board, and, several days later, the ritual of shipboard life truly began. But Natalia did not enjoy herself as she had expected to. Seated at supper, she bristled at Kovalevska's comments. She found Trubecki overly flowery, and Romola altogether unbearable. Boris raised his eyebrows at her, but she merely shook her head despondently. She felt tired, played out.

The scenery of unbroken ocean was restful, and the weather hot. She had lived in the Crimea and should not have minded the heat. She knew Boris wanted her with him, that his exultation would be marred if he knew of the unspoken struggle inside her. She could not help resenting his attitude about her career desires. It was galling to watch him on deck, in his elegant white suit, his face tanning lightly in the bright sun—galling that he always seemed to be holding court, equally with Nijinsky and Romola. An easy friendship appeared to be underway between him and the *danseur*. Irked, she thought: But Vaslav doesn't have a brain in his head! Why is Boris wasting his time? With devastating certainty she knew that she had become jealous of Nijinsky, envious of his preferred status in the Ballet— and that she was seeing her husband's gracious entertainment of him as fawning toward Diaghilev.

Hating herself, she joined the group and smiled politely at something Romola was saying. The Hungarian could not speak Russian, and Vaslav's French was less than adequate, and soon Natalia grew annoyed at Boris for intervening with careful, amusing translations. How the blond girl's eyes were sparkling! Doesn't she know, Natalia wondered with disdain, that Vaslav isn't interested in women? She caught herself and glanced covertly at her husband. People sometimes changed.

Later in the wood-paneled cabin Boris came behind her at the vanity, where she sat brushing her hair, and stilled the frantic pace of her up-and-down motions with his hand. Softly he caressed her neck, her shoulders, where all the tightness was concentrated. She turned slowly to face him, and, inexplicably, shook off his hand. Immediately her lips parted with surprise and shock at what she had done, and she cried out, "I'm sorry—" but the gesture had stunned him, and she could tell from his eyes that he was hurt to the quick. He did not answer her. Instead, his face became rigid, and he left the room. She was shaking, not understanding the tensions within herself.

After that the voyage was not the same. A delicate balance had been upset, and hostilities could no longer be kept hidden under a blanket of pretension. He knew then that she was harboring resentments and that they ran as deep as his own insecurities. Yet pride rose between them like an opaque screen, his pride and hers, evenly matched in their arrogant, useless strength. Each waited for the other to break down, and neither could be the first to do so.

Romola tried to befriend her, but Natala rejected her overtures. There was something vaguely predatory about the beautiful young socialite from Budapest that irritated the dancer. Romola had attached herself to the Ballets Russes where she did not belong, either by craft or by nationality. She was flaunting her wealth by traveling with her maid and seemed charming only as a spoiled child can charm in the beginning. She asked endless questions about Nijinsky's roles, about Diaghilev, about Boris. Natalia had had her fill of them.

At times Boris would absent himself, and in her field of vision there remained Romola, with Kovalevska or Rhené-Baton, and now and then Nijinsky, when he was not practicing on deck to the admiring eyes of the passengers. Natalia practiced in her suite. Boris was ignoring her, and now she felt an overwhelming depression. It was up to her to bridge the gap, to make the first penitent move—but she could not. Something held her back.

She saw him with a young South American diplomat, a lithe, dark man in his middle twenties. Natalia did not like him. She felt repelled by the fluidity of the man's laughter, by his large black eyes that dominated a thin, rather delicate face. Later, in the evening, she said to Boris: "How can you stand him? He's like Swiss chocolate—too much richness turns the stomach!" Her husband stared at her, his eyes a slit of metal, and she felt chilled. But he merely shrugged and left her alone.

Boris climbed on deck, where a light wind had risen, and held the railing with both hands. He could feel something slipping away from him, and thought of Natalia, of the frozen anger in her face. All at once he could not swallow, and the sockets of his eyes started to sting. God almighty, no—

Somebody touched his sleeve, and gratefully, he turned around and saw the tan oval of Armando Valenzuela's face. Like himself, the young man was wearing a tuxedo with a ruffled cambric shirt. "Warm evening," he said, and looked out into the darkness, framed in the golden light from the cabins behind them. Boris nodded but said nothing. He felt a ringing in his ears, a slight breathlessness, and he concentrated on the ocean waves churning beneath him.

Then, in the silence, Valenzuela's long fingers gripped the railing next to his own, and Boris's eyes landed on their delicate slenderness, on the tapered nails. He could not look away. It was as if the other's fingers had intruded on his mind and held it prisoner in a bizarre entrancement. Slowly, then, and with infinite grace, those sensual fingers moved, one inch, two inches, and closed over Boris's right hand. With a slight tremor, the older man turned to the younger, and their eyes met and locked. Boris licked his lips and murmured: "I don't know, Armando. I'm not sure." He could not move his hand.

On August 31 Natalia was awakened by Kovalevska, who said: "I have the most wonderful news! Vaslav Fomitch has proposed to Romola—all through Boris Vassilievitch, of course, since the two young people do not speak the same language! Come on deck. We can see Rio!"

Aghast, Natalia dressed hurriedly and went above. She did not know what to believe, but Boris, looking oddly exultant, made a mock bow to her and approached. "Madame has deigned to join us?" he asked.

"Is it true? That Nijinsky is going to be married?"

"Yes, of course it's true. You weren't stupid enough to think that Romola was really interested in Adolph Bolm, were you? She's had her mind set on our Vaslav from the beginning. I guess the trip was ripe, shall we say?" He smiled ironically.

"Well, I am glad for them," Natalia said dully. "But—Serge Pavlovitch? When Mavrin, his old lover, eloped with Feodorova in '09, he would not even pay him! Why have you encouraged something that is going to make Serge Pavlovitch fit to be tied? I don't understand!"

"No," he remarked dryly, "you don't. But then you never do, Natalia. And in this case, more's the pity, as I was doing it all for you." He turned away.

The view was magnificent, and seeing the Sugar Loaf Mountain soaring up in silent majesty, Natalia felt a lump in her throat. Such beauty—such feelings! Dawn lay over the harbor like a pink cushion upon which lay a perfect jewel. All at once, she felt a tearing pain in her stomach, and gasped, clutching the deck railing. Boris was speaking to the Trubeckis. She tried to call but could not catch her breath. Hot sweat broke out upon her brow. She collapsed on the wooden planks, her hands gripping her stomach, and the last thing she thought was: Am I dying?

Darkness closed over her, and one by one the shining flames of red died out over her closed eyes.

"Tell me. What is wrong with my wife?" Boris asked the doctor.

They stood together outside the cabin door, and Boris, white and tense, could hardly breathe for the fear that had taken possession of him. "She's always been a strong girl," he added lamely. Helplessness sat ill with him.

"Well, there's good and bad, of course," the white-haired ship's doctor said. "You knew that she was pregnant?"

Something caught inside Boris's throat. For a moment he could not think at all. Cold beads of perspiration broke out on his palms, on his temples. "No," he replied. "How long?"

"Only two months. But there is a problem. Some women, my dear Count, have difficulty keeping the fetus attached to the lining of the womb. Your wife nearly miscarried and was very lucky that she didn't. But, in order to have this baby, she will have to spend the next seven months in bed. Do you think you can arrange it?"

Boris shook his head and turned his palms out. "Good God," he said. "What choice do we have?"

"I'm afraid you have none. I haven't mentioned it to her— she seemed frightened enough as it was. I think you should be the one to tell her."

Boris nodded tersely. His mind was a jumble of conflicting thoughts. He was ill at ease in situations that he could not control or even define for himself. The doctor tactfully moved aside, and Boris entered, urgency propelling him forward.

Natalia looked up at him from the small bed, and he saw the terror in her large brown eyes. Coming to her, he cried out: "How could I not have seen it?"

There was a haunted expression in her eyes, on her parted lips. He took the small, cold hand and brought it to his cheek. "I don't know how to ask you to forgive me," he murmured.

Color came to her cheekbones. "Don't!" she said miserably.

"Don't feel responsible, Boris. *I* was in the wrong. I am ashamed. I was afraid that you were never going to return to me. What's wrong with me, Boris?"

He took a deep breath, looked down at her hand, played with the wedding ring on the third finger. "You have no idea?" he asked her.

Her face had become all eyes. She tried to breathe, but instead, little gasps came out in staccato fashion. "I'm so scared," she whispered. "I guess I've almost suspected—but I didn't even want to think it out in words."

"And so that's why you turned against me."

She looked away. "Don't talk about it, Boris," she pleaded.

"But my darling, if you do not want it, you will have to decide now. You can't run away from this. We have to reach an understanding, Natalia."

She uttered a short, half-hysterical giggle. "I've always run away, haven't I? Years ago, from the Crimea— Oh, Boris, what are we going to do? Do you want it?"

Looking at her with a level gaze, he said: "It isn't an 'it,' it's our child, Natalia. If you want it, we are going to have to make plans. The doctor says that this is a difficult pregnancy, and you won't be able to dance—beginning now. That's why I'm afraid it has to be your own decision."

"If I dance, you mean I'll lose the baby?" she exclaimed.

"That's exactly what I mean. We've both put all our hopes into your dancing—you'll never know how much!—but after the baby's born, you would dance again, as before. It's up to you."

Tears came to her eyes. "I didn't think it would turn out this way," she whispered. "Oh, Boris—I do want the baby. I've come to want it very much. A little part of you and me, making us immortal. But I thought I would dance at least till the seventh month! It's so hard—"

He brought her fingers to his lips and said very softly: "Yes, I know. It doesn't seem fair. But what's fair in life, Natalia? I've just realized something: Plans are the greatest absurdity of all in this world, and those who set stock by them are fools. The present moment, Natalia—that's all that truly touches us, isn't it?"

"What are you talking about?" she asked in a whisper.

"Of myself. Building intricate castles with feathers and clouds. Thinking that I was doing it for you, when all along it was to gratify my own sense of importance. I'm afraid you married the most ridiculous court jester of all, Natalia."

She touched his cheeks with trembling fingers. "Tell me," she said.

"There's nothing to tell. You know that Serge will not accept Vaslav's marriage. But I'm afraid this isn't going to turn out quite as I'd wanted it to. I was going to pick up the pieces and branch off into a company of our own—with you and Vaslav as my stars. A silly man, your husband."

"Oh!" she cried. "Oh, Boris. It was for me—of course it was! And I didn't know." She began to weep. "What a wonderful, ambitious project! And how like you to think of it! Serge Pavlovitch, Vaslav—nothing is too much for you to handle, is it? I don't know what to say, except that I don't want it now, this company. I want to have the baby! And then—afterward—we can discuss it again. Oh, Boris—why do I never know what is in your head, and why can't I answer you when I finally do learn what you've done?"

He laughed. "You are sure, about the baby?"

"Oh, yes. Right now, suddenly, I am positive. I want it very much. It's going to be very hard, but I'm going to lie down for the next seven months, and not even think of dancing." She smiled. "And so you're going to have to think up every anecdote you know in order to amuse me! I'm not a good patient, you see."

"*Im*patient, I'd call you."

He bent over her and she placed her arms about his neck. "I'm really happy," she murmured, kissing his earlobe, caressing his golden hair. "I did not think I would ever be happy—I, Natalia. It is rather frightening, this happiness. I do not want to become so happy that you grow bored with me."

Disentangling herself, she asked, knitting her brow: "But what about Vaslav? My God—what will happen to him—?"

Boris shrugged lightly and replied, ironically: "I didn't force his hand with the girl, Natalia. Everyone felt that he'd grown restless. Serge should have realized it and strengthened his own position." He added bitterly: "People fashion their own destinies.

I have created nothing, only encouraged what already lay beneath the surface, waiting to emerge. Don't make me out a god of some sort."

More gently, he kissed her fingertips. With deep, serious eyes, he said, his voice suddenly rich with feeling: "The only thing I've ever created, in these thirty-eight years, is the baby you are carrying for us."

"Then I'm glad we shall have it," she answered, burying her face in the crook of his neck.

PART III

Intermission

Chapter 14

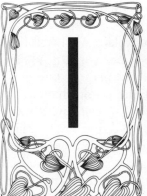

I f one had to live inside the velvet lining of a dream, thought Natalia, then it was only fitting to do so in anonymity. In Zwingenberg, nothing was real—or perhaps it was the true reality, and everything that had come before had been the dream. Her mind floated, rose above her, merging with the clouds, with the soft March breeze. She did not try to call it back but let it take on a life of its own, like the baby.

One could have reinvented the world in Zwingenberg. Boris had chosen this tiny village in the German province of Hesse-Darmstadt because of its physical charm and its total remoteness. It lay twenty-two miles by wooded road from the town of Darmstadt, where the train station stood. Spring had come early. Soft, pine-scented hills alternated with green meadows filled with flowers of every shape and color; there were groves and small forests, and in the fields, often a single majestic tree, always an oak, spreading its unhampered branches to form an uneven ball of leaves. Sometimes one could not even see the grass of the fields for the wildflowers; other places belonged to the lazy cows, which lent an added peace to the landscape. Even during the winter months the loveliness had not lessened: the white-capped hills had had a soothing effect on Natalia, had been a balm on her soul.

Her body was out of control, rebelling. At first terror and rage had filled her, in spite of her desire to have this baby. Something alien was bursting inside her, intruding on her being. Her breasts swelled, hurting, and her stomach pushed out. She felt gross and ugly, a monster. And the pain! After spending a lifetime controlling her body, taking pride in its muscular slenderness, her doe's agility, she now could hardly move. She was not allowed to do so, in any case. But she wanted to escape, to leave behind this grotesque shell that surrounded her. This thing inside constantly reminded her of its presence, making her drowsy when she wanted to stay alert, hungry when she had just finished eating. She had been invaded—but there was no retreat. She was a prisoner of her own body.

She had long since stopped trying to explain what had happened to her. If she had changed, then so be it, and if he had, too, then it was part of the same marvelous plan. If one questioned good things too closely, the mystique would shatter.

She could picture the child in her mind. Inevitably, it was a little girl that resembled Galina, yet Natalia did not want a girl. She wanted a male child, a different sort of being from herself. It would be far more difficult to rear a daughter—she herself had been reared with such lack of care that the mere thought of an infant girl in her arms made her afraid. She could not have explained the rationale behind that fear either, but it had something to do with self-love. Loving a boy would be like loving Boris all over again.

Whenever she thought of Boris, something ached inside her. The whole tenure of their love was like the rarest of crystals, clear and precious and terribly fragile. She did not deserve to be loved this much, nor did she know how to handle these surges of inexplicable emotion for him. Loving him brought out the hidden place where pure joy was so strong that it became like pure sorrow. She was afraid to rest inside this love, oddly afraid to touch it, to trust it.

In many ways this was the honeymoon that they had never taken, for they had not grown together until three years after their marriage, and by then the Ballet had taken precedence over everything else in their lives. She did not know whether the Ballet had pushed them toward each other, allowing them glimpses here and there into each other during the daily workings of an enterprise that consumed them both—or whether it had kept them from discovering what lay behind each of their veneers, because of the constant pressures it had placed on them. She did know this: Under no other circumstance would she have accepted marriage. She had married Boris only because he had not threatened to merge his life with hers; and she was his wife now precisely because they had merged, more perfectly than either would have thought possible.

We have both lived outside society, she said to herself during this final month when Zwingenberg exploded with burgeoning life, and when the life that was taking shape inside her was preparing to be born. They had taken up residence in the sole inn of the village, and there the innkeepers were taking good care of her, knowing only that she was the Russian lady expecting the child, whose handsome, aristocratic husband was apparently a man of means and distinction. This made her smile. She wondered if they had ever heard of the Ballets Russes, these good people, and, if so, whether they knew of her, Oblonova. Sometimes an acute poignancy seized her, unexpected in these soothing surroundings, and she would long to dance again, to be in front of an audience. She wanted to hold onto her dancing, to retain the sharp memories of the stage and the parts she had played, especially the Firebird. Dance was what had made her, and also what had brought her to Boris.

She had learned to put up with her weakness, with her forced immobility, with the constant visits from the doctor in Darmstadt. At first she had been quite ill, her body unsure whether to retain this child or to fight its intrusion. Like my mind, she thought wryly. She remembered Boris sitting with her and holding her hand, worried lines at the outer corners of his eyes. Boris, too, had changed during this pregnancy. He was thirty-nine, and a few strands of silver meshed with his gold hair, but there was a new gravity on his long face, and yet, simultaneously, a joy and youth. He is proud, she realized, more proud than he ever had been of his clever manipulations of people and situations. The simple act of having made a child and knowing he is loved have made him a whole man at last. She was unspeakably moved, as though a door had been opened on a private scene for her eyes only.

Yes, she thought, we have lived outside society, but we have created a society of our own, for ourselves. Now that the child was rooted inside her, now that it was alive and prospering, she felt less pain. Her body, like her mind, had accepted.

Natalia worried that Boris would grow bored in these quiet surroundings; similarly he was certain that she, so quick and vital, was withering from restlessness, too. At least, he thought, I have places to go, things to see. Yet he did not take full advantage of his mobility, for something inside prevented him from breaking the magic of this private time with her.

Images of the SS. *Avon*, of the dark sea and the sensitive face of Armando Valenzuela, now and then intruded on his memory, and then he felt terrible pangs of agony and loneliness—pangs that could be washed away only by her closeness, by the cool reality of her love for him.

Years before, he had met the grand-duke of Hesse-Darmstadt, Tzarina Alexandra's brother, yet now he did not call upon him as he would have under normal circumstances. Sometimes Boris was almost tempted to enter the palace grounds through the grilled gates; the ducal residence was hidden, but one could see the vast park with its great old trees and thick bushes. Still, he wanted no one to know that he was here, that Natalia was going to have her baby in this remote part of the world.

One could almost forget one is in Germany, he thought with some bitterness. Kaiser Wilhelm filled him with disgust and disdain, but also with fear. Madmen, Boris said to himself, were more dangerous than calculating foes. Nero and Caligula had perpetrated more massacres than Caesar or Napoleon! Then, of course, there were the well-meaning fools. Poor Tzar Nicholas! He was limited, narrow, stubborn—yet essentially not an evil man.

Sometimes—more frequently, lately—dark thoughts assailed Boris. Decidedly, he thought with self-deprecation, age is creeping up as I near forty. It was becoming difficult to dispel these attacks, as he called them. He wondered whether Natalia, uncannily perceptive, had sensed them and, if so, had been able to guess at the more troubling aspects of some of his sexual yearnings. Fervently he hoped that he had hidden them from her. No one had been asked to accept more, to forgive and to forget more totally than she; and she had done so without ever looking back. Once she had come to him, she had locked the past behind thick doors. Still, he wondered, perhaps she had placed some of herself in reserve, fearful of committing herself completely. But he detested himself for doubting. It was difficult to trust someone after so many barren years of half-lived existence: He owed Natalia his life, he thought. She had given him the freshness of sharing.

He did a lot of horseback riding through the hills, and between Darmstadt and Zwingenberg. The road was lovely, crossing woods, flowered meadows, and large brooks with rustic bridges. For over a mile the trees on either side were so tall that their branches met over the top of the road, forming a bower of romantic shadows. In his elegant jodhpurs Boris cut a Byronic figure against this natural paradise, alone with his thoughts.

He had been surprised at the intense reaction that he had felt at the news, in December, of Diaghilev's summary dismissal of Nijinsky, and of Vaslav's subsequent difficulties setting up his own production company. The dancer's troubles had been on his mind in a strangely nagging fashion. "Aha!" Natalia had exclaimed, somewhat ironically. "Could it be that you possess a conscience after all, dear heart?" He'd been annoyed, yet he'd had to grudgingly admit that there was some truth to the matter.

"I started the whole damn thing—or rather, as I told you, I helped it along. And now I suppose I should go to Vaslav with some sort of offer. This London season of his isn't working out; you can't have someone like Nijinsky running a company—he's still a child! And the Palace is a variety theatre that puts the dancers between two vaudeville acts: He isn't equipped to handle that the way a hardened professional such as Pavlova could!" Natalia had listened and waited, her large eyes on him. "But the truth is, my heart wouldn't be in it," he concluded. "I want to stay here, with you. My interest in helping Nijinsky would be purely altruistic, and"—he half-smiled, and his eyes twinkled— "you know how poorly altruism fares with me!"

"What has happened to the patron saint of all Russian artists?" Natalia had asked, holding out her hand to him.

"I'm not sure. It does disturb me, I'm afraid. Love does me

244   no good. I've become domesticated, and vastly uninteresting.
But when you dance again, my energies will start to flow once
more, you'll see!"

He also thought about Serge Diaghilev, and old bitterness
flowed into him. If Serge had suffered, well then, so did we all.
People spent their lives zigzagging through dangerous paths between two rows of flaming torches, ending up scorched more
often than not. Diaghilev had never intimated that he had had
the slightest suspicion of Boris's involvement in the matter of
Romola and Vaslav Nijinsky. He had shown a great deal of concern for Natalia and had entreated Boris to continue to help
him in running the company. For all intents and purposes three
associates, two of them longtime friends, had temporarily parted
because of health problems. They would once more join forces
after the birth of Natalia's baby.

How characteristic of us! Boris thought, laughing. Yet we are
and shall always be friends. We have an odd friendship based
on similar traits and a complete lack of trust. Trust could gener-
ate boredom. Only with Natalia was Boris not afraid that this
would develop. One did not become bored with Natalia, for she
never took anything for granted. It was better this way, for if
they trusted the fates as they learned to trust each other, their
lives would fall to ruin and their love would die.

These were strange thoughts for a promenade through the
countryside. Boris could not help being amused at his own som-
berness. He would have to fight this onset of melancholia with
greater self-will. But between moments of sheer joy there were
sharp gaps when his very soul would sink to a purple sadness,
like a sunset. Boris shook his head. His happiness was so deep
that his mind was demanding balance. Hence the sadness. It was
natural, then. He dismissed the guilty feelings toward his wife
and toward Nijinsky, separate but anguish-laden: There was no
time for such futile emotions. Then he kicked his horse lightly
to spur him on, threw back his golden head, feeling energized
by the wind—and laughed at himself, frankly and heartily.

It was the off-season, and, apart from Boris and Natalia, there
were few other guests at the inn. Sometimes after supper Boris
would have Natalia transported to a chaise longue in the sitting
room downstairs, and he would play the piano for her. There

was so little to amuse her. Yet she felt that it would be unfair to make him share the confines of her seclusion, he who cherished the refinements of civilization. Although he said that he did not miss his friends in the Diaghilev committee—Bakst, Benois, Serge Pavlovitch himself, Svetlov, the ballet critic—she knew that he must be padding the truth. Her body was shapeless and distended, her weary face more gray than white, with circles beneath her eyes; she preferred not to be seen by him this way. The end of her term was coming. Since she was convinced that they would be satisfied with a single child, she thought: Thank God, it will soon be over, and I can be myself again, and he can start to breathe again the fresh air of culture. In the meantime, there was the piano.

Natalia was totally unfamiliar with Wagner. "But," Boris told her, "this is as good a place to learn him as any. He embodies the spirit of Germany."

"Play something Italian instead," she suggested.

He smiled. "No, I'm going to initiate you in Wagneriana. It's everything we're not: ponderous, glorious, majestic, and unsubtle. But it must be heard, and then assimilated. You'll learn to understand him." He opened the music cabinet, found some sheets, and arranged them above the piano. Then he rolled back the top and began to play from the first act of *Die Walkyrie*. He started to sing. Natalia leaned on her elbow, fascinated. The innkeepers came in, surprised. Boris possessed an excellent voice, which they had never heard. Even Natalia had not heard it frequently lifted in song. It rang deep and rich, and he sang with complete ease. Sometimes he stopped to repeat a passage to make it more familiar to Natalia. When he stopped, it was late, and he had played through two full acts. The innkeepers were still hovering in the doorway.

With some effort she reached out to him, holding out tremulous fingers. "Please go tomorrow," she whispered. "Go to the opera. I won't have the baby without you. Besides, you've kept me up tonight, and it would do me good to go to sleep early tomorrow."

With a graceful sweep he slipped his arms under her and carried her carefully up the stairs. She was heavy, where before she had been weightless, a flower in the breeze. Or maybe it was merely the mental weight that he had been attributing to the baby. He positioned her carefully on the bed and kneeled down beside her. The little face was still delicate and pale, but it did not seem as frightened as before. He touched her hair and removed one pin, then another, until, free, it fell in soft waves, Madonna-like, around her cheeks and forehead. There was something otherworldly about a woman with child, something poignantly desirable about her intangibility. He drew a line with his fingertip over her nose and chin.

"Sleep now," he said, feeling oddly moved and not at all ridiculous. "My own sweet girl."

The following evening he drove into Darmstadt to go to the opera. He felt exhilarated. Natalia was reading in bed, exhausted after having spent a comfortable day; there was no need to worry. Still, a nagging voice grated within him, telling him that he should have stayed. But she had wanted him to go, and frankly he had longed for such an evening. It was such a beautiful time of year, and Darmstadt was a jewel of a town, so gentle and charming, so *gemütlich*.

Yes, he thought as he entered the opera house and found his reserved seat, she's right, of course, and I've been a fool to deny it: I do miss the productions, the talent, and the creativity. But I also needed this time alone with her, time apart from the pressures of a jumbled existence, time to sort things out, to grow up a little.

At intermission he went out into the corridor to stretch his legs and smoke his pipe. Decidedly, Darmstadt was not a town of elegant people. Boris leaned nonchalantly against a wall and appraised the theatre crowd. The women had thick waists and florid countenances. Their hats were too broad-brimmed to be fashionable. True, there were some aigrettes, plumes of the egret— His eyes began to wander. All at once he abruptly froze.

Boris felt his body tense into a single, taut nerve. His lips parted. Not more than a hundred feet away stood a man in black evening wear, holding his opera hat in one hand and a champagne coupe in another. Boris could feel himself perspiring into his elegant ruffled shirt. He wet his upper lip. Then the man turned, and could not avoid encountering Boris against the wall. Boris saw the crisp black curls, the black eyes that always seemed to possess a life of their own. There was a new crease in the forehead, lines forming at the mouth. No wonder, he's not a child anymore; he's past thirty, older than I was when we met.

Faced with the dark eyes, Boris made an instant decision. He smiled, inclined his head, and raised his hand in an ironic salute. He had caught the other off-guard. Warming slightly after the first shock, Boris took a step and walked with casual grace toward him. Reaching him he said: "Hello, Pierre. I'm afraid you've brought me up short. I can't think of a single clever thing to say."

Pierre Riazhin stared at him, nostrils twitching, the color high on his cheekbones. A sort of grimace playing over his features made him look like a wild beast cornered by a pack of bloodthirsty hunting dogs: angry, rebellious, and aware that the outcome was unavoidable. He said harshly: "What are you doing here, Boris?"

Boris smiled. "Enjoying the opera. *Et toi?*"

Pierre reared his head, and this time Boris was reminded of a black stallion snorting in the open field. It was odd how one thought of animal parallels when standing with Pierre.

"I live here," the young painter said.

"You do? And where, may I inquire?"

"What business is it of yours?" Pierre retorted. The hostility in his eyes was like a sliver of ice thrust into Boris's stomach.

Boris smiled. "Come now, Pierre, such animosity toward an old friend! It isn't becoming. But let's leave all that aside, shall we? What are you saying, you live here? In Darmstadt itself? What on earth for?"

"I live at the *Künstler Kolonie*. It's a good place to work. I've built a house there."

"Indeed?" Boris raised his eyebrows, intrigued. The *Künstler Kolonie* had been set up by the grand-duke from a wooded area, which he had divided into small lots and paved with winding streets. Sculptors, poets, and painters of all sorts had purchased the lots and erected small houses on them.

"Tell me, Pierre. Have you turned your back on Russia?"

"For the moment. I like it here. I have even learned German." Pierre hesitated, then laughed shortly. He coughed and asked, "What are you doing here during this off-season? No ballet?"

There was a moment's silence, then Boris regarded Pierre from narrowed eyes. "Natalia is expecting a child," he said.

Pierre's face became suffused with blood. He made an impulsive motion to spring forward, then caught himself. His lips worked. For a moment Boris felt sorry for the young man. Pierre's black eyes had begun to glow with a strange red glint. "It's been difficult for her," Boris said, to cover the tension. "She's going to give birth any day now, but she hasn't been able to dance for nearly seven months."

Pierre uttered a small noise in the back of his throat, and then burst out: "Difficult? Any day now? Why, you disgusting—" He stopped, took a deep breath, and asked: "Whose is it? Obviously not yours!"

Swiftly, in one movement, Boris closed the distance between them and, before a single person could notice, he slapped Pierre squarely on the cheek. Pierre did not utter a word, but his eyes grew wide, and he seized Boris by the lapels of his dinner jacket and began to shake him. "I'm going to kill you," he said, raising his voice so that several people turned to stare at them.

Boris thrust his shoulders up, making Pierre's hands drop to his sides. "You haven't changed much, Petya," he said. "And that's a damn shame. People change, you know—or they should. They don't necessarily become better human beings, and that's all right. Yet they do change. I'd rather hoped you would have shed your neanderthal behavior in favor of more intelligent ways. But I see it's still eluding you—adulthood, I mean."

They remained staring at each other for a minute. Then Boris slowly turned and walked resolutely into the auditorium. He sat down stroking his mustache and smiled at the old woman seated next to him. But the churning in the pit of his stomach was almost blinding him, and when the curtain rose, red dots still played before his eyes.

Pierre Riazhin stood still in the corridor, clenched fists at his sides. His nostrils flaring with a rising tide of rage, he took the champagne cup, which he had deposited on a ledge, and hurled it against the wall where Boris had been standing. The corridor had been steadily emptying. Before anyone could stop him, Pierre ran out of the opera house, his heart pounding and his throat hoarse from panting.

I'm going to kill the bastard, he thought, his mouth filled with an acrid taste. He tried to think, began to sort out the words. It wasn't true! Fury seized him once again, shook him within its grasp of crimson madness, and he said aloud: "I'm going to kill him!"

Boris could not sleep. His body was alive with tremors that shook him like an ague. His stomach twisted in knots, and disembodied thoughts came at him like screeching trains passing at full speed by a motionless onlooker. At the forefront of his mind lay Natalia, slumbering at his side like a misshapen goddess always hovering on the edge of pain.

He had refused Dr. Fröhlich's suggestion of a clinic. To place Natalia there away from him, to surround her with antiseptic bleakness, filled him with such dreadful feelings that the famous Darmstadt specialist had demurred. Boris had always considered himself an enlightened man—but the idea of a clinic harkened back to inexplicable superstitions: His mother had died in one, of consumption, and Marguerite had been sent to one after a serious mental breakdown. In his mind this Kussov birth, so unexpected at this stage of his life, had become endowed with mystical qualities that he could hardly reconcile with hospitalization.

"Of course, if she or the baby will be in danger otherwise, you must make any arrangement possible," he had added hurriedly, a sense of doom assaulting his insides. But Dr. Fröhlich had compromised: a nurse, Fräulein Bernhardt, was kept on hand in the village of Zwingenberg, lodging at the house of the cabinetmaker during the last three weeks of the pregnancy; and the medical men deemed the enormous bathroom adjoining the Kussov suite at the inn convenient enough for giving birth, with its open space in the center, the tub against one wall, and the sink, table, and chairs on the opposite side.

Boris had never felt so helpless and inadequate in his life. On one elbow he examined Natalia, wondering if she were truly asleep or in that awkward twilight in which she often passed between rest and uncomfortable half-dozing awareness. He reached out to touch her white brow, then held back: He did not want to risk awakening her if she was asleep. Guilt trickled into his consciousness: to have turned this figure of grace and genius into a mountain of flesh, to have placed her wit and verve behind such bars was an appalling selfishness. Natalia had never wanted a child, and now she might die giving birth to one—to his! And yet sheer joy followed lustily on the heels of his guilt. Nina had felt sure that Natalia would want a child. He had never even considered the possibility—how could he? Now it was imminent, and he was overwhelmed with gladness. Gladness, pride, and hope filled him—but also terror at an unknown so dreadful and so vast that it paralyzed his reason.

He had felt sudden fear when he had first become adjusted to the idea of the pregnancy, wondering if the old disgust would surge up again to destroy everything that he had built with Natalia. He had been afraid to come near her, to see her growing stomach become round and fecund and fully female. Somehow she had sensed this and given him space. But with hesitation he had watched the process. Within the first three months she had begun to show the child inside her, and he had been fascinated and touched, awakened to a new level of sensitivity. Their child!

She moved on the bed, and a spasm passed over her pale face. Her eyelids flickered open and she looked at him, her dark eyes alive with questions. Poor angel, my poor sweet girl, he thought. She knows as little about this as I do. We are babes in the wood. He took her hand and found it moist and feverish. She uttered a sharp cry. Alarmed, he rose from the bed and turned on all the lights. "Something horrible is happening," she said, the words like small pointed daggers in the still night air. "My body is ripping open with something—a liquid—"

Boris did not wait. He seized his dressing gown and ran out into the corridor, frantically searching for the room where he knew the innkeepers slept. When he found it, he pounded on the door until a man in an incongruous night bonnet threw it open and stared at him, dumbfounded. "Herr Walter, it's my wife!" Boris said quickly. "Where is Frau Walter?"

The woman was arriving, attracted by the noise. She smiled.

She was large and round, with a creased red face and small brown eyes. Natalia had nicknamed her Henny Penny from a nursery story that she had learned in England. "Go back to bed, Hermann," she told her husband. "Babies are not within your province, as I can see they aren't within the count's."

Boris and the woman did not speak in the corridor, but inside the room she walked rapidly to the bed and turned to Boris. "Please leave us," she said somewhat severely. She gave him a small, unceremonious push, and when he had gone into the small sitting room next door, she threw back the covers. "Ach," she exclaimed, shaking her head, "it's what I thought. The water broke. You're a young one," she said to Natalia, who was looking at her with silent terror. "There's nothing wrong at all. You've just never been through this. I don't think it's time yet to call Fräulein Bernhardt, though I suppose your husband will insist. Men! Useless, if you ask me!"

Unexpectedly, Natalia laughed. Frau Walter smiled back, pleased with their complicity. "We're going to have to change the sheets," she said, and went to the adjoining door. "*Herr Graf*," she called to Boris, "please carry the *Gräfin* to the sitting room while I put clean linens on the bed."

There is nothing like a German *Hausfrau*, Boris thought with some humor. He took Natalia in his arms to the small sofa and sat down near her. Her face seemed brighter, more flushed, and her eyes more alive. "It's all right," she said to him in a strangely normal voice. "The worst is over. The worst was thinking that the baby would die along the way. Now we know it's going to be born." But he thought: What if you should be the one to die, from my selfishness and from my stubbornness concerning the clinic?

Frau Walter settled Natalia comfortably against the pillows and went to telephone Fräulein Bernhardt at the cabinetmaker's in the village. Boris paced the room, thoughts hurtling through his brain. Natalia said evenly: "You're making me nervous. Sit down and read me something, will you? Something not too deep—Turgenev?"

"I'm not a living library, Natalia," he said. "But perhaps you want me to perform a one-man ballet for you. It's too late to cable Vaslav to come."

She bit her lower lip and giggled. "I don't know what else to make you do to stop from fretting. You can't very well play the piano. It must be three in the morning!"

Suddenly she pressed her hands against her stomach and writhed in pain. His face turned white. For a moment she could not breathe, but then, slowly, the color returned to her cheeks. Frau Walter returned with the meticulous Fräulein Bernhardt in a clinical white smock and neat gray bun. "I think I've had a pain," Natalia told her. "Just before you arrived."

Her calm words rang like an alarm in the room. Boris sat down abruptly, all expression vanishing from his face. Frau Walter drew a chair near the bed and took a seat, her knitting in her ample lap. Fräulein Bernhardt, tall and birdlike, hovered between them, attentive. A half hour passed, then another. After two hours Natalia murmured in a small voice: "Must this vigil continue? Please, could I go back to sleep?"

The two efficient women busied themselves in the small sitting room, making a bed for Fräulein Bernhardt on the sofa. "The labor isn't beginning yet, so we should all shut our eyes," the nurse announced. She closed the connecting door, and Boris heard Frau Walter leave the room, presumably to return to her own. He turned down the lights and slipped into bed. But he remained wide awake.

He felt Natalia's small hand slipping into his, tentative and questing. "I'm not going to die," she whispered into the night. "Anyway, the queen mother and the dowager empress in the sitting room wouldn't let me. We have years to spend together, Boris—years! Have you forgotten that you're going to build me a house in the hills of Monte Carlo? With jasmine and mimosa and lilacs in the garden? You can't go back on your promise. It wouldn't be honorable, you know."

He could not find the words to answer her. Nameless oppression lay upon his chest, smothering all sensation.

The next morning she slept. There was no change. Boris dressed quietly and began to pace the floor. Fräulein Bernhardt opened the door connecting the bedroom to the small sitting room where she had slept, and came to him. "There is no purpose in your remaining here, *Herr Graf*," she murmured in her quiet, dry voice. "If the labor begins, I shall send for Dr. Fröhlich. In the meantime, she needs her rest." She hesitated, then continued. "It's an unfortunate timing for the *Gräfin*, but there's to be a village feast here today, with dancing and a band. The Walters tried to stop the players from coming, but they were already on their way. It was too late to warn the villagers. I'm afraid the best Frau Walter can do is to make sure that all the doors are shut to the front room."

An absurd sense of unreality seized hold of Boris. He uttered a short spurt of laughter. "My God," he said, "a band! I suppose I could offer to buy the instruments at a profit, so they won't have to play?"

"Come now," Fräulein Bernhardt remonstrated, a tinge of kindness seeping into her competence. "Why don't you go for a walk or a drive through the countryside? It will do you a lot of good. Babies are born every day, you know. This is 1914—women no longer die in childbirth the way they did years ago."

"But we almost lost this baby," Boris retorted angrily, annoyed at being treated as though he were constantly in the way. A flush spread over his face: "A band! How will she rest in all this noise?"

"I'm certain that the Walters will do what they can. In any case, *Herr Graf*, at this stage she is too exhausted to be deterred by dancing music. She'll be oblivious to it. But she'll sense your nervousness. It will make her very frightened, and then she will not help with the birth and will suffer a great deal more. Husbands' feelings are contagious."

Boris turned away and slammed a fist into the palm of his hand. He seized his riding whip and cap, and, without saying a word, strode out of the suite, into the corridor, and down the stairs. In the large front hall Frau Walter, her husband, and a few chambermaids were setting chairs against the wall and rolling back the carpet. The innkeeper's wife opened her mouth to greet him, but before she could speak, he had left, slamming the door behind him. They stared after him, blinking.

Boris stood uncertainly in the morning air. It was a chilly day, with a strong, bracing breeze. Energy tingled through him, charging him with a heightened awareness of life. Unable to think clearly, he abruptly gave up and walked to the back of the inn, where two horses were hitched in a very small stable. The one he usually rode, Banditt, was a white, nervous stallion that reared his head when he saw Boris. "I suppose you and I are alike, old boy," Boris said, untying him and leading him out to the bridle path. "We don't take well to being caged." He mounted the beast in one swift, graceful motion.

Once on the horse, he felt relieved. He was marvelously one with Banditt, a single male strength and flow, a savage might contained in elegant leanness. He spurred the horse toward the large path that led to Darmstadt, over bridges and under the bower formed by the merging treetops.

He was assailed by conflicting emotions and sensations, but the wind brushed these cleanly from him, making him whole. But something—he didn't know exactly what—kept urging him forward, into Darmstadt itself. Suddenly he knew: He was right on the edge of the *Künstler Kolonie*. For a moment he was angry, and almost turned the horse around; then, with a grim set of his jaw, he directed Banditt onto the winding streets.

Why had he come here? To square away what misunderstanding? Or had he merely allowed his worry over Natalia to raise from his consciousness another worry, caused by his run-in with Pierre at the opera house? He had had his revenge, had ostracized Pierre from the Ballet and from his Petersburg sponsors. Why, then, could he not let go? One simply did not forget past agonies; one had to lay them to rest. He had believed all this to be over. Pierre had proved that it was not. What did he want with Pierre? I want to finish it once and for all, he told himself. I want it finished before the baby's born so that the three of us—she, I, and our child—may proceed without being haunted by the past. I need a resolution.

Suddenly, Boris felt cold sweat on his shoulders, under his armpits. He remembered his first sight of Pierre at the opera, that instant before thoughts had entered his head: that split-second of complete emotion unclouded by reason. What, in fact, had he felt? It would have been better not to have raised the question, not to have analyzed it. Armando Valenzuela had sought him out, recognizing him as one of his own—that had been bad enough. But Pierre had always been with him, a memory to haunt him. He had never really been able to let go, to stop the anguishing treadmill of desire and love: not even converting the love to a vengeful hatred. Not even his love for Natalia, that other love that could bring him peace and self-esteem, had been able to eradicate the memory of his passion for Pierre Riazhin. It was essential that he test it one last time. For his family's sake and his own sanity and well-being.

Halfway up the first street, Boris realized that he had no idea where exactly Pierre lived. He stopped a blond woman walking with a child. "There's a young Russian painter, Pierre Riazhin," he began. "I'd like to find him if you can help me."

"There are no Russians here, *mein Herr,*" the woman replied. "Only Germans. Are you certain he lives here?"

Taken aback, Boris replied: "That's what he told me. He's tall, with broad shoulders, dark curly hair, and black eyes. In his early thirties."

"Oh! You must mean the Swiss man. I'd forgotten about him. His German isn't so good, but it's not bad. He doesn't speak to many of us here, but he's a courteous enough young fellow. He paints beautiful, vivid scenes. Peter Habig, that's his name. I don't know what you called him, but I can assure you he's not Russian."

Utterly bewildered now, Boris merely raised his eyebrows and smiled. "I must have been confused, *gnädige Frau,*" he remarked smoothly. "But tell me, if you will, where I may find this Habig?"

"Up the road, the two-storey house with the semicircular outer staircase," the woman replied cheerfully. Taking the small child's hand, she started down the road once more. Intrigued, Boris spurred Banditt in the opposite direction.

He stopped Banditt in front of a small garden planted with pansies, marigolds, poppies, and short-stemmed daisies. Several pieces of white wicker lawn furniture stood between the flower beds. The house itself was small, like all the houses in the *Künstler Kolonie;* it was boxlike, of white sandstone, with windows of varying shapes. Boris half-smiled and tied his horse to the post outside. With easy grace, he mounted the semicircular staircase to the front stoop, and rang the doorbell.

At the back of his mind he must have wondered whether

Pierre would be the one to answer the door. When it was pulled open, the young painter stood before him in his shirtsleeves, wearing an expression of ill-concealed hostility and outrage. Boris inclined his head and raised one hand. "Don't be banal, my Petya, and ask me how I found you or what I'm doing here. Instead, ask me in, won't you?"

Pierre's black eyes snapped with anger and the muscles in his neck tensed into cords. "What if I killed you right here, with my bare hands?" he whispered.

Boris shrugged lightly and entered. He looked around him. They stood in a small salon adorned with carved ebony furniture lightened by multicolored cushions and a large tapestry on the wall. The chairs and sofa were low and streamlined, of an unusual design. The effect was open, yet busy.

"Since you're here, what do you want?" Pierre broke in.

Boris looked at him directly, coldly. "I'd like to talk to you," he said. "Simply that, without histrionics and physical assault. Is that permissible?"

He scanned the room and went to an armchair by the tapestry and sat down, slinging one leg easily over the other. "You're doing all right, I take it?" he asked.

"Well enough. The disfavor you did me in Petersburg has taken years to mend. It's still not mended, not by a long shot."

"You must learn to accept adversity, Pierre. The past is the past. If you allow bitterness and hatred to consume you, you won't be able to accomplish anything in the future."

Pierre's mouth opened. "And whose advice is this, may I ask?" he cried. "Because it sure as hell isn't yours, Boris!"

Boris laughed ruefully. "No, it isn't. Well done, Pierre. *Touché*. Actually, it's Natalia's. Sound advice, really. You should pay heed to it. So should I, for that matter." A frown marred his smooth brow, and he quickly passed his fingers over his eyes. Then he looked up at Pierre, still standing. "Natalia is going to give birth any moment now. That's why I'm here: This is too damned important a time for her and for me to allow other matters to cloud the issue. If you're here, then so be it. But I don't want you to take it into your head to find her and cause problems. Should you run into us somewhere, I want to make sure you'll behave like a gentleman."

Pierre took a deep breath and opened his mouth to speak, then closed it and sat down opposite Boris. On his knee, his right hand clenched into a fist, then spread out, and became a fist again. Suddenly he looked at Boris and said: "Natalia came to see me three years ago, in Petersburg. After you turned everyone in the committee against me. Did you know that?"

Boris's eyes narrowed. "I suspected it," he answered directly. "But if you'd been a little more secure within yourself, and if you'd capitalized more cleverly on your growing reputation, I could not have harmed you. In a way, Pierre, I hoped that you'd be strong enough to withstand me, and I was disappointed in my easy victory." He sighed. "You haven't lived up to your potential, Pierre. Something is missing inside you: a fibre of determination, a sense of mission. Natalia's always had it about dance. You don't, and more's the pity because you are truly a genius."

Pierre shook his head. "Everything that you touch you contaminate," he said. "I simply wanted a patron. You made yourself much more, more than I'd hoped for, but also more than I really wanted. Why didn't you just leave me to my own devices, Boris? I could have managed better without your playing with my life. It was my life, and you made it your game. Why?"

"Isn't the answer self-evident?" Boris asked. "Don't play the innocent." Without removing his eyes from Pierre's ruddy face, he said: "We're none of us innocents, are we? If we agree to play the game, then it's fitting for us to be graceful losers if such is our fate. You, Pierre, have never learned this."

"I would hardly call you a graceful loser. To have me dismissed from the 'committee'—"

Boris put up a hand. "No, don't confuse the issue. I was not the loser there. The game wasn't over yet. There was still a card left to be played, and I played it." He opened his eyes completely again. "I may win more often than most players, but I'm still human. Nobody likes to be despised and hated. You should have known me well enough to have realized that."

Pierre burst out: "What would you have had me do? Love you? For having cheated your way into Natalia's life—and ruined my own?"

Boris smiled. "Love and war are really not so far removed,

are they? What possible difference can it make who the love object is—man, woman, dog? As long as one can hope for an end to loneliness, love is elevating and sanctified. But once the hope dies, love becomes war. Didn't it occur to you, my young fool, that a man does not turn his life around for another unless love is involved?" He made an ironic, self-deprecating gesture of uplifted palms. "*Mon cher* Pierre, I even married Marguerite Tumarkina, poor ignorant soul, to provide extra funds for the Paris exhibition. I suppose I was the ignorant soul, too, then, wasn't I? But you, my young friend, were merely a self-serving egotist on a treasure hunt. You haven't changed in nine years, have you?"

Pierre's dark eyes flashed with maroon reflections. "And you have? What about Natalia? You married her to take her away from me, and that's all. You can't love her! A man like you doesn't change—and she's as female as they come. I know! Or didn't you know that?"

Boris nodded slowly. "Oh, yes, of course I knew. You don't have to rub it in with such glee, Petya. Your sexual prowess doesn't impress me. Perhaps once it impressed her—I haven't asked. It's not my business. But yes, some people change. I don't say I'd like every woman, or any woman." He laughed shortly. "But the fact is that Natalia is my sort of woman, and we are happy together. I have no idea quite how it happened— only that it did. And that's been my life." He smiled and said: "Now, be a good fellow and tell me how you're doing. Happiness is contagious. It would do me good to think that you had put the past behind you, as well."

A strange smile flitted across Pierre's full lips. "You brought up Marguerite," he said. "Now I'll proceed with her. Did you wonder how I ended up here in Darmstadt? This house belongs to her—to Marguerite von Baylen."

Boris's blue eyes widened, and he threw back his head and burst out laughing. "How marvelous! Marguerite is keeping you? Poetic justice, don't you think? I find this wonderful!"

But Pierre was not laughing. A dark flush had spread over his cheeks. "She isn't 'keeping' me, as you so insultingly put it. I painted her in Kiev several years ago. She liked my work. Some of her Berlin friends liked it, too, and I went there to paint them. More work came my way. It seemed absurd to return to Petersburg—as you know, things were chaotic there for me in every sense—so she suggested that she build me a little house in an artists' colony. As I possessed no reserve funds for such a construction project, I accepted. In return I paint her two large pieces of work a year. So far the arrangement has been satisfactory for both of us—and for the baron, who likes to think that he has become a patron of the arts. The second husband wants to imitate the first."

Boris was still laughing. "Marguerite, a painter's sponsor! She couldn't differentiate between a Gauguin and a Van Gogh! Has she become any better?"

Pierre unexpectedly smiled. "No. She's pleasant enough, in a hysterical sort of way: aristocratically demure, and genteelly uneducated. But I don't expect the fellows from the Foreign Ministry in Berlin notice the lack. They're too busy swaggering with their rows of medals."

Boris's face darkened. "Yes, I see your point. But these days it's men like them who rule Europe. Illiterate, bombastic fools. Someday we shall all die at their hands." He stood up. "Speaking of dying, are you still prepared to kill me, Pierre? Bare hands and all?"

The two men looked at each other. Boris took in the taut, well-built body, the dark curly head, the expressive face with its black eyes. How easy it had been to love him! How easy it would be to love him again. For a moment he hesitated, unable to move. Pierre stared back at him, his own emotions warring inside him: resentment and hatred, but also respect, admiration, bewilderment. How could one simply dismiss Boris Kussov? It was far easier to detest him than to forget him.

Pierre looked away first and said: "I don't know. If I don't, you might destroy me again, this time permanently. Or could you? You already have everything I really wanted: the woman I loved, the child I should have had, and the power to make me famous. I can't say I'm grateful. But it's the old Caesar-Brutus thing, isn't it? Brutus felt guilty once he'd done away with his former mentor—and found himself surrounded by fools."

Boris raised his eyebrows and smiled. "Quite a speech, coming from you, Pierre. Roman history, no less—or are you quoting Shakespeare? I'm quite impressed by the analogy. It lifts me to a level higher than I am usually placed in your estimation, dear boy."

Pierre shrugged moodily. "I'm not entirely without culture," he retorted brusquely.

Boris suddenly stiffened and clamped a fist to his mouth. "Oh, God," he cried. "Natalia! I've got to go, right now. I should have left ages ago!"

"Yes," Pierre answered in a strained voice. "She'd better be all right, or I shall truly kill you, I promise you that."

Boris turned to him at the door, and Pierre was struck by his expression of raw anxiety and anguished concern. Natalia. Pierre opened his mouth and licked his lips. One's whole life— He raised his hand and quickly touched Boris on the arm, then pulled away. His voice cold and distant, he said: "It'll be all right." Then he added, with effort, "Good luck," and turned away from the door.

On his way out, Boris suddenly stopped. "Pierre—why are you living here under a pseudonym?" he asked.

Pierre shrugged, his back still to the other. "I was tired of Pierre Riazhin," he replied thickly. "I was tired of being hurt, too, as Pierre Riazhin, the Russian. Here I am Swiss, and they notice me less. And Marguerite is pleased. Should the Tzar turn against the Kaiser, she will not be embarrassed by harboring an enemy of her adopted country."

With odd warmth Boris said: "Well, Petya, I wish you all the best. Some day you won't need Marguerite, and you won't need me. Perhaps you can join Serge again. Did you know he's rehired Fokine as choreographer for the Ballets Russes? You were good at that kind of artwork—sceneries and costumes. Benois and Bakst liked you. If Serge could rehire Fokine after all their quarrels and bad feelings, he would surely take you back, too. He never had anything against you."

"No," Pierre replied. "Only you did." It was difficult to tell whether his tone held bitterness or simply hard realism. Boris took a deep breath and closed the door behind him. Outside, he mopped his brow. It was over—or as over as it would ever be until he learned to forget Pierre completely.

He unhitched Banditt and swung onto him. But as he started

him off at a brisk canter, his heart knocked within his chest, sending discomforting pulsebeats into this throat, temples and wrist. On the open road he urged Banditt to a gallop. Would she have understood the need to lay this matter to rest? The need to do it now, perhaps while she was having his baby? Another spurt of tender urgency filled him.

Almost as soon as Boris had left the inn, Natalia awakened, and Fräulein Bernhardt plumped her pillows and served her hot tea and toast. "I sent your husband away," she said conspiratorially. "His pacing would have driven you crazy. What a handsome man he is, though, isn't he? Dr. Fröhlich has not told us much about you. Is the *Herr Graf* a diplomat?"

Natalia laughed. "No. He's a patron. He dabbles in all the arts and sponsors many artists of genius. Politics is far too serious for him—" She hesitated, then plunged in: "He helped to sponsor me. I'm a ballerina."

Fräulein Bernhardt's birdlike countenance quickened, and she sat down on the edge of the bed. "Really? Tell me about it. What a life of excitement that must be!"

But all at once Natalia felt a tremendous pain throughout her body. It was far stronger than the one the previous night, and she thought: I am splitting in half. Fräulein Bernhardt's easy, lively words continued to flow, but Natalia's consciousness began to fade. Such awful discomfort had taken possession of her that only the sensations inside her registered on her mind. She was hardly aware of the noise that was coming from the front of the inn and that Fräulein Bernhardt had summoned Frau Walter and gone into the bathroom. Several people entered, carrying pails of hot water and clean white sheets, and then through her dim perceptions she heard a vague commotion in the bathroom. When they brought her in they placed her on a high bed surrounded with iron rails, which had not been there before, in the middle of the bathroom. She saw Dr. Fröhlich and felt him place her fingers over the bars on each side of the cot. She gripped them and concentrated on the pain.

If I try hard enough, I can let myself yield to it, she thought, knowing that her awareness was blotted by the sharp red agony that came and went in waves that grew stronger and stronger.

She thought of the stretching exercises of ballet, of the body's adaptation to new positions and motions. She thought: I am not going to faint. I am going to get through this, I am going to survive no matter what. She bit into a fist, sweat breaking out on her brow.

It was interminable, the pain, the near loss of consciousness, the thoughts that were like hallucinations. She saw a face and shrank, thinking that it was her mother. She panicked and began to cry. Boris was gone, and he was not going to return. Bernhardt had sent him away; he had grown disgusted with her anyway. She was all alone. She screamed and screamed and knew then that surely all her insides must be pouring out of her.

When Boris returned, he left the horse by the front door, calling to a servant to lead Banditt back to the small stable. An incredible din assailed him from the large hall. This was all so unreal—the ride, the interview with Pierre, the worry, the anticipation, the fear—and now all this ungodly noise. He opened the door and found himself facing gaily clad dancers moving to the rhythmic pounding of a large drum and the strident sounds of an accordion. The swirling peasant couples made him blink, and for a moment he was paralyzed, pushed against the door by the joyful confusion.

Then, with a spurt of force, he shoved aside two whirling waltzers and almost ran across the room to the staircase. He took the stairs by threes and, toward the top, was struck by the smell of disinfectants. A piercing female yell tore through him from beyond the partition, freezing his senses and sending him rushing into the bedroom. Frau Walter met him, and when he attempted to avoid her in his path, she placed an iron hand on his arm. "Don't go in there," she warned him. "It's not your business." Her face had lost all its ruddiness and was stark white and lined like sheet music.

In the bathroom the pain was receding, pulling back, and Natalia felt herself slowly slipping into oblivion. The whole bottom half of her body was one gaping wound. But she could hear Dr. Fröhlich saying: "It's a boy, and how like you he looks! He has your big eyes." With desperate effort she tried to raise her head but could not move at all. Weariness swept over her like a delirium. It was over. But he had not shown her the baby. Maybe it had died!

Before losing consciousness, she fought for her grip on reality. The most awful anxiety had penetrated to the center of her being: The baby was dead! She tried to voice her fear but had no strength left. Someone was touching her where it hurt most, aggravating the pain. She made a noise and heard Fräulein Bernhardt say: "It's all right, I'm washing the baby and the doctor is stitching you up. Try to relax!" Stitching her up? Then she had really ripped? A whirlwind of nausea overcame her, and she blacked out the room and its various people.

It was almost an anticlimax when Fräulein Bernhardt came out to the bedroom with the blanket. She was smiling, but Boris could neither speak nor move. He was afraid to look at the small bundle, overwhelmed by a feeling of complete happiness. He could not look at the nurse, but with the most tentative fingers he pushed back the soft cover and peered with wonder at the tiny face. It was not red, as he had expected, but white and unlined, as white as Natalia. Two little fists were balled up near his head, which was matted with dark hair. "You can hold him, *Herr Graf*," the nurse said and handed him the bundle.

In his arms the baby began to writhe, and the softest whimpers came out of him, angry whimpers that made him turn crimson. But they were so soft, compared with adult cries. My son, he thought, a miracle of flesh, so minuscule, so perfect. He could not see for the sudden mist in his eyes, and he turned his back on Fräulein Bernhardt to be alone with his child.

The baby's rage shook his tiny body, stiffening it. Mine. My son, my child. Pulsating with life. I shall remember this day to the end of my life—but what lies in store for you, tiny bit of divinity, miracle of love? I shall take care of you and not let them hurt you, not let them mar your perfection. Boris could not stop his tears from falling on the coverlet, and tried to breathe normally, to regain control.

Discreetly, Fräulein Bernhardt said: "You can go in now. Your wife is ready for you."

In his arms the baby opened his mouth and crammed a fist into it. Then the small body relaxed, and Boris saw that his son was sucking his thumb. A delighted wonder spread through him, a tremendous pride. He looked up, forgetting the moisture on his cheeks, and laughed at the nurse. "He's sucking his thumb!" he cried.

"Well, I've never seen that before," the nurse commented, examining the sight. "At this age!"

All at once reality returned to Boris. Joy was replaced by fear. He had forgotten Natalia! As quickly as he could, he handed the bundle that was his child to the nurse and rushed through the doorway into the bathroom. His heart knocked inside him.

She was so pale, so small, a child also, with a hollowness to her cheeks and purple circles under her eyes. "She's quite all right, just exhausted," the doctor said and tactfully left the room.

They had removed balls of sheets, but in the white bathroom he saw a dark stain of blood. Her blood! A shiver passed through him. He kneeled down next to the cot and touched her forehead. Her eyelids flickered, and the brown eyes suddenly found him, held him. He felt himself drowning in those eyes. The baby, too, had wide, dark eyes shaped like almonds. He opened his mouth but could not speak.

"You came back," she murmured. Color was coming into her cheeks. He took her hand and kissed the fingertips, lightly, gently. Then a spasm passed over her face and she asked: "Have you seen him? Is he alive?"

Boris nodded. How to find the words . . . "He's handsome and well and he looks like you," he finally said, feeling foolish.

She drew away. "But he's not supposed to! I wanted him to be like you—not me!" There was an edge of hysteria in her voice and in her wide eyes.

"But I'm glad. He's exactly what I wanted. What we both wanted, Natalia." He caressed her cheeks, her nose, her temples. He smiled at her, regaining control. "I love you. Thank you for my beautiful son. You'll never know how much I love you both—and everything I want to do for you. Are you all right, Natalia? They wouldn't let me in to be with you."

Then she smiled. "It wasn't so bad, really, darling. But I kept thinking you'd never come back—and that the baby was dead. Don't leave us, Boris. Don't ever leave us. We'll never get in your way, we'll be good. The baby and I shall always love you."

There was a soft knock on the door, and Fräulein Bernhardt appeared with the baby. She brought him to Natalia and deposited him in her arms. Natalia's face bent over her son so that her nose caressed his cheek. "Such a lot of pain you've caused me, little one," she murmured gently. "Such a lot of pain and all those months of boredom. Do you know what that is, boredom? No? Well then, we shall make certain that you never learn, all right? Your papa will keep misery and cold and hunger from you, and I shall keep the boredom away. You're so little!"

"Send up as many bottles of champagne as you've got on hand," Boris said to Fräulein Bernhardt. When she had gone, he placed one arm around Natalia's shoulder and put his other hand on the baby's blanket. "We have to find you a name, little Count Kussov," he said.

Natalia looked at her husband. "We should call him Arkady," she suggested. "For your father's father, the one who bought the Kussov palace on the French Quay. You admired him a lot, didn't you, sweet?"

Boris felt something melting inside him. "Yes. More than anyone, I wanted to be like him. He was a man of honor and of taste—an aristocrat of the heart. I gave up trying to emulate him years ago, but that's an old story. I'm surprised you remembered."

"I remembered. Many months ago I decided that if we had a son, we should give him your grandfather's name. So," she said, "Arkady Borisovitch, how do you like your new identity? Count Arkady Borisovitch Kussov. Such a complicated name for such a tiny fellow."

The innkeeper, Hermann Walter, wheeled in a bucket with a bottle of iced champagne in it. Boris stood up and deftly popped the cork, and in the noise that ensued the baby began to yell in his tiny voice. "Come in, everyone!" Boris cried. "Doctor, Fräulein, Frau and Herr Walter! We must toast Count Arkady Borisovitch Kussov!"

In the background German folk music was playing, the big drum beating and the accordion twanging to a fast-paced marching rhythm. But upstairs in the white bathroom nobody paid attention.

Chapter 15

On either side of Darmstadt stood two sharp cliffs, covered with fields at their base, then rising into blue-green forests scattered with walking trails. These two hills protected the countryside from the harsh north winds of winter, but already now, in late May, the heat was becoming stifling. Only beneath the branches of the pine trees was there a welcome coolness.

Natalia removed her small demure hat with its brim and sat down on a log. She pushed her sleeves up on her forearms and began to fan herself with the hat. Her white and black boots, showing beneath the cotton skirt falling well above her ankles, were tight and painful. It was strange how the mere fact of having a baby changed one's body. She wondered how her feet would have reacted to ballet slippers.

In front of her the child fretted in the perambulator. More and more she felt the need to go alone into the hills with him, taking him away from Mademoiselle Allard, the Swiss nurse whom Boris had hired for Arkady. Natalia needed to be with her son in order to ease the awful sensation of suffocation under which she had been living since the second week of the baby's life. It was a nameless, haunting oppression that prevented her from sleeping and kept tears close to the surface.

It had taken her some time to recover from the birth. At first, Dr. Fröhlich had made her stay on her back, and, unable to fall asleep without turning, she had remained awake, wondering about the child. He was so pale, so fretful, so nervous. She had wanted to take him to her breast and hold him there, to shield him from whatever frightened him, whatever ailed him. He did not seem to like her milk, but when Fröhlich put him on condensed milk in a bottle, he did not accept that any better. Yet, when Boris entered the room, she would look up and smile, presenting him with a radiant face.

But it isn't my imagination, *it isn't,* she now said to herself, beginning to tremble. Dr. Fröhlich, the only doctor of repute in the area, had taken his family to a medical conference in Vienna, and planned to remain there on an extended holiday. He was collaborating on a series of important articles for a journal on obstetrics with a Viennese physician. How can he do this to me, to Arkady? Natalia thought with strident anguish. She rose from the log and pulled back the covers in the perambulator. Her son, who truly did resemble her, stared back at her, stared back at her intelligently. He knows, she thought, he knows he isn't well.

Then she caught herself: Natalia, you are losing your mind, attributing God knows what ridiculous knowledge to an infant only ten weeks old. She touched the frail cheek, smooth and pale like her own, and felt a well of tenderness flowing out to him. Dear little being. I am going to break down completely, she warned herself.

Arkady had her eyes but his father's perfect nose and chiseled lips, her complexion and dark hair but Boris's hands and feet, long and thin. He is not at all like Galina, she thought. At first she had minded his points of resemblance to herself, wishing him instead to be a total Kussov. But no, I'm not so bad, she had finally concluded. That's it! He'll be the new Nijinsky. Vaslav and Romola are expecting their own child at any moment. Perhaps they will have a girl, and then my son and their daughter will dance together as I did with Vaslav. She smiled with self-mockery.

Boris had asked her about that. "When you're completely recovered, shall we try again to form our own ballet company?" he'd said.

But a black cloud of worry had fallen over her, obliterating all other considerations. She had risen with a jerky movement and said, without looking at him: "It's still too soon. Let's discuss it later—when Arkady can hold his head up by himself."

Reading the momentary surprise on her husband's face, she had recoiled from admitting the truth. Let him think that she was merely reluctant to leave the baby. She actually ached for the stage, her young body firm and whole again. In secret she did floor exercises in the room. Had he known, he would have guessed at her desire to resume dancing, and then he would have also realized that she was keeping something from him.

But she could not broach the subject of her anxiety to Boris. As long as she did not say out loud: "My son is not normal!" then it would not have to be faced as a reality, but merely as a mother's hysteria. Besides, she could not do this to Boris—his son was too precious, too miraculous to him. Contaminating his joy would mean contaminating the whole fabric of their existence and of their love.

Bending over the perambulator, Natalia began to weep, very softly. She was alone and no one could help her, no one could see that her baby was ill. No one could tell her what to do.

"It simply isn't like you," Boris countered dryly. They were sitting at a restaurant atop the Ludwigshöhe, one of Darmstadt's hills. He stood up and began to pace up and down in front of her. He is like a nervous racehorse, she thought, suddenly afraid.

The fear flew into her throat and remained lodged there. "Go, if you like, Boris," she said breathlessly. "I understand your boredom here. Go to Serge Pavlovitch—I'm certain he needs you. I'll join you later—with Mademoiselle and Arkady."

"That's ridiculous. Besides, it's the end of June, Natalia. Mademoiselle is due to leave for her month's vacation. If you stay here, who will take care of the boy?"

"*I* shall!" she answered hotly.

He looked at her narrowly, his face masked in shrewd appraisal. "You are treating me like a fool," he said, his cold voice shaking with fury. "Tell me exactly why you insist on staying here. What are you hiding from?"

Half-rising, she cried, "Hiding from? What do you mean?"

His eyes had become slits. His elegant frame stood perfectly still, poised. She forgot her fears for Arkady and concentrated instead on her husband. He was looking at her as if attempting to see through her to her very soul. She had not felt such contained passion inside him since that awful New Year's Day when he had burst upon her in her boudoir to ask about Galina's portrait. "My God," she said in a hushed voice, "what exactly are you accusing me of, Boris?"

I am wrong, he thought, she doesn't know he's here. He breathed in deeply, and touched his forehead. "I don't know," he replied shortly, irritably. "It doesn't make sense, that's all. I'd have thought you, of all people, would have been chomping at the bit to leave this place and move on! The weather's growing unbearably hot and stuffy. If you don't want to join the Ballet again, I'm not going to force you—but I don't understand. You won't tell me what's in your head. How can I be a husband to you when you persist in hiding things from me? But so be it. You don't want to be a dancer anymore. Let's go to Venice then. Or Geneva. Or Timbuktu or the moon. But let's go!"

On a crest of terror, she cried: "No!" Then, blushing, she looked away. "I'm tired," she said. "If you won't stay here with me, I told you, I'll manage. I'm not hiding anything," she added, miserably, seeing the distaste in his eyes.

"Very well, Natalia," he sighed. He called the waitress and asked for the bill, and, while they waited, he shifted in his chair so that he was no longer next to her but facing toward her left. She bit her lower lip to repress a sob.

On the way down to the inn, he refused to speak to her. What was he thinking to make him hate her so? It had to be more than annoyance at her delaying tactics. But he didn't suspect the truth. What truth? Arkady did not suffer from a normal childhood illness. He had no fever, he didn't cough. Was she imagining things? Infants were frequently peevish and colicky.

Leaving Boris at the inn, she ran to the sitting room, where Mademoiselle Allard sat knitting. Arkady's small, insistent wail came from the crib with its cascades of white tulle. She bent down and lifted him up, and he arched his back away from her touch, like a cat. She brought him close and held him against her chest, silently. "He's a complaining boy today, *madame la Comtesse*," the nurse commented mildly. "He hasn't learned his manners, has he? The little love!"

How can this woman be a professional caretaker of children and not see what I see? Natalia cried inside herself. A lump rose to her throat. She heard Boris come in and took the baby to his father. "Here," she said, forgetting their quarrel, "your son." Gently, she held Arkady out to her husband.

On the morning of June 29 Boris rushed into the sitting room like a harsh wind, striding toward Natalia with his outstretched hand clutching a newspaper. She had been reading next to the crib, and his sudden entry, coupled with the excitement in his eyes, made her look up in alarm. They had hardly spoken to each other for several days, but now he exclaimed: "Yesterday the Archduke Ferdinand of Austria was killed in Sarajevo, in Bosnia. There's going to be a lot of trouble this time—with no reprieve in sight."

She stared at him, her eyes wide and frightened. "What does that mean to us?" she asked.

He did not look directly at her. "It means we're going back to Russia," he said.

Her lips parted. She shook her head. "We can't," she whispered. "I can't. You can if you feel you must."

An ugly grimace distorted his features, and he threw the tabloid on the floor. Clenching his fists, he cried: "Don't be ridiculous! If Austria declares war on Serbia, the Kaiser will follow suit and Russia will have to protect its neighbor. You'd be here as an enemy alien. Besides, he's thirty-one years old, young enough to want to go home himself to serve his country!"

"Who? Who's thirty-one, Boris? I don't understand you at all!"

"Then tell me why you refuse to return to Petersburg with me. Give me one good reason that doesn't spell 'Riazhin'!"

Natalia stood up, white and shaking. "Riazhin? Why are you bringing up Riazhin, Boris? He has nothing whatsoever to do with Zwingenberg—or does he?"

Boris compressed his lips into a thin line. He regarded her sharply. "He lives in Darmstadt," he said with disgust. "Isn't that why you want to stay here, on and on? For old time's sake?" The words fell from his mouth with infinite sarcasm, like pellets of hail.

He saw the shock on her face, the horror, the hurt, and turned away, pounding a fist into his thigh. She was completely speechless. Slowly he wheeled back around, chewing on his lower lip. "All right," he said in a low voice. "I was wrong, I behaved like a boor. You would like to slap my face or some such melodramatic gesture of contempt and outrage. But then tell me, tell me what it is, if it isn't our old friend Pierre. How can you blame me for thinking the worst if you will not share the best with me?"

Tears were rolling down her pale cheeks. She could not take her eyes from his face, but the tears would not stop. He took a step toward her, held out a hand. "I was wrong, then?" he murmured abjectly.

She fell backward onto the sofa and dropped her head into her hands. Silent sobs began to shake her. He sat down next to her and put an arm around her frail shoulders. Raising her eyes to him she whispered: "If you so much as mention his name ever again, I shall leave you for good, and you will never see Arkady again. Do you understand me, Boris?"

Her intensity startled him. Reddening, he nodded. "I mean every word of this," she added.

"But you have to explain," he countered. "This is a possible war we're facing—not just a decision about where to go for our next vacation!"

She brought a finger to her mouth and bit it. More tears came, and she blinked them away. "It's Arkady," she said, not looking at him. "I know he's ill. There's something very wrong, and I don't want him exposed to train drafts and discomforts. Oh, Boris, I've been so afraid, so afraid he'd die."

He seized her chin and forced her to face him. "What are you saying?" he exclaimed. He took her by the shoulders and shook her once, twice. "Natalia! Why didn't you tell me? He's my child as well as yours, and if there's something wrong, for God's sake, I want to know!"

"There's something wrong, but I don't know what. Not anything common. He's never comfortable, he almost never sleeps.

I stay awake and go in to him, and usually he's fretting and crying, as if he's in great pain that he can't express. It's awful. But Fröhlich's away, and I'm afraid that if we move him, he won't make it! I mean it—I just don't think he could stand a voyage."

Boris stood up and began to pace the room. "Don't you see?" she cried. "I knew it would be awful for you, the uncertainty. Maybe it's nothing at all—just colic!"

"I doubt it, Natalia," he answered evenly. "You're not a doomsayer. But it was wrong not to tell me. I don't know what to say. This is one hell of a mess we're in. If you'd told me before, we could have sent for Fröhlich by telegram. Now, with this bloody war about to break up every family, he'll want to stay put for a while in Vienna."

"Arkady wasn't born healthy," she said softly. "No one believed me. Fräulein Bernhardt thought I was a hysterical mother."

"For all the good they've been, we could have lived without Bernhardt and Frau Walter! Oh, Natalia, it shouldn't have lain entirely on your shoulders. But of course, I should have noticed. I suppose I was too busy planning how to get you to leave Zwingenberg, the utopia of Western Europe!"

"You couldn't have seen it," she demurred. "The worst part was at night. One of us had to sleep. If he's ill and I've gone mad with insomnia, we shall need your refreshing sanity."

He walked to the crib and lifted the lace curtain. She watched him touch the coverlet with the very tips of his elegant fingers, saw the curve of his agile back, of his graceful neck. A release of love burst inside her and flowed out of her, encompassing him and the baby. Incongruously, Fräulein Bernhardt's words came to mind: "What a handsome man! Is the *Herr Graf* a diplomat?"

Oh Boris, Boris! she thought desperately, now you know we have no choice, we must stay here until Dr. Fröhlich returns to help us. And he will come back, he must! Suddenly she was sick with anguish.

On July 1 Boris sat down on the edge of the bed while Natalia finished combing her hair at the vanity. She could see him through the mirror, his sculptured face pensive, silver strands mingling liberally with the gold of his hair and sideburns. But his body possessed the litheness of a much younger man. In his maroon velvet dressing gown, his reading glasses over the bridge of his nose, he appeared, above all, distinguished—Apollo at bedtime. She smiled at her metaphor and opened her mouth to tell it to him, when he said, very quietly: "Come here, Natalia. We have to talk."

A dreadful sense of foreboding pierced through her. She came to stand in front of him, waiting. "Natalia," he said, his eyes a deep blue as they scanned her face, "I've made some arrangements. Because of Arkady, and the danger. I've spoken with the Walters and given them a handsome sum of money. I've spoken with the mayor of Zwingenberg. I've obtained their assurances—and I do put faith in them, for they are simple, peaceful people who believe in kindness rather than death—that if war breaks out, you can continue to live here, without being reported as an enemy alien and interned. I've had to close out the bank account because as a Russian you wouldn't be able to touch it. But Herr Walter has enough to see you through until the baby's better and we can get you both out of here safely."

"Where are you going, Boris?" she asked, unable to voice her tumultuous thoughts.

For a moment he looked away from her intense brown eyes. Then, softly, he said: "I am going back to Petersburg. Don't laugh too much, my dear, but I'm about to do something as out of character as anything I've ever done in my dilettante's life."

Her ears hurt from the blood beating in them. A spurt of bile swam up her throat, and she swallowed it down. She clasped a hand to her collarbone and sat down next to him, her eyes holding his. "Boris," she asked, "what are you going to do?"

He laughed, but it was not a happy sound. "I've decided to ask Valerian Svetlov to get me into the Division Sauvage. It's his old outfit, you know."

The room was beginning to swim around her head. She could not breathe. "It's something I feel compelled to do, Natalia," he added gently. "I don't like to leave you here, alone with Arkady, worried beyond words about his health. But I don't see a choice. The Kaiser is a madman who will slaughter all of Europe if we let him. I'm hardly what you'd call a patriot—

besides, I'm afraid there's not much hope for us in Russia, either—but I am a human being, and I love the civilized world. If it's to be preserved, we must each do what we can, don't you think?"

"No!" she cried, standing up suddenly, a tower of strength and rage. "I don't think so! Other men, maybe—but not you! You couldn't care less about wars, or armies, or politics! You love music, and the Ballet, and satiric poetry and Renaissance medallions. You are at home in every nation and don't give a damn about preserving Mother Russia! What's gotten into you? Have you gone mad—or is this your idea of a joke?"

He put a hand out to her but she shook him off, her entire body a quivering flame of revolt. "For God's sake!" she exclaimed. "Tell me you don't mean it!"

He said nothing, but his eyes spoke for him. "Boris!" she cried, seizing hold of his dressing gown. "Of course you don't mean it. After all," she said, beginning to giggle, "you're almost forty years old! The Division Sauvage wouldn't consider taking you. Give them a check or something, can't you? As a show of support?"

He threw back his head and burst into peals of laughter. "I'll remember that one, Natalia. Felled by the lethal barbs of a check. *Touché!* But truly, my darling, I'm going. If they don't take me, so be it. I think they will. I've never been brave a day in my life and I may end up shaming the entire outfit—but there comes a moment when a man—a person—has to face his own sense of values. I like the German people well enough, but if Kaiser Willy sets his mind to it, he could convert the whole of Europe into a parade of Prussian soldiers. They'd take up too much space and wouldn't leave enough for Natalia Oblonova and her mercurial feet."

Only then did she begin to cry. She fell face down on the bed and sobbed aloud, like a very small girl. Helpless by her side, he could only stroke her heaving back, caress the soft brown curls on her neck. She sobbed until there were no tears left inside her, but still she sobbed, unable to stop. He removed her slippers and her silk robe, and pulled the covers over her. He turned the lights off and climbed beside her in the bed. She rolled over and said to him, at length: "Don't ask me to understand what you're doing, Boris. You're tearing the heart out of me! What you're doing is so unlike you that I can't think of anything to say."

"I'd rather hoped you'd say something encouraging, Natalia," he countered.

"You're a goddamned hypocrite, Boris!" And then, in a whisper: "When are you leaving?"

"Tomorrow," he answered quietly.

In the darkness she felt her body turn numb. "But perhaps there won't be a war," she said hopefully.

"There'll be a war. Don't hate me so, Natalia."

Like a furtive young animal, her body inched over to the crook of his arm. "But I do," she said. "It's in my character, and I'm not one to change. I don't believe in lying to send you to a glorious death. I want you here, with us. If you're a fool, you'll be one without my blessing. You never listen to my opinions, anyway. Goddamn you!"

"Don't be afraid," he murmured softly, circling her shoulders in a strong grip. "I'm frightened enough for two."

But she could not answer. She was too engrossed in capturing the feel of his arm around her, his smell near her, the sound of his voice. She knew that she would never forget this night as long as there was a breath of life left inside her.

Chapter 16

On July 28, 1914, when Austria declared war on Serbia, with Russia, France, and Britain announcing war against Germany within the following week, Natalia did not feel as shaken as the Walters and the other inhabitants of Zwingenberg did. She simply thought: It has come, and now there is nothing to do but wait. So began a series of monotonous days, an endless procession.

Already Boris seemed like a gilded image to her, highlighted in the rich colors of the Renaissance. She did not want to think of him as flesh and blood, for when she did, nauseous fear swept over her, preventing her from reasoning intelligently. She had received letters until the outbreak of the war, and thus knew that the Division Sauvage had indeed accepted him as an officer among its distinguished corps. Beyond that, Boris's doings remained unknown. Natalia had never been exposed to anything military, apart from occasional encounters with the gentlemen of the Horse Guard, whose garrison in St. Petersburg stood on the same boulevard as the Kussov flat. She had never liked the swaggering officers, had found them pompous and largely useless.

Arkady turned six months old in September. Natalia knew then how right she had been not to leave the Darmstadt area. He was a beautiful child, ethereal and translucent, with brown eyes that encompassed most of his small white face. Gentle brown curls covered his head. He was tall, twenty-seven inches—an inheritance from his father. But he weighed only ten and a half pounds, and his ribs showed pathetically. He simply did not eat enough, and at the age of four months had spent three weeks vomiting after every meal. He almost never lay still, even in Natalia's arms, and he never smiled.

He was intelligent. He liked Frau Walter and looked up brightly if she came in, holding his small arms up for her to take him. But, once held, he was uncomfortable, and she had to put him down. "I've never seen a child like him," the innkeeper's wife said, shaking her head. "It's as if he wants to shed his skin, like a little snake. As if being himself were painful."

"I think it probably is, for him," Natalia replied.

She took him out each day, no matter what the weather, to give him fresh air. She spoke to him—about the ballet, about Paris, about St. Petersburg, about his father, about the little cousin he had never met, Galina. No one in Russia wrote to her for fear, she knew, of exposing her presence to the German authorities. She wished that someone—Nina Stassova, Lydia, Katya—would send her a long, newsy letter relating normal, everyday occurrences: about Galina, or the Imperial Ballet, or Katya's two children. She needed something to reassure her that life outside the Division Sauvage and the prison that Zwingenberg had become was proceeding normally, that all was not as unreal as her own existence.

The Zwingenberg residents treated her with gentle vigilance. Fräulein Bernhardt had told someone that Natalia had been a dancer, and one day Frau Walter brought her a small girl from the village. "For you to teach the steps to," the innkeeper said shyly. Natalia was startled, then delighted. This would provide a welcome break in her monotonous existence. Soon she was teaching three little peasant girls at a makeshift *barre* made from an old staircase banister that Hermann Walter had hooked to one of the walls in the front hall. She sat at the piano herself and poignantly missed Boris more than ever.

Arkady was the center of her life. He had surprised her at five months by saying "Mamamama" and now said it all the time. Perhaps it meant nothing and was only a gurgle that he repeated because it delighted her so. He could crawl, lazily, using only his left leg and dragging the other shamelessly behind him. Natalia had encouraged him by setting some colorful pages of a children's book two feet away from him, tempting him to reach them. Now hc camc aftcr all sorts of lures, his small face squirming with the effort.

But there were no smiles, and many listless, exhausted days when he simply lay in the child's bed that the Walters had found in their attic, hardly moving, constantly whimpering. Natalia sat next to him and wrung her hands.

One day Frau Walter came furtively into the suite and thrust an old periodical in front of Natalia. "We know who you are, *Gräfin*," she said. "You are the famous ballerina of the Ballets Russes, Natalia Oblonova!" She stared at her boarder with unconcealed wonder. Natalia had become as familiar to the Walters as their own daughter—but now the innkeeper's wife looked at her as if for the first time.

Natalia examined the article. It contained sketches of herself, and of Vaslav Nijinsky and Tamara Karsavina. The text spoke of their combined effect on the artistic world of Europe. "We realized it was you when we read that the small one was married to an important count from St. Petersburg," Frau Walter said.

But Natalia was biting her lower lip. "Please," she asked, "don't tell anyone about this. The more people learn who I am, the less chance Arkady and I shall have to escape internment."

"Hermann and I would never speak," Frau Walter retorted indignantly. "But it's such a shame you can't tell the girls' mothers! Some day the little ones would be able to boast that the great Oblonova was their teacher!"

"When the war ends and everything is restored to normal, I promise to send them a pair of ballet slippers from Russia—and I will tell them then," Natalia said with a smile.

But the talk with Frau Walter had made her nervous. If only Arkady would gain weight and start to feel well. If only Boris would return and take them out of this enemy nation. How absurd life was! At any moment Germany, which had lionized her, might declare her and her small son its enemy! The world was a topsy-turvy chaos, changing and churning. Europe was like the Russian Ballet, Natalia thought with a sudden start of amusement; one never knew when one country would suddenly turn against another, just as one could never predict whether Fokine or Benois would decide to quit.

Packing Arkady into the small carriage, she would drive into the hills or into Darmstadt, to change their surroundings for the space of an afternoon. Zwingenberg still employed horse carriages, but in Darmstadt people sometimes stared at her. She thought: So be it. They are taking me for a *Hausfrau* from Zwingenberg who cannot afford a car. The carriage was hardy and inelegant, but it drove well and she could easily handle Olga, the mare. How funny to have a horse with a Russian name, she thought. If anyone gives us away, it will be Olga!

Not far from Steineckerstrasse one of several garrisons of German soldiers were quartered. One day in the middle of September Natalia suddenly realized that, without thinking, she had brought Olga to its place of exercise, a large square, larger than Place Vendôme in Paris, surrounded on three sides by barracks and administration buildings. The fourth side gave onto the street and was separated from it by a tall grilled gate with a large two-paneled door in its center. Through the bars Natalia could see the soldiers exercising in small groups of forty or fifty.

A strange fascination filled the young woman. These men were preparing to leave for the front, preparing to go into battle. She had no idea what Boris was doing, but a palpable anxiety came over her, and she thought: This is what he must be spending his time on! What did it matter that these were Germans and that her husband was a Russian? They were all soldiers in training. The fool, the fool! she cried to herself, hating him with renewed vehemence. She hitched Olga to a post, took Arkady in her arms, and walked to the grillwork. Some soldiers were marching in unison; others were learning to transfer their rifles from their right shoulders to their left. Some were jogging in a group. She saw a double column of men perform a quarter-turn at a sergeant's shout and start off in a different direction. She was hypnotized by this movement, which reminded her in an odd way of a Petipa ballet, with its regroupings and symmetrical formations.

Standing there with the baby in her elegant loose topcoat, her graceful ballerina's ankles exposed in their low kid boots, she resembled a youthful Madonna. One of the noncommissioned officers nudged another, and together they turned to Natalia and smiled. One of them saluted her. They were men, one and all, gallant and lustful. Again she thought, angrily: What difference does it make that they are on the "wrong" side? For she needed to prove Boris wrong, to punish him for what he had done. He'd admitted that it hadn't been an excess of patriotism. Then what? Deep inside she knew there was a human instinct to fight that defied rational explanation, that had made men go to war through the ages, men as blithely disdainful of government as Boris.

She turned away, her heart beating erratically, and took the baby home. But the next day, lured by her obsessive anger at Boris, she returned. The gate was open, and she saw two generals' cars passing through. Arkady's brown eyes, like his mother's, were mesmerized by the soldiers of the Exerzierplatz. So this is why little boys of every epoch have always been fascinated with toy soldiers, she said to herself. But there are no toy wars. She remembered the stilted toy soldier in *The Nutcracker*, dancing for the children at the Christmas party. What shall we be doing at Christmas, my Arkady? For your father has gone off to become a toy soldier with a wooden heart. Wooden hearts don't break, and it's your mama who's the fool.

"Mamama," Arkady said, agitating his small hand. She looked up and saw a German officer coming toward her, with white-blond hair showing beneath his cap and ribbons decorating his broad chest. That's it, they've found us out, and they're going to intern us, she thought with dread. I should never have come here. She raised her head and met his blue eyes without flinching. We don't cower in the Crimea, she thought. We die like Pavlova in *The Dying Swan*, and we remember to be humorous till the end, making silly smiles because we refuse to allow our fear to show. "*Gnädige Frau*," the lieutenant said, clicking his heels and bowing. At least he was arresting them in the style befitting a *prima ballerina*.

She opened her mouth to acknowledge him, but no sound came. He ignored her confusion and said: "We are going to battle in a few weeks, and my men want to know if you will do us the honor of entering the Exerzierplatz and watching us. It would be breaking regulations, but when men are about to risk their lives, a pretty woman does much to encourage them."

But I am your enemy! she wanted to answer. My husband is fighting your own people! My husband might kill one of your men, and one of your men might— "Of course," she replied shortly, her body rigid, her arms wrapped tightly around Arkady.

It was one year now since Natalia had come to Germany, and her command of that language was adequate and well accented. Boris, of course, was fluent and had taught her himself. Frau Walter had taken over. Now Natalia felt infinitely grateful to them, for she could understand the lieutenant and could avoid detection if she made her replies quick and short. He said: "I am Lieutenant Heinrich Püder at your command, *gnädige Frau*." She smiled but did not tell him her own name.

He returned to his men and she stood inside near some grill-work, suddenly awestruck. Once the threshold was crossed, it was bizarre to be so close to the soldiers. Some of the noncommissioned officers cried greetings to her, but after a few moments they resumed their duties and she and Arkady remained alone, watching. One group of men was learning a new movement and could not perform it in unison. The sergeant made them repeat it over and over until everyone had executed it to perfection. Natalia could not take her eyes off them.

Suddenly she froze. A long line of soldiers was marching straight toward her. They marched six abreast and had already drawn so close that there would be no time to run to the end of their row and avoid being crushed. Her face drained of color, and she held the baby in a viselike grip that made him cry out. She felt such panic that she could not even breathe. Where was Heinrich Püder?

Arkady had begun to scream, his small face reddening, his body jerking hysterically in her arms. Six uniformed men with rifles were bearing down on them. She could not think at all, feeling only an overpowering claustrophobia. Then a clipped German voice resounded clearly, and the row, like the Red Sea, parted in the center and marched on either side of her and the child, closing ranks behind her. She remained trembling until the column had gone by, cold sweat breaking out on her brow beneath the small blue hat.

Natalia did not wait to catch Lieutenant Püder's eye. Her arms tightly wound around her son, she ran toward the gate, and out of the Exerzierplatz into the street. Panting, she stood by the post where she had hitched the mare Olga. She was alive! A blinding headache pounded in her head, as she quickly deposited the baby in the carriage.

"I am sorry that you were inconvenienced, *gnädige Frau*," a voice said behind her. She glimpsed the blond lieutenant catching up with her. Now she hated the German army, where before it had seemed composed of fools like the Russians, fools like Boris, playing at a ridiculous war. A jumble of emotions rose inside her, and she wheeled about, her cheekbones red.

"There isn't a man around with any respect for human beings!" she burst out, the German words tumbling out of her, beyond recall. "A bunch of silly little boys in starched uniforms, playing with life! Go away, Lieutenant. Go away before your urge to destroy the earth contaminates my son!"

Heinrich Püder stood in total bewilderment, his jaw dropping. Then, shrugging, he turned and walked back toward the Exerzierplatz. Natalia leaned her head on the post, her breath short and uneven. Of course there is no God, she thought; what God would allow such waste to take place? Women would never have let the world come to this, never. Only the "strong sex," with its absurd delusions of majesty, could cause such misery and confusion.

She was still standing there when someone stopped in front of her. Forced back to the present by this intrusive presence, she shook herself and opened her eyes. She blinked and held onto the post for support. In front of her, his black hair tousled, wearing a light overcoat and no hat, was Pierre Riazhin. Her skin tingled with goose bumps. Boris had said—

"It seems strange not to have run into you before this," he commented without greeting. His face was quick, the eyes sharp and black, the nostrils quivering. He was not a man of repose. Without preamble he added, "But now I must ask why you're still in Germany. Are you here by choice?"

"It's a long story, and I'm exhausted," she replied, without looking at him.

He smiled. "You were never a conversationalist or particularly gracious, though I must say he tried hard enough to turn a sow's ear into a silk purse. No offense, Natalia."

"Your clichés don't bother me, Pierre. I'm sick to death of love and hate and forceful, violent emotions. I just want to go home and have a cup of tea and remove my boots from my swollen feet. Arkady and I were nearly trampled by two hundred German bloodhounds, and I wish to God they *had* trampled me, because suddenly I've ceased to care. I'm too tired."

His features softened. More gently he said: "You remind me of the way you looked waiting for me on my doorstep—tiny, breakable, and very sweaty."

She covered Arkady with his small blanket and turned to look at Pierre. She started to laugh, although reluctantly. "I see," she remarked ironically. "That's how a man speaks to a former love whose faded image no longer inhabits his heart. Your flattery soothes my aching soul."

"Natalia," he asked again, "why are you still here? Enemy aliens can be interned, you know. Or doesn't Boris care about that?"

She looked away. "Boris isn't here," she replied shortly. "He . . . he's joined up with the Division Sauvage—Svetlov's Cossack outfit. I don't want to talk about it."

Pierre's features twisted in disbelief. "Boris? A soldier? I can't believe it! Why, he's middle-aged!" He stared at her, at the small child. "But you—he's left you here, to fend for yourself in a land at war with Russia?"

"He wanted us to come back with him," she said tersely. "But Arkady's sick. I really don't know what's wrong, and I didn't want to take him on any complicated journeys. I was hoping that our physician would return—I had such faith in Dr. Fröhlich!" Her eyes filled with tears of despair, and all at once, pathetically, she began to cry. "But it was such a mistake! Fröhlich won't be back now, not with the military commandeering all the trains. I should have risked a journey as far as Switzerland. There's a specialist in Lausanne of whom I've been hearing—a Dr. Combes, who is even more well known than Fröhlich. He's a pioneer in children's diseases."

Examining the baby, Pierre said in a stilted voice: "He's so like you, isn't he? Boris should never have abandoned him—abandoned you."

"I'm afraid I won't fight you on this," she whispered. "I'm so tired of being brave, and I'm not noble and good and heroic. I'm angry, and I hurt. You've no idea how much I resent Russia for joining the war." She tried to smile and quizzically regarded Pierre a moment. "Well?" she queried. "And why aren't you doing your part for the Tzar and Mother Russia?"

"I don't think this war will last," Pierre replied. "It's based on ridiculous premises. An archduke gets murdered, and the world is turned upside down. I was in The Hague—with Boris, in fact—in '07, and no one there wanted another war. I'm an artist, Natalia, not a fighter. I can't kill Germans just because they carry a different passport. Among them might be a Strauss or a Goethe. My heart's country is composed of creative people who do not waste their energies planning wars—or fighting in them. I'm not a hero, like your husband. And so I'm prepared to hole up here in the *Künstler Kolonie* until all this ends. They think I'm Swiss, anyway, so there's little danger to me personally. No one would think to check on my papers."

"Then your life is the simplest of all," she commented softly. "But then it always was, wasn't it? It never mattered to you how you achieved success, only that you obtained it. Perhaps you're right. What difference will it make a hundred years from now whether or not you were considered a coward by your compatriots? Posterity will only remember you for your great works. At best, you'd make a mediocre soldier, wouldn't you?"

"And at worst, a dead one," he agreed. She had abruptly moved toward the carriage, her face turned away from him, the baby held against her chest. He helped her in, avoiding her eyes. But he could not remove his hand from the horse's flank. Even with this child of another man's lovemaking, he felt, deep inside, a surge of possession for her. She's miserable and doesn't want me, and he'd seduced her emotions in his customary underhanded manner—the manner of an evil genius who alchemizes gold for himself out of another man's lead. But still, inexplicably, she belongs to me. A wave of anger and need passed over him. For a moment he almost jumped astride Olga in order to keep Natalia with him, but he restrained himself and stood aside as she gathered up the reins and drove away.

Pierre sat at his easel, working on a small reproduction of Natalia and Arkady. He had made a sketch of them after returning to his cottage, and now he felt compelled to complete it as a painting. He was angry and rebellious. Until Boris and Natalia he had been a person in his own right, a true artist, but for the last nine years he had been emotionally entangled and artistically enslaved, incapable of leading an independent life. Now he could not function without thinking of his patrons, without their interfering in his life.

Of course, Natalia was right; he had only himself to blame. He had selected his obsession and allowed it to engulf him. He could have parted from Boris in the very beginning. But Boris had shown him a tray of delights, tokens of an irresistible life, and Pierre, although resenting the offering and the obligation it incurred, had not turned away. Boris had danced around him in elaborate courtship, and Pierre had watched, fascinated. He had hated Boris but eventually, he had been conquered by Boris's charm, his brilliance, his money, his connections, and his way of life. Pierre was not guilt-free.

And Natalia? He'd chosen her, as Boris had chosen him. He had selfishly wanted her for himself. He'd felt betrayed by her rejection of him, but Boris had given her understanding and acceptance, which he had not—ever. In the end she had stopped loving him, Pierre, to love the man who had truly known her. Boris and Natalia had both left him because he had never tried to understand them. It hadn't seemed important!

It was a bitter fact. Pierre set down his paintbrush and felt a knot in his throat, pain from behind his eyes. He was miserably alone and angry and could not work. An artist could not produce when his heart was trapped like a hermit in a cave. Somehow, he thought with self-deprecation, I have never loved anyone but Pierre Riazhin, and now no one else gives a damn about me.

The little baby. My God, what a heartrending sight, with his enormous brown eyes, his soft hair, his translucent and pathetic frailty! He was Natalia's child—and the child of Boris Kussov.

Still, Pierre did not want the child to die. Something had to be done.

Pierre rose then and put on his jacket. He would have to try to set his house in order, come what may.

It had been one month since he had seen Natalia. Now, when he entered the inn in Zwingenberg, having discovered Natalia's whereabouts from some villagers, he could hardly think. His mind had given way to feelings of apprehension. Frau Walter seemed pleased that someone had come to visit "the *Gräfin*" and did not hesitate to show him the way to Natalia's rooms. He cleared his throat and asked: "The baby? Is he better?"

Frau Walter looked away, and Pierre felt his stomach sink. "Fräulein Bernhardt doesn't know what to do," the innkeeper's wife said in a muted whisper. "I've never seen a child go through such pain. He's been vomiting for several days now and looks purplish blue in the face. I'm afraid even Dr. Fröhlich, bless his heart, would feel quite helpless. It would take one of the leading medical minds of the century to figure it out—and that's what *she* thinks, too."

"He's that much worse?" Pierre asked in horror.

Frau Walter raised her brows and said nothing. They had arrived at the door to Natalia's rooms, and now the innkeeper knocked and called out: "*Gräfin!* There's a nice young man to see you, from Darmstadt."

She turned the knob and he stood looking at Natalia, his lips parting. She was thinner than he'd ever seen her, and her face was haggard and colorless. She was wearing a housecoat and appeared disheveled, her hair falling haphazardly about her shoulders. The innkeeper had disappeared, and now Pierre took her hands, his heart in his throat. "You're not well?" he murmured, tenderness coursing through him like hot liquid.

"I'm all right. Come in, Pierre." She did not seem surprised to see him, only weary, past caring. Pinpricks of anxiety shivered over him, and he did not know what to say.

Sitting down, she rested her head in her hands. Her voice muffled by her fingers, she said: "I've decided, Pierre. We're going to get out."

"How, Natalia?"

She looked at him, resembling her son in her pallor and ethereal fragility. "I don't know. I'll work it out somehow. But Arkady needs to go to Switzerland. It's no longer a question of whether or not he can stand a train trip. There's no choice: If he doesn't get proper treatment from a specialist like Dr. Combes, he'll die. It's as simple as that."

Her voice reverberated through him, its chilling matter-of-factness piercing through his emotions. He could not answer. She stood up listlessly. "I was such a fool," she said softly, "not to have listened to reason months ago. But no, I was afraid of the voyage. Boris knew better."

"If he did, then why didn't he stay here with you and force you both to leave with him?" Pierre cried out.

She looked at him coldly. "I wouldn't have gone," she replied simply. "God knows he tried to make me."

Pierre rose, and placed his hands on her shoulders. "Perhaps there's something I can do," he said finally. "Give me a few days."

She smiled weakly. "You don't have to, really. It was good of you to come, but we'll manage."

"I know. But I'd like to help."

Before she could reply, Pierre abruptly turned and left the room. An idea had formed, merging with the image of the child and the young mother as he had drawn them from memory. He had to try, even if nothing in his life could be changed by his effort. Love had to mean more than wanting to possess. He had to learn whether he really did love Natalia.

The Baroness von Baylen folded her hands in her lap with haughty impatience. "Pierre Grigorievitch," she said, "you wrote me about a problem. I have come. If you think it was easy—I had to take the car all the way from Berlin because the trains have been commandeered by the military."

"I know, Marguerite Stepanovna. I am most grateful."

"You have already placed me in a most precarious position. My husband is with the War Ministry. I am only a German by marriage and this house is in my name. I could have had you interned months ago, and should have. Now, if you make one wrong move, people here will learn that you are Russian, and it

288   is I who shall be interned as a traitor to my adopted country. My husband does not know that you are still here. When war broke out, I told him that you had not returned from a vacation in Switzerland. I am risking everything in order to protect your safety. What has gone wrong?"

"Don't worry, everything here is all right. People have accepted me a a permanent fixture in the *Künstler Kolonie*. I come and go with nobody paying me the slightest attention."

"At least that's a relief." Marguerite bit her lower lip and rubbed her hands together. She looked around the room. "All this," she murmured somewhat breathlessly, "for a few paintings a year."

Pierre winced. He knew exactly why the baroness had not revealed his identity at the outbreak of hostilities. There was no friendship between them. Neither of them, in fact, possessed any friends. Marguerite was very lonely, and her sponsorship of Pierre was the only reason why Berliners sought her out. True, her husband had an old aristocratic name and was well placed at the War Ministry; but now she had become a *grande dame* in her own right, a patroness. Probably she does not even like my work, and certainly she doesn't understand it, he thought wryly. But she feels that she helped launch me among the German nobility. I am her new toy.

Yet, in spite of his bitterness, he felt sorry for her. She was like a rabbit, ferreting about for a sense of self that would forever elude her. She was spoiled and manipulative, but not very intelligent, and basically harmless. That a person like this had ever yearned for a life side by side with Boris Kussov . . . It seemed incredible. And yet, Pierre knew that after he had left Kiev in 1912, she had written to ask Countess Brianskaya details about him, and that Boris's patronage of him had of course been mentioned. Marguerite had made up her mind then: She had to have Riazhin, to take something that had once belonged to her ex-husband.

So you too, he thought, cannot let go of the Kussov mystique. Aloud he said: "I know what trouble you went to on my account, Marguerite Stepanovna. Sometime soon my work will reward you. I have already begun two large canvases for either side of your mantelpiece in Berlin. I hope you will like them."

He stood up, and she followed him into his workroom, where he pointed to a magnificent landscape of hills and valleys in full summer bloom. She had been thrown off-balance by his change of topic. She blinked, swallowed, and touched her topknot. "Yes," she said, "it's very pretty, Pierre Grigorievitch. The effect is overpowering—one can almost smell the flowers."

He smiled. "Good. That's what I'd planned." He made a gesture for her to return to the drawing room, and she acquiesced, preceding him through the door. Only when they were seated once more did he begin to speak about what was on his mind.

"The problem isn't with me, Marguerite Stepanovna. You have been most good to me. But there is someone else who is in trouble—a young woman, with a sick child. Like me, and like you, too, before your marriage, she is Russian. But she needs to go to Switzerland to consult a doctor there for her son." He licked his lips, avoiding her pale blue gaze. "I thought, perhaps, you might be able to help her."

Marguerite von Baylen stood up, overturning an ashtray on a small side table. Quick color surged to her cheekbones. "Pierre Grigorievitch, you must be mad!" she exclaimed. "I told you—my husband has no idea that you're still here! Why should I help this woman? I don't even know her! And how? What would you have me do?"

"I am certain that among your connections others have helped aliens in similar straits. She would need false papers and transportation. I did not know whom to ask but you. The situation is grave. Wouldn't your husband, such a good man, have compassion?"

Marguerite began to laugh, the breathless, somewhat hysterical sound ricocheting off the walls of the room. "Pierre Grigorievitch, you are so naïve!" she cried. "To think that a member of the War Ministry would put his position on the line to help a total stranger! Truly, you know nothing of politics. My husband is kind, of course. But he has a job to do, and what you ask would be tantamount to betraying his country!"

"A small favor in the matter of a harmless woman and child would be nothing so serious as what you imply," Pierre retorted, his own face flushing. He stood up and began to pace the room, pressing his fists to his sides. Finally he turned to her, his black eyes blazing. "Damn it!" he burst out, "have all decent human beings turned into stones now that some silly men with paper crowns have decided to play King of the Mountain? I'm talking to you about a pathetic child of seven months, a child who may not survive his illness unless he can reach Switzerland in time! And you speak to me of politics! For God's sake, what is happening to everyone? Has the entire world gone berserk?"

She took a step backward, her thin lips stretching over her teeth in a grimace of nervous fear. She shook her head. "No! I can't do anything! I won't do anything! It's bad enough for me, a native of Russia. In Berlin there are those who won't receive me now because they consider me an enemy. It's just the way it was in Kiev, when I returned—from *there*. Nobody wanted to have anything to do with me. I can't have that—not again! Not for you. I shouldn't have come, but I was afraid they'd found you out, that it would get back to Fritz, your being here in this house! Call my chauffeur, Pierre Grigorievitch. I'm leaving now."

In her effort to grab her coat, she pushed past him into a small bedroom, where she had seen him deposit her wraps. There, on the table, stood an unfinished miniature painting of a pale young woman with large, almond-shaped brown eyes, her soft hair in a simple upsweep, a child in her arms, with a similar intense, unsmiling face. Marguerite stood staring at the portrait, her eyes wide. She uttered a small, sharp cry. Then, wildly, she seized the coat, bag, and hat and ran into the front room.

"It's *her!*" she exclaimed. "It was for her that you wanted me to come all the way from Berlin? For her that Fritz should jeopardize his career and I my marriage? And the child? Whose child is it? Pierre Grigorievitch? *His?* Boris's?"

Mutely, he nodded. There was such intense hatred in the baroness's face that he literally could not speak She uttered a quick giggle, like a hiccup, and then, at the door, cried: "I hope the child dies! I hope Germany kills it. Indeed, I know it shall—I'll make certain it does. Boris Kussov and that woman had no right to have a child, and they've no right to keep it!" She opened the door before he could stop her.

He watched from the window as the chauffeur deferentially

helped her into the shining black Rolls-Royce and as the majestic car took off, incongruous on the winding street of the *Künstler Kolonie.* He could hardly breathe for the crushing weight of anger inside his chect. How could he have been so stupid? How could he? But then, one did not often run up against such vengeful hysterics as the Baroness von Baylen. He could not have anticipated her lasting hatred for Natalia. Yet, he had been in Paris in 1909. He should have predicted her reaction.

It was all his fault, he thought and crushed his hands together until the bones of his fingers hurt. He had stupidly endangered Natalia's life! He should have realized that Marguerite was not completely normal, that her hatred of Boris and Natalia had always been tinged with derangement. Why hadn't he analyzed the situation more clearly?

Dear God, he said to himself, I shall have to do something drastic now, or I shall never be able to sleep again.

Chapter 17

Terror had knotted her back into a tense plane, and paralyzed her thoughts. Still, there was no choice. She pressed the button of the enormous gate and waited. There could be no looking back.

It was cold for an October evening, and she pulled the fur hat over her ears, readjusting the collar of her coat. Presently a colossus of a master sergeant came lumbering across the Exerzierplatz and, seeing only a diminutive woman in elegant mink, was momentarily taken aback. Natalia raised her large eyes to him and smiled. "I have come to see Lieutenant Püder," she said clearly, pleasantly, in her best German. "Lieutenant Heinrich Püder."

The sergeant blinked. "And he's expecting you, *gnädige Frau?*"

She nodded agreeably. The large door began to swing open, just enough to permit her access into the military enclave. She passed through and followed the sergeant across the now empty square to one of the low administration buildings. "The lieutenant is probably at dinner," her guide said to her, showing her into a reception hall with sofas, chairs, and a billiard table in one corner. "I can fetch him for you if you'll tell me whom to announce."

Natalia shook her head. "I'd prefer to surprise him," she said, and added quickly: "He didn't know exactly *when* to expect me." She smiled knowingly.

When the master sergeant had retreated, Natalia sat down in

one of the armchairs and clasped her hands in her lap. What if he had her interned at once? She had rehearsed their conversation time and time again, and she felt panic, but also relief that the lieutenant had not already departed for the battlefront. She knew exactly what she would say. Now she needed the strength to carry it off.

All at once, she was drawn from her self-absorption by the sound of heels clicking on the parquet floor. She rose, blushing. Lieutenant Püder stood before her, with his ribbons, his broad chest, his flaxen hair and his eyes of periwinkle blue. He seemed a parody of Boris—a bleached version. He was not an ugly man, but simply a man, whereas Boris was a Machiavellian deity lifted from the Renaissance and ancient Greece. This was a man of today, facing her with surprise, raising his eyebrows.

"I know it was presumptuous of me to think you might remember," she said quickly. "It was in Exerzierplatz—"

A smile spread over his features, and he bowed from the waist, a quick Teutonic bow. "Yes, of course. The pretty lady who was nearly trampled to death. I am surprised, however: I thought that surely you would not wish to see me or my men again."

"I was rude to you," she said, gasping. "I'm sorry." Suddenly she didn't think she could continue this charade, and she waited for the blow to fall from somewhere. But Lieutenant Heinrich Püder motioned for her to sit down, and gratefully she sank into the armchair.

He took a seat facing her on a couch. "I am flattered," he said, "that you recall my name. How is your son? A handsome boy. His father must be proud of him." There was the question, brought into the open but tactfully stated.

She fought back a desire to burst into tears, and, looking at his boots while pressing back the weeping, she whispered: "There is no father. I am a widow. And my son is not at all well. I'm afraid he's going to die, and that's why I came here, bothering you, disturbing the sergeant. I hoped you might help me."

Heinrich Püder said: "I'm sorry about your husband, and about the boy. What can I do?" Clearly, he seemed bewildered that a strange woman from out of nowhere was suddenly appealing to him, and he regarded her with curiosity. "Have I seen you before, *gnädige Frau?*" he asked, narrowing his eyes.

She had built her life around dancing, carving an identity from it, making it her banner. She thought quickly: What can I lose? Perhaps this will help. She cleared her throat and said: "It's possible, if you live in Munich or Berlin and go to the ballet. I am a dancer."

He started to laugh. "But not a German dancer. I would not have remembered you then."

They sat staring at each other, and his smile faded. She said: "A Russian."

"Ah. Your German is good, *gnädige Frau.* I saw the Ballets Russes at the Theater des Westens, in Charlottenburg, in '11. The next year, too. Now since you are not Nijinsky, who are you? Russian names are complicated for us Teutons, especially the female versions."

Behind his easy words she sensed a calculating coldness. She said: "I am Natalia Oblonova. I never expected to be dealing with a balletomane."

"We Germans are not all boors and rustics," he demurred. "But what can I do for you, Frau Oblonova? Why are you in Darmstadt?"

"My son was ill." Aiming her beautiful eyes at him with sudden intensity, she added quickly: "He was born here. I am a Russian—but I suppose he has an option, doesn't he? I mean, later at his majority, he will be able to choose which nationality he wants—won't he? So it's only I who am an enemy alien."

Lieutenant Püder nodded carefully. "Indeed. Why are you telling me this?"

"Because I need to take him to see a doctor in Switzerland—in Lausanne. We must get out, for if we don't he'll die without care. Dr. Combes could save him. We don't have a visa, and besides the trains are no longer at the disposal of civilians, are they? I don't know what to do. Will you help me?" She licked her lips and looked away. "I have money," she added in a whisper.

"Oh? A ballerina's salary?" He seemed amused.

"My husband was a wealthy man." Already she knew what he

was thinking: There had been no husband. The Berliners had treated the dancers like circus acrobats, skilled and beautiful but below them on the social scale. One chose one's mistresses from among the dancers but not one's wife. Suddenly Natalia did not care what Püder thought. The point was that there was money.

"I am desperate," she said. "Otherwise I would not have come to a person I did not know. You struck me as a kind man, Lieutenant. I shall pay whatever you deem necessary for the privilege of space on a train—and a visa. I would give my own life so that my son could reach the doctor, but that would be rather silly, as I need to be alive in order to help him. So I have come to you. If you turn me in to the police, I shall understand."

He stood up and inclined his head. "You are an interesting woman, Frau Oblonova. I don't know how I could do what you ask, but I shan't turn you in. There are men of honor here, too, *gnädige Frau*. Perhaps you would permit me to take you to dinner tomorrow? Our regiment leaves in one week."

She rose then also and felt his eyes appraising her slender figure encased in the expensive furs. She had worn them on purpose, to leave no doubt as to her finances. Now she raised her eyes to his and smiled. "Of course," she replied, extending her hand to him. "I shall be glad to dine with you. I am staying at the inn in Zwingenberg."

Heinrich Püder took the proffered hand and brought it to his lips—another parody of the gallant Boris, this one stiff and formal, whereas the real Boris was graceful and ironic. "Kemmel will escort you out, *gnädige Frau*," he said. "I shall call on you tomorrow, then. *Auf Wiedersehen*."

Turning to leave, she thought: It's done. Even if they come to arrest me tomorrow, I had to risk it.

If Frau and Herr Walter were surprised that, for the first time since Boris's departure, Natalia was going out to dinner—and if their surprise was compounded by the fact that her escort was a German officer—they did not embarrass her with questions. Frau Walter merely came to the small sitting room with her knitting, and sat down near the cot where Arkady slept. She raised her eyes doubtfully to her young friend, as if to say: But you are an illegal alien! But When Natalia pressed her hand and smiled at her, the innkeeper kept quiet.

Lieutenant Heinrich Püder seemed impressed with the loveliness of his companion. He found her waiting for him in a pink hobble skirt revealing dainty ankles and patent leather slippers, and a jacket trimmed with white ermine. Her small hat was tilted to the right and adorned with osprey feathers. At her throat gleamed rubies and diamonds. She took his arm and followed him to the sleek black car in which an enlisted man served as chauffeur, and he drove them to a restaurant on top of the Ludwigshöhe, one of the hills overlooking Darmstadt. "The food is delicious here," he said to her, and she thought, her heart twisting viciously: I've been here with Boris! It was here that he began to hate me, thinking that I wouldn't leave this place because of Pierre—when all along it was because of Arkady. She was miserable, remembering.

Then, abruptly, a new thought jarred her: What if the management remembered her coming with Boris? Who could have forgotten Boris, elegant and distinguished? But perhaps no one would think to remember her. Unlike her husband, she was not striking on first notice. It was only the third or fourth time that people became aware of her subtle beauty.

But the waiters said nothing to distress her. In his stiff style Lieutenant Püder was rather charming. He spoke to her about himself; his uncle had been a career officer, General von Wedekind, and Heinrich had followed in his footsteps. Now this uncle was deceased; still, the family honored his memory. They were well-to-do Prussian burghers, and his mother had been a baroness, a *Freiherrin*. They lived in Berlin in a large gilded mansion on Unter den Linden, the majestic tree-bordered avenue leading to the Brandenburg Gate and the Tiergarten beyond it. He admired Strauss and loved Wagner. He had enjoyed the Ballets Russes of Serge Diaghilev.

He did not tell her about the slim, dark girl called Grethe whom he had loved, and about the time he had taken her to the lodge in the mountains and made love to her. Grethe, who had been a waitress, had run away when she had learned that she was pregnant with his child. He said nothing of his guilt to

Natalia, this cool, sophisticated woman facing him, whose delicate shapeliness, in some small way, reminded him of his lost
love. He'd been so young—a student still, and irresponsible. A
Püder could sleep with Grethe, but never take her home to the
baroness. And Natalia Oblonova? Her child was gravely ill.
Where was Grethe's child—his child? He looked at Natalia and
felt an ache inside, an ache that had slumbered for nearly two
decades. If she offered herself to him later on, he would certainly not reject her—such a beautiful woman!—but it was the
idea of the child that pushed to the forefront of his mind now,
blotting out the other consideration.

He questioned her about St. Peterburg, and she spoke freely
of the people she had met: the Grand-Duke Vladimir; the British ambassador, Buchanan; the Tzarina and the dowager empress; Chaliapin and Kchessinskaya. He was duly impressed.
"All this as a soloist of the first degree?" he asked.

"No," she replied. "I told you I was married. My husband
was a member of the court and also a patron of the arts. But I
prefer not to speak of him; like your beloved uncle von Wedekind, he is gone."

Her words did not brook further questioning: They had
clinched the matter. If he had thought her a wanton woman,
her statement had the effect of dispelling that assumption. But
he had behaved impeccably, and she felt in control. Over dessert she leaned forward and said in a low voice: "Have you
thought about how you might help me, Herr Püder? My son is
very ill indeed."

"There could be a way," he answered, touching his mustache. Boris's mustache was graceful and golden; Püder's was as
stiff as he was. He looked away and continued: "My uncle was a
well-respected man, *gnädige Frau*. He had a daughter. Perhaps
I could obtain false papers in her name—and you would be my
cousin, Hildegard Mannteuffel. In certain cases relations of
officers are allowed to travel in trains normally reserved for the
military. I am the second in command of my company and am
rather junior. But my family connection would help. My colonel might let you and your son on board if I presented him with
an emergency."

She closed her eyes, relief flooding over her. Then, slowly, she reached behind her neck and unfastened the clasp of her necklace. Without a word, she placed it before Püder. Rubies and diamonds sparkled in the soft yellow glow of the candles adorning the table. "Will this be sufficient for the false papers?" she asked. "I would prefer to keep my cash reserve intact, for when I reach Switzerland."

Püder smiled. He picked up the jewels and examined them curiously. "Your husband must have loved you very much," he commented softly.

She winced and looked away. "Yes," she replied. "I think so."

Calmly, he pocketed the necklace and called for the waiter. "I am not money-hungry, *gnädige Frau*," he told her. "But I shall need these to bribe a good printer of identification cards and passports. We—our regiment—are going to the front in eastern France, and there I shall have to make further arrangements for you and the child to reach Switzerland. We will part company, but I shall attempt to find you a car of some sort and a trustworthy driver." He touched his pocket. "These will be most useful then, too. I am going to sell them, if you don't mind. Let me handle the details concerning payments and papers."

"I am most grateful to you," she murmured, tears springing to her eyes. She stood up to leave with him and felt dizzy. Outside the air felt good.

When she entered her sitting room at the inn, she said to Frau Walter: "Everything will be all right. Could you get my money together? Arkady and I shall be leaving Germany within a week. We'll miss you, dear friend—but when this is all over, we will come here again, for a vacation: my husband, my son, and I."

Natalia said to Pierre: "So I have come to say good-bye. All the arrangements have been completed, thanks to Heinrich Püder. I am to travel on the same train as the regiment, in the compartment reserved for family members. I am to be Frau Hildegard Mannteuffel, daughter of the deceased General von Wedekind and the good lieutenant's cousin. His colonel didn't object, and my papers and Arkady's are in order."

"You've taken so much on yourself," Pierre Pierre commented, his brow furrowed.

"I have no choice," she said dryly. They were sitting in his drawing room, on the dark chairs. Looking at him carefully, she added: "And you? Are you going to last the war hiding out in Darmstadt?"

His nostrils quivered slightly, and color rose to his cheeks. "You were going to do the same," he retorted.

He got up and began to pace the room, a panther on the prowl. She saw his strong thighs bristling beneath the broadcloth. Once she had loved him. Now she could hardly remember a life before Arkady, before this wretched war and his growing illness. She had no time for feelings or recriminations. Not even time to think of Boris, to consider him while making her plans.

Pierre stopped abruptly. "I'm glad you're leaving, Natalia," he said. "Maybe I'll have to go as well. The Baroness von Baylen is not happy with me. I—" He stopped. His stupidity was not worth revealing; she would only despise him all the more. Instead, he came to her and took her hand. "When do you leave?" he asked.

"Tomorrow."

She did not withdraw her hand, and he began to caress it rhythmically. Such a small hand, such a small woman. Yet not a helpless one. Nonetheless . . . "Good luck, Pierre," she said. She stood on her tiptoes and kissed his cheek. "Think of us?"

"I won't promise to pray," he said, trying to be facetious. "I know you don't believe in God."

"No. Only in myself. I hope that belief isn't misguided." She smiled and prepared to depart. She did not know that he had been painting her portrait, a third one since the Sugar Plum nine years before, nor that this one also included her son, Arkady. He did not tell her because he intended to keep this picture himself. Instead, he held her coat out for her and walked her to the buggy. Olga, the mare, was waiting.

He knew then what he had to do and was unafraid.

The neat Hessian station was stark in the predawn bleakness. Troops stood about, exhausted from waiting for the train to load, their trim uniforms a sharp contrast to their apprehensive faces. Natalia stood on the platform to the far right of the men, holding Arkady in her arms. She was dressed in a simple woolen coat and a small felt hat. Her furs and jewels had been packed away, and the bags were even now being hoisted onto the train.

Men all resemble babies before they go to war, she thought ironically. She leaned against a pole and shut her eyes. Within the week this would be over. From Switzerland she would write to Nina and her father-in-law, and they in turn would be able to send a message to Boris, to inform him of where she and the boy had gone. He, too, would be relieved to know they were in neutral territory, near a specialist in children's diseases.

She did not see a tall, dark-haired man in a nondescript gabardine coat weaving his way toward the station house. There were so many people on the platform that no one noticed him at all. Unobtrusively he entered the small terminal and looked about him. A small group of engineers, brakemen, and conductors sat drinking coffee and playing cards. He watched them from his position near a rear door by the wall and waited.

Presently one of the brakemen rose from the table and ambled toward the men's lavatory. The man in the gabardine coat followed him. In the small antechamber he stopped the brakeman and said to him: "I am a Swiss citizen, but I've lost my papers. I need to get on this train without anyone's finding out. If you can help me—" He withdrew from his pocket a pair of gold cufflinks with ruby studs, a stick pin encrusted with an enormous black pearl, and a wad of bills.

The brakeman blinked in astonishment. He appraised the man in the gabardine coat: His eyes were black, the pupils merging with the irises. He was swarthy and strongly built, but unquestionably a gentleman. The jewels were magnificent and the wad a thick one. He scratched his head, wondering. If the man were mad, he might kill him with his bare hands; from the look of him he was a veritable bull. But if he were simply a wealthy refugee . . . Wartime had not yet made the Germans prosperous. He coughed. "Maybe," he said grudgingly. "Wait here."

Pierre was left standing in the antechamber. Perhaps, thought the young painter, I am going to be delivered posthaste to the general in charge of this convoy. But I've got to risk it. Besides, *la* von Baylen could hurtle into hysteria and have me arrested. She's hated Natalia because she touched Boris, and why shouldn't she now hate me for in some way touching Natalia's life? He sank against the wall, anxiety penetrating to his very entrails.

But the brakeman was returning, carrying a knapsack. "Here is my change of clothing," he whispered tersely, withdrawing a railroad uniform from the bag. "Change into this, and give me your clothes."

There was no choice. Pierre hastily undressed, handing the man his coat, his shirt, his trousers—and the pocket watch. Clearly this was to be part of the bargain. But when the brakeman was about to pack his things away, Pierre put a hand out to stop him. "There's something I'd like to keep," he said. He fumbled with the inside pocket of his coat and took out the small miniature of Natalia and Arkady Kussov. Unframed, barely finished, it had fit into the pocket without causing him too much discomfort, for it was only five by seven inches. It had been a stroke of luck to make it such a small painting, a private memento.

The brakeman shrugged: This was a madman, all right, hanging onto a reproduction in the midst of a crisis. Madmen came in all shapes and sizes, but some of them had means and could be indulged. The danger was not that great. If someone— a soldier—were to find the man in the railroad uniform, he, Geiser, would simply say his knapsack had been stolen. The only problem lay in getting the man aboard. But he had an idea.

Going out the back door with Pierre in his uniform, Geiser walked to the front of the train under everyone's eyes. Nobody paid attention to these two crew members. Geiser and Pierre climbed aboard. "The fellows would've been the only ones to know you're not one of us," he whispered to Pierre, "and they're still playing cards." They had reached a small door, and now the brakeman opened it, and Pierre saw a cramped men's toilet. "You're going to have to live in here for the next few days," Geiser said. "Now get in. I'm going to find you some food, because once the train starts I won't be able to bring you anything. Too risky."

Pierre walked in, and Geiser shut the door on him and locked it. The crude accommodations stank, and he could hardly stand up because the ceiling was so low. He sat down on the commode and tried to stretch his legs, but could not. Yet, he felt strangely elated. An incongruous vision of himself as a lad in Georgia passed through his mind: of himself on a stallion, riding the winds. Actually, the memory was not so incongruous. This was his life: not the dull propriety of Marguerite's cottage, or even the dinner parties at Boris's flat. He was not a member of the *jeunesse dorée*, but of the Caucasian wilds. This, at least, was a ride to freedom, a risk.

When he heard a key turn in the lock, Pierre reared his head quickly, his adrenaline flowing freely. But it was only Geiser, bringing raisins, water, two lemons, and some dry beef—a paltry supply. "That's all I can get without rousing suspicions," the brakeman said defiantly, as if reading Pierre's mind. "Now listen here: I've put up the 'Out of Order' sign, and I'm going to tell the fellows that we have a backed-up toilet. We're going to have our hands full with this convoy, so I know no one will try to fix it before we reach France. Just don't make any noise."

This time when the door locked, Pierre thought: When I get out, we'll be in the war zone. How will I find out if she's all right? He added to himself: Only in the midst of such a conflict would the meticulous German army accept the fact of a nonfunctioning toilet. When men are about to offer their lives for their country, the indignity of backed-up facilities recedes to a mere inconvenience. He began to laugh, soundlessly.

Boris would have enjoyed the irony of Pierre's predicament. But he, Boris, did not live life, he dabbled in it. It was a game for him, a charade. But for me, Pierre thought grimly, it is simply life.

The train was filled to the brim. Soldiers and officers jostled one another in the hallways and crowded the compartments. At least cattle are incapable of feeling or thinking in their boxcars, Natalia thought with bitterness. With her special military dispensation, she sat in the officers' car, the only woman among a company of two hundred fifty men off to the front in eastern France. Heinrich Püder, next to her, had explained to his comrades that his cousin, Frau Hildegard Mannteuffel, was going to Switzerland to consult a doctor for her child, and so no one bothered her, a concerned, exhausted young mother on a mission of pain and anguish. She was grateful.

There had been a single instant of panic. Püder's own colonel had unexpectedly remained behind, and another, not normally attached to the group going westward, was now at the head of this company for the duration of the voyage. He traveled in a private car, but Natalia had seen him at the station in Darmstadt: a tall, thickset man some forty-five years old, with wiry black hair and small blue eyes like marbles. A paunch struggled beneath the trim uniform. Natalia had seen Püder's surprise and been frozen with terror when the senior officer approached her, clicking his heels and bowing over her hand, his hard eyes glittering at her. He had said: "What a rare pleasure, *gnädige Frau*, to meet you at last! I much admired your father, the great general."

"I could not have known that they would send Lothar Ballhausen," Püder told her afterward in a frantic whisper. "But he can't hurt you if you stay away and don't hold lengthy conversations with him. I knew him in Berlin, and he served for a while under my uncle. He has the reputation of being a highly skilled combat technician."

Damn, she thought. The regular colonel had known nothing personal about von Wedekind, whose exploits had taken him far from this branch of the army, and Püder, her benefactor, had not found it necessary to brief her in particulars concerning her "father." But Heinrich Püder could not always remain by her side. He had to keep an eye on his platoons and report to Ballhausen. It was up to her.

Now she was too numb to feel horror. Fear was such a part of her existence that she could only think one step at a time, one minute at a time. Every nerve ending was alert, every muscle taut. When Püder left, she fell into a kind of stupor and closed her eyes, hoping that the other officers would witness her distress and leave her tactfully alone, without attempting to engage her in dangerous conversation. Why hadn't Püder been a simple lieutenant with undistinguished relatives, instead of a man whose uncle had been a well-known general? She hoped that these men were too young to have known von Wedekind.

Truly, she thought, Püder was a good man. If anyone were to learn of the deception, not only would his career come to an abrupt stop, but he might even be accused of treason. Why was he helping her? He was certainly behaving properly. She decided that this must be the first time a woman in distress had appealed to him—and that few men, especially among those who led lives of rigid conformity, could resist being cast in the role of Sir Galahad. She smiled then, amused in spite of the danger.

Arkady lay asleep in her arms, a restless sleep punctuated by small gasps. The fingers that touched her shoulder startled her, and she looked up, expecting Püder. To her surprise, it was Colonel Ballhausen. Her hand reached out to Arkady's head and remained there, protectively.

"The babe is well?" Ballhausen asked.

Natalia could not speak. Why had Püder allowed Ballhausen to come without accompanying him? She tried to smile. "He just slept for an hour," she replied.

"Then let us step outside for a moment, Frau Mannteuffel. Enlisted men don't crowd the area outside the officers' compartment. We could talk for a while."

Uncertainly, with Arkady in her arms, Natalia rose to follow him into the corridor. His face was square, uncompromising. He leaned against the window and looked at her. A sergeant walked by and she had to move to make way for him, brushing next to Ballhausen in the process. When he had gone, she stepped back, avoiding body contact.

"Heinrich is a fine officer," Ballhausen said pleasantly. "I am lucky to have him so conveniently on board."

"He is a fine man in every way," Natalia said warmly.

Ballhausen smiled. "Ah, yes, of course you would think that, being his cousin. What was it like growing up with him?"

"He was good and kind to me, like an older brother." Natalia spoke calmly, but her throat was constricted with fear, a wild, animal apprehension.

"You must have grieved a long time for your revered father," Ballhausen continued. "General von Wedekind's heart attack shocked everyone."

This time, Natalia turned her face to him and allowed the tears to rise to the surface of her large brown eyes. "Please," she said with genuine pleading, "I would prefer not to discuss it. It is still too painful."

"Naturally, *gnädige Frau*. I am a boor." Ballhausen was silent for a while, and for Natalia, these minutes ticked off into hours, the hours before a certain execution. "The babe is going to Lausanne to see a specialist?" he said at length.

"Yes. It was so kind of you to let us onto the train, Colonel."

"It was a pleasure. Beautiful women adorn a convoy, Frau Mannteuffel."

She smiled wanly, and then, to her infinite relief, Arkady started to toss about in her arms and began to cry. "I'll have to sit down again," she said, holding him tightly and looking nervously at Ballhausen. "It was nice to chat."

"I have a comfortable car. Next time you must allow me to offer you a small collation there. It is less crowded. I take my meals there, with one or two other officers. Do you drink cognac, *gnädige Frau?*"

Without thinking, she nodded, her face white and lifeless. Ballhausen started to laugh. "Heinrich hadn't told me his cousin was spirited!" he cried. "But I like that! I have some marvelous Napoleon: You will enjoy it."

But she had already turned and gone back into her own compartment. He stared after her, the smile fading from his face.

Natalia rocked Arkady in her arms. His face was streaked with tears, and he refused to drink from the bottle of condensed milk. He cried and cried, his whimpers becoming more frenzied. Fear crept up Natalia's chest and rose into her throat, choking her. To reassure him with the sound of her voice, she said, in the unfamiliar German words: "Soon, *Liebchen*, soon. You'll feel better."

This was not good, this crying. Already she had disturbed everyone in her compartment and attracted undue attention. She scooped the frail, struggling Arkady into her arms and pushed into the hall, which smelled of garlic and sausage. Püder was nowhere to be seen.

Outside, the scenery had shifted. The train was slowing down, pulling into a station—Baden-Baden. They were going south into the Black Forest. Natalia looked out the window, remembering how people used to stop here to take the waters. Now she wished they were not stopping at all.

A group of German military police were coming toward the train, and she saw them being directed to Ballhausen's private car. Then, bored, weary and lonely, Natalia looked away, paying them no more attention. Army red tape continued on and on.

Ballhausen's private car was several compartments away, Püder was with him when the knock came, and when he saw the military policemen, he said to his superior: "Whatever it is, I can handle it, sir. Last time we were held up by a munitions check. Shall I see to it?"

"Very well, Heinrich," the colonel replied with some asperity. He did not like being interrupted for technicalities. Püder clicked his heels, saluted, and exited from the car to the corridor.

"Now, gentlemen, let us step outside and discuss your problem," he said. He followed the small group back out to the station platform.

The four members of the military patrol and Lieutenant Heinrich Püder stood directly below Pierre Riazhin's hiding place. One of the men said: "I beg your pardon, sir. This matter is hardly a customary military check, but we've had this letter from the War Ministry, and so we have to comply."

Püder extended his hand and took the paper. His blue eyes scanned it once, twice. "This is absurd!" he said at length. "We're a military convoy on our way to the front. Surely you don't think we could have a woman on board whose presence we knew nothing about? Among two hundred and fifty men?"

"But we were told that you do have a female passenger with you," the military policeman demurred.

"Indeed. My cousin, Frau Mannteuffel, the daughter of

General von Wedekind. She carries a special dispensation. Would you care to check its authenticity?"

The other voice reached Pierre, clear and polite: "Of course not, Lieutenant. Forgive us, but we had to go along with our orders. This paper, signed by Baron Friedrich von Baylen, states that several weeks ago a woman of this description was seen in the company of an officer of your regiment in Darmstadt. Now this woman, a Russian countess, is being sought by the government in Berlin for internment. Her husband is an important man, and it might be possible to negotiate a trade of prisoners with Russia if we can find her. As you've read yourself, sir, she's disappeared with her young son. Our only lead is this officer."

"A German officer would not help an enemy alien," Püder stated dryly. "Certainly no one of this company. Who gave information to that effect?"

"After the arrest report came out, we combed the area of Darmstadt. No one seemed to remember her, except some waiters at a restaurant on one of the cliffs. Two people had dined there, a German officer and this lady. They remembered the insignia of the company on the man's sleeve and although they didn't see a child, the woman they served that evening struck them because of the magnificent jewels around her neck."

"Flimsy evidence," Püder commented ironically. "I myself have taken beautiful ladies for an evening's outing. That is hardly proof of treason."

"I suppose you're right, Lieutenant," the other voice said. Pierre felt the hair on his arms and legs bristle. His throat was knotted. At least, he thought, she has a guardian angel. But why is this man risking so much? I should be taking the risks, not this stranger with the formal Prussian voice! That damned Marguerite! Damned Boris, who started it all! He clenched his fist and felt hot sweat break out under his arms and neck. He couldn't stop his recriminations, the round robin of hatred.

"I understand your predicament," Püder was saying. "Naturally, if you wish to be reassured as to my cousin's identity, you are welcome on board. But she is very tired, so please confine your questions to the minimum."

Pierre was shocked: Why couldn't the man have left well

enough alone? Now the entire group was climbing back into the train. Helpless as a caged tiger, Pierre rammed his fists into the sides of his body and gritted his teeth.

Passing by the colonel's car, Püder saw that the door was ajar. Ballhausen called to him, and he stepped inside. "What's all this about?" his superior asked him.

"Nothing important, sir. A routine check of Hilde's papers. Women," he added with a smile, "don't often travel with military convoys."

"No, they don't." Lothar Ballhausen's small blue eyes stared at him.

Püder saluted and proceeded toward Natalia's car. He encountered her in the corridor, with Arkady in her arms. Her brown eyes widened with unspoken terror. He said gently: "Hilde, my dear, these men don't wish to disturb you. They simply wish to check your military dispensation." As her lips parted, he said to the military policemen: "Now, even my own cousin has brown hair and eyes. Really, your trail of clues is somewhat ludicrous, gentlemen. Will you suspect each German brunette of being a Russian countess in flight?"

Absurdly, while allowing Püder to look through her bag to unearth her papers, Natalia began to laugh. It was a short, hysterical gurgle, more like a death rattle than a sound of mirth. Arkady looked at her, bewildered. She touched the top of his head, so soft and vulnerable, and tried to regain her composure. But the men were examining the documents, and then they nodded and allowed Püder to escort them out to the platform a second time. To Natalia it was a nightmare.

She leaned against the wall, shutting her eyes. Arkady began to cry, her heart was pounding painfully, her knees weakening. Perhaps it would have been better simply to let him die in Darmstadt. Who was to say this voyage, with its unpredictable outcome, might not kill him anyway? I never should have allowed myself to conceive you, she thought with sudden fierceness. I should never have opened myself to Boris, of all men. I did not want to love, I did not want marriage, I never wished for children. Dancing was enough. She looked at the small boy, her heart full of resentment fostered by terror and nervous tension.

"You told me you were a widow, that your name was Oblonova," Heinrich Püder was saying to her in a low voice at her elbow. "Now it seems I have placed myself in jeopardy for a far more important enemy—the Countess Kussova. Why didn't you tell me the truth?"

She looked up at him, her eyes filled with such sadness, such anguish that he fell silent. "It was only a small lie," she said. "But you might not have helped the Countess Kussova, and my son would not now be on his way to safety."

"Helping you was a matter of honor," he said gravely. "Any man worth his mettle would have come to your rescue for the sake of a sick infant. But I am also a romantic: I did not really believe that your son had a father, that the lovely Oblonova was truly married. Women of the stage. . . . How wrong I was, wasn't I?" He smiled ruefully and added: "And I had thought surely that the lovely Oblonova would remember a humble soldier on a train."

Natalia did not answer. Raising herself on tiptoes, being careful not to crush Arkady, she reached Püder's lips and met them with her own in a swift, brief kiss. "How could she not remember?" she whispered.

The note that the young second lieutenant had just handed her read: "Dear Frau Mannteuffel, I should be most honored if you would join me for an aperitif in my compartment. It is the least I can do for the cousin of such a fine officer as Heinrich Püder and for the daughter of my mentor, General von Wedekind." The signature was curiously flowery.

Natalia remained frozen on her seat. "*Gnädige Frau*, the colonel is waiting," the young man said with hesitant insistency.

"I shall have to take the baby," Natalia said. "He can't stay here without me." The lieutenant appeared surprised but said nothing. He held the door of the compartment open for her, and the three of them proceeded down the corridor. She had never seen this officer before, but it hardly mattered.

Natalia knew that now they were speeding westward on the noisy train. Already they had entered occupied France, and the names of the stations had begun to change into that odd German-French blend that characterized Alsace and Lorraine.

310   The lieutenant led the way into a noisy passageway connecting two cars, and Arkady, seeing the rails below his mother's feet, began to screech. She calmed him with a touch of her cool hand.

"Here we are, *gnädige Frau*," the young man said, stopping at a door. He knocked and, upon hearing a voice from inside, opened it, clicked his heels, saluted, and quickly departed. Natalia saw that the car was luxuriously upholstered, like a prewar Pullman. A table had been set up with bottles on it and a tray heaped with small sandwiches. Suddenly Natalia realized how hungry she was. She stopped inside. Her host rose to greet her, smiling. It was difficult to read the expression on his face, which was diffused with small veinules and enlarged pores. Some men did not enter their middle years with grace. "Set the boy down there on the seat, and tell me about yourself. Have you been married long?" He moved aside some papers to make room for Arkady and helped her to settle him on the cushion. He handed her the plate of sandwiches and she selected one, not looking at him.

She had to answer. "Two years," she said.

"And the child is how old?"

"Seven months."

"Ach! So sad that he is ill! But look, he seems happier already. May I pour you a thimbleful of my magnificent Napoleon?"

Mutely, Natalia nodded. Her hand trembled as she reached for the small liqueur glass, and brandy splashed onto her fingers. "I'm sorry," she said. "He's been crying so much, and I'm tired."

"Of course. Tell me, *gnädige Frau*, had your father been suffering from heart trouble all during his last few years?"

Taking a gulp of the amber liquid, she replied: "Yes. But please let us not discuss my father. I told you, Colonel, it is too painful a subject for me."

The thickset man had narrowed his eyes at her. "I can understand that," he said with sudden sharpness, "because General von Wedekind, Heinrich's uncle, did not die of heart failure. He was not your father."

The last five words fell on the room like a tremendous

weight. The red plush seats, the shining bottles, and Colonel Ballhausen's small blue eyes imprinted themselves on Natalia's consciousness with heightened effect. She sat very still, not breathing. Her fear had seeped away and in its place had settled the certainty of inevitable death. It was over. Then her eyes fell on Arkady, and a fierce upsurge of blood coursed through her body, a sudden defiance. She stood up, one hand stretched out to the baby, and said: "What do you want, Colonel? Money?"

Now he rose also and approached her. "Not money. I am a rich man in my own right. But you will do what I ask, or you will never live to see Switzerland. Who are you, *gnädige Frau?*"

It did not matter anymore. If she told him, perhaps he would not harm her, given her status. "I am Natalia Oblonova, the Countess Kussova," she replied. "My husband is Count Boris Kussov of St. Petersburg."

Ballhausen raised his eyebrows. "I'm impressed. A Russian countess. Very touching. But it isn't going to help, *Gräfin.* Your husband is not here to rescue you, and you are an enemy traveling with illegal papers. Heinrich Püder must have received a pretty bribe to do this for you. Strange for such an honest man, and a devoted officer of the German army. But worthier men have succumbed to beauty and charm. You possess both. How did you charm Püder?"

"He agreed to help me because my child was ill. I am not a whore."

He closed the distance between them and placed both hands on the wall on either side of her head, so that she was imprisoned by his body. He was not touching her. She repeated again, coldly: "What do you want?"

From the beginning she had been prepared to sleep with Heinrich Püder to obtain his help. She had coolly considered it and resolved that it would not matter. There could be no question of unfaithfulness in such an act, only of survival for Arkady. Conventional morality had never coincided with her own code of values, and if Püder had wanted a different sort of payment, she would have given it to him. But he had been gentleman enough not to take advantage of her situation. This man, obviously, was not as scrupulous. She knew he would leave her no way out.

A dreadful feeling of claustrophobia assailed her, and her head reeled. He smelled of brandy—expensive brandy, to be sure, but nonetheless he had been drinking, and it sickened her. No, she thought, I can't, I can't! Püder, meticulously clean, young and stiff, would not have hurt her. This man would. Her body recoiled, and her mind balked. "Not that," she stammered. "No."

But he bent toward her, and pressed his lips to hers, parting them with such swift brutality that she started with pain. His tongue probed deep into her throat; her mouth was split open, stretched. She could not breathe. Hysteria overcame her and she began to struggle, attempting to push him off her. She pummeled his shoulders and his chest and tried to raise her knee to reach his groin, and could not. But her fingers encountered something hard at his side, and, with swift realization, she thought: My God, it's his gun!

Now she was more calm. It could be done. She had to make this work. While he crushed her body against the wall, she reached for the holster, found the gun, and pulled it out. With a sudden forceful gesture, she yanked her knee upward and smashed it into his soft testicles. He stepped back, rage and amazement spreading over his face. Now she was free, and the gun was in her hand.

At that moment the train's whistle erupted into a loud wail. In the ensuing din she acted on impulse. She knew how to make a gun work, for Boris had possessed a small pearl-handled revolver he had taught her to use long ago. Now she rapidly cocked the small instrument, aimed it at the roaring Ballhausen—and fired, her eyes wide with fear.

The shot reverberated in the car. The baby started to shriek, but another whistle obliterated all sound, and then the train entered a tunnel, throwing the scene into total darkness. Natalia could not move. She breathed in small gulps, and her hands trembled so much that the gun slipped out of her fingers, bouncing like a toy on the carpet. Light returned, and she saw Ballhausen's ghastly face, his body crumpled on the floor like a mannikin. I have killed a man, she thought, with bewilderment.

A knock on the door suddenly glued her in position. A voice

said: "*Herr Oberst?* Colonel? I wanted to discuss with you about the—" Natalia did not hear the end of the sentence, knowing only that it was Püder's voice, that doom had come to her in the tones of Püder's precise German. He opened the door a crack, then completely. His tall form stood on the threshold of the private car, disbelieving and aghast. She could not speak.

Then, rapidly, Püder entered and shut the door, bolting it behind him. He strode to Natalia and planted his hands squarely on her shoulders, hurting her. "Tell me, Countess Kussova," he said, his breath rasping. "Explain this if you will. Are you a spy?"

Her teeth began to chatter. Püder shook her once, twice, and the pins fell out of her hair one by one. He stepped back, and only then did he notice her torn bodice. "My God!" he cried.

"Are you going to turn me in?" she asked, her voice a whisper in the large car.

Püder glanced at the dead colonel and turned his back on him. He went to Arkady and picked him up, holding him out to his mother. With infinite bitterness, he sighed. "*Gnädige Frau*, I have already risked too much for that. Sit down, and let me think awhile. Thank heavens the train was making noise when you fired that gun. Who'd have thought a little girl like you could kill a man like Ballhausen? But the point is, what now?"

Natalia swallowed. A strange calm had settled over her. "You're going to have to turn me in," she said tonelessly. "What else can you do? But you'll still be blamed for getting me on board under a false identity. What will happen to you?"

"I don't know. I dare not think. But this child still needs a mother. I'm going to get you out of here. In fifteen minutes we're due to pull into Mulhouse. At that time you will calmly exit from this train, as though to take a stroll with your son on the platform. You will disappear. I'm sorry about the jewels and your bags. You can't go back now. If the war ends, I shall try to get those jewels back to you, somehow. That's all I can do for you, *Gräfin*."

"But you?"

Tensing his jaw, Heinrich Püder shrugged. "It will be all right. I shall manage. Hopefully, people won't think to remember where you stepped off the train. I'm going to do my best to spring this murder as a suicide. Our company won't have time to think of you—they'll be too preoccupied with Ballhausen's sudden end."

"Will it work?"

Püder laid his hands palms up in front of him. "Who can tell?" he said.

Natalia was numb with a surfeit of conflicting, overwhelming emotions. She must not look at the dead man, at his grimace of pain. She must not think of what she had done. But Püder! Tears came to her eyes, and all at once she started to sob, with fear, release, and memory. He stood beside her and placed an arm about her, restraining her, calming her. The train was screeching into a station and slowing down.

"It's time," Püder said, in his stiff but kind voice. "Good luck, *Gräfin*."

Natalia took his hand and pressed it to her lips, tears falling upon it. Without looking back, she quickly picked up Arkady, went to the door and unlocked it. She stepped into the corridor and found an exit door. She pulled it open with effort, her whole body trembling with suppressed hysteria. She climbed down the stepladder onto the platform. Mulhouse. Would she and her son ever survive Mulhouse?

Shivering coatless in the wind, Natalia peered about her. No one else stood nearby. In Russian, she said to her son: "Grown men play at being toy soldiers, but in all this confusion one or two keep a human heart. If there were a God, he would protect Heinrich Püder."

She did not know that at a tiny window above her, Pierre Riazhin sat watching her, in bewilderment and horror. But she had seen the blond Lieutenant framed in the window of the colonel's private car. Heinrich Püder watched, and Pierre Riazhin watched, as Natalia and her small son disappeared into the station house, two small, frail figures in the dusk.

Pierre, who above all found constriction hard to bear, now panicked. All the force of his muscles compressed by his cramped position in the lavatory, shivered from the need for release. He stood up and pushed up at the small square window, which appeared to be jammed from disuse. Frantically, he rammed his hands into the pockets of the brakeman's trousers, and there encountered a small metal object. He pulled it out, and to his infinite joy saw that it was a pocket knife. Standing on the commode, he worked the tip of this knife around the edges of the window, to dislodge whatever debris might have been blocking it. Perhaps dampness had glued the paint on the frames to that of the sill. When he next tried to open it, the window gave way. The pane slid upward.

Pierre looked below him. A guard had entered the station house, leaving the platform empty. He appraised the opening before him, and then, desperate for time, hoisted himself to it and threw his powerful legs onto the other side. How would he manage to pass through such a small space? With a superhuman effort, Pierre pushed hard against the top of the window, which blocked his way. The wooden frame broke, and glass fell about him, on his arms and legs, around his head. Concerned with the tinkling noise of the broken pane, he did not feel the shards pierce his skin. Pierre jumped, landing among the remnants of the shattered window. Dusk lay around him like a protective cloak, and the platform was still empty. There was no sign of Natalia and the baby.

Pierre shook the dust, shards, and splinters of wood from his clothing, and ran as quickly as he could to the side of the station house. He could not enter it from the back without rousing suspicion. German voices resounded from the inside. Two soldiers, bayonets on their left shoulders, came out of the terminal, and Pierre hid in the shadows. When they moved away, he slid along the wall of the terminal, making a right-angled turn to the left and at length a second one, until he stood in front of the small wooden shack. He straightened his collar, adjusted his shirt sleeves, and opened the door.

Still no Natalia. With renewed anxiety, Pierre saw that no one was in the station house, and he wondered if perhaps the two German soldiers had killed her and Arkady. How absurd! He had heard no screams, only normal voices raised in conversation. At that moment a door opened along a back wall, and he saw her, small and frail, Arkady rigid in her arms. She saw him at the same instant. Above the door an old French sign read *Dames*. She had been hiding in the women's lavatory and had heard the two soldiers on their way back to the platform.

They remained there for perhaps thirty seconds, relief sweeping over his features while shock froze hers. All at once the back door swung open, and a burly German guard entered on this bizarre reunion. He looked first at Pierre in his brakeman's uniform, noting the tiny cuts on his face, and then at the coatless young woman with the pale, sickly infant. "What's this?" he began, raising his bayonet immediately. He did not finish. Pierre threw himself on the guard, knocking him to the ground with the full force of his strong limbs and the unexpectedness of his assault.

Pierre did not hesitate. He held the guard pinned down, and reached for the brakeman's pocket knife that had already proved so useful. Savagely, he thrust the sharp blade once, twice, three times, into the guard's chest until the man grunted and went limp beneath him. Pierre jumped up, blood all over his trousers and seeping onto the floor of the station house. His face was contorted with violence.

Natalia had stayed to the side, unmoving, unblinking, horrified. When he approached her, she instinctively stepped back, like a woodland fawn taking flight from a wild boar. But he seized her wrist and propelled her into action, forcing her to run with him out the front of the terminal. Arkady wiggled in her arms and her mind was a jumble of clashing emotions, of chaotic sensations. But for Pierre there was no confusion.

Outside it was oddly quiet. Darkness had rapidly fallen on this cold and bleak October day in occupied France. Across the street Pierre spotted an empty cart hitched to a lone plow horse, itself tied to a post in front of what appeared to be a small tavern. He tightened his grip over Natalia's wrist and began to run toward it.

No one had seen them. "Get in," he whispered. While he unhitched the reins of the horse, she hoisted herself and her son into the open wagon. She did not try to understand how Pierre had come to be here, in the middle of her own nightmarish adventure, or why his face was caked with blood and why he was wearing a brakeman's uniform. Her mental faculties were paralyzed; she reacted like an automaton. The child whimpered now, a steady noise, but she did not hear him.

Pierre climbed into the cart, and now the horse started on its way, its uneven canter resounding in Natalia's ears like a kettle-drum on the hard cobbles of the street. It was a charming little town, but she did not watch the houses go by. Pierre had removed his jacket and was laying it over her shoulders. Her teeth were chattering and Arkady had gone completely still, his small face tinged with blue from the cold.

A wooden sign loomed up, indicating directions and distances from Dijon and Baucourt. Pierre pointed to the placard pointing due south: *Frontiere suisse, 40 kilomètres.* "That would be Basel if I'm not mistaken," he said tersely. "That's where we've got to go. Rub his hands and feet, Natalia. Breathe on his fingers. And move your own toes to keep the blood flowing."

She started to cry, small sobs erupting from her uncontrollably. "It's all right," he said, more gently. "I had to kill the bastard, there was no alternative." They had proceeded well away from the station, and the buildings became fewer and fewer. "We're reaching open countryside," he said.

"I shot a man," she intoned dully. "On the train. A German officer. He was going to rape me—"

Pierre turned to look at her, his black eyes alive with mahogany reflections. A spasm contorted his face. She continued, in the same monotone: "Püder will have to pay for what I've done. No one will think it was a suicide—no one."

Pierre did not understand, but he cried out, passionately: "Any man crazy enough to rape a woman could just as easily shoot himself! Stop torturing yourself, Natalia." Giving way to surprise, he said: "*You* killed a man?"

She started to laugh, breathlessly, the sound high and unstrung. "To save my virtue!" she said, giggling, her eyes bright with tears. "Can you imagine? My virtue? Aren't you going to laugh with me, Pierre?" She stopped and bit her lip, her face mirroring her amazement. "Pierre," she said, and it was almost a question. "*Pierre.* Good God, what are you doing here? Why are you dressed like this and what's the matter with your face? It's full of blood!"

Her fingers reached out to touch his cheek, and in his fevered state, their cold tips made him shiver. "It doesn't matter," he answered, looking away, suddenly ill at ease. "I had to come with you on the train. You're still too much a part of my life, Natalia."

"Don't say that. Already a virtual stranger, an enemy officer has risked his career, his honor, and maybe even his life because of me. Not you, too. You mustn't do that, I can't handle it. Think of yourself, Pierre."

"But I am. This is something I needed to do. I don't know about this other fellow, the German lieutenant. Once I fell in love with you at a ballet performance—why couldn't he have experienced the same sudden emotion? Was there anything between you, Natalia?"

"Not at all. I hardly knew him. But he was a man of honor. I suppose war does that to people—it brings out the heroic in them, or the most abject baseness—like the colonel's. When reason steps in, Heinrich Püder will be very sorry indeed that he ever asked me into the Exerzierplatz." She stared ahead of her without expression. Suddenly she burst out: "I can't stand it! I never wanted to owe anybody anything, and now there's Püder, and you. Why couldn't all of you have let us alone, Arkady and me? We would have managed somehow!"

"You don't owe a debt to someone who is repaid by his own desire to give," Pierre replied. Anger suffused his face. "Damn it, Natalia! You always were selfish, weren't you? Nothing ever changes your smugness. We've both killed people and escaped from certain slaughter ourselves. Don't you think this has made us partners of sorts? Püder can take care of himself. He's probably like Boris, a golden boy who can get himself out of any scrape. These men don't deserve your compassion. Reserve it for us in this miserable cart, with this plodding farm horse! We're made of flesh and bone, they aren't! Mercury runs through their veins, not human blood."

She turned to him then, and her resolve started to shake, to come apart. The breath came out of her in small gulps, and the child shook against her in her arms. It was so unreal—a situation of *déjà-vu* because Pierre was here, but otherwise it was wrong, all wrong: the time of day, the clothes, the countryside. "Why have you done this for me?" she cried, suddenly very small and frail. "You know I can do nothing for you in return. I can't even promise you love—that's part of the past for both of us, Pierre." She was too exhausted to reason it out, and besides, they had ridden this merry-go-round countless times before.

In the darkness she saw his face under the ghostly moon and his hands on the reins. Tears streaming down her cheeks, she placed her own hand on top of his. Arkady started to wail, kicking her. No words remained between them now, only the will to survive.

Above them the inky sky spread out like black velvet scattered with myriad sparkling diamonds that were stars. A sliver of moon outlined the countryside. Pierre drove in silence, his lips compressed with tension. Next to him Natalia sat with the baby. She had fed him from the paltry supply that was left of what the brakeman had given Pierre, and they had stopped here and there by a stream to obtain water. But neither adult had eaten anything.

In the middle of the night she finally spoke. "Here, let me take the reins, and you can rest for a while," she said. They had been pushing on at a steady three to four miles an hour, including their stops to change the baby, feed him, and find water. Pierre shook his head and continued to drive.

When dawn pierced the sky, chasing away the stars, he turned to her and announced: "We should be near the border now. Another seven miles or so. I'm going to drive into that clump of woods, and we're going to hide the horse and cart there and walk the rest of the way. Then we're going to sneak across the border if we can."

She nodded. The idea of having to walk three hours with Arkady did not appall her. She had always faced the inevitable with grim determination, undaunted. She had shot Ballhausen and, after this night of sleepless vigil, had come to accept this. It had been unavoidable. Püder's involvement was her only regret, but even then, she thought: I cannot continue to worry. It won't help him at all, and it certainly won't do Arkady any good. He needs me alert, and I need myself alert. Püder is not a sissy; he's a resourceful individual who will make do. I can't worry about Boris, either. The Division Sauvage is beyond my control.

A road sign said that they were approaching Saint-Louis, a small town near the Swiss border. Across it would be Basel, the longed-for haven. When Pierre climbed down from the cart, near some large, tall elms, she followed, holding the child tightly to her. He was sleeping.

They started to walk. Behind them the bewildered horse neighed. There was no time to wonder when someone would find it. Natalia and Pierre did not speak. They synchronized their footsteps, moving slowly because of Arkady's added weight. She carried him at first, then silently relinquished him to Pierre when, exhausted and famished, her body threatened to give way. Her feet, which had danced the Firebird and Giselle, were bruised and blistered. What if she had harmed them permanently? Anguish spread through her at the thought.

Soft, rolling hills curved over this rather flat land. When the sun had fully risen, they saw barbed wire in the far distance. The frontier. Without a word they exchanged a glance, and Pierre nodded. Relief, then anxiety, flooded her: They were so close yet had no guarantees.

From behind some bushes they observed a border patrol, six men carrying rifles. They were so close that their very breathing could be heard. Arkady uttered a sharp cry and Natalia, suddenly frightened, flattened him against her shoulder. But the small squad was moving away, toward the left. Pierre said under his breath: "Now!" He took Arkady from her and broke into a run. She followed, her heart in her throat. She possessed no reserve of strength and this final sprint made her chest constrict and the blood pound in her ears.

At the barbed wire fence they stopped, and with his pocket knife Pierre attempted to cut through the strands of mesh until he had created a hole sufficiently large for her to climb through. He held the wiring apart and she eased through, then stretched her arms through the aperture to grasp Arkady. Pierre could not squeeze past without considerably scratching his limbs and back. His hands were dripping with blood from every knuckle, the nails ripped in broken zigzags over the ragged skin. Once on the Swiss side, he pointed to an embankment with underbrush on their right, and they ran toward it, away from the returning border patrol. They collapsed among the heather, sounds of

German voices echoing in their ears. The squad was going by and had missed their odyssey.

"Look ahead, Natalia," Pierre said. "See that city? That's Basel, Switzerland. We've arrived in one piece!"

She looked at him, at his sweaty, tanned face, at his brilliant raven's eyes, at the curls that tumbled messily over his wide brow. His clothing was torn, and stained with perspiration. Arkady had soaked his diaper and the woolen jumpsuit he had been wearing, and that in turn had wet the whole front of her dress. She had not put back the pins that Heinrich Püder had shaken from her in the colonel's compartment. Her brown hair lay tangled about her shoulders. Dark circles made half-moons under her eyes. Suddenly laughter came rolling out of her, hysterically. She rocked back and forth on her haunches, tears streaming down her face. The last forty-eight hours poured from her in this stream of cascading mirth, and she could not restrain herself, now that they were safe at last.

Pierre watched her, his own energy finally yielding. Around him the countryside took on the colors of a dreamer's landscape, in purples and oranges and burnished golds. Her wild laughter pierced his consciousness and became maniacal. He tried to stand up and steadied himself against her shoulder. Then her laughter died in one spurt, and there was a strange silence in the heather. His arms went round her, avoiding the baby lying on the soft earth before her. She looked at him, her eyes wide. Then, almost violently, he bent down to kiss her, drowning out the sharp cry beginning in her throat.

A ray of warm sunshine fell across Arkady's vision, and the baby uttered an angry wail. From the damp grass her arms slid from his shoulders, rose between them like a wall, and pushed him away. She stared at him, the breath caught in her chest, and for a moment they remained frozen in position, her skirt pushed up to her knees, his hands still touching her sides. Then, her hair falling in her eyes, she swiftly scooped the child into her arms. "Let's go," she said. "Arkady's hungry, and we must find refuge."

Chapter 18

The Russian consul in Basel, Nicolai Medveyev, said to Natalia: "It won't be easy, but, given who you are, I think we'll be able to help you. I am familiar with your financial situation. Several years ago, when I was at the Consulate in Geneva, I had occasion to discuss some of the particulars with Boris Vassilievitch. He wanted our people to be aware of how he had disposed of his funds, so that, should a problem ever arise to place you in a difficult position, we would know how to assist you. I think," he added with a smile, "that this moment has come."

"The bulk of our fortune is in Paris," Natalia said.

"Indeed. But the Swiss have always been excellent bankers. Boris Vassilievitch has set up a cache for you in Geneva. You should be able to live off it for some time. You see, when war was declared, a freeze was placed over all bank accounts in France, and so that much more considerable reserve cannot be touched."

"Nicolai Petrovitch," Natalia said, passing her tongue tentatively over her upper lip, "what about my legal status here? That is my real problem, isn't it?"

The consul coughed. "Yes. For you see, the Swiss are neutral and cannot act as a haven for Russian refugees. Had you actually been here when the war broke out—that would have been a different question. What I shall have to do is have some documents made up to prove that you entered Switzerland—in July, shall we say? With your son."

"You would do this for me?" Natalia asked.

"I could not turn away Oblonova," Medveyev said, bowing. "You are one of our national treasures. We diplomats can perform feats of magic, and in your case it would be my pleasure. I used to watch you at the Mariinsky, but I made a special trip to London for the Coronation gala to see you in Diaghilev's company. I have seen you twice in Paris and once in Rome. My wife and I found you exquisite in *The Firebird*, especially. Besides, your husband is a powerful man. Turning away Count Boris Kussov's wife and child would hardly sit well with the Tzar."

Natalia was seated on a chaise longue in the Consulate's library. There were bandages around her feet, and a quilt covered her limbs. Her pale face seemed translucent, her eyes enormous, like burnt topazes. She looked away, wringing her hands. "Another kind person to risk something for us," she said miserably. Glancing at her feet, she added, "You compliment me, Nicolai Petrovitch. But after tramping through the countryside, I have doubts about my ability to dance again."

"We shan't ask you to perform tomorrow, dear Natalia Dmitrievna. Now listen to me—I have sent word to Russia about you. The Division Sauvage is at present in the Caucasus Mountains, protecting the area from Turkey. Your husband will be able to write you here, as he was not able to when you were hiding in Darmstadt. But the child must go to Doctor Combes in Lausanne. I agree with you, he is a fine specialist, worth your odyssey. And"—Medveyev examined his hands—"you should not waste time. I've already made arrangements to have work begun on your papers. But, since you foresee a lengthy stay, your status as a visitor could be improved if you purchased a piece of property, Natalia Dmitrievna. Then you would have little trouble having your status changed to resident. At that point we could all stop worrying."

Natalia nodded. Her lips were tightly drawn. "As soon as I have spoken to Combes, I'll start to look for something in Lausanne, perhaps a small house near the hospital. Thank you, Nicolai Petrovitch. I am more grateful than you'll ever know."

"I must say we were quite amazed when you arrived on our doorstep, with the baby and that young man, Pierre Riazhin—

he's a painter, isn't he? I thought the name sounded familiar. But imagine our wonder upon discovering that the bedraggled girl in the soiled clothing was our own Oblonova! A fairy tale, my dear, to brighten our rather drab existence, don't you think? You're quite a courageous woman, Natalia Dmitrievna. A tribute to the Russian spirit."

"You overwhelm me, Nicolai Petrovitch. I only did what had to be done. Arkady is quite ill." Gulping down the tears that were rising to her eyes, she leaned forward and said: "Pierre Grigorievitch—you'll be able to help him, too? He did a wonderful thing, hiding on that convoy train and then driving me and my son to safety. Can you arrange to have papers prepared for him as well?"

"Certainly. He's a friend of yours, isn't he?"

Her brown eyes met the consul's, and she answered unflinchingly: "Of my husband's too. Boris would want me to do something behind the scenes to make things easier for Pierre. Maybe you could assist me again. I should like to transfer some of the funds that are in my name to a new account to be set up in the name of Pierre Riazhin. But I don't want him to learn of this. Perhaps you could inform him that my husband had done this years ago, in a gesture of friendship? Boris was Pierre's first patron," she added staunchly.

Medveyev's brow wrinkled, then smoothed out. "Of course, Natalia Dmitrievna. This can be managed quite simply. I'll send Bunin to you in a moment, for details as to amounts, and so on. Pierre Grigorievitch is resting upstairs and won't know a thing about this kind gesture of yours."

"I shall be forever in your debt," Natalia answered. As Medveyev prepared to depart, she closed her eyes. Another hurdle had been crossed.

Pierre said: "So you go to Lausanne tomorrow. After all we've been through, you might let me come with you, Natalia."

"No. This doesn't concern you," she replied, biting her lower lip. "I don't want to prolong this, Pierre. I'm here to consult Dr. Combes for my son. You and I have no further need to continue together."

"You're afraid to be alone with me," he said, his black eyes flashing. "You're afraid that you won't be able to control your feelings—that you'll discover what a farce your marriage really is! Tell me the truth!"

"Arkady is my son and I want to take care of him," she replied. "Right now he's the only link I have to Boris. I want them both back, to health and to me. You are not a part of our life. Don't you understand that? You bring back painful memories for me, for Boris. I wish it weren't so. Maybe in twenty years the three of us shall be able to remove the barriers around us and forget the bad times. I have the man I love, but it's still fragile, still tenuous—and when you're around I'm afraid. But not in the way you think."

"It's jealousy, then! You're jealous of me!" He stood up again and began to pace the room." "I can't believe it," he added.

"But it's true. I am jealous, I admit it! You came first for so long in Boris's life! Don't make me speak about it, Pierre: It's too cruel of you. We've built a house of love, stone by stone, and it means everything to us because it was gained at such cost. I'm jealous of you, but do you know what it would do to Boris to learn that you were here, accompanying me to the doctor, holding his child? He'd suspect the worst—he'd think we'd become lovers again! Because you came first for me, too, and he's more jealous than I! I don't want that, Pierre! It isn't worth it to me. I'd rather never see you again because he means life itself to me—he, and my son, and the dance! Please, Pierre, go your own way! You don't need us."

The young painter stopped in his tracks, wheeled about, and looked at her.

His own anger was such that he did not see the wretched expression in her eyes, her frightened mouth. Under the brave front Natalia was quaking, her world uncertain, threatened. Toward the end there had been something in Boris that she had not understood, a desperation, and now it was she who was desperate. "You don't need us," she repeated, but her lips quivered.

"No," he said. "It's time I learned the truth of that. You're right, Natalia. I don't want to be a part of this sordid little

326   *ménage à trois.* It disgusts me! But don't worry, darling: If your husband finds the temptation too great to resist, it won't be with me that you'll discover him! I was never one of his little boys, in spite of what you believe. You go to Lausanne, and I think I'll go in the other direction: to Locarno, perhaps. It has beautiful landscapes, a marvelous lake." He glared at her: "And what's this about Boris setting up an account for me here? That's ridiculous! I don't believe it!"

Defiantly, she cried: "I don't care what you believe! Boris once loved you, and thought of your well-being. You can take the money or not, as you so choose. I don't give a damn!"

"Unfortunately, that's all I possess in this country at this moment. Of course I'll take it. But I'm going in the opposite direction from you—you can bet on that!"

For a moment their eyes locked, hers proud, his furious. He turned his back on her and left the small sitting room. When Madame Medveyeva came in, she found Natalia with her head in her hands.

Dr. Louis Combes was a bony man with a sallow complexion. Natalia had first heard of him years before, in St. Petersburg. He had cured a little girl of a stomach ailment, and the mother had brought back songs of his praises. Afterward she had heard many other tales of miracles performed on children's small bodies, and even on those of larger adults. Now she sat in his spacious office overlooking Lake Geneva. She said: "At first I refused to have him transported out of Germany. Then I knew I had to risk a journey, to bring him here. What do you think, Doctor?"

Combe's mournful face took in her elegance, her anxiety, her exhaustion. "My dear Countess, don't blame yourself. You did the right thing. None of this is your fault. It's too early to tell, but I suspect a kidney deficiency. It was probably congenital."

Natalia's eyes filled with animal fear. "The kidneys? What can you do about it?"

Combes said: "I'm going to hospitalize Arkady, keep him on a special regimen under constant care and surveillance. But I must warn you: Kidney problems are very hard to treat. I must run tests on him. He's terribly thin and underweight, but he's been retaining water. Edema, Countess. Have you ever suffered from edema?"

She shook her head, her breath coming in little gasps. "Should I have?" she asked. "Has all this come from me? It's my fault, isn't it, Doctor?"

"No, no, don't think this way. We shall find a method by which to treat Arkady. My secretary tells me you are looking for property? Around here? A wise decision, my dear lady. This way you can come to see the child each day, yet live in a house of your own. May I suggest Sauvabelin Hill? You will find it lovely. But you know this already, for aren't you at the Hôtel du Signal?"

Natalia regarded him with amazement. He was about to separate her from her son, and he was speaking of properties and hotels? Blinded by tears, she rose quickly, tripping over the foot of the chair. "May I see him?" she whispered.

Combes stroked his chin carefully. "I'm afraid not, Countess. I had him taken directly to the children's wing. The nurses are feeding him now."

She blinked. Just like that. Her hands began to tremble, and she took a deep breath. Arkady had to improve. He had to grow strong and healthy. Otherwise she would lose her grip on reality. This was her fault. Edema. Kidneys. Congenital defects.

When she was once more outside, having left her child in the hands of these strangers, she allowed a hospital attendant to call a cab for her to drive her back to the Hôtel du Signal. But her mind was a blur of horror.

She was thinking of Boris. How will he feel, thinking that if he'd stayed away from me, none of this would have happened? Will he leave me? I am defective, I am not whole. I should not have been permitted to have this child, to bear him only so that he might suffer.

In her hotel room she could not sleep. Clenching her fists so tightly that her nails dug into the soft palms, Natalia scourged herself with recrimination and anguish. She had never been superstitious or moralistic. But now she thought: My father was a bad man, an evil man. My mother was a total weakling.

Something bad came to me from them, and now I have passed it on to Arkady. And there is nothing I can do but wait and trust the doctors.

She remained dry-eyed. Even the catharsis of tears, she thought, was more than she deserved.

Lausanne was built on the side of a hill, and all its streets, even those parallel to the crest and to the lake, went up and down unevenly. After crossing the Bessière Bridge, which straddled a large and deep ravine, the road continued to climb until it reached the University. Beyond the school was a plateau with fields, villas, and gardens, but to the left a steep cliff rose, the Sauvabelin. Here Natalia purchased a small house on some wooded land.

One could climb to the top of Sauvabelin in a cablecar, by driving up a winding road, or even by following a path on foot. At the edge of a vast blue-green forest stretched a magnificent panorama of Lausanne below, with the lake at its feet. Across the lake the white peak of Mont Blanc rose into the crisp fall sky.

There were no luxurious shops there, only the comfortable Hôtel du Signal, where Natalia had stayed upon arriving in Lausanne. There was no other distraction or entertainment. But the small forest, now adorned with its mantle of snow, contained its own minuscule lake, with rowboats for hire. As winter approached, the lake froze and became a skating area for the local villagers. Not far from the lake was a vast space enclosed by wire, where deer ran free. They could be fed by hand, and would stretch their velvet lips through the trellised fence. These were Natalia Kussova's surroundings.

Her house was really a chalet, with a gingerboard façade and a peaked roof, and, inside, paneled walls and hardwood floors. She took only a single maid, a Swiss girl from Lausanne, Brigitte. The latter cooked and cleaned, and her husband, Alfred, occasionally tended the grounds. Wrapped in fur, Natalia spent her days waiting. She took walks to the forest and walks into town. She wrote letters to Boris, letters to Nina and Galina Stassova, letters to Lydia Brailovskaya, letters to Diaghilev, to

Karsavina, to Benois and Bakst. She wrote and wrote in order not to think, to put off sorting through her reactions to her son's illness. She carefully avoided writing to anyone about the slow erosion of her heart because of his condition.

At the beginning of November, Dr. Combes had said to her: "There's more and more protein in his urine. The kidneys are degenerating, Countess. It's nephrosis."

She nodded mutely. What was there to say?

Natalia practiced ballet movements in her living room several hours a day. Only then did she feel lifted out of herself, out of this baser being that had engendered nephrosis in a newborn child. These were her only moments of peace.

Her worst times came when she received a letter from her husband. They had only just begun to reach her and took so long in arriving that the news was already stale by the time she received it. Boris, however, came alive for her through his words. Better not to have been so acutely reminded of his reality.

"My love," he wrote,

If you still hate me for having abandoned you, then you'll be maliciously pleased at my discomfiture here. I had imagined battles filled with blood and glory, with your humble servant—what an inappropriate epithet!—leading a battalion forward, bayonets pointing to the morning star. Instead, I am attached to the Headquarters of the Division Sauvage, where the closest I come to a bayonet is when I sharpen a pencil. A truly creative endeavor.

Because of my title and standing—which seem to throw the rest of humanity into quite a turmoil, both good and bad—I am at present the bearer of the rank of major. Like my golden hair, it's only a façade, however. Svetlov got me in, and my fellow Sauvages are loath to trust me. What do I know of the trenches, I, dilettante *par excellence?* Who can blame them for their lack of enthusiasm? But at Divisional Headquarters I do the same paperwork as I used to do for the Ballets Russes, and our heroic savages are less entertaining than Serge. I wax impatient by the minute and squirm at the vision of your superior disdain as you read this woeful missive. Perhaps I was a fool after all, Natalia.

I wonder if Arkady remembers me. Of course I know this is absurd. I am relieved beyond words to know that you are both in Switzerland, on neutral ground, and that Dr. Combes is taking care of our son. When I think of him, I cease to care what they will do with me here and remain quite content with my ineffectual activities among the pencils. For then I start to care about life as never before. He is so small, so frail, and he does need me. Even you, Natalia, are strong and independent, and will never need me as that little creature already does. How we two cynics, we two atheistic sinners ever came to form him, to bring forth the miracle of him, is still to me the greatest wonder of all. I shall have lived for something, after all.

The story of your adventures leaving Darmstadt frightened me more than the nearness of the Turks to Tiflis, where we are stationed. Only you could have managed such an escape and survived. You're right, I am despicable, to have left you to your own devices. Still, you have to admit that those devices were ingenious and worthy of all my faith in you. You are the better part of me, without doubt. But even so, is that a good thing? Before you I was without conscience, outlined in black. But if Pierre were to paint me now, in spite of your softening influence, he'd still omit pure white from his palette.

It is natural that I think of him now and then, darling, for I am in his native habitat here in Georgia. This is where he played and romped and had his black-haired maidens. How strange life can be, setting me down here of all places!

Tiflis is a beautiful city, but our patrol squads travel far out to peer over the crested mountains. I envy them! A Turk would lend more color to my existence than those bloody pencils—pardon the pun. For you, in Lausanne, it must be the same: Boring routine and the same faces, no?

We shall have our summer home in Monte Carlo. Plan

its decor. It's about time you worked on a house, isn't it? Every place we've had is imprinted with my ineffable good taste, and people have begun to wonder just how bad yours might be. Gossip can kill a marriage: Prove them wrong, my darling, and then we can pick up the pieces of our life.

Seriously, seriously, that's what I want: to pick up the jagged puzzle pieces and put back our life, yours and mine and Arkady's. The Caucasus has brought out an oddly annoying sentimentality in me. Learn to overlook it, will you? I love you and belong to you forever, if you'll still have me. I can't go on too much longer without you.

How to survive such letters? How to read them without starting to tremble, without weeping? But she wasn't weeping. Her tear ducts appeared to have dried out from worry about Arkady. She wrote to Boris because it would have been unthinkable not to—what would he have thought, so removed from the mainstream of life? That she no longer loved him? Or that something truly tragic had occurred? She knew that he loved the boy more than he had ever thought he would be capable of loving another human being. Sometimes she even felt jealous of her own son. To relate the illness, the progressive degeneration that Combes did not seem able to stop, would have been sadistic: One did not pull the life out of a man so close to combat. Besides, if she refused to acknowledge the nephrosis, perhaps it would go away.

Pierre did not write and did not come to see her. She had learned from Medveyev that the painter had moved to Locarno, on the Lago Maggiore. She remembered when she had written to break off their relationship in St. Petersburg, six years before. He had succeeded in shutting her out completely. He thought that she and Boris had each played with his life, pushing him in and out of their own lives at will. Perhaps he was right. Threesomes don't work, she thought. We can't love you, Pierre. We can only love each other. Had we lived in an enlightened society, the three of us might have tried to love each other and live together in understanding. But it wouldn't have worked! Somehow, some way, someone would have felt forced out, loved less.

By December, when the small lake had thoroughly frozen

over and Lausanne was indistinguishable from every other Swiss town beneath its hood of snow, Natalia's existence had become regulated by her routines. Outside of them, her mind did not function. She rose and went to the hospital, saw Arkady, went home, exercised, went for a walk, and returned to eat and write meaningless letters. She could not even read through the nonsense of others' missives. She read only Boris's. Sometimes she would bite her lip until it bled to drown out the pain. Then she would eat a light supper and go to bed. She had forgotten that she had ever danced on a stage or been married to a man of flesh and blood.

Dr. Combes worried about her. "You're wasting away," he said gently. "Are you still not sleeping?"

"On and off. I have nightmares. I see Arkady's face. All I can see is the eyes, and they're eating me alive."

"Have you been taking the pills I ordered for you?" Combes asked.

"No. I don't care anymore whether I sleep or not."

But the Swiss physician frowned and said: "Punishing yourself isn't doing the child a bit of good. Do you want to let yourself die?"

Natalia's enormous eyes, so like her son's, fastened on his thin, craggy face. "Because that's what's happening to him, isn't it?" she said dully. "He's dying." And then, in a sudden wail: "You're letting him die! Why, Doctor, why? Why don't you just inject him with poison and be done with it?"

Combes did not answer. Slowly Natalia's eyes filled with tears, and the tears overflowed onto her thin, colorless cheeks. "I never wanted a child," she said.

A week before Christmas 1914, Natalia arrived early at the children's wing of the hospital. She walked into Arkady's room, for which she was paying a small fortune. He was so tiny among the white sheets, in a child's bed, which was too large for him. Why hadn't they simply put him in a crib? His small body was turned to her, and he was sleeping. She sat down on the edge of the bed and looked at him. All alone, covered with patches where the needles had been inserted, he slept, his features drawn. They had to feed him through tubes now, but today he was singularly free of them, alone in the cot, almost normal in his stillness. Natalia touched his forehead and could not breathe.

My child, my own, myself. Do something, do something! Children your age crawl everywhere. I saw one at the lake yesterday; he made me think of you. He was just beginning to walk. You're nine months old now; maybe you'll walk soon. Why don't you open your eyes and say my name, Arkady? "Mama." My name.

Why don't they paint the children's rooms a different color? Something bright and cheerful to encourage you to live. Your papa, whose bright joy you are, would hang this room with Lyon silk, but I'd have my say, and pick something plebeian, such as checkered wallpaper. To make you laugh. Or smile, at least. Why can't you smile? You've never once smiled at me. Am I such a bad mama that I don't deserve a smile?

She kneeled down to stare at the sleeping face and touched the tip of his nose. When are they going to put the tubes back in and feed you? How much do you weigh now? They don't tell me anymore; they're afraid I'll become hysterical.

Natalia sat, mesmerized by the sleeping child. Why was no one there? No nurses, no doctor. She stood up, unsteadily, and moved to the open door. No one was in the corridor. Then she heard a small whimper and started. The child on the bed had moved, spasmodically. She ran to him and took his hand. It was limp. She stroked his forehead again. Then, wildly, she began to scream: "Somebody, somebody come! Somebody come now!"

A nurse, clothed in the standard white uniform, brushed past her into the room. She went to the cot and sat down. Natalia saw her expert hands feel his face, his pulse, his chest. Slowly she turned to Natalia and regarded her without saying a word. She was a plump, middle-aged woman, and now her chin trembled.

But Natalia did not tremble. She asked: "Why was no one here? Why weren't the tubes in?"

The nurse shook her head listlessly from side to side. "Countess, Countess. Dr. Combes told you last week that we were stopping the intravenous feedings. I'm so sorry."

But Natalia couldn't remember. "Dr. Combes? He said that? Really? But why?"

Now the nurse looked away at a speck of dirt on the wall. Her voice was so low that Natalia had to strain to hear it. "Because," the nurse answered, "nothing was doing him any good anymore."

Natalia blinked. She stood before the nurse, a diminutive figure in a cape of black sable. "So what are you going to try now?" she asked in a cold, matter-of-fact voice.

The nurse seemed taken aback. She twisted her hands together. Then she cried out: "I'm so sorry, Countess! Your son is dead. He just passed away. I thought you were aware of it, and that this was why you'd summoned me. I—"

"He isn't dead," Natalia stated firmly. Her eyes appeared totally vacant. The nurse reached for a cord above the bed and pulled on it frantically. She had seen many cases of grief prostration, but never such a calm, assured denial. Natalia sat down on the chair that faced the bed and said to the nurse: "Of course he wouldn't die, just like that. I've never been sick in my life, and my husband is as healthy as I. Our child is still alive, and you will be fired for lying to me this way. Dr. Combes will be shocked that you could be so cruel for no reason. I have never disliked you, Nurse Trévin. Why do you hate me, then?"

But Dr. Combes, roused by the alert, had entered the room. He went first to examine the baby and exchanged glances with the nurse. Then he placed his hands on Natalia's shoulders, looked into her glassy eyes, and said: "Countess Kussova, this is dreadful for you. Dreadful for all of us. Please, let me keep you in the hospital tonight, under sedation. You haven't slept in days."

Suddenly she sprang up, throwing off Combes's hands. Her face was alive again and twisted into a grimace of total horror as, finally, the truth hit the bottom of her soul. "You want me to stay here, where you have killed my child?" she exclaimed. "Here? Do you think I shall let you kill me, too? You are all butchers and murderers, and one day you will pay for this! One day you will awaken in hell, and—and—"

She collapsed on the floor, her face drenched with tears, and Combes and Nurse Trévin watched in shock as she began to tear out her hair in clumps. The doctor kneeled down and took hold of her hands to restrain her. She spat in his face. Then, just as suddenly as this had begun, her paroxysm of hatred and self-loathing died down. Her eyes closed, and she lay back, unmoving. Nurse Trévin began to cry.

Several hours later Natalia regained consciousness in a small, white hospital room. She was in a large cot, in infirmary clothes. She got out of bed and swayed unsteadily on her feet but went to the chair where she had noticed her clothes. Silently she dressed. She pulled the cord to summon a nurse. "Please inform Dr. Combes that I'm going home," she said to the bewildered young woman. "I'm going home and I shall never come back again. Let him make all the arrangements. I shall pay the bill, but I don't ever want to see him again—not ever."

"The doctor?" asked the young nurse.

Natalia shook her head impatiently. "No, my son," she replied. "From now on I've never had a son. The doctor was going to take care of him, so I'm going to let him: He can take better care of him now than he could when he was alive. Tell him that for me."

She adjusted the collar on her sable cape and walked out.

Chapter 19

Pierre Riazhin slammed the fist of one hand into the palm of the other. "I'm not the one to do it," he said. "I'm sorry you've wasted your time coming out here."

Nicolai Medveyev, the Russian consul from Basel, scratched the top of his head and sat pensively in front of the fireplace. They were in the living room of the small chalet that Pierre was renting in Locarno, in Italian Switzerland. "Still," he insisted, "it's imperative that Boris Vassilievitch be told. For such a delicate task, only someone close to the Kussovs should be chosen. She refuses to write to him about their son, but he has a right to know."

"If she refuses, then it is her decision. I no longer wish to involve myself in their affairs. This story, tragic though it may be, does not concern me." Pierre sat down abruptly in front of Medveyev.

"You are a hard man, Pierre Grigorievitch. If you had only seen her! She's moved out of the villa in Lausanne, and that's understandable, given the suffering she's had to endure in that city. She's taken up residence in Geneva. I fear for her sanity."

A spasm of emotion passed over Pierre's face, but when he turned to look at his guest, there was only grim resolution in his black eyes. "Nicolai Petrovitch," he said slowly, "you could not possibly understand why I don't choose to go to Natalia Dmitrievna. Each person has his own anguish to bear, and I've had mine. She's a strong girl. I've known her a long time, and she's never lost her hold on reality. As for her husband, there could not exist a less feeling individual on the face of this earth. Write to him. He'll survive. Little children die every day, and they're two healthy people. When he returns home from his dabble in heroism, he can make her a number of other babies."

Medveyev stood up, his drawn features white, his frame shaking with suppressed indignation. "You are not a man, Pierre Grigorievitch," he whispered. "Have you no heart? A vague acquaintance should not be the person to write to a father about the death of his only son. If you will not do it for the count, or for her—then you owe *me* this favor. I took you in, I arranged to obtain false entry papers for you, a resident's visa—and in return I ask only this."

Pierre sat down, the muscles in his legs visibly twitching beneath the broadcloth trousers. "Very well!" he cried, color flowing into his cheeks. "I'll write the damned letter for you. But don't ask anything else of me, Nicolai Petrovitch. Don't ever ask it!"

The brilliant sunlight made tiny dots, like golden buttercups, on the white snow and on the blue tips of the pine trees. Pierre looked out the window over the large Lago Maggiore, almost purple in its depth, and ran his fingers through his thick curls. Perspiration ran in rivulets down his temples, and the whites of his eyes were shot with red. The Kussovs always came out the winners, he thought, resentment swelling again within him. Even when they lost, he lost even more.

These people have invaded my life, my soul, my consciousness, he thought. The golden count and his dancing Sugar Plum Fairy. They had excluded him and made a cocoon to protect themselves from the world, shutting him out, hating him.

Blood throbbing in his throat, Pierre raised his head and examined the vellum in front of him. Boris would be doubly hurt at receiving word through Pierre, and this, then, would be justice. He dipped his pen in the inkwell and began to write. Words had never come easily to Pierre, and he tried to imagine Boris in the Caucasus, reading about his son's death and his wife's withdrawal. An unexpected stab shot through his middle. He couldn't picture the child dead, not when he'd held him in the heather, when he'd risked his own life to help save him. Suddenly he felt the pain of Natalia's loss, imagining her arms hanging limp without Arkady.

"Boris:" he began stiffly:

Consul Nicolai Medveyev suggested that the task of writing to you should fall on me as a friend of the Kussov family. You needn't be told that I demurred. Our friendship came to an end long ago. But Medveyev does not know the particulars.

First of all, I do wish to assure you that what I am about to relate came to me through Nicolai Petrovich Medveyev, and not firsthand. For whatever it's worth to you, Natalia hasn't loved me for a long time. I helped her to escape from Germany in memory of the past. There is nothing whatsoever between us. This said, the news I bring is bad—the worst, I'm afraid.

Little Arkady passed away. He'd suffered all his life from faulty kidneys, and his death was no more painful than the nine months that he was alive. Natalia, Medveyev tells me, could not write to you about it. He says that she has gone to Geneva, and I'm certain you can reach her at the address he's given me, which I'm enclosing. She's distressed and refuses to see the Medveyevs, who had been friendly to her since her arrival in Switzerland. Probably a letter from you would help her to adjust. She is afraid that all this is her fault and that you won't forgive her. There's nothing I can hope to accomplish on her behalf, so I will not go there to call on her. But if she needs a friend, Igor Stravinsky is in Switzerland too, I've been told. She is your wife, and I have finished meddling in her life and yours.

I must add that I am truly sorry. Words, as usual, fail me totally. Whatever ill feelings may have passed between us, I don't think even you deserve to be hurt this way. No human being does, and having been the one to convey this message has helped me to understand how truly wrong war is to separate families and countries from each other. Arkady is the first war casualty for whom I have wept.

Pierre laid down his pen and shut his eyes. If the letter sounded dry, heartless, and inarticulate, then so be it. He'd done the best he could, under the circumstances, and damned be the Kussovs and Medveyev.

In the late fall of 1914 an exchange of gravely wounded prisoners had been established between the Allies and members of the Central Powers. Convoys of French as well as German veterans passed through Geneva on their way home. Each night at midnight and again at three in the morning, a train would stop on either side of the tracks at the large terminal. Women in Red Cross uniforms would wait on the platform and dispense bandages, chocolate bars, and coffee. Society ladies who had volunteered as nurses would come to help, bringing the treats onto the trains to the soldiers. A crowd always gathered to watch, to see how bad the gaping faces looked, but also to lend support to those who had lost limbs for their various countries.

The hospitals from which the prisoners came were short of bandages, medicines, and disinfectants, and those on convoy trains suffered most from this scarcity. In Geneva the halt at the station took a long time, while officials checked papers and went over formalities. The nurses, therefore, could take their bundles onto the train cars at leisure and sit in turn by each patient, changing dressings and administering tranquilizers, helping the men to drink hot coffee, and leaving them chocolate bars and cigarettes. The military commander of the Place de Genève, a Swiss colonel named Rodolphe Senglet, was in charge of these proceedings. It was his duty to make certain that all went smoothly.

When Natalia left Lausanne, she went to the nearest city that was large enough to guarantee her anonymity but familiar enough to make her adjustment relatively easy. Her bank account was in Geneva, and there was sufficient activity to drown out her thoughts. She had trouble finding a hotel that could accommodate her, but at length she was given a comfortable room at the Hôtel Metropole. She did not care about the opulence of her surroundings because she had really ceased to care about herself, but the Metropole was centrally located, and she needed that so as not to feel isolated.

The town, though busy and filled with foreigners who had been caught there by the outbreak of war, was operating in slow motion. It had become a women's town. The Swiss men had been mobilized to ensure their country's neutrality, by protecting its frail borders. The old, the weak, and hordes of female citizens and visitors had taken over their soldiers' previous occupations. Natalia was in shock, and saw this different Geneva without interpreting how its changed aspect might affect her. Nothing was real to her anymore. If she encountered Boy Scouts throughout the city streets, running errands on their bicycles, they were not worth considering—just another volunteer group helping to keep the city alive and functioning.

Natalia went at once to sign up for nurse's training. In the hospital she made herself look straight at the white walls and learned to wear the starched uniform as a punishment. She felt fundamentally unclean and guilty, and this service, she thought, would be her expiation. She believed that blood cleansed blood, that only by immersing herself in the suffering of others would she be able to forget the suffering of her son. She had always faced the inevitable with uncommon staunchness; now she attacked the healing profession in the same indomitable manner. The doctors and other trainees found her oddly unflinching—even in the worst of circumstances.

In January the group in which Natalia was training began to greet the convoy trains of the gravely wounded. It was extremely cold, and patches of ice lined the platform on which she stood with the other volunteer nurses. Over her uniform Natalia wore a long velvet cape of dusky rose, with silver fox trimmings at the collar and hem. She felt goose bumps shiver over her skin but ignored them as she did all physical discomforts. The more her body ached, the more vindictive she felt against her own infirmities.

The crowd was loud and dense that night. Young boys and girls tense with wartime excitement shouted in the darkness. Old men and women peered about them with owlish fascination. A train pulled in, whistling shrilly, and a sudden pain shot through Natalia as a picture of the dead colonel flashed through her mind. This was a French convoy, and the Swiss, who were francophiles, ran up to the cars and waved, their handkerchiefs and scarves dancing in the cold winter wind, banners of joy. Natalia took her bundle of foodstuffs and dressings and climbed aboard.

In the first compartment she paused in the doorway for a quick intake of breath. The face staring at her drained the color from her cheeks. One round eye, its brow and eyelid burned away, regarded her from one of the bunks, its mate completely swathed in dripping red bandages. From somewhere else a French voice called her, but, mesmerized, Natalia went toward the ghastly sight and sat down on the edge of the bunk. In a low, confident voice she said: "Hello. I'm Natalia Oblonova. What's your name?"

"Antoine Mayard. You're a beautiful lady. I haven't seen anyone like you in months."

He sounded so young! "Shall I change your dressing?" Natalia asked, realizing how banal her words were, compared with the courage of his statement. Her staunchness began to give way. With increasingly trembling fingers, she unpinned the bandage around his head and saw a hole where the other eye had been. She could feel her stomach slowly turning, felt herself begin to gag. Then she thought: Who am I to be disgusted? His wounds are on the outside, while no one can see mine. But they're there, and they made Arkady die! She controlled her nausea, washed the blood from the empty socket, and applied a new gauze bandage.

Gently, she raised Antoine Mayard's head so that he could drink from a cup of hot coffee. Both his hands had dressings wrapped around them. Natalia wanted to weep. She felt like crying out: Why are you fighting? Why did you give up one of your eyes? Is the Archduke Ferdinand really your intimate concern, that you and my husband and Heinrich Püder should all be willing to die because of him? But Arkady had died for no reason, and Natalia remained silent.

When she climbed off the train, one of the Swiss nurses, Louise Dondel, said to her: "How can you do it? I saw him—such a dreadful wound. Did it make you sick to have to change it?"

"Yes," Natalia replied in a soft, even voice. "That young man is in such pain, and there was so little I could do. Death and maiming make me sick, Louise. Because we can't control what happens to us."

Another train was pulling in, this one with the German colors on it. All at once the crowd appeared to swell and began to roar. Next to Natalia, Louise had blanched, and Natalia heard her mutter: "The damned pigs! It's all their fault. Well, I'm not going. No one can make me!"

Horrid faces stared from the compartment windows, faces as ghastly as those of Antoine Mayard. The Swiss crowd was now hurling insults and obscenities at them, waving not banners but clenched fists. Rodolphe Senglet was pacing frantically about and shouting admonitions in a frantic effort to control the partisan feelings among his countrymen. In his colonel's uniform, with his trim mustache and Van Dyke beard, he resembled an elegant Swiss monkey. No one paid any attention to him.

Natalia stared at the frightened faces of the German prisoners. One of them had raised a handless arm to protect his eyes, as in the line of fire. Her heart, so often closed these days, suddenly burst open like a dam, and nameless fury shook her. She seized Louise Dondel by the arm and propelled her forward. "We are nurses, for God's sake!" she cried. "Get on that train or I shall push you onto it myself!"

Several startled faces turned to her. Natalia made her way to the stepladder and climbed to the train level. She stood above everyone else on the platform and placed her hands around her mouth to form a sound tunnel. "I can't believe it!" she exclaimed. "The Swiss are the only nation with an ounce of sense in this war. You, of all people, should understand that where a wounded man comes from is immaterial! He's wounded, and he needs care—and the rest simply doesn't matter! My husband is fighting on the Russian front, and so I have more reason to hate the Germans than you do. But I don't. I was helped once by a noble man, and he happened to be a German officer. So I'm going to go up there with bandages and coffee and some good words, and I'll be damned if I'll be the only one to go. We need every nurse on this platform!"

Hypnotized, the crowd had frozen, looking up at the tiny fig-

ure in rose with her large eyes. Colonel Senglet took advantage
of the sudden calm. He waved to his soldiers, and they, in turn,
dispersed the angry bystanders. Louise Dondel took one small
step, then another, toward the train. She was the first of the
Swiss nurses to climb up the ladder behind Natalia.

When the three-A.M. trains had departed, and it was time to
return to the Metropole, Natalia noticed that her velvet cape
was besmirched with blood. She could not control the nerves
that twitched in her hands and shoulders, but, for the first time
since Arkady's death, it was the stench on the outside of her that
rose to the surface of her brain. The cape, and not her womb.
The blood of others, and not of her son. Pressing trembling
fingers to her brow, she began to weep.

At the beginning of February the Headquarters of the Division Sauvage was stationed on the outskirts of Tiflis, capital of
the Caucasus. The Caucasus constituted a veritable barrier between Europe and Asia: High, steep, and jagged, its mountain
range rose like a solid wall, beginning west at the Black Sea and
stretching east to the Caspian. Its peaks were abrupt and majestic, their ragged crests like boar tusks on the horizon. Boris Kussov saw this view daily.

He was living at Division Headquarters, attached to the support staff of General Baranov. The men of this Cossack division
were all bold and daring, having selected this branch of the
army because of its reputation for heroic endeavors and great
risks. Boris, too, had found the atmosphere exhilarating in the
beginning. In his uniform he appeared particularly distinguished, like a modern swashbuckler. The tunic, with its large
trousers stuffed into boots, was black with a silver cartridge belt
and white buckles and buttons, unlike the other Cossack uniforms which were red, maroon, or royal blue with black accou-
trements. With his tall, slender figure and golden hair, Boris
seemed cut out for action—but instead of spending his days on
a horse fighting in the mountains he sat behind a desk battling
piles of paperwork.

He had been made a major. Baranov was a thickset man of
advancing years who had known the old count, Vassily Arkadievitch. The younger soldiers had certainly heard of the gal-

lant, courtly Boris as well. Everyone seemed to know that he had married Natalia Oblonova, and it made Boris smile to think how much her reputation had enhanced his own so close to the front. Any man who could pick for a wife one of the leading ballerinas of the Mariinsky was indeed worthy of the Division Sauvage. And so they drank with him, told him stories, and listened mesmerized to his anecdotes. But still, they were loath to let him near the battlefront.

"Everyone knows you don't know anything about maneuvers and strategy," Baranov told him one evening over coffee and cigars. Brandy would come later; there were as yet no shortages among this division of wealthy rogues. "Let's face it, you pulled strings to get in, and others have had to sweat through the ranks. Entrusting a mission to you, my dear Boris, would be tantamount to committing suicide. Perhaps next year."

"I should have stayed with my wife," Boris said bitterly. "Somehow, there's always been something I could do that was unique—even if it was only to manage the financial aspects of a ballet company. Surely you can find me something besides organizing the filing system."

Baranov puffed on his cigar and closed his eyes beneath the bushy brows. "You're that restless?" he asked, his rasping voice sympathetic.

"Yes. I'd be elated to go with a company patrol, as an observer—I'm certain the junior officer could give me something to do to help. I could carry the water flasks, maybe? Or sing Wagner to egg the troops on to battle?"

"That isn't funny, Boris. But I do see your point. Perhaps I could work something out. From Headquarters we have been sending out three regiments toward the Turkish border; these regiments web out into twelve battalions, containing forty-eight companies of some two hundred ten men each, with a staff support system of forty per company. Stretching even farther out are small platoons of seventy men, including staff. Our patrols go out by squads of fiteen under a sergeant. The purpose of webbing out this way—"

"—is to make certain that no Turks can invade our frontier. And the small squads are our exploratory force?"

"Yes. Would you like to participate in one of these patrols? I could attach you as an observer to a platoon headquarters, and you'd go out with the men. Hardly a brilliant venture, but necessary and dangerous. And you'd learn, my boy. There's nobody like a sergeant to teach you."

Boris smiled. "I'd be delighted," he said. "Thank you, Anton Alexandrovitch."

But Baranov sighed. "We have problems in the mountains, Boris. Revolting Cossacks. Oh, don't remind me that we're a regiment of Cossacks ourselves, because our being on the same side doesn't seem to matter a damned bit. It isn't that they want to go over to the Turks—it's that they're fierce and proud and refuse to be dominated by anyone. They feel we've been disturbing their life."

Boris narrowed his eyes and fingered his mustache. "Our men have not always behaved honorably," he said. "They've raped and plundered villages. The Cossacks are quite naturally angry. Under the best of circumstances, they are an unruly lot. They'd kill a man for looking at a woman that wasn't his. Think how justified they now feel to hate our soldiers! Not every last Sauvage knows how to be a gentleman."

Baranov set down his cigar and motioned to his orderly for cognac. "The Cossack women are beautiful, indeed," he murmured. "And now we'll drink to your new activity. And to little Arkady in Switzerland, who may yet join our ranks someday!"

No one at platoon headquarters knew quite what to make of Major Count Kussov. He was a splendid man, graceful and easygoing, with impeccable manners, a charming man who seemed to know how to speak to the lowliest soldier. But did he know how to fight? Did he even know how to protect himself? Doubtful eyes exchanged glances, which were averted when the major appeared on the scene. But worried thoughts continued.

They were encamped some miles to the southwest of Tiflis— seventy men comprising three squads and a support staff. Each of these squads went on an exploratory trail for two days, then was off patrol for four. For the first six days Boris had stayed in camp with the remainder of the staff. He was getting to know the men, the three sergeants and the lieutenant in charge of the platoon, a small muscular man from Kiev by the name of Ivan

Outchakov—or Vanya, as he was called. Ivan was suspicious of Boris. Although he was learning to enjoy smokes with the Division major, he still wondered what Boris wanted. Adventure? Color? "And why not, Vanya?" Boris asked easily. "Why should that trouble you?"

"War isn't a game, Boris Vassilievitch. Above all, it's not a parlor game."

"So I'm told, repeatedly. How the hell am I to prove you right or wrong if I'm forever kept on the periphery of things? I am not a voyeur, *mon cher.*"

To Boris's amused surprise, the young lieutenant blushed a deep scarlet. Boris threw back his head and laughed.

The next morning he awoke before Outchakov. A creeping restlessness and dissatisfaction had kept him up most of the night, and now he washed and dressed and wandered out of the tent that he shared with the lieutenant. The panorama, so rugged and lonely, struck him like a blow. In front of him the Elboruz and Kazbek peaks, covered with snow, stretched their jagged tips toward the dawn skies. He felt a burning in his stomach, the old pain reviving. It did so now and then. What was he doing here? Playing "parlor games"? Certainly not what I came here to do, he thought angrily.

Then reveille sounded, and the camp came alive. Boris went to the mess tent and had his breakfast among the enlisted men. Natalia's father had been such a man, he thought, curious about her background. Why had he never insisted on meeting her family? She'd hated them, but still— He had, as usual, done what came easiest.

But Natalia had not been easy. She had come more than halfway. He'd doubted her, over and over, accusing her of seeing Pierre, degrading her, even after Arkady's birth. Suddenly he felt hot with shame. He was a grown man nearly forty years old, still entertaining the silly jealousy of a teen-ager.

In the middle of the morning the rider came with the mail pouch from Tiflis. Natalia hadn't written in an age—what could have happened? His sister Nina hadn't heard from her either and had been concerned. Now there was a letter from Switzerland—but not in her hand. Boris raised the envelope to the light and started. From Pierre? Fear, anger, and remembered pain shot through his chest and stomach, knocking the breath out of him. He regained his composure and strode with casual grace toward the tent to peruse his missive in private. Inwardly his body was churning.

He sat down at the small folding table and put on his spectacles. She's getting a divorce, he thought, his throat constricting, and she's made him write the letter because she can't even face me on paper. Then, outraged, he heaped scorn and contempt upon himself. He must never let her know that his absurd fears still refused to die. He took his letter opener and meticulously inserted it into the corner of the envelope to quiet the snare drum that his heart had become. There it was, short and to the point. He leaned back to read it at leisure.

He read it once, the words making no sense. Then a second time, and a third. He could no longer hear his pounding pulse nor feel his extremities. His mind seemed to float above reality, in a strange amniotic fluid. The first paragraph registered perfectly well—but from there the logic short-circuited.

Boris felt his fingers lose their grip on the flimsy vellum, which dropped to the edge of the table. He looked at his hands with great, detached curiosity: They shook uncontrollably. He opened his mouth to laugh but found that his lips, too, refused to obey his command. Why had lightning pierced his stomach, gashing through his entire body like a tree on a stormy day?

Now he could no longer see, for a thick fog clouded his vision. He remained this way for an indeterminate length of time: It seemed like hours, days. When Outchakov entered the tent, Boris had to blink to make him out, and then he realized that his face was wet, that tears were overflowing into his mustache, onto his trembling fingers.

"My God!" Ivan Outchakov cried. "What's happened, Boris Vassilievitch?"

Boris was surprised at how calm his voice sounded when he attempted to speak. "Nothing yet, Vanya," he replied. "But tomorrow I shall go on the first patrol. Make the necessary arrangements, will you? I've had enough waiting."

If it were ever possible to set grief aside, the place to do so would be the Caucasus. The squad with which Boris traveled

348   contained thirteen enlisted men plus a corporal and a sergeant. They rode on horseback, the cold wind in their faces, prickles of anticipation running across their skins. The countryside was stark, and they climbed ridges and patrolled from their flatter tops, looking out toward Turkey. If the enemy traversed the boundaries, they would be able to send back warnings through the elaborate protective system set up by Baranov and the others at Division Headquarters in Tiflis. From platoon to company to battalion to regiment, the Division Sauvage's intricate network would be prepared to receive the Turks and push them back.

The sergeant was older than most men of his rank. He was a dark-faced Georgian with hairy hands, a tall build, and black eyes that reminded Boris of Pierre. He was thirty years old, and his name was Lev Grodin. His corporal, almost a decade his junior, was a young Armenian from Yerevan, with a sweet face and a gentle demeanor. Mikhail Bogdanian was softly unassuming and bore the brunt of Grodin's abuse. Boris wondered at their odd partnership and decided that they complemented each other in their dealings with the men. Grodin issued orders and Bogdanian made certain that the soldiers followed through; morale remained high because the poor corporal received the brunt of Grodin's rage, and not them. Armenians, thought Boris wryly, had never fared well at the hands of Georgians. How had two such different peoples managed to coexist in the Caucasus for so many centuries?

The immensity of the spaces around them touched Boris deeply. He tried not to think of Arkady, but the burning in his stomach reminded him that eventually he would have to deal with his son's death. To Grodin the major appeared a brooding, remote, and handsome man, perhaps imperiously conscious that the men in the squad were below him on the social as well as the military scale. Yet this was strange: At the platoon headquarters, Major Count Kussov had laughed with the soldiers, sat with them, and told them bawdy stories. To be sure, his stories were different from theirs—but still, he had mingled quite charmingly. Now he seemed absorbed in something far away, and the excitement of anticipation was the only point of connection between the noble observer and the rest of the squad.

The top of the mountain range was sharp and barren, offering

a panorama of vast loneliness to Boris. No wonder Pierre had
always been so sullen, so bristling with rebellion. He had grown
up in this open land where man and beast could ride as one,
feeling the elements. Boris smothered his pain in the vista
below. His own mount pawed the red earth of the hilltop, as
nervous as he was himself.

"We're descending now, Major," Grodin announced. "Time
for a watering stop." He began the single file climb down from
the promontory. It was late; they had traveled twenty miles out
from platoon headquarters, then patrolled back and forth among
the ridges twice already; ten miles in each direction. An orange
sun illuminated the peaks of the tallest mountains, dancing over
the tips of snow. They would patrol the heights one more time,
and then camp overnight on the flank of a hill.

Below them flowed a small river, which had started its trip
high above them and would at length hurl itself furiously into
the Black Sea. It was an impetuous torrent that roared over the
stones and gamboled at the bottom of a deep and narrow gorge.
Lev Grodin led the way down to it, and Boris followed, with the
men behind him and little Bogdanian making up the tail. "I
certainly am thirsty, Excellency," Grodin said conversationally.
His wide shoulders were sagging, from fatigue, Boris thought.
Amicably he patted the man's shoulder and reined in his magnificent black stallion to again follow in the leader's tracks. The
men didn't know what to call him: Sometimes they stuck to
military terms, and at others they reverted to a class-conscious
"Excellency." Boris was amused and a little touched. To the
Turks we're one and the same, he thought—the enemy.

His horse suddenly stiffened, and Boris turned back in his
saddle, curious. A black mass was moving toward them, and all
at once his muscles tensed and his entire body became poised
for action. He cried: "Lev, look—over your shoulder, there—
Do you think they're Turks?"

Grodin stopped, and the enlisted men did likewise on the
other side of Boris. The tall sergeant began to shout orders. The
intruders raised their rifles; shots rang out. Boris felt an exhilaration that drove all the anguish of Arkady's death from his body
and mind, an exhilaration that was more elating than anything
he'd experienced in his forty years. Youth flowed into him, and

intense virility. Next to him, firing on the approaching mass, Grodin had thrown back his head and was laughing, his face flushed. "Turks?" Boris called to him.

"No. We'd have seen them, Major. These must be Cossacks—guerilla fighters. But if we don't kill them, they'll slaughter us. There must be a villageful, and we're only sixteen men!"

Briefly Boris felt disappointment, but Baranov had warned him of these Cossacks. Now *they* were the enemy. Boris turned for a split second to address Grodin, when he saw the sergeant open his mouth and fall forward in his saddle, clutching his stomach from which red liquid was spurting. Boris's throat went dry. He swerved to the right and saw that the men had witnessed Grodin's fall and that panic was spreading through the line. "Forward!" he cried, not certain of the validity of his order, but knowing that only by propelling them onward at this very moment could he possibly prevent chaos from taking over. The young coporal, Bogdanian, looked at him in surprise, then raised his arm and spurred his mount toward the Cossacks. Boris followed suit.

In the mêlée that ensued, Boris saw the angry men throw themselves into the fray, shooting the guerillas with fierce resolution. Only one young soldier fell from his horse. Boris held the reins of his stallion in one hand and was preparing to reload his rifle, when something grazed his temple and he wheeled about, bewildered. His eyes were seeing double images of horses and Cossacks and his own men, firing. The sky was tinged with gold from the setting sun. A blinding pain made his eyes water, and he touched the side of his face. When he looked at his fingers, there was blood on them.

"Major, are you hit?" Bogdanian called, his voice sounding far off, as if from a dreamland. Boris supposed he was wounded. His body was collapsing because he could feel himself falling from his horse, and the fall took forever, like a ballerina's movement in slow motion. He must have hit the ground because his blurred vision was jarred. He could see hooves and boots and the red-brown earth. But where was Natalia?

Now there was cotton in his head, wads of it in his mouth and ears. "Natalia?" he said. "Natalia?" A face with dark eyes bent over him, and he said: "Pierre?" Then he couldn't see at all, and he supposed they'd gone into the baby's room, to fetch Arkady. He smiled: Arkady, his son. And then the sky disappeared behind his horse.

It was chilly when Natalia entered the lobby of the Metropole. She had spent a wearing day at the hospital, and her calves ached from standing. Her muscular frame could support physical hardship, but, as a dancer, she had been accustomed to regulated periods of rest. Now there was dull, endless toil without respite. No rest and no glory and no joy, only wrecked human bodies and her own exhaustion. She wanted to throw herself on her bed and forget dinner. Who could eat after seeing what she had seen?

The desk clerk stopped her on her way to the elevator. "Letter." He held an envelope out to her, and she went to pick it up. She was too tired to see whether it came from Boris. She wondered if her marriage would ever be the same after the war, if the resentment would ever fade. She did not allow herself to consider Arkady, and the fact that she would have to face her husband's grief, making her own resurface. Accepting, she knew, would be the hardest adjustment of all.

She unlocked her bedroom door. The soft lights had been turned on by the floor chambermaid, and the bed lay invitingly open, welcoming her. She unhooked her cape, removed her skirt and blouse, and tossed off her hat. Her bathrobe lay on the bed, and she slipped it over her tired limbs. I need to practice longer on my basics, she thought with irritation: Her muscle tone was disappointing these days. She was twenty-five and no longer in perfect form: She hated to see her hard-won muscular control slip away.

Only then did she look at the envelope. It had come from the Caucasus, and on the back, in a strange hand, was the name of the sender: General Anton Alexandrovitch Baranov. Boris had written to her about this man, one of the leaders of the Division Sauvage. All at once she knew what his message contained.

Natalia felt very cold. She rang for room service, then lay down on her bed, facing its foot. Two medium-sized, "modern" cubes adorned either side, like two pedestals guarding the bed. Natalia had always hated that footboard with the ungainly flat cubes. They were a stupid decorating notion that Boris would have laughed it. Boris. She felt her throat begin to beat, and waited. Presently the maid knocked, and entered. Natalia said: "Bring me a bottle of Napoleon cognac and a snifter."

The maid curtsied, then hovered near the threshold of the room. "That's all," Natalia said calmly. The young Swiss girl quickly exited, somewhat startled. What an odd request from the Russian lady!

Only when a busboy came in with a tray did Natalia look up. "Put it there," she said, indicating one of the cube tops to the right of her. It would make a perfect little table. The boy did as he was told and went out, closing the door behind him noiselessly. Now Natalia was alone.

With steady fingers, she poured herself a snifterful of brandy and unsealed the envelope. Baranov's decisive handwriting stared at her, and she perused it thoroughly. He was attempting to make the news more bearable by telling her about her husband's courage, about his heroic leadership that had lived up to the "traditions of the Division Sauvage." So. Fine traditions. And I am to be healed by reminding myself that my dead husband was true to these fine traditions?

She sipped the golden liquid and felt it coursing down her throat into her stomach. He'd always suffered from burning in his stomach but had never kept to a diet. She waited, but nothing came—no tears, no wild eruption of her body, no uncontrolled shaking. She reread the letter and poured another glass of Napoleon. Napoleon—another bloody fool for whom other fools had died. Fools such as Boris.

All at once cold anger began to tremble within her. He had lived up to the traditions of the Division Sauvage! What a joke! He hadn't lived at all. You may be fooled, General Baranov, but I'm not, she thought. Boris is, as Pierre says, a manipulator, and he's manipulated me once again and changed my life by his actions. That's right—he's dead and I'm still alive, and our son is dead too. He's won even in this. And I'm supposed to accept this victory, and not fight back? Oh, God, how *can* I fight back, what can I do? I have to win this one away from you, I can't just let you die and laugh at me from your grave. But maybe you don't even have a grave. Those rebel Cossacks who killed you surely didn't bury you. They didn't know about you, about your mystique and your charm and your ironic mind. They thought you were only a man, an undistinguished major accompanying his squad. The idiots! They failed to recognize the great Boris Kussov, before whom all men trembled—and all women. Isn't that the greatest irony of all, my darling? Carry that wherever you are, my own true love. You can't win with everyone.

She was beginning to feel tipsy, but she treated herself to a fourth glass of brandy and raised it to the empty room. "To your health, my dear husband." It was ludicrous, ludicrous. I have never hated anyone so much as I hate him, for doing this to me, she thought. And now if there's a place where dead men go, he's found Arkady, *my* son, *my* child, part of *my* body. I'm glad you're dead, Boris Kussov, because it saves my having to leave you upon your return. Though I always knew you'd never come back. I knew it that night in Zwingenberg, when you told me of your absurd decision. You made a fool of me even then! You've always made a fool of me. Even when you said you wanted a child, you were making a fool of me. You who knew everthing, didn't you have any idea he'd die, too?

Goddamned Boris Kussov, she thought, pulling the bedspread over her. And goddamned Natalia Kussova. God has damned us all. And then, starting to sob, she thought: But I'd forgotten, there is no God! We have damned ourselves.

Chapter 20

ierre held Diaghilev's letter to the light and took a deep breath. In Viareggio the Russian impresario had learned of Boris's death and wondered whether Pierre had seen Natalia. The war had separated the various members of the Ballets Russes from one another; it had caught Serge Pavlovitch and his new *premier danseur* and favorite, Leonid Miassin, in Italy. Pierre wondered exactly how much Diaghilev knew—or had inferred—of his relationship to both the Kussovs.

Pierre had renewed his acquaintance with Stravinsky, who lived in Morges, near Lausanne. Through the composer he had learned that Diaghilev had signed a contract with the Metropolitan Opera in New York to appear there next year, in April 1916. "Karsavina's in Russia; he'll have to get Natalia and find some way of enticing Nijinsky for the North American season," Stravinsky had told Pierre. "The New World wants to see the main attractions of the old Ballets Russes." But Pierre had known that Natalia was tied to her sick baby and that Nijinsky and his wife and small daughter had been caught in Hungary when war was declared and were now interned in house arrest at the home of her mother, Emilia Markus.

Later, when Arkady had died, Pierre had written to Stravinsky, asking the composer and his family to call on Natalia. But she had refused to see him. I'm not going to her, Pierre had thought fiercely. If she needs me, let her send for me.

He had met a young woman from Locarno, Fabiana d'Arpezzo, and had moved her into his rented house overlooking the Lago Maggiore. Fabiana was dark, laughing, and compliant, a good model and a fine cook. I don't need Natalia, or her problems, he had said to himself. Life is sweet this way. I'm not expected to love, and I'm not looked upon as a commodity. I can devote my energies to painting, and Fabriana does not wreak havoc on my nerves or make demands of my very soul. I am free of her at last, free of Natalia.

Then Medveyev had shattered his peace by announcing in a letter that Boris had been killed in the Caucasus. An inexplicable tightness had gripped Pierre's throat and brought the taste of salt to his mouth. Somewhere at the back of his life there had always been Boris. Now there was emptiness and the certainty of never encountering him again, of having no one left to hate, no force against which to battle. Boris Kussov has been my albatross, Pierre thought, and he has been my Satan. But while he was my mentor, I escaped mediocrity, and since then my potential has never been fulfilled.

She will have to make the first move, he had also thought. She's lost her husband and her son, but why should that matter to me? She loved him. It's time I faced reality: Natalia's love for me was the quick infatuation of a schoolgirl. The woman Natalia wanted another man because I had become commonplace. I don't want to win her by default because he is dead and she is distraught. I shall stay away.

Now Diaghilev was asking him questions. Evidently, Pierre concluded, he had written to her and not received an answer. Stravinsky had made another attempt to see her and had reported to Pierre that for a while she had remained closeted in her hotel, receiving no visitors. Then she had resumed her work as a nurse and had sent him a brief note: "Igor Feodorovitch, I am touched that you wished to see me. But right now I cannot face old friends. Please do not begrudge me my seclusion." Pierre chewed on his lower lip. It was so difficult to understand things from a distance. But he was afraid to come closer, afraid to confront what she had become and too proud to overcome his fear.

There is nothing to cling to, Natalia thought. There is no core to Natalia Oblonova. The Countess Kussova was a dream, a fairy tale, and getting married was the greatest mistake of my life. Anger once again paralyzed her emotions. She had been angry since reading Baranov's letter, angry that the little Crimean waif had allowed herself to become vulnerable. Boris had seized on each person's vulnerability, had twisted and turned others' lives into cruel parodies of existence, and she, fool that she was, had allowed him to do this to her own life.

Damn you, damn you, I won't mourn you! she thought for the hundredth time as she arrived at the train station for duty. Station duty provided a means of escape; she always returned to the hotel too exhausted to think. Now she squeezed her eyelids tightly shut, holding back the agony that had to be anesthetized each day anew. Why couldn't you have stayed out of my life, Boris Kussov? Why did you have to help me make a baby? Why did you ever love me?

"The trains are late tonight," Louise Dondel said, her teeth chattering. It was March and the nights were still frosty. The young Swiss girl looked at Natalia and was startled. Natalia's face beneath the hood of her thick cape appeared white and stark and totally devoid of emotion. Louise bit her lip, shocked. She liked the Russian woman but found her increasingly strange, since her husband's death. She should have expressed her tragedy, wept, and broken down, but instead she came faithfully, night after night, but with that cold, expressionless face, that alabaster remoteness that discouraged all sympathy. How could she help a woman like Natalia? Or perhaps she had never cared for her husband and now had no reason to grieve.

The first evening, after Louise had learned of the count's demise, she had said to Natalia: "I am so sorry. I have never been married—" She would have continued to explain why words were failing her, but the other had turned to her with an intense light in her brown eyes and whispered:

"Neither have I. We are born alone and we die alone, and in between we do what we can to prevent pain. Let's never discuss this, Louise."

She had looked, Louise Dondel thought, as if she had actually hated her husband and believed that he had deserved to die in combat.

This March night the trains eventually arrived. The women

waited in chilled silence on the platform, then tended the wounded and administered care, coffee, and medicines. Louise lost track of her Russian companion. When the whistles resounded as wails in the black, frosty air, Louise hastened toward the warmth of her waiting car. Natalia, she thought, had probably accepted a ride from another volunteer. Louise went home.

At the first whistle Natalia had found herself still mopping the brow of a very young Prussian lad whose left leg had been amputated. She'd nearly had to force the coffee down his throat to revive him. But she did not allow his pain, his wracked, limbless body to register on her emotions. Competently she wiped the perspiration from his brow. When he relaxed, she set his head down on the bunk and made her way out of the train. She stepped from the ladder seconds before the last whistle emitted its shrill elegy. The other nurses were already leaving the platform.

Natalia was lost in thought and hardly noticed the piercing cold that surrounded her. The young soldier had finally ceased to writhe, had calmed down. His other leg had stopped twitching. They said that missing limbs often felt more acutely painful than wounds on the living flesh. She had accomplished something, getting him to lay his head down peacefully. Now she would be able to sleep, too. No one had done that for Boris.

She froze and could not walk: No one had done that for Boris! The horror penetrated like a searing blade slashing through her, and she bent over, sickened. Now she knew why she continued to come here, night after endless night: to prevent another man from dying alone. Natalia shook the thought from her but could not remove the bitter intensity of her pain. I am atoning for letting him leave, for letting him die alone, she thought. She could picture herself spending the rest of her life plodding to the Geneva train station to mop fevered brows, to whisper words of encouragement to total strangers in the middle of the night. Hers would be an endless expiation.

Natalia's eyes filled with tears, and she missed a step. She felt herself slipping into a puddle, felt the clammy cold of the sloshy water on the platform. But she could not rise. Utter exhaustion had come over her, enveloping her reflexes in a narcotic stupor. She thought: This too is death. Boris died alone and now I am paying for it. Her head lolled back and hit the pavement as she fainted.

Pierre sat in the wing chair by the bed and watched the little heart-shaped face delineated against a mound of white pillows. She is the love of my heart, he thought, and felt a rush of anger at his own weakness. She breathed with difficulty. The feather-soft brown hair formed a halo around her pale features, suggesting to him her sudden vulnerability.

She stirred, and her eyes fluttered open like tentative butterflies poised over honeysuckle. "Natalia," he said. He moved his chair closer to the bed and took the small hand that lay on the coverlet, its palm perspiring. "You slept a long time."

She turned her face to him, her eyes wide and surprised. "You?" she whispered. She was too weak to speak up and too limp to sit. "Who let you in?"

He smiled. "The nurse. She needed some time off. I took over, if you will. Do you mind?"

She shook her head. "I don't care, Pierre. But don't feel sorry for me. It doesn't matter anymore." She swept the room with her eyes, then looked at Pierre again, insistently. "Who told you?" she asked.

He shrugged lightly and smiled. "Stravinsky. You probably don't even remember that he came to see you while you were in the hospital. You were at your worst then, after they found you frozen to the pavement of the train station in a pool of ice. You were lucky to have escaped with pneumonia."

"Incredibly lucky," she said ironically. Shiny dots of fever marked her prominent cheekbones, and on the coverlet her hand trembled, its blue veins marbling the white skin. Suddenly, her face contorted with anguish, and tears streamed from her eyes. "I wish you would let me die," she whispered.

He turned away, overcome by what he had seen. Regaining control with effort, he said, "I didn't come to let you sink into abject self-pity, Natalia. I know what that's like: It's death-in-life, and I've succumbed to it more than once myself. I didn't make the journey to come to a funeral, either."

"Well, why did you come?" Her pupils had enlarged, and in her glowing, excited face they shone strangely. Suddenly she said, in small gasps: "Show me what it is to live, Pierre! You used to love me!" She was trying to sit up, her lips parted, her breath rasping. The cover fell from her armpits to her waist, revealing her nightgown open to her cleavage, which had never been deep but which, to Pierre, was riveting now. The beginning of her two firm apple breasts stared at him, glistening with moistness. She did nothing to hide them.

He stood up and began to pace the room. At length he stopped in front of her, and placed his hands on her shoulders as if leaning on her for support. She raised her hands to his, looking at him through her shining eyes. "It wouldn't work, Natalia," he said finally. "I'm not a substitute. A man has to be loved for himself alone—at least, this one does."

They stared silently at each other. Then Pierre said: "Diaghilev is planning to come to Lausanne with Miassin, to set up a new committee. For the North American season next year. He needs you, Natalia."

She closed her eyes and breathed deeply. "Thank you," she said and pressed his hands with her own.

In the fall of 1915 Natalia received Serge Diaghilev in her suite at the Hotel Metropole. After the chambermaid wheeled in a tray of teacakes, Natalia herself, Russian fashion, poured him the scented brown infusion into a cup of the most delicate Meissen porcelain. He smiled beneath his thin mustache. "Tea in a cup—it seems barbaric, does it not, my dear?" he remarked.

"I have lost touch with Russia, Serge Pavlovitch. Somehow I do not care anymore. Lydia, Katya—they are friends of the past. My life no longer touches theirs, and I have no desire to reintegrate the country of my birth."

"And I? Am I another 'friend of the past'?"

"In two years a lifetime can go by," she said, and then, hearing her own words, she turned aside and bit her lower lip.

"Indeed. Natalia—you must realize how much I miss him, too. We weren't always on the same side, but we were always friends—ever since I first arrived in Petersburg, at eighteen, and he, at sixteen, was still at the May gymnasium. Not even Serov's death affected me so deeply."

"It does no good to talk about it," Natalia said sharply. She breathed quickly in and out and looked at Diaghilev. "I didn't mean to be rude to you, Serge Pavlovitch. But I don't want to hurt anymore. I have nothing left of him except material things—possessions—and so I'm going to pick up from 1908, when I was alone with my talent and my ambition. This may sound hard to you, but I've always been a hard woman. I don't wish to relive my experience of him."

Her clear brown eyes were fastened on him with an intensity that belied the coldness of her words. He could not meet her gaze and examined his finely manicured nails instead. "Natalia—I am reassembling the Ballets Russes," he said. "The war nearly broke us totally. The company won't have many of the same people, as you can fathom. I have Miassin; he could become as great a choreographer as Fokine when properly launched. He doesn't dance like our previous male star, but in his own way he parallels Nijinsky. I have excellent artists, a young Russian couple, Gontcharova and Larionov. They've worked for me before, but now they've given us a new perspective. I also hope to rekindle the interest of Pierre Riazhin. Will you join us?"

Color rose to her checks, which were still wan from her illness. "I want nothing else," she answered simply. She smiled. "And Pierre—I'm certain he'll be enthusiastic. He hasn't done anything these past years to equal the work he did for the Ballets Russes, and before that, for the Paris Exhibition."

Raising his brows, Diaghilev said: "Very true. He had an inspiration then—the Sugar Plum Fairy. But I had nothing against the young man—I believe it was Boris who dropped him from the committee."

"None of this was my concern," she replied quietly. Her hands lay folded in her lap, and she sat erect and sylphlike in the armchair. "Will I be dancing my old roles, Serge Pavlovitch? Or something new?"

"A bit of both, of course. We are attempting to conjure up the miracles needed to have Nijinsky released from his political internment. Then you and he can conquer America. The Firebird, Natalia. Otto Kahn asked me to bring him the Firebird. We each see you in a different role: Pierre as the Sugar Plum,

Kahn as the Firebird—and I rather fancied you as Tahor. You are a multifaceted dancer, *ma chère*. A treasure."

"Thank you, Serge Pavlovitch."

He scratched his chin and regarded her directly. "One final question, Natalia. Indelicate but necessary. May I ask it?"

"Please do. But I shan't promise to answer you."

"You are a wealthy woman. We have our usual financial dilemmas, only worse, because of the impossibility of performing in London and Paris last year and this. Would you provide us with some backing, Natalia?"

The fingers stiffened in her lap. "I do not want to step into his shoes," she said in an undertone. "I am a dancer. Let me dance for you—but do not use me to take his place. Someone not long ago told me that no man could accept being a substitute. No woman can, either. Besides, my assets are for the most part tied up in France, and I couldn't get them out because of the war. Maybe later, if no one else can aid your enterprise." She coughed and looked at the cup of tea in front of her. "I need to recapture Oblonova," she said, "and to forget the Countess Kussova."

"Of course, my dear." Diaghilev rose and bowed over her hand. "Rehearsals will be starting soon. And we shall expect you to participate in our committee meetings at my house in Ouchy."

She stood up, too, and now a surge of hope pierced through her, a burst of energy and courage. Looking into his massive dark face, she said, somewhat breathlessly: "I would be honored, Serge Pavlovitch. But there's something else—something that I'd discussed with Boris long ago." She hesitated, losing her nerve, then resolutely plunged in: "I should like the opportunity to choreograph a ballet. You know I could do it!"

He gave her a piercing stare, cocking his head to one side. Then he patted her arm. "Sweet Natasha," he replied, smiling, "a child must learn to walk before it can run. It's been a long time, hasn't it? Ease your way back in, like a good girl."

Maybe he was right, maybe it was too soon. When he had left her alone, she walked pensively to the window. Ouchy was a mere village by Lake Geneva, directly below Lausanne. Could she summon enough courage to open up her house on Sauvabelin? Even if she didn't now, wouldn't she eventually be forced to confront that city?

She went to her secretary and rolled back the top. On a piece of strong vellum she began to write, dipping her quill in the sunken ink-well. "Pierre," her note read:

> If both of us are to move to Lausanne to rejoin Diaghilev's Ballet, I shall have to take up quarters in the house I own there. You will need to live somewhere, too. Come as a guest in my home, and I shall be grateful for your presence. By myself I could not leave Geneva.

Her head sank softly onto her outstretched arms, and she closed her eyes. There was never any respite from the pain. It lurked in each corner of her existence and laughed at her like an evil spirit, a Caliban. But I need to dance, she thought desperately. I shall have to go.

Nothing had remained static. Natalia felt like a woman who had awakened in the dark and had to blink to get her bearings; her world was like a kaleidoscope that had been shaken, all the colored pieces reassembled into a different landscape.

Pierre's presence in the chalet was disconcerting. He was so large, so vital, that she felt him in the house even when he was elsewhere. It even smells of him, she thought, recalling in a flash the distinctive scent of his bedroom. He had begun to work with Larionov on a new ballet of Miassin's composition, *The Midnight Sun*, and there were pots of paint and canvases all over the living room. Brigitte was frightened of him and went scurrying to Alfred in the garden, telling stories about the black-haired, savage-looking painter from the Caucasus. Had the countess taken leave of her senses, inviting such a man as a guest? And what was worse, without a chaperone? But Natalia was thankful for Pierre's presence and indifferent to convention.

Pierre, on the other hand, was caught up in his work. For the first time he would actually sign his name to a set design. He and the Muscovite Larionov spent hours sketching, then painstakingly converting their drawings to models, or copying back cloths. They were making a huge sun with a backdrop of the deepest blue, almost black. High-strung and ebullient, Pierre sustained Natalia's strong attention. It was as though life had taken his shape, and was being held up in contrast to her own haunted nightmare of death.

Bakst often came to see Pierre at the chalet, and sometimes the committee held meetings there. Natalia sat silently among old and new associates, listening to plans. Ideas were fermenting around her, and the American season was imbuing everyone with nervous expectancy. New York had witnessed Pavlova's classical dancers, and also Lydia Lopokhova, who would join her old company there. But the magic virtuosity, the opulant rush of style characteristic of the Ballets Russes, would be a totally new experience for this young nation. Conversely Natalia did not know what to expect of America. Once, a decade ago, she had viewed France through new eyes, too. How long ago that seemed now!

Rehearsals began, and so did the most excruciating physical ordeal of Natalia's life as a dancer. Her muscles ached as though she had never exercised them before, for her months of inactivity, with only isolated hours of solitary practice, had left her body unused to such travails. The younger dancers watched her with awe as she perspired and strained at the *barre*, cords standing out in her throat—for, at twenty-five, she was the sole representative of the prewar Ballet and its only star. But she huffed and puffed with greater determination than any of the newcomers, as though her very life were on the line.

December came, and finally, at long last, she was ready. Diaghilev set up some charity matinées for the Red Cross, and Natalia danced the *Blue Bird pas de deux* with Adoph Bolm. If anyone remembered that this was the anniversary of Arkady's death, not a word was mentioned. Natalia would not have allowed it. Pierre watched her anxiously from the wings, and thought: She has never been so lovely or danced so superbly. But when he took her home afterward, he did not break her silence. Her eyes glistening, her chin firm, Natalia shut away her feelings with a furious, driving determination. She had never had a son, never lost her husband. She had always been Natalia Oblonova, alone and proud.

364   But when she went to bed that night, she could not control the trembling in her hands. Her teeth were chattering. New York! That's what I need, she thought, a place as far removed from Boris as snow is from the Equator. A place where I won't have to remember.

PART IV

Curtain on a Changed World

Chapter 21

rom Bordeaux to New York the ship took twelve days. Natalia's last sea voyage had been physically uncomfortable and emotionally tense. Now she let her mind float away with the seagulls, let it sink beneath the turgid green-gray waters of the ocean. She didn't want to feel. Since the journey took place at the start of the new year, 1916, it was too cold to stay on deck. Natalia enveloped her consciousness in the rolling motions of the ship and slept a great deal.

On January 12 she had her first glimpse of New York. The Statue of Liberty, immense and rigid, filled her with a sensation of powerlessness. This country would overwhelm her, she thought. Yet, once on land, she had to concede that New York was not altogether the barbaric hell she had imagined. Fifth Avenue was a majestic stretch of road bordered by stone mansions not unlike those of Paris, and the neat brownstones on the cross streets of Manhattan's East Side showed restrained good grace, like London's squares. The stores were enormous, filled with furs and jewelry, and the people always appeared briskly jovial and were forever in a hurry. Natalia thought: I can immerse myself in this city, in its bustle and its fanfare, and then I won't have to think about myself.

The first week she did not have much time to think in any event. She rehearsed continuously for the two weeks' worth of performances that were to be given at the Century Theatre on Central Park West. Then the troupe would travel to Boston and continue from there on a tour of sixteen cities. Finally, in April they would return to New York, this time to fulfill their engagement at the Metropolitan.

Natalia was disappointed. Once again, things seemed to have changed, and yet, at the same time, to have stayed the same. The ballets in which she was appearing were all familiar and the limited repertory saddened her. Yet for the most part, the dancers were new, and their work did not live up to the exceptional talents displayed by Karsavina and Nijinsky. Flore Revalles, a French opera singer whom Diaghilev had hired to add an exotic flavor à la Ida Rubinstein, did not exude the Moscow Jewess's sensual flow. Miassin, whom his mentor had renamed Massine for simplicity, was competent, even inspired—but hardly the innovator that Fokine had been, with his poetic insights. It's odd, she thought, but I wish Pierre were here. Somehow he would add a feral element that is missing in this uninspired group. New York is too conventional, and I feel trite in my old roles. Perhaps, after all, I have outlived my prime. Yet I *know* I could put together a wonderful new ballet.

Increasingly, she was relieved at the idea that Pierre was working in her house in Lausanne. There was something reassuring about his presence: He, at least, would keep the world, her world, from disappearing behind a cloud. They had helped each other, openly and behind the scenes, enough times over the years to have convinced her of his permanence. He was not the brilliant magician that Boris had been, or as complex a man. But he was living in her house, preventing it from collapsing, preventing her from collapsing. As a young woman she had been afraid of Pierre's sexual power; now she felt impervious to it. She did not want another man, ever—sexually or emotionally. Pierre was simply a blood brother of sorts—her family, for who else was there?

She did not think much about Pierre, actually. At night, wracking dreams still possessed her, waking her just before an imaginary death. Once she dozed off in the early morning and touched the pillow next to her, gently, then frantically: the old familiar gesture. She sat up, her eyes distended with sorrow, and stared at the pillow. With a scream, she hurled it to the ground, her throat constricting with anguish. She did not cry. She washed, ate breakfast, and went to rehearsal.

Eventually New York cheered her. Its citizens had been disappointed by Nijinsky's absence, but not as much as the Europeans had been. The American public, moralistic and prudish, found it easier to accept female dancers than tightly clad *danseurs*. Natalia, small, strong and infinitely graceful, a passionate Tahor and a palpitating Firebird, was fêted.

"It's essential that you go to the receptions," Diaghilev admonished her with some asperity. "You are our star. In essence, you are today's Ballets Russes. I need you among the bankers and stockbrokers, *ma chère*."

And so she went. Her slim body sheathed in simple evening gowns of graceful design, bands of material brought from the sides to the back of her skirt in the draped fashion that was popular, Natalia moved listlessly among New York's elite. Their English baffled her. She had learned the language in London, and Boris had spoken in an impeccable Oxford accent, indistinguishable from that of the highest British aristocracy. The men of New York shook her hand vigorously and did not kiss it. But Natalia did not pass judgment on them. She merely thought: This is the place to forget an airy, lighter world in which I was vulnerable to life and love.

She felt more lonely than ever but did not want to break out of the loneliness, so the new dancers of the company found her aloof. When the Ballet was invited to the magnificent Vanderbilt mansion on Fifth Avenue for an important evening reception, she escaped to the vast window and peered curiously toward Central Park. Voices dimmed around her. She fingered the tassel of the draperies and thought: The park is beautiful. But I could never slip out of this mausoleum without arousing the anger of Serge Pavlovitch, who watches me like a hawk. She licked her lips and did not move. I shall not mingle, she said defiantly to herself. He can make me come, but he can't force me to live a lie.

"You're weary of us?" a man's voice resounded in a low tone from behind her. Not wanting to turn around, she bowed her head, hoping he would tiptoe away and not intrude further. But he continued: "I have some champagne. Would you care to join me?"

She looked at him then and saw a man of some six feet, with brown hair rising like a crown over a wide brow. He had a square jaw, a firm straight nose, a rather large mouth, and a thick mustache. The eyes that probed her own from beneath thick brows were an unusual gold-green hue, an arresting color. Dressed in a rather shabby evening suit, the man appeared to be in his late thirties. Surprised, Natalia smiled. "You're not what I expected," she said. You're not quite a gentleman, she thought.

In his right hand the man held a green bottle of Dom Perignon, and between the fingers of his left hand were twisted two tall crystal glasses. When he smiled, he displayed large white teeth. "I'm Stuart Markham," he told her. "Here—hold these, will you?" He handed her the coupes. The bottle had been uncorked, and as she held out the crystal, he poured bubbling yellow froth into it. Looking around him furtively, he laughed and deposited the bottle behind a table. "Cheers," he said, moving with her to the window.

She sipped the champagne, and suddenly bitterness enveloped her, tightening over her throat. Champagne had been *his* drink. "I prefer cognac," she said to the man and then wondered why she had spoken at all. He seemed content simply to watch the park below them, as she had been.

"And I prefer whiskey," he countered. "But what's to be found among these bloated, self-important money-makers? Madame, one imbibes champagne in Paris—the Vanderbilts would do no less in New York."

"You don't like them much," Natalia commented with amusement. "Who are you? Why did you come?"

Stuart Markham nodded pensively. "A good question. I'm somebody's dissipated younger brother, you see. I get taken along now and then, in an attempt to civilize me. You see, I'm a writer—a novelist. The other two boys in the family are an attorney and a dentist. Hardly the stuff of novels, I'd say. We don't fit at all into one another's lives. The attorney is about to run for political office—and I think that's the most ridiculous profession of all. Kissing babies isn't my idea of a good time."

Tears suddenly rose to her eyes. She bit her lip and forced them down. "There," he said. "I've already managed to bore you. I saw you today in *The Firebird*. Now you, gracious lady, are the stuff of novels. Or of poems. 'Ode to a Ballerina,' by Stuart Markham. Not my usual style, but we'll see!"

She could not help smiling. "You liked *The Firebird*. I'm glad, because I didn't perform well this evening. I haven't performed well since I arrived. I'm sorry. I'm cheating everyone, I suppose. Poor Diaghilev! He must be seething beneath his elegant broadcloth jacket."

Stuart Markham raised his eyebrows quizzically but said nothing. They drank in silence. Then he said: "Look, let's take a walk in the park, shall we? D'you have a warm coat?"

Before she could reply, he had begun to propel her toward a back door. They edged their way past one salon and into a hallway. At an open door he whispered: "Show me your coat," and entered a well-lit room where wraps of every sort lay draped over chairs, on an enormous bed, and on hangers in a special armoire. Natalia found her sable, and Stuart helped her into it. "It makes you look like a ball of fur," he remarked, pushing her softly in front of him down the corridor. There was a back staircase, and they descended on tiptoes. Natalia thought: I am doing what I want, and Serge Pavlovitch be damned! Then she wondered why she felt comfortable with this stranger.

Stuart took her arm, and together they went past the two butlers by the door, which gave onto a side street. Outside a gust of wind lifted his hat off his head, and he clamped it back down over his brow. They found their way to Fifth Avenue and up several blocks before crossing the street. Only then did he speak again. "Coach ride or walk?" he asked.

"I'd rather walk. I'm a Russian, remember? This is nothing compared with our own winters. We have to stuff cotton between our inner and outer walls to prevent freezing inside our homes. This wind is a sweet balm, Mr. Markham."

They entered Central Park. All at once, beneath the trees and the black sky scattered with its confetti stars, Natalia knew why she liked this man. He was neither condescending nor threatening to her, and he was of her own world: irritated by his brothers' lives, yet clearly cultured, educated. They walked at a brisk pace to outdistance the wind, and, bending toward his beaver collar to be heard, she said: "Why haven't I read anything by you yet?"

He laughed. "Fame doesn't come easily, Madame Oblonova. I've published countless short stories about disenchanted young iconoclasts, and two novels. One was about the disillusioned upper classes of America, whose members don't care to read about themselves. The second was a better book, and dealt with a more worthwhile subject. It was about a woman's reaction when her husband kills himself. A grisly topic—but real."

Natalia had stopped in her tracks, her eyes wide, one hand at her throat. "What's wrong?" he asked, peering into her white face. "Did my story offend you? Death, you know, is part of life. Art that doesn't have a life of its own can't touch us at all."

"It's death that shouldn't touch us," she whispered. The wind blew a small twig across her cheek, and he brushed it away with the back of his hand. Tears filled her eyes. "Stop it," she said. "Don't talk anymore. I can't listen to what you're saying."

"You haven't read my book," he countered gently. "There's nothing further to say about it. I prefer that people read my work rather than listen to me describe it. I'm not that interesting. Let's talk about you."

"No! Let's not talk." Natalia did not look at him, but when he placed a firm hand under her elbow, she did not shake him off. They walked on the dark pathways in complete silence, but her pounding heart seemed ready to burst while her mind and body struggled to control it. She had once seen a teacup of bone china shatter from contact with too hot a liquid, and now she thought: That is what is happening to me!

Panic overflowed from inside her, and once again she stopped, pressing her hands to her thighs. Purple shapes danced on the backs of her velvet eyelids. A sound began in her chest and started to rise, but she stifled it, holding her lips tightly over her teeth in a white line. Stuart Markham put his hands on her shoulders and kept them there, firmly but without pressure. She thought: If he were Pierre, I'd run away; I'd never want to see him again! But then her lips parted, and a deep wail escaped from the pit of her stomach, a wail that became a sob.

Tears rushed from her eyes, splashing haphazardly over her

cheeks, mingling with the fur of her collar. She started to fall, but Stuart caught her, steadied her, and folded strong arms around her shaking body. Against his large chest she screamed and sobbed, unable to regain her breath, blinded by the tears that had been released at last. She sensed that he had begun to walk with her, but she hardly felt her own legs, until he sat her down somewhere and she was dimly conscious that it was a park bench. Her face protected by the lapels of his coat, she wept and wept until she had cleansed the panic from her gut and could breathe again.

When at last she could speak, she looked into his eyes and asked: "What was her reaction? Your woman?"

Calmly he brushed strands of clammy hair from her face, his fingers lingering on her soaked cheeks. "My widow? At first she wants to die, too, because she can't cope. With the guilt, you see. Who was he?" he added gently. "Your husband?"

Natalia nodded and felt fresh tears sting her eyelids. "He didn't really commit suicide. But for me he did. It was a stupid war death, and I should never have let him go. He was almost forty years old!"

"What was he like?" Stuart Markham asked.

"Like no one else. Different people might tell you different things about him. I don't care! Whatever he did, he did it brilliantly and with grandeur. He was supremely selfish, but it didn't matter to me after a while. He hurt people, but only because they were weak and let him do it. He had no right to be a hero—it didn't fit in the least into his way of life, into his morality. But then, *I let him leave.* It was my fault."

"It wasn't anybody's fault. How could you have held onto a man like that? A strong, willful individual? It's not the same as watching a man go to pieces in front of your eyes, without lifting a finger to help him. Natalia—may I call you Natalia?—you have to accept that he's gone. Then you can learn to mourn him."

"But it wasn't only Boris!" she cried. "There was the baby first. Our baby died, Stuart—and I shall never learn to mourn for him because his life spanned too short a time! Who can grieve for an infant who could not speak, who could barely say, 'Mamamama'?" She turned away and bent over, hugging her knees. Sobbing gasps escaped her. He touched the back of her neck, but she jerked up and confronted him. "Why are you doing this to me? You don't know me, and you're twisting a knife inside my heart. Why didn't you leave me alone by the window?"

Tilting her face up with his hand, he murmured: "I'm not sorry. You were killing yourself. No wonder you don't think you're dancing up to your usual standards! There's no soul left in you! A person has to let go of his dead, Natalia. Do you think you're helping your husband, or your child, by throwing yourself on their funeral pyres? If your husband loved you, this kind of death-in-life would make him lose respect for you."

"But I hated him so," she said. "For dying. For going to war. For wanting me and loving me and making this defective baby with me. I was glad he died—or I would have left him."

Stuart Markham shook his head. "No, you wouldn't have. You loved him, and there's no reason to stop loving him because he's dead. You've forgiven him a lot—forgiven him for betrayals and God knows what else. Your husband didn't plan to die, Natalia. Forgive him and forgive yourself."

He handed her a clean linen handkerchief, and she pressed it to her eyes, cheeks, and mouth. "I don't want to die with him," she murmured.

"That would truly be cheating the public," he said. Then he cupped her small, tear-streaked face in his two large hands and held it for several moments. He kissed her lips, softly, then more fully. "Do you want to stay alone tonight?" he asked her.

A shiver passing over her spine, Natalia simply shook her head no.

It isn't just the deaths, Natalia thought: It's the feeling of being part of a closed triangle, unable to break loose. She looked at Stuart Markham and was grateful. He had never known about the convoluted relationships in her life; he had not known Boris. Stuart Markham listened to her speak about her husband and accepted what she told him, without question. Natalia Oblonova had been married to a brilliant man, a complicated man, a patron of the arts throughout Europe—but beyond those facts he could add nothing to his own opinion. He could help her to begin the healing process because her past was not his past; none of his emotions was tied to her previous experience. I can be clean with him, she thought. Pierre is too involved, and so I could not bear him and had to run away. With Stuart, Boris and Arkady remain my own: I do not have to share my memories of them or edit my conceptions to conform with his outlook.

She was beginning to realize that her grief would not be exorcised until she allowed herself to truly explore its depths. There were so many hurts. To lose a man like Boris had brought to the surface myriad smaller pains. She could remember the good, the ineffably sweet, but also the insecurity, the lack of self-esteem that had characterized some of their earlier dealings. She said softly to Stuart: "The most difficult thing to accept is that I shall never learn whether he loved me most. If we had been able to continue to live together, perhaps I might have come to know. As it is, I think he loved me, but maybe he loved Pierre more. But I suppose it doesn't matter. The point is that he did love me, and our baby."

She had been spending most of her free time with the American writer. Ten days before, at the end of January, the Ballets Russes had finished their engagement at the Century Theatre in New York. Natalia had looked at Stuart and thought: I can't leave again so soon; I can't be alone with the pain. Impulsively, she had asked: "Why don't you come with us on tour?"

"Is that what you want?" he had countered.

"Yes. I really do." Natalia's eyes had met his, and she had felt the soft pressure of his fingers on her arm. He was a warm man who would give her complete freedom to be her own person but still be supportive next to her. He liked her and seemed to expect nothing in return. She was not ready to let him go, not well enough adjusted to stand her ground without his help.

"My editor isn't exactly pounding the pavement in front of my door," he said with a light laugh. "I'll come. Why not? You need a guide to this strange country, Natalia. I'll bring along my manuscript and work while you rehearse."

And so he had accompanied the Ballet on its tour. When they stopped to perform in Boston, he took her to Harvard Square in Cambridge to show her where he had studied for four years. They strolled arm in arm among the brick buildings, facing the statues of his early youth. "I'm glad you're here," she murmured. "I've never had many friends, but you're my friend. I haven't known you long—why are you with me?"

"I like you, Natalia. You're not like the women here. You're solid and real. You have a goal, and you're not afraid to feel."

"But I am. I've always built walls to protect me from myself. And you? What do you feel?"

"I'm neither happy nor unhappy. Maybe I'm too selfish. I never cared much what people thought of me—my family, my professors, my publisher. I never tried too hard, either. Not like you, with ballet. I write because there's something inside pushing its way out, and because I suppose I'm good. Apart from that, I live a fairly good life, but I'm rather restless. I don't inspire myself."

He laughed then, but she was silent. He did as he pleased and apologized to no one. Did she not profess to do the same? She had read some of his work in New York: pages typed on onionskin, corrected in a sprawling hand. He liked himself, liked what he did. Stuart Markham, she had learned, was the youngest of three sons of a Philadelphia surgeon, and he had been reared in a traditional upper-middle-class manner. His father had give him an excellent education, first at the Andover preparatory school, then at Harvard. But there he had discovered, he had told her with amusement, that he was like a dandelion shooting up in a garden of well-tended roses: thoroughbred roses, to boot. "But then," he had added, "there is no such thing as an American thoroughbred."

He was right, she thought. America was a strange country, a conglomeration of immigrants and sons of immigrants who had sought refuge from famines and pogroms, or had been tempted to conquer new, raw lands. A land of rugged imperialists, of harsh industrialists with little culture, a land of children waiting to be shown new ways and softer manners—a land of modest, puritanical dreamers, of debutantes who danced in honky-tonk hideaways, of frightened followers as well as bold creative geniuses such as she felt sure Stuart was.

Natalia was still amazed by the audience for which she danced. Their jewels glittered and their mansions were enormous. Yet underneath that veneer of splendor lurked the virgin minds of children. They did not know how to judge a ballet, let alone a Diaghilev production. They possessed no background of general culture on which to fall back to form an artistic opinion. Now Natalia could understand why America had adopted Anna Pavlova without question. Brilliant though she was as a performer, Natalia's old rival from the Mariinsky had come to America as she had previously come to England, then equally unprepared for the complexity of Russian dance. Now Pavlova's little troupe was composed mainly of lesser dancers from Britain. She had not attempted any choreographic innovation, because all dance to the Americans was totally novel. She had distinguished herself in her individual performance, relying on her repertory of classical and romantic roles. Europe would have demanded bolder strides, new directions, and more virtuosity from the *corps*.

"Diaghilev's productions are too complex for us," Stuart explained to Natalia. "We love you because you are accessible: You're small, and lovely, and vulnerable. You're a good actress; Tahor makes the women weep. But dance is seen as recreation, like the movies."

Natalia was amused. He had taken her to see a moving picture in New York, and she had been filled with wonder. How odd that Serge Pavlovitch, always so interested in new artistic media, had steadfastly refused to involve his ballet in film. "Perhaps," she said, "the public would prefer to see us in a movie theatre. I wouldn't mind: If I missed a step, it wouldn't be the end of the world. I could redo it in as many takes as I needed to achieve perfection. I wish we could go to Hollywood and watch a film being made."

He regarded her with his green-gold eyes and stopped walking. "I wouldn't mind at all if you stayed in this country," he said, his voice low and melodic, like a trembling cello. He was like an oak, strong and brown with touches of color, she thought. His writing possessed that same male quality, punctuated with points of intuition. He never condescended, hardly ever passed judgments. He sometimes lived his life haphazardly, but he recognized his limitations without regret. Pierre had been forever embittered by his failures, forever envious of more successful artists. Boris, on the other hand, had turned his life into a work of art, fashioned with the easy grace of a Benois and the heightened vividness of a Bakst landscape; but he had dabbled at the venture without ever grasping its essential earthiness. Life, after all, belonged to the earth, just as, Natalia thought, did Stuart. This notion reassured her.

"But I would have no place here," she countered gently, surprised at the unexpected tug that had pulled her closer to this man, this virtual stranger. "I need to dance."

"Maybe someday you will merely *want* to," he remarked, circling her shoulders with his arm and starting once more to walk. She nodded, wondering, and then dismissed the strange idea and put her head on his shoulder. The only way to assimilate the loss of a man was by allowing warmth, another man's warmth, to penetrate inside. This man seemed prepared to allow her privacy: the privacy of her past, the privacy of her professional needs. For the first time she did not stop to wonder about the future: Stuart Markham was part of today, comfortably entrenched in the present.

Beside them strolled the students, young men with blazers, straw hats and books; young men with crew cuts and no hats. Such young men! She was twenty-six already. Suddenly she sighed and felt old. "What did you mean, someday I shall merely want to dance?" she asked.

"You still use dance to make yourself feel whole," Stuart answered. "But when I write, I'm trying to establish a line of contact between myself and the rest of the world. One day soon, Natalia, you'll dance because you have something to say and not merely something to prove."

She was stunned and immediately angry. Tears came to her eyes. "I want to live," she said, "and I'm only alive when I dance. That's just how I am."

"But you don't really like yourself the way you are," Stuart said.

Later, when he took her to a gentle hill overlooking the lazy Charles River, she said to him: "You can't set me down in your gracious Boston landscape, Stuart. I don't belong. When you studied here, there were New England debutantes in their pantalettes to court. Why didn't you marry one of them?"

"I almost did," he replied, smiling slightly. His mouth was large and well shaped beneath the mustache. It was an unapologetic mouth, she thought, just as Pierre's was sensual and Boris's ironic. "She was the only daughter of one of my professors," Stuart explained, "a very sweet, intelligent girl, who went to the Episcopalian church and attended meetings of the Junior League. A very proper girl. But there wasn't an artistic bone in her. She thought the word *create* had to be followed by *havoc.* I gave up on gracious Boston ladies after that."

She laughed, but when he took her chin in his strong fingers, she shook her head. Below them the river wound its blue ribbon much as, three years before, the Mediterranean had unfurled its current over the rocks of the Bay of Monaco. She had promised Boris to make that year memorable. They had created Arkady. Stuart's girl was right: In some cases, the things that one created broke up one's world. "Let's get out of here," she said.

She was bewildered by the newspapers. Reporters assailed her in hotel lobbies, in Cincinnati, in Chicago, in Kansas City. They printed terrible stories about "the Countess Kussova, so tragically widowed," and pictured her, small and sad, "her arms bereft of her child." At first she was dreadfully hurt, and Diaghilev upbraided the reporters for their crudity. But she knew he would never risk offending the press on behalf of any individual. Much as he had loved Boris and felt protective of her, one of his prized dancers, he realized that any publicity was good and would draw a crowd at the box office. He told her, gently: "Ignore them, my dear. They are adolescents at heart. This is a nation of adolescents, and, like most adolescents, they are fundamentally kind but impossible to handle."

Actually, the bitterness of her loss was seeping out of her, little by little, town by town on this extensive tour. Now, when a baby was wheeled near to her, she no longer recoiled in agony but only trembled slightly on the inside. With Stuart she was careful to keep an emotional balance. When talk veered toward the future, she steered it at once back to the present. Unlike Pierre, Stuart did not insist. She did not know whether she would like to see him in Europe; this rough and energetic country was a part of him, and she could not imagine his attending a Diaghilev committee meeting. That was her other life.

In Chicago a story appeared about them, and Diaghilev burst into her hotel suite at the Ritz, brandishing the offending tabloid. His large bulldog's face was contorted with rage. "Where are you, Natalia?" he shouted, and then, noticing that the door to the bathroom stood ajar, he pushed it open without knocking. His single lock of white hair trembled over his forehead. She was in the tub and started to laugh, unself-consciously: He was not, after all, a man to take notice of a woman's nudity.

"You and this man are not discreet!" he cried. "Look at this: 'Natalia Oblonova, America's darling, is being escorted through sixteen cities by a somewhat controversial writer, Stuart Markham, best known for his novel of suicide, *Tomorrow's Girl*. Does this mean that, for him, Natalia, the diminutive Russian Countess, has become the girl of today?' That is vulgar, Natalia! One does not flaunt one's bedside partners in a country like this!"

"Balletomanes have followed their favorite dancers for centuries!" she retorted angrily. "And I flaunt nothing. We don't live together openly, and you know that. I am discreet, as you say. What I choose to do in private is my business, isn't it?"

"We are not in Italy, or even in France. What is all this about, Natalia? Are you infatuated with this man? I've checked on him—his book is fairly good, but hardly the penstroke of a genius. He drinks too much, on occasion. His family doesn't think very highly of him. He dresses carelessly, and his manuscripts are always behind schedule."

"And you, of course, are today's innocent, Serge Pavlovitch?"

She met his furious stare with an equally angry glare of her own. "You mix yourself so easily into my business," she said. "But for you I am only a commodity. Why, then, will you not make the best use of me that you can? When will you let me do what Massine does—create a ballet for you?"

"When the gossip columnists cease to make you an object of scandal," he replied evenly.

Abruptly, she rose and stepped lightly out of the tub, her naked body dripping over the bathmat at his feet. "You're intruding, Serge Pavlovitch," she announced coldly. "Please leave."

Before returning for its engagement at the Metropolitan in New York, Diaghilev's company stopped in Washington, D.C., to give a special performance attended by President Wilson. Natalia was enchanted with the capital, arranged as it was in the French architectural style. But at the start of April she and her colleagues came back to their starting point, completing the tour of America. New York's elite was in a fever: Nijinsky was to meet his old company, having at last been released from internment in Hungary.

Pierre had written to Natalia about the Nijinskys, after seeing them when they had passed through Switzerland: "He is very nervous, and she most resentful of Serge Pavlovitch for having dismissed Vaslav." Now Natalia did not know whether she should first call upon her onetime partner, or whether she should let him come to her. They had all suffered, but now, she said to herself, I am healing. She went to see the Nijinskys at Claridge's.

His Mongol's face appeared tightly drawn, and there were circles under his eyes. But: "Serge Pavlovitch met us at the ship," Nijinsky said brightly. "He brought flowers for Romola." Apparently, he was still hopeful of reconciliation—a naïve child, like the Americans. They would adore him. Natalia wondered how long the truce would last between Vaslav and his former protector and felt ill at ease.

"We could not contact you when we learned," Romola murmured. "We—"

"Thank you, Romola Karlovna. It's over now." But it would never be over, never. Too brightly Natalia said: "Where is your little girl, Kyra?"

An embarrassed silence fell over the room. Romola called out, and a governess entered, holding the hand of a small, chubby, pretty girl with large, shining eyes. Arkady's eyes had shined like that. Arkady would be walking now, too. Arkady, I shall never heal, I shall never forget. She held her hands out to the child, who smiled and came running. It can't continue this way, Natalia thought, and this time tears rolled down her face and fell heedlessly over the small girl's fingers. "Why was the nice lady crying?" Kyra asked when Natalia had made a hasty retreat.

"Her little boy is gone," her mother answered gently.

The night of April 12 the most elegant New Yorkers came by the dozens to witness the true wedding they had been expecting: Nijinsky partnering Oblonova on stage. The two stars danced *Petrouchka*, and *Le Spectre de la Rose*. But Natalia noted Nijinsky's anxiety, his irritability, which had not been evident before the voyage on the S.S. *Avon*. As she danced with her old partner, as she watched his face and made her own familiar movements, drawing the same tumultuous applause as they always had in Europe, a sadness enveloped her that did not match the brittle excitement of the audience. She knew then that she needed to confront Diaghilev one more time, because the past was not enough, dancing itself was no longer enough. After the celebration supper, she went to see him in his suite at the Ritz.

"Too excited to sleep, Natashenka?" Diaghilev asked her pleasantly. Since their confrontation in the bathroom in Chicago, they had not bridged the gap of coolness between them. "Sit down. What's on your mind?"

"It's very simple," she said. "I want to know once and for all whether you plan to give me the chance to choreograph a ballet of my own."

His brows shot upward. "But you are a great ballerina. An interpreter, not a choreographer."

"Choreographers aren't born that way. They dance and then they develop their own ideas and methods after much experience. I'm twenty-six, not twenty, like Leonid Massine. If he can do it, so can I. You can have more than one choreographer in the same company. It's my turn, too."

He noticed the stubborn tilt of her chin, the hardness in her brown eyes. Then, gently, he laughed. "No, my Natalia. They have not made choreography a woman's profession. Not yet. Perhaps one day soon, though."

She wet her lips and stood up. "Very well, Serge Pavlovitch.

I've asked you three times. We have only a verbal contract. I am breaking it, as of this minute. I am returning to Switzerland."

Outraged, he rose with a single swift motion and took her by the shoulders. "You can't be serious!" he exclaimed. "For God's sweet sake, Natalia! Over this? Over this silly issue?"

"Over this and over things that do not concern you. Lopokhova is here, and now Vatza. You don't need me. I need to live my own life, Serge Pavlovitch. Good-bye now."

Calmly she looked at his face, contorted with fury. "I need my freedom," she added clearly. "I've never had it before, but now I want it. I want to dance, and I want to compose ballets, and if not with you, then with another company—my own company. If Pavlova can do it, why shouldn't I?"

She turned away from him, avoiding the expression in his eyes, an expression of murderous hatred that shook her deeply.

Natalia sat down softly on the bed, her eyes enormous in the pale oval of her face, and took Stuart's hand gently, almost absently, stroking the fingers rhythmically. "It isn't you," she murmured. "You're the best of all men, too good to be true. Too good for me, in fact." She turned to look at him, and shook her head. "It's my own life that's made us impossible. I wasn't being fair—I never really loved you in the way you deserved. You're the dearest friend I've ever had."

"Why?" he asked. His large face crested by the brown, vital hair, was marked by lines of anxiety and the beginning of despair.

"I wanted to escape from my past, from the pain of Boris, and from my confused feelings about Pierre Riazhin. But I can't escape, Stu. I find America wonderful—but I can't forget that there's something to deal with in Switzerland. If I stayed with you, then you would never know how much was really forgotten—or how much was lying, festering, beneath the surface of my emotions. I have to talk to Pierre."

Her mouth was beginning to quiver, and she said: "Stu—please don't hate me. I tried not to be dishonest with you—I never pretended—I really did care, *do* care!"

"Yes, yes, I know. You're a good girl, Natalia, and I was

starting to fall in love with you. It hurts—of course, it hurts. But I'm not going to forget you, and we'll try to be friends, won't we? Come on, don't cry. In any case, Diaghilev and I share a common disaster: We'll both be left behind by the most interesting little countess that ever stepped on a stage." He put a finger beneath her chin and added: "Laugh a little now, darling, for the camera!"

Chapter 22

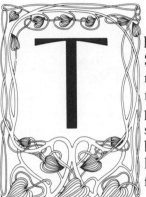

The full bloom of spring had settled on Sauvabelin Hill. Violets, crocuses, and a myriad wildflowers were scattered beneath the trees around the Signal outpost, overlooking Ouchy and the sapphire lake. To Natalia, this scented beauty was like a heady cloud: It took her mind off herself and allowed her to feel instead of think.

Alfred had worked wonders with the garden. Fruit trees stood strong and young in the morning breeze, their buds still tight on the swinging limbs. The gravel path was clean and well tended, and her feet crunched on it with sudden haste. She did not wait to ring for Brigitte but opened the front door herself with her key. On the floor, at her feet, she saw a startling sight: a layer of bright red cloth woven with gold thread spanned the area like a gigantic carpet.

Natalia found herself face to face with an attractive young woman of her own age, with large black eyes and shiny black hair that hung straight down her back like the Mona Lisa's. The young woman was tall and full bosomed, and when she smiled, her white teeth were large and glistening. Her skin was a dark ivory tint. "Yes?" she said, inquiring of Natalia and barring the way.

"I am the Countess Kussova," Natalia declared, taken aback. "And who are you? Where is Brigitte? And Monsieur Riazhin?"

At once the woman held the door wide, and then bent to the floor to push aside the red material. "Pierre!" she cried. "It's the countess!" She extended her hand to Natalia. "I'm Fabiana d'Arpezzo," she said. "I'm helping Pierre."

"I see." Natalia sidestepped the odd carpet and allowed the other woman to shut the door. This was her house, but Fabiana appeared to be the hostess, the one in charge. A slow anger began to creep into Natalia—not directed at the young Minerva who stood graciously before her, but at Pierre.

Fabiana was on the floor, rolling up spools of silk threads. She showed Natalia a sleeve being cut out of the shiny material. "It's Monsieur Diaghilev," she said conspiratorially. "He's commissioned Pierre to design some costumes for a ballet. His next stop will be Spain, you know. But of course, you would know—you're Oblonova!" She smiled delightedly at Natalia.

"Yes, I'm Oblonova," Natalia echoed, wondering why this girl made her feel as if they were rehearsing a dream sequence.

"Pierre thought it would be easier to compose this costume if I could actually cut it up according to his direction," Fabiana enlightened her. "It's been rather fun. But this cloth is so heavy—I don't see how one could dance inside it. What do you think?"

"I think that Pierre's turning *couturier* is rather amusing," Natalia remarked. Or ridiculous, she thought. Aloud she said: "Excuse me, mademoiselle," and before Fabiana could continue her conversation, she left the room and went into the hallway toward the bedrooms.

As she had expected, Pierre was in her own room, arranging two pieces of cloth on the bed. He was on his knees and raised his head sharply when he heard someone enter. His face reddened. His lips parted. How much he and that girl look alike, Natalia suddenly thought. He has found his eternal partner, his *âme soeur*. Nameless fury rose into her throat, flushing her cheeks.

"Natalia! Why didn't you warn me that you were coming back?" he asked.

"I didn't know myself. What would you have done differently if you'd been prepared?" Her brown eyes bored into his, and he turned away, fumbling with the cloth. "Does she live here, the pretty Madonna? Your assistant, I mean?"

Pierre laughed abruptly. "Fabiana. Yes, she does. But she's

very clean, Natalia. She hasn't made a mess of the house. Don't be concerned."

"Oh, I'm not! I like her. She's pleasant and attractive. But this is a small house, my house, and there's no room left in it for me. Is anyone else staying here, Pierre?"

The cutting edge of irony was so light that he hardly felt it. Nevertheless he rose quickly, his thigh muscles tensing, and, compressing his own rising anger, he said: "What the hell do you mean, Natalia? What are you implying?"

"That I am paying two servants to take care of this house, entirely as a gesture of friendship to you. That Fabiana d'Arpezzo was not part of the arrangement. This is not a house of assignations, Pierre. Nor is it a haven for unemployed *couturiers.*"

They faced each other, trembling. His features twisted into an ugly grimmace, and he cried: "You aren't Boris Kussov, keeping some kind of pet! I am a free man, Natalia, and an employed man. Shortly I shall be going to Spain to join Diaghilev. Fabiana is my guest, and she'll be coming with me. You offered me your house—she has done more to keep it clean and well-functioning than that idiot Brigitte. You should be grateful to her—instead of resentful."

"Get out now!" Natalia said. Tears came to her eyes, and she brushed them furiously away. "I bought this house for my family: It's Boris's house, and Arkady's, not yours! Not ever yours! I wanted you to use it because of him—because he once loved you! But I'm through—through!"

He uttered a short laugh. "Dear, kind, generous Boris. And how did you remember him, my love? Don't you think I read the papers? Oblonova's American shadow—how charming, how touching! Another one of your pets, darling?"

She took two steps forward to stand in front of him and raised the flat of her hand to his cheek. Just as it was about to hit him, he grabbed her wrist and twisted it until she cried out and fell on the bed, writhing. He did not let go, but continued to twist, until sobs escaped her and her face was bathed in tears. Then he released her, and stood above her threateningly.

She began to rub her wrist, crying, biting her lip. He loomed above her like a poised panther, his muscles tensed for action. Suddenly he put his hands palms down on the coverlet, on either side of her body, and leaned over her. She recoiled, bewildered but also expectant, her eyes wide, her nostrils quivering. Neither of them spoke.

She watched his face, his red cheekbones. His eyes reflected back her own image, crouching frightened on the bed. Yet, in the cocoon of her terror lay a thrill, an excitement, long buried but suddenly resurfacing. She could feel the pulse beating painfully in her throat, drowning her like the waves of a rushing surf.

All at once, without premonition, he moved his hands and fell with full force on her, breaking his fall at the last second to keep from smothering her below him. She breathed his own particular smell, which gave her the same weightless feeling as champagne. She was suffocating. She tried to cry out, but his lips found hers and pressed the cry back like a quail frightened by a hunting dog. His fingers streamed through her hair, over her scalp, scattering the pins about the untidy coverlet. Little shivers brought goose bumps to her skin, to the softness of her temples. She felt light, swallowed, submerged, and shut her eyes against the dizziness. Her own arms went to his shoulders, his neck, and finally they too mingled with the black curls on his head.

Natalia felt the sheer weight of him, and her own smallness beneath him. In the daylight his shoulders appeared broad and swarthy, and now, as they fumbled to undo buttons and tear off their clothes, she could see the taut pectoral muscles tapering down, the dark nipples ringed with tendrils of black hair. Then she saw nothing, for he was kissing her neck, biting her lightly, then sucking in her tongue in that fierce way of his that left her possessed and robbed of all control. He entered her when she was least expecting it, when she had become almost numb with his kisses—and yet this time, her body was better prepared for the onslaught, ready to receive him. She had become a woman and was no longer the eighteen-year-old virgin whose skin had felt torn and bruised by the reality of a man's desire.

More than eight years had passed since their first encounter, but this time urgency overwhelmed them so that neither had time to think things through, to absorb the changes. It happened with such rapidity, such readiness, that neither thought at all until it was over, and he fell beside her among their mound of clothes. At last, however, thought caught up with feeling, and, once again, she was Natalia, fully aware. She burst into tears and sobbed, covering her face. She could not stop sobbing.

Tentatively, afraid of his own gentleness, he touched her naked shoulder. "It's all right," he whispered. "It's all right—isn't it?"

From the living room they heard Fabiana laughing, and Brigitte's voice. Filters of yellow sunlight streaked across her back, a glistening alabaster smoothness turned away from him. He felt helpless and confused. "You're not ashamed, are you, Natalia?" he asked.

She shook her head. "Not ashamed. Not that." But still she would not look at him.

He rose then and wrapped himself ludicrously in the material with which he had been working. He resembled a tall, well-built Indian, or a Roman senator sheathed in a toga. "I'll tell her to go," he announced.

At last she turned her head and took in the absurd attire. She twisted her hands together and bit her lip. "If that's what you want," she said.

But he was sinking to his knees before her, and laying his chin on her lap. "I'd like to tell them all to go so we could be alone," he answered. And all the ghosts, too, my beloved, he thought. And all the ghosts that plague us, haunting our present. But, wisely, he did not say the words.

Some men, thought Pierre Riazhin, take progressive steps that lead, at their prime, to a kind of peak. His life had never before been so predictable, or so organized. He felt as though he had burst forth upon the earth, a splash of color on the Caucasian horizon, his talent a bright banner raised above the everyday in a gesture of defiance. Then he had met Boris Kussov, and for a moment he had possessed genius. Mirrored in the eye of his mentor, Pierre had lost all touch with the loathsome quagmire of normal existence. He had also met Natalia and made her his muse. Then the two had turned away and forgotten him. His splash of brilliance had lost the echo of their admiration. Without them he had found himself sapped of all but the most abject mediocrity. He was only now beginning to rise again, to set aside the blanket of common boredom that had been wrapping his fine instincts in dreary hopelessness.

He was happy, as only Pierre Riazhin knew how to be happy. The ecstasy of his flesh had pierced through to his spirit, for in Pierre heart, body, and mind tended to merge together. He was a mystic of sorts who, when transported, lost footing on the ground. Like all mystics, he believed in something beyond the earthly. As a child he had called this force God; now, he was not so sure. But he had not forgotten the icons of his youth.

"I have loved you since before I was born," he would say to Natalia. She found this somewhat embarrassing. Being loved by Pierre was like delving into a box of rich, exotic Turkish delight or like taking a bath in gallons of bubbling champagne: It was tinged with the indecency of excess and, therefore, of decadence. Always a spare person whose desires and feelings rose to a pure point, this sensation of overflowing, boundless emotion staggered her. Yet she knew that she was only the focal point of a greater, all-encompassing enthusiasm: Pierre's creativity was flowering into a riot of smells, sights, and sounds, and, to give it a name, he had called it Natalia.

This frightened her. It was exactly Pierre's disorganized, devouring adoration that had kept her away in their younger days. She had wanted a more focused involvement, not this deification, this aggrandizement that was, essentially, not her at all. Pierre did not know her. He thought that he was grasping the essential core of her, but her mind lay unassimilated on the side. He considered her thoughts and beliefs simply beside the point. Why should he humanize an elemental passion that was also an adoration of divinity?

I could not have stood this as a young girl, Natalia thought, lying in bed covered only by a sheet. The evidence of her naked limbs was like the proof of a dreaded force unleashed from within herself. It did not matter, at this point, that she was not understood: for in a way she was more understood than ever before; she had been broken open and left to spill out. Pierre was offering her a barbaric feast, a splurge of creative bounty. She could lose herself in it, forgetting the fears and the hurts and the losses by drowning in a sea of sensations. There was truly no comparison between this love and that which she had shared with Boris—or even the dalliance in which she had partaken with the American writer. Someday, she said to herself, to reassure her conscience, which quaked at the back of her mind, someday I shall awaken replete and seize the reins to my own life again. But right now she could not: The reins still dragged in the dusty gutter while the horse galloped straight ahead, oblivious of obstacles in its way.

The house was a splurge of color that matched the summer splendor of the out of doors. The woods were filled with dark blueberry bushes, and strange birds made sharp sounds among the boughs. In the garden Alfred's roses climbed strong and round, their velvet petals every shade of pink, red and coral, with sometimes a pale yellow head peeking among the thorns. The phlox, timid blue, and the tall gladioli seemed to have sprung up wild—which vexed the temperamental gardener. Inside, draped over every piece of furniture, Pierre's designs were hung to dry, their magenta and deep gold tones creating a constant center of attention.

Natalia went through the house like a little girl, laughing, picking up strands of imitation pearls or wide-plumed hats, and trying them on. Pierre was making designs for the ballets that Diaghilev and Massine were now putting together in Madrid. Then softly, gently, he would lift her up to his chest and carry her to the bedroom, and there, banging the door shut with the back of his foot, he would make love to her in front of the open window, pushing aside the soft material of the costume that she had donned in merriment.

He was a wonderful lover, holding back the moment of fulfillment to be sure her pleasure was as great as his. If he was impatient, it was only in wanting to possess her often, over and over. She loved being exhausted by his passion, being filled with him again and again. When he worked on his designs, she followed him, suddenly very young and insecure, needing to be near him, to touch him, to smell him—for he overpowered her senses in every way.

He was amused by this new dependency but also startled. It

was an odd reversal of their previous roles. I suppose I was right, he thought, when years ago I wanted her to stop dancing, to be my wife. Once he lay down his paintbrush and, searching her face for signs of trouble, asked: "Shall we get married, Natalia?"

She cried then, pressing her fingers against her eyes. "Marriage! I *hate* being married! Then the loving stops and you begin to own each other. I never want to be married again—do you hear me, Pierre?"

"But I love you. I want the world to know how much I love you. Are you ashamed of me—or do you just want to remain Countess Kussova?"

The pain on her face made him feel instant guilt. "You see?" she exclaimed. "It's already starting—your wanting to own me!"

"But isn't that the way love goes, Natalia? When someone is as much a part of the other as of himself—isn't that ownership? What's wrong with that?"

"Everything! You wouldn't understand, Pierre. If we were married, you would love me less freely, and obligation would enter into it. We both care too much about our freedom to allow this to happen. No 'musts,' no 'duty.' Oh, my beloved Pierre, is it so bad to want to be happy, without looking back and without looking ahead?"

She touched his sleeve and felt the tension go out of his arm as he fought the impulse to rebel against her fears of the future. He would take the horror out of loving for her; he would soothe away whatever crept up between them now and then, the specter of Boris Kussov, of his death, of the baby. He knew exactly how but this was not the moment, not yet.

"I shall have to go to Spain soon," he said to her one evening. She turned to him, and he saw her dismay, the small helpless opening of her mouth, the way her hands moved to her breasts as if to protect herself. Had she been that badly wounded, then? "Come with me," he suddenly cried. "Pack a bag and come! You'll love Spain, and the king will love you, too. The court is like a Velázquez painting, all baroque pageantry. It will be fun!"

"I can't," she replied, her eyes filling with tears. "Diaghilev—

I don't want to see him, Pierre. I know you work for the Ballets Russes, and you and Massine have become work friends. But that dreadful scene in New York—"

"Do you want me to have a talk with Serge Pavlovitch?" Pierre offered.

"What's to be said? He's broken with Nijinsky for the second time, and now he's broken with me. Or rather, I've broken with him. He'd be only too glad to watch me hanging on the outskirts of his organization. I don't ever want to see the man again, Pierre."

"You never talk about it, but you miss it, don't you?" he asked, a sinking feeling in his stomach. "It isn't enough, then— us?"

She rushed to him, and he could see the pulse beating in her delicate throat, an exposed vulnerability that suddenly moved him. "Oh, my darling!" she cried against his chest. "I miss nothing! I just don't want you to go. I don't want fo be alone, I don't want to be robbed of you."

"But I'll come back," he murmured gently, stroking her hair. "There's no war in Spain, only a work project!"

The way she reared her head, the shock in her eyes, told him how tactless his words had been, and he threw his hands up in despair, shaking his own head helplessly. "Damn it, Natalia," he began, and then his own emotions dissolved in the shaking of his knees, the realization that he loved her more than he had ever thought it possible to love another person. "Forgive me, forgive me," he whispered, tears of contrition mixing with her tears of fear and pain. And then she uttered a small tremulous laugh, and he knew it was going to be all right, this new, this half-formed love of theirs, this passion and this caring.

During his absences she remained for hours at the window, smiling in bemused fashion, counting the hours that remained until his return. She hated the bed that was empty without him, hated and conversely loved the workroom with his paintbrushes and palettes, with his bolts of colored cloth and his many easels backed one against the other. She hated him for being gone and yet loved these small and large reminders of his imminent return. Sometimes she prepared Russian pastries and *zakuskis*, which she knew he loved. When he came home, she placed platters of his favorite food before him and watched him eat them morsel by morsel, each one a testimonial of her love for him, of her devotion.

Pierre adored these demonstrations, which she had never shown toward the aristocratic Boris Kussov, who had taught her to be a lady but had never quite been able to obliterate the simple Russian girl from her heart. He was very happy. He was thirty-three, and his career was soaring; recognition had at last come to him. In Spain his designs were bringing him fame, and in Switzerland he lived with the girl he had always loved. The only problem lay in the fact that Diaghilev was constantly failing to fulfill his contract and paying him far less than had been promised. But money was not a problem, for Natalia lavished the good life on him, spoiling him shamefully when he was home. He only wished that she would come with him and forget her quarrel with the Ballets Russes.

In September a change came over her, and she began to watch herself with a dreadful sense of calamity. Her fingers were swelling, and her breasts had grown tender and large. She measured her waist and was seized with panic at its increased size. Wringing her hands, she sat down on the bed and cried, then made an appointment to see Dr. Combes. Pierre, thank God, would not be back for several days.

When he came home, she could not face him. Hearing his voice in the hall, all at once she felt overwhelmed with anger and resentment. He had done this to her! Then she thought: No, he has only loved me, again and again, and when one wants to be loved as much as I did, something is bound to happen! It was I who was crazy, I who threw all caution to the wind. Her misery was enormous, palpable, and she stayed in the bedroom, one hand on her offending stomach. I don't know what to do, she thought. I don't know what to do!

Panic-stricken, she rang for Brigitte to tell her to keep Monsieur away, to find some reason—logical or not—to prevent his coming in to find her. But before the maid could answer her call, Pierre's hand was on the doorknob and he was entering, his body framing the doorway, his curls atumble from the wind, a package in his arms. She stared at him, appalled and frightened.

Pierre burst into the room, throwing the package on the bed and moving toward her, enveloping her in his embrace, crushing her. His forcefulness pushed her fear to the surface and she began to cry, at first small sobs, then more insistent, hysterical ones. Amazed, he dropped his arms to his sides and asked: "What happened, Natalia? Tell me!"

She could not speak. She could only turn away, bending over in her grief and helplessness. "You can't have missed me all that much," he teased her softly. "Come now—what's so bad?" He was becoming caught up in her despair, and a dull warning was spreading over the joy of seeing her, like a chilling blanket of ice.

Finally she wheeled about and pointed at her stomach. "That's what's wrong!" she cried. "Look what we've done, Pierre! Two irresponsible fools! I'm going to have a baby, that's what! And I can't have another baby! I can't! What are we going to do?"

Tremendous relief flooded over him, then quick joy. Taking her hands, he raised them to his lips, his smile illuminating his handsome, dark features. "But that's wonderful!" he exclaimed. "That isn't a reason to cry, my sweet! We shall get married at once. Is that the only problem? That we're not married? You silly girl!"

Her sobs increased, and now she said: "No, Pierre! I don't want to marry you, and I don't want to have this baby! Don't you understand? The nephrosis—that was probably something Arkady was born with! I can't take the risk of having another child, not ever! What was Arkady's short life but a nightmare of incessant pain, for him and for me? I can't go through it one more time!"

He could not help it then and said to her harshly: "But you know what Dr. Combes has told you, many times! That you were in no way responsible for Arkady's illness. Have you spoken to him about this pregnancy? Hasn't he been able to reassure you?"

"But there are no guarantees!" she cried.

"No guarantees? What guarantees are there to any part of our lives? I only know I love you and that I will not have you abort this baby out of overblown fears! It's time you grew up, Natalia."

"If I have this child, it won't ever be the same between us, Pierre," she told him. "I shall have to marry you, and that will destroy the spontaneity of our love. And what about dancing? I've been away from it now for a number of months—this will keep me away for nearly eight more! Is that fair, Pierre?! You won't have to carry this baby, and it isn't going to stop you from painting. But for me it will be different."

He said, slowly: "You would abort our baby for eight months of ballet? Then Arkady was just an excuse? All this time when I thought we were happy, you were really missing the dance and planning to go back?"

She shook her head from side to side, tears streaming down her cheeks. "No. I don't honestly know what I was planning to do. But I wasn't planning to have a baby. I never wanted to have Arkady, but when I did, I loved him—and he died, and I don't ever want to suffer like that again, ever again! The dance is something else; it just came up because it's true, I suppose I have missed it, and never realized it. I always thought I would start my own company and ask you to work with me—to make a company with me, *our* company! I didn't see that my resuming dance would separate us. On the contrary, I thought it would bring us closer together. You wouldn't have to work for Diaghilev anymore. You wouldn't have to leave me like this—"

She fell back against the bed, small and grief-stricken. "I don't understand," he murmured, standing in front of her. "I don't understand any of this. I only know that you don't love me enough if you can even consider aborting my baby. Oh, certainly, Dr. Combes will explain to me about Arkady and tell me that there is medical precedent for such a drastic measure. But you know as well as I that this baby will be well because there is nothing wrong with either one of us."

She raised her head, an expression of amazed horror on her face at the implication. "You can't live in the past!" he cried out then, taking her head and pressing it against his thigh. "You can't deny us, Natalia, and destroy the life we've created together. If you do, I swear to you I'll go, and this time, I won't ever return!"

He felt her wet tears through the cloth of his trousers, and laid a hand on the top of her head. Perhaps the timing for this baby was wrong, but having it would chase away her ghosts by replacing them with life.

Chapter 23

She twirled the name in her mind as if it were a ring on her finger: "Natalia Riazhina." It brought to mind string instruments and Russia, as "Kussova" had suggested an arrow, powerful and direct, and "Oblonova" graceful curvature, voluptuous and honeyed. Names had always held a magic for her. "Natasha" had been in the prison of her youth, harsh and barren, and that was why she seldom used it.

Riazhina. She would not have married Pierre but for this baby. The pregnancy enveloped her as compressed heat does a hothouse flower. She fought its smothering effect, and yet her own self, Natalia, kept being pushed back, choked down by this invasion, which she resented even more than she had resented Arkady's. She thought: They have conspired against me, Pierre and his child. In her heart she reared her head and cried out her rebellion, her feeling of doom. The child was killing the woman, as once before the woman had thought she had killed a child.

This pregnancy had taken well. This time the fetus was firmly embedded in her womb, and, after much hesitation, the doctor had pronounced her fit and able to lead a normal life. She was even proceeding with her former ballet exercises. When Pierre was home in Lausanne, he walked erect and proud, as though, she thought with pain and a resulting anger, to show that *his* child was not harmful to her, that *his* child would be born whole and well. She hated him then and could not speak to him. It was as though the pregnancy had made Boris resurface in both their minds, bringing back old pains and frustrations— and on Pierre's part, mixed feelings toward his old mentor.

The double-edged quality of Pierre's feelings for Boris came up more strongly now, in Rome, when Diaghilev and all the artists congregated in the impresario's apartment. Pierre realized that Boris was still a part of the discussions. He had been much admired. Without him Diaghilev was like a boat with only half a rudder. One found oneself looking over one's shoulder, expecting the blond phantom of Boris Kussov to materialize and participate in discussions of new projects. Something was missing. Pierre thought: The best years of my life are gone because the friction of his opinions will be forever lacking from what I do. We can all function, but without a mind such as Kussov's, the ultimate finesse escapes us all.

Under Boris's helmsmanship, the Ballet's financial situation had fared impeccably. Boris Kussov had had an astuteness that had been absolutely necessary to the group. Pierre sensed its absence and raged that he should now be making his artistic mark at a time when Boris, his evil genius, was already dead.

Pierre was in the center of a new movement, one of the changes in the wind that Diaghilev, by wetting his index finger and holding it to the air, had been able to predict and abet. With the absence of Nijinsky, Karsavina, who was still in Russia, and Natalia, the Ballets Russes had to make do with lesser dancers. The new stars that were emerging, therefore, consisted of designers, composers, and librettists. Pablo Picasso, the Spanish painter, had enthralled Pierre with the cubic shapes that peopled his works. And he had renewed an old friendship with the French poet and humorist Jean Cocteau.

Sometimes Pierre took long walks, to clear his mind, to revive his body. One afternoon as he climbed down to the Coliseum, the relic of a civilization killed by excess, a deep depression settled into his bones. He clambered onto the ruins and sat down where, more than a thousand years before, other men had gone to distract themselves from the weight of their worries. He felt an overwhelming sadness. Often before, when this black cloud had descended, he had busied his hands with work. But now he found that they were trembling in his lap.

He did not notice the young woman who sat down not far from him. The enormous crumbling structure could seat thousands. But, after a while, the afternoon sun went below a wall of the stadium, and Pierre glanced about him. The young woman inclined her head, graciously. He remembered that she was a dancer, an English girl whom Diaghilev had recently hired. Her name was Jacqueline Vendane, but Serge Pavlovitch, who turned all his dancers into Russians, had changed her name to Vendanova. Pierre had no idea what they called this girl among the *corps*, but all at once he found her proximity warming.

She was a tall, willowy girl with pale skin like Natalia's and brown eyes smaller and less distinctive in their shape than those of his wife. But Natalia was twenty-seven. This girl was perhaps twenty, or twenty-one. Oddly, in spite of her tall stature, he was reminded of Natalia during the early years, when they had both been striving, unknown, and lovers. Jacqueline stood up, and he smiled. She came toward him, and he rose instinctively. "It's pleasant to be out in the afternoon," he stammered lamely.

She laughed—a clear, tinkling, self-assured laugh—and sat down beside him. "But your thoughts weren't pleasant ones, Pierre Grigorievitch," she countered. "Aren't you happy here?"

There was nothing like a dose of English straightforwardness, he thought. He shrugged lightly. "Rome is magnificent," he said. "But you've heard it all before." Then, all at once, almost angrily, he turned to her and said: "No, I'm not happy. Not at all."

"I dare say." Her small mouth made a circle of wonder, but she remained agreeably distant. "Perhaps you miss your wife? I should like to know her. She has become a sort of myth. You know—Oblonova. And also: Countess Kussova. But oh—I say—I'm terribly sorry! That was untactful in the extreme, wasn't it?" She flushed scarlet and examined her shoes.

The girl's words and embarrassment pierced through him to a rare reserve of humor. He chuckled. "In the extreme, my dear. But everybody does it. They must think Natalia has gone down a peg, marrying me after Count Boris Kussov. He cut quite a figure."

"And you don't?" It was a straightforward question, without

pity, without cruelty, without false reassurances. She had felt the hard bitterness beneath his light tone.

Pierre turned away. "God knows," he answered. "I'm still covered with morning dew. A babe in the woods."

"You're only thirty-four. I think you're accomplishing a good deal, actually. Couldn't your wife—Natalia—be with you here?"

He had always begged Natalia to come to him, to mend her relationship with Diaghilev, but all at once Jacqueline's question jarred him, unearthing new feelings within him. He turned to her, startled. "This will sound crazy to you," he said, "but suddenly I know I don't want her here. I love her more than the world—but I don't want her to come here now. Not now! Do you see—in any way—what I mean?"

The last words hit him with their absurdity, their childishness. But Jacqueline placed a smooth white hand on his arm, and squeezed it lightly. "Yes," she replied. "I think I do. This is your world. If she came, you'd be afraid she might preempt it. How can you live with that? Doesn't she feel how it tears you apart? Even I can feel it—and I barely know you. Mostly I know you through Olga—Olga Kokhlova, Picasso's girl. Picasso feels that Natalia robs the creativity out of you."

Pierre turned away. "There's nothing to be done about it," he said, but his voice trembled slightly. "I found I could not live without her. And now—"

"You can't live with her. Maybe she feels the same way."

They did not speak. A light breeze rose from the stadium, and lifted Jacqueline's skirt to her knees. She bent to smooth it, but all at once Pierre seized her hand. Jacqueline looked up, startled, embarrassed. She saw the strange expression on his face, the black eyes like smoldering coals, the curls tumbling over his wide brow, the lips parted over white, glistening, savage teeth. He frightened her, but she could not pull away. She closed her neat brown eyes against the sight of him.

When he kissed her, she did not resist. He found her pleasantly compliant, not a virgin, and tender enough to bring a cool balm to his sores. He was grateful to her for the calm understanding, for the lack of fuss. Although something within him ached for Natalia, he also knew that he had not done this to wreak vengeance on her: He had done this only for himself, to make the passage less rough.

It took several weeks for news to reach the Ballet that the Tzar's government had been overthrown and that the reign of the Romanov dynasty had come to an end. Then pandemonium broke loose. Each Russian ran to the post office to send frantic telegrams, inquiring as to what had happened to members of his particular family. Pierre could discover no news of his mother. But she had not been wealthy, or prominent, and in the outlands fewer massacres had occurred. He presumed her shaken but alive.

In Lausanne Natalia was nearing the end of her term. After the first fleeting thought, she did not even consider her mother and father. She had never really known her sister. Instead, she speculated about Nina and Galina Stassova, and Lydia Markovna Brailovskaya, and Katya and her parents and small children. Natalia sat frozen in fear, uncomprehending. Had Boris been there, he would have explained, cleared up the confusion, and succeeded in finding everyone of importance to her. She wondered what had become of Tamara Karsavina, of whom she had grown so fond. It was awful, not knowing.

In March Natalia had been forced to endure Arkady's birthday. Before that there had been her own, shrouded in the anniversary of Boris's death. She had never thought herself fatalistic, but now she admitted that a deep, pervasive Russian gloom had seized her. Natalia wept with worry about Nina and Galina, last ties of blood to Boris Kussov. She sent Brigitte to the post office for several days, and mailed long letters to Medveyev, now no longer employed. She did not weep for her country. The Tzar's court had truly been corrupt, and monarchs, after all, had to be held accountable to their people.

After a week Natalia said to Dr. Combes: "I am going to Rome. I've never cared about this baby the way I did about the first—oh, don't pretend you're shocked! The trip won't harm me. But I need to be with my husband. We've always been vagabonds, in the service of the Ballet—but now we're truly homeless. When the roof blows off, the inmates of the house must huddle together for warmth and safety."

In the face of her stubbornness, the Swiss doctor yielded. Natalia packed a light suitcase and had Alfred drive her almost at once to the station. "Why the master can't come home, I don't know," the gardener said to his disapproving wife. The doctor would have been forced to agree with him. Combes had telegraphed a colleague in Rome to make certain that, if worst came to worst and Natalia did not return on time, there would be somebody on hand to deliver her baby. Why Natalia had not thought this through was utterly beyond his comprehension. It was almost as though she had ceased to care: about herself and about the child.

When Natalia arrived in the lobby of Pierre's hotel, it was late at night. Bulging with her pregnancy, ungainly and exhausted, she nearly collided with the elegant figure of Diaghilev, young Massine by his side. Natalia felt a moment of shock. She leaned against a tall marble pillar and fanned herself. Let him think what he wants, she thought miserably. Let them both think what they want. I am fat and ugly and I haven't worked in ages, and now I'm here for God knows what reason. I don't remember, I don't want to remember. She hoped that because of their last interview Diaghilev would pretend not to notice her.

But, naturally, he did not comply. He was too well educated and always enjoyed an obvious upper hand. He came to her with a sprightly step and kissed her on both cheeks. "*Ma chère!* I've missed you. We've all missed you," he said. She noted the undertone in his voice and realized he was having an even better time of this than she would have predicted.

"I came because of the news," she said. "I felt frantic and helpless. How did your people fare, Serge Pavlovitch?"

"Well enough," he replied. "And yours? The Princess Stassova?"

"I am most worried about her. She was truly my sister. *Is* truly. What am I saying? I'm so tired, Serge Pavlovitch. Could we speak in the morning, after I have rested?"

Diaghilev smiled and inclined his head, that large oval with the streak of white in the dyed black of his hair. "Natalia, Natalia," he intoned. Then, suddenly sharp, he asked: "This baby—it's due soon?"

She colored, feeling undressed and exposed in her whalelike proportions. No wonder this man preferred other men: They did not bulge out, become obscene fertility goddesses. She had become a veritable horror, a freak. "It's due any time," she stammered miserably, looking at Leonid Massine with mute appeal: Make him go away, she thought. Don't let him take such pleasure in my grossness. "I shouldn't have traveled," she added to fill the silence. "My physician was furious."

"Hotel lobbies are quite unsuitable for this sort of thing, I quite agree," Diaghilev remarked with amusement. "But I'm asking for a reason. Picasso and Pierre are working with Leonid on some marvelous new ballets. It would be wonderful to have you with us again, my dear."

Natalia's hands began to tremble. To steady them, she clasped them together over the mound of her stomach, covered with the fur of her coat. She lifted her chin resolutely to regard her old employer. She smiled. "You flatter me, Serge Pavlovitch. But not enough. Not quite enough. If Boris were alive, I would have outmaneuvered you somehow—but alone, you know, I can't. You two were a perfect match for each other. I can't compete."

Diaghilev licked his fleshy lips. "And your new husband, Pierre? You don't trust him to bargain for you?"

"It is not his business to do so," she replied calmly. "Good night, gentlemen."

In the scented night air, waiting for their car, Diaghilev said to his *protégé:* "There goes a great lady, a brilliant dancer. With her in a company of his own, and with Vaslav, Kussov would have dominated the entire world of ballet. As it is, I feel immensely sorry for her."

"Why is that?" Massine asked.

Diaghilev merely shrugged and lifted his hands palms up in the air.

Natalia said to the desk clerk: "You can bring the bags up. Right now I simply need to be directed to my husband's room."

Still small, her face ringed by curls under a high-crowned velvet hat, Natalia seemed oddly proportioned. The rest of her was trim, petite, and elegant. Her skirt peeked from beneath her fur coat, eight inches from the ground, and her small buttoned boots of ivory patent leather gleamed attractively below it. The clerk looked at her with appreciation, but when his glance wandered to her midpoint, his eyes became worried. Not here, he silently begged.

The bellhop escorted Natalia to a baroque elevator, behind grilled doors. Halfway down the final hallway, a feeling of suffocation grasped Natalia's throat, and she laid a nervous hand over the young man's uniformed arm. "Wait," she breathed. She fumbled in her purse and withdrew some lire, which she pressed into his hand. "Just give me the key," she told him. "I can proceed from here."

He retreated at once down the dark corridor with its tapestried walls and deep crimson carpet. She remained hesitant, and felt light-headed. It was just a feeling, and she tried to shake it off reasonably. But in the recent past, logic seemed to have deserted her completely: The events in Russia, the confusion of her own sentiments, and the pregnancy appeared to have chased order away with a cudgel. She held the key tightly in her gloved hand and arrived at the door.

Should she knock or simply open it? She did not wish to intrude upon Pierre. She had come on impulse, without warning. She had always prized a separate niche for her professional life, a kind of neatness that did not brook intrusion. She was a private person. She knocked.

It was close to two in the morning. Diaghilev and Massine had undoubtedly been on their way home from one of their late suppers. Natalia was very tired now that she had reached her destination: She did not even want to have to explain to Pierre. Let him merely hold me, she thought, which was as close to a prayer as she could come. With a stab of pain, she thought: But what am I to him now? He can't touch me the way I am. I'm simply a nuisance, in the way.

The door swung open on its well-oiled hinges and Pierre stood staring at her, squinting. He was wrapped in a large towel, from which his naked legs, powerfully muscled, emerged forlornly. The thick curls on his head fell over his eyes, and he reminded her of a young child awakening. All he needed was to rub sleep from his eyes with pudgy fists to complete the image.

She touched his cheek and smiled at him, tenderness flowing into her heart. "It's all right," she reassured him with amusement. "I'm real. I had to come, Pierre. The loneliness was unbearable, since the news of the Revolution."

He was not reacting. His eyes had enlarged, but he stood like a statue before her, disconcerting her. He was also blocking the doorway. Feeling ridiculous with her bulging stomach, Natalia uttered a short, embarrassed laugh and squeezed by him into the room. It was dimly lit by a single lamp, and she could see the patterned carpet, the elaborate, ornate furniture: a table, two chairs with elaborate scrollwork, a portmanteau. To the far right was a large, unmade bed. The bedspread lay entangled with cover and sheet, and the pillows were scattered about. Pierre had always been disorderly.

"Natalia," Pierre said. She turned to him, totally exhausted, ready to collapse. The smile was slipping off her face from sheer lack of strength. He appeared fully awake now, and she could not understand the expression: concern, anger, bewilderment, resentment, embarrassment? Not now, she answered mutely. *Not now.*

He suddenly reached out and touched her arm, his grasp strong and imprisoning. "You're hurting me," she said with some exasperation. "The bags should be arriving at any minute now. Put something on—or go back to bed."

Then, she followed his gaze to the bed itself, and her extremities, fingers and toes, began to tingle with numbness. Her lips fell open. An overwhelming lethargy robbed her of rational thought. She could make out the form of someone in the bed, moving on the pillows, a young woman, wearing a white nightshirt trimmed with lace. I have one almost exactly like it, Natalia thought stupidly. She watched the girl descend from the bed, her graceful feet touch the floor. She is a dancer, Natalia thought, like recognizing like. The girl's hair was brown and shone from the soft yellow glow of the lamp. Her face was very pale and oval, a cameo.

Pierre did not move, and Natalia could not breathe. The girl stepped resolutely across the carpet toward them. She was young and pretty, though not beautiful. Neither am I, Natalia thought wryly. She had never seen the woman before and knew at once that she was not a Russian. "I don't know you," Natalia intoned, and there was an odd note of wonder in her voice.

The woman regarded her quietly. "I'm not important, Madame Riazhina," she replied. "I am sorry."

"I am sorry, too. But he is a most compelling man. I do understand."

The girl blinked. Tears came to her eyes, and she looked away. But Natalia's brown eyes pursued her relentlessly. Her gloved hand reached out to touch the other's arm. "Please tell me who you are," she asked.

"Diaghilev calls me Vendanova. My name is really Jacqueline, Jacqueline Vendane. If I had known you—"

"Yes, well. I don't own my husband. We are all individuals, Miss Vendane. We are born alone and we die alone, a cliché but nevertheless a fact. Another is that we must live with what we do. You went into this with a clear conscience: Who could be hurt? Live with it, my dear. I don't pretend not to be hurt, but it's hardly the end of the world. Good night, then."

Jacqueline Vendane burst into tears, her cool composure falling away like a molting skin, and she ran into the adjoining bathroom. Why is this happening to me? Natalia wondered dully. She went to the nearest armchair and fell into it heavily. Pierre still stood mutely staring at his wife. She could not look at him.

The bathroom door opened, the young British dancer stepped out, dressed and coiffed. She passed in front of Natalia without meeting her eyes, but when she walked by Pierre, he siezed her arm, and her face, frightened and wondering, turned fully toward him. Pierre's dark eyes seemed to bore into her, devouring her. She shook herself loose, but he blocked her passage with his absurdly clad body. She waited for him to speak, as Natalia had waited before her. But he simply squeezed his hands into two fists and pounded them into one another in frustration. His eyes were bloodshot.

When the girl had left, Natalia sank her forehead into her right hand. The room was dancing around her in all its baroque bad taste. Finally she raised her head with extreme will power and looked at her husband. "This has been going on a long time?" she asked, in a calm but weak voice. Only her fingers continued to tremble.

He chewed on his lower lip. "Do you intend to keep seeing her?" she added. "Tell me, for God's sake!"

Pierre shook his head. "Stop it. Don't question me now. If you do, I'm going to leave, Natalia. I can't stand this!"

"*You* can't? It's a pleasant diversion for me, then? Are you going to blame *me* for this? Or maybe Boris? Is that it, Pierre? All this—Vendanova—is because of your hatred for Boris Kussov? You are retaliating by humiliating me, by stripping me of all dignity, because of a dead man?"

Her voice had taken an edge of hysteria. Now Pierre walked over to her, looming above her, his jaw tensed, his eyes cavernous and gleaming. "You're always holding back from me because of that man. You take and take and take and never give me what I need. Jackie demands nothing. She's uncomplicated. I don't love her, but I don't know whether I'm ready to give her up. What a relief it is to be with a woman who's foremost a woman, and a dancer second, who doesn't have the mentality of a goddamned *prima ballerina!* You have no idea."

Natalia's fingers twirled into her hair and tightened until the curls cut off her circulation. Her scalp burned, and she was grateful for this physical pain that obliterated her other emotions. Her face still turned to him, she said: "I have no idea. You're right. But I shall never forgive you. It isn't *la* Vendanova—she's actually immaterial. I can't forgive the hatred. You hate me, Pierre. But you don't like yourself much, either, or you wouldn't hate me so. You're a weak, twisted man—an incomplete man, half a person."

She looked away then, her eyes filling with tears. I can't cry in front of him—not now, she thought. And then: This is worse than the last time, when I found him with Boris. Last time I needed to learn the truth. But now? This?

She felt his hands on her shoulders, his arms wrapping around her torso. "God, how we do this to each other," he murmured, his voice breaking, as he buried his face in the crook of her neck. She felt his wet tears. "Don't turn away," he pleaded. "Don't let me hate you. Please, Natalia, help me to be a husband to you."

"But I never wanted you to be my husband," she whispered. "I only wanted you to love me. To love me—not to bind yourself to me in any fashion. I did not make you send Fabiana away. You chose to do so. Don't resent me for this marriage—it was of your own doing."

"But not yours! How do you suppose that's made me feel? Generally when a man wants to marry a girl, he doesn't have to wait eight years! And when the woman becomes pregnant, it's usually the man who is defiant. Honestly, Natalia, don't you ever imagine what it must feel like to live inside this damned skin and know, truly *know*, that the woman I love never wanted to marry me, but that there was another man whom she accepted as a husband?"

"I did not marry Boris that way," she protested lamely. "You know that the marriage came before the love. If anyone should have been jealous, it should have been Boris. I still loved you when I became his wife. That all changed later."

"And it's never changed back! If there hadn't been the pregnancy, you would never have agreed to a wedding. I can't be grateful, Natalia. Every day I am with you you make me feel that you regret being my wife, that you think I forced you into having the child and marrying me. I own the most precious gem on earth but am not free to remove it from its case and wear it openly."

"I am not a gem, Pierre. I'm a woman. Are things so bad between us that you need other women? Will you always need them?"

"This simply happened. Don't go into it, Natalia. I am a man—incomplete as you think I am. You are never with me."

"But do you really want me along? In the beginning you were right, I did not want to come. But now I feel it's you who don't want me—you who don't include me in your plans!"

"It's you who don't wish to be a part of them," he retaliated. "You who quarrel with Serge Pavlovitch. I am a member of his company now. I like it. For the first time without the help of kind and not so kind mentors. I'm thirty-four years old. Isn't it right that some sort of sunshine falls on me, Natalia? What do you want?"

"I want you to love me. I want you to understand me. I want us to know each other, Pierre." Her brown eyes sought his, and she touched his cheek. "I want your success. But I don't want to be swallowed by you, to be second to you. There should be room for us to walk beside each other without resentment."

He stood up abruptly, the towel at last falling from him and showing him splendidly naked, the muscles glistening with perspiration. "Words," he said. "Words! I need to feel you, Natalia, to know you are my wife! I can't continue to live in shadows. You're killing me every moment we're together. You suffocate me, tear the heart right out of me. You make me become that incomplete man, that half a person."

In the silence that followed, Natalia's throat was clogged and she could only draw small, strained breaths. At last she cried out: "But how? Tell me how, Pierre. Indict me, for both our sakes!"

He sank to his knees and enveloped his arms around her legs, laying his head on her lap. "I do love you," he said, beginning to weep. "I do love you!"

But her face above him was ghastly, pallid, and hollow and full of anguish. She could not reach out to touch his hair, to mingle with his pain. At that very moment her own first sharp pain had pierced through her abdomen, the pain of her labor. "You never share," he was accusing her. "You are always apart, always alone!"

Chapter 24

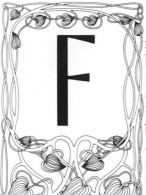

From the beginning Natalia felt excluded by Pierre and his little daughter. Tamara was plumper, stronger, and more colorful than Arkady. She lay next to her mother like a foreign object: her black curls, black eyes, and small red cheeks so totally unlike Natalia that her mother found it difficult to relate to her. She was a little Tcherkess baby, a female Pierre. Tamara Petrovna, Natalia thought. Another name, this one evocative of a Russia now torn in pieces. Thamar, fittingly, had been a ruthless, lustful Caucasian queen.

Natalia had named her daughter after her much admired friend, the dancer Karsavina. But that had been her single contribution to the child since her birth. Tamara had been born in the hotel—am I destined to keep delivering in rented bathrooms? Natalia had wondered—under the care of Dr. Combes's associate, the tall, gallant Dr. Contini. The labor had been short: She had known what to expect this time, in spite of the suddenness of the initial pains. Perhaps this baby had pushed its way out with greater impatience, already possessing the will to live.

Natalia touched the child, the small crinkled fists, the tiny toothless mouth, like that of an old crone. Arkady was smoother than you, she thought. He was more noble, more subtle. He was fine and weak and translucent, and the world was too much for him. I had him once inside me, then in my arms. Once, too, I walked beside his father and we shared a bittersweet, poignant romance, fragile and tinged with ironies—a romance that sprang up unknown to us, a romance that enveloped us even as we still refused to believe in its possibility. Now I have a new family: you, my little one, and your father. Yes, you shall live: I have no doubt of that. You will cling to the pleasures of the flesh the way your father does, always clamoring for more. And I will always feel that in some measure I will not fill your needs. People like me never have enough to give to those like you.

When Pierre swept into the room, his face was ecstatic, his cheekbones flushed, his eyes glowing. He was like a tornado entering Natalia's presence. He delighted in the child but not in the same way that Boris had delighted in Arkady. To Boris, his son had simply been a miracle. He had been awed, touched, and grateful to her for having brought to life his unformed dreams. Pierre, on the other hand, relished Tamara as if she epitomized all earthly joys. She was his, and he burst with love for her, with the need to possess her and merge with her. Natalia felt that in his excitement he had forgotten her part in the formation and birth of this baby. She was jealous. At three days old, her daughter had already become the Other Woman.

Pierre was at the bright center of joy. He was happy with his creative endeavors on the ballet *Parade*, and now his daughter had completed his nerve-tingling awareness of the world. In this state of mind he was open to all things and all people. Those who had once found him sullen or moody now saw an ecstatic Pierre, not quite human but touched with the sublime. Natalia saw him, too, and recognized the young artist who had fallen in love with her and waited for her at the back entrance of the Mariinsky: an unreasoned young man, full of verve and imbalance, full of poetry, revelry, and mysticism. He had frightened her then; now she was disconcerted. Between his black brows were two strong lines etched in experience, and between the black curls were strands of gray, noticeable only when one stood close to him. She would wonder: How many see him from this close? And the agonies of her eighteenth year would return to haunt her. Could one ever trust a man like Pierre when he claimed to love a woman? Or was there simply too great a need to possess, too great a need for novelty and exploration?

She hated herself for these doubts. But her daughter's birth had left her in pain. It was taking her longer to shed the weight than the first time. Natalia went to the vanity and examined the fine, feathered lines around her large eyes. She had not done anything with her life in so long—the American interlude had been her single season, brief as it was, since 1913. To rely on one's past reputation for that long was unhealthy. A dancer's body began to change by the time she turned thirty; at twenty-seven, Natalia was nearing that, and because she had had such scant exposure to the stage in four years, she knew that her performance skills had decreased to a perilously low level. Her only exposure, in fact, had been outside of Europe. She realized all too well that she had become a legend, almost forgotten.

As soon as she could walk, she went to the company rehearsals at the Costanzi Theatre. At the end of May, they were to travel to Paris for some other performances, including Pierre's *Parade.* Meanwhile Natalia sat in the front row, silent and still, watching the present production of *The Good-humored Ladies,* a paeon to eighteenth-century Venice choreographed to music by Scarlatti. It was a gay, carefree production, based on the play by Carlo Goldini. The action revolved around a series of pranks, mistaken identities, and joyful lovemaking. Massine's dances were filled with the essence of *joie de vivre.* Nevertheless, illogically, Natalia's throat constricted. The quickly paced musical phrases, rolling in repetitive motifs, sentimental and courtly, reminded her of Boris. He had never particularly admired the Scarlatti family. But for her, right now, the expert simplicity of the toccatas and small sonatas rang true of him: all flowing charm on the surface, all cunning imagination underneath. For him, life had been a clever game of chess, which, ultimately, he had lost.

The only dancer whom she knew well in this production was Lydia Lopokhova. They had been together at the Imperial School and in New York. Now Natalia watched the other small dancer, married to one of Diaghilev's secretaries, Barocchi, and sudden anguish seized her. Lydia had always been the lesser known of the two, an excellent dancer but not quite on Natalia's level. Now Natalia thought: She is superior. Shall I ever equal her again? It was not envy, but self-doubt and self-deprecation. She had allowed her career, her better, unique self, to fall by the wayside. Now she was suddenly afraid of becoming like other women, women she had always despised for the narrow scope of their existences, women such as her mother.

She sat in the theatre and ached. She hurt because she felt shut out from her chosen life, set aside by her husband and unwilling to be bound by her little baby. Perhaps I've been wrong about Serge Pavlovitch, she thought, angry at herself for indulging in self-pity. It would have been wonderful to choreograph a ballet, many ballets. But to give up dancing in a fit of pique—I must have been mad!

On stage, Lydia Lopokhova noticed her and bent down to wave. Natalia held her hands up and made a clapping gesture in mime. Bravo, my dear. If no one cares about Oblonova, it's because Oblonova doesn't deserve it. She hasn't really cared about herself. She's become a relic.

Pierre could not sort through his feelings. He knew that she was attending the rehearsals, that she even joined the soloists when they held their practice classes. Maestro Cecchetti had told him—she had not. Pierre chewed on his lower lip and paced the floor. He took long walks. He went to the hotel and startled the nurse by seizing Tamara and bringing her with him to the workrooms. People smiled at him but were also bewildered. Pierre Grigorievitch was behaving erratically again. His exuberance would give way to anger, which in turn became a pure fount of exquisite joy. If he could combine Tamarotchka and the paint pots, he was supremely himself, a man fulfilled—almost.

One afternoon Diaghilev came upon him with Tamara in the hotel gardens. Amiably, the impressario fell into step beside him, and for a moment they ambled companionably together, smiling at the tiny infant in her red nightshirt. Then Diaghilev motioned to a bench, and they sat down, Tamara in Pierre's arms. "She is very lovely, your daughter," the older man commented.

"I wish my mother could see her," said Pierre. "And I wish Tamara could see our country. But Rome is a good city in which to be born—it's a city with a heart, a city for artists."

"They call it the city of lovers," Diaghilev said indifferently, but his sharp eyes scrutinized Pierre as he held the child, supporting her flaccid neck. He saw Pierre's cheek twitch.

"You are hardly the simpleton you allow others to make you out to be," Diaghilev suddenly remarked. "You are certainly not a man of words, but genius has many languages, don't you think?"

Surprised and wary, Pierre stared at him with his deep black eyes. "What do you mean, Serge Pavlovitch?" he demanded. Somehow he knew that this had some bearing on Natalia. His body went rigid.

"I helped launch you. I like you and I find your work outstanding. I am proud to call you my friend. Once, too, I was Natalia's friend. I had a father's affection for her."

Pierre's jaw set, and over his daughter's body his fingers were clamped together, white at the knuckle. "I wish to God you had put it to her in those very words," he finally said.

"I felt like a father to her—a guide, a mentor," Diaghilev continued. "She is still dear to me in those ways. But she rejects my overtures at reconciliation. You know of our old quarrel?"

"Quarrel? Oh yes, certainly I knew of it, Serge Pavlovitch. I am sorry if my wife has offended you. I'm certain she meant nothing of the kind. Natalia is very proud—"

"Yes, she is. It is a Kussov trait never to forget the smallest slight. You and I both had the ill luck to find ourselves more than once on the wrong side of the cannon in the Kussov camp. Of course, Natalia is only—a Kussov in-law. But don't worry: I am not insulted by her behavior. I am merely concerned. Natalia is no longer a young girl—for a ballerina, that is. Unless she dances soon, she will never again live up to her name. Do you want her to dance again, Pierre?"

The painter was startled by the directness of this query. He licked his upper lip. "Frankly, I don't know," he replied. "There's Tamara. I want my daughter to have a mother. And I want to have a wife."

"Most of my dancers are wives, my dear boy. One hardly precludes the other. The point is, Natalia wants to dance again. Any day now she will ask me to take her back. I'm not certain what my answer will be."

416 Pierre's jaw dropped in frank amazement. "You're not? But no one is a better ballerina!"

Diaghilev inclined his massive head. "True. But right now you are the Riazhin that I need more. There are Lopokhova, Sokolova, Chabelska. But I cannot continue these ballets without my Riazhin. You are necessary to me, Pierre."

"Thank you, Serge Pavlovitch. I am most flattered."

"And I am most sincere. My single problem has to do with financing. Always, always the same rigamarole, the same convoluted entanglements. That was where Boris was most useful to me. I am sorry, dear boy, to keep bringing up his name, as I'm aware that you two had your share of disagreements. But during these lean times I am constantly reminded of how precious all that Kussov savoir faire was—not to mention the money."

"For a profligate hedonist, he managed it quite well," Pierre remarked coldly.

Diaghilev laughed. "We are all profligate hedonists, aren't we, though? Now that you are a wealthy man yourself, aren't you the least bit of a spendthrift?"

Pierre's hands began to tremble slightly. "I am not a wealthy man. My wife, as you well know, is a wealthy woman."

Diaghilev's eyebrows shot up quizzically. "But I didn't know. Surely all's equal between a man and his wife?"

"I could not take the Kussov money," Pierre said. "It would not have been right. Our marriage contract specifies a separation of goods. Natalia still controls her inheritance. Now, of course, she's one of the few wealthy Russians left. Boris Kussov had his funds transferred to France and Switzerland years ago."

"I see. You are a generous man, Pierre. I trust that Natalia appreciates that. Most people would be shocked to hear that you are not a joint tenant to her estate. After all, you are the head of your family. And, as I stated before, you are far from being a fool." He started to chuckle, shaking his head amiably from side to side. "You will now judge me to be the fool. For you see, I was going to come to you on bended knee to beseech you to invest some of your money in the Ballet. Now I fear that the money I plead for is not yours to offer."

White-faced, Pierre rose, his daughter clutched in his arms. "I shall speak to Natalia," he said shortly. "If, as you say, I am

no fool, then she will do as I ask. After all, the Ballet may be
yours, Serge Pavlovitch, but it is also mine. I could not let it go
to ruin because of foolish—yes, foolish—pride. Kussov or not,
the money is solvent."

"And if she truly wishes to rejoin our company, a father's
arms will, of course, be wide open. I do not generally allow
older stars to make comebacks—but for Oblonova, I might
make an exception. If she works very hard, and if her husband
gives her his permission."

The teasing irritation in Diaghilev's voice finally made Pierre
angry. The painter's cheeks reddened, and his muscles tensed.
"That's enough, Serge Pavlovitch," he said in a furious undertone. "Or I shall know once and for all how much of a fool you
deem me."

Tall and massive, he turned on his heel and marched away
toward the hotel. The baby began a bleating refrain of protest,
but for once he ignored her totally. His mind had become a
churning tide of fury. But, oddly enough, the focus of his
hatred was, once again, Boris Kussov.

Natalia leaned her head on her arms and closed her eyes.
The letters and business documents she had been working on
were starting to depress her and she was trying to avoid despondency by keeping safely to the factual and the obvious. How
strange, she thought, that I have thus turned out to be a financial manager—I, who wanted only to dance! But someone had
to keep track of the family estate. Pierre had neither the head
nor the inclination for it, and in a way she was relieved. Doing
things herself had always been her particular approach to life,
apart from the few years when Boris had been there to do them
for her.

Boris. How long ago that had been! She wondered briefly
what he would have thought of the new ballet, *Parade*, that had
premièred hours before at the Châtelet in Paris. From her box
she had watched those strange, modernistic, cubelike figures
drawn by her husband: the Stage Managers. He had worked on
the designs in conjunction with Pablo Picasso, the Spanish artist, and she remembered how difficult it had been for them to
paint the huge curtain, which had dwarfed them. Tonight she

had seen it rise majestically before the public, its painted guitar player a living example of the triumph of art over the limitations of time and space. She had been proud of Pierre Riazhin, proud to be his wife.

It was May already, springtime. Yet how few young men had sat in the audience! They had all gone to war, all wasted their lives. Natalia felt herself harden and thought: Somehow, there is never enough protection against pain. She looked at the assembled legal papers and said to herself: Boris wanted to be a hero, and all I have left of him are these. And Pierre? What had he been trying to prove, with Vendanova? Had he hoped that his conquest would make him more of a man in her eyes?

The door opened noiselessly, and a sliver of golden light streamed over her shoulder, falling on the paper in front of her. Pierre stood framed in the doorway in his bathrobe of crimson silk, a man of rich tastes and rich colors, with boundless, gluttonous needs. He looked well there, framed by the luxury in this house. It was her house, her riches, her husband—yet not hers, never fully. Did he know that Boris had bought and furnished this Paris house for him, as a gift of love?

"You are not coming to bed?" he asked.

She hesitated. He occupied the master bedroom in style, his paintings on the wall, his bottles of scent on the dressing table, his cravats scattered over chairs and small stands. He had taken possession of it with riotous joy, another expression of his hedonism. Now she avoided going there at night, seeking to oppose his magnetism in any way she could—the only way she knew how. There was pain there and she could not give to him, could not let him love her. I shall not fight for him that way, Natalia thought with sudden, defiant anger. He must come to me of his own accord.

"I still have work to do," she answered quietly, avoiding his bottomless black eyes. It was better if she did not look at him. She could pretend to be calm if she did not look. His face, his eyes were the keys that unlocked an unbearable vulnerability in her. His own weaknesses were less discernible these days. Pierre seemed more a man and less an impetuous child—and therefore more complex, less understandable.

"I wanted to talk to you," he said. He came into the room and sat down on the low, ornamented sofa. "Do you have time?" he asked.

She nodded, and pushed aside the stationery. "Of course."

"It's the Ballet. You know Diaghilev's in financial trouble, don't you? This damned war has taken every last sou, every last kopek, from the reserve of funds."

She uttered a short, harsh burst of laughter. "What reserve? Serge Pavlovitch has never had any reserve of funds, my dear Pierre. Has he been wheedling you about it now?"

His body tensed. She could see the undulating muscles tighten under the silk of the bathrobe. "Give me more credit than that, Natalia. The company's in trouble and I'm aware of it, all right? Why couldn't you help? It's my future—my present."

"And my past."

Their eyes met now, cold and level, and she raised her chin. He stood up and began to pace the room. "You're hurting me, do you know that? Hurting me, as a by-product of some silly game with Serge Pavlovitch, left over from the days of Kussov versus Diaghilev. That's childish, Natalia. To hurt your own husband and to stamp out his future because of false pride. How can you expect things to work out between us?"

"I don't expect them to," she replied, surprised by the cool clarity of her response. He turned around then, his eyes widening with amazement, and she continued hotly: "Pride! What do you know of pride, Pierre? It's one thing you've never had, not now, not ever! 'Take care of me, Natalia,' you always say. And who will take care of Natalia? Jacqueline Vendane? Serge Pavlovitch?"

He closed his eyes on her anger, and she saw shame and contrition on his face, but also outrage. Her own fury burst out of her then with a ferocity she could not restrain. "You want to be the golden boy in Diaghilev's stable. With my money! You still despise Boris Kussov, yet you expect that his funds will save your work, will make magic for you! And that you won't have to pay, because you're a genius! Well, I'm sick of it, sick to death of it! What pretensions you have, because you're an artist! The world owes you nothing—not one thing. I owe you nothing. Because you see, Pierre, you give me nothing in return! In life one has to pay. Learn that, once and for all."

"I have paid," he said quietly. "For years and years I paid, in waiting. I'm not going to wait anymore, Natalia. Everything you give me you consider a favor. I am not a protégé, begging. I came to ask you as a man, as a husband. Well, I don't want your favors anymore."

The words resounded with odd strength in the small room. Natalia's lips parted. She rose, a terrible cry tearing through her chest but never quite making it to her mouth. I shall not lose my pride to him, or whatever's left of it, she thought. He will not strip me of my dignity, he will not. "Pierre," she asked, and he barely heard her, "what do you mean?"

"I'm through, Natalia. Through with not being loved enough."

"Not loved enough?" Again she was outraged. "Not loved enough. You can speak to me this way, after everything? After Tamara? I had her for you, for God's sake. You were the first man I loved, and the one I came back to. But when I did come back, I truly *came back*. There is no one else for me, Pierre. No one backstage, no one to prop me up, to stroke my hand. I don't care about the marriage vows, but I do care about the commitment. Without commitment love has no meaning. Why, Pierre? Why Vendanova? Why the need for a Vendanova, whoever she may be?"

The answer came to her in his eyes. She said, "Are you that much in need of constant reassurance? Of—of applause?"

"I have to get it somewhere," he retorted, his hand on the doorknob.

"Please go away," she whispered. "Go now, Pierre."

When he had left, she sank back into the pillow. We all need reassurance, she thought miserably. We all need applause.

Too much had been said, and yet not enough. When June came, Pierre went to Spain with Diaghilev and the Ballet, and Natalia remained alone in Paris. More than ever, she missed her profession, and in the house on Avenue Bugeaud, she practiced until her aching muscles glistened with sweat, until she had exercised her yearning for Pierre out of her very consciousness. Summer passed, and then fall.

World events began to intrude on the life that Natalia was carefully erecting for herself and her small daughter. In November Lenin's Bolsheviks took over Russia, driving out the more moderate Provisional Government of Alexander Kerensky. Suddenly the March Revolution paled by comparison, and Natalia sat home and trembled, wondering what could have happened to her family and friends. There seemed no adequate way to find out, and in her isolation she imagined the worst. More than ever during these days of estrangement from Pierre, Natalia thought of Nina Stassova and her daughter, Galina. Nina had been Boris's favorite sister, she and her daughter had become Natalia's only family. Now she felt as if part of herself were somewhere in Leningrad—her St. Petersburg—hiding from the Bolsheviks. What else would a wealthy aristocratic family be doing during these troubled times filled with rumors of bloodshed?

But, much as her thoughts converged on her native country, another revolution became a more pressing concern. In the winter Diaghilev and his small band of followers found themselves in Lisbon, a city under civil strife. As she read the news, Natalia saw Pierre's image vividly in her mind. She sat in the English-style parlor of her elegant stone house on Avenue Bugeaud and pictured her husband cowering behind barricades, or walking across a street, calm and majestic in his dark solidity, being hit by a volley of exploding shells. Crumpling, crumpling. The male beauty of him destroyed, bloodied. Her fingers trembled so that she could no longer hold the newspaper, which was illegible through the curtain of her tears.

She did not know how to wire him for news, as there was no Russian embassy in Lisbon. She waited, adding this fear to the others. Yet all the while she persisted in thinking stubbornly: If he's all right, I shall not communicate with him.

The defiance in her heart strengthened when Diaghilev finally wrote to her from Madrid. Somehow he had succeeded in evacuating them from Portugal, but his plans for a season in Barcelona had been canceled. "We are desperate, my Natashenka," he explained in his letter. "We have absolutely no funds, not enough to eat. We can't get out, and I can't pay anyone, and so we shall be disbanding in an attempt to survive, each in his own fashion." Clearly, she thought, Pierre is too proud to communicate at all. Well, if that's the case, I'll be damned if I'll help him.

Still, regret seeped through her bitterness. Boris would have done anything to keep his company together. If I don't owe it to anyone else, she thought, I do owe *him* the effort to sustain Serge Pavlovitch. Leaning her head face down on the blotter of her secretary, she wept with frustration and wrote out a large check to the order of the impresario. She mailed it to Madrid.

When a letter arrived in Pierre's handwriting, she felt the bottom fall out of her stomach, and her hands begin to shake. He had sent her only a few lines, but when she read them, tears blinded her.

> We're still alive, and Serge Pavlovitch is terribly grateful. But I've missed you, missed Tamara, and wondered how a man can survive if he is not forgiven. We can't continue apart, Natalia. Is there no way to mend fences with Diaghilev, to have you work alongside me in the Ballet? I think he would be ready to take you back on your own terms.

But the accompanying missive from the director himself was not as encouraging. Diaghilev thanked her for her financial help but explained that the crisis was far from resolved. Only the promise of a solid engagement would save the Ballet from total collapse, and at the moment no European impresario was willing to take a chance on the Diaghilev dancers. He had been trying in vain to strike a bargain with Sir Oswald Stoll in London—and could report little progress in the negotiations. He was at his wits' end.

Boris would have known what to do, Natalia thought, suddenly grim. She called Tamara's nurse and said to her: "I shall have to go to England tomorrow. But only for a few days, so you and the baby should remain here." As she packed, she knew that she was making the only possible decision. Her marriage and her career both depended on it. On the train to Calais, on the ferry to Dover, and later on her way to London, she thought through what she would say, how she would look, how she would sound.

Once in the British capital, she went directly to Claridge's and telephoned Sir Oswald Stoll, inviting him to tea the following day. She received him in her suite, in an afternoon dress of ivory wool with wide sleeves and a low waist. "I hear that you are negotiating with Serge Pavlovitch Diaghilev," she said, pouring tea for him in the hotel's fine china. "He is a desperate man."

"And have you rejoined him, Madame Riazhina?" the impresario asked with a distinguished and subtle smile.

"That's what I wished to discuss," she replied, looking at him with quick coolness. "You are planning to book the Ballet into the Coliseum, between vaudeville acts? Would you have me perform Armida between the talking dogs and Lockhart's elephants?" She smiled at him then, the most charming, unprepossessing smile that he had ever seen, and she knew at once that he had noticed, close up, the unmistakeable aura of her beauty.

"I am a businessman first, a balletomane second," he demurred.

"Of course. And we are infinitely grateful. London is special to us. I shall never forget the year of the Coronation Gala, Sir Oswald. The British have been most gracious to us. And so I have a proposal for you. Offer Diaghilev a contract, the contract he wants, and I shall pay you the sum of the advance. Between you and me."

Sir Oswald coughed, his eyes betraying deep surprise. "Oh, don't worry," Natalia continued sweetly. "I have the Kussov fortune at my disposal. I cannot finance the entire Ballets Russes from my own purse, but I can help from time to time." She regarded him directly. "But you see, I too have become something of a businesswoman. Diaghilev must not know of this, or it would lower my value as a performer in his estimation. A man must pay for quality, or he comes to disregard its inherent price. My late ex-husband, Count Boris Kussov, was a patron of the arts by profession. I'm not and must be considered no differ-

424   ently from any other aspiring choreographer. Because that is my
goal, you see."

The impresario began to smile and raised his teacup in appreciation. "My dear madame," he declared, "I hope that we shall have the pleasure of a long and fruitful association."

hen Natalia returned from London, she found Pierre in the Paris house, feeding his baby daughter. He appeared more gaunt than before, and there were lines of fatigue etched around his dark eyes. For a moment stubborn pride fought for control, then it dissolved, and he came to her, burying his lips in her hair. She rested limply in his arms, exhausted from the worry and the trip, wanting to be made whole again, wanting to obliterate her pain in his sensuality. But *he* was seeking help from *her*, forgetting that he had left her, that, like Boris, he had disappeared from her life and not she from his. "It doesn't matter," she whispered. "It doesn't matter as long as we love each other, does it, Pierre?"

But there was so much for each of them to forgive. There were all the years when she had belonged to someone else, and then there had been Vendanova.

The reunion with Diaghilev proceeded with infinite smoothness. He simply accepted her back as *prima ballerina*, and she mentioned nothing about choreography. At this point, all she wanted was to dance again on a stage, and she received this opportunity at Sir Oswald Stoll's arrangement. The Ballets Russes were booked into the Coliseum for six months in 1918, and the Riazhins took Tamara and her nurse to London with them. On November eleventh of that year, Pierre hoisted his small daughter to his shoulders in Trafalgar Square, and they danced in the streets with the British to celebrate the Armistice. But afterward

Pierre said harshly: "How nice for the British! I wonder, however, if an armistice can occur in a civil war. Until such an event, we will all be exiles from our own mother country, won't we?"

His wife clasped her hands together, thinking of a man who had been senselessly murdered by his countrymen even before the outbreak of the Russian Revolution.

Several months later Natalia received a letter from Romola Nijinskaya, in Switzerland. Vaslav had been committed to the Sanatorium Bellevue Kreuzlingen for treatment of a condition labeled "schizophrenia." Too many people had played with this man's life, tampering with the delicate balance of his sanity. Natalia felt sad, anguished at the remembrance of times spent onstage with him and of the parallels in their lives. His daughter, Kyra, would have been Arkady's age—and hadn't Boris turned to a woman in the same way that Vaslav had? But Boris had virtually abandoned the Nijinskys after helping to arrange their coming together on the S.S. *Avon*, and Natalia felt a stab of bitter shame. As for Diaghilev, he had never overcome his need to avenge his lover's "betrayal." Had it been like that between Boris and Pierre, with her at the center of their conflict?

That spring, a new and even lengthier London season began, this time at the Alhambra. Natalia could never come to the British capital without being reminded of the summer of 1911, when Boris had finally made love to her at Ashley. But now Tamara Karsavina, who had been caught in Russia during the dreadful last months of 1917, unable to escape until now, rejoined the Ballets Russes in London. She told Natalia and Pierre about the Bolshevik takeover of the Russian capital, about the bloodshed and terror that had paralyzed the city. All the Kussov property had been destroyed.

"And the family?" Natalia asked. "My father-in-law? Nina and her daughter?" She felt her throat tightening and looked at her friend, her eyes insistent.

Karsavina glanced at the carpet, at her fine kid boots. "No one has learned anything about Princess Stassova and the girl. They weren't in Petersburg—Leningrad—when the riots broke out on November 8. But the others—the old count, and his two other daughters, and their husbands and children—they were

all killed in the old man's home. There had been a christening,
I think—Liza was visiting from Moscow—"

Pierre saw Natalia collapse in her chair, all color drained
from her face. After he had put her to bed, he sat beside her,
unable to read, unable to think. Their Russia had become a
nightmare of bloodlust, its people brutal and depraved. And yet,
in his profound shock, he could not help feeling a twinge of
animal excitement at the notion that Boris's fine people, with
their august lineage, had been crushed without regard for their
special status, just as Boris himself had been. In death the great
fell with their inferiors, and breeding counted for nothing.

In the months that followed, he sometimes wondered if the
little princess, Galina Stassova, had been able to survive the ordeal. He had never quite forgotten the golden perfection of her
features, which he had painted with the love that artists always
bear the objects of true beauty.

In June of 1919, Tamara watched her mother perform in *La
Boutique Fantasque.* The girl of two stood up in her seat to see
the mechanical can-can dancer who wore a short, flouncy skirt,
and could not understand how this live doll onstage could be
her actual Mama, as her nurse was telling her. But she clapped
and clapped with her chubby hands, giggling aloud, and afterward she was taken backstage. There, approaching her, came
the mechanical doll herself! Tamara was filled with wonder.
Bending toward her, the doll said: "Did you enjoy it, sweetheart?" and then the little girl knew, really knew, that this was
Mama! She went home bewildered and excited, and before
going to sleep, she hugged to her breast one of Natalia's old
ballet slippers.

When Tamara turned three, she was already strong and willful, a tiny replica of her father, with black curls circling a round
face endowed with black eyes and long lashes. She had her
mother's graceful, sloping shoulders, her delicate hands. She
was a little princess, conscious of her domain, already able to
manipulate the young nurse who took care of her. Natalia spoke
to Pierre about her development. "She needs to be taken firmly
in hand," she said, "and we can't do it, working such long
hours as we do. Tamara needs a governess, and she needs a
home, not a hotel suite. I'd like to send her back to Paris and

hire a French or a Swiss governess to take care of her and begin her lessons."

"But I don't want her away from us," Pierre countered abruptly. "No one knows how long this British season will last."

"No, and where will we go from here? We're traveling minstrels, Pierre. A child can't traipse around the world with people like us. She needs to put down roots, to have a country. Since we can't send her back to Russia, the best we can do is to settle her in Paris, the nearest either of us comes to having a real home! And besides, London isn't far. We can visit her whenever we want!"

"You find her a burden," he tossed at her, but he could think of no valid argument with which to counter hers. To Tamara's dismay, they took her back to Paris and hired Mademoiselle Pichenet, a middle-aged matron from Normandy with the beginnings of a mustache on her upper lip. Chaillou, the white-haired butler who presided over the house on Avenue Bugeaud, declared himself delighted to have part of the family back again. Pierre missed his daughter and blamed Natalia, but he was silent, and the child, ever sensitive to the moods of the grown-ups closest to her, absorbed his resentment and hoarded it in the secret part of herself. Mama had shoes of magic, but she was also a tyrant, to be opposed.

Natalia was in Paris to prepare for Christmas. It was snowing outside, and this year, 1920, marked the sixth anniversary of Arkady's death. Had it been up to her, she would never have celebrated the holidays again, for the pain of loss made her want to sleep and forget, to obliterate this part of her past that was still with her. But for Tamara she had to push on, to make plans that were abhorrent to herself.

Pierre had fallen in love with her during a Christmas season fifteen years before, a lifetime ago, she thought, touching her hair, which she now wore clipped in a bob. She was sitting in the cheerful parlor, her favorite room of the house, and now she laid down the large print sheet of winter fashions that she had been perusing and thought: But we were all in love that year, each of us hopeless and each of us in the throes of anguish! Somehow this made her smile, and she felt a little better. It could only have been resolved this way, she said to herself—with her and Pierre together. What would have happened if Boris had not died? Horrified, she laid her head in her hands and shivered. But I wanted him to live, and I did love him!

"Mama, I don't want to go for another walk in the Bois!" Tamara was crying, bursting into the room, her curls tumbling over her shoulders. In her fur coat she resembled a small, fluffy rabbit. "I won't go! Tell Ma'zelle I don't have to go!"

"You most certainly do have to," Natalia said sternly. "Go to your room and apologize to Mademoiselle and tell her that I have something to discuss with her. Then you two will take your walk and work up an appetite for tea. Don't forget to put on your hat before you leave."

The child glared at her and opened her mouth to protest. But her mother stood up and propelled her out of the room, pushing her gently but firmly ahead of her into the hallway. When she had gone, Natalia returned to the sofa and picked up her fashion tabloid, sighing deeply.

She heard Chaillou coughing delicately, and looked up, startled. "There is a letter for Madame," the old butler said, carrying it to her on a silver tray. "It is addressed to the Countess Kussova."

Natalia raised her eyebrows and smiled. "Ah? That's interesting. For some the appeal of a title is irresistible, although one would think it might have less value now, since the outpouring of exiled Russian nobility into France."

She took the heavy, soiled envelope, and Chaillou unobtrusively turned on his heel and left the room. Natalia fingered the envelope, examining the large round handwriting with which she was not familiar, and the postmark from Constantinople. The letter had obviously traveled far and taken its time to reach her. She slit it open and withdrew a series of folded sheets. Inexplicably, foreboding seized her, and she felt her fingers begin to tremble. She started to read, her heart palpitating in her throat and echoing in her ears. She was so intent that she did not hear the governess enter, discreet in her soft-soled shoes.

"Darling Aunt Natalia," the letter began, and she experienced a profound shock upon assimilating these words:

It also strikes me that if you don't remember who I am, I can't possibly blame you. The last time you saw me was seven years ago, when I was eight. But I remember you so well—you were my most special aunt. My mama loved you too, and that is why I've decided that since I need to ask for help, I should turn to you.

I shall backtrack now and explain how I have ended up in Turkey. When Uncle Boris was killed at the start of '15, my mother was beside herself with grief. She adored him, if you recall. Everyone tried to be strong, especially Grandfather, but it really didn't do Mama any good. She couldn't make effective contact with you at the time. Your little boy had died, and you were not up to writing anybody. Then one day, in 1916, while you were still in America, Mama received a letter from a man in a small Caucasian village just south of Tiflis—Tbilis they call it today. He claimed that he had been harboring an officer of the Division Sauvage who appeared to have lost his memory after having been seriously wounded in the head. Instead of going to the divisional commander, this Caucasian man, who resented the intrusion of the Cossack division almost more than he feared the Turks, had decided to write to Mama, for among the things that he had found on the person of the amnesiac officer had been an old envelope bearing her return address. Did she have any notion as to who this man might be?

You can imagine how long she hesitated before going to the Caucasus. Perhaps half an hour. She did not want to raise Grandfather's hopes, or Aunt Nadia's and Aunt Liza's. Papa had gone to Kiev to conduct some business, and so she decided that I would travel with her. I'm still not exactly sure why she made this decision: It was wartime, and if you remember, 1915 had been the worst year for the Russian front. A year later everyone still talked about the fearful losses, and no civilian approached a war zone. Mama never did explain why she chose to risk two lives, and why she burdened herself with an unruly child on such a delicate mission. But the fact remains that she did—thank God for my sake!

When I think about it a lot, as I am doing now, it seems to me that Mama must have possessed a strange premonition and did not want to be separated from me for the slightest reason—even an obvious one such as safety. Or else it was because she always thought I should have been Uncle Boris's daughter, even more than hers: She found my resemblance to him so very remarkable. In any event, we hastened onto a series of trains, squashed among traveling soldiers, and then, from Tiflis, we hired a car and driver. Mama didn't even want to stop to talk with General Baranov, whom she had known when she was a girl and who had commanded Uncle Boris's division. She had to learn if the wounded man in the hilltop village was her brother.

We were able to locate our correspondent, who was a leather-faced old man of Tcherkess blood, fierce as the devil in person but evidently kind to the bone. He had been feeding and tending this officer for months now, not knowing who he was. We went to see him—the officer— and no, it wasn't Uncle Boris, although we think it was one of his men because of the letter from Mama which he had apparently picked up somewhere. War is such strange business.

We had planned then to return to Petersburg, which by then had become Petrograd, but we couldn't seem to find a driver to take us back to Tiflis. Mama wrote Papa—but because of the intense confusion generated by the war, he never received our message, or else he would have come for us, wouldn't he? We didn't want to risk our lives again this time. It had been one thing to come here on the double, thinking we might find Uncle Boris. But knowing now that it wasn't he, we were going to use caution in returning. Only we never did—the March Revolution came, and Mama was afraid, and no one at home was sending for us. She thought perhaps they'd all been killed, and so we stayed put in the village. Everyone was most kind to us, since we were harmless enough, and we helped care for the officer.

Mama had changed a lot by then. She'd grown very frightened, and nervous. The disappointment of not having found her brother alive had hurt her very much. She couldn't sleep, didn't really want to go back to Petrograd. She seemed happy enough in the village, where we were left alone and she could think and brood. But I missed Papa, and my lessons, and the aunts. It was as though Mama wished to remain lost. Maybe you too felt like that after you heard of Uncle Boris's death, right on top of Arkady's. I was still too little to have known how to mourn or even whom to mourn for—Uncle Boris had been like a golden image, not truly real to me.

Then, early in '18, after the November Revolution, Mama caught the cholera. There was a dreadful epidemic and no way of curing it in our primitive village—no doctors, no medicines. She simply died. It seems so cold, so abrupt, to write it that way—but I've had to learn to deal with that fact over the years, and that's really what happened. She grew sick and died. We'd always been together, more like sisters than mother and daughter—and then she died and I was all alone among strangers, in a remote part of the country, and no one at home knew that I was there, or how to reach me. You can't possibly imagine how broken down communication systems were at that dismal time in our Russia!

I was able to survive. The Tcherkess family took me in, though there was almost no money left, for Mama hadn't been able to bring much of her own along. Then, in '19, I found a way to reach Tiflis—Tbilis by then—and started sending messages to Papa and Grandfather. That's when word reached me through various sources about the deaths and the burning of the house. All of them killed! (You had learned of that, hadn't you, Aunt Natalia? That our whole family was murdered by some rioters, in November of '17?) But I took that news better than Mama's death. Somehow I'd expected it. I'd been alone so long, I'd known that I'd have to remain that way. I'd long since stopped hoping that Papa would be around to save me.

Then I found some other refugees in Tbilis—a charming town, full of good people—and we tried to put aside some funds to escape from the Bolsheviks. One of the girls was a *tzigane* from Moldavia, with a wonderful rich voice, and she taught me to sing the way they do, wrenching your heart and guts out as you do it. We used to go to local *traktirs*, simple provincial eateries, and sing for the clients, and the owners would pay us a few kopeks, which we then put away. I wasn't very good, but life was manageable. And it wasn't difficult to learn how to repel the advances of drunken men. One learns quickly about such matters— even a little princess from the Boulevard of the Big Stables, who's only fourteen!

Yes, my dear Aunt Natalia, I've changed! I'm almost sixteen now, but I feel as if I've grown up very fast, much faster than I would have in the capital. Do you realize—I wouldn't even have come out at my début yet? Oh, I know—Papa had such dreams for me: presentation at court, then a brilliant marriage. But do you know, I'm not half sorry that these things won't ever take place? I've seen a part of the world, and I don't know what's meant by "brilliant marriage" anymore. You made one, that's for sure; Uncle Boris was very special, very—well, glowing. But it was you who brought the "specialness" out in him. He needed you, because you were an artist, one of those unique individuals who defies class distinctions and brings some of God's magic to the poor earth. Maybe I can do something special myself, someday. I don't know—I'm not certain I possess any gifts. I sing, but not that well, as I've told you. And my education stopped when we came to the Caucasus. So about dance, or painting, or formal musical training—what can I say?

Recently we have come to Constantinople, my friend and I. We crossed the mountains with some hardy people, mostly other *tziganes* whom Irina knew. The *tziganes* are accustomed to moving around the face of the earth, knapsack in tow. We found our way—I shall skip the trials and tribulations—to this strange Turkish city, overrun by foreigners of all types and races—Greeks, Armenians, Jews, and now hordes of emigrated Russians. Irina and I are renting a room and singing again, by night.

And so, Aunt Natalia, I need you. You are my only living relative, so I am not going to pretend to false pride with you. I don't want to spend the rest of my life all alone in Turkey—I want to come to Paris, to you! If you will have me??? I shall need a visa and the money for a train ticket. Someday I shall find a way to reimburse you. I promise not to be a burden in your life—only let me come and have a family again!

Your loving niece,
GALINA ANDREIEVNA STASSOVA

"Is Madame all right?" Mademoiselle Pichenet demanded, placing a hand on Natalia's shoulder. But when the young woman turned her face up, the governess blinked, taken aback. Tears were streaming down Natalia's cheeks, silent tears that dripped down her chin in haphazard rivulets, falling on the sheets of paper in her hand.

"Yes, I'm fine," Natalia answered softly. "Just fine, mademoiselle."

Finally, at thirty-one, Natalia had been given her chance to plan a work of dance. Leonid Massine, following in the footsteps of his predecessor, had succumbed to the charms of a woman and had been dismissed from the Ballet. Diaghilev had been about to launch into a remake of the Mariinsky's classical extravaganza *The Sleeping Beauty*—a remake he was calling *The Sleeping Princess*. For this adaptation he had turned to the only person present who could fill the shoes of a choreographer: Natalia. Pierre was working on costumes and set designs, and once again they were in London, living in a suite at the Claridge Hotel.

She had never known how difficult it would be to move from

individual interpretation of a character to the planning of a whole ballet. There was no well-developed system of notation, nothing like the bars and notes a composer used or the mock-ups that Pierre and Bakst could produce on a moment's notice. She had worked with the stylized choreographers of the Imperial Theatres, where she had watched Petipa follow the music with a sheet of notes on what he thought the dancers should be doing. Fokine had danced in front of his people, working from a half-formed idea, derived from the music he was using. Massine had been very precise, expecting each interpreter to follow his directions to the letter—there was to be little individual acting, for he as creator knew every gesture that had to be made. Nijinsky had proceeded from a vague idea of a frieze, of the primitive. But all of these choreographers had not compounded their work until the dancers were at hand.

Natalia, however, had devised a different working method. At first she sketched her ideas and sometimes played with candlesticks on a large expanse of desk representing the stage. She moved them about, interrupting herself to dance out a phrase. Then she would try to remember how Petipa had arranged his *Sleeping Beauty*. She would ask the accompanist to play a few bars for her, and she would write down what she could still visualize from the Imperial Theatres. Then she would think of ways to change this, to soften the acrobatic nature of some of the steps, to weld Diaghilev's ideas and her own into a whole. Only after this could she walk into a rehearsal room and see if the dancers could follow her train of thought. Sometimes, with their bodies in front of her, knowing their individual limitations and strengths, she would change a routine, redo a passage, smooth out an *enchaînement*. It was an endless task.

There were also some unresolved problems between her and Pierre concerning the costumes. He had designed splendid extravaganzas, baroque full-length finery that flowed thick and richly textured, but which made it difficult for the dancers to move. "How can any ballerina worth her mettle execute a *jeté* when she's carrying twice her own weight?" she had cried to Diaghilev. Pierre had stormed from the rehearsal room, angered that she had complained about his work to the director. But

Diaghilev had not supported her practical objections. He had been most enthralled by Pierre's and Bakst's designs.

They were together in their hotel suite when the telegram was delivered. He took it eagerly from the bellhop, tearing at it with his customary impatience. "Ah!" he cried. "She has come at last, our little princess!"

Natalia grabbed the paper from his hand, restraining a momentary flare of resentment. He was appropriating something not rightfully his—something from *her* past, not his, not theirs together. Galina had never been a member of his family. She scanned the words. "Natalia darling: I'm here! Visa took own sweet time, then I became sick. But I'm in Paris, Tamara's beautiful. Where are *you?* Love, Galina."

Something warm dissolved inside her, and she smiled at the excited confusion of the telegram, at this proof that Galina had reentered her life. "We must go home and greet her," Pierre was saying.

Natalia wheeled about. "No, I must go by myself. Darling, Galina hardly remembers *me*, let alone *you!* It wouldn't be right. Besides, she doesn't even know that I've remarried."

"It wouldn't be right not to come with you to welcome her. You're forgetting, Natalia, that she'll be a guest in what's also my house."

She could feel his eyes boring into her, daring her to challenge this statement, and now she felt like lashing out that Galina would be no one's guest, that as Boris Kussov's only descendent, she actually belonged there more than they, the Riazhins. But she said nothing. Her heart was knocking in her chest. "I'm tired," she whispered. "Dear God, I'm so tired. Please pour me a glass of brandy, Pierre, and let's sit down. So much is happening to us all at once."

She was thinking of Galina, remembering her as a child, wondering if she had changed. How like Boris she had looked! Natalia pressed her fingers to her eyes and felt the old deep pain of loss, the disorientation of *déjà-vu*. A breathlessness had come upon her, and she thought: But Galina is hardly more than a child—and I'm not very good with children! What have I opened up—what have I done to my life, accepting this responsibility? Then a rush of passion flowed out of her, the need to care for this little remnant of her lost husband, of the father of her son. Arkady would have been—*had* been—Galina's cousin.

But Galina had resembled Boris far more than Arkady had. In a sense *she* had been his *daughter*—the first child to have touched both their lives. Had she then not also been a kind of daughter to Natalia herself? The feeling of dislocation between past and present, between real and imagined, persisted, and she took the brandy snifter from Pierre with trembling fingers.

"I still think we should both go to Paris," he said. "We should all be there together for this first reunion—Tamara, too, will need to adjust. You must think of her also, Natalia."

"Tamara! You see her alone all the time!" She was referring to the trips he often took across the Channel, "to see my child," he claimed. In reality Natalia felt that he was escaping Diaghilev's pressures and their own more and more frequent disagreements. She said: "Let me make the trip once on my own—my daughter thinks I'm a stranger, and it's not fair. Serge Pavlovitch can spare you far more easily than he can spare me in our day-to-day operations, but Tamara has no way of understanding that!"

"You don't go because the ballet is more important to you than she is," he countered roughly, suddenly turning away. "Now you will go for Galina's sake, without even considering Serge Pavlovitch!"

Natalia bit into her knuckle, welcoming the pain. "I'm going because this is an emergency," she said in a low, tense voice. She took a swallow of brandy, then another, some of it spilling onto her fingers. "Think a little, Pierre! Galina has suffered a tremendous shock—the loss of her whole family, of her country, of her money. She watched her mother die. How can you be so callous as to compare her needs at this time with those of our daughter, who is healthy and happy in her own home?"

"A home composed of servants," he said sullenly.

"It's a better solution than to spend one's childhood surrounded by four hotel walls!" she cried. She bit her lower lip and then thought: What the hell, he deserves it, and added: "Besides, I don't want my daughter to grow up to be an English miss, as cool and calm about sleeping with another woman's husband as she might be about eating someone else's cold porridge! Oh, God, Pierre, she couldn't even dance. Why did you pick her? Why did you do it?"

Now she wanted to catch the damaging words and stuff them back inside herself. Vendanova had long since left the Ballet. Why had she dredged up this old incident? It was not simply because of Pierre—it was because of Serge Pavlovitch; it was because of the construction crews, the *danseurs*. She had grown unforgiving, tired perhaps from the extra work, tired also of the years when one thing or another had held her back, had made a mockery of her, had hurt her.

Once their bitter quarrels had led to a kind of physical confrontation, when she would tremble with fear as he bore down on her, his fists clenched. But instead, the compressed energy would be released in another sort of physical climax, a ferocious lovemaking, the passion surging through them like cleansing fire, scorching and blistering but also healing. Then she would think, aghast afterward at the violence inside them: He wanted to hurt me, and I too could have hurt him! She would tremble slightly, horrified but also fascinated by this side of them that defied civilization. Their love was like a pagan ritual from which one emerged bruised and spent but also renewed. Then would follow a period of intense sweetness, of gentleness, of consideration.

Now when the moments of rage began, one of them would leave the room, walking or running outside to drive away the tension, while the one left vented his anger on pillows, newspapers, and haphazard cups and saucers. Natalia waited now, watching Pierre. Who would leave this time? Nameless anguish rose in her throat. This hatred, these accusations were not right—just as the war that had slaughtered millions because of the pompous pride of a strutting Kaiser had not been right. My God, my God! Is this, then, what we've come to? she inwardly cried. Mutual destruction? And for what, for what?

She grabbed her coat and ran out of the suite.

Together they went to the front door, feeling the February wind on their shoulders through their fur wraps, each involved in his own emotions. Natalia was seized with a wordless anticipation: to see Galina again, after all these years! Pierre was curious. He remembered Galina, of course, from that long-ago time when he had painted her. Painting Galina Stassova had initiated the rebirth of his career: Baroness von Baylen had seen the painting—or had it been her friend, the Countess Brianskaya?—and had commissioned one of herself. Then had come those years at the *Künstler Kolonie*, in Darmstadt—years best forgotten, years of dry bitterness, of loneliness, of rejection. But Galina had been a lovely, lively child. She'd also been Boris's niece, his look-alike. Pierre had painted her with fierce resentment, frightening her. Actually, he'd wanted to become her friend and hadn't known how.

The front door opened and Chaillou bowed graciously, smiling imperceptibly. Everything about the man is imperceptible, Pierre thought with wry amusement. But Natalia was pushing past him, her face coloring with expectation.

"Where are they?" she asked.

"Mademoiselle Tamara is having her tea, with Mademoiselle Pichenet," the old butler replied. "The princess . . ." His white brows shot up with the merest hint of quizzicality. "The princess is in the parlor, waiting."

In the hallway sudden shyness took hold of Natalia. In the parlor so carefully put together by Boris sat his only living descendent, the child who had helped to cement their relationship, who had unconsciously prepared Natalia for having a child of her own. As she hesitated, Pierre strode forward, until he had crossed the threshold and stood framed in the doorway, eyeing Galina Andreievna Stassova.

His strong footsteps had startled her. Expecting Natalia, ill prepared for this tall, wide-shouldered, dark man, her face registered bewilderment and even fear as she looked at him as at an apparition. She had been sitting on the sofa, her long legs crossed, her slim fingers resting in her lap, her torso upright with apprehension. The exclamation of welcome died on his lips. She was so poignantly beautiful, so startling in her eerie resemblance to her uncle, that he could not speak, could not breathe normally for a full few seconds. He could only gaze at her in amazement.

He could not discern how tall she would be when she stood

up, but the legs which she displayed were lanky and well molded, partially hidden by a hideous cerise skirt that had definitely seen better days on another, shorter person. The color was wrong, but the girl was right. She was long-waisted and her breasts were full and high, pushing slightly against the soft wool of the cream blouse. Cascades of hair, blond and glowing, spread over her shoulders, unrestrained by pins, totally unseemly and out of fashion in this day of crimped bobs, yet completely bewitching. The face was a gentle oval, the nose perfect and straight, the mouth large, chiseled and somewhat chapped, and the eyes—he had never seen the likes of them, not in thirty-eight years of existence, most of them spent in quest of subjects to commit to paint and canvas.

What met her own sight was a man, pure and simple. Galina had seen few of them like Pierre, elegant in a robust, sensuous fashion. The dark azure of her magnificent eyes went to his face like scared rabbits, and she took in the unruly black curls heavily interspersed with premature gray, and beneath them the wide brow, the high cheekbones, the full lips. Her eyes encountered his, and she read the admiration in them. He was appraising her as if she belonged to this room, as if she were a work of art, an antique, a treasure. She blushed and looked uncomfortably away. All at once nameless misery had invaded her spirit, and she was thinking: It was a mistake, I shouldn't have come!

And then she saw Natalia, who was entering the room with her small, quick steps, the same agility of a doe in flight, the same lovely heart-shaped face that had bent over her as a child—the pale beauty that she remembered, the overwhelming brown velvet eyes. She stood up and Pierre saw that she was indeed tall, tall as befitted a Kussov. She threw her arms around his wife with a small cry, and tears streamed down her face as they rocked together back and forth. Then she and Natalia sat down side by side on the sofa, very close like schoolgirls, their fingers intertwined. Still he had not spoken. He felt as though he had intruded on a private scene—two Kussovs meeting—and yet he could do nothing to bridge the gap, to welcome Galina. Her sheer beauty had mesmerized him.

Tamara's entrance forced him to react. The little girl burst into the room, calling: "Papa! Mama!" and jumped into Pierre's arms, her small, firm legs locking around his torso, her laughing face close to his, merry, boisterous.

"Well, princess!" he ejaculated, and then, looking at Galina, he caught himself, suddenly foolish. "I don't suppose we should call you that anymore," he said to Tamara, coloring. "After all, we have a real princess living with us now."

But Galina's blue eyes caught him, and she said: "Come now! We're old friends by now, you know. Aren't we, Tamarotchka? And besides"—and suddenly her eyes turned to slate, hard and old—"nobody cares anymore about old titles. Prince taxi drivers are just as eager for a tip as all the others."

"Nevertheless," Natalia inserted with a sly grin, "Chaillou is delighted to have a princess under the roof. No one is a greater snob than he."

"The household misses the days when Natalia was a countess," Pierre remarked, bitterness seeping into his tone.

Galina blushed. "You must ignore Pierre when he turns sourpuss," Natalia said gently, taking her hand. "You'll become used to him in minutes. We both looked forward to your coming, dear."

"Yes, we did," Pierre added with forced brightness. But still Galina could not bring herself to look at him. "Well," he commented and sat down abruptly.

"I don't know what to call you," Galina said in her low, tremulous voice. "It all seems so bizarre, really. All this— luxury—after years in the village, and then in Tbilis and Turkey. I didn't know that you had remarried, Natalia. And I didn't know it would be you," she added lamely, finally regarding Pierre.

Natalia's lips worked, and she stroked Galina's hand with a smooth, soothing gesture. She felt their mutual discomfort, and knew it was up to her to resolve it, to restore ease and flow. "Pierre was an old friend of your uncle," she began, the words quiet in the hush that ensued. "Long ago, when he graduated from the Academy, he went to see your Uncle Boris—plain Boris, I should say, for you're not a child anymore. Boris became his sponsor, his mentor, and introduced him to many men of influence that could help a young painter. That was around the time that I met both of them—Pierre and Boris. I met them separately, but we all knew one another, we all had common interests in the ballet, in the arts. When your uncle married me, we didn't see much of Pierre any longer. Sometimes people go their different ways. It happens especially when they marry and form a home of their own. By odd coincidence, however, Pierre was living in Germany near where we went when I was expecting Arkady. When Boris enlisted in the Division Sauvage, and Arkady was ill and needed to see a doctor specialist in Lausanne, it was Pierre who helped me. He helped Arkady and me out of one of the most difficult situations I have ever found myself a part of—someday I shall tell you about it. But then, when Boris died, when Arkady died, when there was no one at all—Pierre reappeared. And I realized that being his wife was the only thing that made sense now—for the woman I'd become, and for the girl I'd been. I didn't remarry because I'd forgotten Boris. Actually, I married Pierre for Pierre's own sake, but also because he'd been Boris's friend. Does this make sense to you, Galina?"

Looking at them both on the couch, Pierre saw the same grave expression on their faces, the same tears in their eyes. He wanted to draw near them, to touch them. Galina was saying: "Yes, Natalia. I'm glad for you, that you found Pierre Grigorievitch."

She's a child, still, thought Natalia with quick compassion: a child half the time and a woman old beyond her age the other half. Now she wants to trust, to belong. "You're part of us, too," Natalia said. "Don't ever feel a burden, as you wrote in your letter. First of all, we love you. I loved your mother, I loved you. Pierre wanted to love you when he painted you. And then, let's be fair: You're Boris's niece. Your place is here."

"Yes, it is," Pierre said and was surprised that he meant it, that in his mind's eye he could see her there, this little girl with the woman's body, this pathetic little refugee with the bearing of an Olympian goddess. He was surprised above all by his acceptance of this reminder of Boris Kussov, of his appreciation for the heir of his nemesis, the thorn of his life. He lowered Tamara to the floor and went to them then, to the two women, and kneeling in front of them, placed their hands in his own palm, smiling.

"As long as you don't pretend to be our daughter, we'll get along perfectly," he said. "We're much too young to be your parents, Galina! What are you, our step-niece? It doesn't matter now, does it? You're our friend."

"Thank you," she replied and looked at him seriously, her eyes shining like jewels. He licked his lips and shook his head and started to laugh, all at once conscious of the tension in him.

Then she laughed too, the woman-child, absurdly joining in. It's a strange world, Natalia thought: We laugh at the wrong moments, when we're feeling nervous. "I shall have to take you shopping, my friend," she said to Galina. "For spring. You, and Tamara."

"That's true, I have no clothes," Galina replied with an embarrassed giggle.

But Tamara did not agree. "I'm a child, Mama," she said earnestly. "Galina's a lady. You can't take us both shopping at the same time!"

"Oh yes, I can!" Natalia countered, and then she shivered, for her own voice had rung clear and forceful in the small room, surprising everyone by its intensity. She rose and took her daughter's hand, and stood uncertainly by the sofa. "Come, Pierre," she said gently. "We have to unpack, and Galina needs to regain her bearings in this strange household."

Chapter 26

ierre reveled in this new decade, the 1920s. He had felt uncomfortable in St. Petersburg, where Diaghilev's intimates had tended to be highborn and admitted to court, thereby revealing to him his own lack of sophistication. He had been very young, with raw talent and tongue-tied emotionalism. Now, in his late thirties, he had acquired a certain polish—not of the perfect gentleman, or of Boris Kussov's eclectic Renaissance prince, but rather a stylistic conscience that expressed itself primarily in his work but also in his dealings with other people. He had gained in stature. He felt totally at ease within his medium, knew where he was going and how far he could tempt fate into accepting new forms. Neither a Dadaist nor a cubist, he was able to maintain his own perspective, his own style, at all times and in each endeavor. Diaghilev had helped give him confidence. But now, at thirty-eight, Pierre had achieved self-integration such that he no longer needed the Ballets Russes to bolster his reputation. In the Europe of the twenties the works of Riazhin were as appreciated as those of Derain, Picasso, Utrillo, Modigliani. His contributions to the Ballets Russes were therefore less frequent, and his relationship with Diaghilev had reached that level of near-equality that characterized Serge Pavlovitch's dealings with Larionov, Bakst, and Benois—when they were not on the outs with the impresario.

Above all, he loved Parisian life. More and more, while Natalia worked in London on the new version of *The Sleeping*

Beauty, renamed *The Sleeping Princess*, to be shown to the British that coming winter of 1921–22, Pierre took small trips to Paris to see his daughter and immerse himself in the artistic atmosphere there. His lack of formal education, which Natalia had obtained through the Imperial School of Ballet, no longer bothered him. Boris had given him a large enough base from which to build his own aesthetic. In fact, Pierre had said to Galina: "The problem with Boris was that he was too knowledgeable. There was no area of intellectual life with which he was not totally familiar. At his fingertips lay the wealth of the ages. How, then, could such a man ever hope to create, to form his own way through this morass of superlatives? I'm luckier—I know' less and therefore can make up my own mind. There's less clutter, and I feel less dwarfed by comparison with centuries of worthier artists." Instead of the past, which Boris had revered, Pierre felt that today was what mattered—the changing world, the changing art, the changing morality.

He had become accustomed to Galina's presence in the house on the Avenue Bugeaud and had come to regard her as a part of the family. Or almost. There was still a strange aura that surrounded her for him, and which created a distance between them, unbridged by words. When he came to Paris, he would burst into the house, a whirlwind of gay energy, and sweep into Tamara's room, uttering Georgian words of endearment that delighted the little girl. Often Galina would be there, quietly playing a game with the child. Pierre would become conscious of her presence, unobtrusive but not quite retiring, and he would feel before he saw those great eyes on him. Her habit of looking at him, frankly appraising him in her serious manner, disturbed him, although deep down he felt a flicker of pleasure. He was not certain why she regarded him this way, but after an initial resentment and defensiveness he had begun to feel flattered by the attention.

When she looked at him from the corner of Tamara's room, he would put the child down with self-consciousness, a red flush rising to his cheeks. "Ah, our little princess," he would say in a bantering voice intended to dispel his own uneasiness, quick defiance kindling in his black eyes. Instead, what he wanted to say was: What's there to stare at? He did not seem able to forget the fact that she belonged to one of the oldest aristocratic families of Russia; in her presence he could not help feeling plebeian, as though her being there cast the shadow of his humbler roots on his present standing. When he was prey to these emotions, he actually found himself disliking Galina. But he could not blame the girl for a problem that was not her fault—and something about her touched him, so that he expressed his insecurities only through veiled teasing. "We have a real princess living with us now, you understand," he had murmured in jest to the painter Derain. "So I must watch my table manners." Both Galina and Natalia found these jokes embarrassing, for different reasons.

Natalia knew that when Pierre behaved like this around Galina, he was taking revenge on her uncle, Boris. She was ashamed for his sake. He was demeaning himself in everyone's eyes by speaking this way. But to Galina, these references to her birth were a source of pain. Her family had died, horribly murdered, and the Stassov and Kussov names were now ridiculous reminders of how little the past had to do with the present. Calling attention to her being a princess only underscored the fact that she was penniless and poorly educated, a relic of a lost civilization, the last living member of an obsolete, extinct species. She did not understand why Pierre resented her or her family. But she did feel his insecurity, and after the hurt had worn off the first few times, she felt pity for him, and even wonder. Why wasn't he completely at ease? After all, he was one of the foremost painters of the day, a great man—and, she was convinced, a true genius.

Pierre spent only enough time with Galina to acquire an impression of her. When he was in Paris with Natalia, the young girl spent her time with his wife. Endless hours, he sometimes thought, with bewilderment and irritation. Natalia's relationship with her niece had sprung up so suddenly that it had taken him aback. His wife had never had close female friends. Katya had been simpleminded, more of a burden than a confidante; and Lydia Brailovskaya had been a model, whose wry wit and worldliness Natalia had looked up to. Nina Stassova had been dear to her because of Boris, and because of her essential kindness—no one could have disliked Nina, not even Pierre himself when he most bitterly resented the Kussovs. But Galina had come into Natalia's life and taken root there, like an edelweiss on a barren mountain slope.

For Natalia, Galina had calmly opened the door and entered the room of her heart: a familiar and loved person from the beginning. The girl had come to them at fifteen. Quiet, steadfast, she nevertheless had impressed Natalia with her wisdom, the sort that can only come from life itself, from adaptation and resolution. The older woman was reminded of herself at that age—the age when she had first danced the Sugar Plum Fairy at the Mariinsky. Galina's experiences in the Caucasus village, then with the *tziganes* in Tbilis and later in Constantinople, had matured her early, marking her with indelible scars. There had been no one to help her, no person on whom to rely. Natalia essentially understood what Galina must be feeling: She had felt the same way herself.

Yet there was another side to Galina, equally important but totally contrasting. She had been born an aristocrat, with centuries of breeding flowing through her veins. For the first eleven years of her life, years that Natalia had spent growing up like a weed on the Crimean farm, Galina had lived like a fairy-tale princess, reared by a German governess and surrounded by works of art, priceless and unique. She had seen the Ballet and spoke the flawless French and German of the Russian nobility. She could play the piano, not elaborately but the proper way, her knowledge of the instrument built on a sound foundation. All of Galina Stassova had been built on a sound base: a base of good taste, quality, and refinement. Life had come later, superimposing its harshness over this base, but never destroying it. More of Boris was in his niece than what had so obviously been stenciled on her oval face.

Natalia did not feel disloyal when the thought came to her that, truly, Galina represented a perfect merging of herself and Boris. Had Arkady lived, he would have been like Galina: fine, intelligent, discriminating, with an awareness of life's ironies and the ability to cope with them. Tamara, on the other hand, was a spoiled little plebeian. Natalia could not help noticing the difference, but it enabled her to love her more by understanding her better. Galina had come to them a lady born and bred, but without the advantages that Tamara took for granted. But Tamara would never be a lady. And neither shall I, her mother thought wryly.

Pierre had discerned Galina's innate breeding, and after his initial resentment he had come to be fascinated by it. The girl was so unassuming! She fit into the house like a bright, beautiful object, shy but observant, her mind always working. The few times he had truly engaged her in conversation beyond a humorous query here and there, he had found her intelligent, with a mind of her own, clear and curious. Once in a while she made a remark that startled him: an ironic comment that came unexpectedly into the conversation, a reflection on life that seemed too hard, too precise, for someone so young and so gentle. Galina usually reminded Pierre of Nina, her mother. But when the rare dry comments fell, he could not help but think of Boris.

Pierre had begun to feel vaguely jealous of Galina. Natalia spent so much time with this girl, who, after all, was no direct relation. There was such an easy communication between them, whereas between him and Natalia there had always been an undercurrent of strife, even at the beginning. Galina was a little sister to Natalia, an older sister to Tamara. Natalia had hired a tutor to fill the gap in Galina's education, which had come to such an abrupt halt in her eleventh year. A music master also came, and Natalia herself had begun to coach Galina in dance. In a sense, she was repaying a debt to Boris through the girl.

And yet sometimes Pierre caught a flicker of amusement in Galina's serious eyes. All at once he thought he understood her better than his wife did, and he was brought up short, and at the same time excited. Galina was indulging Natalia out of affection, but she was already beyond this, beyond adolescence. She was a woman who had lived through an inferno of her own, and who did not care whether it was Aristotle or Aristophanes who had written a play called *The Frogs*. He looked at her and smiled. She did not know why, but it seemed to her then that a sympathy had sprung up between them, that they had found a piece of common ground.

It had been so easy for Natalia, Tamara, and the servants.

Galina's role in their lives had defined itself. But between her and Pierre there was an unspoken barrier of the uncomfortable unknown. At thirty-one, Natalia could hardly have been Galina's mother. But at thirty-eight, Pierre could definitely have been her father. She did not know how to treat him and did not feel at ease in this roleless position. Everyone else "belonged," played a part. Yet in his own house he was an outsider—once again. He could not help feeling a surge of antipathy toward both Galina and Natalia: They were locking him out, not defining his place in their relationship. And yet he liked Galina, in a strange way. He might have resented some aspects of her presence, but not her presence itself.

In August of 1921, just before Galina turned sixteen, Pierre felt that he could no longer bear the oppressive heat of London, where he had been working with Léon Bakst on *The Sleeping Princess*. Bakst, it seemed to him, had never recovered from the bitter aftermath of his quarrel with Diaghilev over the scenery for *La Boutique Fantasque*. He had become more sensitive, more irritable. Since Pierre had eventually taken over the commission for the *Boutique* decors, Bakst had been on edge with him, too. But Pierre was also annoyed because there was never any time to be alone with Natalia: Whenever they drove into the countryside, they would return to find Diaghilev in front of their suite at the Claridge, distraught over some problem or other. It had not seemed worth Pierre's time to stay in the heat, caught between differing sets of ill humor. A short trip home was in order, a change of atmosphere.

He never discussed these brief stays with Natalia. She knew that when he could no longer remain in one place, he replenished himself by going to Paris. In a sense this relieved her of a nagging guilt toward Tamara. Pierre would see their daughter, bridge the gap. But Natalia was also annoyed. He was a child, really, allowing petty problems to irritate him. The free spaces of his Caucasian childhood, then the confinement of his years in Germany during the war, explained this claustrophobia without justifying it. She was left behind, expected to continue, to take care of things.

So, once again, Pierre had come home to the house on Avenue Bugeaud. When Chaillou opened the door to him, it was early evening and Tamara was having her bath. Pierre bounded into the large tiled bathroom, and the little girl, covered with suds, stood up in her pink nakedness and stretched out her plump arms to him in ecstasy. "Papa's home!" she cried.

Mademoiselle Pichenet regarded him with ill-concealed disapproval. "Isn't she too old to be seen in the tub?" she demanded.

Pierre burst into loud laughter. "Really, Mademoiselle! She's my baby girl, aren't you, lovey?" He scooped her in his arms, allowing her soapy wetness to stain the entire front of his suit and tie. She wriggled merrily, a sensuous child.

"Hello, Pierre Grigorievitch," Galina said in her calm, low voice. He had not noticed her before, for she had entered after him, carrying fresh towels, and was now standing beside him.

"Why, hello, *Principessa.*" All at once it seemed foolish to be holding the wet child, and he handed Tamara back to her governess.

"Chaillou's put out some tea," she said. "Will you come?"

He smiled at her. "Only if you join me. It's been so long since anyone's talked to me—really spoken with me. You can't imagine! Natalia's choreographing, you know, and Bakst—well, we will skip Bakst, won't we?"

They were walking into the parlor, and she sat down first in front of the fine Meissen teapot. Her long fingers, tapered like her uncle's, moved deftly, yet with a tiny hesitation. "Not like our samovars, I'm afraid, or our Russian glasses," he commented gently.

She looked up, startled. "Yes, I've often thought so." She fell silent, abrupt, embarrassed. She poured his tea into a cup, adding the two cubes of sugar on the saucer. He was impressed: She always remembered everyone's preference.

"You were speaking of Bakst," she said suddenly. "I am very interested in what you are doing, Pierre Grigorievitch. Yet you so rarely discuss it with me."

"I had no idea you really knew what it is I do," he replied, amused.

"But I'm not a child. Of course, I know. I know what set designs are. In fact"—she grew shy all at once, averting her clear blue gaze from him—"I have been trying to paint in my spare time. Oh, I'm hardly talented—but I've been thinking about what you do, and that sort of work appeals to me."

He arose with one bold gesture and pulled her up with him. "Then you must show me!" he exclaimed. "Really, Galinotchka—Natalia never said one word to me about this!"

But she drew away frantically, her golden hair falling into her face. "Oh, no, Pierre Grigorievitch! Natalia doesn't know, and I don't want you to see it! Not yet," she added more quietly.

He shrugged lightly, releasing her hands. "Very well, I don't want to force you. But don't you think it's time you stopped calling me Pierre Grigorievitch and began callimg me simply Pierre? You make me feel old, and on the outside."

She laughed breathlessly, still overcome by her sudden terror. "I thought you rather liked it that way," she said.

He could not help blinking. Actually, he had found it quaint, charming, and oddly ironical. A princess whom he called by her first name, or by a familiar diminutive, who persisted in this courtly formality. Once Boris had said nearly the same words to him about using the patronym toward him. Galina was a strange girl: astute and naïve, very young or quite old, a lady by birth or a woman of the streets. In some ways Natalia had become a woman of similar contradictions, after her years with Boris Kussov. But this girl was not in the least like Natalia.

"Tell me about *The Sleeping Princess*," she was saying. "Is it strict Petipa classicism or a Bakst fantasy?"

"What can I say? You will have to see for yourself. In fact, we must arrange for you to do so, if you are truly interested. The decor is romantic. The Forest of the Lilacs is green and mauve, which hints at wistfulness. The stairway is classical, with a romantic glimpse of the white castle walls. But there are purple trees and a blue foreground and those are modern touches."

"Impressionistic," she interjected. Her oval face was very grave and attentive, like that of an earnest student.

He laughed. "You make me feel like the master lecturing a disciple," he remarked. "But the costumes are airy and colorful, an overstatement of the characters of the ballet. Aurora's is wispy, classical, ending at midcalf. Aurora should be danced by you, really, Galina: She's so engaging, so young and lovely and innocent in the beginning. But then you're not those things anymore, are you, my dear?"

"I don't know. Am I?"

"You are still a mystery. I'm hardly a subtle man, Galina. It isn't in me to read character. The Queen has a red train—highly dramatic. But what does that really say about this woman? Red is the color of lust, and of anger, and of tragedy."

"It's also a beautiful color in and of itself. Would you like more tea . . . Pierre?"

He sighed, shook his head, rose and stretched. "No, *mon enfant*. I'm off—to the Jockey Club, I think. To hear some jazz. It soothes one's nerves after so much Tchaikovsky."

"Have a pleasant evening," she said, remaining seated. He inclined his head briskly and left the room. Sometimes he likes me, other times he doesn't at all, she thought with wonder. Yet it was the first real conversation they had ever had, and she relived it in her mind, somewhat bemused. He was a puzzling individual, with a sea of hostilities brewing under the surface. Some of the hostilities were in some way connected with her, but she did not understand why.

When Pierre returned from his evening's outing, the house stood in total darkness but for a tall lamp in the entrance gallery, at the foot of the stairs near the bronze statue and the potted plants. He took his moccasins off, removed his wraps, and went to the sideboard in the large living room. From a decanter of Armagnac he poured himself a thimbleful and took it to the window overlooking the neat garden. It was comforting to gaze out to green bushes, to trim but joyfully arranged flower beds. French gardens all possessed the feeling of not having been formally cultivated, of having sprouted up naturally—and yet he knew how carefully they were tended, this one above all. He had loved this house since the beginning, since that summer of '06 with Boris. He realized now that Boris had bought it with him in mind, as a gesture of wooing. Yes, Boris had known how to love him totally—more than Natalia could ever learn to love him, in all the years of her life.

Suddenly he was weary, demoralized. Why couldn't life develop normally, like a French garden? Why did the sexual tension never abate, pulling apart and then throwing together? He sat down and pressed his fingers to his temples. He had never felt so alone in his life.

A series of piercing shrieks wrenched him from his reflections, sending adrenaline through him like mercury, and beads of sweat broke out over his chest, around his neck, and under his arms. Tamara! With a leap he rushed from the salon and up the stairs, his heart pounding. The door to the child's room stood ajar, and he pushed it open and turned on a light. In the second bed the governess had risen to her elbow, covering herself demurely. "Oh, it isn't the babe, it's the princess," she told Pierre hastily. "Don't worry so, monsieur. The princess has these bad dreams now and then. We're all used to it."

Horror-stricken, Pierre studied the woman's face and blinked. "The Princess Stassova? Nightmares? Why weren't we told? Shouldn't a doctor—?"

"Oh, doctors wouldn't help. She hoped you wouldn't find out. Tamara sleeps through the screams now. But the poor little princess. It's that dreadful time she had, when her mother died."

Pierre turned away, shutting off the light. In the hallway he hesitated. Then, resolutely, he walked to Galina's door and knocked once, softly. "Who is it?" she asked, her voice trembling.

"Me, Pierre. May I come in?"

"Please, it's all right," she said miserably, her tone pleading. But he had already turned the knob and stood on the threshold, looking into the small bedroom.

The lamp had been switched on by the large canopied bed, with its rose silk hangings. Sitting on it was Galina, in her frail cotton nightgown, shivering. Tears were drying on her cheeks, which were totally devoid of color. Pierre came to her, but she refused to look at him. "I had to check," he said lamely. "To make sure you were all right. Mademoiselle told me . . ."

"I'm sorry. Did I waken you?"

"Of course not. I hadn't even gone to bed, I'd just come in. What frightened you, Galina?"

"It was nothing," she stammered.

Pierre bent down on one knee, and gazed at her squarely.

"It's all right," he said softly. He tucked his fingers under her chin, and raised it to his eye level. "Don't be afraid," he said. "We're all here. I'm here."

Then she burst into tears, like a small child, and threw her arms around his neck, sobbing onto the side of his shoulder. "I saw Mama dying," she cried, "and the officer who'd lost his mind, crawling on all fours, drooling like an animal. And then there was a fire, and Papa was caught in it, struggling, screaming—and I was outside and couldn't reach him! I couldn't get to him, I was helpless, I was letting him die!" She lifted her tear-stained face to his, terror in her eyes. "Don't you see? I let my own mother die in that awful village, with no care, no medicines. I thought only of myself. I should have walked to the nearest town, found help—"

"Stop it!" Pierre pushed her from him and took her by the shoulders. "No wonder you have nightmares. Such foolishness! Your mother was a big girl, she went to the Caucasus of her own free will. It's terrible that she was struck with the cholera. But it wasn't your fault! Listen to me, Galinotchka—there's nothing you could have done for her that you didn't do. Not one damn thing! You were there when she died. She didn't have to die alone. Think about that!"

She nodded. "Not like Uncle Boris," she added in a hushed voice.

"That's right."

They remained silent, their eyes on each other, intent and sober, drained of their emotions. He drew back the sheet and patted the mattress, and she lay down, and he covered her lightly, for it was hot and humid. "Go to sleep now," he said. "I'll stay right here. Nothing bad will happen, Galina. You're with us now, you're safe."

But her eyelids had already closed. He touched the velvet coverlet, and noticed with surprise that his hand was trembling. He could picture Boris receiving his own dry, cold letter about Arkady's death, and all at once shame flared up inside him. To die alone . . . He glanced at the sleeping girl and sighed, a sigh that was like a wrenching sob. Yet he did not know for whom that sigh was intended.

The Sleeping Princess didn't feel right to Natalia. She had many conflicting thoughts about this production, her first effort as a choreographer. Through these many months of life in Great Britain after the war, she had come to understand the cultural climate of its inhabitants. Reserved in their emotions but open-minded in their acceptance of new art forms, they had responded with discreet enthusiasm to Diaghilev's aesthetic. Fokine's graceful ventures into lyricism, into exoticism, had charmed them; the traditional romanticism of *Giselle* had left them cold. The British defied one's preconceptions: They tolerated novelty when it was couched in good taste but did not always respond to tried and true staples. How, then, would they react to a revival of a Petipa classic?

The old masters of the Ballet Russes were showing a middle-aged lack of vision, she thought to herself. Bakst was ill, she could see it. There had been quarrels with Diaghilev, strained moments with his former disciple, Pierre. She had watched with discomfort and sadness. Serge Pavlovitch presented a different problem. Too much time in England, sandwiched between vaudeville acts, which he found degrading to the Ballet, had dimmed some of his acute perceptivity. Turning back the clock to the Mariinsky—to *The Sleeping Princess*—had not been an altogether good idea. Perhaps, she surmised, he had wanted to make a statement: that Russia, imperial Russia, was not dead after all.

But it was dead, Natalia thought stubbornly, with a kind of desperation. The Russia of Nicholas and Alexandra, and even of Boris Kussov, had died a bloody death in November of '17, exactly four years before. To attempt to resurrect it for the intellectual, skeptical British, made pragmatic by four years of war and by King George, was an error in judgment. Bakst and Pierre had created beautiful decors, splendid costumes of airy gauze suggestive of fairyland. Two older *grandes dames* of the Imperial Ballet, Svetlov's wife, Vera Trefilova, and Lubov Egorova, would take turns with Natalia herself in dancing Princess Aurora. Lydia Lopokhova would be the Lilac Fairy, and Prince Florimund, a role of the traditional male supporter, was to be portrayed by another Mariinsky *danseur*, Vladimiroff. All of these dancers had been formed by the Imperial School, all possessed a solid base in classicism. Stravinsky was orchestrating the Tchaikovsky scores, interspersed with music from another classic, *The Nutcracker*. The ballet would be a mixture of the tried and true that was supposed to result in an innovative whole flavored with old favorites.

It has been so long since the Diaghilev dancers had put on a classical show! How ironic, really! Their master had initially rebelled against what he had considered stale: the formality of Petipa's choreography. Now he was honoring his nemesis, in time for Petipa's commemorative hundredth birthday in '22. There were other ironies as well: Natalia had been born the same year as the original production of *The Sleeping Beauty* at the Mariinsky, and although she had never danced Aurora, she had appeared in the role of the Lilac Fairy before. The introduction of the *Nutcracker* music, of course, brought to mind her first real success as a soloist. In a sense, then, it was appropriate, after all, for her to have been chosen to choreograph this ballet.

She was exhausted. The summer had dragged on, with Diaghilev spending more and more money on loan from the impresario Sir Oswald Stoll. She had said to Diaghilev, with irritation: "Isn't it enough that neither Pierre nor I is being paid a full salary? I have a growing niece to educate, as well as my daughter! Surely you can learn to curb your spending!" It was good that he had no inkling of her previous transaction with Stoll.

Why wasn't Pierre worrying about this financial question? Natalia sat in the sitting room of her suite at the Claridge, perspiration seeping through her bangs, her fingers trembling as they twirled through her hair. It was always like this—always! Pierre concerned himself with materials, with cardboard props, with color schemes, and could stay up for nights in a row, infused with the creative urge, which animated him as nothing else did. Then, when he grew impatient, he would take the ferry across the Channel to spend a few days in Paris, vacationing. He would blithely take his four-year-old daughter to the Tour d'Argent for luncheon, tipping the waiters lavishly. There was always a matinée at the Comédie Française, and lately he had begun taking Galina to some of the places where he spent his evenings: cafés in Montparnasse or the Île-St.-Louis, clubs in Pigalle, outdoor restaurants in the Place du Tertre near the Sâcré-Coeur in Montmartre. He seemed to share Diaghilev's illusion that her funds were limitless.

Summer evolved into fall, and it was now November. On the night of the première Natalia herself was to dance Aurora. Yet she felt heavy with depression, with unfair responsibilities and strange misgivings. Galina had come for the occasion, and Natalia wished for the girl's sake that she could feel more festive and less out of sorts. They took a short drive to Ashley on the weekend, just the two of them, without Pierre. "Now you're really my sister," Galina murmured with her odd maturity. "But when I was a child here, you were like my mother, the mother one dreams of having: talented, independent. You led such a romantic life then, didn't you, Natalia?" She had not called her "Aunt" since she had arrived from Turkey; they had never spoken of it, yet the term of deference had been dropped in favor of the more equal, less formal given name.

"Yes," she answered, her eyes misting over suddenly. "Those were good times."

For a minute Galina was silent. Then she said: "Pierre does not like England."

"Oh, I don't know if that's it, or if he just misses Paris. He's not at home in this logical, intellectual country. Paris suits him now—with the American expatriates, who demand nothing more than a rollicking good time, and all the exiled Russian noblemen in quest of the past. He's a child too: His eyes are still full of the wonder of bright, new things." She said this with some asperity.

"But that's what makes him different," Galina countered gently. "Yes, he is a child. I've seen that side of him, too. But in this world different people are born to play different roles. There are those who toil endlessly to keep civilization alive and working. And then there are others—the da Vincis, the Van Goghs—and even the Riazhins. The price we pay to keep them happy is reimbursed to the entire world, when they produce their miracles!"

Natalia stared at her then, a hard, flat stare, and shrugged her delicate shoulders. Unkindly she remarked: "You're a child, too, if you think that way, Galina. But then what else could I have expected of you? One forgets that you're just sixteen."

Galina's posture straightened, her eyes darkened, and her regal young face set. That's it, I've hurt her, Natalia thought with exasperation. But that absurd defense of Pierre, of his lack of responsibility . . .

At the dress rehearsal everything failed that could fail. The work crew was having problems setting up the stage. Props were not standing up. Just when Natalia was ready to scream, her tutu caught on a nail. Pierre came running, his long strides dwarfing the romantic designs, and forcibly yanked her up from the floorboards like a recalcitrant flower. When he set her down abruptly, she saw how red his eyes were. There was an unhealthy flush in his cheeks. "Goddamn it!" he shouted, not so much at her as at the entire Ballet.

"Don't forget that this is my first production," she whispered to him ferociously, her brown eyes gleaming. "You've had many ventures, but this one is mine—especially mine! Don't steal it from me!"

A group of dancers, lighting men, and prop men were staring at them, their breaths held. Any excuse was good enough for gossip, especially if a married couple were involved. Pierre glared at Natalia and moved away without answering.

After the rehearsal everyone came to her dressing room: Diaghilev, Pierre, and Galina in a blue wool tailored dress that matched her eyes. "A disaster, a bloody disaster!" the impresario was saying, waving his monocle.

"We did the best we could," Pierre countered angrily.

"The best you could? Because of you and Bakst I've overextended myself again! Stoll will confiscate the costumes—"

"—which were poorly made to begin with," Pierre interrupted. "Don't blame us, Serge Pavlovitch. We ordered all our materials through you!"

Natalia walked up to her husband and squeezed between him and Diaghilev. Both men were tall, massive, furious, and flushed. She wondered whether Pierre had been drinking. In a low, trembling voice, she said: "Stop it! The last thing we need now is a volley of accusations. We're all in this together. Let's pick up the pieces and go home. There is still tomorrow to get through."

Every muscle taut with unexpressed tension, she silently changed, folding her costume carefully. Galina had come to help her. They had not spoken much since Ashley. Natalia could feel the girl withdrawing, as if she were physically moving away. We all must grow up sometime, Natalia thought with irritation. I can't continue to wet-nurse her forever—the way I do Pierre. He's another sensitive one—sensitive to himself, primarily. He had disappeared after the argument—she vaguely wondered where or with whom.

Later, as she undressed in the hotel suite, she had to sit down, because her head was swirling with anxieties, fears, and loneliness. The door that connected to the bathroom, which they shared with Galina, swung silently open, and she saw the girl, her blond hair falling in thick waves over her shoulders and breasts. Something inside her unknotted and relaxed. She looked up and Galina looked back, her face grave, unsmiling. "You're right," she said to Natalia. "He is a child. You know him better than I do. I'm sorry." She sat down beside Natalia and took her hand.

They sat this way for a while, their fingers entwined, and Galina leaned her head on Natalia's shoulder, her hair caressing Natalia's neck, warming it. Then Galina spoke again. "But you *must* love him. He needs you so much!"

Natalia could not reply and simply raised her hands helplessly, shaking her head. "I love you, Natalia," Galina said. "Don't be unhappy."

Natalia's throat tightened, and warm salt tears filled her eyes. Galina's hold around her waist grew stronger. She could feel the young girl's own tears on her shoulder, seeping through her chemise. She put an arm around her, stroked the blond hair. "I'm glad you're here," she whispered. "Truly glad, inside."

"Me, too. You're my family. You, and Tamarotchka—and Pierre." She said this with some hesitation, then added more confidently: "The three of you belong to me now."

Natalia sighed and looked away: "Sometimes I think you're my only family," she murmured. "So many mistakes, so many false impulses . . . I gave up my real family when I was ten and never wanted another one. Then, of course, it came anyway: Boris, Arkady." She shut her eyes on the sweetness of pure pain. "But there, too, it was wrong. We poisoned each other."

"What do you mean?" Galina asked.

"Nothing you could possibly understand. Boris wanted to love me, wanted our child—but I don't think I made him happy. Something was missing that I couldn't provide. He was always going from one experience to another, seeking some kind of validation—the Ballet, me, Arkady, the Division Sauvage. I failed him, or he wouldn't have gone into the war." Her voice caught. "But I can't keep blaming myself! I did the best I could! For years, I preserved his feelings, I cared for his needs—I was there for him, always! I couldn't be all that he wanted because he wanted too damned much! I was only one woman, one human being."

"And was Pierre simply a substitute?" Galina asked, her clear tone carrying a certain sharpness.

"Pierre? Of course not. Pierre was my first love. Every young girl should fall in love with a Pierre Riazhin: wonderful, impossible Pierre, who lives in a different world from mine, and who probably has his share of regrets, too. Don't listen to me, Galina, I shouldn't be speaking this way to you, I know I shouldn't—but you're a little bit me, aren't you? More than Tamara will ever be, I'm sure of it. There's no one to talk to, ever!" she added bitterly.

"We can talk to each other," Galina replied. "Between us we've lost everyone there is to lose. You've lost a husband and child; I've lost my parents and my grandparents and my aunts and uncles and cousins. But Natalia, we both have Pierre. Don't discount him!"

Natalia turned to look at Galina and was struck by the intensity of expression in the large blue eyes. She said nothing, but her lips parted. She closed them, freed herself from Galina's embrace, and placed her hands on the girl's shoulders. She scrutinized the young face and then sighed, shaking her head. "Don't count too much on him, lovey," she said with muted harshness. "He can be very thoughtless. And he's impatient:

When he breaks something, he doesn't always bother to pick up the pieces. But still, he's a remarkable man."

She pressed her lips together, and her eyes grew cloudy.

Galina watched from the stall, her long hands folded neatly on her lap, a line of apprehension on her high forehead. Being here felt so unreal to her, so artificial. She was wearing a simple ivory-colored gown, with a neckline that revealed the graceful line of her throat, where a single strand of pearls was the sole decoration. Her skin glowed pink and slightly moist. The pearls had been Natalia's gift to her for her sixteenth birthday, and Galina knew that Boris had made a present of them to his wife many years before. This made the girl vaguely ill at ease. It was as though Natalia sought to make her a Kussov in spite of herself—whereas, in actual fact, the real Kussov was Natalia.

Galina's mother, Nina Vassilievna, had been quiet, composed, and gentle, a retiring but charming lady. Did I ever really know her? Galina asked herself, touching the pearls. She remembered best those moments of physical closeness, moments she knew Tamara, for one, rarely shared with Natalia. Galina had often settled snugly in the crook of her mother's arm and listened to her speak to a guest, or to her father. What had the words been? She couldn't recall, and it didn't matter. Nina's scent had mattered: jonquils and lilacs and apricots. Later there had been the war and the death of Uncle Boris. Nina had been nervous, inconsolable—but still the same pervasive mother, with time for a touch, with a backward look that signified: "Coming?" They had truly never been apart.

But had her mother been "a Kussov"? Galina doubted it. Nina had blended so well into her husband's family, the Stassovs. Galina had known that her mother belonged to a great family, refined, cultured, and influential. But these words had meant nothing special to her. Everyone among their set had borne those qualities. Her grandfather, Vassily Arkadievitch Kussov, had been gruff and elderly, a *bon vivant* who had reveled in good food and an occasional hunting expedition: a kind man, but not one who stood out from the grandfathers of other girls; apart from a perfunctory question or two about her doings, he had generally not paid her much attention. He had been a man's man, with little time for the frailties of women and small girls. He had seemed very different from her mother, and therefore it had been all the more difficult for Galina to conceive of that elusive quality that might have distinguished Nina and made her first and foremost a Kussov.

There had been Boris, golden, elegant, an arbiter of taste. But he had been the only real Kussov! Whatever the Kussov mystique had been, he alone had created it—and perhaps his own mother, whom Galina had never known, and his grandfather Arkady, dead long before her own birth. Boris had been a dream and had created himself. He had chosen a bride who had been plucked from the very earth, a girl without antecedents but who had been extraordinary in her talent, in her unique grace and ambition. He had created her, but her own inborn gift had helped to make him complete. They had been the Kussovs: Boris and Natalia, above society, above culture, above mere talent. They had been the Kussov mystique—not she, Galina Stassova, who was neither particularly brilliant nor particularly distinctive. Natalia had not owed her a thing!

And how had Pierre fit into this scheme of things? Why did both Pierre and Natalia cling to this absurd fantasy of her being the true heir of Boris Kussov? She was only herself, and it would have been better simply to forget her useless relatives, who hung as an albatross around her neck. She wished she could push this dubious inheritance all away.

She looked around her cautiously. They had surrounded her with illustrious people, wanting to make the evening perfect for her. Just as they'd like to be able to erase my past and mold my future to a beam of perfect light, she thought with amusement. She sighed. Sometimes their dreams were a burden to her. She was so ordinary—couldn't they see it, and leave her to develop as she wished? She wanted only to learn how to draw better so that some day she might be able to assist in the building of theatre sets and costumes. She enjoyed bringing imaginary worlds to life—but she had no special ambitions to become the next Léon Bakst! Galina chewed on her lower lip. At least Natalia is sensible, she thought. She'd like to make my life perfect, but she also knows that it's *my* life, and that there's very little she can do for me. But Pierre . . . he thinks that by showing me Paris by night, he will prevent my nightmares from recurring. How can I make him understand that I simply enjoy being with him, learning from him, but that what I saw really happened, and that no paint can cover the dark areas of experience? I can't ever tell him! Unlike Natalia, he believes in magic, in his own magic.

They had placed her there in the most elegant stall with Tamara Karsavina and her husband, Henry Bruce, here for a brief vacation from his diplomatic post in Bulgaria, and with the economist Maynard Keynes, who was in love with Lydia Lopokhova. Those strange Sitwells were there too: Dame Edith, and her brothers, Sir Osbert and Sacheverell. They were all poets, all highly intellectual and erudite; Edith was also a critic, Osbert an essayist, and Sacheverell (Galina could never remember his name) an art critic. Karsavina was Tamara's godmother, Galina knew—and of all these people, she spoke most easily with Galina, and not as though she were a hundred years old. "I remember when your aunt was sixteen," she said to her. "She appeared in the school production of *The Daughter of Pharaoh* and made such an impression that the Tzarina came to see her, and your uncle, too. That was how they met."

Galina smiled. "That's like a fairy story," she commented.

"Perhaps. The Tzarina brought her an enamel portrait of herself—and do you know what Boris Vassilievitch gave her? A necklace of pearls, with a ruby clasp! She was so overcome that she burst into tears."

Galina's eyebrows rose, and her mouth widened with amazement. She touched the jewels around her neck shyly. "You mean—these?" she asked.

Karsavina was amused. "Ah, she gave them to *you!* Well, now you know their origin."

"But Tamara should have them, not I," Galina protested.

Karsavina shook her head. "Tamara was not Boris's niece," she replied. Again the Kussov obsession, that immaterial, essential aura that had been placed around her. Galina looked at Keynes and at Dame Edith: Then they, too, saw her only as the niece of that illustrious balletomane Boris Kussov. As if reading her thoughts, Karsavina said: "Boris Vassilievitch did much for the Ballets Russes. We all thought highly of him. He was a friend to most of us. He understood artists, and he loved them. It's a shame you didn't know him well."

Galina wet her lips. "Perhaps I didn't, but I don't think I'll ever be able to escape him."

Then the curtain rose, and wonder replaced the vague self-consciousness that she had been feeling. Pierre's curtain . . . She really knew so little about the ballet, its history, its trends and countertrends. Unlike the people in the stall with her, she was ignorant, alone with her own opinions, rough-hewn and untested. But Pierre had told her that sometimes that was a good thing, not to know too much. Then one's creative ideas could rise up fresh and personal, not borrowed or planned. She sat back, folding her legs carefully so that they would not catch on the hem of her skirt. She watched the stage, wide-eyed.

The music was lovely—an enchantment really. She had heard it before, in her parents' house, bits of it on the piano, and at the Saturday matinées at the Petersburg symphony. But the costumes were wonderful, all ribbons and flounces. And Natalia moved so exquisitely, so small and dainty and flowing, capturing youth and hope. Galina felt a momentary flush of pain. Innocence! That was what Natalia was embodying: innocence, a floating quality that no longer existed on this earth. Natalia had never been innocent—and she herself had lost her innocence long ago. But there were still some innocents: Pierre was one, incontestably. Dear Pierre, the dreamer, forever angry because life did not meet his exalted expectations!

Oh, God, she thought fervently, wincing slightly, let them stop! Let this tension break between them, let them not fight, let there be peace this one time. She closed her eyes to the beauty onstage, reliving the ugliness of reality. It pierced her own body when they argued, so bitterly, so cruelly—yet she could not assign blame to one or to the other. I wish I could escape it all, she thought and then bit her lip. Oh, no, I don't wish that! If I were not there, God only knows that they'd do to each other.

She remained immersed in her thoughts until Tamara Karsavina leaned over to point something out to her, and then she thought, ashamed: This is Natalia's clever arrangement; it is she who has created this Dance of the Three Ivans, accompanied by the coda to the *grand pas de deux*. And here I am, not looking. She raised her opera glasses to the stage, where three robust Russian *danseurs* were offering their energetic homage to Aurora and Florimund. Galina smiled: This, then, was Natalia's ovation to her husband. She had taken his essentially Russian force of life and transposed it into this virile dance at the end of a classically perfect, rather feminine ballet not of her own true making. She stood up, forgetting Maynard Keynes behind her, her young face flooded with light and hope.

Later Galina did not understand the atmosphere of tense despondency that seemed to permeate the members of the Ballets Russes. She had gone backstage at once and found everyone in an uproar. "A failure, a total failure!" Diaghilev was exclaiming, cursing in French and Russian. Natalia was sitting on a low stool, her face very pale, her eyes enormous. Pierre stood in a corner, his hands balled into fists.

"Well, there's nothing to be done about it now," Natalia said to Diaghilev. "We can only continue, for as long as they will let us. Classicism leaves them cold, Serge Pavlovitch. They want a short burst of exoticism, the sort of diet that Fokine fed them."

"A fine time to say that!" he retorted.

She stood up then, frail and delicate. "I said it before," she stated succinctly. "Don't you remember, Serge Pavlovitch?" Before he could answer, she left the area, her light footsteps carrying her like a billow of gauze away from his recriminations.

Galina did not know what to do. She felt out of place, unsure of what had happened to mar this perfect evening. No one was explaining anything to her; no one had even noticed her. Pierre and Natalia had probably completely forgotten her existence! She saw Pierre stride over to the backdrop of the Enchanted Forest and kick it savagely. She rushed up and laid a hand hesitantly on his arm, restraining him. For some reason no one but she had found his outburst extraordinary. "Please," she whispered urgently, "don't destroy your work! It was so beautiful—a real magic wood. What's wrong, Pierre?"

"The whole damned thing's wrong!" he cried. "Bloody trees wouldn't rise, nothing worked! Magic that didn't succeed. But what's to be expected? Nobody cared enough! Everybody was too busy blaming everybody else! Even Natalia had stopped caring!"

"No, she hadn't at all. I thought she was lovely. Didn't you?" she added with dismay.

He gave her a look of pure disgust. "Lovely. My wife hasn't been lovely in fifteen years. Don't talk to me of loveliness, Galina. Natalia is a workhorse, and a good, competent dancer. But she's dried up inside along the way, and it shows! She's simply not the same—in any way!"

Galina was profoundly shocked and swallowed her terror. She looked around her and saw that small groups had formed, and that, once again, no one was near them. "Look, Pierre," she murmured, "let's go for a walk, shall we? Please, you can't just stand here like this, all wound up, ready to kill someone."

He uttered a short laugh, like a gasp, and once more she was frightened. So much was compressed inside this man—so much that she did not understand! How could she help him? He had helped her, again and again. Embarrassed at his display of mounting hysteria, she took his arm and gently but surely propelled him outside, away from the noise and eyes of curious onlookers. He was all hers now, to somehow repair.

It was very cold outside, and she shivered in her gown. He walked at a fast pace, and although her legs were long for a girl's, she had difficulty keeping up with him. Finally he stopped in the amber light of a streetlamp. Leaning against its post, he regarded Galina as if noticing for the first time that she had come with him.

"Ah," he said, blinking in some bewilderment. "Galinotchka. Why did you follow me?"

"I didn't follow you. I had to lead you out before you destroyed the sets. Why was this such a failure, Pierre? I don't understand. I thought the production was marvelous."

"But you were never here for a real success! Then, my dear, you would have been struck by the amazing difference. Tonight's audience was bored and disappointed. Revamped Petipa isn't for Londoners. They liked Fokine too much. Even Massine."

Galina wrung her hands and looked away. "Poor Natalia," she said. "Her first choreography—"

"She'll do many more. No one is blaming her. Her dancing was perfect, the arrangements were good. It was my sets that didn't work! But she will not let me forget this. I ruined her first show. Mark my words, sweetheart, she will never allow me to live this one down."

"You're wrong!" Galina retorted angrily. "How can you speak of her this way? You act as though you hate her! Why, you're a selfish, cruel man, Pierre Riazhin! All these years she loved you, and took care of you, and paid your bills! And yet you accuse her of—of unmentionable insensitivities."

He started to laugh, and she stopped, overcome with anguish and horror. She stepped back and he bent over, clutching his stomach. "Ah, my pet, the bills, the bills!" he exclaimed between gusts of bitter merriment. "Have you known all along that she was 'keeping' me? She doesn't love me and never did. I serve a purpose, though God knows what it is at this point, because *I* don't!"

As he continued laughing, Galina began to cry. Tears streamed down her cheeks, and small sobs came to her lips. She brought her hands to her face, and held them there. "Come now, I can't be that evil," Pierre said, and he was not laughing any longer. His face was serious and drawn, the cheekbones well defined in the changing light.

"If my mother and father had lived," Galina whispered fiercely, "they would have known how to love each other. You and she—you are criminals! Yes, criminals—I'm not exaggerating. People who waste love, who distort it the way you do, both of you . . . Oh, Pierre, why do you do it? Is it really so hard to love someone, to cherish that person and treat her well, to fill one's home with harmony and joy, instead of this endless wounding? You are two emotional assassins. I don't know why I stay with you, I really don't!"

But he had seized her hands and was caressing them softly. "You stay because we need you," he replied quietly.

In February Natalia was visited in her suite at Claridge's by Serge Diaghilev, around whose eyes deep circles had been etched. He appeared old, and his massive bulk seemed proportionately shrunken. A hardness came into Natalia and, as she offered him tea and crumpets, she thought: He feels I have been forced on him, he's never liked me. And yet how hard I've tried for him—every time!

"Are we floundering badly?" she demanded, sitting across from him and cupping her chin in her hand.

"Box office receipts are disastrous. You know what's been happening, *ma chère*. *The Sleeping Princess* is simply not being accepted by the London public. Sir Oswald Stoll is threatening to seize everything because we have not recouped his advance."

More kindly she said: "You can't be right every time, Serge Pavlovitch. It's a lovely ballet—in spite of our calamity on opening night, when Pierre's Enchanted Forest creaked and groaned and didn't rise. Nobody could have helped that."

"But you were right. It was the wrong public for it, the wrong time." His eyes sought hers, and he smiled slightly. "We're going to have to close, Natalia. Just like that. There's no other option at this point. Do you see one?"

"Frankly, no. We are none of us Croesus, Serge Pavlovitch. The best I can do for you is one thousand pounds."

"Thank you, my dear. It will help. I shall repay you."

She shook her head, all at once angry. "No. Use it to quell some of the troubled waters around you. All the artists who haven't received any of their salaries. The Ballet is disbanding, Serge Pavlovitch, because you were too extravagant on the decor. Yet this is a ballet for dancers! If anything, Petipa's works should have proven that to you. Above all, *The Sleeping Princess*, like *The Sleeping Beauty*, on which it is based, displays the plastic arts first and foremost. But if you insist on paying more for an Enchanted Forest than for a Florimund—what can I say?"

Diaghilev's brow shot up quizzically, and he touched the white lock of hair mingling with the dark on his head. It was always carefully dyed and had earned him the nickname Chinchilla. "My dear Natalia," he declared, irony seeping into his voice, "surely you cannot begrudge me Fokine's three *sine qua nons* for a good ballet: the music, the setting, and the choreography in equal proportions? Come now!"

"I begrudge you nothing at all," she answered sweetly. "It is

Sir Oswald who does the begrudging, and your company of dancers. Pay them, Serge Pavlovitch. And pay my husband. But do not tell him at any time that I gave you this check. I don't want him thinking that I pay his emoluments."

"I would try to be nice to Natalia, my dear boy," Diaghilev warned Pierre. "Sometimes you are impatient and cause her pain. I am concerned about her."

Something in the director's undertone caught Pierre off-balance. He glanced quickly at Diaghilev, then turned away, and a sudden flare of anger swept inside him. "A few years ago you were informing me that Riazhin was more important to you than Oblonova," he said, his voice compressed with resentment. "Now you are reprimanding me! Why, Serge Pavlovitch? Because she is the financial backer, and I am the one responsible for the unenchanted forest? Well, it was not my fault. Blame the English machinery, but don't lecture me about my own wife!"

"Easy, Pierre. I was merely cautioning you. Natalia is a charming girl and you have not always been considerate—shall we say?—of her sensitivities. I like you both, dear boy. There is no other purpose on my part. Only sympathy."

Pierre stood very straight, his black eyes wide with anger, and regarded Diaghilev with the most profound hatred possible. But the director laid a hand on his arm and said, quite softly: "I mean it, Pierre. No false moves, no bad feelings. We are about to crumble to ashes, and that means your reputation as well. Oswald Stoll is closing us down."

"Then I shall do what others have done in this company!" Pierre cried. "I shall go to Massine at Covent Garden and join him!"

Diaghilev's eyes, fishlike and shining, grew narrow. "He wouldn't want to take you right now, my boy," he said in an almost singsong undertone. "I'd take another risk with you, but he isn't in that position. Think it through, my impulsive young mustang. Think it through. Because Natalia's absolutely right: Her choreography was perfect, and I allowed your work to overshadow it. My mistake, it would appear."

"May you both be damned!" Pierre exclaimed and strode

from the room. As he passed across the threshold, he nearly collided with Natalia, whose face looked white and pinched and whose eyes he avoided with a flush of shame, hostility, and embarrassment.

Sir Oswald Stoll regarded the check in Natalia's hand and smiled delicately. "I'm sorry to say that this won't cover my expenses," he said in a tone of deep regret. "I am truly sorry, Madame Riazhina, but your Serge Pavlovitch has been intractable. He's been refusing to pay the tradesmen, and his credit is nil. What can I do? I told you, I am a businessman, not a high-spirited creator."

Natalia sighed. "I understand. But it will have to do, Sir Oswald. This is as far as I am willing to go. I own two houses and am supporting, in effect, two daughters—my own and my niece. I do not want the Ballets Russes to disband. But I cannot be the dishrag that cleans up every spill."

"Then I shall have to seize the properties, the costumes, and the scenery," the impresario said in a dull voice.

Natalia looked at him carefully. "Do that," she said.

Diaghilev was irrepressible, and, like a small boy in search of allowance money, he was soon in contact with former backers on whose resources he had not drawn in recent months. Like the boy whose father is annoyed by his spendthrift habits, he went to one of his godmothers—this time the Princesse de Polignac, in Paris. But the sets of *The Sleeping Princess* could not be recovered. The best that Diaghilev could hope for was the possibility of another season—which in light of his bankruptcy had seemed out of the question. Natalia had predicted this outcome and thought: At least this time he has had to face some of the consequences himself.

Shortly after the debacle in London Diaghilev met with the Riazhins in Paris. "I have a project for both of you," he announced, his cold eyes appraising them from behind the façade of his smiling countenance. "It originated as a score by Igor Stravinsky—*Les Noces*. Massine and Nijinsky both wanted to produce it during the war. But I can't see their work in this, my dears. It bears Natalia's stamp. A Russian peasant wedding without pageantry. Instead of joy, there is the heaviness, the sadness of a prearranged ceremony—the couple as objects. Come—we must listen to the music together."

The impresario noted the spark of interest in Natalia's eye, a quickening of color in her cheeks. He turned to Pierre, whose face was already lit with inner passion. They were sitting in the Riazhin salon, and now Diaghilev rose, and, withdrawing some sheets of annotated music from his coat pocket, he settled himself at the shining grand piano. The strains that emanated from his fingers brought rural Russia to Natalia's mind. The percussive notes, the asymmetrical bars evoked the traditions of the Russia of her childhood, where one merely survived, with little individual freedom of choice. But now and then something gay pierced through—a wedding, after all, was one of the events at which a peasant could relax, dance, and revel.

"I see it in four scenes, each delineated by Igor Feodorovitch's music," Diaghilev said when he had finished and was rolling down the piano cover. "The benediction of the bride; the benediction of the groom; the departure of the bride from her parents' home and her resultant despondency; and finally, the wedding celebration. What I'd like to see first of all, Pierre, are some sketches. Then we can set Natalia to work and unite you both with Stravinsky."

Natalia's lips parted, and a spark of defiance flashed through her eyes. But she nodded. "Very well," she agreed. "I see something very stark, very simple. I'd like to have an idea of what to expect—I could work with Pierre—"

Diaghilev's eyes narrowed, and he shook his head. "No. Pierre must think through his own ideas, Natalia. Think about the choreography, but give him the chance to reach his own conclusions. Husbands and wives can sometimes impede one another's progress—it isn't a usual sort of collaboration. The ballet is of primary importance—not your feelings, or his."

He knows, Natalia thought. He knows about Sir Oswald Stoll. He must know, or suspect, that I allowed him to seize the costumes and sets. He is threatening me with this—threatening my marriage. If Pierre knew I had let him take his favorite decor—his beloved models of *The Sleeping Princess*—he would never forgive me. But Diaghilev and Pierre were wrong about the ballet! Both of them, in their own selfishness, are seeking to push me down.

During the weeks that followed, she did not see Pierre's work. He hid himself among his sketch pads and his paints, and she sat in her boudoir, thinking of the new ballet that would be the supreme challenge of her career. She drew on large pieces of cardboard massive formations that merged and reformed. Group dancing. Ritual heaviness. When at last Diaghilev called them together he looked first at the piles of designs that Pierre had prepared. "These are perfect," he said. Only then did he allow Natalia to peer at them over his shoulder.

She saw the brilliant peasant headdresses, the colorful skirts, the gay costumes, and slow rage began to gather inside her chest. "You're not exhilarated by these boyar celebrants?" Diaghilev demanded. Her husband's beautiful black eyes were riveted on her face, and she saw in them expectation, joy, pride. She swallowed and held her hands together in front of her.

"Serge Pavlovitch," she murmured softly, "what we have here is from the same genre as the exuberant dancer of *The Midnight Sun*. Or another Polovtsian Dance from *Prince Igor*. I can't work with these ideas. First of all, I want visual uniformity—this isn't a true celebration, it's a ritual, a rite. I want something more subdued. I want to be able to group and regroup, so that the eye is caught by the movements of the *corps* rather than by the flashy costumes. Oh, Pierre! They're beautiful, they're splendid! But this ballet demands something else— something simpler."

Pierre stood up, and two of the drawings fell to the floor, fluttering down like dry autumn leaves in the light breeze. His cheeks scarlet, he exclaimed furiously: "You're doing this on purpose, aren't you, Natalia? To demean me in front of Serge Pavlovitch. To devalue me as an artist. You simply can't bear the thought of sharing credit for this production. It galls you! Ever since *The Sleeping Beauty*, you've criticized all my ideas— and yet one day, those very designs are what will be most remembered! Heavy or not, they were beautiful!"

"And none of us could move around in them! You had us weighted down as if we were construction workers! These"—and she pointed at his sketches on the table—"are just as heavy, just as impractical. You forget for whom you are working, Pierre! You're working for a ballet production! For men and women who need to move, above all! Don't you understand how well a dancer needs to know his own body—its weight, its leverage?"

"Well, I haven't forgotten that I'm not working for you!" Pierre retorted angrily, his eyes unfocused, his nostrils dilating. "We're equals, Natalia—equals, not boss and underling, for God's sake!"

"You are both working for *me*," Diaghilev said in an even, sweet-tempered voice. His stare bored into Natalia, then into her husband. "And this time I shall make the final decision. Pierre's designs have enchanted me and will enchant Igor Feodorovitch Stravinsky. Perhaps," he added coldly, "someone else should choreograph *Nes Noces, ma chère* Natashenka. I'll reserve another piece of work for you."

Pierre's look of intense exaltation was the last thing she saw as she turned to leave the room, making certain that her head stayed tilted proudly upward. But when she had calmly shut the door behind her, she fled into the bathroom and stood shaking by the sink.

Chapter 27

In the spring of 1923 Tamara turned six, Natalia was thirty-three, Galina was not quite eighteen and Pierre had made the precarious jump to age forty. Diaghilev seemed to have abandoned the idea of producing Stravinsky's *Les Noces*; after a financially unstable season in London, the Ballets Russes had entered into a quasi-partnership with the Opéra of Monte Carlo, which was housed in the ornate Casino, its cupolas encrusted with turquoise and gilt. Every winter, beginning with the coming one, during Monaco's opera season, the Russian dancers were to provide accompaniment to the singers; and every spring, the Diaghilev Ballet was to play its own repertory in the sumptuous Salle Garnier, all golden curlicues and frescoed ceilings. The company became the Ballets Russes de Monte Carlo, under the direction of Serge Diaghilev. This left six months for holidays and any other engagements, in Paris or abroad, while also ensuring the dancers and artists time and space in which to compose and practice their new productions.

Looking at Natalia, Galina thought that for her, at least, the change would be beneficial. She admired her aunt tremendously: Natalia's compressed energy, her never-ending creative fire and discipline, her artistic vision that shone like a beam of pure light, unimpeded by outbursts and histrionics. She had seen Natalia at her worst, in London when *The Sleeping Princess* had failed so miserably, and memories of this haunted Galina as part of the kaleidoscope of nightmares from her past.

It hurt her physically to remember Natalia's exhausted yielding to tears, the nakedness of her misery: she, a woman who was so reserved, so controlled in her emotions. Natalia was neat and whole, and her art was biting and satiric but never strident, never overdone. In the clean lines of her dancing, Galina saw the same form as in Natalia herself. Galina, tall and statuesque, with cascading waves of brilliant blond hair and eyes of an arresting sapphire blue, thought that there could be no greater loveliness, no finer elegance than that which was embodied in her aunt.

Galina's eyes followed Natalia round a room when she walked, always delicately poised and yet strong, ever a dancer. She envied the older woman's small stature, her sloping shoulders—her own shoulders were so straight, so imposing, almost square, and Galina was ashamed of them, finding her bearing masculine. Natalia's hair, soft and brown, was still bobbed, emphasizing the heart shape of her face, with its great deep eyes, eyes that missed nothing, eyes that expressed love and hate far more eloquently than did her words. Natalia's dainty carriage was ideal for the new fashions, the low-waisted tubular dresses that displayed her slim legs and boyish grace. Everything about Natalia was easy, lithe, airy, yet modern, whereas Galina felt big, awkward, overflowing into unfashionable generosities of breast, hair, and feet.

The move to Monaco would be a good one. Natalia had accepted it with a clearing of her brow, a relaxation of her features that had interested Galina. It was as though Diaghilev's announcement had relieved her, calmed her. She herself knew nothing of Monte Carlo, but in her heart there was a flutter of wistfulness for Paris, for the excitement of its cosmopolitan atmosphere. She had been taking drawing classes at the Académie des Beaux-Arts on the Left Bank, because Natalia had made her promise to "develop her technique" before allowing Pierre to teach her the intricacies of set and costume design. They had disagreed about this, he insisting that Natalia knew nothing about art but that Galina was already talented and capable, and that her interest should not be made to lie fallow for the sake of a conventional education. Natalia had argued that if Galina wished to be an artist, she should at least be given the option of

476 choosing which sort of artist, even if today she had her heart set on the theatre. Galina had said quietly that this was her life and that Natalia had a point, but perhaps Pierre might, in his spare time, begin his coaching? She had started her lessons at the Académie the preceding year and had simultaneously begun to study with Pierre.

Galina loved Paris. She had to admit that Pierre's own love of this city had certainly been an inspiration to her. He had made himself her guide as well as her teacher, and in her heart Galina was both touched and amused. She had been told that Boris had introduced Pierre to the French capital many years ago, dutifully showing him how to appreciate this city. Maybe she was, then, a bit like her uncle. But Pierre took pride in reversing the situation and helping her along as Boris had once helped him. She thought: Everyone feels he or she has a debt to pay to this man, my mother's dead brother, and each one is attempting to do it through me.

"Why don't you want me to be a set designer?" she had once asked Natalia. The other woman had been startled. "No, really—I can tell," she added. "For some reason, I'm disappointing you by choosing that profession."

"It isn't that, lovey. It's simply that I know what sort of life theatre folk live, and it's so easy to starve. Pierre's career has gone up and down and then up again. In between the good times there were moments when he thought he would go mad—with boredom, and with poverty, and with humiliation. A woman can't be sure what will happen to her: You can't count on getting married or on marrying a wealthy man, Galina. In Paris today there are a hundred Russian princesses for every bourgeois nincompoop from Rheims. You need to find a career."

"Such as what?" Galina interposed.

"I don't know. It has to be something meaningful to you. Dance was, to me. And we received good, solid contracts at the Imperial Theatres. Today dancers are not as lucky or as safe."

Galina had remained quiet. It presented a delicate matter, this selection of Pierre's own field. Had she announced that she had chosen set design in order to emulate Benois, Larionov,

Bakst, or Gontcharova, instead of their colleague Riazhin, would Natalia have shown the same reluctance to support her? But I enjoy drawing, Galina thought, and that's what's important. At least her forced exile at the age of eleven from the Russian capital had made one thing obvious to all: Her knowledge of ballet was so minimal that a career in dance was out of the question. She had not been compelled to choose between her aunt and her aunt's husband. Her choice had been made freely and not at all to please or flatter Pierre.

It would have been difficult to explain to Natalia that her world, that world she had so carefully created, composed of Firebirds and Sugar Plums and bold new steps, was so essentially her own world that no one else, least of all Galina, could have entered it without trespassing. Galina thought herself clumsy, and all she knew of dance was that it enchanted the spirit of its spectators while exerting impossible demands on the bodies and senses of its actors. She had been present at some of Natalia's rehearsals, had seen her create—and had found it magic. How could she have explained that Pierre's work was simply more understandable, that it involved the tangible: canvas, paint, materials, measurements? That for a person essentially earthbound, less visionary than literal, his art possessed the appeal of being grasped at once?

For Galina, Natalia was unattainable, a woman like herself but more than she could ever be—whereas Pierre had the simplicity of a man, the genius in him born of energy and color and space, his reactions those of a child who has not yet learned to assimilate and digest. They were equals, he and she—whereas Natalia stood above them, radiant in her clean, intellectual scope, in her ability to synthesize across media and through the bodies and ideas of other people.

Nineteen twenty-two had been a hard year for Natalia. She had ideas and a technique as well as the steady discipline to accomplish great works, but Diaghilev's financial fiascoes had robbed the Ballet of its security. By herself she could not bail it out. "You mistake me for Boris, because he left me his fortune," she had told the impresario. "But Boris was much more than a wealthy man. He was a financier: He knew who else had available funds and how to trick money out of misers. I am only a dancer!" Galina had overheard this exchange, had caught the passion in Natalia's tone, the entreaty to be understood and accepted as she was and not as her first husband had been. She cannot live him down either, the young girl had thought.

But '22 had also been the year of *Renard*, which had held its première at the Paris Opéra on May 18. Men of intellect had praised Natalia's simple, sharp choreography of this short Russian burlesque folk tale about a fox intent on capturing and killing a cock. The vastness and splendor of the Théâtre de l'Opéra were not, however, conducive to this terse, ironic rendition of a popular farce. The cleverness of Natalia's fox, who disguised himself as a nun and was eventually outwitted by the cock's cohorts, a cat and a goat, could not be clearly discerned by all the spectators.

Natalia herself had danced the fox, her small, agile body ideal for the role. Pierre had worked on the scenery with Larionov and Gontcharova. Galina had gone to watch them, fascinated. The four characters they had designed were stark and simple, as befitted the rough, clear minds of the people who had passed this story down through the generations. The cat was blue, the goat yellow, the cock had slitty eyes above a V-shaped beak, and the fox had a huge snout, a black-visored cap and a nun's drooping black veil. The barn in which they attempted to outwit one another was a wooden A-frame of rough planks. Galina thought that she had entered a sideshow on the main street of a small village in the outlands of Podolia or in the Steppes.

On the whole, Natalia had been pleased. The production had been a good one, achieving what it had set out to do. If the spectators had been less responsive than to the pageantry of *Schéhérazade*, which had startled them and raped their very senses, nonetheless it had provided her with a proper introduction to the Parisian public as an innovative and intelligent choreographer. Galina had been struck then by the differences between Pierre and Natalia: He always expected the world to offer him its riches, and, when it failed to do so, his disillusionment was abysmal and self-punishing; whereas she expected life to be a never-ending struggle, with few if any gifts along the way, and none that was not earned. Each half-step upward constituted a grim victory for her. Why was it then that during the spring, Galina was afraid for her aunt? Afraid for all of them?

The young girl found her answer when Natalia took her to Monte Carlo, hoping to rent a house for the family to live in during the approaching ballet season. During the first day Natalia had taken her niece to the quaint, yellow harbor, and to the Palais-Garnier, which was the Casino. They had sat at outdoor cafés and looked at the turquoise sea. Now it was evening and Galina was ready for dinner. She went to find her aunt.

When she opened the door to Natalia's hotel room, it was dark but for one lone light by the roll-top secretary. She saw the older woman, wreathed in the shadows of the spreading dusk, seated on a stool with her head in her hands, bending over something. Galina entered the room, and Natalia looked up. She was holding something crumpled in her hands. Galina swallowed, feeling like an intruder, and her blue eyes met Natalia's brown ones, and she licked her lips, ready to make a discreet exit.

But in a quiet voice Natalia said: "You can't forget, can you? Those dreams of yours, they still come, don't they?"

Galina nodded. "Sometimes. Less and less, but still."

Natalia turned aside, and Galina could see her clear, delicate profile below the mesh of the bangs. "For me it's more and more." She held out her hand, and Galina took the crumpled object and examined it with hesitant fingers. It was a tiny infant's woolen booty, dirty with age.

"Why here?" Galina asked.

"Because this is where we discovered we wanted him. I fought wanting him. I had always rejected motherhood, but when he came, it was different, somehow. I should have listened to my earlier self."

Galina took a step forward, until she was facing Natalia. "But you can't live in the past!" she cried passionately. "Especially not you, of all people! You're a woman of today, one of those people who can create the future! Why are you destroying yourself, Natalia?"

"I am not destroying myself," Natalia replied bitterly. "I am merely allowing the illusions to destroy themselves. We'd all be better off if we were born hopeless, as well as naked."

She tossed the dirty woolen garment with a clean sweep of her arm out the open window, through which the scent of fruit trees had come wafting.

Galina watched, motionless, and then, holding her head up, she said: "If you're through caring, there isn't anything I can do. I can't help you anymore, Natalia." She walked away while the other woman stared after her in stunned silence.

We have reached the end of this stage in our relationship, Natalia thought, suddenly afraid. She isn't my little sister anymore. Something has changed, in her, in me. Does she think I'm through caring for *her?* Anguish filled her chest, pushed up into her throat. Doesn't she understand that if I can let Arkady go, it's because of her, because of what she's come to mean in my life?

In the adjoining room Galina sat on her bed, her large eyes limpid and clear, but her breath quick and uncomfortable. There's nothing more that I can do, she thought. I can't try to merge with her, she's too independent, and so am I. I've tried to love her, more than my own mother. I don't know what she wants, what she needs. She's too complex for me. Her suffering is too much like mine; I can't live hers too as well as my own. There has to be a life here for *me*, for myself!

Abruptly, her heart constricted with hot pity. Poor Pierre, she thought, poor, simple, joyful Pierre, and poor Tamara.

Natalia and Galina returned to Paris shortly thereafter. They had found a pleasant house for rent in Monte Carlo, and it was time to go home. On Avenue Bugeaud, without its ever having been discussed, Natalia had taken to sleeping more and more frequently in her boudoir. At first Pierre had been bitterly resentful; then, half from spite and half as a practical measure, he had made the adjustment. Somehow the large master bedroom with its molded ceiling had evolved into his room, and he no longer felt apologetic about enjoying its size and decorations. She had always seemed to prefer the smaller chamber that she had occupied when she first came there in the summer of

1909—and her boudoir had become her personal enclave. Now she stepped into Pierre's room, her slight figure draped in a silver-toned dressing gown trimmed with Brussels lace, her soft hair like a cap around her young girl's elfin face. He was sitting on the large bed, removing a shoe.

Raising an eyebrow, he said, "Ah, Natalia." He did not know how else to hide his embarrassment, for he had no idea why she had come, and the budding expectation was dangerous, treacherous, as past disappointments had taught him. They fenced with each other now, protecting themselves from any possible attack on their respective vulnerability. They were like two wounded warriors sheathing themselves in yet another coat of mail.

Natalia twisted her wedding ring on her finger. She had not entered of her own accord in a long time. Since Monte Carlo she had found it difficult to sleep, remembering Galina, the impenetrable quality of the girl's judgment of her as Pierre's wife. Clearly, to the younger woman, Natalia had failed, giving up her marriage in a bitter, self-pitying fashion. Was this, in fact, true? She looked at the floor, emotions sweeping with a flush over her breasts and shoulders, up into her face. He was still wearing his evening jacket, and she remembered how he had looked that night in Petersburg long ago when she had waited for him outside his door, like the Little Match Girl. He did not invite her to sit down, to stay. "You had a pleasant evening?" she asked, her voice low and tentative.

"Yes, very. Our people are finally making a mark on this city. The Pigalle area is becoming infested with Russian nightclubs. You should go some time. The Château Caucasien has a wonderful *tzigane* chorus and Caucasian dancers. I felt right at home."

She could feel his eyes on the point between her breasts, could almost touch the challenge in his words. She looked at him fully and smiled. "You're right. I should go. You should have asked me tonight."

He allowed the shoe to drop and leaned back on the bed, resting on his elbows. A slow smile spread across his face, and he nodded. She was such a part of his life, such a beautiful woman, that even now, at thirty-three, she surpassed any other female he knew. He had loved her forever. But then a grim line formed between his eyebrows, and he bit his upper lip with caution. "You know why I didn't, Natalia," he said dryly.

He saw her wince, but instead of the usual flare of responsive anger, her face only registered a moment of mute hurt. "Please, Pierre," she murmured, "not tonight. We're still so young! We have a lifetime stretching before us, don't we? You were the first man I ever loved. And I still love you. We're at the peak of our careers, we have a child we cherish. I'm trying to put the past away in a box, but you haven't let me, all these years. It's as if now that you have me, you've decided you don't need me anymore. Our lives have become so separate that we might as well not be married. Is this what you want for us?"

"I honestly don't know," he replied, looking away, away from the pale, tender throat, from the parted lips and the large brown eyes. "Why are you speaking to me about this now? Why now?"

"Does it matter?" She sat down on the bed beside him but did not touch his hand, so close to her on the bedspread. "So much doesn't really matter! I don't care whether there ever was a Vendanova, or what truly took place between you and Boris. I do know he loved you—he loved us both. In my heart I've come to feel that he would want us to be together. As long as he lived, he wanted us apart, but now he would wish for us to merge, the two people he most loved, apart from his son. It gives me peace to think this way. I know that it would give you peace as well. We have each other, and Tamara, and Galina. Now."

"But you've never loved Tamara," Pierre retorted. His entire body was drawing into itself, pulling away from her nearness, which was making him tremble.

"She's never liked me," Natalia answered. "You've always put yourself between us, so that by comparison I seemed the mean one, the dictator, the one who punished and took away privileges. You've never been a father to her, Pierre, only a kind of youthful Father Christmas, present at the good times but never at the bad. I watched Arkady die, and I shall not allow my daughter to be lost as well, through your spoiling. She is like a small animal, without conscience and responsibility!"

"Maybe so," he answered wearily. His surge of hope was

quickly dying down, like a graying ember. Nothing was different, then.

"Don't give up," she said, and placed her hand on his. "Don't throw me away, Pierre. I love you, I want to try to make you happy. Don't tell me I'm too late."

But to his amazement, all he could feel was a pervasive, sickening numbness. She was bending over him, her lovely face closing in, her scent erotic, making his head swim. He felt exhausted, depressed, cold, and impotent. Slowly, trying not to hurt her, hurt him, he turned on his side and sank into the coverlet, shutting his eyes. He felt tears sting his lashes, but no sound could rise from his lips, and he could not move.

The last thing he heard was the door opening and shutting. The next morning she had left again for Monte Carlo, leaving him a note that read: "I've decided to go to the new house, which needs renovation. The owners are causing some small problems, and I want to talk to them in person. I've taken Tamara with me. It's time she got to know her own mother. Take good care of Galina."

He crumpled the piece of vellum into a small ball, and hurled it to the floor with a hoarse cry that Galina, who was walking quietly past, interpreted as one of pain and fury. Later, when he had gone, she went into the room and found the remnants of the note, worried lest the servants discover it first. She had heard him and seen his face, and now concern overrode common ethics in her mind, and she smoothed out the paper to see what it said. Her smooth oval face set in grim lines, and, tearing the note into tiny pieces, she said aloud, her voice trembling slightly: "Damn Natalia."

Several days later, Pierre received a letter from Serge Pavlovitch in Monte Carlo:

"Dear Pierre," the letter said,

I have given *Les Noces* careful consideration this past year, and have been thinking over Natalia's suggestions. Perhaps her ideas are more on target after all. Stravinsky seems to believe that they are. A ballet that pulls and tugs, with the same sort of ponderous ritual as the *Song of the Volga*

Boatmen. And for this, she's right, we'd need stark costumes and a sparsely furnished set, something rather *functional*. For at heart this wedding is functional. One can almost feel the fathers discussing the dowry of two heads of cattle.

Therefore, I have invited Natalia once again to participate in this project. She seems delighted. I hope you will be pleased to be collaborating once again—you worked so well together on *Renard*. When I return to Paris, I shall expect your reworked sketches.

Pierre's hand began to tremble slightly, but he stilled it with the strong fingers of his other hand. He was tired, so very tired.

Sometimes Galina felt caught on a precipice between two worlds, in a no-man's-land where she would begin to wonder who, in fact, she was. There was the world of the Riazhins: bright, artistic, unpredictable, and temperamental, with immense riches in the background. These people were the geniuses of the world. They created colorful new worlds of their own, which defied measure and containment. These were the gods of today's society: Natalia, Pierre, Diaghilev, Stravinsky, and their cohorts. They were never conventional or dependent on society. Then there was a cruder world, that of the strugglers, the mediocre. She had lived among them in Tbilis and in Constantinople, and, in many respects, still believed that she was one of them rather than a part of that other, more unique realm governed by her step-family. Among this other set the *tziganes* and the less talented painters' models had achieved success—while the rest of them were still anonymous, still barely surviving. Yet Galina had been born into neither of these worlds. She had participated in both, but had been reared in yet another environment, altogether different in its values and precepts: that of the most elite Russian aristocracy, with its Christian Orthodox outlook and its arrogant sense of self-sufficient *noblesse oblige*.

No wonder then that Galina did not always feel at home within her own skin. Her experience, and her observant mind that weighed and judged carefully before reaching a decision, allowed her to see good and bad in each segment of society with which she had been in contact. She hesitated most about judging herself. Galina thought that she could learn to become a stage designer, but that she lacked the special gift that might otherwise have propelled her to become a great one, like Pierre or Gontcharova. She had come to respect the Moldavian *tziganes*, with their particular, inimitable brand of music. If she had found herself unable to sing well among them, it had been because of her upbringing, she thought. As a well-controlled young princess from St. Petersburg, she had been taught to tame the wilderness from her heart—and it was precisely this wilderness, voiced in snatches of song and in the twang of violins, that the *tziganes* expressed to their listeners, reaching inside themselves to connect with other men and women through a common, basic humanity, animal and divine at once. Galina found herself healed by their music, although she could not have explained why.

Sometimes, when she felt betwixt and between, unsure and prey to nagging doubts, a scorching loneliness would set in. It was particularly bad that spring of '23, with Natalia and Tamara gone. Galina was a practical girl and had often occupied herself with projects that turned her away from herself, from her concern with her own mental state. For Galina the best outlet was being with Tamara, playing with her or showing her how to do things. Now, with the small girl gone, the gray moments came more frequently and proved more difficult to chase away.

The house was empty most of the time, except for the servants. Uneasily, Galina prowled from room to room, wondering about Pierre. Whenever she thought of Natalia's note, a hot flush would rise within her, and something inside her constricted for Pierre. She worried about him. He was gone so often, without explanation. True, he was master of the house and of his own life, and he owed her nothing. But there was an abstraction about him when he was with her that bothered her, an abstraction compounded with fierceness that kept her from approaching him for fear of intruding on a personal sadness. Then she would silently curse Natalia again, blaming her for what she saw as Pierre's unhappiness.

Galina missed Pierre. If anyone could have understood her

vague feelings of alienation, surely he could have. She longed to sit with him in the comfortable semidarkness of a late afternoon, to tell him quietly what she felt and thought. She had sensed in him a dichotomy of self similar to her own. She understood his Caucasian pride, his flares of sudden temper, his passionate nature, for she had lived among people like him long enough to grasp their essence. She also saw his need for beauty, his struggle as an artist to wrench from himself the vague ideas that were born every minute of every day, seeking expression incoherently. On top of that was the sense of style that Boris Kussov had given him, the final polish that had turned him from an elemental painter into a master of universal scope, a pace setter as well as an unabashed explorer. He was a primitive who had risen above himself without denying his own uniqueness.

After all these months she had discovered that Natalia was not the only one who had found it impossible to put Boris safely away in the past. Galina had methodically pieced together certain inferences about Pierre, certain bits of information provided by Natalia, and other odds and ends that had wafted her way, and reached the conclusion that Pierre had resented his mentor for the control that he had exerted over Pierre's life and career, while at the same time grudgingly admitting that no man had so thoroughly touched his soul and influenced his art. Sometimes the young girl actually caught a glimpse of Boris in Pierre: his love of opaline lamps from China, for example, or a particular way of nonchalantly crossing his legs. She could understand how such a man such as her uncle might have branded the lives of others who had intimately known him.

At first Pierre had taken her to the cafés of Montparnasse and the Île-St.-Louis, but, beginning the preceding fall, he had introduced her to something quite different: the Russian cabarets. There were several of them, modeled on the all-night restaurants that had abounded on the outskirts of Moscow and St. Petersburg, each with its chorus of *tziganes*, with its atmosphere of outrageous risk, where vast, limitless fortunes could be lost in an evening. She had found it fascinating to watch Pierre's face, especially at the Château Caucasien where Tcherkess tribesmen would perform the *lezhinka* of his youth, the dance of the daggers. There had been something almost sexual in the rapt attention that Pierre gave to these fierce Cossacks, as if they had unlocked his heart in front of a room full of strangers. Yet she had also thought of her Uncle Boris in his costume of the Division Sauvage. She'd seen him in Petersburg before he had been sent to the Caucasus, resplendent in his black and silver uniform, and had found this image of him the most compelling one of all.

Now, wandering through the magnificent house where only the maids crossed her path, Galina felt a powerful urge to find something familiar, something to draw her out of her gloom. She had come home from the Académie des Beaux-Arts, swinging her portfolio in the balmy spring air, raising dust on the bridges and the quays as she stopped to peer into the open bookstalls by the banks of the Seine. She was tired but felt revived by the sun, by this city that she had grown to love, by the beauty of her fellow students' work. It was evening now, and still she was alone. When Chaillou came to ask her if she cared to have supper, she shook her head with sudden impatience. Tonight she would not be the genteel young princess, controlled and wise. "I'll just take a bite before I leave," she told the startled old man and smiled warmly to dispel his shock. Then she threw off her afternoon's clothes and put on a cool cotton middy blouse and a pleated skirt. Before leaving, she seized a long strand of colored beads.

In the kitchen she sat down and ate two apples and a piece of Dutch Gouda cheese, to the consternation of the cook and two maids. "If Monsieur comes home before I do, just tell him not to worry," she said lightly and touched the cook on the shoulder. "Mmm . . . very good, those apples." Then she took her flowered shawl from the wardrobe in the entrance gallery. She let herself out with a little sigh of infinite relief. Since Tbilis, she had found certain atmospheres confining, claustrophobic. Being alone in the lilac-scented Paris night was like floating on a pool of clear, cool water after a hot day.

Sometimes Galina was cerebral, weighing matters carefully; but there was another side of her, that half that gave itself up to sensation, unimpeded by thought. In the taxi she simply knew that she would spend the evening at the Château Caucasien, that this was where it would feel good to be. She was not embarrassed about being alone; at nearly eighteen, Galina had experienced sufficient adventure not to feel the need to be chaperoned, as befitted her station as an unmarried girl of good family. Paris was full of unmarried Russian girls, and of American girls and French girls. The flapper generation was in full swing.

The cabaret had been built on three levels, so that its patrons might enjoy three kinds of entertainment. It was early yet, and Galina went to listen to the *tzigane* chorus and its soloist, Nastia Poliakova. The large floor was dotted with small tables and was shaded to reflect yellow lights. The effect was intimate and rich. Galina ordered something to eat and sat back, her golden hair falling thickly about her shoulders. She looked around as the music enveloped her, transporting her above Paris to some remote region beyond sight and sound.

It was intriguing, from an artistic point of view, to watch the patrons here. There was a table filled with young American girls, their hair bobbed and their hands studded with rings. They laughed, their rouged lips parted, and they spoke in a strange twang, slouching in their seats. Brand-new mink adorned their collars, and their hair shone with cleanliness. Their lovely legs were sheathed in colored hose, and when they regarded the chorus, it was not Nastia who caught their eyes but the male *tziganes*. Galina was rather amused at their open flirtation: They wanted to appear so worldly, in such control.

A *tzigane* would gently mock them behind their backs while smiling at them with his limpid black eyes.

To Galina's left sat an unusual woman, with a tower of red hair and lashes ringed in kohl. The girl judged her to be at least sixty years old. Pear-shaped diamond earrings dropped dramatically from her flaccid lobes, and age spots and emeralds stood out on her hands. "That's the Countess Tereshenko," the waiter whispered to Galina. "She can't believe that here in Paris she's a nobody." Galina looked away from her, embarrassed.

In the dark but joyful room Galina lost her awareness of time. The American girls were joined by some young men, beardless, hatless, and sporting crew cuts that she found very unattractive. The young men ordered whiskey. Then the *tzigane* chorus disappeared and was replaced by the Tcherkess dancers. In their white tunics and dark pants, a cartridge belt slung around each of their chests, these incredibly tall men and their serious women silenced the assembled patrons by their entrance. Galina ceased to notice anyone but them.

Pierre had told her that his mother had been born within the Tcherkess tribe. As a child, he had often watched the men and women dance, the men hitting the floorboards with their heels, and throwing daggers within inches of the women's moving feet. The women danced on, nobly confident that the daggers would miss them each time. The frenzied pace of the clicking boots and flashing daggers brought a kind of animal tension to the room, a tension that Galina could now breathe. A jeweled dagger fell in front of her, and she raised her eyes to one of the magnificent dancers. He had intended this gesture to show homage to her for her great beauty, and she blushed, immensely embarrassed.

When the show was over, the aura of feral danger, of suppressed violence and sexuality, still lingered, indefinable in the night. The Countess Tereshenko narrowed her eyes and beckoned with one gnarled, jeweled hand to a young waiter with wide, dark eyes, who came to sit with her at her table. Galina felt someone near her, and looked up, surprised. Two of the American men were standing in front of her, wobbling slightly in their well-cut gray suits, their faces glistening with youthful perspiration. One was massive and blond, with a crew cut, and the other was dark, with curly hair and a wiry body. "Buy you a drink?" one of them asked, winking. His French sounded slurred.

She shook her head, the muscles tightening in her arms, legs, and neck. A vivid image passed through her mind of herself fighting off a large drunken client at one of the *traktirs* of Tbilis. The curly-haired one, who seemed more a boy than a man, now blinked and pulled up a chair, falling into it with a small giggle. "Pretty girl like you shouldn't drink alone," he remarked.

This was not going to be pleasant. Galina rose and in one swift motion scooped up her bag of Moroccan leather. But the man with the crew cut seized her other wrist and held it down on the table. "We don't mean any harm," he said softly. "What are you, anyway? Russian?"

"Let me go," Galina said, trying to pull away.

"Lots of li'l Russian gals around, these days. Here, I'll bet that's what you are—look, Louie—costume jewelry. This one's poor, too." With his free hand he held up Galina's necklace. "Come on," he added, "we'll treat you nice. Take you to the Ritz. Bet you haven't eaten well in years. That right?"

Looking first at one man and then at the other, Galina said in a low, guttural voice: "God—damned—bastards, leave me alone, or I will scream and have you thrown out!"

The young waiter with the countess was looking at them, squinting. Cold sweat began to trickle down Galina's temples, under her arms. That was it, he didn't see that she didn't want them, didn't want this. In Paris the Americans reigned supreme, gave the best tips and propositioned countless willing Russian princesses. Nobody cared about the Russian patrons, their funds were nonexistent compared with those of the Americans. Some of the Russian princesses were, in fact, surviving by going from one American bed to another. She could feel tears forming at the base of her throat, and she swallowed hard to press them down. "Go away," she pleaded.

To her amazement a third party pushed his way among them, and the young man with the crew cut dropped her wrist and backed away, blinking. Galina stared into an unknown face, older, some forty-five years of age. He had a straight nose and thick brown hair. The gold and green eyes surprised her by their beauty, for he was not a handsome man, but rugged and lively. A gold pocket watch caught her eye, and a signet ring. He turned to the small, dark youth and seized the lapels of his neat jacket. Shaking him, he brought his face close and said: "You no-good son of a bitch, get the hell out of here before I call the cops!" This time he had spoken in English, and Galina, who did not understand it well, could only gather the gist of his words through the harshness of his tone and gesture.

"Look here—" began the man with the blond crew cut. He poked the bearded man in the ribs. "This' our gal, you go get your own!" Without warning the older man swung at him with his right fist and smashed him wordlessly in the jaw. The youth crumpled to the floor, whimpering, and the older man offered his hand to Galina, saying quickly, in French: "Get your wrap, mademoiselle, and I'll take you home."

Without pausing to consider, Galina tossed her shawl over her shoulders and accepted the man's proffered hand. The commotion had finally begun to draw waiters and other clients around them, but the bearded man cleared a path through them and led her away, down the stairs. She was breathing in small, swift gulps, her face red with tension and embarrassment and the haste of their exit. On the street it was cool, and she stopped to look at her savior. "I can't thank you enough," she said gravely. "But I've ruined your evening."

He laughed, a low, gentle laugh. "I apologize for my inebriated countrymen, my dear. By the way, it isn't really safe to go out alone like this, you know. I'm not a prude, so don't look at me like that. But men can be quite nasty sometimes. I know," he added, shaking his head humorously, "because I'm one myself. Now—shall we take a taxi? I'd like to see you safely home."

In the taxicab they did not speak. She was still breathless and somewhat disoriented, and when they reached Avenue Bugeaud, he helped her out, told the driver to wait, and walked with her up the steps to the front door. He took the key from her trembling fingers and unlocked the heavy wooden panels, then escorted her inside the entrance gallery. As she turned to thank him, he suddenly scratched his head, and said: "You know, there's something familiar about this house. I know I've never been inside it, but I believe it may have been described to me once. Tell me, you're a Russian, aren't you?"

She nodded. "Yes. Galina Stassova."

He shook his head. "No. Not Stassova. Only a Countess Kussova. But that was years ago, in the States. Natalia Oblonova, the dancer. You wouldn't happen to know her, would you? One Russian to another?"

Galina smiled. "Oh, yes. She's my aunt. You see, my mother was a sister to Count Boris Kussov, Natalia's first husband. But"—her smile dimmed—"she's in Monte Carlo right now."

The man sighed. "Ah well, such is life, *c'est la vie*, and so on, and so on. It was a pleasure rescuing you from those college-boy Don Juans, I assure you. But mind what I said: Wait for your aunt to return and go out with her!"

Galina laughed and offered him her hand. He took it, shook it gently, and then bent down and planted a small kiss on her forehead. At that moment they both blinked, disoriented by the strong beam of light that had been turned on overhead. The bearded man stepped back, and she instinctively drew her arms to her sides, rigidly. Pierre stood framed in the doorway of the darkened salon, dressed in his shirt sleeves, his hair tousled, a haggard expression in his bloodshot eyes. "What's this?" he demanded, his voice harsh and aggressive.

"I was just leaving," the brown-haired man said tactfully. "I'm Stuart Markham, and there was a bit of unpleasantness, nothing serious—"

"What are you talking about, and who exactly are you?" Pierre demanded.

Galina blushed, and stepped between the two men. "Mr. Markham's been so helpful, and so kind, Pierre," she said in her clear, pure voice. "There were two drunken boys who were bothering me, and he pushed them out of the way and brought me home." Looking directly into Pierre's face, she added, "We should be terribly thankful to him, shouldn't we?"

"Yes, well, I'm leaving now, the taxi's outside waiting," Markham demurred, and Galina quickly held the door open for him. He patted her shoulder once, eyed Pierre, and darted outside to the taxi. It whirred its motor and started off, and Galina shut the door and leaned against it, looking at Pierre. Something was not right, and she felt on edge, from the American boys and now from this head-on encounter between the nice man and Pierre, whose mood she could not read.

"Where were you?" he asked, and she could see the cords standing out on his powerful neck. He was still framed in the doorway, and beyond him she could make out the sofa, a coffee table, the piano. She felt the threat of his anger, and suddenly sensed the lack of reason behind it.

She stiffened. "I went out, to the Château Caucasien."

"Alone? Are you mad, Galina?"

His eyes were wide. She took a deep breath and met them with her own level blue gaze. "No," she answered quietly. "I'm not mad at all. Just lonely. You go out—all the time, it seems. What's wrong with my doing the same thing? You forget that before I came to you and Natalia, I'd been on my own for years! I am not a child, Pierre."

"No," he said, "you are not a child." Then his voice rose: "Perhaps if you were, it would be safer! Don't you understand, Galina, that you're a very beautiful young woman, and that any man would be justified in making advances toward you? Don't you see yourself at all?"

"It's you who are mad!" she cried out then and started to walk up the stairs, bending her head in a sudden clash of emotions. "Sometimes I don't like you, Pierre, sometimes you are unfair and cruel and you degrade me! Leave me alone—I don't want to speak to you. You were so rude to that poor man, that nice good man, when if you love me, you should have been grateful! I don't understand you, not at all!"

"That man was kissing you," Pierre retorted savagely, taking her arm to prevent her from running up the stairway.

"Kissing me? As a friend, as a brother! Don't make it sound so sordid and shameful, Pierre! For God's sake, you're behaving as if—yes!—as if you were jealous! Jealous of some stranger who was kind, who—"

"I don't want to hear another word about your stranger! Not one word, Galina! Jealous? Yes, yes, of course, I'm jealous! What do you expect me to be?"

Slowly she wheeled about, and her pocketbook fell to the bottom of the stairs, unnoticed. Her oval face shone white and stunned in the light, her lips parted and her blue eyes intent on his face, which she seemed to be seeing for the first time. He took a half-step backward, color rising to his cheeks, his eyes staring at her with a kind of wild agitation. It was as if he suddenly was realizing what he had said. She did not move, and his arms began to tremble, his breath to come in staccato gulps.

For a moment they remained frozen in space, the girl and the man, and neither one could think or act. Then he clenched his fists and pounded them together, and compressed his lips. She whispered, "I—" but the words stopped coming, and her

494   face flooded with shame, with horror. But she could not look away from him, or he from her, from the riveting azure blue of her eyes.

Then at last she made a furtive movement and turned her back on him, fleeing up the stairs, her blond hair bouncing in back of her like a mantle of fur. Only then did tears well up in his eyes and spill down his cheeks.

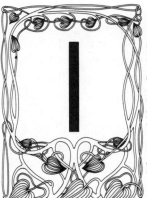

Chapter 28

I shall have to deal with it later, Natalia thought, annoyed with herself, with Galina, with Diaghilev, and with Pierre. Demands on her were pressing from all directions, and there seemed to be no reserve for herself in which to regain her peace of mind. She was preparing *Les Noces*, trying to work her ideas into Stravinsky's composition, but finding that, although his music was the perfect inspiration, its stops and starts, its breakdown in structure, were contrary to the continuous flow she wished to achieve. At least Pierre's new designs were what she wanted: simple, stark. The set was to be a white stage with a door to the back, through which the public would catch glimpses of the nuptial bed heaped with pillows. The costumes were two-toned, breeches and tunics for the men, and shirts and jumperlike dresses for the women, all purely functional.

Natalia understood the point of Stravinsky's music, of his decision to include only percussion instruments. Singers would be raised to the stage like a kind of chorus, to echo the mood of the theme. Natalia had seen peasant weddings in the Crimea, hence her tableaux had a bitter reality, which Diaghilev had envisioned when first discussing the ballet with her. Life flowed through the wedding preparations: a continuing, fatalistic life, with its brief climax of festivity. To those who ran a farm, who toiled incessantly to grow vegetables and raise livestock, a wedding was functional, not the culmination of romantic love.

For Natalia, everything came down to weaving and interweaving groups of dancers: the bride's friends, the groom's cohorts, the older marriage guests. She could imagine the girl's family, resigned to yielding their daughter to the groom's, and the bride's own fear as she prepared to leave their loving cocoon. The bridegroom, who was insecure: What did having a wife really mean? The couple as objects of a tradition, marrying a person chosen by the parents. The bride's friends moving around her on either side, bending inward as if braiding her long tresses in a touching ritual of female caring. The boy's male friends forming two lines encircling him, their hands meeting over his head to form a passageway: homage to the one who was about to enter matrimony. An older couple warming the nuptial bed. This was a wedding symbolic of illiterate rusticity, yet beautiful in what it said about the continuity of life among those who worked in routines of drudgery. Natalia planned her groups, her floor patterns, her gentle pulling apart and juxtaposing in geometric arrangements. This, finally, was imagination: the assimilation of reality into an artistic expression.

Bending over the sheets of paper on which she would diagram her desired positions, Natalia worked day after day in Monte Carlo. Tamara was with her, as was Mademoiselle. Natalia was truly making an effort with her daughter, to include her in her plans, to take walks with her, to teach her simple dance steps based on the five positions, which the small girl had learned at four.

Still, it did not go well. It was as if Tamara, her black eyes defiant, was punishing her mother for months and months of involvement elsewhere. "No, I don't want to dance now," she would say irritably. "Mama, this is my time to swim, don't you remember?"

Natalia would look guiltily at Mademoiselle, whose raised eyebrows were a clear indication that the child, not the mother, was right again. Children, my dear madame, need their routines.

At night Natalia would silently tiptoe into Tamara's room and watch her sleep. She would sit on the small bed, her heart flowing with sudden tenderness, and her fingers would touch the peach skin, the soft black lashes. My child, my child. I do love

you, even if I can't always show it the way you want. How little
I know you! How little we know each other, or forgive each
other. Maybe someday . . . But it had to be today, didn't it? Or
it would be too late.

There was a desperation about Natalia that spring, a nervous
frenzy of love that Tamara could not understand. She did not
know how to handle it. A baby still, flailing about in the sea of
human emotions, she did the only thing she knew how to do:
She tensed against this outpouring, hardened herself against her
mother. More than ever, Natalia felt totally rejected by her.

Then Galina unexpectedly arrived at the rented villa, adding
her own confusion to the general chaos in the household. "For
God's sake," Natalia muttered, dropping her pen and diagram
on her secretary and coming out into the hall. Then she saw
Galina's face, her willowy body huddled oddly upon itself like a
frightened animal.

"Will you let me stay?" the girl pleaded, shyly averting her
hurt eyes.

"Yes, yes, how can you ask?" Natalia answered, putting her
arms around her. "Tamara will be so glad to see you." This
remark proved painfully true. That same day Natalia saw them
walking hand in hand in the garden, stopping once in a while
for Galina to point something out to her small playmate.

Tamara said later to her mother: "Do you know what I love
best about Galinotchka? She hugs so well. We hold and we
hold and we hold, and she never goes away."

Natalia cried silently into her pillow that night, not knowing
that Tamara, shivering, had gone into Galina's bed whimpering: "I missed you, I missed you. Mama always wants to talk to
me when I'm playing, or she wants to play complicated games
when I feel like being by myself. I don't always like Mama,
d'you know, Galina? I don't always like Mama."

When Natalia returned to Paris with her daughter and niece,
Pierre's presence in the house could be felt in every room.
Natalia saw signs of his restlessness in the half-finished painting
on an easel in the master bedroom, could feel his spirit needing
to break out in the very chaos of his closet, where ruffled shirts
lay scattered in a litter of reckless hedonism. He's been doing

the cabarets, she thought, reliving his golden youth in St. Petersburg, spending money as casually as if he were a young prince of high standing at the Tzarist court. She saw evidence of his confusion and despair, and it reverberated inside her. He's gone away from me, she thought. Something has come to take him away from his very self, something cataclysmic.

Galina saw all this, too, in her own way. She saw it, felt it, and crept away, as if Pierre's sickness were catching, as if she was afraid of him. But he ignored her. Sometimes at breakfast she would announce plans to have dinner with a friend—and sometimes, too, she would throw in the name of some young man, looking at Pierre from under her golden lashes. He shrugged it off. You're a big girl. Amuse yourself the way you see fit, his eyes told her, their cutting edge a singularly painful blow.

Then, one afternoon, he entered Tamara's room, where Galina had come to put away the small girl's sweater, and there was no avoiding him. Birds chirped evening songs outside, young buds on the trees threw long, dappled shadows on the soft carpet. It was a lazy afternoon, and the oddly empty house seemed lazy, too, with Tamara and her governess out, Natalia at a rehearsal, and the servants otherwise occupied. Galina felt her mouth dry up, and she pressed her hands together. "They're at the Bois de Boulogne," she said aimlessly, staring at his feet, resplendent in shiny black moccasins.

"So where are you going? Plans for tonight, my sweet?"

Her eyes filled with tears at his tone of bitter irony. Why do you hate me? she thought, although deep inside she already knew the answer. It was inescapable. "We used to be such good friends, Pierre," she murmured in misery. "Let me go, please."

He opened his hands, palms up, and smiled. There was no mirth in his face. "I'm hardly holding you, am I?" he said.

The strong blue of her eyes suddenly shone at him. She was speaking through those extraordinary eyes, saying—saying what? Resenting him. "Look," he stated, anger forming deep within him and slowly rising, "you're the one who ran off to Monaco, weren't you? Playing all those silly games, day after day? Do whatever you want, Galina, but don't involve me. Your Uncle

Boris was the game player, not I. I don't give a damn whom you see—whether you sleep with every male friend you have—"

"Stop it!" She had balled her hands into fists and stood shaking. "Don't say anything. Just—don't *say* it!"

"Fine," he answered shortly, "I won't." He turned around and walked out, and she continued to stand, trembling. Then suddenly he was back, framed in Tamara's doorway. "I want *you* to tell *me* what it is you want," he said.

"I want it to be the way it was before," she replied, looking at him again. "I want you to care."

"You want a perfect world." He stepped inside the room, and now his voice was warmer, less hostile.

She bit her lower lip and absently picked up Tamara's sweater. She said nothing and instead tried to leave the room. He caught the sleeve of her blouse and stopped her. "Don't tease me," he said, very softly now, drawing her to his chest and enclosing her within his arms. He rested his chin on the top of her head and said again: "Don't tease me. I'm too old for that, and it's hardly fair. But if you do sleep with anyone, I don't want to know, I'm not that kind of friend. You can't have it both ways, Galina."

Gently but firmly, he pushed her away from his chest, tilted up her chin. She was tall, a golden tulip, he had often thought. His finger caressed her cheek, drew an outline of her brow. There was so much sadness in his face that she had to look aside, suddenly overcome with embarrassment. He looked so old, so . . . *old*, and his face was a living wound.

"I must go," she said, and pushed past him hurriedly.

On the evening of Bastille Day, July 14, *Les Noces* premièred at the Théâtre de la Gaîté-Lyrique in Paris. Natalia did not dance in her own production this time. It was too important; too much needed to be supervised at the last minute. Her ballet, with its chorus seconding the dancers, was unfolding as planned on Pierre's plain stage with walls giving onto a door through which the spectators could see a bed strewn with pillows. The groups of wedding guests and family members moved with a graceful heaviness, in one direction and then another, meshing together in clusters. Natalia watched from the sides, her heart pounding in her throat, fear and excitement drying her lips and moistening her palms. More than the ill-fated *Sleeping Princess*, presented at the wrong time to the wrong audience, more than *Renard*, a tiny jewel hidden in the vastness of its setting, this production would establish or destroy her reputation as an innovative choreographer. So much depended on this performance.

When it was over, Natalia knew that she had scored a triumph. The Parisians greeted her work with unabated enthusiasm, and she felt her fear dissolve, joy replace it.

The stars of the Ballet had been invited to a party given by some brilliant young American expatriates. Now she encouraged Galina to join the group. Pierre said nothing. Hesitantly, like a scared rabbit, Galina looked up at him and then down at her feet. "I'm too young, and I'd be out of place," she said awkwardly.

"Let her go home if she wants to," Pierre cut in abruptly, rearing his head in a gesture of annoyance, contempt. He began to move away, and Galina suddenly looked up into Natalia's face and colored brightly:

"All right," she said, somewhat breathlessly. "I'll come!"

During the drive Pierre's mood began to worry Natalia. After all, *Les Noces* had been his victory as well as hers: He had designed the sets! "We've won, darling," she whispered to him, but in his preoccupation he seemed not to have heard. Something lurched in her heart.

At the party it was even worse. Natalia saw him move toward a back room just as she was being surrounded by their old friends Stravinsky, Gontcharova, Diaghilev, and Georges Auric, who had been playing one of the four pianos that had accompanied the singers and dancers. Through the crowd she could see Pierre's retreating back, his bent head. The joy died inside her, and her eyes began to glitter with a kind of brittle pretense. This was her night, a celebration. All her life she had been waiting for this, all the long years. "Yes, give me more champagne," she said and heard the false excitement in her voice and hated it, hated herself, hated him, and was afraid.

She looked around for Galina, suddenly apprehensive lest the girl feel left out, unwanted. "Has anyone seen my niece?" she asked.

"Not since we came in," Diaghilev replied. He was smiling at her, his monocle reflecting her own small self, clothed elegantly in a long, straight gown of metallic blue, strands of pearls around her neck falling to her waist. "It's remarkable," he continued, "how much she is like Boris. Tonight in that black outfit she was more like him than ever."

"So young to mourn," Auric said with a half-smile.

"Not really. She has many for whom to mourn," Natalia countered. "But somehow I don't think that's why she chose the black. I think Galina's trying to tell us something: 'Look out, people, I'm grown up now!' "

Someone was edging his way into the group. Natalia looked over the rim of her *coupe* and saw the brown hair rising like a crest over a high forehead with rugged lines, saw green-gold eyes, and parted her lips with an expression of joy and a small tingle at the bottom of her spine. "Stuart!" she cried. "You're here?"

"To gratify Monsieur Diaghilev, I should answer, 'No, I'm his shadow,' " Markam replied, laughing. He bent over and kissed Natalia on the cheek, then turned to greet the impresario. But now there was a new dynamic to the group, and it began to reform. Diaghilev, his sharp eyes appraising the American writer and his choreographer, was repositioning himself so that now he, and not Natalia, was at the center of the group. The dancer and her friend stood on the outside, smiling at each other.

"So we always meet by the champagne bucket," he said. "It was a wonderful ballet, Natalia. My general impression is that you finally changed the old tiger's mind and proved to him that a woman can do it better, after all."

She took his arm, and they walked to a corner of the enormous reception room. "I met your niece a few months ago," Stuart said. "Did she tell you about it? At the Château Caucasien? I even saw your house and had a brief encounter with some man whom I assumed to be your husband. Tell me, does he always greet his guests with scowls and shouts of anger?"

"I don't know anything about this," Natalia said, feeling suddenly cold in the warm room.

"Oh? Well then, I assume it wasn't very important. How are you? Apart from the stage, I mean."

"I'm quite well. All right. But what's this about Galina and Pierre? And why didn't you come to see me if you were in Paris all this time?"

He raised his eyebrows quizzically and shook his head. "I helped Galina rid herself of some silly college boys, and Pierre was not amused. I don't think he took my chivalry the way it was offered. As for you, my dear—I've followed you about in the papers, and I've always been proud of your accomplishments. But it's not easy to forget. A friendship such as ours leaves its share of scars. I did love you, you know. Now it's been seven years, and no, I haven't moped about playing the romantic young fool, beating his breast while another man makes off with his fair maiden. But still, Natalia, you can't expect it not to hurt, being in the same city and being reminded daily that you are here with someone else."

She bit her lower lip, suddenly embarrassed. Wordlessly, she shook her head. He patted her shoulder and said, with amusement: "It's all right. Life goes on. This Trojan prince never did get his Helen, but think of the carnage we avoided! We'll always be friends, Natalia. That's one of the reasons why I came tonight. I wanted to congratulate you, and to see you again. But for a girl who's just won at bingo, you don't look very happy. What's up?"

"I don't know," she answered, looking at him with her large brown eyes. "Maybe Serge Pavlovitch was right. Maybe a woman can't handle this sort of thing—you tell me, Stu."

He started to laugh. "But I'm not an oracle," he demurred. "Wrong profession. How can I help?"

She held out her glass. "You can refill this and tell me all about your new book," she said brightly. "I loved *Night Before Sunburst*. But your last one—*Toys That Don't Work*—that was so sad, so terribly depressing, Stu. So much waste among the rich set in your country."

"For a Russian *contessa* without a country of your own, you are an arrogant one, aren't you?"

"But really now. Isn't there any hope at all? Can't there at least be one toy that functions properly?"

He poured amber champagne into her raised *coupe* and met her intense brown eyes with playful green ones. "Oh, come on, Natalia," he commented lightly, "this is a party, remember? And in any case, you know I'm not a prophet, as I said earlier. I just chronicle what I see. But here's to us, and to the Ballet, and to your success! Drink up and be merry."

In the back of the room Galina saw Stuart tilt up Natalia's chin and place one quick kiss on her lips. She shivered and walked away. She could not see the tears that glistened in Natalia's eyes, could see nothing but what lay inside herself. Suddenly it had become imperative that she leave, that she take her bag and coat and go home. Here the world was askew, here she would find no questions answered. She opened the door into the hallway behind her, and walked with long, rapid strides to the room where she had seen the maid place the wraps.

Galina stood alone in the dimly lit room and glanced at her reflection in the full-length mirror. She had designed this outfit herself and had it made by Natalia's seamstress. It was a long tunic that billowed out over tight pants, all black silk. The dainty fashions do not fit me, I am too big, she had thought. This will be "me." Now she admitted that this parody of the masculine tuxedo was exactly what she'd needed. It made her look distinctive, setting off her tall structure as proud rather than awkward. As usual, her blond mane flowed over shoulders and breasts; and she wore no makeup. The Americans, she knew, had found her odd.

Ah well, she thought, suddenly amused. What difference can all this possibly make: who I am, what I look like? But the door was opening, and with quick embarrassment, she seized her black cape and her small bag. She moved into the shadows and watched to see who would emerge, hoping it would be a total stranger.

But it was Pierre, still in his evening suit, his ruffled white shirt emphasizing his darkness, his broad, sharp maleness, his quickness of gesture. She felt her throat beginning to swell, her ears to hurt from the beating pulse. "I'm going home now," she stammered. "I don't know a soul here—"

"You know me," he retorted sharply, unkindly.

"I can't always stay with you and Natalia. I must get out on my own. You can see that, can't you?" she asked. "In fact, I've been mulling over an idea. I'd like to find an apartment of my own, as well. I need the space."

"Need the space? God, Galina, Bugeaud has space enough for ten of us, plus servants! Don't be ridiculous!"

"I'm an artist just as much as you are, Pierre," she said coldly. "I'd be more comfortable by myself, in an attic somewhere, overlooking Paris. Luxury isn't everything, you know!"

"No," he repeated softly and looked at her. "It isn't everything."

They remained standing apart, their eyes on each other. Then, his voice so low that she could hardly hear him over the strains of music from the party room, he asked: "What are we going to do, Galina? We have to do something."

"But there's only one thing to do: I shall go and find another place to live," she answered, suddenly relieved, calmed, now that it was out in the open.

"That's no solution. When the wound is bad, you amputate the limb, not bind it in gauze. Eventually, bandage or none, the limb falls off."

"But if I go, that's exactly what will happen," she countered. "The limb will have fallen off by itself and cause no more pain."

He came to her and tried to take her hands, but she motioned for him to back away from her. "Don't," she said in her clear, grave voice. "Don't do this. Just say whatever it is you feel should be said, and then I'm going to leave."

"I can't tell you strongly enough how sickened I am by your solution. It's ghastly, Galina. And it's childish. Just because you'll sleep elsewhere isn't going to remove the problem. She'll still want to see you. If, that is, she ever lets you go in the first place. She loves you more than anyone on earth, more than Tamara, more than . . . me."

"Yes," Galina murmured. "I know. And it hurts. The whole thing hurts, it hurts us all. At least if I go, you two will keep on, and then later, when I've married, I can come back to you—to both of you."

"When you've married? You can speak so blithely about this when you know how it is . . . between us?"

She twisted her hands together and looked away. "Nothing lasts forever," she said bitterly. "Life, love—you know that, too. You loved her all these years—all these years—and now suddenly you think you love me, and I don't know if it's true, I don't know! The point is that one day I shall wake up free of you, as she did once also, and I shall be glad, and love another man who will be able to love me, with his whole heart. For as long as it lasts."

"But I can't let that happen, Galina," he said. He placed his hands on her shoulders and kept them there, looking into her face, so close to his, so pure and pink, the eyes so magnificently proud and azure, the eyes of a goddess. "I want to live with you, I want to be the one that loves you. You were a child when you came to us two years ago. And yet, not a child. You saw how things were—between her and me. How could you seek to preserve—that—to the detriment of—this, which is good, young, healthy? She never really loved me, or it wouldn't have gone bad. It was always Boris! And for me—I can't put it into words. It was a kind of possession. I wanted her and I couldn't have her, and I wanted what the world had, I wanted to devour her talent and make it mine, too. Oh, I don't justify any of this—or rather, of course, I do, but it's so bloody complicated, and your handling it as if it were a simple case of jumbled ABC's doesn't help us at all, not at all!"

Slowly he let his hands drop and sat down on an ottoman to the right of her. She watched him, motionless, as he pressed his fingers to his eyes. She watched him with a kind of eerie fascination, her emotions frozen inside her. "Do you know," she finally said, "I understand her better than I do you. She and I are alike. We've lost so much, we've lost our very worlds, and yet, somehow, we managed to survive when others didn't. But you—you don't know what it's like to lose anything!" Her blue eyes widened, the pupils dilated. "And yet you're one of these people who shouldn't suffer, who should always be protected. I wish . . . I wish I could stay to protect you, Petya, but I can't, I can't. For you see, I must survive this, too, like the death of my mother, like my family being burned alive. I have to make this love die inside me, so that I can keep on."

He raised his head and saw that she had swung the cape

around her like a cloak of gloom. Her blond hair cascaded over it, and she opened the door, a tall, black figure with yellow hair, leaving the small room. He wanted to rush up behind her, to crush her to him, to preserve her for himself forever—but he willed himself to sit still, to watch her depart.

She had called him Petya, like Boris Kussov.

"So," Natalia said, massaging her ankles, "you pack the next day after my biggest success. Do you think *Les Noces*, and the silly reviews in the newspapers, will compensate me for the loss of you, my dear, sweet child?" There was a faint glimmer of amusement in the brown eyes, but also something else, more remote, more faint.

"It isn't as if we won't see each other," Galina said, sitting down. They were in Natalia's Chinese boudoir, the scene of so many of their intimate talks, and this made the girl acutely uncomfortable, watching her aunt.

"Stay, and then I'll help you find that blessed artist's garret," Natalia suggested. "But this way—where are you going, Galina?"

"To a friend's, from the Beaux-Arts. I'll be eighteen in two months, and at my age you'd been living on your own for a full year."

"Ah, yes. With Lydia . . . I can't deny you your independence, Galinotchka. I was the same at your age, and I'm not so old now that I can't remember that. It's just that—well, this is so sudden. What's really wrong, dear?"

Galina shook her head and looked away. "Nothing. I don't want to live in your shadow anymore. You've done so much for me, Natalia! You've been so dear to me, so generous, so loving! And all I've done is take! Now I'd like to see what life is really like, without help from anyone."

"You saw what it was like in Tbilis, and in Constantinople," Natalia retorted dryly. "And it wasn't very pleasant. We don't spoil you unnecessarily, Galina. Pierre does that to Tamara, but then that's a different story." Her eyes fastened on the girl. She breathed in rapidly and said sharply: "It's Pierre, isn't it? Stuart

Markham told me about a quarrel, some kind of problem. Did you quarrel with Pierre?"

"Yes," Galina answered, much too quickly. She held her hands immobile in her lap, like dead weights. "Ask him, you'll see that it can't be mended—"

There was something in Galina's eyes, in the eager expression on her face that Natalia recognized, that pulled at her with such sudden force that for a moment she could not breathe at all. "Galina," she said. A vein was throbbing on her temple. "Galina, no!"

The girl stood up, upsetting a book that her aunt had been reading. "I've got to leave now," she stammered.

Natalia's eyes held her. "Not this," she finally said. Tears came to her eyes, and she brushed them impatiently away. "Galina, sit down. Listen. You're eighteen. Your father was far away from you, then he was dead—and so of course now there's Pierre. It's normal, all girls feel this way! We grow up loving our fathers because who else can a little girl love? It's my fault for not giving you a proper début, for not introducing you to interesting young men! Pierre was all you had! For God's sake, Galina!"

Galina began to tremble. Natalia could see her whole body starting to shake, as though she had the palsy. "Darling, he doesn't know this, does he—how you feel?" she asked the girl.

Galina blinked, and tears fell on her cheeks. "He does know," Natalia intoned, and all at once her limbs were cold, and her heart was numb. "He knows. So if he knows and hasn't told me—then that means—" She fell silent, and now she too started to tremble uncontrollably. Galina continued to weep and Natalia turned on her, blood rushing to her cheeks. "Galina," she said, and her voice cracked slightly. "Galina, don't be a fool. He doesn't love you, except as a child, his own child—or as a young sister whom he cherishes. You've grown up, you're a woman now, at least physically—but you're not ready for a serious involvement, least of all with a man like Pierre."

"Yet you were at my age!" Galina exclaimed suddenly. "You were even younger than I, weren't you? Do you think you know him so much better, that you can make him so much happier than I could? What makes you believe that, Natalia? You've hurt him and slighted him and God knows what else, and now you want to tell me that he's too much for me—but not for you?"

Natalia hid her face in her hands, and Galina saw tears trickling through her fingers and waited. "Yes," the older woman sighed, "he's too much for you. Don't avoid the obvious. When I was seventeen and fell in love with him, he was twenty-four years old! Now he's a man of forty, Galina, a man with a lifetime of disillusionments, of despairs and glories. I can understand him because I've watched him grow, and because I've learned to be with him. I've earned that right!"

"But now he doesn't love you anymore," Galina said quietly.

The finality of her words, their gravity, slapped against Natalia like a corded whip. She blinked and wet her lips. It was all so simple for Galina, so irrevocable, so black and white. "No matter what he said to you," Natalia said in a dead voice, "it isn't you he loves. It's himself. He loves himself, Galina. He hated Boris because he couldn't control him, and he hates me for the same reasons. He wants to create his own universe, and if a woman fits into his picture, he seems pleased enough. But that's not love! All these years, whenever there's been another woman, I've known it wasn't love, and I've stood by. Don't let him make a fool of you, the way he did that nice little English girl, Vendanova, or the Swiss one, Fabiana. They meant nothing to him. I was always there since the beginning!"

"But love is like life, it sometimes ends," Galina declared. She spoke softly, almost gently, and yet resolution pierced through her blue eyes, beyond her tears. Then she added in the same tone: "And he can't make a fool of me. You can't turn someone into what she isn't, and I'm no fool."

Natalia burst into the harshest laughter that Galina had ever heard.

He did not knock on her door but opened it noiselessly and entered, with a care that was contrary to his habit. She was lying on the bed, fully clothed, her face buried in her arms, and when she looked up at him suddenly, he stepped back instinctively. Her small face stared at him with tears bathing the hollow cheeks, unashamed and haggard. He raised his hand to his mouth and nervously bit his forefinger.

As he stood before her, she could not help seeing the broad shoulders slightly straining his jacket, the still slim waist, the strong legs beneath their broadcloth. His face had thickened slightly in recent months, from drinking a bit too much, she thought. But the eyes held her with the same magnetism as before, and if there was considerable gray among his tight curls, it was all the more becoming. "You haven't changed," she told him with a bitter smile.

"In what way?" The comment had startled him, quickened his response.

"In every way. What do you want now, Pierre? Haven't you caused enough damage in this household?"

He stiffened. "What I want is a divorce, Natalia." He kept his face averted to the ground, counting the seconds as they ticked by.

Finally she asked: "Just like this? No regrets, no apologies whatsoever? Just 'I want a divorce, Natalia,' as if you were saying, 'I want roast pork for dinner'? Isn't that a bit crass, even for you, Pierre?"

His black eyes flew to her face in a flare of emotion. "It was you who willed this," he said tightly.

"I? It was I who seduced a young girl in my own house, who turned her life into a positive hell? I who broke up a marriage of seven years? Who split apart a family, separating two women who loved each other?" Her tears were flowing again, and Natalia did not brush them away.

"Nobody breaks up a marriage, you know that! Our marriage was ruined almost from the beginning because you didn't want it, didn't want our daughter, and didn't love me! As for Galina's being split from you—about that, of course, I'm sorry. You were really good with her, good for her. But she had nothing to do with this. She didn't plan this. We didn't deceive you, either one of us. I never once touched her, and she loves me. And I intend to marry her, as soon as you give me this divorce. I intend to marry her in the Orthodox Church, to be my wife forever under God—in whom you profess not to believe."

"No," she cried, her voice rising with passion. "I do not

believe in Him! How could a God, any deity, have allowed a man such as you to exist, breaking everything in your path, hurting others guiltlessly? There can be no God!"

He took a deep breath, clenched and unclenched his fists. "Please," he said. "We need to discuss Tamara. Of course you know I want her with me."

"A divorce takes a long time!" she cried, sitting up completely. "And while you wait for the final decree, do you plan to rear your daughter all by yourself, or put her between you and your mistress? Did you suppose for a single minute that I would not fight for her?"

The muscles in his jaw tensed. "Galina isn't going to be my mistress," he countered brusquely. "And I'm going to use every bit of influence I can get to speed up the divorce. One year! I promise you that in one year, we won't be married even on paper! As for Tamara," he continued, looking away from Natalia, "I can give her love, which is what she needs most of all."

"You know nothing of love," she said, beginning to scream. "Tamara is one part of me you will never touch. Get out of here, Pierre! Get out of my room and get out of my house, and leave me and my daughter alone from now on!"

He watched her for a moment, watched the fevered cheeks, the brown eyes flashing with hysteria, and then he turned his back to her. His hands were trembling. "Natalia," he said quietly, "can't we keep the hatred out of this? For Galina's sake?"

"For Galina's sake. Oh, I don't hate Galina, she's only another one of your victims. I can see through you, Pierre, but she's still young and immature, in spite of having had to grow up faster than most of us. You see her as the ultimate revenge on me—it all boils down to that. She is the last remaining Kussov, and you think that by taking her from me, you have evened the score with Boris for having taken me from you. All those years of courting patrons—even Marguerite—were your manner of showing me that you too could find one of them, a Kussov to protect you! And now you have this fine young girl, the last one of the lot, and she wants you and wants to make the world fit again for you, the way Boris started to do when he cared for you! Only this time there won't be money involved, because

Galina's penniless! Nevertheless, she will protect you because you're weaker than she is, despite her youth. Boris lives on through her, and now you have her and I don't, and in this final competition you've come out the winner!" She thrust her face out at him, her eyes wild. "You see," she said breathlessly, "our marriage was a ridiculous farce. You married me to prove that you could defeat Boris on his own ground. I was the pawn in your childish chess game with a dead man. But now you've found an even more clever gambit. Not content to have surpassed him once, you've found Galina, his own flesh and blood—a girl he helped to rear, whom he cherished. What irony! Pierre has finished with the Kussovs by marrying a Kussov."

"You're mad," he said, gaping at her. "Quite mad."

She uttered a small laugh. "No," she answered. "I'm saner than you are. You're the greatest fool of them all, Pierre Riazhin. Don't you see? Don't you see at all that Boris is winning after all, you stupid man? A Kussov is going to enter your bed, is taking over your life. That's what he wanted, more than anything else in the world! Can't you hear him laughing at you from the grave? That's what comes of playing games with a master, when you're only an inept amateur."

When his hand reached the doorknob, she said, suddenly very cold: "If, however, you wake up to a life that doesn't suit you, I shall expect better behavior out of you than I received. You will not flaunt your other women, Pierre—not to Galina! She will never be subjected to the same humiliation to which you submitted me, for it isn't in her to overlook them. Don't hurt her, Pierre. Don't you dare hurt her."

When he left the room, her eyes were dry, and her lips were twisted into a grimace of complete disdain.

Chapter 29

ou were right after all," Natalia wrote on the back of one of her visiting cards to Stuart Markham, who had taken up residence at the Ritz. "The world is filled with toys that don't work, beginning with myself."

In the wake of the disaster with Pierre she spent no time delving into the whys and wherefores. It was simply over, a part of her life had ended, the way it had when Boris and Arkady had died, leaving her alone. But now she was at the helm of her own ship, in spite of the terrible storm that threatened to drown her. This time she was at the peak of her career, whereas then she had been far removed from the world of dance which made her function.

She threw herself into the creation of ballets with a new frenzy. She needed her work, hung onto it for sanity, to sustain her battered self-esteem. It was most difficult not to think of Galina. In her boudoir Natalia could not avoid the thoughts, the pain, the bitterness, the feeling of rebellion against what had happened. Galina! She had loved her, educated her, confided in her as in no one before or since. Once Boris had understood Natalia without words. Later it had been his niece. But then, Galina had not fully understood Natalia, for if she had, she would have known how very much, beneath the surface anger, Natalia had loved Pierre and needed him. No, Galina had stopped short of understanding. She had stopped short in order to feel justified in allowing what had happened to . . . happen.

Galina had passed judgment on Natalia and blamed her, and then placed her own needs first because of Natalia's mistakes.

Galina came to see her one afternoon, and Chaillou said to Natalia, averting his eyes and coughing slightly: "The princess wishes to see you, madame. What shall I tell her?"

Natalia eyed him levelly and replied: "Tell her to go to hell and not to return. This isn't her home any longer."

The old butler departed, his head wobbling like that of an ancient marionette. Natalia went to the window, parted the curtains, and looked out. Dressed in a tailored linen dress, Galina was emerging from the front stoop, her left hand over her face, the right across her breast. "Cry, then," Natalia said sarcastically, but as soon as the tall figure disappeared behind a clump of maples, her own tears came and her face twisted with blind yearning—for her or for him, she was not certain.

It was a strange adjustment. She wandered through the house, hating it for its emptiness, for the closets that held no remnants of his suits, none of her dresses. She searched for Galina's creams, for Pierre's pots of paint—and yet, deep inside, she knew that if she had found those small traces, she would have thrown them out of the window, would have sent them crashing to the floor. But still—not to have left her the slightest memento—something tangible to hate—that was the supreme insult on their part, and her frustration was nerve-rending and crimson in its vehemence.

She realized that she could not continue this way, that she must somehow pull herself together. There was her work. But how to avoid him—or how, on the contrary, not to avoid him, to search his face for clues as to what he was feeling, hoping that he would be missing her, and yet, defying all the rules, also hoping that he would make Galina happy, because in spite of everything, Galina's happiness mattered? Crazy, crazy thoughts. Natalia squeezed her hands together until the knuckles had gone very white, until the nails had gashed the soft skin. Damn her, damn them both!

At first the Riazhin scandal sent ripples of shock into the artists of the Ballet. Natalia went among them with her head held high, trying to smile. But everybody talked, whispered, wondered. Nobody knew how to behave. Smooth and debonaire, Diaghilev placed a hand on her arm and said: "Don't worry, my dear. We have no Riazhin productions on the books for the winter season."

"It wouldn't matter if you had," Natalia countered dryly. "For me he simply doesn't exist."

"He has burned all his bridges behind him, it appears," the impresario said.

"He's a stupid man," Natalia commented. But she wondered: Have they all turned against him because of me? Or is there more to it? Serge Pavlovitch has never liked me, and he does like Pierre.

Tamara was beginning to be a problem. One day, retaliating after a punishment, she burst into tears and cried: "Oh, it's your fault, I hate you. It's all because of you that Papa and Galina have left us, that they don't want to live with us anymore! They hate you, too!" Her words tore deeply into Natalia's heart.

That winter she took Tamara to Monte Carlo and set to work on a new ballet called *Les Biches*. It was a modern *Sylphides*, with no plot save that of flirtation among the idle, fashionable classes. Her young people teased and played in their pastel-colored outfits, gracefully belying the seriousness of life. Oh, Galina, Natalia thought bitterly, why didn't you tease and play with the casual ease of your generation?

Before leaving Paris she had signed the divorce agreement, which guaranteed her custody of her daughter against her promise not to contest the proceedings. She had heard that Pierre was renting a small apartment for Galina on the Île-St.-Louis so that she would be close to the Académie des Beaux-Arts, and that he himself was living in a studio in Montparnasse. Ah, so he had not yet taken her as his official mistress, Natalia had thought. He had had no such compunctions where she herself had been concerned, in Lausanne. Then he had moved into her house, purchased with Boris's money, and had fathered Tamara out of wedlock as if it were the most natural thing in the world.

Suddenly Natalia felt old, abused, emptied of all illusion and hope. Where had they all gone, the dreams and the promises that she had once held in the palm of her hand, promises fashioned by the optimism of youth and ambition? She had achieved stardom, had collected the bouquets and reappeared

for endless curtain calls. But once she had wanted the un-
knowable glory of tomorrow. Now it was Galina who felt this
way, Galina who wore Boris's pearls around her neck, who wore
Pierre's love around her heart. Galina had also stolen from
Natalia that marvelous quality of expectation. Rage shook Natalia—impotent rage. Life didn't bring its promised gifts; instead, it robbed one even of the will to hope.

She returned to Paris in the late spring, feeling aggravated
and weary and hopeless. Chaillou had kept the house going
beautifully, and all the vases had been filled with spring flowers.
But the old butler too seemed sad, listless. I have tried, Natalia
thought. I've worked and I've parented and I've entertained, but
still the core of me is burned out, dry as bone or ashes.

Chaillou brought her tea in the small parlor and her mail on
a silver tray. Tucking her feet underneath her, she slit open the
envelope from her lawyer. The final divorce was about to be
pronounced. Could it be that almost a year had passed already?
Natalia let the paper slip to the floor and held onto her china
cup with shaking fingers. Ah well, old girl, you knew it was in
the offing. But there was such a sense of the irrevocable, of the
official now. What do I do? she thought. Where do I go?

On the morning of the divorce hearing she dressed carefully,
finally deciding on a tubular navy dress that displayed her slenderness and her appeal. It was not truly the color of mourning,
but almost. She selected a broad-brimmed hat adorned with a
large navy ribbon and set off. Think about something else,
Natalia, she admonished herself. Don't think about seeing him,
what that may do to your precarious sanity. Don't wonder if
she'll be there. Oh, damn, why didn't I ask Stuart to come with
me? Stuart may not love me anymore, but he cares, he's my
friend.

At the courthouse she mounted the steps, feeling caught up
in something beyond her control, beyond her understanding.
The May sunshine filtered through the dirty casement windows,
but it was chilly inside the marble rooms. Am I in someone
else's ballet, dancing steps I don't know? she wondered. She
could feel panic swelling within her, pushing upward, upward.
She went to the bench outside the hearing room and sat down,

clutching her thin alligator bag. Her solicitor walked up, shook her hand—am I not pretty enough to him to kiss it?—and she stood up next to him, finding it difficult to breathe normally.

She felt him before seeing him, as she had done so many times before during their life together. Life together: What a farce that had been! she thought with a sudden surge of hatred. She looked up then, her lips parted over her handsome, even teeth, a female animal provoked. He was mounting the steps alone, in a gray suit, his gold watch chain elegantly dangling from one vest pocket to the other. There were slight pouches beneath his dark eyes. He seemed ill at ease, like a boy in man's clothing.

When he caught her regarding him, he stood in position, his body awkwardly rigid. Suddenly, stupidly, tears began to form in her eyes, and she swallowed hard, seeking to dispel them before they could fall. Tamara's father, her beloved father. Goddamn him to hell for all eternity.

"Natalia," he said stiffly, at length walking up to her.

"Pierre." Her eyes said, outraged: Leave me alone! What do you want?

"Natalia." The awkwardness persisted. He chewed on his lower lip, fumbled with his signet ring. She noticed that he was no longer wearing his wedding band and thought with quick, self-directed anger: But I, the fool, am still wearing mine!

"Well?" she said sarcastically. "What is this message that ties your tongue in knots?"

"I'm sorry," he stammered, reddening. "That's all, really, Natalia. I didn't mean for it to be this way between us."

She shrugged and raised her eyebrows. "How else could it be? Did you hope for my blessing?"

"Don't. Don't tease the wounds the way you always do. I just wanted to say—it's sad, isn't it, the death of a marriage?"

"Tragic. So said Henry VIII when word reached him of the execution of Anne Boleyn. And so much for clichés. You were never good with words, my dear."

They were silent, her face alive with resentment, his with acute discomfort. At length he said, almost shyly: "Natalia, she misses you. I wanted you to know that. Sometimes she wakes up crying in the night—"

An ironic light glinted in her eyes then, and they widened. "So the chaste interlude has come to an end," she murmured, the corners of her mouth turning upward. "Bravo, *mon cher.* Virgins have always been your specialty, haven't they? Beginning with me."

His face had become congested. "Shut up, Natalia!" he cried. "Don't be vulgar! If you're so curious, then I'll tell you, I'll tell you all about it, so that you won't judge her this way when she doesn't deserve it. She's terribly lonely, Natalia, and she's a mess of nerves because of you, thinking she's the cause of your pain. She felt so guilty that she hasn't been able to sleep, to function properly. And so I've spent a few nights in her living room, to be with her when she awakened, to make certain she was all right."

"How touching! I'm gratified that one of you still has a conscience. It's also nice to know I wasn't the only one who couldn't sleep. And were you there to hold my hand, Pierre? Did you ever hold my hand? Do you remember the night of Tamara's birth? Did you even feel the slightest twinge of guilt that time?"

"Why bring this up now?"

"Because you make me sick, that's why," she replied, placing her hands over her throat to contain her exploding hatred. She could feel the cords standing out on her neck, knew that she had started to sob, that more sobs were coming that seemed to scream out of her like a siren, a siren that continued even though she was certain she had shut her mouth. The solicitor was kneeling in front of her, holding her arms, and still she was shouting something, she couldn't hear what—

Pierre had disappeared into the hearing room, and the lawyer was repeating gently: "Come now, it's our turn."

To make her life worse, Natalia ran into problems with Diaghilev. He had set to work rehearsing a new ballet, *The Blue Train;* his mind could not remain for long on a certain style, and now he appeared to chase each new trend, seizing on the modern to the detriment of substance. This was an acrobatic ballet to display the charms of his new lover, Anton Dolin—and so she was parodying the sports of the twenties, as she had parodied the party habits of its young generation in *Les Biches*. Diaghilev had commissioned one of his friends, the *couturière* Chanel, to make up the bathing costumes, since the action was taking place on the beach.

She could feel the director's cold eyes on her during the rehearsals, and then the quick glances to her star, Dolin. With a start she thought: Of course! He wants Anton to take over my position. He has always wanted to turn his dancers into choreographers—the ones who slept with him, that is. She clenched her fists and took a deep breath to calm the angry feelings inside her.

She did not have much time left before the première on June 20. But she had problems in her private life. Since the divorce, a terrible nervousness had beset her. She could not sleep and her stomach would not digest a single morsel. At odd times her hands would start to shake, and sometimes she could not control her speech and uttered choppy phrases of garbled words. She was plagued with blinding headaches. But with the inevitability of the oceans' tides, deadlines pressed upon her. She did not care anymore whether the dancers and prop crew knew of her distress, whether they gossiped about it on their own. It only mattered that she continue to arrive on time at rehearsals so that Diaghilev would not have reason to smirk. This became her obsession: to keep up the façade for his sake, to protect her last remnant of self-respect. If she did not yield, it had to mean that she was not a failure.

She was lying on her bed, a cold compress over her eyes, when the door creaked open and Tamara poked her head into the semi-darkness. She had grown into a very vivid girl of seven, leggy and well balanced, with her father's proud carriage and his fine black eyes and tumbling black hair. Her complexion was swarthy but touched with a rich coral glow, and her full lips pouted above the small, delicate chin, the sole heritage from her mother. She was an intelligent girl but an obstinate one, who learned only when she wanted to, and only what interested her. Natalia saw in her daughter the same quick temper that Pierre had: With the least provocation, she could enter into a towering rage, the rage of the self-centered.

That afternoon Tamara came in on tiptoe, and Natalia felt

rather than heard her by the side of her bed. "Are you sick or sleeping?" the girl asked.

"I'm all right." Natalia sat up and took the girl's hand and smiled.

"No, you're never 'all right' anymore. You're either sick or busy, and Papa doesn't come as often to visit anymore. I'm lonely with Mademoiselle." The girl chewed sullenly on the in-side of·her mouth.

Natalia felt a rush of blood to her face, a sudden thudding in her chest. She said carefully: "I didn't know he'd ever come to visit you. Why didn't you tell me, darling?"

Tamara looked away, all at once embarrassed. "Because he asked me not to tell you. He told me it would cause all sorts of problems. But *why?* He's my father!"

Natalia's free hand lay clenched in her lap, the nails digging into her palm. "I never sent your father away," she said. "He's the one who left and who broke up the family. I don't think he should be allowed to come and go here as he pleases. It's not his home anymore—and I'm not his wife."

"But I'm still his daughter! And I want to see him! Sometimes he only comes to pick me up, and we go for a drive, or out to tea or to a matinée at the Comédie Française. You're not being fair! I don't want to lose him!"

Tamara's voice had grown sharp with suppressed sobs, and now Natalia raised her hands to her temples and, shutting her eyes against the pain, cried: "I didn't want to lose him either! Do you think *he* was being fair?"

But Tamara was running from the room, and Natalia thought: What have I done? What damage have I now compounded in this little girl?

A week before the première, Natalia came home early from a rehearsal. Perhaps, she thought, her hands trembling with this added despair, perhaps if I give her time, listen to her, try to talk with her. . . . But it had been so many years since she had been Tamara's age. She simply did not remember how it felt to be seven and to feel betrayed by one's parents. A deep, gnawing frustration permeated Natalia's whole being.

She was never mine to begin with but always Pierre's, Natalia　•

admitted, allowing Chaillou to remove her coat and handing him her little felt cloche. What use is it, she wondered dryly, to keep up with fashions when on the inside everything has been stripped? But the old *maître d'hôtel* was rubbing his chin, and murmuring: "*She*'s here, madame. We . . . I couldn't . . ."

"The princess? You let her in?" Just as he had let Pierre in behind her back?

Chaillou simply turned his eyes to a speck of dirt on the floor. He had always held a soft place in his heart for Galina, ever since her arrival over three years before. Natalia took a deep breath, steadied herself, and said: "Very well, Chaillou. Where is she?"

"She . . . they . . . are in the parlor, madame."

I have to learn to control myself better, Natalia thought as she hastened away. In front of the servants . . . no pride. . . . And all for a chit of a girl who thinks she's a woman!

She wound her way to the parlor door, which stood open. Natalia's face whitened. Tamara was sitting on an ottoman, her head in Galina's lap, and the older girl was saying, softly: "Nobody's right and nobody's wrong, my darling. In the grown-up world people don't really lie. They see the same thing differently, sometimes. Nobody hurts another person on purpose. Nobody wanted to hurt you."

"My mother doesn't love me," Tamara said.

"Yes. She loves you. She loves you and she needs you. Tamara, don't take sides. It isn't fair to anyone."

"I don't care! Mama doesn't have time for me. You always had time. Oh, Galinotchka—why can't I live with you? I want to so much!"

Galina raised the child's face with her index finger. "I want it, too. But I'll come to see you. And someday you can come see us."

"Don't play the saint, Galina," Natalia cut in sharply, entering the room. Galina reached for her purse and clutched it to her knees defensively, and Tamara jumped up and ran out, brushing past her mother on the way. Natalia did not sit down but remained, examining Galina, whose rigid, white face seemed frozen. She was trapped by the other woman's brown eyes riveted on her.

"Why did you come here?" Natalia asked, her voice a low tremble.

Galina said nothing, but her eyes filled with tears, and her knuckles on the bag were white with tension. Finally she said: "I wanted to see you."

"Is anything wrong?" For an instant, the briefest instant, Natalia's face betrayed the old concern, and Galina's lips parted, suddenly hopeful. Then the older woman looked away and reached for an enamel box on the coffee table. She sat down on the sofa and extracted a cigarette, then carefully lit it. The habit was still new and shocked her niece. Silently, Natalia took a puff and regarded Galina with expectation.

"I came to tell you something," Galina said. Her eyes went to the carpet and remained there, abstracted. "We—Pierre and I—are going to Brussels next week. The banns. . . . You only have to live there six weeks."

"So. You're going to be married."

"Yes." Galina looked at Natalia then and stopped trembling. "I felt that you should know," she added.

"Well. That was very brave of you, Galina." Natalia could feel the pulse beating in her throat, heard a din in her ears, and she closed her eyes and brought the cigarette gratefully to her lips. Then a scarlet anguish rushed into her, and she sat up brusquely, her eyes widening. "Damn it, Galina," she cried, "why couldn't you have been this brave before? Why couldn't you have told me in the beginning, when you first thought you were falling in love with him?"

"I thought that I would be able to handle it myself," the girl said miserably.

"Yourself! Look what a mess you've made of things, handling them yourself!" Natalia felt tears coming and brushed them angrily aside. "Oh, God! If you felt you loved him that much, why didn't you just sleep with him and leave his life alone? Like that little English dancer? She had him, I suppose he liked her well enough—but she didn't break open his marriage. She had the courage to stay on the outside!"

"He didn't want me that way," Galina responded dully, numbed by Natalia's vehemence.

"Don't be so sure. Pierre's a very sensual man, and I don't

think he'd turn any woman away from his bed if she were attractive. No—admit it, Galina—*you* were the one who wanted marriage. And Pierre, like any middle-aged fool, felt absurdly flattered by how much you cared for him. He didn't consider his daughter, or—or me! Because Pierre *did* love me, Galina. And love like that doesn't evaporate in one day."

"You had your chance to make him happy," the young woman said, and now tears streamed over her cheeks. "Don't make me out the only bad one in this. You're the one who made Pierre sneak behind the scenes to be with Tamara. Is that fair to *her?*"

They were both standing now, staring at each other, bathed in tears. Natalia shook her head, threw up her hands—and stepped toward Galina. The young woman began to sob, almost hysterically now, and Natalia pressed her arms around her, held Galina's head against her own neck, felt the other girl's tears. Then she pushed her lightly away. "God, God," she whispered. "Get out of here, Galina. Get out and get married and live happily ever after. But get out *now* . . . please."

When she heard the front door closing, Natalia fell across the sofa and smothered her face in the bright cushions so that Chaillou and the other servants would not hear the shattering expression of her grief.

Natalia was tired after the première of *The Blue Train*. Dolin had performed remarkably well: "Beau Gosse," the libretto had called him, "the handsome kid." Now all of Parisian society would nickname him this. And he had managed to tell her, somewhat shyly, that he had no desire to encroach on her new profession: "I shall always be a dancer," he'd said. "I can't make ballets."

Now Natalia sat alone in her dressing room, removing her makeup. She had danced the part of a tennis player in the production, and was still clothed in the short tunic outfit. There was a soft, discreet knock on the door, and rather irritably she said: "Yes, yes, come in!" She was seated at her makeup table removing the paint on her face and turned to look at her intruder. Her hand, holding a cotton wad, remained in midair. Pierre had slid into the small room, a strange figure whose black suit made the silver in his hair all the more startling. He was somewhat pale, holding a walking stick in both his hands and twirling it nervously.

"You came to the show?" she asked, amazement overcoming her other emotions. "But—why?"

"Out of habit, perhaps?" He seemed uncomfortable as he sat down, so she turned back to the vanity and applied cold cream to her cheeks. "You're the best ballerina alive today," he added.

"Damn it, Pierre! Couldn't you have had the common decency not to show yourself? Everyone must have seen you come into this room!" Her brown eyes were blazing at him from the mirror. She was starting to tremble, and now she breathed once, twice to control herself. "Of course, our colleagues all think there's something romantic about your situation, don't they? I mean, here you've left one woman, whom they've all known for years, for that same woman's young and well-born niece, the niece also of their onetime co-director. It's made you quite the dashing figure of a modern Casanova, hasn't it?"

He shifted uncomfortably on the chair, but without taking his eyes from her. Then he shrugged. "I didn't want that," he declared, a roughness in his throat. "It never had to come to that."

She closed her hands together and turned slightly, raising her brows. "Oh? You mystify me."

Color rose in his cheeks, and he stood up, clenching his fists to his thighs. "You made it all so easy!" he cried. "You never— you never fought, never fought for me, never asked me not to leave! It all seemed a confirmation of what I'd been thinking: that actually, I hadn't meant all that much to you, that you could let me go with such . . . such a lack of passion. And if she loved me and you didn't—"

The words hung in the moist, hot air between them. Then she said in a clear, crisp voice, applying a sterile wad of cotton to the tip of her nose: "You'd better go, Pierre. Galina tells me you're leaving tomorrow for Brussels. I suppose she's home packing and could use your help."

"You're not going to say anything to me about my wedding?" he asked, hovering near the door.

Her resolve broke then, and she whispered: "What more can

possibly be said between us at this point, Pierre? I'm the woman who didn't love you enough."

Diaghilev's London agent, Wollheim, wrote in his letter: "My dear Natalia, my discussions with Sir Oswald Stoll concerning the liquidation of the Ballet's debt and the instigation of a new season this coming winter are stalling badly. For some reason with which I am not familiar, he has indicated that he would consider dealing with you. Can you come?"

She smiled. Boris would be amused, she thought: I am wanted as a diplomat in the affairs of Serge Pavlovitch. But Paris was beginning to drain her, and this would be a good way to clear the air between her and Diaghilev. If need be, she could make herself as indispensable to the Ballets Russes as her first husband had been. She could match wits with Diaghilev— or with Oswald Stoll.

In London she had lunch with Sir Oswald at the Savoy Grill. It was the first time she had seen him since her divorce, and she had dressed with casual elegance to demonstrate that she did not care what he might have learned about her rather sordid situation. She would appear free of stain, above it all. She wore a simple pleated skirt with a cowl-necked blouse and long gold chains: fashionably understated, and perfect for a British mind.

"Our last venture was a disaster," Stoll said, carefully dissecting a piece of châteaubriand. "Seizing the properties hardly helped me at all, my dear Madame Oblonova. Why should I consider another season? Diaghilev is a madman. He distrusts the carpenters and the costume makers, and he pays none of them for fear of being cheated. And so, in the end, it is my reputation that suffers—as well as my bank account."

"I understand. But Serge Pavlovitch can deliver a good product. I believe he's grown wiser these past few months. Still—he must be made to reimburse you. You can make him do so from the receipts of the new ballets. Another season with you would help considerably to reestablish the financial balance of the Ballets Russes." She dabbed at her lower lip, took a swallow of wine, and said, smiling: "But Sir Oswald, I am not going to do business with you in secret this time. I shall not offer you money, which Diaghilev would discount at once if he knew of it. No. I shall act quite openly, and he will have to take notice. I shall offer you my house in Lausanne as collateral. If he fails to repay you for his previous debt, and if he cannot recuperate a new advance for this coming season—then by legal contract between you and me, you will seize my Swiss property. How does that suit you?"

"You are either extremely confident in Monsieur Diaghilev, or your devotion is beyond reason," Stoll commented. He regarded Natalia with a level gaze. "But I cannot believe that you, madame, ever lose sight of reason. Therefore let me tell you that your faith has convinced me."

"My faith . . . and my house," she added, raising her glass.

Then she thought, narrowing her eyes: Our lives are separate now for good, Pierre Riazhin—both in the professional and private sectors.

Chapter 30

"adame is practicing in the rehearsal room," Chaillou announced in a tone of slight disdain. Stuart Markham smiled beneath his mustache. It was evident that to Chaillou the American writer, whose suits were always one year out of fashion, was not on a par with Count Boris Kussov (whom Chaillou had known only by reputation) and that flamboyant painter of the *tout Paris*, Natalia's ex-husband, Pierre. To Chaillou their divorce had been tantamount to the Dreyfus Affair or the scandal caused in English circles by Alfred Douglas and Oscar Wilde: It was unspeakable and would never be lived down.

The rehearsal room, so elegantly named by Chaillou, was simply the converted master bedroom, which Natalia, with a dual objective in mind, had equipped with two *barres* and a floor that tilted upward like a ballet stage. She had needed a room in which to practice and choreograph, and now that Tamara's dance lessons had increased in length and frequency, this need had seemed more urgent. She had also felt compelled to cleanse herself of Pierre, to rid the house of any last reminders of his previous presence there. And so the rehearsal room had come into being. Stuart now went there, oblivious to Chaillou's shocked stare: Madame was practicing with Mademoiselle Tamara!

Through the open door Stuart saw Mademoiselle Pichenet at the piano, giving a less than inspired rendition of a Chopin nocturne. He stopped and watched. Tamara, black curls falling

down her neck in childish disarray, was standing at the lower
barre, her small body gracefully erect, the round buttocks firm,
the waist already defined, her right arm extending out, the
fingers relaxed. She was wearing a red leotard and red woolen
leg warmers.

"All right now, *tendu,*" Natalia said. She stood in front of
Tamara, and Stuart could see her face, its large, deep eyes
gently on her daughter, her hair youthfully bobbed, her skin
pale, almost anemic. There was something nakedly vulnerable
about watching her when she was unaware, her brown leotard
molded to her small, slender form like a second skin, more real
than the first. The absurd black leg warmers made her appear
bottom-heavy, a common pitfall of all dancers.

Natalia cocked her head to one side as Tamara pointed her
right foot out, and Mademoiselle's music started up again.
Then the mother held up her hand, and the piano stopped.
"Look now," Natalia said. "Your turnout isn't quite strong
enough. Here"—and she went behind the child and took hold
of her calf, repositioned it, and laid the small foot back on the
hardwood planks. "All right?"

Tamara nodded, and Natalia motioned for the governess to
resume her playing. But at that moment Stuart decided to break
the atmosphere and entered the room. He saw the startled, then
suddenly joyful look on Natalia's face, a quick flush in her
cheekbones, and then the quiet grace of her steps to him, the
small kiss on the cheek. "We didn't hear you," she said, smiling. She always conveyed an unspoken aura of intimacy, of
having let him into a private circle, that had lately made his
stomach contract at odd times.

Tamara's face turned toward him, too, and he was once more
confronted with the child's vivid beauty, so dark, so alive. He
read initial gladness followed by uncertainty, and then she too
came to him, almost shyly. "Hello, Mr. Markham," she said.
"Did you see me dance?"

"Yes, I did," he replied, mingling his fingers in the curls on
her head, while Natalia watched, stabbed suddenly by the poignant memory of her own oft-repeated gesture with Pierre's
hair. "You're very serious, aren't you, Tam, about becoming a
ballerina?" he asked.

The child's features broke into a wide, toothy grin. "Oh, yes," she said. "When I'm ten, I'm going to try out for the *petits rats* at the Opéra. But Mother says I must be very good. It's almost as hard as when she went for her entrance exams at the Mariinsky!"

"That, Stu, is our favorite bedtime story," Natalia said and laughed. "Now come along, Tamara. It's tea time."

"Do I have to take it alone in my room with Mademoiselle?" Tamara asked, flashing her mother a look of sullen rebelliousness. "Can't I have it in the parlor with Mr. Markham?"

Natalia hesitated. "I don't want any white mustaches," she remarked. "And you were messy at lunch. But it's all right," she said, her voice catching. "Wash your hands and come."

When Tamara had eagerly scampered out with her governess, Stuart took Natalia's face in his hands and examined it, raising his brows. She laughed, shaking herself free. It was always this way: tentative, questing, unsure, sparring. Now he took her by the shoulders and did not let go. Slowly the laughter, the playfulness died away. Her white face seemed to recede, to close off. Her eyes gave off an unreadable glow. He pulled her toward him and she did not resist, but neither did she respond. Finally he dropped his hands to his sides and shook his head. Taking his hand, she whispered: "Don't go away."

"Not without my tea," he retorted, squeezing the cold fingers. "And besides, Tam's expecting me. For some reason the little ruffian likes me."

"Both of us do," Natalia answered quietly. Her fingers twitched slightly in his hand, and then she extricated them and made a pretense of scratching her collarbone. She pushed open the door to the parlor and cried, suddenly very brightly: "My! This is wonderful. Look, Stu! Chaillou has made a new fire for us!"

"My, my, indeed. Miracles never cease in this household, do they?" he commented, his green-gold eyes twinkling, but though she colored somewhat, she did not acknowledge his remark. She concentrated with great seriousness on slicing a thick, marbled pound cake.

Tamara came in, dressed in a new, frilly outfit of lace and flounces, her black hair in ribbons. "Oh!" she exclaimed, throwing herself with a startling lack of grace stomach first on an ottoman. "My favorite! D'you like it too, Mr. Markham? Our cook makes it. It's chocolate and rum-flavored."

"I'm starved, too," Natalia said. "Be careful this time, won't you? Be a lady!"

She served her guest and her daughter, then sliced a thinner piece for herself. From beneath her eyelids she watched them, watched the warm colors of the room swirling around her. Tamara was saying to Stuart: "You know what's nice? When you promise to come, you always do. Some grown-ups promise lots of things that never happen. If I did that, Mother would punish me. But who punishes a grown-up?"

"Some people think there is a special being called God, and that He punishes us all. I don't really know, Tam. I suppose all unkind people are eventually punished by their own bad consciences. Something inside them doesn't let them forget."

"My papa and my friend Galina are going to have a baby," Tamara declared. She spooned some cake onto her fork with abrupt belligerence, and the crumbs flew off her plate. Natalia did not say a word, but her eyes remained on her daughter's face, watchful.

"Let's all go ice skating tomorrow," Stuart suggested. "What do you say, ladies?"

"Mama and I aren't real ladies," Tamara interposed. "We just pretend, don't we?" She had said "Mama," not the more distant, adult "Mother," which she most often used.

Natalia started to laugh. "Too bad for our gallant Harvard blue-blood," she said. "He'll have to put up with us all the same."

Natalia adjusted the netted veil over her small face and made certain that the little black velvet hat fit her perfectly. For this strange occasion she had carefully chosen a gray wool suit bordered with silver fox fur and ankle-strap high heels of black patent leather. She had told her driver to wait in a café and had walked up to the tall house on the narrow Rue de Lille, across the Seine on the Left Bank. It was a long, picturesque street filled with small arches, balconies with flowers, and old restaurants with antique signs jutting above them. These Left Bank streets made one think back to the lusty days of France, the days of Louis XIII and Richelieu, of wenching and duels, of pestilence and sweat and plots and counterplots, of peasants and illiteracy and the intrigues of the court. Natalia's heel caught on a cobble, and then she pressed a shining brass button and passed through a heavy black wooden carriage entrance into a small courtyard, somewhat dismal but well kept and also cobbled. In front of her was the house: the apartment was on the third and top floor. She now rang the doorbell.

A rather dour-faced maid, in bombazine and white lace, let her in. "Madame is expecting you, but she is resting. If Madame will follow me?" Natalia nodded, and looked around her. They were standing in a beamed, white hall, adorned with four large, antique mirrors. In the corner was a Chinese vase filled with dried wildflowers, arranged to greet the eye with a splash of color. Natalia walked behind the servant into a dark passageway, hung with blue and gold wallpaper, and into a large, airy salon, where she was left alone.

The salon had one enormous window, all of stained glass. Below it was a bench upholstered in green velvet, and to the left an alcove where a wide couch of lighter green stood flanked by tiny English Queen Anne tables. On each one lay a special knickknack: an antique music box, a cut-glass paperweight, and a miniature globe. Over the mantlepiece was another mirror and two vases from Thailand, adorned with coiling dragons. A bookcase was enclosed on either side behind glass panels. Natalia sat down on the sofa and tilted her head to examine the painting above it. Yes, of course, that was natural: the mermaid on her rock, overlooking the emerald sea, was perfect, her blue eyes mirroring joy, and peace, but also a certain fear and shyness, evidenced by the waves of golden hair that covered one round breast ever so gently, leaving only its twin exposed to the rays of the setting sun. How could he have failed?

She heard a rustling noise and looked up. Galina stood holding on to the doorjamb, and something caught in Natalia's throat. The girl's eyes were on her, large and full of that old serenity, the age-old wisdom of the elderly and those who have borne witness. Beneath a new coiffure of upswept hair that coiled into a full chignon on top of her head, her face appeared less round, more linear. The willowy shape, in its simple tailored dress of royal blue, only hinted at new plumpness just below the bustline. Where we all first show, Natalia thought. Three months . . .

She rose suddenly and took two steps toward Galina. For a moment they stared at each other, each hesitating. Then, without looking at Galina's face, Natalia pressed her arms around her, held her—and quickly released her. "You're not doing so well?" she asked.

Galina uttered one short nervous giggle, then stopped it with a hand to her throat. She shook her head lightly. "It's nothing. It's worth it, Natalia. Just dizziness, nausea. I'll be fine next month, you'll see."

"Have you informed your doctor about your mother? Her pelvis was very small. That's why she was told not to have other children after you were born."

"It'll be all right, really. I'm not worried. I want this child, Natalia," The blue eyes were gently reassuring, bright with serene joy. Natalia bit her lip and said nothing. "I want this chold." How he must have exulted, hearing these words! Another one of my mistakes, she added bitterly.

"That's wonderful, Galina," she said. "You're very good with children. And Pierre will take care of you." Her eyes blinked rapidly, like fluttering butterflies. "Galina," she continued, "it's about a child that I've come today. You must have wondered why this sudden visit."

"I was happy that you had at last decided to come. It didn't matter why. When I came to you last time, I had hoped . . ." She let the sentence hover in midair.

Natalia shrugged. "Well. You must understand, Galina, that there's been no person in my life about whom I've felt so good and so bad at the same time. I loved you the way a woman can only love another woman. I trusted you. And then, of course, I hated you. Now . . . well, things are different. You can't expect the good to return to the way it was. I wish you all the best, but our lives don't touch anymore, except in a single area. And that's Tamara. That's why I came."

Galina's face had set, a glaze had come over her eyes. Now her mouth worked, and she leaned forward. "What's wrong with Tamara?" she asked.

"Everything. She feels betrayed, Galina. You know how she always felt about her father: He was perfect, brilliant and perfect; and I was human, and negative, and strict. You were her older sister. When Pierre . . . left me, she wanted above all to go live with you, her two favorite loves. I was the mean one, the barrier. I suppose I'm much to blame, because I was never a mother by choice, and because I had my own life to deal with. But I did try. It's difficult to keep trying when a child resists you and prefers the other parent, the one who's hurt you beyond all hurts, torn up your self-esteem. Still, I tried, because I loved her and she was my child. And very slowly she's come around. She's disoriented and afraid and confused, but at least she no longer detests me. We dance together. She wants to become a *petit rat*. When we don't quarrel about the mess in her room, we even get along fairly well together. So you see, here we've been attempting to rebuild our lives, the two of us, but rather in vain: She feels that you and Pierre have abandoned her, that there's no room in your lives for her anymore, now that you're expecting a baby of your own."

Natalia had been speaking fast, the words pouring out, for she had been afraid to pause, afraid that if she did, her courage would vanish, her resolve seem silly, and her presence here, in this apartment where he now lived and which they had turned together into a home, would make her ill. "Tamara misses her father," she added. "I know I resented his visits when I first learned of them. But I never told him not to come! It was his idea to go behind my back, to hide his comings and goings from me. Still—I didn't think he would drop her, just like that!"

"Pierre adores her, he always has," Galina said, her tone somewhat hurt and defensive. "He used to go to the house, to see her, as you know. But then after the marriage it was more difficult. We had to move into—this place. Then I became pregnant. He's had commissions, right now this canvas for Winnie de Polignac—and then, too, Natalia, your attitude was less than encouraging."

"Then he should have written me, or called me. She is more important than my feelings, or his, or even yours. Why didn't he get in touch with me or inquire about his daughter? Why didn't you?" Now Natalia's face had reddened.

"Because your words to me, that last time in your house, were plain enough. You thought that I was bad for Tamara!"

Natalia swallowed. "All right. Look. Enough of that. I was bitter, you were offended. Do you or do you not wish to be involved in Tamara's life? Because if you do, this is the moment to step in. It can't wait any longer."

Galina pressed tremulous fingers to her forehead and closed her eyes. She looked suddenly very frail, exhausted. Natalia sighed and rose, and went to her at the opposite end of the long sofa. She bent over her and touched her face, with quick, deft strokes. Galina looked up, but Natalia tossed her head impatiently. "Lean forward," she said brusquely.

Then, climbing behind the girl onto her knees, Natalia applied her fingers to the nape of Galina's neck, and began to massage her, smoothly, rhythmically. Silent tears welled into the blue eyes, fell on her folded hands. Natalia rubbed between the shoulder blades, applying soft pressure. She moved down to the small of Galina's neck, made little circles up and down, Something seemed to break inside Galina, and Natalia felt rather than heard the sob, through the tense muscles. Her hands stopped moving, remained poised over Galina's shoulders.

Natalia felt paralyzed by Galina's tears, by the force of her distress. She wanted to pick up her bag and run, forgetting Tamara, forgetting everything. What was she doing in their home, anyway? She felt ashamed, embarrassed, afraid. Flee, Natalia, this is not your concern, she thought, and then, all at once, she realized that she was lifting Galina backward, toward herself, that her hands were firmly locked around the girl's waist, that Galina, like a child had sagged against her breast, and that she was rocking with her back and forth, back and forth, in the eternal gesture of comfort.

"It's all right, my darling," Natalia whispered. "It doesn't matter anymore, it doesn't matter. You can love him freely. I don't love him anymore, it's all right." She buried her chin in Galina's hair, kissed it soothingly, and repeated, with muted wonder: "I don't love him anymore."

Hours later, when dusk had filtered through the brilliant panes of indigo and gold, Pierre came home and went to the salon to find his wife. The sight which met him glued him in place, stupefying him. Galina lay sleeping in Natalia's arms, her face strangely restful, and Natalia, her arms around her, was silently waiting, immobile. He noticed her almond eyes first speaking to him, holding him at bay.

Later he thought to himself, resentful again: It was like being an intruder in the Amazon, where no man is welcome.

Natalia was packing. First she would be going to Monte Carlo, and then to London. In the spring the Salle Garnier in Monaco's turretted Casino belonged exclusively to the Ballets Russes, but in winter it belonged to the opera, when, by their contract, the Russians lent their dancers to operatic productions in return for a "home" in which to rehearse for their own spring shows. This season Diaghilev would be putting on two operas by Gounod, *Doctor in Spite of Himself* and *Philemon and Baucis*, and it had fallen to Natalia to choreograph them. After that she would join Diaghilev in London, where he was preparing a season of ballet at the Coliseum.

It was one week since Pierre had come upon Natalia in his apartment, and now he strode into her house, using his old key. Chaillou greeted his master with timid glee and told him where to find Natalia, in her boudoir. It did not occur to the old butler that to send Pierre thus unannounced to his mistress was no longer his job.

It jolted Pierre to walk in on Natalia while she stood holding up colored hose, and asking her maid to pack them for her. There were beads of perspiration on his ex-wife's upper lip, and she was clad only in her dressing gown, the Chinese one with the embroidered dragons woven into it. He stood incongruously aside and coughed.

Natalia turned around, and so did the maid, who clapped a hand to her mouth. Natalia's lips parted, the color leaving her face; then she appeared to regain her composure and said briskly, "You may come back later, Giselle." The girl left the room and Natalia sat down in an armchair, swinging one leg over the other. When the dressing gown slid from her knee to reveal one clear, bare leg, she ignored it and asked: "What brings you here?"

"You're leaving for Monaco, aren't you?" he asked rather roughly. He sat down on the edge of her bed, feeling ridiculous in this room, which literally breathed of her, which had seen so many nights with her, witnessed such violent arguments. The contact with her bed, her sheets, burned him. He rose and began to pace the room to relieve his nervousness. He could not look at her and knew that she was enjoying his discomfiture. Suddenly his hatred flared up and he cried: "How could you claim that I've stopped loving Tamara? It's you who never wanted her!"

"That's old news, Pierre. Can't we progress from that point? She's here, and she's ours, and we both love her. How many babies do you think are conceived as she was, haphazardly, unplanned? Hundreds of thousands, in and out of wedlock! But most of them are loved, nevertheless! You say that she's so precious to you: Prove it then."

"I intend to. First of all, when you go to Monte Carlo and then to London, I'd like to take her. I'm entitled to her, damn it! She'll see a great deal more of me and Galina than she would of you, with all your bloody rehearsals. And that American fellow, what's his name? The one you spend your time with. I don't want him alienating Tamara from me, d'you understand? She's not to be a part of that!"

"A part of what, Pierre?" Natalia asked icily.

"You know what I mean! The man was your lover years ago. It's obvious he's fit right back into his old shoes, that you kept them for him in readiness, dusted and shined in your closet."

Natalia started to laugh, succumbing with sensual abandon to the ripple of mirth that cascaded out of her. Finally, she said, gasping: "My gentle Stu! He has 'been here' for Tamara, has come to watch her dance, has taken her to tea and to matinées of children's plays." Then, regarding him with infinite disdain, she remarked: "It's not your business what I do. I'm not your wife. But I am Tamara's mother, and I've thought of her. I don't know how I feel about your taking her. She hardly knows you anymore. Stu knows her better!"

White-faced, his black eyes glittering, Pierre said from between clenched teeth: "Why are you taunting me, Natalia? Why now?"

She rose and shook herself easily, the folds of the gown slipping back into place. It was a graceful gesture of nonchalance, which caught at his throat the way only small gestures can. She looked up and was startled, for he stood poised, like a leopard ready to pounce, his eyes glued to her, eager to devour. She could not move. Then he seized her around the waist and pulled her to him, his fingers hurting the small of her back, her heart beating against him. He parted his lips over the white perfection of his large teeth, and drew nearer. Inside she felt as though a hot liquid were running through her veins, and still she could not move, stood dumbly in his arms.

And then, abruptly, she stepped back and slapped him directly across the face, so hard that her fingers made a red imprint on his cheek, while he reeled sideways, blinking tears. "I am not Vendanova," she said, her voice like a cutting blade. "Just because your wife is pregnant . . ."

Turning away, his hand on his cheek, he murmured in a monotone: "I'm sorry, Natalia. It wasn't that. It wasn't that at all. It was this room, it was . . . us, you. I can't put it all away behind us. It's there, inside me."

"Well then, you will have to learn to exorcise it by yourself," she declared. "You've made your bed, now don't go sleep in someone else's. You're out of my life, Pierre, blessedly out of it. Now stay out!"

"I wish you'd never existed, Natalia," he said and opened the door.

I am not "I" anymore, I am "we," Galina thought, holding her hand over the budding growth of her stomach. We. . . . He has given me of himself, and I have put my own self in, and the seed has grown and will be a person in his own right, in her own right. She breathed the winter air in deeply, trying to feel it, trying to sense the elements through her pores, so that this moment would last forever.

"I wish it could be like before," Tamara said to her, taking her hand. "You and I, and Papa and my mother. When you have this baby, what will it be? My brother? Or some kind of cousin?"

"Your half-brother or half-sister. Will you help me take care of it, Tamarotchka?"

The little girl shrugged and kicked a stone. "I don't know. Babies are boring." She looked into the distance, her eyes narrowing. "But maybe this one will die, like my brother Arkady."

Galina stopped in her tracks, her feet crunching the gravel of this forgotten path in the Bois de Boulogne. She blinked slowly. "Tamara, that's a dreadful thought. Why were you thinking it?"

"Papa often told Mother that Uncle Boris—was he my uncle, too?—carried weak blood. Well, you're part of his family, aren't you? The Kussovs. Everybody talks and talks about them. Papa said that about his blood, so why not yours, too?"

Galina's heart was pounding ferociously, and without thinking, she backtracked to a small bench and fell into it, unseeing. Tamara ran up to her, suddenly contrite. "I'm sorry, Galinotchka," she said, putting her hand on the older girl's arm. "It was just something I heard."

But Galina could not answer. A horrid fear had taken hold of her, was pushing into her, toward the core of her being. To Pierre she was in many ways only a Kussov, a symbol. A symbol of what, though? If Tamara could remember isolated phrases, why couldn't Galina? A word here and there among Pierre and his various associates: Bakst, Benois, an irritated Igor Stravinsky, Diaghilev. Yes, something like that. A comment about Diaghilev? No, it hadn't been that at all, it had been Cocteau, teasing Pierre one evening at Weber, just the two of them sketching amusing things on a tablecloth. They hadn't seen her coming, and Jean had said, laughing: "Well, our immaculate count certainly had us fooled when he married Natalia. We'd always rather supposed that he was keeping you!" Pierre's features had darkened, grown that purplish crimson hue that always frightened her, and then Cocteau had lightly shrugged and said:

"Come now, there are worse fates for a man than to be kept by Boris Kussov."

I didn't understand. I never thought to ask about this, Galina now realized, horror-struck. Pierre and her uncle, Natalia's husband. But now it made sense, it fit, somehow. Boris Kussov, the missing link. He loves me because of Boris, she thought, despair filling her, her hands pressed together inside her muff. He wanted something out of the Kussovs. Boris is an obsession to him—because they were lovers, or because one of them wanted it and the other didn't? But—which one? Did it matter? I don't care! Galina cried silently. I don't give a damn if he slept with Boris or with Natalia, or with twenty men and two hundred women. But I care about us, about him today, about whether he still loves me, or whether I have already disappointed him. If he married me to make a child with the Kussovs, then it isn't me, it isn't me he loves, but a false, gilded image of me! An image that is bound to be better, more perfect than I am.

He has never stopped loving Natalia. I should have known. He thinks he loves me, but he loves her and wants to be with a Kussov so desperately that he'll take me, because I'm the only one left! He wants to make a Kussov baby. But I love him in spite of this, I love him with all my heart, I love him even if his own love for me is flawed and incomplete.

Tamara was tugging at her sleeve, and Galina looked down at the small girl in her red woolen coat and fur hat, from which black curls were tumbling. She was so like her father! Galina's heart rose on a pure wave of love, and she touched Tamara's cheek. "It's boring just to walk," the little girl said. "Let's do something!"

But Galina, heavy and frozen by her thoughts and feelings, could not form the words to answer. Tamara made a face and sat down beside her, fussing with her buttons. She looked around her, at the bleak sky, at the tops of the pines and naked maples. "Hey!" she suddenly cried, "I have an idea! I'll bet if I climbed that tree—the tall one over there—I could see all of Paris!" Her face looked alive and quick, and then it fell, moodily. "But you won't be able to come with me," she said. "Then it won't be so much fun."

Galina blinked, feeling dizzy and disoriented, and Tamara

took her hand and pressed it. "That's all right, Galinotchka," she said. "I know you're not feeling good. I'll climb up all by myself. Watch me!" She jumped up in a burst of enthusiasm, slid on a patch of ice, and ran toward a tall pine tree laden with powdery snow. She waved to Galina and began to hoist her agile form up the corrugated trunk.

Bewildered, Galina looked at the red coat, at the curls, and rose unsteadily. "No!" she called out. "It's dangerous, Tamara! Come back here!" but the words whistled away on a gust of wind, and the child continued to climb with the ease of her strong dancer's body. Galina walked over to the tree and stood below it, dark in her mink coat and hat sprinkled with white snowflakes. Above her Tamara was swinging gracefully from limb to limb, moving up just in time to avoid snapping off the weaker branches. Snow fell all around Galina as Tamara shook it off the tree.

"It's fun up here!" Tamara cried. She threw her fur cap down in triumph, and a twig caught it, balancing it precariously. Galina shivered inside her coat and drew it more closely around her. "Come back down!" she shouted.

Then, all at once, she heard a piercing shriek: "GALINA!" and saw Tamara flailing her arms wildly, her body toppling backward, the branch cracking in the bleak light. "Grab the next one!" Galina cried, but Tamara could not hear her, she was falling, her voice one long wail of terror. Her foot caught on a limb, her hand seized a dead two-inch outgrowth, and it snapped off, falling to the ground at Galina's feet. The red coat appeared among the green pine branches and the white snow, and Tamara was tossed down like a bird catapulted from its nest, crimson like a cardinal.

Galina began to scream, slipped on the ice and remained there, unable to move. Tamara's horrible cries had stopped now, and someone was holding Galina, trying to raise her from the frozen patch of grass and mud. Somebody else had run to the back of the tree, was kneeling down.

"Pierre! Pierre!" Galina cried, and only then did tears start to form in the corners of her eyes, wide with shock.

PART V

Encore

ven before she opened the telegram, Natalia knew that it would mean a loss, still another loss, another calamity. She stood in the large rehearsal room of the Salle Garnier in the Monte Carlo Opera House, in leg warmers and a long-sleeved leotard, and set down her baton to tear open the envelope. Around her the dancers scattered to the walls, feeling the tension, the scent of disaster.

At the last moment before reading it, she turned to Serge Diaghilev who stood behind her, and, her back gracefully erect, she handed the paper to him. As if from a far distance, she saw him approach the *chef d'orchestre*, who was standing by the piano, and speak to him *sotto voce*. He caught her looking at him and averted his eyes in sudden discomfort.

Naked dread filled her then. Outside it was lightly snowing, but the Riviera scents assailed her nevertheless: jasmine, sea kelp, lavender. Diaghilev was gently but firmly pushing her into his car.

Natalia said nothing. When Diaghilev was ready, he would speak to her, she knew. As the driver wound down toward Beaulieu, the impresario removed his monocle, polished it, reinserted it, and said: "She's alive, Natalia. That's the important thing. She fell from a tree, your little Tamara—but she's still alive. They have her in the hospital at Lariboisière now."

"My God!" she cried. Somehow she had not thought it might be Tamara. Not Tamara, who was so healthy, so sturdy, so resilient. So much like— "How bad is she?" she whispered.

"Not good, Natalia. Broken arm and leg, concussion. Three damaged vertebrae."

Natalia swallowed. Examining the windowpane through a blur, she said almost inaudibly: "The spine. Will she be paralyzed? And a concussion? Tell me, Serge Pavlovitch!"

Placing a firm hand on her shoulder, the impresario simply shook his head. "We'll have to see when we get there," he told her.

They left the taxicab in the Rue Amboise Paré and walked through a carriage entrance. The first courtyard was large and square, with a center stage surrounded by flowers in a trim enclosure. All around it the building rose to three stories, the first an open gallery supported by narrow pillars and giving the impression of a cloister. The windows were large, painted white.

Natalia absorbed these images without thinking, but, once at the office of registry, her face went dead white and her lips took on a blue, pinched look. Diaghilev tightened his arm about her and said in a low voice: "It's all right. This isn't like Arkady. You have to face this, Natalia. You have to face it now." But it was the same! she thought. Couldn't he see that?

"Why did you accompany me all the way to Paris? All the way here?" she asked him hoarsely.

"I wanted the personal satisfaction of knowing that you were going to pull through. Old friends are important to me, Natashenka."

She blinked at him, unbelieving. "Old friends?"

He smiled then. "We'll discuss it later," he said smoothly.

They walked to the second floor, through an enormous white room filled with narrow metal cots and sick people, at whom Natalia could not look. Her legs carried her out of fear, out of panic that if she did not hurry, she would be ill in the common room. Diaghilev kept pace with her. To the right were two small private rooms, and a nurse, looming out of nowhere like a ghost, ushered them into the farthest one. Diaghilev remained discreetly outside. He, too, abhorred the sight of blood and found it difficult to deal with.

The room was small, painted ivory more than halfway up the walls, then white, with a thin red stripe separating the two colors. Natalia took note of these details, as well as the neat white lacquered side table, the wooden chair, and the wicker armchair. Then her eyes moved up to the cot, and they widened, her lips parting dryly. Tamara was not lying on the bed, she was suspended just above it by a series of pulleys, and her black eyes were bruised, and in her skull were two screws.

Natalia uttered a small cry and then, to Diaghilev's horror, she slid noiselessly to the floor.

She sat on the chair, her hands folded quietly, watching the unconscious girl in her odd contraptions. Of course, she'll make it, she thought. She'll make it because she's my daughter, because we're stronger than that, both of us. Then Natalia glanced at the legs, and winced. *Petit rat!* If she did not move for many weeks, if she remained perfectly still, Tamara might be lucky enough to learn once more how to use her lower limbs. If . . . But she'd wanted to dance!

The dance. How it saved me, how it destroyed me too! Natalia thought. It made me want to live, to rise, to become a person in my own right, an artist. But it also made me overlook you, my little one. It's true, what Pierre has said through the years: I didn't want you. But then I never wanted Arkady either, and yet how much I loved him while I had him. He had seemed like such a miracle to us, to Boris and to me, whereas you, my sweet, were just a mistake, an impulsive, childish mistake. "But I always loved you," she said aloud. "I always did. It's been difficult between us, and we've both felt rebuffed, alienated. But lately it has been quite good, especially those last few months, the two of us dancing, and Stu . . ."

"Hello, Natalia," Pierre said. She had been speaking very quietly, and now she blushed, and jumped up, embarrassed. Had he been listening? But then, why not? She was his daughter, too. Their daughter.

"Hello, Pierre." She tried to smile but couldn't make the corners go up. He sprawled into the wicker armchair, crossed his legs, laced his fingers together. His face was thinner, more drawn, and there were bags under his eyes. A wave of feeling swept over her, and she placed a hand quickly over his, then withdrew it. "You look awful," she murmured.

"And you. But she'll be all right. You'll see—" His voice rose, trembled, dropped.

She picked up the cue, almost without thinking. "Yes, dear. She'll be all right. How is Galina?" she asked, steadying her voice.

"Fine, fine." His eyes were focusing improperly, and he rubbed his temples. "Not so fine, really. None of us is 'fine,' of course, Natalia. God is punishing us."

She started and sat forward, suddenly lively. "What? Are you mad, Pierre?"

But his voice droned on, weary, self-flagellating. "Punishing us all. I've done many reprehensible things, you know that. Nobody knows it better than you because you're the one I wronged the most. Not just because of Galina—also before. I shouldn't have forced you into having Tamara. And then, Jackie Vendane. I behaved despicably, putting you through that for so long. The night of Tamara's birth—I'm paying for it now, and you're paying for your denial of motherhood, and Galina's paying for her own involvement, for—whatever. It's God's way, Natalia. What the hell!"

"You always were somewhat of a mystic, Pierre, but never to this extent. Take hold of yourself! You're starting to sound like Vaslav before his mind completely deteriorated." Oh, God, she thought, closing her eyes, isn't it enough that I have Tamara to pull through? Why is it always my job to help Pierre, even now? But she was too tired, too depressed to turn on him, and so instead she sat in silence, staring at the small, bound figure on the bed. My daughter, my heart. My piece of immortality. Which we all want, don't we?

Pierre was holding his head in his hands and softly weeping. She looked at him and did not move, sat back and watched, her hands folded. Oh God. She rose and kneeled by the armchair, pried the fingers away from his eyes, and stared into them, an intense light burning in her own. Her strong hands held his on his thighs. "Damn it, Pierre," she said in an undertone, "don't you understand? I've lost a son in one bloody hospital, and I'm not about to relinquish my daughter—our daughter—to another. I've had my fill of disinfectants, and if I never wear the color white again, you'll know why. I don't know what was wrong with Arkady's makeup, but I'm through blaming myself. And this—it was an accident, for God's sake, an accident! There's nothing mystical about that, it isn't retribution, it's simply a terrible fact that they are going to try to correct, right here in this place that I detest, that makes me think of a living tomb."

Her voice began to break, and she added: "Do you realize that this is Christmas again? If your God existed, He wouldn't have done this to me, would He now? But do you know what, Pierre? I'm glad we have a daughter and not a son. Women are stronger than men, women are survivors!" She turned her face away, deep sobs breaking from her in the silence of the room.

She felt his fingers tighten over hers. "Maybe you're right," he said. "Maybe you're right."

"It's going to be months, Serge Pavlovitch," Natalia said, offering him a snifter of Napoleon. She stretched out her legs in front of her, under the coffee table in the parlor. "I don't know what to do. I don't know what to do."

"You're not to worry, to start off with."

"She wants to be a ballerina! God knows if she'll ever walk again. It's funny, my life. Nothing good ever lasts. But then I hardly expect it to. I suppose Tamara thinks this way, too. She had a mother she never saw, and a father she adored. Then the father left and she had a very nervous mother with whom she didn't get along. Then there was another upset, and her father reappeared. And now this. Pierre thinks the heavens are falling down on us."

"Pierre is an adorable child, Natalia. But you are not a child."

She sighed. "I wish I could be." She laughed nervously. "Then someone else could take care of me for a change."

"We shall miss you," he said. "You're like Lopokhova, popping in and out of the Ballets Russes, like the prodigal son.

Still—we'll find it very difficult to survive without you. You've been one of our best choreographers, and you've proved me wrong."

"It's good of you to say so. However, you can't fool me, Serge Pavlovitch. These past few months I haven't been blind to the fact that Serge Lifar, our new *danseur* from Kiev, has been practicing his own ideas with you. It's a game I haven't enjoyed, to tell you the truth. People are pawns to you, Serge Pavlovitch, and when you're through with them, you discard them."

"Not always. I rehired Fokine, remember? Now when I go to London, I intend to rehire Massine, too. Enticements abound. You judge me too harshly, my dear."

"Survival of the fittest? Let the Nijinskys go mad?"

He looked down at the floor, kicked lightly at the Aubusson rug. "That was a tragedy over which I had little control. I won't say no control. But there were other factors, Natalia."

"I know. And you've never fogotten that Boris played a role."

"Yet, in Boris's place I would have acted as he did. All I can say in defense of my own behavior is that, as far as you've been concerned, I always knew with whom I was dealing. You may not have thought yourself Boris's equal, but I did. You were always an interesting woman."

"Thank you, Serge Pavlovitch."

"You've been a friend. I've counted on you many times, and you've been there. The Ballet won't be complete without its Oblonova."

She smiled wryly. "Certainly it will. I was speaking to Benois, and he feels that he is no longer useful to you, that his style is *dépassé*. With me it isn't exactly the same thing. I simply see your enthusiasm lying elsewhere than in the plastic arts. For you the Ballets Russes have come to mean a compendium of all the new trends in the arts, a receptacle of all that hasn't quite yet been discovered, but which will dictate the new style in music, painting, sculpture. Novelty upon novelty. I want room. I want space, to create unencumbered by the myriads of brilliant minds who surround your own brilliance. Our objectives aren't the same anymore, but that's all right. There's room on this earth for us both, I have no fear."

He took her hand and kissed it. "You're a lovely lady, Natalia," he said. "Good night."

Afterward, holding her brandy snifter to the light of the fireplace, she thought: He is the only man who has ever seen me first and foremost as Oblonova—not as the Countess Kussova, not as Madame Pierre Riazhina. If it weren't for Tamara, I would stay to witness the last splendid burst of flame from this great giant, the Ballets Russes, which cannot last much longer now that it lacks a solid base. I would stay, even though this is the time to leave, my time to say "so long," because I'm almost thirty-five and need to be on my own.

To do what? she wondered. But she was not afraid in the still night, not afraid for herself. She was only frightened for her daughter, for what would become of those lovely legs, of all those dreams with which she, Natalia, was so familiar.

"It's your turn now, Tamara," she whispered to the gold-red flames. "I'm not going anywhere until you're better, and then we're going to go together."

Galina sat in the narrow chair, reading aloud. "It's all right, " Tamara said. "I'm tired of Gulliver. Tell me one of your old stories, Galinotchka. Remember? About what it was like in the Caucasus, and also about Petersburg when you were a child. I prefer that, anyway."

"You should ask your father to tell you about the Caucasus. He was very happy there. I wasn't, you know."

"It wasn't nice what I told you about the baby, the day I fell."

Galina's eyes filled with tears. Her fault, everything her fault. "I understand," she murmured. "You were afraid we didn't love you very much, and that it was the baby's fault."

"What's going to happen to me?" Tamara asked, her voice suddenly very young and scared. "I want to be a dancer. Now I can't even move my neck."

Galina pressed her hands together over her small stomach. "It's going to take some time, Tamarotchka. It will all work out."

"How do you know? Did the doctor promise?"

"Tamara, stop it!" Galina rose in one swift motion, her face bright and moist. She sat down again. "I'm sorry, sweet. It's just that we've . . . we've all . . ." She broke down, rocking back and forth, sobbing. Tamara watched her silently from her hooks and pulleys, as immobile as a statue.

Someone had entered the room, and from her cot Tamara said, "Hello, Mother." Natalia stood uncertainly on the threshold, then resolutely made a small kissing gesture toward her daughter and went to her niece. She pressed a firm hand on Galina's shoulder. "Let's go outside," she said tightly.

When they had walked down the corridor toward the empty laundry room, Natalia said: "Don't do this, Galina. You're not helping her to fight. She's not even eight years old, for God's sake! If she sees you breaking down, she'll assume it's hopeless. You're as bad as her father. He *does* think it's hopeless."

But Galina could not stop. Leaning against the wall, she wept soundlessly now, her face covered with red splotches. Natalia began to tremble. "She's a difficult child," she said. "She's not what you once were as a child. You were charming and pliable and well mannered and considerate. Tamara is selfish, indulged by her father since she was born; and she's also confused. I told Diaghilev I wasn't coming back, that I needed to stay here with my daughter, to spend time mending with her, reestablishing a sense of trust, of fairness. You're going to have a baby in several months. Take care of yourself and avoid this sort of strain. It isn't good for you, and it isn't good for Tamara."

"You're telling me not to come to see her?"

Natalia regarded the tall, lovely form of Galina Riazhina, her fine golden hair, her wide azure eyes—the eyes of Boris Kussov, but guileless. Galina felt the appraisal and flinched. I am not part of them, she thought. I am the outsider, the one whose stupidity caused all this—and so much more besides. "Pierre looks at me like that, more and more often," she said in wonder, her voice quivering.

Natalia raised her eyebrows. "Oh?" She sighed and stroked Galina's cheek. "He doesn't mean to. Neither do I. My darling girl, in many ways it was easier to lose Arkady, because there was nothing I could have done. This is limbo. We don't know what's going to happen. And somehow, we all feel responsible. Don't let us both hurt you by interpreting our nervousness as rejections. But we're all human. Under stress we each react with a minimum of thoughtfulness. That thoughtfulness should be reserved for Tamara."

Galina ran out of the secluded hallway, down the corridor, and out of the hospital. Natalia pressed her forehead against the coolness of the wall, thinking: She can't afford the luxury of guilt. It costs too much.

Several days later when Pierre came to the hospital, Natalia was blocking the way to Tamara's room, her face white and thin, deep circles under her eyes. "They aren't letting us in," she declared in a dead tone. "The doctor's told me she has a fever."

Pierre's eyes widened, and two lines stood out around his lips. "A fever?"

"Come," she said wearily, "let's take a walk. Outside, in the courtyard—anywhere but here." She pulled the veil down over her face, adjusted the egret feather on her hat, and took a few steps ahead of him. For a minute he simply stood in place, mesmerized, watching her small, graceful form from the back: the gray coat trimmed with fur, the shapely legs, the kid boots. She was so infinitely pathetic, so tired and hopeless and dragging. Yes, dragging, even old-looking. An indefinite feeling passed over him like a wave, and he caught up with her and took her arm. She did not resist. It was as if, finally, she had given up the fight.

In the cloistered courtyard they began to march dully around the statue. "Bakst is dead," she finally sighed. "Serge Pavlovitch sent me a message from London. Fine New Year's gift, don't you think? Dear old Léon Nicolaievitch. I liked him well. It seems as though the world is preparing for a giant mourning. Everything around us is falling apart."

"That's what I told Galina. She thought I meant—" He stopped suddenly, embarrassed. "I'm sorry about Bakst. He was one of my first mentors. I preferred him to the more refined snobs in the group. He and Serge Pavlovitch hadn't been on friendly terms for a while, had they?"

"No. The Ballet has changed. Diaghilev's cohorts are growing younger and younger. Even I felt outdated." She smiled, but he could see that her eyes were not smiling. "But it's going to be all right for him. He's just hired a brilliant young choreographer from Russia, Yuri Balanchivadze. He's twenty-one!"

"So what are you going to do?" Unspoken lay the question: If . . .

She stopped, and he stopped with her. Overhead the clouds were gathering for a storm, and a kind of dusk had fallen. "Maybe I'll go to America and make a talking movie in Hollywood. Who knows? That would be exciting. Something new."

His mouth worked, and he laid his hands on her arms. "You can't do that," he said simply.

"Why not? It's exactly what I'm searching for: a way to express myself artistically, without growing moldy and repetitive. Stuart's been offered a chance to write the screenplay for *Toys That Don't Work*. He asked me to go with him."

"But you don't love him!"

"I care for him, I'm attracted to him, I like him. Why shouldn't that be enough?"

"Because it never is!" he cried, tightening his hold on her arms. He dropped them and sighed. "Nothing ever is. We wake up too late."

She looked up sharply, then continued to walk. "We are both fools," she said. "Talking to fill the space of our fear. This fever—America! I might have told you I was going to the moon, to allay my own fear of the fever. They wouldn't let me see her. There's an oxygen tent over her, they said."

"The only good that ever came of our being together," he said, his voice catching in his throat. "But she is good, isn't she? Isn't she the most beautiful little girl you've ever seen? And she has your chin."

Natalia shook her head and laughed, without much joy. "She is good, I'll grant you that. But Galina was as pretty. Maybe you'll have another daughter, Pierre. Would you like that? Or do men always want sons?"

Without looking at her, Pierre said: "I honestly don't care. Since Tamara's accident I haven't really thought one way or another about the new baby. It's left me indifferent. Perhaps we all feel a special something for our first. I remember you in Germany, with Arkady. I thought then that you loved him because of Boris, and that if you cared less about Tamara, it was because you never could love me as much as Boris. But now I realize it's not that. You do love Tamara—only she's less of a miracle to you because you've gone through the process before."

She regarded him from her clear brown eyes and reached up to touch his cheek. She smiled. "Thank you, Pierre," she murmured. "It means a lot to hear you say this."

He caught her fingers in his and pressed them to his lips. "I should have thought to say it long ago. I should have done a lot of things I didn't do, long ago."

She took back her hand and stuffed it in her pocket, and they walked silently back into the hospital. They had not seen Galina, who had entered through the heavy carriage door. Trembling in the cold, she watched them disappear inside the building and continued to stare toward the statue, her blue eyes slowly filling with tears. Then she shook herself and briskly crossed the courtyard toward where Pierre and Natalia had preceded her.

From the atelier one could glimpse the rooftops of Paris, their tiled gables, slate gray, and their iron balconies hung with flowerpots. Inside were eaves and attics and student rooms hardly bigger than closets. From them one could see the Seine, wide and green-gray, with the bookstands lined on its quays, and its elegant bridges.

Pierre had bought the top floor of an apartment building on the Left Bank, and had knocked out the walls separating each of the students' and maids' rooms from its neighbors. This had provided him with a large work area overlooking Paris, the windows tilting down in a charming way. He came there each day, and sometimes when Galina went there to visit him, she would find his friends there too: Picasso, Braque, Man Ray, who had photographed her with her hair down over her shoulders. Now there was no one, and Pierre threw the brush down angrily at his feet, where it splattered green paint in an absurd pattern.

"I can't seem to work," he said moodily, looking beyond her out the window. "I can't think of anything except that she may never lead a normal life, that she may be a cripple forever! I feel like a failure, suddenly. It's as if everything else were paper trinkets piled up in a child's room: all the triumphs, all the commissions, all the good reviews." He sighed, licking his lips, and murmured: "I can understand Boris now, what impelled him to go to the front line. It must have been my letter! It must have been! There's nothing quite like losing a child. Nothing can ever fill that void again, no other child. Part of oneself dies, a part of oneself that was better than you, more than just you. You and someone else, the best of both of you."

Galina watched him carefully, fingering the wide gold band on the ring finger of her left hand. She was silent, her eyes enormous. "Natalia and I wrought a lot of damage," he said in a husky voice, balling his hands into fists. "Tamara is the single thing that we truly built rather than destroyed. I can't bear it, Galina—to imagine her crippled. Because she's the only one that will ever be—the only child to come from her and me, with whatever we have of good and the towering amount we certainly have of defects and vices."

Galina breathed deeply and, with the barest tremble in her voice, asked: "Why did you leave her, then? Natalia?"

He wheeled around, his dark eyes flashing. "What are you saying? I left her because of you, because I wanted you! Have I ever given you reason to be jealous of Natalia?"

She shook her head slowly. "No. But I thought you had left her first and foremost because you no longer loved her, that it was only because your feelings for her had died that you were able to come to me, a free man. I did not want to take you from your wife. I thought it was over between you."

He turned away from her, picked up his brush, and dipped it angrily into a pot of paint. "The palette's dry," he said with disgust. "Nothing works anymore."

"We do, don't we?" she asked softly. "Don't we?"

"What's that supposed to mean, Galina? I'm talking about the paint, for God's sake!"

"Don't be annoyed, answer me. Sometimes I think you're not really with me, that you're still . . . a little in love with Natalia. Tell me!"

The blue eyes held him. Suddenly he was filled with nameless anger, and he cried: "Leave me alone, Galina! Natalia is—my past. She's a reflex action! Can't you be sensitive enough to understand that and not read any more into it? Natalia has been part of my thoughts, of my whole life, since I was twenty-two. That was the year you were born, Galina. So all the years of your life Natalia has been with me, in some way or another. Nineteen years! She's also the mother of my child— my child, who can't even turn over in bed by herself, my child, whom I think of day and night! Of course, I can't get rid of Natalia! Of course, I will wake up and say her name first—out of bloody habit! There—are you satisfied?"

She stood quietly, unflinching, her blue eyes like mirrors of the sky. "Pierre," she murmured, "if I had been anyone else but Boris Kussov's niece, would you have cared for me?"

"Look, Galina, I've had enough. I'm trying to work. Why do you harass me?" He set the brush down again, sighed, left his stool and walked up to her. "Galina. If, if, if. I've never heard anything so ridiculous in all my life. If you'd had hairy moles all over your face, and if you'd weighed two hundred pounds, would you have been my girl? And if I'd been an uneducated, evil-smelling, eighty-year-old peasant from the Upper Volga, would you have slept with me? You are who you are. And among the things you are, you are Boris's niece. All right?"

"Tell me about you and Boris—my Uncle Boris. I'd like to know."

For a moment there was an odd light in Pierre's eyes, a flicker of red. His nostrils flared. She stepped back, instinctively, all at once afraid. "You've been seeing Natalia," he said in a low, tense voice. "What has she told you? Why can't you let well enough alone?"

"I haven't discussed any of this with Natalia. But I'm your wife, Petya. You must talk to me. Why is it so terrible for me to ask about Boris? Is it true, then? That you and he were lovers?"

"No!" he shouted, a purple flush mounting to his cheeks and forehead. "But only Natalia could have told you that—she's always believed it! God knows who else she's convinced over the years! And yet she should have known, after all our years together, that there was no way, no way I could have slept with a man, not ever! And now you doubt me too."

Galina's eyes filled with tears, and she shook her head rap-

556   idly. "No, no, of course I don't doubt you. And I don't care! It's all in the past, I wouldn't have cared however it had been! I asked you only because I love you and want to understand you in every way. I want to be a better wife, to learn why Boris upset your existence, to see that no one ever upsets it again. Don't you see that, darling?"

But his black eyes were unseeing, and his face grew more congested. He took her by the shoulders, and she could feel his fingers pressing down, bruising her. "All I can see," he said, a note of hysteria in his voice, "is the face of Boris Kussov taunting me, taking from me all I had, playing with my life as if he were God—laughing, laughing! I believe in the demon because I have seen him, and I still see him now, in your own face, his face! Oh, I wouldn't be surprised to learn he was your father, that he committed incest along with everything else! The damned Kussovs, with their aristocratic inbred genes and their immaculate beauty, with all their riches and their degenerate life-style. You asked me if I would have loved you if you'd been someone other than a Kussov relation? For a while I was fooled into loving your outside, your beauty, your gentleness. But now that I have lived with you, I can see chinks in your armor. I can see weakness, I can see evil! You are not who you seem! You're like all the rest, a jealous woman, jealous of Natalia and of Tamara! And like Boris you want to destroy me, you want to degrade me—"

She cried out then, pushing him away and collapsing against the wall. All at once he went completely still, the color draining from his cheeks, his arms hanging limply at his sides. He covered his face with his hands. "Oh, God," he moaned, "what have I said? Galina, my darling—I didn't mean it, not any of it! Please—"

She lay huddled on the floor, staring at him like a bewildered child. He crouched down, took her in his arms, started to caress the thick blond hair. "My darling, my little love," he said softly, tears falling from his eyes. "You're the only pure and lovely tree in my garden, the only encouragement I have to become a better man. It wasn't I speaking to you. It was a man who hasn't been sleeping nights, who's been worried sick about a child. You must forgive me, Galinotchka, you must."

"But it's my fault that you haven't been sleeping," she said in her clear, low voice. "It's my fault that you've begun to hate me, not Boris Kussov's or your own. Tamara fell because of me, and neither you nor Natalia will ever be able to look me in the eye again without feeling some kind of terrible resentment. Try to tell me, Petya, that I'm wrong—that things haven't started to change between us already!"

Clinging to her, tangling her hair with his fingers, he cried: "No, no, my dear sweet love. Nothing has changed. I promise you." He pulled her up, and pressed her to his chest, where she rested like a child. He sighed, a sigh that pierced his entire body. And then he straightened up and said, without looking at her: "You'd better go now, Galina. I must try to work here."

Galina waited in the apartment, knitting by the fire, tears splashing unheeded over her fingers. All afternoon she had been profoundly chilled, but now she was too hot. There's nothing I can do, she was thinking, desperation knotting her throat. Pierre's violent words, his distorted features, reappeared before her mind's eye over and over. Dusk came at last, and when the servants inquired after Monsieur, she dismissed them for the evening. Her teeth were absurdly chattering. It was no use. Natalia had been right that day at the house: She had made a sorry mess of things, and now Tamara was at her worst and this was her fault, too.

She got up abruptly and went to the large window. Why wasn't he coming home? Had he become so bored with her that he could be happy only when she was out of his sight? Or was he simply a man who could never be happy? She felt her clothes clinging to her and shivered.

A nameless terror took possession of her, and she went to the telephone and lifted the receiver. She must call Natalia, ask her to come and talk to her, to fill the space with words, with life. I'm going to have a baby in less than six months, she thought, but already I know that he has ceased to care. I'm not enough for him. And he blames me.

He blames me because he never really loved me. He still loves Natalia. It isn't possible to be "civilized," to love the same man and to share him. It will always be she against me, and I against her. And now he feels responsible to me, and to our baby—but it's Natalia he loves, and Tamara, *their* daughter.

Galina went to the mirror and stared at herself with growing revulsion. She was so vivid, so oversized! He had told her once that she was too perfect to be painted accurately. Galina began to sob. She'd been a symbol: the princess, Boris's niece! Oh, I hate you, Boris! she cried to herself. Why couldn't everyone have forgotten you?

She felt her forehead and realized that it was hot and damp, that she was shaking. The room oppressed her to the point of strangulation. Without thinking, she threw down her knitting and went into the hallway. Take a walk, get some cool air, she thought, and heaved a sigh of relief. Yes, that would do it, would ease the pressures building up inside her. She would leave him a note in case he came home while she was out.

Her breath coming in constricted gasps, Galina opened the door and ran down the stairs into the cobbled courtyard. This was much better. Without even feeling the December wind, she allowed it to propel her forward into the street. She had forgotten to bring a wrap, but it hardly mattered. Her skin was burning, and her eyes were stinging. She realized she had not left Pierre the note, but what difference would that make? He didn't love her. He was probably somewhere with Natalia.

Natalia . . . Galina had wanted to call her on the telephone, to see her. Well, she would walk there. She had never walked from the Left Bank clear to the Bois, but why not now? Exercise was good for expectant mothers.

For a moment she stopped, her mind reeling, feeling more intensely dizzy than she had ever felt in her life. "I must be very sick," she said aloud, hugging herself in the afternoon dress. "I don't know where I am anymore, and I can't stop shaking and shivering."

Overpowered by nausea, she stood against a gaslamp and vomited, aware that night had fallen and that she was alone in the street. The wind blew ominously around her, lifting her skirt, and she felt the sharp drizzle of hail. She began to panic. She could not remember why she was out in the storm, why she was trembling, why every limb of her body ached with throbbing pain. She would soon awaken, and her mother would be there, and Pierre. With supreme effort she forced herself onward, into the street, blinded by darkness and a stinging cascade of hail.

She was beginning to stumble, and thought: It's all right. I can't walk anymore, I'm going to lie down. I'm going to lie down and go to sleep, and then Pierre will find me. Pierre loves me. She closed her eyes and felt her body slide to the rough ground, not sensing the moment of impact. Pierre! Galina felt for her wedding ring, touched it, and remembered in one flashing moment that it was over, everything was over, Pierre would never love her again because she had trapped him, hadn't slept with him before their marriage—and what else? She had forgotten, but this afternoon he had told her: She was like Boris Kussov, a user, a depraved individual, and *what else?* Why was it so essential to remember this now? But it was, it was!

Galina heard the screeching of the tires and huddled on the ground like a baby. Her dress was soaked through with hail and perspiration, and her hair lay matted on the cobbles. She heard the tires and put her hands over her face and felt the colliding shock of the rubber against the soft part of her stomach, where the baby was. She opened her mouth to scream: *Pierre!!!* but before the sound came, she saw the red spots over the blackness, felt the searing pain. There was no time to think, I am Galina Stassova Riazhina, the princess, beloved wife of the painter Pierre Riazhin— soon to be the mother of his child—

"It's a very young woman," a man was saying in the night. "But with the storm I couldn't see her at all, officer. I'm afraid she's dead."

Natalia refused to admit Pierre into the house but threw herself vehemently against Stuart Markham, pounding on his chest with her fists until, in pain, he let her go. Then she fell into a chair and doubled over, her teeth clamped together and her lips pulled up. He could see her swaying back and forth but was afraid to touch her again, knowing that she would lash out and strike him. Instead he sat down in front of her and waited, watching this display of violence with discomfort and awe. It occurred to him that women, in their grief, came closer to pure agony than men ever could.

After a while she began to breathe again, in deep dry sobs. "He murdered Galina, he murdered her! I don't know what he said to drive her out into the night during the worst storm of the year—but he murdered her as surely as I live!"

Then her voice broke as she was stunned with the realization. "My little girl," she whispered. "He killed my little girl, my sister, my child." She fell forward onto the carpet, her fingers in her hair, gasping for air as tears clogged her throat and the dam was at last released.

Stuart went into the entrance gallery and saw old Chaillou, tears in his eyes, and the figure of Pierre Riazhin, his face haggard, the muscles slack in his cheeks and jaw. Pierre took one giant stride toward him and asked: "Will she see me?"

Stuart licked his lips and examined the man before him. Something inside him was infinitely moved, and he wanted to break the shock, help alleviate the anguish. But then he remembered the woman on the floor in the parlor, gagging with grief. He straightened his shoulders and said evenly: "You'd better try to forget about Natalia. I don't know if she'll ever receive you again."

Feeling a presence, he turned around and saw her, disheveled and wild-eyed, in the doorway of the living room. He remembered how the young blond princess had regarded Pierre the night he, Stuart, had found her in the Château Caucasien with the American boys. The memory was painful: Galina so vivid, so alive, so golden and azure, and Pierre, unable to contain an unreasonable fury. Had he already been in love with her?

Abruptly, Stuart wiped his eyes with the back of his sleeve, and stepped toward Natalia. But she did not see him, was not conscious of him or the aged butler. Looking at Pierre through narrowed eyes, she spoke to him alone, her voice suddenly high and shrill:

"Murderer!"

Chapter 32

On the glistening hardwood floor the girl stood in fifth position, her head held proudly on the long neck, her hands low in front of her, palms up, fingers relaxed. She was tall for her ten years, and her black curls were held in a cluster by a ribbon at the back of her head. She was a striking child, with a chiseled, up-turned nose, a small, well-molded chin, high cheekbones, and enormous black eyes ringed by curling lashes. Her skin glowed a healthy peach tone, only barely moistened from exertion.

When the piano started to play, she slid her right foot forward on *pointe*, shifted to the *pointe* itself, and made a half-turn to the right, bringing her left foot quickly on *pointe* in front of the right, and finished the turn in the same place that she had begun it. Without missing a beat, she repeated the *déboulé* a second time, retaining her momentum. She spun around, her dark head the topmost peak of the axis, her arms constant, a flush spreading to her cheeks. Then, gently, she lowered her feet to the floor, made an automatic *plié* in first position, and slumped forward like a ragdoll. "Uh!" she groaned.

Natalia said evenly: "That was excellent, Tamara. You've really mastered it this time. I'm very pleased."

"Are you?" The dark head shot up quickly, the eyes bright and hopeful. Tamara rubbed her forehead roughly with her knuckles and then scampered on *demi-pointe* to her mother, making amusing faces. "Am I going to be good enough for the Opéra audition?"

"We'll see. Remember that they sometimes have five hundred young people trying out and only some thirty or forty openings."

"But you're Oblonova," Tamara countered. "Everybody knows you!"

Natalia nodded and smiled. "Maybe so, but nobody knows Tamara Petrovna Riazhina. I'll put on my blond wig to take you there!"

They laughed, but Natalia sensed her daughter's bristling. She chose to ignore it. Companionably, they sauntered out of the practice room and went into the parlor, where Chaillou had put down the tea tray. Natalia poured their cups full and then sat back, wryly amused. Another audition! How long it had been since 1900, when she had gone with Masha into the Imperial School, for her first examination. It was now 1927, and she was thirty-seven years old. Twenty-seven years.

"What are you thinking about, Mother?" Tamara asked.

"Oh, odds and ends. How strange it feels that my recalcitrant young daughter has opted for a career in dancing. But I'm so glad, darling. In all my life ballet has been my single constant friend, the one thing that's kept me going. I hope that it will bring you joy, but I don't want it to be your whole life. There are other things, too."

"There is nothing else for you," Tamara countered.

"There's you."

Tamara bit on the end of her index finger and thought about that. Then she nodded, and her bright black eyes flicked to her mother's face. "That's true. I didn't always think I was that important to you."

"I didn't, either," Natalia said softly.

"But I remember thinking when I had the accident that it was always your face that was there—you know what I mean?— when I would wake up. And then when I was so ill—I can't think back too clearly on that—you'd take my hand, and it felt so good, your cool, firm hand. I didn't think I'd ever be able to feel anything in my legs at all. Then when Galina died—" Her eyes filled with sudden tears, and she looked away, embarrassed. "That's when I really had only you, wasn't it? Papa just fell to pieces and stopped caring."

"Sometimes," Natalia said, her eyes focusing on a point above the door frame, "even the strongest man feels that his container is too full for another drop. We all have our breaking point. Your father reached his when Galina died. It was such a horrid way for her to have died—such a waste! And for him two beloved people died in one—Galina and the baby."

Tamara blushed and looked at the floor. "I wasn't very nice to her about her baby. I told her that it might not live, like Arkady. That was the day I fell, remember? But I didn't want her baby in our family. I didn't want Papa to prefer it to me."

"It's all right, darling. I didn't particularly like her baby, either—for different reasons that were just as selfish. Let's not think about it anymore. It doesn't do us any good. Drink your tea, and I'll give you another cupful."

"I miss her," Tamara murmured. "Don't you?"

Natalia bit down hard on her lower lip and concentrated on pouring the hot beverage. She nodded silently. Yes, she thought, of course I miss her. But did any of us ever really know her? Didn't she finally die of loneliness, that night in the storm? It isn't only Pierre—we were all guilty, all responsible. I won't remember, I can't, not now. Now I have what I have, a tenuous thread, a hope, a . . . something. I can't lose it now!

Tamara gulped down her tea and cake and stood up, suddenly just a child again, a young foal on uncertain legs. "I have to go diagram three irregular verbs," she said, kissing her mother with buttery lips. "See you later? At dinner?"

"Mm. Yes. Of course." Natalia watched her leave and thought: Lately she's known I'd be there every night. She pressed her fingers over her eyes and sighed. No, it was better not to think about the options. There were none at this point, anyway. She had burned her bridges, made a decision, and at heart she knew that it had been for the best. When Tamara had been released from the hospital, it had seemed so unlikely that she would ever use her legs again, but it had been such a miracle that she had survived at all that Natalia had refused all offers of engagements in France or abroad and had concentrated, instead, on caring for her daughter. It was she who had implemented the difficult physical therapy outlined by the physicians at the hospital, she who had urged, cajoled, and browbeaten

Tamara into using first crutches, and then, painfully, tentatively, her own legs. Now, two and a half years later, she was walking perfectly, dancing, pirouetting, as if this brush with a crippled life had made her earnest desire a bright banner for which to fight, a goal as essential as the Holy Grail. And that's been good, Natalia thought. Thank heaven for dance! It has made us both survive all the bad times.

She rose and went to the small English secretary in the left corner and rolled down the top. There, neatly folded together, lay the letters. Natalia could feel the constriction in her chest, the moisture suddenly bursting onto her palms and forehead. She took the small pile to the sofa and sat down again. On the coffee table, beside the silver tea tray, her reading glasses were waiting. She had first needed them the year before, now used them daily. She slipped them on, unfolded the first letter, and began to reread it.

But she had already committed it to memory, and now only snatches of phrases jumped out at her, twisting her inside. "My lovely Natalia: Hollywood rises out of tropical hills, a fake paradise of back-lot castles juxtaposed with skyscrapers." And then; "The silent-screen stars aren't doing so well in the talkies. They aren't used to having to watch their inflections, their accents. . . . One wonders sometimes if the real world exists outside of sand and sun and drunken screenplay writers from the East, and cigar-brandishing, agate-eyed moguls from small towns in Poland and Serbia." The part that was becoming blurry said: "Where are you now in Tamara's development? You know I think of you, but once before you made a decision, and it was not in my favor. I understood it then, I understand it better now, knowing you better and caring for that little tomboy of yours in my own way." Natalia put the letter down in her lap, and said aloud: "I don't want to be your friend, Natalia, my love. It isn't enough. I understand, but I can't risk allowing you to use me as a shoulder to cry on. You don't need that anymore, and I don't particularly relish that role. I'd rather remain in a small corner of your mind as a remembered joy."

She folded up the letter and set it down on the coffee table. The next one was less troublesome but made her shift restlessly in her seat. Something vague in this letter from Michel Fokine tugged her out of her self-absorption. At that time he had been mounting a production in a New York film theatre. "The Americans relish our exoticism," he had written. "It is virgin ground broken by few, and we've enjoyed it, Vera and I. New York bristles with energy. The jazz is mesmerizing, the landscape quite unreal, like Pierre's American Stage Manager in *Parade*. There is no true aristocracy here, only money and the power that it creates." Old words, old thoughts. Old friends.

I don't have a life anymore, Natalia thought, startling herself. I am thirty-seven and live the life of a recluse, remembering dead dreams, dead husbands, dead children, and finding hope only in my one living child. It isn't good—it isn't good for her, and certainly not for me. Fokine appears to have adjusted to traveling from country to country, a homeless artist; Kchessinskaya thinks she'll be happy teaching a ballet school here in Paris, but I am nervous, like a reined-in horse. What can I do?

There was a photograph on the secretary, of Boris and Arkady in Germany, an old photograph that she had forgotten about, which the Zwingenberg innkeeper, Hermann Walter, had snapped several weeks after her son's birth. Some months ago a newspaper columnist had interviewed Natalia, and an article had followed that had been reprinted in various foreign tabloids, about Oblonova, who had chosen seclusion in order to teach her daughter how to use her legs again, and how to dance. Then she had received a letter, postmarked Munich: "Dear little *Gräfin*, As you see, we have moved, sold the inn after the war. But we shall never forget that we had the privilege of helping you to deliver your precious son." They hadn't even known. They hadn't suspected how much that resurrected photograph would hurt, would rub her raw. They hadn't known, the two old people, that Arkady and his father had both passed away, so shortly after she had left the inn.

The Kussovs were all a dream, she thought, clenching her hands together. They touched my life like spiritual beings, and I was the solid earth, unmoving. One by one they brought their starshine and I closed my eyes, believing them, pretending that I was the sun. One by one they were extinguished in a burst of grandiose sparks—Boris, Arkady, and then Galina. In the end I have survived them all, I the peasant, the earthling. I and my solid daughter, my girl-child. We were not meant to peter out like comets, but to endure like the earth itself.

Still, what shall I do? Diaghilev predicted this, too, that I would withdraw until it was too late. I didn't want to be a mother, but I gave up my career three times, each time for a child. I never had a chance to be Arkady's mother, and I lost my chance the first time around with Tamara. The accident provided the last possible opportunity, and it's worked out—at least I think it has.

Natalia stood up, shivering suddenly, and whispered: "Nevertheless, a child's a child, and I'm grown up. We were not meant to be each other's keepers, she and I. She's on the brink of something wonderful. And I? Who would want a ballerina long past her prime, another relic from the Mariinsky?" The empty room filtering the afternoon sunlight did not answer her. Yet that's hardly true, her mind rebelled: I have as much inside me that is strong and unique as Diaghilev's young prize, Balanchivadze—"Balanchine" now.

She sighed and took off her spectacles and brought the folded old letters back to the secretary. Someday, she thought with quick amusement, I shall have to compile my memoirs, someday when I am very, very old, and my feet are crippled with arthritis. *Oblonova Remembers*. But that will be when my eardrums have caved in, and I can't hear the beat of the piano, except as it reverberates through my mind.

The body, she thought wryly, touching her stomach, isn't so bad after all. But when she smiled, her lips felt like plastic, stiff and false.

Natalia sat at the vanity in her boudoir, brushing her soft, glowing brown hair. It was December again, and the cold and gray outside seemed to seep into the marrow of her bones. Three years since Tamara's accident, since Galina's death—why did her catastrophes tend to cluster around the holidays, and always come in twos? Arkady and Boris, Tamara and Galina. But her daughter had recovered and broken the spell. And actually Christmastime had not always been the harbinger of death and disaster: It had also been the beginning, that glorious Christmas of 1905, when she had danced the Sugar Plum Fairy

and triumphed at the Mariinsky for the first time. She laughed
in self-mockery.

Outside her door she could hear the sounds of the servants
busying themselves, and then a sudden joyful voice, Tamara's.
Natalia looked up, suddenly alert, and waited for the door to be
flung open. Tamara was so much like her father! "Oh, Mama!"
the girl cried, tossing her dancing shoes with buoyant care-
lessness on Natalia's bed. "Guess what happened today after
class? They selected dancers for the Christmas matinées of *The
Nutcracker!* Your own wonderful daughter, Tamara Petrovna, is
going to be one of the Claras! Alternating with two other girls,
of course, to 'rest' us."

"Darling, that's grand news!" Natalia exclaimed, and her face
lightened into that of a very young girl, color rising to her
cheeks. "That's marvelous! But I'm amused: In my day only the
greatest stars were 'rested'—Nijinsky, for instance, because he
exerted himself so much executing his *jetés.* Is the director of
the Opéra a more lenient man than Teliakovsky? It would appear so, anyway."

Tamara giggled. "Teliakovsky was a mean old bear, wasn't
he?"

Natalia smiled. "Not such a mean one, really. But very strict.
The Tzar could not have been stricter. But lovey, I'm delighted!
Tell me more about the ballet, about you—"

Tamara threw herself down on the floor, and, playing with a
tassel on Natalia's hemline, began to recount in a singsong
voice, tinged with unsuppressed excitement, what had happened and how she had been chosen. Her mother listened, but
part of her watched her child's eyes, examining Tamara with
great care. There is my determination there, she thought, and
Pierre's immense hunger for life. There is the spark of creativity, but also my own follow-through. She won't let down
until she has what she's set her mind to capture. Right now she
only wants one thing, to shine as a ballerina. Natalia felt her
eyes fill with sudden tears.

"What's the matter, Mama?" Tamara asked, interrupting her
narrative. "Is it that you miss the Mariinsky?"

Natalia laughed. "Heavens, no! I was done with it years ago."

"Still," Tamara persisted, biting her nail, "I feel it's strange, being a Russian and not knowing my own country. You don't miss it at all, ever?"

"The Russia of my early days is no longer there, dear. We're not really Russians, actually. I mean, we wouldn't want to go back and be a part of what it's become—and the old Russia had to die, it was corrupt and rotted through."

"Then, what are we? French?"

"I'm not sure." Natalia scrutinized her own reflection in the mirror and remarked: "I don't think I am. You, yes. You've always been a little Parisian. Even professionally you'll be formed by the French, whereas I may love it here, but I came as a foreigner and shall always be one to a certain extent. I don't quite know where I belong. Perhaps nowhere!"

"We have this Russian lady in the costume department, and she was somebody's wife—a grand-duke or something—in Moscow, and she's always throwing up her hands and rolling her eyes and telling us how nothing, nothing will ever replace her beloved country. She smells of dust and dead things, and people laugh at her behind her back. But I find her sad. I'm glad you're not that kind of Russian exile, Mother. I feel sorry for her."

"They take all forms—the Russian exiles, I mean," Natalia reflected. "I saw Mala Kchessinskaya today. She's in Paris for a brief visit and asked again if I won't help her open a new ballet studio here. She's a grand lady. But still . . . there are plenty of other Russian dancers who can do this as well as I could. Mala's a classical ballerina in the Petipa mold, primarily. Teaching her skill here will be an ideal outlet for her—less so for me."

Tamara raised her eyes to the ceiling. "But I'll be a classical dancer, Mother," she said with the forced patience of the very young. "Isn't there anything that tempts you? People ask me, you know. 'When's Oblonova going to dance again? What does she have planned?' It's embarrassing!"

Natalia rose then, regarding her daughter with a strangely quizzical narrowing of her eyes. She went to her bedside table and pulled out a drawer, which was full of letters. Sitting on the coverlet and picking one up from the top of the pile she said: "Listen to this, Tamara. It's from Sol Hurok—you know, the Russian-born impresario in America, who arranges tours for

concert artists: pianists and dancers and what-not. I received this
two days ago:

> Dear Madame Oblonova,
>
> Perhaps you remember me from 1916, when you were
> in New York with the Ballets Russes. My purpose in con-
> tacting you is that you are one of the few dancers today
> whose name is a known entity at the box office and who is
> still remembered with affection as a pet of the United
> States public.
>
> Since you are no longer a member of Diaghilev's illustri-
> ous company, I should like to issue a proposal to you. I
> have successfully booked tours for many of your col-
> leagues, among them Pavlova herself, who is so popular in
> our country. I would like to arrange for you to appear again
> in various cities throughout America, dancing your favorite
> pieces as well as some of your own compositions. Our au-
> diences appreciate one-woman shows such as this.

Then he continues on and on about finances: who backs him,
what he can guarantee, etc., etc. But that, my dear, sparked my
interest."

Tamara said warily: "I didn't think you liked America. Didn't
you find it uncivilized in '16?"

"Yes, but since then eleven years have gone by, almost
twelve. And there's a staleness here in Europe that is rather
depressing, at least to me, right now. I'm ready to tackle the ridiculous small towns with their puritanism and their general
stores. Actually, they can be quite an experience to a seasoned
dancer. When I was there last, I was still quite young, and I arrived expecting the Opéra or the Mariinsky. Now I know better.
America wants to have its eyes opened artistically—and I think I
can be one of those to accomplish this."

"In one short tour?" Tamara asked.

Natalia shrugged lightly. "Who knows? Anything's possible.
Go on, now, Clara—it's time for your bath, isn't it?"

Her daughter gave her a sour look and grumpily picked up

her shoes from the bed. Then she walked out, exaggerating the heaviness of her step. Natalia sighed. I am being watched, she thought, to see how I can be manipulated. But don't be so certain it will work, Tamarotchka. There are two strong-willed women here, and I'm older and more adept at defending my position.

Natalia bit her lower lip with nervousness. In her short bob and bangs, her full skirt cinched by a wide black belt that made her waist appear childlike, she looked like a waif caught on the pages of a fashion tabloid. She could not sit down but paced the floor of the formal salon, walking back and forth in front of the deep windows overlooking the garden.

Chaillou entered unobtrusively, wheeling in the tray of caviar, smoked salmon, *foie gras*, and pumpernickel rounds, and the heavy bucket in which the magnum of Moët et Chandon was chilling. "You and the others can leave now," she informed him, unexpectedly touching his arm with a small, graceful gesture. "It's late, and all of you are tired. I can let Monsieur in myself."

But when he turned to leave, she felt a quick pinch in her chest, as if his presence had somehow been warm and reassuring. Tamara was practicing for the Christmas ballet at a friend's house, and suddenly Natalia missed her. She ran her fingers through her hair, still surprised after seven years by its shortness. Then the doorbell rang, and she went out to open it, a quick flush rising to her forehead and cheeks.

"Good evening, Pierre," she said as he passed into the entrance gallery. He paused for a moment before removing his topcoat, and she saw the slight heaviness in his jowls. The salt and pepper of his hair had lightened considerably, but she thought it attractive, softening his predatory appearance.

"Natalia." She took his coat, hung it in the wardrobe by the potted palm, and turned quickly into the salon, where Chaillou had discreetly turned on the low lamps before taking his leave. She knew that Pierre, like her, had no desire to linger in the entrance hall, where, the last time he had set foot in the house, she had called him a murderer. It was a scene best forgotten, yet impossible to forget.

She sat down in one of the Louis XIII armchairs and folded her hands in her lap. "I'm glad you could come," she said. "There's something I need to discuss with you. Would you like some champagne?"

"Champagne? Are we celebrating, Natalia?"

She read the hostility in his eyes and looked at once at the tray. Pouring the golden liquid into fluted glasses, she said: "That's vulgar. Even from you."

"You've always thought me vulgar. But I wasn't thinking of Galina. Do you think I could ever forget that she died this month?"

"I'm sure you couldn't. None of us can." A tense silence hung between them, and she handed him his glass and began spreading caviar onto a round of black bread. "The champagne isn't to celebrate. It's merely a courtesy on my part toward you because it always was your favorite drink. Was I wrong?"

"Oh, no, Natalia, you're never wrong. No, indeed." He sat back now, accepted the caviar, and bit into it with appreciation. "That's very good. Things are always very good here, though, aren't they? The ghost of Boris Kussov hovers over us, replenishing our glasses like the best of butlers."

"Don't make me angry, Pierre. I wanted to talk to you about Tamara." Natalia looked at him now, and the directness of her gaze made him uncomfortable all at once. "I've decided to take a trip to the United States," she announced evenly. "Sol Hurok is going to book a tour for me. I'll go at the beginning of the year—if you'll take Tamara, that is."

He allowed the coolness of her tone, the fact of her declaration, to sink in, and then he leaned forward, and his jaw worked. "How long will you be gone?" he asked.

"I'm not certain. Two months, six months. Tamara can't come with me because of her training, and she'd like to stay with you. In fact, lately, she and I have been together too much. Symbiosis isn't good for either of us, and a short break could benefit us both."

"Six months isn't a short break!" he exclaimed.

"Will you or will you not take her?"

His face colored, and he breathed in deeply, two lines jutting out around his lips. Her brown eyes still held him, not letting him avoid their searching light. "Why are you going?" he asked, but this time his voice was pitched low and intense.

"Because I'm suffocating. It's no one's fault but mine, but I have no life of my own right now, and I can't live through Tamara as if I were eighty years old. There's still so much I want to show the world—there's still so much in me! I remember," she added wryly, "when Diaghilev first told me that he was going to show Europe the manifold riches of Russia. I didn't understand the need to do this. Now I've come full circle. Who knows? I might even decide to stay!"

He blinked slowly and said: "Stay? In that godforsaken country?"

"How do you know it's that? You've never even been there," she retorted, but without bitterness. Pausing between words, she said: "It's what I want. Tamara understands that; why can't you? I'm not going to abandon her. I'll be home shortly, and if I do go back to stay, I'll return here regularly to see her. And she'll be able to visit me there. I'm not leaving her behind out of neglect. She *wants* to stay, to complete her years at the Opéra. That's her choice, and I respect it. But I must do what's best for myself, too."

"How can you be so sure, Natalia?" Pierre suddenly rose and came around to her armchair. "Natalia, we haven't exactly been friends since before Galina's death. Even when Tamara was in the hospital, I know you blamed me in your heart for that senseless death. And you were right. Every day of my life these past three years, I've blamed myself, scourged my heart with memories of that last day and what I said to her. It doesn't really matter what I said—just that I felt the need to hurt her, to crush her. She was so beautiful, so pure and strong, and yet so vulnerable, so breakable. I'd wanted to mold her, to protect her, and also to be loved and cherished by her, in that soft, warm, comforting way of hers. But it didn't work out like that, Natalia. Or rather, it did, but I was disappointed. Galina wasn't enough—you know I still wanted you!"

"No," she said. "You've always wanted what you couldn't have. You'd stopped loving me. Whether or not you were the right man for Galina is immaterial, but you didn't love me. You despised me. Afterward, if you missed something, it was just a memory—the early memory of us when we were young, in Petersburg. Twenty years ago."

"But the truth is that I've always loved you. During the bad times I overlooked it, and yes, I even hated you. But I hated you for hating me! You were too strong for me, you cared about other things too deeply. I wanted you to be my girl, and you were always first and foremost your own girl."

She smiled ironically and raised her eyebrows. "What's the point of all this reminiscing? Galina was a tragedy that could have been avoided, like Boris's death. But I couldn't influence him the way you could her! That's why I blamed you. However, it wasn't fair. She was your wife, she was carrying your child. I forgot that for a while and remembered only my own grief, my own guilts. It's so easy to blame someone else for one's own failings. Let's leave all that behind us now, shall we? For Tamara, because she needs us both."

"You can say that, and still think of leaving?" He put one knee on the floor and gazed at her earnestly, his nostrils quivering. "Natalia, I feel as though we've just crossed an ocean toward each other—don't cross one away from me again! I love you, Natalia. You should never have let me go when you did because if you'd only said: 'Don't leave,' I would have stayed with you!"

She looked at him in disbelief. Slowly she took a sip of champagne, then said: "But you wanted to make a new life with another woman. What nonsense you speak: 'Don't leave!' How simple you make it sound, how ridiculously simple! As if Galina didn't matter at all, as if we two had simply had a lovers' quarrel. But she did exist, and she pointed out to me how right I'd been, years ago, when I refused to marry you in Petersburg. We were wrong for each other, Pierre! Certainly then—and as for now, how can you think of it, after so much has happened to prove otherwise?"

"We're violent people, Natalia. Galina got crushed between us without understanding, and for that I can't forgive myself. But I can't continue to deny the obvious, out of a sense of guilt for somebody we both loved but who's dead and can't be helped any longer. We've always loved each other, Natalia. Face it with me!"

"Oh, Pierre!" she cried, rising and clasping her hands together. "Look, my darling, I will tell you how it is for me, since you insist. All my life until Galina, I lived for the moment, knowing inside that whatever happened, Pierre Riazhin was somewhere in the world, loving me. I carried this certainty in my subconscious, like a talisman: Pierre loves me! Then you broke away and took my good-luck charm away from me, leaving me only with myself. I was downtrodden and miserable, and for the first time in my life, I didn't really care whether I lived or died. It took Tamara's accident to bring me around again. I thought: This isn't so bad, this self I'm stuck with, my one and only wealth. So now it doesn't matter if Pierre Riazhin loves me or not. I don't need his love to keep me alive!"

She turned to him, her elfin face aglow in the soft lights, her eyes all at once bright with triumph. He stood up and approached her, towering above her, tall and broad, and she did not step back. He hesitated, and she could feel the electric tension in the space between them, could almost hear its crackle. He took her hands and kissed them, and still she regarded him with that same expression, ardent and unafraid.

He dropped her hands and suddenly took her in his arms, holding her frailty close to him, so that she could hear the enormity of his beating heart. When he kissed her lips, she parted them swiftly, and thrust her hands into the curls of his hair. In front of the large bay window he tilted her back onto the thick Aubusson carpet, where she gazed up at him in an apricot flush, her eyes half-closed and luminous, her mouth slowly curling into a smile. They undressed without taking their eyes from each other for a single moment, and then, with urgent need, came together on the floor in a magnificent tangle of limbs.

Her skin felt the same as in the first flush of youth, but the tender softness of her breasts was of a different texture than he remembered: like the softness of feathers, where before all had been taut and firm. Suddenly desperate, he thought: This is what I want, this is how I prefer her. Not a girl, not a young bride—but a woman in the middle of her life, who would accept my own imperfections. She smiled at him and ran her hand gently over his stomach, silken reminder that he had changed, too, from the days of their marriage. It did not matter. It was still his strength that drew her, the large broad shoulders, the muscular calves and thighs, all the same but altered. Maybe the attraction lay half in the past and half in the newness: They had never before made love knowing that time had left its mark on each of them and that the world would never be for them what it had been before. In the early days life had been unknown and wonderful and frightening—and so had Pierre been to Natalia, and she to him.

Later, they lay silently entwined, and she could hear his breathing. She knew its very cadence, had been rocked to sleep hearing it against the softness of her hair time and time again. But now he did not shift her face against his chest, preparing her for rest. Instead, he sat up, leaning on his elbow. His dark eyes probed her. "So?" he asked, with a hint of tension. "You won't be going now, will you, after all?"

Pressing a finger to his lips, she shook her head. "I'll go. This was my farewell to you, my darling Pierre."

"Is it Stuart Markham?" he demanded.

She shrugged sadly. "Stu is living his own life. I had two chances with him. Even if I could still choose him, I'm not certain I love him. I have to go for my own sake, because I want to dance, and this seems like the right opportunity at this moment. But who knows what could happen? I did receive some interesting offers. To go to San Francisco and form a ballet company. Another was to go there and open a studio for the daughters of the wealthy matrons of Nob Hill. Or—to go to Hollywood, and make a talking movie. Dancing, of course!" Her eyes flashed merrily now and then rested on his face with sudden gentleness.

"Don't begrudge me my life, Pierre," she murmured. "Tell me to leave and to be happy."

"But that is more than I can do," he replied, rising swiftly and going to the window. She watched the well-muscled back and bit her lower lip. "It would kill me to send you away from me. You'll never return!"

"Oh, yes," she said. "I have a daughter, and I shall return. But not to you, Pierre. We've had our chance, and now it's finally over. Now we can finally stop hating each other, my dear. All the years of pain came about through the love, our hurtful, barbed, obsessed passion for each other. Now at last we can breathe again, without love, without hatred. We can see each other as people, Pierre, and not as demon angels. We can go on from here."

She stood up, diminutive and naked, and went to him at the window. "I want you to move back here when I'm gone, to live in this house," she murmured, draping her body gracefully across his back. "It's only fair. Boris wanted *you* to have it, not me. And Tamara loves it and wouldn't want to leave it. Galina," she added in a soft, wistful tone, "was also happy here. Come, then. While I'm on this tour."

He moved aside and let her step beside him, and together they looked out into the snow-covered garden. Behind them the lamps cast a burnished gleam over the varnished piano, over the armchairs and the little tables. The champagne glasses stood in shimmering grace near the uneaten canapés, and somewhere a clock chimed, sonorous and plaintive. She smiled, remembering, and then tears replaced the smile, and she swallowed them down.

"The spell of the Firebird," she said. "One magic feather and all the monsters disappeared. Do you believe that such a thing can happen? A world without monsters?"

"A world of Sugar Plums," he sighed. "That's how it all began, wasn't it? For all of us?"

She did not reply but turned around and started to pick up her clothes from the floor.

On the enormous stage of the Opéra, the ten-year-old Clara stood out from the other children in the Party scene. She was tall and slender, with a fluid but stately form, well-molded shoulders and graceful hands. Black curls tumbled over her neck, held back by a ribbon and velvet flowers. Her long dress with its wide skirt was deep yellow, trimmed with lace and a border of fur. To Natalia she suddenly appeared older, a presage of the dancer she would be in later years. Not an elf, like Lopokhova, nor an intellectual beauty, like Karsavina, but rather a flowing, sensuous power, a magnetic personality with regal charm.

Natalia sat in the red velvet box, her hands clasped in her lap. Beside her was Pierre, but she could not turn to look at him, for her throat had suddenly constricted and tears had come into her eyes. It felt so strange to be observing rather than performing in this grand but familiar opera house, stranger yet to be watching another woman, who was part of herself and yet not herself. She wanted to cry out, to merge with Tamara on the stage, and yet something held her back.

The music rose, and Clara stood back in awe at the nutcracker that her godfather, Councilor Drosselmeyer, was giving her for Christmas. She moved with ease in the thick dress, her arms flowing in a single, fluid line, her throat young and stately as she drew back her head. *She's good!* Natalia cried inside, her feelings soaring with an intense emotion that startled her in its vehemence. She's good, she'll be all right, she's going to be all right from now on, my daughter, my own heart!

Slowly she turned to Pierre and saw that his eyes were wide with concentration and luminous with wonder. All at once she touched his hand, softly, quickly. She could imagine him at the Mariinsky, watching her on the stage, watching and wanting her from that very moment. Perhaps, right now, in this theatre in another capital, twenty-two years later, a young man was falling in love with Tamara. Oh, God, no, I don't want that for her, Natalia thought. She's still a child, and I don't want her to repeat my life.

How odd it is, she mused then, that we have somehow come together, she and I! She is going to be a ballerina, not for my sake, not to please me, as I once feared. She is dancing to prove to herself that she is not afraid to compete on my territory. Oh, the battles aren't over, not nearly so. She still resents me for going to America next month, for not placing her ahead of my personal needs. And she still prefers her father; he is the bright god in her existence. But that's all right; I have no wish to be a goddess, only her mother. In the long run she and I are quite close. We understand each other and will not destroy each other in the process of loving.

I have had a son, and loved him, and now I have this beautiful young daughter, who has risen from myself and Pierre, and from the untamed passion that we thought was love. But look at her! She is whole and she is lovely; she radiates the best of him and maybe a little bit of good from me.

Clara was sinking softly, delicately into sleep on the sofa, while the Christmas tree was growing, growing. Yes, Natalia thought, her Clara is wise and naïve at the same time, a true woman-child. Where had Tamara found this interpretation? And then, with a momentary wrenching of her heart, Natalia remembered golden hair and a look of pure, azure sky: Galina! So Galina lives again, through Clara, through my own Tamara, she thought.

Pierre's eyes had filled with tears, and tactfully Natalia concentrated on the stage to give him his privacy. So he's seen it, too. Well, that is good. I'm glad. So long as we're alive, none of the others will be dead, for we shall not forget.

She fumbled with the clasp of her purse and removed from its depths a dry and withered flower. For a moment she hesitated. Then, gently, she tapped Pierre on the arm and showed it to him. It was one of the rosebuds that Boris had thrown to her at the première of *The Nutcracker* in 1905, a flower that had been a promise, the promise of glory and of love. It had come in a tight bouquet and landed at her feet, telling her of curtain calls to take, of certain encores that would be shouted to her from the stalls. Tonight she would lay it on her daughter's pillow. For as long as a dancer lived, there had to be an encore.